CLASSIC

The classic comedies selected for this single-volume collection of plays capture the enduring elements of comic theater, from the fast-paced satire of Greek Old Comedy to the scathing social farce of George Bernard Shaw. The complete English texts of plays by Shakespeare, Jonson, and Shaw, and outstanding translations of plays by Aristophanes, Plautus, Molière, Gogol, and Feydeau, provide a rare opportunity to trace the Western comic tradition from its roots. This collection helps to identify the characteristic word play, themes, and denouements that appear in the romantic comedy of Shakespeare and Feydeau as well as in the darker comic drama of Jonson and Molière.

These seven plays represent the best work of some of the world's greatest playwrights. Here is the bawdy audacity of *Lysistrata,* as the women of Athens go on strike against their men; the broad slapstick of mistaken identity in Plautus' *The Menaechmus Twins,* a story of twins of the ancient Roman Empire adapted centuries later in Shakespeare's early *Comedy of Errors*; and the naughty peccadilloes of Feydeau's husbands in *A Fitting Confusion.* Often ribald, always lively, these are masterpieces that remain fresh and contemporary.

MAURICE CHARNEY is a professor of English at Rutgers University. He is the editor of *Timon of Athens* in the Signet Shakespeare edition and has published eleven other books.

CLASSIC COMEDIES

EDITED AND WITH AN
INTRODUCTION BY
Maurice Charney

A MERIDIAN BOOK

MERIDIAN
Published by the Penguin Group
Penguin Books USA Inc., 375 Hudson Street, New York, New York 10014, U.S.A.
Penguin Books Ltd, 27 Wrights Lane, London W8 5TZ, England
Penguin Books Australia Ltd, Ringwood, Victoria, Australia
Penguin Books Canada Ltd, 10 Alcorn Avenue, Toronto, Ontario, Canada M4V 3B2
Penguin Books (N.Z.) Ltd, 182–190 Wairau Road, Auckland 10, New Zealand

Penguin Books Ltd, Registered Offices: Harmondsworth, Middlesex, England

Published by Meridian, an imprint of Dutton Signet, a division of Penguin Books USA
Inc. Previously published in a Signet Classic edition.

First Meridian Printing, October, 1994

10 9 8 7 6 5 4 3 2

ACKNOWLEDGMENTS
LYSISTRATA by Aristophanes, translated by Douglass Parker, edited by William
    Arrowsmith. Copyright © 1964 by William Arrowsmith. Reprinted by
    arrangement with New American Library, New York, New York.
THE MENECHMUS TWINS from SIX PLAYS BY PLAUTUS, translated and edited
    by Lionel Casson. Copyright © 1960, 1963, by Lionel Casson. Reprinted by
    permission of Doubleday & Company, Inc.
THE MISANTHROPE from THE MISANTHROPE AND OTHER PLAYS BY
    JEAN-BAPTISTE MOLIÈRE, translated by Donald Frame. Copyright © 1968
    by Donald Frame. Reprinted by permission of New American Library, New York,
    New York.
A FITTING CONFUSION by Georges Feydeau, translated by Norman R. Shapiro.
    This play is fully protected, in whole, in part, or in any form throughout the world
    and is subject to royalty. All rights, including professional, amateur, motion
    picture, radio, television, recitation, public reading, are strictly reserved. For
    professional and amateur performance rights all inquiries should be addressed to
    Samuel French, Inc., at 25 West 45th Street, New York, N.Y. 10036, or at 7623
    Sunset Boulevard, Hollywood, Calif. 90046, or to Samuel French (Canada) Ltd.,
    80 Richmond Street East, Toronto, Ontario, Canada M5C 1P1, or to Samuel
    French Ltd., 26 Southampton Street, London WC2E 7JE, England.
THE INSPECTOR GENERAL by Nikolai Gogol, translation by Robert Saffron;
    copyright © 1962 by Robert Saffron and reprinted by his permission. All rights to
    produce, perform or reprint this translation are fully protected and extended by
    the new copyright laws. Application for any such use, by amateurs or professionals,
    should be addressed to Robert Saffron, 41 Fifth Ave., New York, N.Y. 10003.
CANDIDA by Bernard Shaw. Copyright © 1898, 1913, 1926, 1931, 1941 George Bernard
    Shaw. Copyright © 1905 Brentanos. Copyright © 1958 The Public Trustee as
    Executor of the Estate of George Bernard Shaw.
"Laughter" by Henri Bergson was originally translated by Cloudsley Brereton and
    Kenneth Rothwell and appears in COMEDY with an Introduction by Wylie
    Sypher, which is published by Doubleday and Company, Inc.
"Errors in Comedy: A Psychoanalytic Theory of Farce" by Barbara Freedman appeared
    in SHAKESPEAREAN COMEDY edited by Maurice Charney and published
    by the New York Literary Forum.

LIBRARY OF CONGRESS CATALOGING IN PUBLICATION DATA

Classic comedies / edited and with an introduction by Maurice Charney.
        p.   cm.
    Originally published: New York : Signet Classic, 1985.
    ISBN 0-452-01143-4
    1. Comedy.   I. Charney, Maurice.
    PN1922.C43   1994
    808.82′523—dc20
                                                              94-18222
                                                              CIP

Printed in the United States of America

CONTENTS

v

INTRODUCTION:
THE WORLD OF COMEDY

TRAGEDY HAS ALWAYS enjoyed spectacular cultural advantages over comedy. It is considered a higher genre, more serious, and more worthy of study, especially in schools and universities. Comedy is popular, it makes us laugh, it is not intellectual, it does not deal with fundamental issues of life and death, and, therefore, although we may enjoy it personally, it is not thought to be a fit subject for study and contemplation. These are the prejudices about tragedy and comedy that everyone takes for granted in our society, and these are the obstacles with which we must begin. Among literary and dramatic critics comedy is said to improve in status insofar as it resembles tragedy and is not mere farce or something we laugh at. Critics as well as directors have been especially keen to ally Shakespeare's comedies with Shakespeare's tragedies, and they have invented terms to improve the lowly status of comedy: "autumnal" comedy, "bittersweet" comedy, "problem" comedy, "dark" comedy.

But comedy doesn't need all this support. It is a form of expression quite different from tragedy, although comedy and tragedy overlap at many points. Once we can start thinking of comedies as autonomous creations, we don't need to invoke tragedy at all. In point of fact, the number of comedies is vast whereas the number of tragedies is small. Once we get down to the question of what is a true tragedy—whether it conforms to the precepts of Aristotle's *Poetics*—the sum total of authentic tragedies shrinks even further.

In the essays in Part Two I have included selections from two of the most powerful thinkers about the comic experience: Henri Bergson and Sigmund Freud. Although Bergson and Freud had very different interests, they nevertheless agree on one important point: the close relation of comedy to dreams. Freud came to his book on jokes fresh from *The Interpretation of Dreams* (1900), and he applies to both the distinction between the surface appearance or symbolism—the manifest content—and what the joke or dream really means—the latent content. In other words, the comic expresses meanings hidden deep in our consciousness. It may express them in a disguised form that seems lighthearted, trivial, frivolous, and pure play. Barbara Freedman argues that the real purpose of farce is to mask aggression, both to exhibit it and to punish it at the same time in a manner that is purposely irresponsible and dreamlike. Bergson puts a strong emphasis on

the power of the intuition to protect us from becoming inhu
manly stiff, mechanical, and absentminded. In other words,
laughter releases our awareness that we are becoming automa-
tons. The world of dreams is intended to preserve the free flow
of energy that makes us characteristically human.

All the plays in this anthology have a strong element of
fantasy and wish fulfillment. The women's sex strike in *Lysistrata*
has little relation to the subordinate position of women in Athenian
society. It is, rather, a grand imaginative gesture that manages to
create peace between Athens and Sparta. In the symbolic style of
the dreamer peace is personified as a beautiful, naked young girl.
The twins in both Plautus's *The Menaechmus Twins* and Shakespeare's *Comedy of Errors* create illusions, coincidences, and
deceptions that can only be explained as mental events because
the twins and the world in which they function are determined
never to recognize the obvious reality that surrounds them. There
is a commitment to error that is surprising—we think of it as a
kind of comic stupidity. The impenetrability of the disguises
suggests that the strength of comic illusion does not depend on
the practical world of everyday reality.

Molière's *Misanthrope* is so extreme and so exaggerated as to
be almost lovable. He is a nonpareil of misanthropy, and we are
impatient when he is not on stage dominating the action. He is a
dreamlike figure in the sense that he is so fully imagined; he is
not the garden variety of misanthrope of our ordinary experience.
It is easier to identify with rational, commonsensical, unheroic
characters like Philinte and Éliante. In *The Inspector General*
Hlestakov is also an "impossible" figure who has no physical
resemblance at all to what an inspector general is supposed to look
like. He is, in fact, gawky and ungainly but gifted with a powerful imagination. He is the supreme example of wish fulfillment
among our protagonists because he always says what people want
to hear, even to the intimate details of the luxurious and romantically boring life one is forced to lead at the court of St. Petersburg.

Feydeau's Doctor Moulineaux is as much in flight from reality
as Hlestakov. The doctor would be the first to acknowledge that
he has a beautiful and attractive young wife, but his philandering
is a self-perpetuating autonomous system without any clearly
defined relation to goals. Feydeau cleverly detaches consummation
from seduction, thereby preserving comic energy that would otherwise be squandered. Frustration is the most powerful plot mechanism
in Feydeau, as if all the furious activity would cease immediately
once desires were satisfied and therefore ceased to exist.

Shaw was also fascinated by erotic games. In *Candida* everyone is playing some imagined version of his or her self, but no

one is more histrionic than the young, upper-class poet, Marchbanks. He is dreamlike in the sense that the rhetoric he is spouting—abortive poems—can have no conceivable relation to actual conversation. He is in the enviable position of being able to live out his fantasies. But everyone in the play is more or less living out a fantasy, and Shaw is wise enough at the end not to convert his characters to the humdrum world of everyday existence. We may not know what secret is in the poet's heart, but we may not want to know either—and Shaw is certainly not about to tell us.

All of our plays are strongly anchored in farce. The characters are not intended to be believable, rounded, psychological persons but are rather a collection of extravagant and turbulent energies that are set off by a complex plot full of disguises and coincidences that make it possible for anything to happen. Farce emphasizes quirks and eccentricities of behavior and tends to exclude such worthwhile human emotions as tenderness, sensitivity, sympathy, and compassion. Bergson is thinking primarily of farce in his theory of comedy, especially in the notion that comedy demands an "anesthesia of the heart." Horace Walpole's famous dictum is relevant here: "The world is a comedy to those that think, a tragedy to those that feel." Not that comic characters are thinkers in any intellectual sense, but feelings are generally excluded from farce. It sets up relations and establishes a world that we would consider hard, abstract, and possibly even cruel. The hardness is mitigated, however, by the sense of detachment we feel for experience set apart from ordinary concerns. Farce is the purest comic product of our fantasies and wish fulfillments.

Plautus is the model for most subsequent farce, and his plays tend to define the genre. There is little romantic love interest in Plautus, but money plays a large role in the engineering of his plots. The young are set against the old, and, in *The Menaechmus Twins*, the twins, through the force of circumstances, seem to be set against each other. The action is highly artificial, yet we are willing to accept it not because it is plausible but because it is surprising and entertaining. We enjoy the perturbations the twins undergo because of mistaken identity. By doubling the twins, Shakespeare can also, in *The Comedy of Errors*, multiply possibilities of error. That seems to be a positive dramatic value because the more knots that are tied, the more knots there will be to untie at the end. We enjoy the undoing of the plot because it is so ingenious, especially because the twins are so reluctant to greet each other and acknowledge consanguinity. Beatings are another aspect of farce we delight in, mainly because the blows don't hurt. Farce promotes the notion of comic invulnerability—or at least impenetrability in a literal sense. In an irrational world of wandering twins who will not stay put, what other form of protest is there except to beat at the inexplicable reality?

Feydeau is directly influenced by Plautus, but the love interest is much more important in his plays. Not really love, but rather sex, and the plot itself resembles the strange and unpredictable meanderings of desire. Lust is a powerful motive, especially if it will never be fulfilled (and thereby weakened). Providential accidents are constantly preventing consummation, which is all to the good, since obstacles keep the characters lively and in pursuit. Identity tends to be rather shaky in Feydeau, and one woman like Mimi in *A Fitting Confusion* can appear as one's long-lost wife; the mistress of one's youth; a respectable, upper-middle-class married woman; an available *cocotte*; or a total stranger. It is these shifts of identity that make *A Fitting Confusion* so sinuous and so hilarious. It as is if anything is possible in farce, despite the middle-class, drawing-room solidity (with plenty of doors) in Feydeau's stage sets.

Gogol's inventiveness and originality are well displayed in *The Inspector General*. Amidst all the tawdry details of petty bureaucracy, one feels a frantic, hysterical energy driving this play. Gogol is a master of snowballing. In other words, the illusion of Hlestakov's magnificence is built up piece by piece almost by geometric progression, so that we feel an intense effect of acceleration until the grand anticlimax that marks the entrance of the real inspector general. The illusion is much more convincing than the reality since that's what everyone wants to believe in anyhow. Money, for example, plays a surprisingly vague role in the play. It is a figment of Hlestakov's intoxicated imagination. Being a total impostor, he is thus free to make promises based on fantasy rather than on the size of the bribes offered.

The Misanthrope is farcical in its wild exaggeration. We cannot believe in Alceste and his lofty ethical ideals. In a more realistic play he would have been shown up as a hypocrite, but that is not the point at all in Molière. Alceste is not pretending to virtue, as Arsinoé clearly is; rather, he is making impossible demands on life. Of course, Célimène would make a splendid wife for him, but it is impossible for him to marry at all or to tolerate the company of his fellow human beings. If Alceste were more human, then the farcical aspect of the play would be diminished and the whole action would be more rational and believable. In Alceste's intransigence also lies his comic magnificence. He is grandly unlike us and therefore worth paying attention to and imitating.

The situation in *Lysistrata* is also farcically impossible. Who ever heard of a viable sex strike on the national level? No union has ever dared to threaten it. Lysistrata is the spokesperson for all our fantasies of speaking out when we're so angry that we can't take it anymore. She is the ideal representative of women oppressed by stupid male domination. The farce is the result of the working out of an ingenious idea: what would happen if . . . ? I remember a production of *Lysistrata* in New York with Melina Mercouri that was specifically directed against the Greek military dictatorship of the time. There were many Greeks, especially Greeks in exile, in the opening night audience, and I was impressed by how easily the sexual farce was translated into a politically potent message. Sexual revolution is an analogue of political revolution. The groaning, bursting phalluses of the men are produced not so much by the sex strike itself as by the alienation from everything that is most characteristically human. Peace restores sex and the spirit of comedy.

Shaw's *Candida* is not usually considered a farce, yet it seems to me that this play, and many other early works of Shaw, are wonderful examples of what Walpole literally meant when he said that "the world is a comedy to those that think." Shaw was eminently a comic thinker. Candida controls the play, and she graciously mocks the foolishness of both her husband and Marchbanks. Morell is absurdly self-important. He cannot recognize the difference between rhetoric and conversation, so that he makes the constant error of addressing everyone as if they were his audience. What makes Candida so wise? In her brilliant intuition she is not a farcical figure at all, but she understands the farcical pretensions of various men in the play, including her own father. There is a sense that the play turns on exposure; that is, the difference between what characters profess and what they really mean. Their mouthings expose them to the withering mockery of others. Shaw seems to move between the isolation and solipsism of his characters and the social milieu in which they move and must be judged. As theater pieces comedies are social by definition; there can be no world apart in comedy as there is in tragedy.

The relation of the plays we are reading to farce should not imply that they are in any way lacking in complexity. There is a mistaken notion that farce is always simple, if not simplified. Feydeau's plots, for example, are enormously intricate, and they involve bringing a whole series of unexpected characters together in an unlikely place in an intrigue that baffles probability. In *A Fitting Confusion* Feydeau hardly intends the transformation of Dr. Moulineaux into an Italian dressmaker to be believable. Yet he manages to hold his own even against his formidable mother-in-law, who is metamorphosed into the Queen of Greenland. We enjoy the complications for their own sake.

Farce and paradox go hand in hand, especially for Molière's Alceste, the misanthrope, and Shaw's Reverend Morell, the misunderstood husband. These are complex characters whose virtues are strangely mixed together with their vices. Alceste's honesty with the world is also a form of aggressive self-indulgence. By freeing himself from social restraints and the normal demands of politeness, Alceste can set himself up as moral tutor to mankind. His assumption of moral superiority is oppressive, particularly to his friends. With Célimène he has an inherent conflict between being a lover and being a pedagogue. Audiences tend to like both Alceste and Morell because we sympathize with their fallibility. Both seem to know nothing at all about love, and they both put an excessive emphasis on speech. They are extravagant figures without knowing it, boys who have never grown up, with an infinite need for mothering. Their ranting and raving and their frenzies of moral indignation mark them off as comic heroes impervious to reality.

I am trying to argue that farcical comedies can also present unresolvable problems. Twinning in Plautus and Shakespeare produces a whole series of deceptive illusions, and both *The Menaechmus Twins* and *The Comedy of Errors* depend heavily on dramatic irony. The audience is trusted with knowledge not allowed to the characters on stage. They are the arbiters of the farcical misunderstandings that occur so naturally and so frequently. In *Lysistrata*, too, everything depends on the triumph of a crazy and impossible idea. As a matter of fact, actual events in ancient Greece took an entirely different turn from the play, and the glorious city-state of Athens eventually succumbed to Sparta. Aristophanes seems to be the comic voice crying in the wilderness with no power to influence political life. If we examine the political implications of *The Inspector General*, everything moves in the opposite direction from comedy, and the real inspector general at the end strikes awe and terror into his audience. This is that hard part of reality that cannot be manipulated. And Hlestakov must be forgiven because his sudden grandeur is so forcibly thrust upon him. He makes no deliberate attempt to deceive but is puffed up by the cringing pettiness of the town, whose need to create authority figures before whom it can grovel is pitiful.

The values of comedy are obviously not those of tragedy, nor are they the exact opposite, either, just as laughing and crying are not physiological opposites but independent systems of expression. Comedy celebrates life and the life processes, and it usually ends with feasting, drinking, revelry, and the promise of offspring. The young are reconciled with the old, and love triumphs over money. Eating, drinking, and sex are comic values not so much for their own sake as for their affirmation of life. Wish fulfillment and fantasy gratification prevail over the limitations and meanness of ordinary life. There is something grand and transcendent in the happy ending of comedy. It is necessary because it is demanded by the genre. None of the problems or paradoxes disappears at the end; they are merely replaced with a sense of festivity and symbolically appropriate rewards. Women play a large role in the happy ending because they function as preservers of comic values in a way that men don't. In a typical comic ending, as in *Candida,* the male characters ally themselves with the spontaneous and intuitive values of the women, which have been asserted throughout the play.

Finally we must pay tribute to the splendor of language in all our plays. Our comic heroes are all grand talkers and are not to be put down by the intrusion of mere reality. It is only when Hlestakov, in *The Inspector General,* begins talking that his authority asserts itself. He speaks with mad conviction, so that it is impossible for anyone to contradict him or question his credentials. Lysistrata, too, displays a wild energy and frenzy that cannot be denied. The power of language is also, magically, the power of truth, and that is enough to defeat the male warriors. Why does everyone want to befriend the misanthropic Alceste if not because he is so audacious and speaks with such flamboyant ease? Everyone wants to hear him talk. The play flags when he is not on stage, and we wonder for how long Alceste will be able to flee mankind. Where in the wilderness will he be able to find listeners for his moral exhortations?

In *The Comedy of Errors,* Antipholus of Syracuse speaks for all comic protagonists when he agrees to forgo his own identity and to assume the person that everyone is thrusting upon him in Ephesus:

> Am I in earth, in heaven, or in hell?
> Sleeping or waking, mad or well-advised?
> Known unto these, and to myself disguised?
> I'll say as they say, and persever so,
> And in this mist at all adventures go. (II.ii.213–17)

"I'll say as they say" is the exact comic equivalent of entertaining "the offered fallacy" (II.ii.187). Antipholus of Syracuse is ready to receive all the good things that life has to offer him. And for the comedian, as for Hamlet, "the readiness is all."

—MAURICE CHARNEY

PART ONE

THE
COMEDIES

Aristophanes
LYSISTRATA

ARISTOPHANES WAS THE first great comic playwright of Western literature. He flourished in Athens in the late fifth and early fourth centuries B.C. (about 445 to 385 B.C.). His eleven surviving plays are more like review sketches than comedies with plots. Typically he engages important contemporary issues such as peace versus war or the old learning versus the new, and attacks literary and political figures directly. His plays are highly formalized. There is usually an *agon*, or debate, setting forth the pros and cons of the ideas on which the play turns. There is also a *parabasis*, in which the leader of the chorus directly addresses the audience. This is clearly a comedy of intellect and ideas, and it is not difficult to perceive affinities with the comedies of George Bernard Shaw.

Lysistrata, produced in 411 B.C., addresses itself to the grinding war between Athens and Sparta, which was bleeding Athens and would lead to its eventual subjugation. But the real war becomes a projection of the false male values that are ruining Athens. The war is a product of mindless machismo that can only be corrected by the powerful sex strike that lies at the heart of the play. *Lysistrata* is a tribute to the power of women, but this, too, is fantasy because women had very little power in Athenian society. Aristophanes likes to mingle the most urgent political issues with fantasy, wish fulfillment, and farce. He seems to be saying that the present situation is now so grave that only something so radical as a sex strike can save Athens.

The slogan "Make Love, Not War" seems to be the guiding principle of the play. The men are hopelessly teased and taunted, if not actually routed in battle. Why is sex so powerful? It represents the instinctual life, the irrepressible id, pleasure and self-expression that cannot be denied. The patriotic slogans of the military leaders are ruining the quality of life in Athens. Peace is strongly associated with sex. It is the good life of eating, drinking, and the indulgence of the senses. But it is also the foundation of family life, a point much emphasized in

3

Lysistrata, which concerns itself almost exclusively with husbands and wives. Peace means fertility in many senses of the term. Sex is the vehicle of love, a condition nurtured by peace but destroyed by war. Sex is also necessary to establish the civic, communal, and family values of the Greek city-state. War is solitary, savage, and antithetical to happiness and civility. In the play peace is personified by a beautiful young girl who appears naked on stage. As in modern burlesque, her nakedness is completely irresistible to all of the males, Athenians and Spartans alike.

Lysistrata is the sort of protagonist that Aristophanes particularly likes. She is an ordinary woman, undistinguished and unheroic, who suddenly can't take it anymore. She is fed up with the war and resolved to do something about it. Comedy is especially concerned with heroines like Lysistrata, who have a folk wisdom and driving energy that make them overcome all obstacles. Lysistrata is so attractive just because she is so much like us. Her speeches are much more practical than intellectual. In her great plea for peace, she develops the analogy to wool at great length: "Consider the City as fleece, recently/shorn. The first step is Cleansing: Scrub it in a public/bath, and remove all corruption, offal, and sheepdip." This is not complex reasoning, but that's not what's needed here. The simple moral point is driven home with great force.

Lysistrata's explanation of how she came to organize the women's movement is also practical and not at all either abstract or intellectual. It is a form of spontaneous politics: "When the War began, like the prudent, dutiful wives that/we are, we tolerated you men, and endured your actions/in silence." But the frustration of the women at their husbands' boorish stupidity gradually mounts until it can no longer be contained. The women's revolution comes as the climax of a long period of silence: "To keep us from giving advice while you fumbled the/City away in the Senate. . . . But this time was really too much." The women "have valuable advice to impart," which the men refuse to hear. This irreconcilable conflict between male and female values erupts in the sex strike.

Male values in the plays are graphically represented by the phallus, a more-than-lifesize penis made of leather, which appears quite often in Greek comedy and is strongly associated with the god Dionysus and the fertility rites connected with his worship. The painful erections of the Spartans are grandiosely indicated by the phallus. As Douglass Parker so felicitiously puts it in his translation: "Hit ain't the heat, hit's the tumidity." The leader of the male chorus speaks with compassion of the men's plight:

> Behold our local Sons of the Soil, stretching
> their garments away from their groins, like wrestlers.
> Grappling with their plight. Some sort of athlete's disease,
> no doubt.
> An outbreak of epic proportions.

The extremely farcical scene between Kinesias and his wife, Myrrhine, is also specifically tumescent, a kind of endless striptease that will never reach consummation. Horniness undermines the military virtues. Lysistrata is definitely right in her assessment of men.

Earlier in the play, the chorus of men present the hunter Melanion as their masculine ideal. He is much like Shakespeare's Adonis (in the poem *Venus and Adonis*) in his coy and skittish flight from female pursuers. Melanion is pursued by women intent on marriage, but he flees to the woods to trap rabbits:

> He stuck to the virgin stand, sustained
> by rabbit meat and hate,
> and never returned, but ever remained
> an alfresco celibate.

The "alfresco celibate" suggests an affinity between Aristophanes and musical comedy. The strong emotions of the plot are mitigated by song and dance, especially by the chorus.

Lysistrata ends as a festive comedy with reconciliation, revelry, and the promise of sexual indulgence. Peace is, after all, a beautiful naked girl. By celebrating sex the play is also celebrating the power of women, who are never seen with the painful erections that convert the men totally and grotesquely into creatures of need. Aristophanes was very conservative politically. He was certainly no feminist, yet his play is a tremendous tribute to women, who are the peacemakers and the bearers of good tidings. Lysistrata enunciates the moving force of the play:

> Of course. What did you expect? We're not slaves;
> we're freeborn Women, and when we're scorned, we're
> full of fury. Never Underestimate the Power of a Woman.

In his important *Essay on Comedy* (1877), George Meredith insists that there can be no comedy without the presence of "freeborn Women":

But where women are on the road to an equal footing with
men, in attainments and in liberty—in what they have won
for themselves, and what has been granted them by a fair
civilization—there, and only waiting to be transplanted from
life to the stage, or the novel, or the poem, pure comedy
flourishes. . . .

Meredith might have been wrong about the actual position of
women in the Athenian society of Aristophanes' time, but in
Lysistrata Aristophanes postulates a free society in which women
are the moral arbiters who call men back to their senses. This
pun points to the union of sexual and political meanings in the
play.

LYSISTRATA

TRANSLATED BY DOUGLASS PARKER

CHARACTERS

LYSISTRATA
KLEONIKE } *Athenian women*
MYRRHINE
LAMPITO, *a Spartan woman*
ISMENIA, *a Boiotian girl*
KORINTHIAN GIRL
POLICEWOMAN
KORYPHAIOS OF THE MEN
CHORUS OF OLD MEN *of Athens*
KORYPHAIOS OF THE WOMEN
CHORUS OF OLD WOMEN *of Athens*
COMMISSIONER *of Public Safety*
FOUR POLICEMEN
KINESIAS, *Myrrhine's husband*
CHILD *of Kinesias and Myrrhine*
SLAVE
SPARTAN HERALD
SPARTAN AMBASSADOR
FLUTE-PLAYER
ATHENIAN WOMEN
PELOPONNESIAN WOMEN
PELOPONNESIAN MEN
ATHENIAN MEN

SCENE: *A street in Athens. In the background, the Akropolis; center, its gateway, the Propylaia. The time is early morning.*[1] *Lysistrata is discovered alone, pacing back and forth in furious impatience.*

LYSISTRATA:

Women!

Announce a debauch in honor of Bacchos,
a spree for Pan, some footling fertility fieldday,
and traffic stops—the streets are absolutely clogged
with frantic females banging on tambourines. No urging
for an orgy!
                    But *today*—there's not one woman here.

(Enter Kleonike.)

Correction: one. Here comes my next door neighbor.
—Hello, Kleonike.[2]

KLEONIKE:

                    Hello to *you*, Lysistrata.
—But what's the fuss? Don't look so barbarous, baby;
knitted brows just aren't your style.

---

[1]The play's two time scales should be noted. By one, its action encompasses a day, beginning at dawn and lasting until after sundown; by the other, its events logically occupy a period of weeks, if not months—not that this sort of logic has much to do with the case. At no point is the play stopped to indicate the passage of time.

[2]This is to adopt Wilamowitz' conjecture for the *Kalonike* of the manuscripts, without accepting his views on the character's age. Kleonike's actions approach those of the stock bibulous old woman too closely to indicate a sweet young thing. She is older than Lysistrata, who fits comfortably on the vague borderline between "young matron" and "matron." Quite a bit younger are Myrrhine and Lampito.

LYSISTRATA:

It doesn't
matter, Kleonike—I'm on fire right down to the bone.
I'm positively ashamed to be a woman—a member
of a sex which can't even live up to male slanders!
To hear our husbands talk, we're *sly*: deceitful,
always plotting, monsters of intrigue. . . .

KLEONIKE:

(Proudly.)

That's us!

LYSISTRATA:

And so we agreed to meet today and plot
an intrigue that really deserves the name of monstrous . . .
and WHERE are the women?

Slyly asleep at home—
they won't get up for anything!

KLEONIKE:

Relax, honey.
They'll be here. You know a woman's way is hard—
mainly the way out of the house: fuss over hubby,
wake the maid up, put the baby down, bathe him,
feed him . . .

LYSISTRATA:

Trivia. They have more fundamental business to engage in.

KLEONIKE:

Incidentally, Lysistrata, just why are
you calling this meeting? Nothing teeny, I trust?

LYSISTRATA:

Immense.

KLEONIKE:

Hmmm. And pressing?

LYSISTRATA:

Unthinkably tense.

KLEONIKE:

Then where IS everybody?

LYSISTRATA:

Nothing like that. If it were,
we'd already be in session. Seconding motions.
—No, *this* came to hand some time ago. I've spent
my nights kneading it, mulling it, filing it down. . . .

KLEONIKE:

Too bad. There can't be very much left.

LYSISTRATA:

Only this:
the hope and salvation of Hellas lies with the WOMEN!

KLEONIKE:

Lies with the women? Now *there's* a last resort.

LYSISTRATA:

It lies with us to decide affairs of state
and foreign policy.
The Spartan Question: Peace
or Extirpation?

KLEONIKE:

How *fun!*
I cast an Aye for Extirpation!

LYSISTRATA:

The Utter Annihilation of every last Boiotian?

KLEONIKE:

AYE!—I mean Nay. Clemency, please, for those
scrumptious eels.[1]

LYSISTRATA:

And as for Athens . . . I'd rather not put
the thought into words. Just fill in the blanks, if you will.
—To the point: If we can meet and reach agreement
here and now with the girls from Thebes and the

---

[1] The constant Athenian gustatory passion, rendered sharper by the War's embargo: eels
from Lake Kopaïs in Boiotia.

<u>Peloponnese,</u>
<u>we'll form an alliance and save the States of Greece!</u>

KLEONIKE:

Us? Be practical. Wisdom from women? There's nothing
cosmic about cosmetics—and Glamor is our only talent.
All we can do is *sit*, primped and painted,
made up and dressed up,

   (Getting carried away in spite of her argument.)

                              ravishing in saffron wrappers,
peekaboo peignoirs, exquisite negligees, those chic,
expensive little slippers that come from the East . . .

LYSISTRATA:

Exactly. You've hit it. I see our way to salvation
in just such ornamentation—in slippers and slips, rouge
and perfumes, negligees and décolletage. . . .

KLEONIKE:

                                             How so?

LYSISTRATA:

So effectively that not one husband will take up his spear
against another

KLEONIKE:

                   Peachy!
                         I'll have that kimono
dyed . . .

LYSISTRATA:

       . . . or shoulder his shield . . .

KLEONIKE:

                                   squeeze into that
daring negligee . . .

LYSISTRATA:

       . . . or unsheathe his sword!

KLEONIKE:

                                 . . . and buy those
slippers!

LYSISTRATA:

Well, now. Don't you think the girls should be here?

KLEONIKE:

Be here? Ages ago—they should have flown!

(She stops.)

But no. You'll find out. These are authentic Athenians:
no matter what they do, they do it late.

LYSISTRATA:

But what about the out-of-town delegations? There isn't
a woman here from the Shore; none from Salamis . . .

KLEONIKE:

That's quite a trip. They usually get on board
at sunup. Probably riding at anchor now.

LYSISTRATA:

I thought the girls from Acharnai would be here first.
I'm especially counting on them. And they're not here.

KLEONIKE:

I think Theogenes' wife is under way.
When I went by, she was hoisting her sandals . . .[1]

(Looking off right.)

But look!

Some of the girls are coming!

*(Women enter from the right. Lysistrata looks off to the left
where more—a ragged lot—are straggling in.)*

LYSISTRATA:

And more over here!

KLEONIKE:

Where did you find *that* group?

---

[1]This rendering follows, with Coulon, Van Leeuwen's emendation at 64—τἀκάτειον
"sail"—while suggesting that the pun plays on the unmetrical reading of the Ravennas,
τἀκάτιον "skiff," as a name applied to a woman's shoe. It is tempting to return
to an old proposal of Biset and read τἀκάτιον ἀνήρετο.

LYSISTRATA:

> They're from the outskirts.[1]

KLEONIKE:

Well, that's something. If you haven't done anything
else, you've really ruffled up the outskirts.

(Myrrhine enters guiltily from the right.)

MYRRHINE:

> Oh, Lysistrata,

we aren't late, are we?
> Well, *are* we?
> > Speak to me!

LYSISTRATA:

What is it, Myrrhine? Do you want a medal for tardiness?
Honestly, such behavior, with so much at stake . . .

MYRRHINE:

I'm sorry. I couldn't find my girdle in the dark.
And anyway, we're here now. So tell us all about it,
whatever it is.

KLEONIKE:

> No, wait a minute. Don't

begin just yet. Let's wait for those girls from Thebes
and the Peloponnese.

LYSISTRATA:

> Now *there* speaks the proper attitude.

*(Lampito, a strapping Spartan woman, enters left, leading a
pretty Boiotian girl [Ismenia] and a huge, steatopygous
Korinthian.)*

And here's our lovely Spartan.
> Hel*lo*, Lampito

dear.

---

[1]Literally, "from Anagyrous," a rural deme of Attika which took its name from the
plant *anagyros* "the stinking bean-trefoil." Kleonike's riposte puns on this by
reference to an old proverb: "Well, the *anagyros* certainly seems to have been
disturbed" = "you've really stirred up a stink" = "the fat's in the fire." Here, as often
when geographical names are involved, it is more important to render the fact of a pun
than the specifics of the original.

Why darling, you're simply ravishing! Such
a blemishless complexion—so clean, so out-of-doors!
And will you look at that figure—the pink of perfection!

KLEONIKE:

I'll bet you could strangle a bull.

LAMPITO:

I calklate so.[1]
Hit's fitness whut done it, fitness and dancin'. You know
the step?

(Demonstrating.)

Foot it out back'ards an' toe your twitchet.

(The women crowd around Lampito.)

KLEONIKE:

What unbelievably beautiful bosoms!

LAMPITO:

Shuckins,
whut fer you tweedlin' me up so? I feel like a heifer
come fair-time.

LYSISTRATA:

(Turning to Ismenia.)

And who is this young lady here?

LAMPITO:

Her kin's purt-near the bluebloodiest folk in Thebes—
the First Fam'lies of Boiotia.

LYSISTRATA:

(As they inspect Ismenia.)

Ah, picturesque Boiotia:
her verdant meadows, her fruited plain . . .

---

[1]In employing a somewhat debased American mountain dialect to render the Laconic
Greek of Lampito and her countrymen, I have tried to evoke something like the
Athenian attitude toward their perennial enemies. They regarded the Spartans as
formidably old-fashioned bumpkins, imperfectly civilized, possessed of a determined
indifference to more modern value systems.

KLEONIKE:

(Peering more closely.)

Her sunken
garden where no grass grows. A cultivated country.

LYSISTRATA:

(Gaping at the gawking Korinthian.)

And who is *this*—er—little thing?

LAMPITO:

She hails
from over by Korinth, but her kinfolk's quality—mighty
big back there.

KLEONIKE:

(On her tour of inspection.)

She's mighty big back *here*.

LAMPITO:

The womenfolk's all assemblied. Who-all's notion
was this-hyer confabulation?

LYSISTRATA:

Mine.

LAMPITO:

Git on with the give-out.
I'm hankerin' to hear.

MYRRHINE:

Me, too! I can't imagine
what could be so important. Tell us about it!

LYSISTRATA:

Right away.
—But first, a question. It's not
an involved one. Answer yes or no.

(A pause.)

MYRRHINE:

Well, ASK it!

LYSISTRATA:

It concerns the fathers of your children—your husbands,
absent on active service. I know you all have men
abroad.
          —Wouldn't you like to have them home?

KLEONIKE:

My husband's been gone for the last five months! Way up
to Thrace, watchdogging military waste.[1] It's horrible!

MYRRHINE:

Mine's been posted to Pylos for seven whole months!

LAMPITO:

My man's no sooner rotated out of the line
than he's plugged back in. Hain't no discharge in this
     war!

KLEONIKE:

And lovers can't be had for love or money,
not even synthetics. Why, since those beastly Milesians
revolted and cut off the leather trade, that handy
do-it-yourself kit's *vanished* from the open market!

LYSISTRATA:

If I can devise a scheme for ending the war,
I gather I have your support?

KLEONIKE:

                    You can count on me!
If you need money, I'll pawn the shift off my back—
     (Aside.)
and drink up the cash before the sun goes down.

MYRRHINE:

Me, too! I'm ready to split myself right up
the middle like a mackerel, and give you half!

LAMPITO:

Me, too! I'd climb Taÿgetos Mountain plumb
to the top to git the leastes' peek at Peace!

LYSISTRATA:

Very well, I'll tell you. No reason to keep a secret.

[1]Or perhaps treason. The Greek refers to a General Eukrates, who may be the brother of the
illustrious and ill-starred Nikias. If so, he was put to death by the Thirty Tyrants in 404.

(Importantly, as the women cluster around her.)

We can force our husbands to negotiate Peace,
Ladies, by exercising steadfast Self-Control—
By Total Abstinence . . .

(A pause.)

KLEONIKE:

From WHAT?

MYRRHINE:

Yes, what?

LYSISTRATA:

You'll do it?

KLEONIKE:

Of course we'll do it! We'd even *die!*

LYSISTRATA:

Very well,
then here's the program:
Total Abstinence
from SEX!

(The cluster of women dissolves.)

—Why are you turning away? Where are you going?

(Moving among the women.)

—What's this? Such stricken expressions! Such gloomy
gestures!
—Why so pale?
—Whence these tears?
—What IS this?
Will you do it or won't you?
Cat got your tongue?

KLEONIKE:

Afraid I can't make it. Sorry.
On with the War!

MYRRHINE:

Me neither. Sorry.
On with the War!

LYSISTRATA:

This from
my little mackerel? The girl who was ready, a minute
ago, to split herself right up the middle?

KLEONIKE:

(Breaking in between Lysistrata and Myrrhine.)

Try something else. Try anything. If you say so,
I'm willing to walk through fire barefoot.
                                      But not
to give up SEX—there's nothing like it, Lysistrata!

LYSISTRATA:

(To Myrrhine.)

And you?

MYRRHINE:

Mé, too! I'll walk through fire.

LYSISTRATA:

Women!
Utter sluts, the entire sex! Willpower,
nil. We're perfect raw material for Tragedy,
the stuff of heroic lays. "Go to bed with a god
and then get rid of the baby"—that sums us up!

(Turning up Lampito.)

—Oh, Spartan, be a dear. If *you* stick by me,
just you, we still may have a chance to win.
Give me your vote.

LAMPITO:

Hit's right onsettlin' fer gals
to sleep all lonely-like, withouten no humpin'.
But I'm on yore side. We shore need Peace, too.

LYSISTRATA:

You're a darling—the only woman here
worthy of the name!

KLEONIKE:

Well, just suppose we *did*,
as much as possible, abstain from . . . what you said,
you know—not that we *would*—could something like
that bring Peace any sooner?

LYSISTRATA:

           Certainly. Here's how it works:
We'll paint, powder, and pluck ourselves to the last
detail, and stay inside, wearing those filmy
tunics that set off everything we *have*—
                      and then
slink up to the men. They'll snap to attention, go
absolutely *mad* to love us—
                but we won't let them. We'll Abstain.
—I imagine they'll conclude a treaty rather quickly.

LAMPITO:

  (Nodding.)

Menelaos he tuck one squint at Helen's bubbies
all nekkid, and plumb throwed up.

  (Pause for thought.)

                 Throwed up his sword.

KLEONIKE:

Suppose the men just leave us flat?

LYSISTRATA:

                 In that case,
we'll have to take things into our own hands.

KLEONIKE:

There simply isn't any reasonable facsimile!
—Suppose they take us by force and drag us off
to the bedroom against our wills?

LYSISTRATA:

                 Hang on to the door.

KLEONIKE:

Suppose they beat us?

LYSISTRATA

          Give in—but be bad sports.
Be nasty about it—they don't enjoy these forced
affairs. So make them suffer.
            Don't worry; they'll stop
soon enough. A married man wants harmony—
cooperation, not rape.

KLEONIKE:

Well, I suppose so. . . .

(Looking from Lysistrata to Lampito.)

If *both* of you approve this, then so do we.

LAMPITO:

Hain't worried over our menfolk none. We'll bring 'em
round to makin' a fair, straightfor'ard Peace
withouten no nonsense about it. But take this rackety
passel in Athens: I misdoubt no one could make 'em
give over thet blabber of theirn.

LYSISTRATA:

They're our concern.
Don't worry. We'll bring them around.

LAMPITO:

Not likely.
Not long as they got ships kin still sail straight,
an' thet fountain of money up thar in Athene's temple.[1]

LYSISTRATA:

That point is quite well covered:
We're taking over
the Akropolis, including Athene's temple, today.
It's set: Our oldest women have their orders.
They're up there now, pretending to sacrifice, waiting
for us to reach an agreement. As soon as we do,
they seize the Akropolis.

LAMPITO:

The way you put them thengs,
I swear I can't see how we kin possibly lose!

LYSISTRATA:

Well, now that it's settled, Lampito, let's not lose
any time. Let's take the Oath to make this binding.

LAMPITO:

Just trot out thet-thar Oath. We'll swear it.

[1] In the Opisthodomos, at the back of the Parthenon, was kept the reserve fund of one
thousand silver talents established at the beginning of the War twenty years before.
Since the fund had been dipped into during the previous year, Lampito's expression
constitutes more than a normal exaggeration.

LYSISTRATA:

                                        Excellent.
—Where's a policewoman?

(A huge girl, dressed as a Skythian archer [the Athenian police] with bow and circular shield, lumbers up and gawks.)

                              —What are *you* looking for?

(Pointing to a spot in front of the women.)

Put your shield down here.

(The girl obeys.)

                              No, hollow *up!*

(The girl reverses the shield. Lysistrata looks about brightly.)

—Someone give me the entrails.

(A dubious silence.)

KLEONIKE:

                              Lysistrata, what kind
of an Oath are we supposed to swear?

LYSISTRATA:

                              The Standard.
Aischylos used it in a play, they say—the one where
you slaughter a sheep and swear on a shield.

KLEONIKE:

                                        Lysistrata,
you *do not* swear an Oath for *Peace* on a *shield!*

LYSISTRATA:

What Oath do you want?

   (Exasperated.)

                         Something bizarre and expensive?
A fancier victim—"Take one white horse and
disembowel"?

KLEONIKE:

White horse? The symbolism's too obscure.[1]

---

[1]This sentence may seem a startling expansion of the word *poi* (literally, "Whither?"; here, "What is the point of . . . ?"), but is in a good cause—an attempt to explain and

LYSISTRATA:

> Then how
> do we swear this oath?

KLEONIKE:

> Oh, *I* can tell you
> *that*, if you'll let me.
>   First, we put an enormous
> black cup right here—hollow up, of course.
> Next, into the cup we slaughter a jar of Thasian
> wine, and swear a mighty Oath that we won't . . .
> dilute it with water.

LAMPITO:

> *(To Kleonike.)*
>
>   Let me corngratulate you—
> that were the beatenes' Oath I ever heerd on!

LYSISTRATA:

> *(Calling inside.)*
>
> Bring out a cup and a jug of wine!
>
> *(Two women emerge, the first staggering under the weight of a huge black cup, the second even more burdened with a tremendous wine jar. Kleonike addresses them.)*

KLEONIKE:

>   You darlings!
> What a tremendous display of pottery!
>
> *(Fingering the cup.)*
>
>   A girl
> could get a glow just *holding* a cup like this!
>
> *(She grabs it away from the first woman, who exits.)*

motivate the darkest white horse in literature. The sequence is this: Lysistrata, annoyed at the interruption, sarcastically proposes a gaudy sacrifice; Kleonike, whose mind is proof against sarcasm, points out that it has nothing to do with the matter at hand. For the rationale, I am indebted to Wilamowitz, though he assigned the lines (191–93) differently. Other explanations, in terms of Amazons, genitalia, or lovemaking blueprints, are, albeit venerable, obscure in themselves. One sympathizes with Rogers, who translated, "grey mare."

LYSISTRATA:

(Taking the wine jar from the second serving woman [who exits], she barks at Kleonike.)

Put that down and help me butcher this boar!

(Kleonike puts down the cup, over which she and Lysistrata together hold the jar of wine [the "boar"]. Lysistrata prays.)

> O Mistress Persuasion,
> O Cup of Devotion,
> Attend our invocation:
> Accept this oblation,
> Grant our petition,
> Favor our mission.

(Lysistrata and Kleonike tip up the jar and pour the gurgling wine into the cup. Myrrhine, Lampito, and the others watch closely.)

MYRRHINE:

Such an attractive shade of blood. And the spurt—
pure Art!

LAMPITO:

> Hit shore do smell mighty purty!

(Lysistrata and Kleonike put down the empty wine jar.)

KLEONIKE:

Girls, let me be the first

(Launching herself at the cup.)

> to take the Oath!

LYSISTRATA:

(Hauling Kleonike back.)

You'll have to wait your turn like everyone else.
—Lampito, how do we manage with this mob?

> Cumbersome.

—Everyone place her right hand on the cup.

(The women surround the cup and obey.)

I need a spokeswoman. One of you to take
the Oath in behalf of the rest.

(The women edge away from Kleonike, who reluctantly finds herself elected.)

The rite will conclude with a General Pledge of Assent by all of you, thus confirming the Oath. Understood?

(Nods from the women. Lysistrata addresses Kleonike.)

Repeat after me:

LYSISTRATA:

I will withhold all rights of access or entrance

KLEONIKE:

I will withhold all rights of access or entrance

LYSISTRATA:

From every husband, lover, or casual acquaintance

KLEONIKE:

from every husband, lover, or casual acquaintance

LYSISTRATA:

Who moves in my direction in erection.
—Go on.

KLEONIKE:

who m-moves in my direction in erection.
Ohhhhh!
—Lysistrata, my knees are shaky. Maybe I'd better . . .

LYSISTRATA:

I will create, imperforate in cloistered chastity,

KLEONIKE:

I will create, imperforate in cloistered chastity,

LYSISTRATA:

A newer, more glamorous, supremely seductive me

KLEONIKE:

a newer, more glamorous, supremely seductive me

LYSISTRATA:

And fire my husband's desire with my molten allure—

KLEONIKE:

and fire my husband's desire with my molten allure—

LYSISTRATA:

But remain, to his panting advances, icily pure.

KLEONIKE:

but remain, to his panting advances, icily pure.

LYSISTRATA:

If he should force me to share the connubial couch,

KLEONIKE:

If he should force me to share the connubial couch,

LYSISTRATA:

I refuse to return his stroke with the teeniest twitch.

KLEONIKE:

I refuse to return his stroke with the teeniest twitch.

LYSISTRATA:

I will not lift my slippers to touch the thatch

KLEONIKE:

I will not lift my slippers to touch the thatch

LYSISTRATA:

Or submit sloping prone in a hangdog crouch.

KLEONIKE:

or submit sloping prone in a hangdog crouch.

LYSISTRATA:

> **If I this oath maintain,**
> **may I drink this glorious wine.**

KLEONIKE:

> *If I this oath maintain,*
> *may I drink this glorious wine.*

LYSISTRATA:

> **But if I slip or falter,**
> **let me drink water.**

KLEONIKE:

> *But if I slip or falter,*
> *let me drink water.*

LYSISTRATA:

—And now the General Pledge of Assent:

WOMEN:

A-MEN!

LYSISTRATA:

Good. I'll dedicate the oblation.

(She drinks deeply.)

KLEONIKE:

Not too much,
darling. You know how anxious we are to become
allies and friends.
Not to mention *staying* friends.

*(She pushes Lysistrata away and drinks. As the women take
their turns at the cup, loud cries and alarums are heard
offstage.)*

LAMPITO:

What-all's that bodacious ruckus?

LYSISTRATA:

Just what I told you:
It means the women have taken the Akropolis. Athene's
Citadel is ours!
It's time for you to go,
Lampito, and set your affairs in order in Sparta.

(Indicating the other women in Lampito's group.)

Leave these girls here as hostages.

(Lampito exits left. Lysistrata turns to the others.)

Let's hurry inside
the Akropolis and help the others shoot the bolts.

KLEONIKE:

Don't you think the men will send reinforcements
against us as soon as they can?

LYSISTRATA:

So where's the worry?
The men can't burn their way in or frighten us out.
The Gates are ours—they're proof against fire and fear—
and they open only on our conditions.

KLEONIKE:

Yes!
That's the spirit—let's deserve our reputations:

(As the women hurry off into the Akropolis.)

UP THE SLUTS!
WAY FOR THE OLD IMPREGNABLES!

(The door shuts behind the women, and the stage is empty. A pause, and the Chorus of Men shuffles on from the left in two groups, led by their Koryphaios. They are incredibly aged Athenians; though they may acquire spryness later in the play, at this point they are sheer decrepitude. Their normally shaky progress is impeded by their burdens: each man not only staggers under a load of wood across his shoulders, but has his hands full as well—in one, an earthen pot containing fire [which is in constant danger of going out]; in the other, a dried vinewood torch, not yet lit. Their progress toward the Akropolis is very slow.)

KORYPHAIOS OF MEN:

(To the right guide of the First Semichorus, who is stumbling along in mild agony.)

Forward, Swifty, keep 'em in step! Forget your shoulder.
I know these logs are green and heavy—but duty, boy, duty!

SWIFTY:

(Somewhat inspired, he quavers into slow song to set a pace for his group.)

>   I'm never surprised. At my age, life
>   is just one damned thing after another.
>   And yet, I never thought my wife
>   was anything more than a home-grown bother.
>   But now, dadblast her,
>   she's a National Disaster!

FIRST SEMICHORUS OF MEN:

>   What a catastrophe—
>   MATRIARCHY!
>   They've brought Athene's statue[1] to heel,
>   they've put the Akropolis under a seal,

---

[1] Not one of Pheidias' colossal statues, but the old wooden figure of Athene Polias ("Guardian of the City") in the Erechtheion.

they've copped the whole damned commonweal . . .
What is there left for them to steal?

KORYPHAIOS OF MEN:

*(To the right guide of the Second Semichorus—a slower soul,
if possible, than Swifty.)*

Now, Chipper, speed's the word. The Akropolis, on the
     double!
Once we're there, we'll pile these logs around them, and
     convene
a circuit court for a truncated trial. Strictly impartial:
With a show of hands, we'll light a spark of justice under
every woman who brewed this scheme. We'll burn them
     all
on the first ballot—and the first to go is Ly . . .

(Pause for thought.)

                                        is Ly . . .

(Remembering and pointing at a spot in the audience.)

is *Lykon's* wife—and there she is, right over there![1]

CHIPPER:

(Taking up the song again.)

          I won't be twitted, I won't be guyed,
          I'll teach these women not to trouble us!
          Kleomenes the Spartan tried
          expropriating our Akropolis[2]
               some time ago—
               ninety-five years or so—

SECOND SEMICHORUS OF MEN:

          but he suffered damaging losses
          when he ran across US!

---

[1] I have given the Koryphaios a bad memory and placed the object of his anger in the audience to point up what is happening. Rhodia, wife of the demagogue Lykon, was a real person, frequently lampooned for her morals. In a not unusual breaking of the dramatic illusion, her name occurs here as a surprise for the expected "Lysistrata." Some commentators, disliking surprises, have decided that Lysistrata is the wife of someone named Lykon—thus managing to ruin a joke and import an obscurity without the change of a word.

[2] Kleomenes' occupation of the Akropolis in 508, high point of his unsuccessful bid to help establish the Athenian aristocrats, lasted rather less than the six years which the Chorus seems to remember. The actual time was two days.

He breathed defiance—and more as well:
No bath for six years—you could tell.
We fished him out of the Citadel
and quelled his spirit—but not his smell.

KORYPHAIOS OF MEN:

That's how I took him. A savage siege:
                                        Seventeen ranks
of shields were massed at that gate, with blanket infantry
    cover.
I slept like a baby.
                    So when mere women (who gall the gods
and make Euripides sick) try the same trick, should I
sit idly by?
            Then demolish the monument I won at Marathon!

FIRST SEMICHORUS OF MEN:

  (Singly.)

            —The last lap of our journey!
            —I greet it with some dismay.
            —The danger doesn't deter me,
                                        —but
it's uphill
        —all the way.
—Please, somebody,
                —find a jackass
        to drag these logs
                        —to the top.
        —I ache to join the fracas,
                                —but
        my shoulder's aching
                        —to stop.

SWIFTY:

            Backward there's no turning.
            Upward and onward, men!
            And keep those firepots burning, or
            we make this trip again.

CHORUS OF MEN:

  *(Blowing into their firepots, which promptly send forth clouds
  of smoke.)*

                With a puff (pfffff). . . .
                and a cough (hhhhhh). . . .

The smoke! I'll choke! Turn it off.

SECOND SEMICHORUS OF MEN:

(Singly.)

    —Damned embers.

              —Should be muzzled.

—There oughta be a law.

—They jumped me

         —when I whistled

             —and then

they gnawed my eyeballs

         —raw.

—There's lava in my lashes.

—My lids are oxidized.

—My brows are braised.

         —These ashes are

volcanoes

     —in disguise.

CHIPPER:

    This way, men. And remember,
    The Goddess needs our aid.
    So don't be stopped by cinders. Let's
    press on to the stockade!

CHORUS OF MEN:

(Blowing again into their firepots, which erupt as before.)

    With a huff (hfffff). . . .
    and a chuff (chffff). . . .
    Drat that smoke. Enough is enough!

KORYPHAIOS OF MEN:

(Signaling the Chorus, which has now tottered into position before the Akropolis gate, to stop, and peering into his firepot.)

Praise be to the gods, it's awake. There's fire in the old
    fire yet.

—Now the directions. See how they strike you:

                     First, we deposit

these logs at the entrance and light our torches. Next, we
    crash

the gate. When that doesn't work, we request admission.
    Politely.

When *that* doesn't work, we burn the damned door
  down, and smoke
these women into submission.
                              That seem acceptable? Good.
Down with the load . . . ouch, that smoke! Sonofabitch!

*(A horrible tangle results as the Chorus attempts to deposit the
logs. The Koryphaios turns to the audience.)*

Is there a general in the house? We have a logistical
problem. . . .

(No answer. He shrugs.)

Same old story. Still at loggerheads over in Samos.[1]

(With great confusion, the logs are placed somehow.)

That's better. The pressure's off. I've got my backbone back.

(To his firepot.)

What, pot? You forgot your part in the plot?
                              Urge that smudge
to be hot on the dot and scorch my torch.
                              Got it, pot?

(Praying.)

              Queen Athene, let these strumpets
              crumple before our attack.
              Grant us victory, male supremacy . . .
              and a testimonial plaque.

*(The men plunge their torches into firepots and arrange them-
selves purposefully before the gate. Engaged in their prepara-
tions, they do not see the sudden entrance, from the right, of
the Chorus of Women, led by their Koryphaios. These wear
long cloaks and carry pitchers of water. They are very old—
though not so old as the men—but quite spry. In their turn,
they do not perceive the Chorus of Men.)*

KORYPHAIOS OF WOMEN:

(Stopping suddenly.)

What's this—soot? And smoke as well? I may be all wet,

·[1]Most of the Athenian fleet was at the moment based in Samos, practically the only
Ionian ally left to Athens, in order to make ready moves against those states who had
defected to Sparta in 412 after the Sicilian fiasco.

but this might mean fire. Things look dark, girls; we'll
have to dash.

*(They move ahead, at a considerably faster pace than the
men.)*

FIRST SEMICHORUS OF WOMEN:

(Singly.)

Speed! Celerity!	Save our sorority
from arson. Combustion.	And heat exhaustion.
Don't let our sisterhood	shrivel to blisterhood.

    Fanned into slag by hoary typhoons.
    By flatulent, nasty, gusty baboons.
      We're late! Run!
      The girls might be done!

(Tutte.)

Filling my pitcher	was absolute torture:
The fountains in town	are so *crowded* at dawn,
glutted with masses	of the lower classes
blatting and battering,	shoving, and shattering
jugs. But I juggled	my burden, and wriggled
away to extinguish	the igneous anguish

    of neighbor, and sister, and daughter—
      Here's Water!

SECOND SEMICHORUS OF WOMEN:

(Singly.)

Get wind of the news?	The gaffers are loose.
The blowhards are off	with fuel enough
to furnish a bathhouse.	But the finish is pathos:

    They're scaling the heights with a horrid proposal.
    They're threatening women with rubbish disposal!
      How ghastly—how gauche!
      Burned up with the trash!

(Tutte.)

Preserve me, Athene,	from gazing on any
matron or maid	auto-da-fé'd.
Cover with grace	these redeemers of Greece
from battles, insanity,	Man's inhumanity.
Gold-browed goddess,	hither to aid us!
Fight as our ally,	join in our sally

    against pyromaniac slaughter—
      Haul Water!

KORYPHAIOS OF WOMEN:

(Noticing for the first time the Chorus of Men, still busy at their firepots, she cuts off a member of her Chorus who seems about to continue the song.)

Hold it. What have we here? You don't catch true-blue patriots red-handed. These are authentic degenerates, male, taken *in flagrante*.

KORYPHAIOS OF MEN:

                    Oops. Female troops. This could be upsetting. I didn't expect such a flood of reserves.

KORYPHAIOS OF WOMEN:

                              Merely a spearhead. If our numbers stun you, watch that yellow streak spread. We represent just one percent of one percent of This Woman's Army.

KORYPHAIOS OF MEN:

Never been confronted with such backtalk. Can't allow it. Somebody pick up a log and pulverize that brass.
                                        Any volunteers?

(There are none among the male chorus.)

KORYPHAIOS OF WOMEN:

Put down the pitchers, girls. If they start waving that lumber, we don't want to be encumbered.

KORYPHAIOS OF MEN:

                              Look, men, a few sharp jabs will stop that jawing. It never fails.
                    The poet Hipponax swears by it.[1]

(Still no volunteers. The Koryphaios of Women advances.)

KORYPHAIOS OF WOMEN:

                    Then step right up. Have a jab at me. Free shot.

[1]The Greek refers to one Boupalos, a Chian sculptor mercilessly lampooned by the testy poet until, as a doubtful tradition has it, he hanged himself. The only surviving verse of Hipponax which bears on the subject ("Hold my clothes; I'll sock Boupalos in the jaw") does little to establish the tradition—or, indeed, to dispel the feeling that Hipponax was about as effective a boxer as the Koryphaios.

KORYPHAIOS OF MEN:

>*(Advancing reluctantly to meet her.)*

>>Shut up! I'll peel your pelt. I'll pit your pod.

KORYPHAIOS OF WOMEN:

The name is Stratyllis. I dare you to lay one finger on me.

KORYPHAIOS OF MEN:

I'll lay on you with a fistful. Er—any specific threats?

KORYPHAIOS OF WOMEN:

>*(Earnestly.)*

I'll crop your lungs and reap your bowels, bite by bite,
and leave no balls on the body for other bitches to
gnaw.[1]

KORYPHAIOS OF MEN:

>*(Retreating hurriedly.)*

Can't beat Euripides for insight. And I quote:

>>>>*No creature's found*

so lost to shame as Woman.[2]

>>>>Talk about realist playwrights!

KORYPHAIOS OF WOMEN:

Up with the water, ladies. Pitchers at the ready, place!

KORYPHAIOS OF MEN:

Why the water, you sink of iniquity? More sedition?

KORYPHAIOS OF WOMEN:

Why the fire, you walking boneyard? Self-cremation?

KORYPHAIOS OF MEN:

I brought this fire to ignite a pyre and fricassee your
friends.

KORYPHAIOS OF WOMEN:

I brought this water to douse your pyre. Tit for tat.

[1] I here adopt John Jackson's transposition of line 363 to follow 367 (*Marginalia Scaenica*, p. 108).

[2] The observation is clearly offered as an illustrative quotation, and the sentiment is certainly Euripidean. But the extant tragic line nearest it in expression is Sophokles *Elektra* 622.

KORYPHAIOS OF MEN:

You'll douse my fire? Nonsense!

KORYPHAIOS OF WOMEN:

You'll see, when the facts soak in.

KORYPHAIOS OF MEN:

I have the torch right here. Perhaps I should barbecue *you.*

KORYPHAIOS OF WOMEN:

If you have any soap, I could give you a bath.

KORYPHAIOS OF MEN:

A bath from those polluted hands?

KORYPHAIOS OF WOMEN:

Pure enough for a blushing young bridegroom.

KORYPHAIOS OF MEN:

Enough of that insolent lip.

KORYPHAIOS OF WOMEN:

It's merely freedom of speech.

KORYPHAIOS OF MEN:

I'll stop that screeching!

KORYPHAIOS OF WOMEN:

You're helpless outside of the jury-box.

KORYPHAIOS OF MEN:

(Urging his men, torches at the ready, into a charge.)
Burn, fire, burn!

KORYPHAIOS OF WOMEN:

(As the women empty their pitchers over the men.)
And cauldron bubble.

KORYPHAIOS OF MEN:

(Like his troops, soaked and routed.)
Arrrgh!

KORYPHAIOS OF WOMEN:

/ Goodness.
What seems to be the trouble? Too hot?

KORYPHAIOS OF MEN:

Hot, hell! Stop it!
What do you think you're doing?

KORYPHAIOS OF WOMEN:

If you must know, I'm gardening.
Perhaps you'll bloom.

KORYPHAIOS OF MEN:

Perhaps I'll fall right off the vine!
I'm withered, frozen, shaking . . .

KORYPHAIOS OF WOMEN:

Of course. But, providentially,
you brought along your smudgepot.
The sap should rise eventually.

(Shivering, the Chorus of Men retreats in utter defeat.)

(A Commissioner of Public Safety[1] enters from the left, fol-
lowed quite reluctantly by a squad of police—four Skythian
archers. He surveys the situation with disapproval.)

COMMISSIONER:

Fire, eh? Females again—spontaneous combustion
of lust. Suspected as much.
Rubadubdubbing, incessant
incontinent keening for wine, damnable funeral
foofaraw for Adonis resounding from roof to roof—
heard it all before . . .

(Savagely, as the Koryphaios of Men tries to interpose a
remark.)

---

[1]That is, a *proboulos*, one of the ten extraordinary Athenian officials appointed in 413
after the Sicilian catastrophe as a check on legislative excesses. Chiefly responsible for
drafting the agenda of Senate and Assembly, the commissioners were drawn from men
over forty years of age. The two whose names we know were well along: Hagnon was
over sixty, Sophokles (if the poet is meant, a matter not absolutely settled) eighty-two.
But these instances scarcely prove Wilamowitz' contention that decrepitude was a
necessary qualification for the office; and Aristophanes' Commissioner, for all his
choleric conservatism, is marked by vigor and intellectual curiosity.

and WHERE?
                        The ASSEMBLY!
Recall, if you can, the debate on the Sicilian Question:
That bullbrained demagogue Demostratos (who will rot,
  I trust)
rose to propose a naval task force.
                        His wife,
writhing with religion on a handy roof, bleated
a dirge:
        "BEREFT! OH WOE OH WOE FOR ADONIS!"
And so of course Demostratos, taking his cue,
outblatted her:
        "A DRAFT! ENROLL THE WHOLE OF
  ZAKYNTHOS!"
His wife, a smidgin stewed, renewed her yowling:
"OH GNASH YOUR TEETH AND BEAT YOUR
BREASTS FOR ADONIS!"
And so of course Demostratos (that god-detested blot,
that foul-lunged son of an ulcer) gnashed tooth and nail
and voice, and bashed and rammed his program through.
And THERE is the Gift of Women:
                        MORAL CHAOS!

KORYPHAIOS OF MEN:

Save your breath for actual felonies, Commissioner;
see what's happened to us! Insolence, insults,
these we pass over, but not lese-majesty:
                        We're flooded
with indignity from those bitches' pitchers—like a bunch
of weak-bladdered brats. Our cloaks are sopped. We'll
sue!

COMMISSIONER:

Useless. Your suit won't hold water. Right's on their side.
For female depravity, gentlemen, WE stand guilty—
we, their teachers, preceptors of prurience, accomplices
before the fact of fornication. We sowed them in sexual
license, and now we reap rebellion.
                        The proof?
Consider. Off we trip to the goldsmith's to leave
an order:
        "That bangle you fashioned last spring for my wife
is sprung. She was thrashing around last night, and the
  prong

popped out of the bracket. I'll be tied up all day—I'm
boarding the ferry right now—but my wife'll be home.
If you get the time, please stop by the house in a bit
and see if you can't do something—anything—to fit
a new prong into the bracket of her bangle.''

                                                    And bang.
Another one ups to a cobbler—young, but no apprentice,
full kit of tools, ready to give his awl—
and delivers this gem:

                        ''My wife's new sandals are tight.
The cinch pinches her pinkie right where she's
    sensitive.
Drop in at noon with something to stretch her cinch
and give it a little play.''

                                        And a cinch it is.
Such hanky-panky we have to thank for today's
Utter Anarchy: I, a Commissioner of Public
Safety, duly invested with extraordinary powers
to protect the State in the Present Emergency, have
    secured
a source of timber to outfit our fleet and solve
the shortage of oarage. I need the money immediately . . .
and WOMEN, no less, have locked me out of the
    Treasury!

    (Pulling himself together.)

—Well, no profit in standing around.

    (To one of the archers.)

                                        Bring
the crowbars. I'll jack these women back on their
pedestals!
    —WELL, you slack-jawed jackass? What's the
attraction? Wipe that thirst off your face. I said *crow*bar,
not saloon!—All right, men, all together. Shove those
bars underneath the gate and HEAVE!

    (Grabbing up a crowbar.)

                                        I'll take this side.
And now let's root them out, men, ROOT them out.
One, Two . . .

    *(The gates to the Akropolis burst open suddenly, disclosing
    Lysistrata. She is perfectly composed and bears a large spin-
    dle. The Commissioner and the Police fall back in consternation.)*

LYSISTRATA:

> Why the moving equipment?
> I'm quite well motivated, thank you, and here I am.
> Frankly, you don't need crowbars nearly so much as brains.

COMMISSIONER:

Brains? O name of infamy! Where's a policeman?

(He grabs wildly for the First Archer and shoves him toward Lysistrata.)

Arrest that woman!
> Better tie her hands behind her.

LYSISTRATA:

By Artemis, goddess of the hunt, if he lays a finger
on me, he'll rue the day he joined the force!

(She jabs the spindle viciously at the First Archer, who leaps, terrified, back to his comrades.)

COMMISSIONER:

What's this—retreat? Never! Take her on the flank.

(The First Archer hangs back. The Commissioner grabs the Second Archer.)

—Help him.
> —Will the two of you kindly TIE HER UP?

(He shoves them toward Lysistrata. Kleonike, carrying a large chamber pot, springs out of the entrance and advances on the Second Archer.)

KLEONIKE:

By Artemis, goddess of the dew,[1] if you so much
as touch her, I'll stomp the shit right out of you!

(The two Archers run back to their group.)

---

[1]That is, Pandrosos, one of the daughters of Athens' legendary King Kekrops. A tutelary divinity in her own right, she had a shrine in the Erechtheion—and was never identified with Artemis. Having said this, I follow in the translation an unprovable theory of Rogers': that *pandrosos* "all-bedewing" just might be an epithet of the moon-goddess, classical antiquity's best-attested virgin, who is otherwise invoked here in three out of four instances.

COMMISSIONER:

Shit? Shameless! Where's another policeman?

(He grabs the Third Archer and propels him toward Kleonike.)

Handcuff *her* first. Can't stand a foul-mouthed female.

(Myrrhine, carrying a large, blazing lamp, appears at the entrance and advances on the Third Archer.)

MYRRHINE:

By Artemis, bringer of light, if you lay a finger
on her, you won't be able to stop the swelling!

(The Third Archer dodges her swing and runs back to the group.)

COMMISSIONER:

Now what? Where's an officer?

(Pushing the Fourth Archer toward Myrrhine.)

                        Apprehend that woman!
I'll see that *somebody* stays to take the blame!

(Ismenia the Boiotian, carrying a huge pair of pincers, appears at the entrance and advances on the Fourth Archer.)

ISMENIA[1]:

By Artemis, goddess of Tauris, if you go near
that girl. I'll rip the hair right out of your head!

(The Fourth Archer retreats hurriedly.)

COMMISSIONER:

What a colossal mess: Athens' Finest—
finished!

(Arranging the Archers.)

       —Now, men, a little *esprit de corps.* Worsted
by women? Drubbed by drabs?
                     Never!
                       Regroup,
reform that thin red line.
               Ready?
              CHARGE!

---

[1] I here assign two lines in Attic Greek (447–48) to a Theban hostage, for no better reason than symmetry.

(He pushes them ahead of him.)

LYSISTRATA:

I warn you. We have four battalions behind us—
full-armed combat infantrywomen, trained
from the cradle . . .

COMMISSIONER:

Disarm them, Officers! Go for the hands!

LYSISTRATA:

(Calling inside the Akropolis.)

MOBILIZE THE RESERVES!

(A horde of women, armed with household articles, begins to pour from the Akropolis.)

Onward, you ladies from hell!
Forward, you market militia, you battle-hardened
bargain hunters, old sales campaigners, grocery
grenadiers, veterans never bested by an overcharge!
You troops of the breadline, doughgirls—

INTO THE FRAY!

Show them no mercy!
Push!
Jostle!
Shove!
Call them nasty names!
Don't be ladylike.

(The women charge and rout the Archers in short order.)

Fall back—don't strip the enemy! The day is ours!

(The women obey, and the Archers run off left. The Commissioner, dazed, is left muttering to himself.)

COMMISSIONER:

Gross ineptitude. A sorry day for the Force.

LYSISTRATA:

Of course. What did you expect? We're not slaves;
we're freeborn Women, and when we're scorned, we're
full of fury. Never Underestimate the Power of a Woman.

COMMISSIONER:

Power? You mean Capacity. I should have remembered
the proverb: *The lower the tavern, the higher the dudgeon.*

KORYPHAIOS OF MEN:

Why cast your pearls before swine, Commissioner? I know
    you're a civil
servant, but don't overdo it. Have you forgotten the bath
they gave us—in public,
                                    fully dressed,
                                                    totally soapless?
Keep rational discourse for *people!*

*(He aims a blow at the Koryphaios of Women, who dodges
and raises her pitcher.)*

KORYPHAIOS OF WOMEN:

                                        I might point out that lifting
one's hand against a neighbor is scarcely civilized
behavior—and entails, for the lifter, a black eye.
                                        I'm really peaceful by nature,
compulsively inoffensive—a perfect doll. My ideal is a
well-bred repose that doesn't even stir up dust . . .

(Swinging at the Koryphaios of Men with the pitcher.)

                                        unless some no-good lowlife
tries to rifle my hive and gets my dander up!

*(The Koryphaios of Men backs hurriedly away, and the Cho-
rus of Men goes into a worried dance.)*

CHORUS OF MEN:

(Singly.)

> O Zeus, what's the use of this constant abuse?
> How do we deal with this female zoo?
> Is there no solution to Total Immersion?
>   What can a poor man DO?

(Tutti.)

> Query the Adversary!
> Ferret out their story!
> What end did they have in view,
> to seize the city's sanctuary,
> snatch its legendary eyrie,
> snare an area so very
>   terribly taboo?

KORYPHAIOS OF MEN:

(To the Commissioner.)

Scrutinize those women! Scour their depositions—assess their
  rebuttals!
Masculine honor demands this affair be probed to the bottom!

COMMISSIONER:

(Turning to the women from the Akropolis.)

All right, you. Kindly inform me, dammit, in your own words:
What possible object could you have had in blockading the
  Treasury?

LYSISTRATA:

We thought we'd deposit the money in escrow and withdraw
  you men
from the war.

COMMISSIONER:

The money's the cause of the war?

LYSISTRATA:

And all our internal
disorders—the Body Politic's chronic bellyaches: What
causes Peisandros' frantic rantings, or the raucous cau-
cuses of the Friends of Oligarchy?[1] The chance for graft.
But now, with the money up there,
they can't upset the City's equilibrium—or lower its balance.

COMMISSIONER:

And what's your next step?

LYSISTRATA:

Stupid question. We'll budget the money.

COMMISSIONER:

You'll budget the money?

LYSISTRATA:

Why should you find that so shocking?
We budget the household accounts, and you don't object at all.

---

[1]This expansion makes more explicit a reference to the political clubs or *synōmosiai*,
who caucussed and combined their votes to gain verdicts and offices, thus paving the
road for the oligarchic upheaval in May of 411.

COMMISSIONER:

That's different.

LYSISTRATA:

Different? How?

COMMISSIONER:

The War Effort needs this money!

LYSISTRATA:

Who needs the War Effort?

COMMISSIONER:

Every patriot who pulses to save
all that Athens holds near and dear . . .

LYSISTRATA:

Oh, *that*. Don't worry.
We'll save you.

COMMISSIONER:

You will save us?

LYSISTRATA:

Who else?

COMMISSIONER:

But this is unscrupulous!

LYSISTRATA:

We'll save you. You can't deter us.

COMMISSIONER:

Scurrilous!

LYSISTRATA:

You seem disturbed.
This makes it difficult. But, still—we'll save you.

COMMISSIONER:

Doubtless illegal!

LYSISTRATA:

We deem it a duty. For friendship's sake.

COMMISSIONER:

Well, forsake this friend:
I DO NOT WANT TO BE SAVED, DAMMIT!

LYSISTRATA:

All the more reason.
It's not only Sparta; now we'll have to save you from you.

COMMISSIONER:

Might I ask where you women conceived this concern about
War and Peace?

LYSISTRATA

(Loftily.)

We shall explain.

COMMISSIONER:

(Making a fist.)

Hurry up, and you won't
get hurt.

LYSISTRATA:

Then *listen*. And do try to keep your hands to yourself.

COMMISSIONER:

(Moving threateningly toward her.)

I can't. Righteous anger forbids restraint, and decrees . . .

KLEONIKE:

(Brandishing her chamber pot.)

Multiple fractures?

COMMISSIONER:

(Retreating.)

Keep those croaks for yourself, you old crow!

(To Lysistrata.)

All right, lady, I'm ready. Speak.

LYSISTRATA:

I shall proceed:
When the War began, like the prudent, dutiful wives that
we are, we tolerated you men, and endured your actions
   in silence. (Small wonder—
   you wouldn't let us say boo.)
                          You were not precisely the answer
to a matron's prayer—we knew you too well, and found
   out more.
Too many times, as we sat in the house, we'd hear that
you'd done it again—manhandled another affair of
state with your usual staggering incompetence. Then,
masking our worry with a nervous laugh,
we'd ask you, brightly, "How was the Assembly today,
   dear? Anything
in the minutes about Peace?" And my husband would
give his stock reply.
"What's that to you? Shut up!" And I did.

KLEONIKE:

   (Proudly.)

                                   I never shut up!

COMMISSIONER:

I trust you were shut up. Soundly.

LYSISTRATA:

                          Regardless, *I* shut up.
And then we'd learn that you'd passed another decree,
fouler than the first, and we'd ask again: "Darling, how
did you manage anything so idiotic?" And my
husband, with his customary glare, would tell me to spin
my thread, or else get a clout on the head.
And of course he'd quote from Homer:
                   Y^e menne must husband ye warre.[1]

COMMISSIONER:

Apt and irrefutably right.

LYSISTRATA:

               Right, you miserable misfit?
To keep us from giving advice while you fumbled the
City away in the Senate? Right, indeed!

[1]*Iliad* 6.492 (Hektor to Andromache).

But this time was really too much:
Wherever we went, we'd hear you engaged in the same
  conversation:
"What Athens needs is a man."[1]
                    "But there isn't a Man in the country."
"You can say that again."
                    There was obviously no time to lose.
We women met in immediate convention and passed a
unanimous resolution: To work in concert for safety and
Peace in Greece. We have valuable advice to impart,
and if you can possibly deign to emulate our silence,
and take your turn as audience, we'll rectify you—
we'll straighten you out and set you right.

COMMISSIONER:

You'll set *us* right? You go too far. I cannot permit
such a statement to . . .

LYSISTRATA:

             Shush.

COMMISSIONER:

                    I categorically decline to shush
for some confounded woman, who wears—as a constant
reminder of congenital inferiority, an injunction to
public silence—a veil!
Death before such dishonor!

LYSISTRATA:

(Removing her veil.)

                    If that's the only obstacle . . .
I feel you need a new panache,
so take the veil, my dear Commissioner, and drape it thus—
                    and SHUSH!

*(As she winds the veil around the startled Commissioner's
head, Kleonike and Myrrhine, with carding-comb and wool-
basket, rush forward and assist in transforming him into a
woman.)* Cross-
          dressing

[1] Traditionally interpreted (perhaps with too much enthusiasm) as a reference to the
longing of the Athenian commonality for the return of glory-and-shame Alkibiades, who
obliged the following summer.

KLEONIKE:

Accept, I pray, this humble comb.

MYRRHINE:

Receive this basket of fleece as well.

LYSISTRATA:

Hike up your skirts, and card your wool,
and gnaw your beans—and stay at home!
    While we rewrite Homer:
    Y^e WOMEN must WIVE ye warre!

*(To the Chorus of Women, as the Commissioner struggles to
remove his new outfit.)*

Women, weaker vessels, arise!
                    Put down your pitchers.
It's our turn, now. Let's supply our friends with some
moral support.

*(The Chorus of Women dances to the same tune as the Men,
but with much more confidence.)*

CHORUS OF WOMEN:

(Singly.)

Oh, yes! I'll dance to bless their success.
Fatigue won't weaken my will. Or my knees.
I'm ready to join in any jeopardy.
    with girls as good as *these!*

(Tutte.)

A tally of their talents
convinces me they're giants
of excellence. To commence:
there's Beauty, Duty, Prudence, Science,
Self-Reliance, Compliance, Defiance,
and Love of Athens in balanced alliance
    with Common Sense!

KORYPHAIOS OF WOMEN:

(To the women from the Akropolis.)

Autochthonous daughters of Attika, sprung from the
soil that bore your mothers, the spiniest, spikiest
nettles known to man, prove your mettle and attack!

Now is no time to dilute your anger. You're
running ahead of the wind!

LYSISTRATA:

We'll wait for the wind
from heaven. The gentle breath of Love and his Kyprian
mother will imbue our bodies with desire, and raise a
storm to tense and tauten these blasted men until they
crack. And soon we'll be on every tongue in
Greece—the *Pacifiers*.[1]

COMMISSIONER:

That's quite
a mouthful. How will you win it?

LYSISTRATA:

First, we intend to withdraw
that crazy Army of Occupation from the downtown
shopping section.

KLEONIKE:

Aphrodite be praised!

LYSISTRATA:

The pottery shop and the grocery stall
are overstocked with soldiers, clanking around like
those maniac Korybants,
armed to the teeth for a battle.

COMMISSIONER:

A Hero is Always Prepared!

LYSISTRATA:

I suppose he is. But it does look silly to shop for sardines
from behind a shield.

KLEONIKE:

I'll second that. I saw
a cavalry captain buy vegetable soup on horseback. He
carried the whole mess home in his helmet.
And then that fellow from Thrace,

---

[1] In the Greek, *Lysimachas* "Battle-settlers," a pun on the name of the heroine; also, if D. M. Lewis is right, a reference to her real-life model Lysimache—in 411, priestess of Athene.

shaking his buckler and spear—a menace straight from
   the stage.
The saleslady was stiff with fright. He was hogging her
   ripe figs—free.

COMMISSIONER:

I admit, for the moment, that Hellas' affairs are in one
hell of a snarl. But how can you set them straight?

LYSISTRATA:

                            Simplicity itself.

COMMISSIONER:

Pray demonstrate.

LYSISTRATA:

                It's rather like yarn. When a hank's in a tangle,
we lift it—*so*—and work out the snarls by winding it up
on spindles, now this way, now that way.
                    That's how we'll wind up the War,
if allowed: We'll work out the snarls by sending Special
   Commissions—
back and forth, now this way, now that way—to ravel
these tense international kinks.

COMMISSIONER:

                 I lost your thread, but I know there's a hitch.
Spruce up the world's disasters with spindles—typically
woolly female logic.

LYSISTRATA:

                If *you* had a scrap of logic, you'd adopt
our wool as a master plan for Athens.

COMMISSIONER:

                      What course of action
does the wool advise?

LYSISTRATA:

                Consider the City as fleece, recently
shorn. The first step is Cleansing: Scrub it in a public
bath, and remove all corruption, offal, and sheepdip.
                    Next, to the couch
for Scutching and Plucking: Cudgel the leeches and

similar vermin loose with a club, then pick the prickles
and cockleburs out. As for the clots—those lumps
that clump and cluster in knots and snarls to snag
important posts[1]—you comb these out,
twist off their heads, and discard.

                      Next, to raise the City's
nap, you card the citizens together in a single basket
of common weal and general welfare. Fold in our loyal
Resident Aliens, all Foreigners of proven and tested
friendship, and any Disenfranchised Debtors. Combine
  these closely with the rest.
Lastly, cull the colonies settled by our own people:
these are nothing but flocks of wool from the City's
fleece, scattered throughout the world. So gather home
these far-flung flocks, amalgamate them with the
  others.

                  Then, drawing this blend
of stable fibers into one fine staple, you spin a mighty
bobbin of yarn—and weave, without bias or seam, a
cloak to clothe the City of Athens!

COMMISSIONER:

                    This is too much! The City's
died in the wool, worsted by the distaff side—by women
who bore no share in the War. . . .

LYSISTRATA:

                None, you hopeless hypocrite?
The quota we bear is double. First, we delivered our
sons to fill out the front lines in Sicily . . .

COMMISSIONER:

              Don't tax me with that memory.

LYSISTRATA:

Next, the best years of our lives were levied. Top-level
strategy attached our joy, and we sleep alone.
                  But it's not the matrons
like us who matter. I mourn for the virgins, bedded in
single blessedness, with nothing to do but grow old.

---

[1]Most of this rather torturous allegory is self-explanatory, but the "clumps" are the
political clubs, or "Friends of Oligarchy," mentioned earlier.

COMMISSIONER:

Men *have* been known
to age, as well as women.

LYSISTRATA:

No, not as well as—better.
A man, an absolute antique, comes back from the war,
    and he's barely
doddered into town before he's married the veriest
    nymphet.
But a woman's season is brief; it slips, and she'll have
no husband, but sit out her life groping at omens—
    and finding no men.

COMMISSIONER:

Lamentable state of affairs. Perhaps we can rectify
    matters:

(To the audience.[1])

TO EVERY MAN JACK, A CHALLENGE:

ARISE!
Provided you can . . .

LYSISTRATA:

Instead, Commissioner, why not simply curl up and *die?*
            Just buy a coffin; here's the place.

(Banging him on the head with her spindle.[2])

I'll knead you a cake for the wake—and *these*

(Winding the threads from the spindle around him.)

        make excellent wreaths. So Rest In Peace.

KLEONIKE:

(Emptying the chamber pot over him.)

        Accept these tokens of deepest grief.

---

[1]Or, possibly, to the Chorus of Men. I do not accept Van Leeuwen's emendation here
(598), but I do follow him in taking the line to be an interrupted exhortation to all
available and qualified males.

[2]Here and earlier, the women are certainly armed, but with what? The pronouns
supplied by the Greek are tantalizingly specific in gender, but in nothing else; solutions
usually bring out the worst in interpreters. I have tried to assign appropriate weapons
early, and continue them to this denouement—but visualizers (or producers, if any there
be) are at liberty, as elsewhere, to use their imaginations. One caveat: the Greek will not
bear a direct repetition of the bath given earlier to the Old Men by the Old Women.

MYRRHINE:

> *(Breaking her lamp over his head.)*

>> A final garland for the dear deceased.

LYSISTRATA:

>> May I supply any last request?
>> Then run along. You're due at the wharf:
>> Charon's anxious to sail—
>> you're holding up the boat for Hell!

COMMISSIONER:

This is monstrous—maltreatment of a public official—
maltreatment of ME!
>> I must repair directly
to the Board of Commissioners, and present my
colleagues concrete evidence of the sorry specifics of
this shocking attack!

> *(He staggers off left. Lysistrata calls after him.)*

LYSISTRATA:

You won't haul us into court on a charge of neglecting
the dead, will you? (How like a man to insist
on his rights—even his last ones.) Two days between
death and funeral, that's the rule.
>> Come back here early
day after tomorrow, Commissioner:
>> We'll lay you out.

> *(Lysistrata and her women re-enter the Akropolis. The
> Koryphaios of Men advances to address the audience.)*

KORYPHAIOS OF MEN:

Wake up, Athenians! Preserve your freedom—the time
is Now!

> *(To the Chorus of Men.)*

Strip for action, men. Let's cope with the current mess.

> *(The men put off their long mantles, disclosing short tunics
> underneath, and advance toward the audience.)*

CHORUS OF MEN:

This trouble may be terminal; it has a loaded odor,
an ominous aroma of constitutional rot.

My nose gives a prognosis of radical disorder—
  it's just the first installment of an absolutist plot!
      The Spartans are behind it:
      they must have masterminded
some morbid local contacts (engineered by Kleisthenes).
      Predictably infected,
      these women straightway acted
to commandeer the City's cash. They're feverish to freeze
      my be-all,
      my end-all . . .
      my *payroll!*[1]

KORYPHAIOS OF MEN:

The symptoms are clear. Our birthright's already
  nibbled. And oh, so
daintily: WOMEN ticking off troops[2] for improper etiquette.
WOMEN propounding their featherweight views on the
  fashionable use
and abuse of the shield. And (if any more proof were
  needed) WOMEN
nagging us to trust the Nice Spartan, and put our heads
in his toothy maw—to make a dessert and call it Peace.
They've woven the City a seamless shroud, bedecked
  with the legend
DICTATORSHIP.
              But I won't be hemmed in. I'll use
their weapon against them, and uphold the right
  by sneakiness.
              With knyf under cloke,
gauntlet in glove, sword in olive branch,

  (Slipping slowly toward the Koryphaios of Women.)

              I'll take up my post
in Statuary Row, beside our honored National Heroes,
the natural foes of tyranny: Harmodios,
              Aristogeiton,
              and Me.[3]

[1]The *triobolon*, the three-obol per diem wage for jury duty, which often constituted the only income of elderly men. It would naturally be stored inside the Citadel in the Treasury.

[2]Emending πολίτας at 626 to ὁπλίτας.

[3]The reference, to a famous statuary group by the sculptor Kritios in the Athenian Agora, picks up an earlier quotation from a popular *skolion*, or drinking-song, on the assassination of the tyrant Hipparchos: "I'll carry my sword concealed in a myrtle bough. . . ." The translation expands on the idea, but hides the quotation in the familiar "sword in olive branch."

(Next to her.)

Striking an epic pose, so, with the full approval
of the immortal gods,
> I'll bash this loathesome hag in the jaw!

*(He does, and runs cackling back to the Men. She shakes a fist
after him.)*

KORYPHAIOS OF WOMEN:

Mama won't know her little boy when he gets home!

(To the Women, who are eager to launch a full-scale attack.)

Let's not be hasty, fellow . . . hags. Cloaks off first.

*(The Women remove their mantles, disclosing tunics very like
those of the Men, and advance toward the audience.)*

CHORUS OF WOMEN:

We'll address you, citizens, in beneficial, candid,
    patriotic accents, as our breeding says we must,
since, from the age of seven, Athens graced me with a
    splendid string of civic triumphs to signalize her
        trust:
            I was Relic-Girl quite early,
                then advanced to Maid of Barley;
in Artemis' "Pageant of the Bear" I played the lead.
    To cap this proud progression,[1]
    I led the whole procession
at Athene's Celebration, certified and pedigreed
            —that cachet
            so distingué—
            a *Lady!*

KORYPHAIOS OF WOMEN:

(To the audience.)

[1]Since this passage is frequently cited as primary evidence for the *cursus honorum* of a high-born young girl in fifth-century Athens, here are the steps set forth a bit more explicitly: (1) *arrêphoros* ("relic-bearer") to Athene, one of four little girls who carried the Goddess' sacred objects in Her semi-annual festival of the *Arréphoria*; (2) *aletris* ("mill-girl") to the Founding Mother (doubtless Athene), one of the girls who ground the meal to be made into sacrificial cakes; (3) *arktos* ("she-bear") at the *Brauronia*, a festival of Artemis held every fifth year at Brauron in Attika, centering on a myth which told of the killing of a tame bear sacred to that goddess; and (4) *kanêphoros* ("basket-bearer"), the maiden who bore the sacrificial cake and led the procession at Athens' most important festivals, such as the City Dionysia and the Great Panathenaia.

I trust this establishes my qualifications. I may, I take it,
address the City to its profit? Thank you.

              I admit to being a woman—
but don't sell my contribution short on that account.
It's better than the present panic. And my word is as
good as my bond, because I hold stock in Athens—
stock I paid for in sons.

(To the Chorus of Men.)

—But you, you doddering bankrupts, where are your
shares in the State?

(Slipping slowly toward the Koryphaios of Men.)

Your grandfathers willed you the Mutual Funds from
   the Persian War[1]—
and where are they?

(Nearer.)

             You dipped into capital, then lost interest . . .
and now a pool of your assets won't fill a hole in the ground.
All that remains is one last potential killing—Athens.
Is there any rebuttal?

*(The Koryphaios of Men gestures menacingly. She ducks down,
as if to ward off a blow, and removes a slipper.)*

             Force is a footling resort. I'll take
my very sensible shoe, and paste you in the jaw!

(She does so, and runs back to the women.)

CHORUS OF MEN:

             Their native respect for our manhood is small,
             and keeps getting smaller. Let's bottle their gall.
             The man who won't battle has no balls at all!

KORYPHAIOS OF MEN:

All right, men, skin out of the skivvies. Let's give them
a whiff of Man, full strength. No point in muffling
the essential Us.

---

[1]This money originally made up the treasury of the Delian League, an alliance of Greek
states against Persia formed by the Athenian Aristeides in 477; following its transfer, for
safety's sake, from the island of Delos to Athens in 454, it became for all practical
purposes Athenian property, supported by tribute from the Allies. Athens' heavy
expenses in Sicily, followed by the Allies' nonpayment and defection, made this
question all too pointed in early 411.

(The men remove their tunics.)

CHORUS OF MEN:

> A century back, we soared to the Heights[1]
>> and beat down Tyranny there.
> Now's the time to shed our moults
>> and fledge our wings once more,
> to rise to the skies in our reborn force,
>> and beat back Tyranny here!

KORYPHAIOS OF MEN:

No fancy grappling with these grannies; straightforward
    strength. The tiniest
toehold, and those nimble, fiddling fingers will have their
foot in the door, and we're done for.
               No amount of know-how can lick
a woman's knack.
         They'll want to build ships . . . next thing we
    know,
we're all at sea, fending off female boarding parties.
(Artemisia fought us at Salamis. Tell me, has anyone
caught her yet?)
         But we're *really* sunk if they take up horses. Scratch
the Cavalry:
         A woman is an easy rider with a natural seat.
Take her over the jumps bareback, and she'll never slip
her mount. (That's how the Amazons nearly took
    Athens. On horseback.
Check on Mikon's mural down in the Stoa.)
               Anyway,
the solution is obvious. Put every woman in her place—
stick her in the stocks.
         To do this, first snare your woman around the neck.

---

[1] To Leipsydrion, in the mountains north of Athens, where the besieged Alkmaionid exiles held out for a time against the forces of the tyrant Hippias. Since this siege, ever after symbolic of the Noble Lost Cause, took place in 513, commentators find it necessary to point out that the Chorus of Men couldn't *really* have fought in a battle 102 years before; that they are pretending, or speaking by extension for the Athenian Fighting Spirit, or whatever. Seemingly, this goes without saying; actually, it is dead wrong. Dramaturgy has little to do with geriatrics; Aristophanes needed a Chorus of Men old enough to be hidebound, decrepit, so old that they would first see the Women's Revolt, not in terms of sex, but of politics—the recrudescence of a personally experienced tyranny. He was cheerfully prepared to have them average 120 years of age, if anyone cared to count. The critical attitude gives one pause: A modern American playwright who composed a fantastic comedy, set in the present, featuring a Chorus of GAR members—would he be greeted with a flourish of actuarial tables?

(He attempts to demonstrate on the Koryphaios of Women. After a brief tussle, she works loose and chases him back to the Men.)

CHORUS OF WOMEN:

> The beast in me's eager and fit for a brawl.
> Just rile me a bit and she'll kick down the wall.
> You'll bawl to your friends that you've no balls at all.

KORYPHAIOS OF WOMEN:

All right, ladies, strip for action. Let's give them a whiff
of *Femme Enragée*—piercing and pungent, but not at
all tart.

(The women remove their tunics.)

CHORUS OF WOMEN:

> We're angry. The brainless bird who tangles
> with *us* has gummed his last mush.
> In fact, the coot who even heckles
> is being daringly rash.
> So look to your nests, you reclaimed eagles—
> whatever you lay, we'll squash!

KORYPHAIOS OF WOMEN:

Frankly, you don't faze me. *With* me, I have my friends—
Lampito from Sparta; that genteel girl from Thebes,
    Ismenia—
committed to me forever. *Against* me, *you*—permanently
out of commission. So do your damnedest.
                                        Pass a law.
Pass seven. Continue the winning ways that have made
your name a short and ugly household word.
                                        Like yesterday:
I was giving a little party, nothing fussy, to honor
the goddess Hekate. Simply to please my daughters,
I'd invited a sweet little thing from the neighborhood—
    flawless pedigree, perfect
taste, a credit to any gathering—a Boiotian eel.
But she had to decline. Couldn't pass the border. You'd
    passed a law.
Not that you care for my party. You'll overwork your
    right of passage
till your august body is overturned,
                            and you break your silly neck!

(She deftly grabs the Koryphaios of Men by the ankle and upsets him. He scuttles back to the Men, who retire in confusion.)

(Lysistrata emerges from the citadel, obviously distraught.)

KORYPHAIOS OF WOMEN:

(Mock-tragic.)

*Mistress, queen of this our subtle scheme,
why burst you from the hall with brangled brow?*

LYSISTRATA:

*Oh, wickedness of woman! The female mind
does sap my soul and set my wits a-totter.*

KORYPHAIOS OF WOMEN:

What drear accents are these?

LYSISTRATA:

The merest truth.

KORYPHAIOS OF WOMEN:

Be nothing loath to tell the tale to friends.

LYSISTRATA:

'Twere shame to utter, pain to hold unsaid.

KORYPHAIOS OF WOMEN:

Hide not from me affliction which we share.

LYSISTRATA:

In briefest compass,

(Dropping the paratragedy.)

we want to get laid.

KORYPHAIOS OF WOMEN:

By Zeus!

LYSISTRATA:

No, no, not HIM!
Well, that's the way things are.
I've lost my grip on the girls—they're mad for men!
But sly—they slip out in droves.
A minute ago,

I caught one scooping out the little hole
that breaks through just below Pan's grotto.[1]
                                          One
had jerry-rigged some block-and-tackle business
and was wriggling away on a rope.
                              Another just flat
deserted.
          Last night I spied one mounting a sparrow,
all set to take off for the nearest bawdyhouse. I hauled
her back by the hair.
                    And excuses, pretexts for overnight
passes? I've heard them all.
                        Here comes one. Watch.

(To the First Woman, as she runs out of the Akropolis.)

—You, there! What's your hurry?

FIRST WOMAN:

                                  I have to get home.
I've got all this lovely Milesian wool in the house,
and the moths will simply batter it to bits!

LYSISTRATA:

                                      I'll bet.
Get back inside.

FIRST WOMAN:

                      I swear I'll hurry right back!
—Just time enough to spread it out on the couch?

LYSISTRATA:

Your wool will stay unspread. And you'll stay here.

FIRST WOMAN:

Do I have to let my piecework *rot?*

LYSISTRATA:

                            Possibly.

(The Second Woman runs on.)

SECOND WOMAN:

Oh dear, oh goodness, what shall I do—my flax!
I left and forgot to peel it!

[1]A cave on the Akropolis containing a shrine to the god, outside the Citadel wall, which
it adjoined on the northwest.

LYSISTRATA:

Another one.
She suffers from unpeeled flax.
—Get back inside!

SECOND WOMAN:

I'll be right back. I just have to pluck the fibers.

LYSISTRATA:

No. No plucking. You start it, and everyone else
will want to go and do their plucking, too.

(The Third Woman, swelling conspicuously, hurries on, praying loudly.)

THIRD WOMAN:

*O Goddess of Childbirth, grant that I not deliver
until I get me from out this sacred precinct!*

LYSISTRATA:

What sort of nonsense is *this?*

THIRD WOMAN:

I'm due—any second!

LYSISTRATA:

You weren't pregnant yesterday.

THIRD WOMAN:

Today I am—
a miracle!
Let me go home for a midwife, *please!*
I may not make it!

LYSISTRATA:

(Restraining her.)

You can do better than that.

(Tapping the woman's stomach and receiving a metallic clang.)

What's this? It's hard.

THIRD WOMAN:

I'm going to have a boy.

LYSISTRATA:

Not unless he's made of bronze. Let's see.

(She throws open the Third Woman's cloak, exposing a huge bronze helmet.)

Of all the brazen . . . You've stolen the helmet from Athene's statue! Pregnant, indeed!

THIRD WOMAN:

I am *so* pregnant!

LYSISTRATA:

Then why the helmet?

THIRD WOMAN:

I thought my time might come while I was still on forbidden ground. If it did, I could climb inside Athene's helmet and have my baby there.
The pigeons do it all the time.

LYSISTRATA:

Nothing but excuses!

(Taking the helmet.)

This is your baby. I'm afraid you'll have to stay until we give it a name.

THIRD WOMAN:

But the Akropolis is *awful*. I can't even sleep! I saw the snake that guards the temple.

LYSISTRATA:

That snake's a fabrication.[1]

THIRD WOMAN:

I don't care *what* kind it is—I'm *scared!*

(The other women, who have emerged from the citadel, crowd around.)

---

[1] By inserting this speech (and the reply to it) I do not wish to make Lysistrata a religious skeptic, but to point out the joke. No one had ever seen the snake; even its most famous action, that of assisting Themistokles to persuade the Athenians to abandon the city before the battle of Salamis, had been accomplished by its nonappearance.

KLEONIKE

And those goddamned holy owls! All night long,
tu-wit, tu-wu—they're hooting me into my grave!

LYSISTRATA:

Darlings, let's call a halt to this hocus-pocus.
You miss your men—now isn't that the trouble?

(Shamefaced nods from the group.)

Don't you think they miss you just as much?
I can assure you, their nights are every bit
as hard as yours. So be good girls; endure!
Persist a few days more, and Victory is ours.
It's fated: a current prophecy declares that the men
will go down to defeat before us, provided that *we*
maintain a United Front.

(Producing a scroll.)

                    I happen to have
a copy of the prophecy.

KLEONIKE:

             Read it!

LYSISTRATA:

                Silence, *please:*

(Reading from the scroll)

**But when the swallows, in flight from the
    hoopoes, have flocked to a hole
on high, and stoutly eschew their
    accustomed perch on the pole,
yea, then shall Thunderer Zeus to
    their suff'ring establish a stop,
by making the lower the upper . . .**

KLEONIKE:

Then *we'll* be lying on top?

LYSISTRATA:

**But should these swallows, indulging their
    lust for the perch, lose heart,
dissolve their flocks in winged dissension,
    and singly depart
the sacred stronghold, breaking the
    bands that bind them together—**

**then know them as lewd, the pervertedest
    birds that ever wore feather.**

KLEONIKE:

There's nothing obscure about *that* oracle. Ye gods!

LYSISTRATA:

Sorely beset as we are, we must not flag
or falter. So back to the citadel!

(As the women troop inside.)

                                And if we fail
that oracle, darlings, our image is absolutely *mud!*

(She follows them in. A pause, and the Choruses assemble.)

CHORUS OF MEN:

                I have a simple
                tale to relate you,
                a sterling example
                of masculine virtue:

The huntsman bold Melanion
        was once a harried quarry.
The women in town tracked him down
        and badgered him to marry.

        Melanion knew the cornered male
        eventually cohabits.
Assessing the odds, he took to the woods
        and lived by trapping rabbits.

        He stuck to the virgin stand, sustained
        by rabbit meat and hate,
and never returned, but ever remained
        an alfresco celibate.

        Melanion is our ideal;
        his loathing makes us free.
Our dearest aim is the gemlike flame
        of his misogyny.

OLD MAN:

        Let me kiss that wizened cheek . . .

OLD WOMAN:

(Threatening with a fist.)

A wish too rash for that withered flesh.

OLD MAN:

and lay you low with a highflying kick.

(He tries one and misses.)

OLD WOMAN:

Exposing an overgrown underbrush.

OLD MAN:

A hairy behind, historically, means
   masculine force: Myronides
harassed the foe with his mighty mane,
   and furry Phormion swept the seas
     of enemy ships, never meeting his match—
     such was the nature of his thatch.

CHORUS OF WOMEN:

       I offer an anecdote
       for your opinion,
       an adequate antidote
       for your Melanion:

       Timon, the noted local grouch,
       put rusticating hermits
   out of style by building his wilds
       inside the city limits.

       He shooed away society
       with natural battlements:
 his tongue was edged; his shoulder, frigid;
       his beard, a picket fence.

       When random contacts overtaxed him,
       he didn't stop to pack,
 but loaded curses on the male of the species,
       left town, and never came back.

       Timon, you see, was a misanthrope
       in a properly narrow sense:
 his spleen was vented only on men . . .
       we were his dearest friends.

OLD WOMAN:

(Making a fist.)

Enjoy a chop to that juiceless chin?

OLD MAN:

(Backing away.)

I'm jolted already. Thank you, no.

OLD WOMAN:

Perhaps a trip from a well-turned shin?

(She tries a kick and misses.)

OLD MAN:

Brazenly baring the mantrap below.

OLD WOMAN:

At least it's *neat*. I'm not too sorry
to have you see my daintiness.
My habits are still depilatory;
   age hasn't made me a bristly mess.
      Secure in my smoothness, I'm never in doubt—
         though even down is out.

(Lysistrata mounts the platform and scans the horizon. When her gaze reaches the left, she stops suddenly.)

LYSISTRATA:

Ladies, attention! Battle stations, please!
And quickly!

(A general rush of women to the battlements.)

KLEONIKE:

What is it?

MYRRHINE:

What's all the shouting for?

LYSISTRATA:

A MAN!

(Consternation.)

Yes, it's a man. And he's coming this way!
Hmm. Seems to have suffered a seizure. Broken out
with a nasty attack of love.

(Prayer, aside.)

O Aphrodite,
Mistress all-victorious,
mysterious, voluptuous,
you who make the crooked straight . . .
don't let this happen to US!

KLEONIKE:

I don't care who he is—*where is he?*

LYSISTRATA:

(Pointing.)

Down there—
just flanking that temple—Demeter the Fruitful.

KLEONIKE:

My.

Definitely a man.

MYRRHINE:

(Craning for a look.)

I wonder who it can be?

LYSISTRATA:

See for yourselves.—Can anyone identify him?

MYRRHINE:

Oh lord, I can.

That is my husband—Kinesias.[1]

LYSISTRATA:

(To Myrrhine.)

Your duty is clear.

Pop him on the griddle, twist
the spit, braize him, baste him, stew him in his own
juice, do him to a turn. Sear him with kisses,
coyness, caresses, *everything*—

but stop where our Oath

begins.

MYRRHINE:

Relax. I can take care of this.

---

[1] A perfectly good Greek name, but in this context it evokes a pun on a common sexual
application of the verb *kinein* "move."

LYSISTRATA:

>   Of course
you can, dear. Still, a little help can't hurt, now
can it? I'll just stay around for a bit
and—er—poke up the fire.
>   —Everyone else inside!

*(Exit all the women but Lysistrata, on the platform, and
Myrrhine, who stands near the Akropolis entrance, hidden
from her husband's view. Kinesias staggers on, in erection
and considerable pain, followed by a male slave who carries a
baby boy.)*

KINESIAS:

OUCH!!
>   Omigod.
Hypertension, twinges. . . . I can't hold out much more.
I'd rather be dismembered.
>   *How long, ye gods, how long?*

LYSISTRATA:

(Officially.)

WHO GOES THERE?
>   WHO PENETRATES OUR POSITIONS?

KINESIAS:

Me.

LYSISTRATA:

>   A Man?

KINESIAS:

>   Every inch.

LYSISTRATA:

>   Then inch yourself out
of here. Off Limits to Men.

KINESIAS:

>   This *is* the limit.
Just who are *you* to throw me out?

LYSISTRATA:

>   The Lookout.

KINESIAS:

Well, look here, Lookout. I'd like to see Myrrhine.
How's the outlook?

LYSISTRATA:

                    Unlikely. Bring Myrrhine
to you? The idea!
                        Just by the by, who are you?

KINESIAS:

A private citizen. Her husband, Kinesias.

LYSISTRATA:

                               No!
Meeting you—I'm overcome!
                        Your name, you know,
is not without its fame among us girls.

    (Aside.)

—Matter of fact, we have a name for *it*.—
I swear, you're never out of Myrrhine's mouth.
She won't even nibble a quince, or swallow an egg,
without reciting, "Here's to Kinesias!"

KINESIAS:

                         For god's sake,
will you . . .

LYSISTRATA:

    (Sweeping on over his agony.)

                  Word of honor, it's true. Why, when
we discuss our husbands (you know how women are),
Myrrhine refuses to argue. She simply insists:
"Compared with Kinesias, the rest have *nothing!*"
Imagine!

KINESIAS:

Bring her out here!

LYSISTRATA:

                  Really? And what would I
get out of this?

KINESIAS:

You see my situation. I'll raise
whatever I can. This can be all yours.

LYSISTRATA:

Goodness.
It's really her place. I'll go and get her.

*(She descends from the platform and moves to Myrrhine, out
of Kinesias' sight.)*

KINESIAS:

Speed!
—Life is a husk. She left our home, and happiness
went with her. Now pain is the tenant. Oh, to enter
that wifeless house, to sense that awful emptiness,
to eat that tasteless, joyless food—it makes
it hard, I tell you.
Harder all the time.

MYRRHINE:

(Still out of his sight, in a voice to be overheard.)

Oh, I *do* love him! I'm mad about him! But he
doesn't want my love. Please don't make me see him.

KINESIAS:

Myrrhine darling, why do you *act* this way?
Come down here!

MYRRHINE:

(Appearing at the wall.)

Down there? Certainly not!

KINESIAS:

It's me, Myrrhine. I'm begging you. Please come down.

MYRRHINE:

I don't see why you're begging me. You don't need me.

KINESIAS:

I don't need you? I'm at the end of my rope!

MYRRHINE:

I'm leaving.

(She turns. Kinesias grabs the boy from the slave.)

KINESIAS:

        No! Wait! At least you'll have to listen
to the voice of your child.

(To the boy, in a fierce undertone.)

           —(Call your mother!)

(Silence.)

                . . . to the voice
of your very own child . . .

       —(Call your mother, brat!)

CHILD:

MOMMYMOMMYMOMMY!

KINESIAS:

Where's your maternal instinct? He hasn't been washed
or fed for a week. How can you be so pitiless?

MYRRHINE:

Him I pity. Of all the pitiful excuses
for a father. . . .

KINESIAS:

        Come down here, dear. For the baby's sake.

MYRRHINE:

Motherhood! I'll have to come. I've got no choice.

KINESIAS:

(Soliloquizing as she descends.)

It may be me, but I'll swear she looks years younger—
and gentler—her eyes caress me. And then they flash:
that anger, that verve, that high-and-mighty air!
She's fire, she's ice—and I'm stuck right in the middle.

MYRRHINE:

(Taking the baby.)

Sweet babykins with such a nasty daddy!
Here, let Mummy kissums. Mummy's little darling.

KINESIAS:

(The injured husband.)

You should be ashamed of yourself, letting those women

lead you around. Why do you DO these things?
You only make me suffer and hurt your poor,
sweet self.

MYRRHINE:

       Keep your hands away from me!

KINESIAS:

But the house, the furniture, everything we own—you're
letting it go to hell!

MYRRHINE:

       Frankly, I couldn't care less.

KINESIAS:

But your weaving's unraveled—the loom is full of
chickens! You couldn't care less about *that?*

MYRRHINE:

               I certainly couldn't.

KINESIAS:

And the holy rites of Aphrodite? Think how long
that's been.
       Come on, darling, let's go home.

MYRRHINE:

I absolutely refuse!
          Unless you agree to a truce
to stop the war.

KINESIAS:

       Well, then, if that's your decision,
we'll STOP the war!

MYRRHINE:

         Well, then, if that's your decision,
I'll come back—*after* it's done.
           But, for the present,
I've sworn off.

KINESIAS:

      At least lie down for a minute.
We'll talk.

MYRRHINE:

      I know what you're up to—NO!
—And yet . . . I really can't say I don't love you . . .

KINESIAS:

                          You love me!
So what's the trouble? *Lie down.*

MYRRHINE:

                Don't be disgusting.
In front of the baby?

KINESIAS:

          Er . . . no. Heaven Forfend.
(Taking the baby and pushing it at the slave.)
—Take this home.
(The slave obeys.)
          —Well, darling, we're rid of the kid . . .
let's go to bed!

MYRRHINE:

       Poor dear.
               But where does one do
this sort of thing?

KINESIAS:

         Where? All we need is a little
nook. . . . We'll try Pan's grotto. Excellent spot.

MYRRHINE:

(With a nod at the Akropolis.)
I'll have to be pure to get back in *there*. How can I
expunge my pollution?

KINESIAS:

         Sponge off in the pool next door.

MYRRHINE:

I did swear an Oath. I'm supposed to perjure myself?

KINESIAS:

Bother the Oath. Forget it—I'll take the blame.

(A pause.)

MYRRHINE:

Now I'll go get us a cot.

KINESIAS:

                No! Not a cot!
The ground's enough for us.

MYRRHINE:

                I'll get the cot.
For all your faults, I refuse to put you to bed
in the dirt.

(She exits into the Akropolis.)

KINESIAS:

          She certainly loves me. That's nice to know.

MYRRHINE:

(Returning with a rope-tied cot.)

Here. You hurry to bed while I undress.

(Kinesias lies down.)

Gracious me—I forgot. We need a mattress.

KINESIAS:

Who wants a mattress? Not me!

MYRRHINE:

               Oh, yes, you do.
It's perfectly squalid on the ropes.

KINESIAS:

              Well, give me a kiss
to tide me over.

MYRRHINE:

       Voilà.

(She pecks at him and leaves.)

KINESIAS:

        OoolaLΛlala!
—Make it a quick trip, dear.

MYRRHINE:

(Entering with the mattress, she waves Kinesias off the cot and lays the mattress on it.)

Here we are.
Our mattress. Now hurry to bed while I undress.

(Kinesias lies down again.)

Gracious me—I forgot. You don't have a pillow.

KINESIAS:

I do *not* need a pillow.

MYRRHINE:

I know, but *I* do.

(She leaves.)

KINESIAS:

What a lovefeast! Only the table gets laid.[1]

MYRRHINE:

(Returning with a pillow.)

Rise and shine!

(Kinesias jumps up. She places the pillow.)

And now I have everything I need.

KINESIAS:

(Lying down again.)

You certainly do.
Come here, my little jewelbox!

MYRRHINE:

Just taking off my bra.
Don't break your promise:
no cheating about the Peace.

KINESIAS:

I swear to god,
I'll die first!

[1]In the Greek, Kinesias compares his phallus to "Herakles at table"—a stock comedy bit wherein the glutton hero, raving with hunger, is systematically diddled of his dinner by his hosts.

MYRRHINE:

(Coming to him.)

Just look. You don't have a blanket.

KINESIAS:

I didn't plan to go camping—I want to make love!

MYRRHINE:

Relax. You'll get your love. I'll be right back.

(She leaves,)

KINESIAS:

Relax? I'm dying a slow death by dry goods!

MYRRHINE:

(Returning with the blanket.)

Get up!

KINESIAS:

(Getting out of bed.)

I've been up for hours. I was up before I was up.

(Myrrhine spreads the blanket on the mattress, and he lies down again.)

MYRRHINE:

I presume you want perfume?

KINESIAS:

Positively NO!

MYRRHINE:

Absolutely *yes*—whether you want it or not.

(She leaves.)

KINESIAS:

Dear Zeus, I don't ask for much—but please let her spill it.

MYRRHINE:

(Returning with a bottle.)

Hold out your hand like a good boy.

Now rub it in.

KINESIAS:

(Obeying and sniffing.)

This is to quicken desire? Too strong. It grabs
your nose and bawls out: *Try again tomorrow.*

MYRRHINE:

I'm *awful!* I brought you that rancid Rhodian brand.

(She starts off with the bottle.)

KINESIAS:

This is just *lovely.* Leave it, woman!

MYRRHINE:

Silly!

(She leaves.)

KINESIAS:

God damn the clod who first concocted perfume!

MYRRHINE:

(Returning with another bottle.)

Here, try this flask.

KINESIAS:

Thanks—but you try mine.
Come to bed, you witch—

and please stop bringing
things!

MYRRHINE:

That is exactly what I'll do.
There go my shoes.

Incidentally, darling, you *will*
remember to vote for the truce?

KINESIAS:

I'LL THINK IT OVER!

(Myrrhine runs off for good.)

That woman's laid me waste—destroyed me, root
and branch!
       I'm scuttled,
            gutted,
                 up the spout!
And Myrrhine's gone!

(In a parody of a tragic kommos.)

      Out upon't! But how? But where?
      Now I have lost the fairest fair,
      how screw my courage to yet another
      sticking-place? Aye, there's the rub—
      And yet, this wagging, wanton babe
      must soon be laid to rest, or else . . .
      Ho, Pandar!
             Pandar!
                 I'd hire a nurse.

KORYPHAIOS OF MEN:

      Grievous your bereavement, cruel
      the slow tabescence of your soul.
      I bid my liquid pity mingle.

      Oh, where the soul, and where, alack!
      the cod to stand the taut attack
      of swollen prides, the scorching tensions
      that ravine up the lumbar regions?
        His morning lay
        has gone astray.

KINESIAS:

(In agony.)

      O Zeus, reduce the throbs, the throes!

KORYPHAIOS OF MEN:

      I turn my tongue to curse the cause
      of your affliction—that jade, that slut,
      that hag, that ogress . . .

KINESIAS:

                 No! Slight not
my light-o'-love, my dove, my sweet!

KORYPHAIOS OF MEN:

> Sweet!
>   O Zeus who rul'st the sky,
> snatch that slattern up on high,
> crack thy winds, unleash thy thunder,
> tumble her over, trundle her under,
> juggle her from hand to hand;
> twirl her ever near the ground—
> drop her in a well-aimed fall
> on our comrade's tool! That's all.

(Kinesias exits left.)

(A Spartan Herald enters from the right, holding his cloak together in a futile attempt to conceal his condition.)

HERALD:

This Athens? Where-all kin I find the Council of Elders
or else the Executive Board? I brung some news.

(The Commissioner,[1] swathed in his cloak, enters from the left.)

COMMISSIONER:

And what are you—a man? a signpost? a joint-stock
company?

HERALD:

>   A herald, sonny, a honest-to-Kastor
> herald. I come to chat 'bout thet-there truce.

COMMISSIONER:

. . . carrying a concealed weapon? Pretty underhanded.

HERALD:

(Twisting to avoid the Commissioner's direct gaze.)

Hain't done no sech a thang!

---

[1] I maintain the Commissioner as Athens' representative in this scene (980–1013), not primarily because of the testimony of the manuscripts (shaky support at best), but from the logic and structure of the speeches themselves. Coulon assigns them to a *Prytanis*, or member of the Executive Board. In this he follows a whim of Wilamowitz, who took a hesitant suggestion by Van Leeuwen and exalted it into a new principal character in the play—one of the unhappiest changes ever made in an Aristophanic text. The caution of Van Leeuwen, who usually knew no fear as an editor, should have given anyone pause.

COMMISSIONER:

Very well, stand still.
Your cloak's out of crease—hernia? Are the roads that
  bad?

HERALD:

I swear this feller's plumb tetched in the haid!

COMMISSIONER:

(Throwing open the Spartan's cloak, exposing the phallus.)

You clown,
you've got an erection!

HERALD:

(Wildly embarrassed.)

Hain't got no sech a thang!
You stop this-hyer foolishment!

COMMISSIONER:

What *have* you got there, then?

HERALD:

Thet-thur's a Spartan *epistle*.[1] In code.

COMMISSIONER:

I have the key.

(Throwing open his cloak.)

Behold another Spartan *epistle*. In code.

(Tiring of teasing.)

Let's get down to cases. I know the score,
so tell me the truth.
                 How are things with you in Sparta?

HERALD:

Thangs is up in the air. The whole Alliance

---

[1]Correctly, a *skytalê*, a tapered rod which was Sparta's contribution to cryptography. A
strip of leather was wound about the rod, inscribed with the desired message, and
unwound for transmission. A messenger then delivered the strip to the qualified recipient, who deciphered it by winding it around a rod uniform in size and shape with the
first. Any interceptor found a meaningless string of letters.

is purt-near 'bout to explode. We-uns'll need barrels,
'stead of women.

COMMISSIONER:

What was the cause of this outburst?
The great god Pan?

HERALD:

Nope. I'll lay 'twere Lampito,
most likely. She begun, and then they was off
and runnin' at the post in a bunch, every last little gal
in Sparta, drivin' their menfolk away from the winner's
circle.

COMMISSIONER:

How are you taking this?

HERALD:

Painful-like.
Everyone's doubled up worse as a midget nursin'
a wick in a midnight wind come moon-dark time.
Cain't even tetch them little old gals on the moosey
without we all agree to a Greece-wide Peace.

COMMISSIONER:

Of course!
A universal female plot—all Hellas
risen in rebellion—I should have known!
Return
to Sparta with this request:
Have them despatch us
a Plenipotentiary Commission, fully empowered
to conclude an armistice. I have full confidence
that I can persuade our Senate to do the same,
without extending myself. The evidence is at hand.

HERALD:

I'm a-flyin', Sir! I have never heered your equal!

*(Exeunt hurriedly, the Commissioner to the left, the Herald to
the right.)*

KORYPHAIOS OF MEN:

> The most unnerving work of nature,[1]
> the pride of applied immortality,
> is the common female human.
> No fire can match, no beast can best her.
> O Unsurmountability,
> thy name—worse luck—is Woman.

KORYPHAIOS OF WOMEN:

> After such knowledge, why persist
> in wearing out this feckless
> war between the sexes?
> When can I apply for the post
> of ally, partner, and general friend?

KORYPHAIOS OF MEN:

> I won't be ployed to revise, re-do,
> amend, extend, or bring to an end
> my irreversible credo:
> *Misogyny Forever!*
> —The answer's never.

KORYPHAIOS OF WOMEN:

> All right. Whenever you choose.
> But, for the present, I refuse
> to let you look your absolute worst,
> parading around like an unfrocked freak:
> I'm coming over and get you dressed.

(She dresses him in his tunic, an action [like others in this scene] imitated by the members of the Chorus of Women toward their opposite numbers in the Chorus of Men.)

KORYPHAIOS OF MEN:

> This seems sincere. It's not a trick.
> Recalling the rancor with which I stripped,
> I'm overlaid with chagrin.

---

[1]The ensuing reconciliation scene, with its surrogate sexuality, is one of the most curious in Aristophanes. It is not lyric; yet both its diction, oddly diffuse and redundant, and its meter, a paeonic variation on a common trochaic dialogue measure which paradoxically makes it much more regular, seem to call for extensive choreography. I have tried to hedge my bet by stilting the English and employing an irregular scheme depending heavily on off-rhymes.

KORYPHAIOS OF WOMEN:

> Now you resemble a man,
> not some ghastly practical joke.
> And if you show me a little respect
> (and promise not to kick), I'll extract
> the beast in you.

KORYPHAIOS OF MEN:

(Searching himself.)

> What beast in me?

KORYPHAIOS OF WOMEN:

> That insect. There. The bug that's stuck
> in your eye.

KORYPHAIOS OF MEN:

(Playing along dubiously.)

> This gnat?

KORYPHAIOS OF WOMEN:

> Yes, nitwit!

KORYPHAIOS OF MEN:

> Of course.
> That steady, festering agony . . .
> You've put your finger on the source
> of all my lousy troubles. Please
> roll back the lid and scoop it out.
> I'd like to see it.

KORYPHAIOS OF WOMEN:

> All right, I'll do it.

(Removing the imaginary insect.)

> Although, of all the impossible cranks. . . .
> Do you sleep in a swamp? Just look at this.
> I've never seen a bigger chigger.

KORYPHAIS OF MEN:

> Thanks.
> Your kindness touches me deeply. For years,
> that thing's been sinking wells in my eye.
> Now you've unplugged me. Here come the tears.

KORYPHAIOS OF WOMEN:

> I'll dry your tears, though I can't say why.

(Wiping away the tears.)

> Of all the irresponsible boys. . . .
> *And* I'll kiss you.

KORYPHAIOS OF MEN:

> Don't you kiss me!

KORYPHAIOS OF WOMEN:

> What made you think you had a choice?

(She kisses him.)

KORYPHAIOS OF MEN:

All right, damn you, that's enough of that ingrained
   palaver.
I can't dispute the truth or logic of the pithy old proverb:
> *Life with women is hell.*
> *Life without women is hell, too.*

And so we conclude a truce with you, on the following
   terms:
in future, a mutual moratorium on mischief in all its
   forms.
Agreed?—Let's make a single chorus and start our song.

(The two Choruses unite and face the audience.)

CHORUS OF MEN[1]:

> We're not about to introduce
> the standard personal abuse—
> the Choral Smear
> Of Present Persons (usually,
> in every well-made comedy,
> inserted here).
> Instead, in deed and utterance, we

---

[1]Coulon, with most other modern editors, assigns the two strophes here (1043–57, 1058–71, pp. 84–85), plus the two which follow the subsequent scene (1189–1202, 1203–15, pp. 94–95), to the entire Chorus, which thereby demonstrates its new-found unity. This seems possible, but unarticulated; even in this play, antistrophic responsion does not necessarily indicate opposition. By paying attention to the matter of this Indian-giving, I have tried to indicate the appropriate diversity within unity: here, first Men (money), then Women (cooking); following Lysistrata's address, first Women (dress and ornament), then Men (grain). In any case, the manuscript indications, giving the first two strophes to the Women and the last two to the Men, appear impossible.

shall now indulge in philanthropy
    because we feel
that members of the audience
endure, in the course of current events,
    sufficient hell.
Therefore, friends, be rich! Be flush!
Apply to us, and borrow cash
    in large amounts.
The Treasury stands behind us—there—
and we can personally take care
    of small accounts.
Drop up today. Your credit's good.
Your loan won't have to be repaid
    in full until
the war is over. And then, your debt
is only the money you actually get—
    nothing at all.

CHORUS OF WOMEN:

Just when we meant to entertain
some madcap gourmets from out of town
    —such flawless taste!—
the present unpleasantness intervened,
and now we fear the feast we planned
    will go to waste.
The soup is waiting, rich and thick;
I've sacrificed a suckling pig
    —the pièce de résistance—
whose toothsome cracklings should amaze
the most fastidious gourmets—
    you, for instance.
To everybody here, I say
take potluck at my house today
    with me and mine.
Bathe and change as fast as you can,
bring the children, hurry down,
    and walk right in.
Don't bother to knock. No need at all.
My house in yours. Liberty Hall.
    What are friends for?
Act self-possessed when you come over;
it may help out when you discover
    I've locked the door.

(A delegation of Spartans enters from the right, with difficulty. They have removed their cloaks, but hold them before them-selves in an effort to conceal their condition.)

KORYPHAIOS OF MEN:

What's this? Behold the Spartan ambassadors,
  dragging their beards,
pussy-footing along. It appears they've developed
  a hitch in the crotch.

(Advancing to greet them.)

Men of Sparta, I bid you welcome!
                                    And now
to the point: What predicament brings you among us?

SPARTAN:

We-uns is up a stump. Hain't fit fer chatter.

(Flipping aside his cloak.)

Here's our predicament. Take a look for yourselfs.

KORYPHAIOS OF MEN:

Well, I'll be damned—a regular disaster area.
Inflamed. I imagine the temperature's rather intense?

SPARTAN:

Hit ain't the heat, hit's the tumidity.
                                    But words
won't help what ails us. We-uns come after Peace.
Peace from any person, at any price.

(Enter the Athenian delegation from the left, led by Kinesias.[1] They are wearing cloaks, but are obviously in as much travail as the Spartans.)

KORYPHAIOS OF MEN:

Behold our local Sons of the Soil, stretching
their garments away from their groins, like wrestlers.
Grappling with their plight. Some sort of athlete's disease,
  no doubt.
An outbreak of epic proportions.
                                    Athlete's foot?

---

[1]So I assign the leadership of the Athenians in this scene. Coulon follows Wilamowitz in allotting it to the latter's beloved "Prytanis." The manuscripts commit themselves no further than "Athenians," which is at least safe. It is definitely not the Commissioner.

No. Could it be athlete's . . . ?

KINESIAS:

(Breaking in.)

Who can tell us
how to get hold of Lysistrata? We've come as delegates
to the Sexual Congress.

(Opening his cloak.)

Here are our credentials.

KORYPHAIOS OF MEN:

*(Ever the scientist, looking from the Athenians to the Spartans
and back again.)*

The words are different, but the malady seems the same.

(To Kinesias.)

Dreadful disease. When the crisis reaches its height,
what do you take for it?

KINESIAS:

Whatever comes to hand.
But now we've reached the bitter end. It's Peace
or we fall back on Kleisthenes.

And he's got a waiting list.

KORYPHAIOS OF MEN:

(To the Spartans.)

Take my advice and put your clothes on. If someone
from that self-appointed Purity League comes by, you
may be docked. They do it to the statues of Hermes,[1]
they'll do it to you.

KINESIAS:

*(Since he has not yet noticed the Spartans, he interprets the
warning as meant for him, and hurriedly pulls his cloak
together, as do the other Athenians.)*

Excellent advice.

SPARTAN:

Hit shorely is.
Hain't nothing to argue after. Let's git dressed.

[1]See Glossary, s.v. "Hermes."

(As they put on their cloaks, the Spartans are finally noticed by Kinesias.)

KINESIAS:

Welcome, men of Sparta! This is a shameful
disgrace to masculine honor.

SPARTAN:

                  Hit could be worser.
Ef them Herm-choppers seed us all fired up,
they'd *really* take us down a peg or two.

KINESIAS:

Gentlemen, let's descend to details. Specifically,
why are you here?

SPARTAN:

            Ambassadors. We come to dicker
'bout thet-thur Peace.

KINESIAS:

            Perfect! Precisely our purpose.
Let's send for Lysistrata. Only she can reconcile
our differences. There'll be no Peace for us without her.

SPARTAN:

We-uns ain't fussy. Call Lysistratos, too, if you want.

(The gates to the Akropolis open, and Lysistrata emerges, accompanied by her handmaid, Peace—a beautiful girl without a stitch on. Peace remains out of sight by the gates until summoned.)

KORYPHAIOS OF MEN:

Hail, most virile of women! Summon up all your
   experience;
Be terrible and tender,
               lofty and lowbrow,
                      severe and demure.
Here stand the Leaders of Greece, enthralled by your
   charm.
They yield the floor to you and submit their claims for
   your arbitration.

LYSISTRATA:

Really, it shouldn't be difficult, if I can catch them
all bothered, before they start to solicit each other.
I'll find out soon enough. Where's Peace?

       —Come here.

 *(Peace moves from her place by the gates to Lysistrata. The
 delegations goggle at her.)*

Now, dear, first get those Spartans and bring them to me.
Take them by the hand, but don't be pushy about it,
not like our husbands (no savoir-faire at all!).
Be a lady, be proper, do just what you'd do at home:
if hands are refused, conduct them by the handle.

 (Peace leads the Spartans to a position near Lysistrata.)

And now a hand to the Athenians—it doesn't matter
where; accept any offer—and bring *them* over.

 *(Peace conducts the Athenians to a position near Lysistrata,
 opposite the Spartans.)*

You Spartans move up closer—right *here*—

 (To the Athenians.)

           and *you*
stand over *here*.

     —And now attend my speech.

 *(This the delegations do with some difficulty, because of the
 conflicting attractions of Peace, who is standing beside her
 mistress.)*

I am a woman—but not without some wisdom:
my native wit is not completely negligible,
and I've listened long and hard to the discourse of my
elders—my education is not entirely despicable.

             Well,
now that I've got you, I intend to give you hell,
and I'm perfectly right. Consider your actions:

           At festivals,
in Pan-Hellenic harmony, like true blood-brothers, you
 share
the selfsame basin of holy water, and sprinkle
altars all over Greece—Olympia, Delphoi,
Thermopylai . . . (I could go on and on, if length

were my only object.)

But now, when the Persians sit by
and wait, in the very presence of your enemies, you fight
each other, destroy *Greek* men, destroy *Greek* cities!
—Point One of my address is now concluded.

KINESIAS:

(Gazing at Peace.)

I'm destroyed, if this is drawn out much longer!

LYSISTRATA:

(Serenely unconscious of the interruption.)

—Men of Sparta, I direct these remarks to you.
Have you forgotten that a Spartan suppliant once came
to beg assistance from Athens? Recall Perikleidas:
Fifty years ago, he clung to our altar,
his face dead-white above his crimson robe, and pleaded
for an army. Messene was pressing you hard in revolt,
and to this upheaval, Poseidon, the Earthshaker, added
another.

But Kimon took four thousand troops
from Athens—an army which saved the state of Sparta.
Such treatment have you received at the hands of Athens,
you who devastate the country that came to your aid!

KINESIAS:

*(Stoutly; the condemnation of his enemy has made him forget
the girl momentarily.)*

You're right, Lysistrata. The Spartans are clearly in the
wrong!

SPARTAN:

*(Guiltily backing away from Peace, whom he has attempted to
pat.)*

Hit's wrong, I reckon, but that's the purtiest behind . . .

LYSISTRATA:

(Turning to the Athenians.)

—Men of Athens, do you think I'll let *you* off?
Have you forgotten the Tyrant's days,[1] when you wore

---

[1]The reign of Hippias, expelled by the Athenians in 510 with the aid of Kleomenes and
his Spartans, who defeated the tyrant's Thessalian allies.

the smock of slavery, when the Spartans turned to the
spear, cut down the pride of Thessaly, despatched the
friends of tyranny, and dispossessed your oppressors?

Recall:

On that great day, your only allies were Spartans;
your liberty came at their hands, which stripped away
your servile garb and clothed you again in Freedom!

SPARTAN:

(Indicating Lysistrata.)

Hain't never seed no higher type of woman.

KINESIAS:

(Indicating Peace.)

Never saw one I wanted so much to top.

LYSISTRATA:

(Oblivious to the byplay, addressing both groups.)

With such a history of mutual benefits conferred
and received, why are you fighting? Stop this wickedness!
Come to terms with each other! What prevents you?

SPARTAN:

We'd a heap sight druther make Peace, if we was
indemnified with a plumb strategic location.

(Pointing at Peace's rear.)

We'll take thet butte.

LYSISTRATA:

Butte?

SPARTAN:

The Promontory of Pylos—Sparta's Back Door.
We've missed it fer a turrible spell.

(Reaching.)

Hev to keep our
hand in.

KINESIAS:

(Pushing him away.)

The price is too high—you'll never take that!

LYSISTRATA:

Oh, let them have it.

KINESIAS:

What room will we have left
for maneuvers?

LYSISTRATA:

Demand another spot in exchange.

KINESIAS:

(Surveying Peace like a map as he addresses the Spartan.)

Then you hand over to us—uh, let me see—
let's try Thessaly[1]—

(Indicating the relevant portions of Peace.)

First of all, Easy Mountain . . .
then the Maniac Gulf behind it . . .
and down to Megara
for the legs . . .

SPARTAN:

You cain't take all of thet! Yore plumb
out of yore mind!

LYSISTRATA:

(To Kinesias.)

Don't argue. Let the legs go.

(Kinesias nods. A pause. General smiles of agreement.)

KINESIAS:

(Doffing his cloak.)

I feel an urgent desire to plow a few furrows.

---

[1]Puns on proper names, particularly geographical ones, rarely transfer well, as the following bits of sexual cartography will show. "Easy Mountain": an impossible pun of Mt. Oita, replacing the Greek's *Echinous*, a town in Thessaly whose name recalls *echinos* "hedgehog"—slang for the female genitalia. "Maniac Gulf": for Maliac Gulf, with less dimension than the Greek's *Mêlia kolpon*, which puns both on bosom and pudendum. The "legs of Megara" are the walls that connected that city with her seaport, Nisaia.

SPARTAN:

(Doffing his cloak.)

Hit's time to work a few loads of fertilizer in.

LYSISTRATA:

Conclude the treaty and the simple life is yours.
If such is your decision convene your councils,
and then deliberate the matter with your allies.

KINESIAS:

Deliberate? Allies?
                    We're over-extended already!
Wouldn't every ally approve our position—
Union Now?

SPARTAN:

                    I know I kin speak for ourn.

KINESIAS:

And I for ours.
                    They're just a bunch of gigolos.

LYSISTRATA:

I heartily approve.
                    Now first attend to your purification,
then we, the women, will welcome you to the Citadel
and treat you to all the delights of a home-cooked
banquet. Then you'll exchange your oaths and pledge
your faith, and every man of you will take his wife and
depart for home.

(Lysistrata and Peace enter the Akropolis.)

KINESIAS:

                    Let's hurry!

SPARTAN:

                    Lead on, everwhich
way's yore pleasure.

KINESIAS:

                    This way, then—and HURRY!

(The delegations exeunt at a run.)

CHORUS OF WOMEN:

> I'd never stint on anybody.
> And now I include, in my boundless bounty,
>> the younger set.
> Attention, you parents of teenage girls
> about to debut in the social whirl.
>> Here's what you get:
> Embroidered linens, lush brocades,
> a huge assortment of ready-mades,
>> from mantles to shifts;
> *plus* bracelets and bangles of solid gold—
> every item my wardrobe holds—
>> absolute gifts!
> Don't miss this offer. Come to my place,
> barge right in, and make your choice.
>> You can't refuse.
> Everything there must go today.
> Finders keepers—cart it away!
>> How can you lose?
> Don't spare me. Open all the locks.
> Break every seal. Empty every box.
>> Keep ferreting—
> And your sight's considerably better than mine
> if you should possibly chance to find
>> a single thing.

CHORUS OF MEN:

> Troubles, friend? Too many mouths
> to feed, and not a scrap in the house
>> to see you through?
> Faced with starvation? Don't give it a thought.
> Pay attention; I'll tell you what
>> I'm gonna do.
> I overbought. I'm overstocked.
> Every room in my house is clogged
>> with flour (best ever),
> glutted with luscious loaves whose size
> you wouldn't believe. I need the space;
>> do me a favor:
> Bring gripsacks, knapsacks, duffle bags,
> pitchers, cisterns, buckets, and kegs
>> around to me.
> A courteous servant will see to your needs;

he'll fill them up with A-1 wheat—
    and all for free!
—Oh. Just one final word before
you turn your steps to my front door:
    I happen to own
a dog. Tremendous animal.
Can't stand a leash. And bites like hell—
    better stay home.

(The united Chorus flocks to the door of the Akropolis.[1])

KORYPHAIOS OF MEN:

(Banging at the door.)

Hey, open up in there!

(The door opens, and the Commissioner appears. He wears a wreath, carries a torch, and is slightly drunk. He addresses the Koryphaios.)

COMMISSIONER:

               You know the Regulations.
Move along!

(He sees the entire Chorus.)

            —And why are YOU lounging around?
I'll wield my trusty torch and scorch the lot!

(The Chorus looks away in mock horror. He stops and looks at his torch.)

—*This* is the bottom of the barrel. A cheap burlesque bit.
I refuse to do it. I have my pride.

(With a start, he looks at the audience, as though hearing a protest. He shrugs and addresses the audience.)

                —No choice, eh?
Well, if that's the way it is, we'll take the trouble.
Anything to keep you happy.

(The Chorus advances eagerly.)

---

[1]This stage direction, and what follows it, attempt to make sense of a desperate situation in the manuscripts, whose chief accomplishment is to differentiate between Athenian and Spartan. In the passage 1216–46, I assign to the Commissioner those lines given by Coulon to the "Prytanis," and to Kinesias those he assigns to "an Athenian," with the following exceptions: the Koryphaios of Men receives 1216a ("Prytanis," Coulon) and 1221 ("Athenian," Coulon); the Commissioner receives 1226 ("Athenian," Coulon).

KORYPHAIOS OF MEN:

                    Don't forget us!
We're in this, too. Your trouble is ours!

COMMISSIONER:

(Resuming his character and jabbing with his torch at the Chorus.)

                              Keep moving!
Last man out of the way goes home without hair!
Don't block the exit. Give the Spartans some room.
They've dined in comfort; let them go home in peace.

(The Chorus shrinks back from the door. Kinesias, wreathed and quite drunk, appears at the door. He speaks his first speech in Spartan.[1])

KINESIAS:

Hain't never seed sech a spread! Hit were splendiferous!

COMMISSIONER:

I gather the Spartans won friends and influenced people?

KINESIAS:

And *we've* never been so brilliant. It was the wine.

COMMISSIONER:

Precisely.
          The reason? A sober Athenian is just
non compos. If I can carry a little proposal
I have in mind, our Foreign Service will flourish,
guided by this rational rule:
                    No Ambassador
Without a Skinful.
                    Reflect on our past performance:
Down to a Spartan parley we troop, in a state
of disgusting sobriety, looking for trouble. It muddles
our senses: we read between the lines; we hear,
not what the Spartans say, but what we suspect

---

[1]This rendering of 1225 in dialect, and the reading of 1226 as an ironical question, is prompted by a notion of Wilamowitz', to whom an uncommon verb form seemed clear enough evidence of Spartan to warrant a native informant on stage 18 lines early. I am not sure of the validity of his perception, but it allows other solutions, such as the present one: Kinesias is awash with wine and international amity, and the Commissioner is amused.

they might have been about to be going to say.
We bring back paranoid reports—cheap fiction, the fruit
of temperance. Cold-water diplomacy, pah!

                                        Contrast
this evening's total pleasure, the free-and-easy
give-and-take of friendship: If we were singing,
> *Just Kleitagora and me,*
> *Alone in Thessaly,*

and someone missed his cue and cut in loudly,
> *Ajax, son of Telamon,*
> *He was one hell of a man—*

no one took it amiss, or started a war;
we clapped him on the back and gave three cheers.

(During this recital, the Chorus has sidled up to the door.)

—Dammit, are you back here again?

(Waving his torch.)

                                        Scatter!
Get out of the road! Gangway, you gallowsbait!

KINESIAS:

Yes, everyone out of the way. They're coming out.

(Through the door emerge the Spartan delegation, a flutist, the Athenian delegation, Lysistrata, Kleonike, Myrrhine, and the rest of the women from the citadel, both Athenian and Peloponnesian. The Chorus splits into its male and female components and draws to the sides to give the procession room.)

SPARTAN:

(To the flutist.)

Friend and kinsman, take up them pipes a yourn.
I'd like fer to shuffle a bit and sing a right sweet
song in honor of Athens and us'uns, too.

COMMISSIONER:

(To the flutist.)

Marvelous, marvelous—come, take up your pipes!

(To the Spartan.)

I certainly love to see you Spartans dance.

(The flutist plays, and the Spartan begins a slow dance.)

SPARTAN:

> Memory,
> send me
> your Muse,
> who knows
> our glory,
> knows Athens'—
> Tell the story:
> At Artemision
> like gods, they stampeded
> the hulks of the Medes, and
> beat them.
>
> And Leonidas
> leading us—
> the wild boars
> whetting their tusks.
> And the foam flowered,
> flowered and flowed,
> down our cheeks
> to our knees below.
> The Persian there
> like the sands of the sea—
>
> Hither, huntress,
> virgin, goddess,
> tracker, slayer,
> to our truce!
> Hold us ever
> fast together;
> bring our pledges
> love and increase;
> wean us from the
> fox's wiles—
>
> Hither, huntress!
> Virgin, hither!

LYSISTRATA[1]:

(Surveying the assemblage with a proprietary air.)

Well, the preliminaries are over—very nicely, too.
So, Spartans,

---

[1]Coulon, following Wilamowitz' ungallant suggestion, takes this speech from Lysistrata (1273–78) and gives it, plus the dubious line following the choral song (1295), to the "Prytanis"—thus crowning the play and turning a superfluous man into an unnecessary hero.

(Indicating the Peloponnesian women who have been hostages.)

take these girls back home. And *you*

(To the Athenian delegation, indicating the women from the Akropolis.)

take *these* girls. Each man stand by his wife, each wife
by her husband. Dance to the gods' glory, and thank
them for the happy ending. And, from now on, please be
careful. Let's not make the same mistakes again.

*(The delegations obey; the men and women of the chorus join
again for a rapid ode.)*

CHORUS:

> Start the chorus dancing,
> Summon all the Graces,
> Send a shout to Artemis in invocation.
> Call upon her brother,
> healer, chorus master,
> Call the blazing Bacchus, with his maddened muster.
>
> Call the flashing, fiery Zeus, and
> call his mighty, blessed spouse, and
> call the gods, call all the gods,
> to witness now and not forget
> our gentle, blissful Peace—the gift,
> the deed of Aphrodite.
>   Ai!
> Alalai!   Paion!
> Leap you!   Paion!
> Victory!   Alalai!
> Hail!   Hail!   Hail!

LYSISTRATA:

Spartan, let's have another song from you, a new one.

SPARTAN:

> Leave darlin' Taygetos,
> Spartan Muse! Come to us
> once more, flyin'
> and glorifyin'
> *Spartan* themes:
> the god at Amyklai,
> bronze-house Athene,

Tyndaros' twins,
the valiant ones,
playin' still by Eurotas' streams.

Up! Advance!
Leap to the dance!

Help us hymn Sparta,
lover of dancin',
lover of foot-pats,
where girls go prancin'
like fillies along Eurotas' banks,
whirlin' the dust, twinklin' their shanks,
shakin' their hair
like Maenads playin'
and jugglin' the thyrsis,
in frenzy obeyin'
Leda's daughter, the fair, the pure
Helen, the mistress of the choir.

Here, Muse, here!
Bind up your hair!

Stamp like a deer! Pound your feet!
Clap your hands! Give us a beat!

Sing the greatest,
sing the mightiest,
sing the conqueror,
sing to honor her—

Athene of the Bronze House!
Sing Athene!

(Exeunt omnes, dancing and singing.)

GLOSSARY

ACHARNAI: Largest of the rural demes of Attika, located about seven miles north of the city of Athens.

ADONIS: Mythical youth of marvelous beauty, beloved of Aphrodite, early cut off by a boar. His death was regularly bewailed by women of Greece and the East at summer festivals.

AISCHYLOS, AESCHYLUS: The great Athenian tragedian (525–456 B.C.).

AJAX, AIAS: Greek hero of the Trojan War, son of Telamon of Salamis.

AKROPOLIS: The citadel of Athens.

AMAZONS: The mythical race of warrior-women, said to have invaded Attika in heroic times to avenge the heft of their queen's sister, Antiope, by Theseus of Athens.

AMYKLAI: A Lakedaimonian town, traditional birthplace of Kastor (q.v.) and Pollux, site of a temple to Apollo.

APHRODITE: Goddess of beauty and sexual love.

ARISTOGEITON: Athenian hero who, with Harmodios, assassinated the tyrant Hipparchos in 514 and was put to death. With the expulsion of Hipparchos' brother Hippias four years later, the tyranny of the Peisistratids came to an end. Statues to Harmodios and Aristogeiton were erected in the Athenian Agora.

ARTEMIS: Goddess of the hunt and moon, sister ðf Apollo.

ARTEMISIA: Queen of Halikarnassos, who, as an ally of the Persian King Xerxes in his invasion of Greece, fought with particular distinction at the sea battle of Salamis in 480.

ARTEMISION: Site on the northern coast of Euboia, off which the Athenians defeated the Persians in a sea battle in 480.

ATHENE, ATHENA: Goddess of wisdom and war; patroness of Athens, and thus particularly associated with the Akropolis (q.v.)

BACCHOS: Dionysos, the god of vineyards, wine, and dramatic poetry, celebrated at Athens in a series of festivals, among them the Lenaia (January–February) and the City Dionysia (March–April).

BOIOTIA: A plentifully supplied state directly northeast of Attika, allied with Sparta during the Peloponnesian War.

CHARON: A minor deity in charge of ferrying the souls of the dead to Hades.

DEMETER: The Earth-Mother; goddess of grain, agriculture, and the harvest.

DEMOSTRATOS: A choleric Athenian demagogue, first to propose the disastrous Sicilian Expedition of 415–413.

EROS: God of sensual love, son of Aphrodite.

EURIPIDES: Athenian tragedian (480–406 B.C.), whose plays and private life furnished Aristophanes with endless material for ridicule. Euripides' determinedly ungallant representation of women (Phaidra in *Hippolytos*, for instance), alluded to in *Lysistrata*, becomes the basis for Aristophanes' next play, the *Thesmophoriazusae*.

EUROTAS: A river in Laconia, on which is located the city of Sparta.

HARMODIOS: Athenian hero; assassin, with Aristogeiton (q.v.), of the tyrant Hipparchos.

HEKATE: Goddess of the moon, night, childbirth, and the underworld.

HELEN: Daughter of Leda and Tyndaros, wife of Menelaos of Sparta. Her abduction by Paris of Troy furnished a *casus belli* for the Trojan War.

HERMES: God of messengers and thieves; in Athens in every doorway stood a statue of Hermes (i.e., a *herm*, usually a bust of the god surmounting an ithyphallic pillar), protector of the door and guardian against thieves—it takes one to know one. The wholesale mutilation of these statues by persons unknown, just before the sailing of the Sicilian expedition in 415, led to the recall of Alkibiades—and thus, perhaps, to the loss of the expedition and ultimately of the war.

HIPPONAX: A satirical iambic poet of Ephesos (fl. 540 B.C.), noted for his limping meter and his touchy temper.

KARYSTIAN: From Karystos, a town in Euboia allied to Athens, whose male inhabitants enjoyed a seemingly deserved reputation for lechery.

KASTOR: Divinity, son of Leda and Tyndaros, or of Leda and Zeus; twin of Polydeukes (Pollux), with whom he constitutes the Dioskouroi. These twin gods were particularly honored by their native state of Sparta.

KIMON: One of Athens' greatest generals (died 449 B.C.); in the years following the Persian Wars, principal architect of the Athenian Empire—an activity abruptly interrupted by his ostracism in 461.

KLEISTHENES: A notorious homosexual; on that account, one of Aristophanes' favorite targets for at least twenty years.

KLEOMENES: Sixth-century king of Sparta, whose two Athenian expeditions had rather different results: The first, in 510, materially assisted in the expulsion of the tyrant Hippias; the second, in 508, failed to establish the power of the aristocratic party led by Isagoras.

KORINTH: Greek city allied to Sparta during the Peloponnesian War; situated on the strategic Isthmus of Korinth.

KYPROS: A large Greek island in the eastern Mediterranean, especially associated with the goddess Aphrodite, said to have stepped ashore there after her birth from the sea-foam.

LAKONIA: The southernmost state on the Greek mainland, Athens' principal opponent in the Peloponnesian War. Its capital city is Sparta.

LENAIA: An Athenian Dionysiac festival, celebrated in January–February.

LEONIDAS: Spartan king and general, who led his 300 troops against Xerxes' Persian army at Thermopylae in Thessaly (480).

MARATHON: A plain in eastern Attika; site of the famous battle (490 B.C.) in which the Athenian forces under Miltiades crushingly defeated the first Persian invasion of Hellas.

MEGARA: The Greek state immediately to the west of Attika; also, its capital city.

MELANION: A mighty hunter, evidently proverbial for his chastity. Probably not to be identified with Meilanion (Milanion), victorious suitor of the huntress Atalante.

MENELAOS: Legendary king of Sparta; husband of Helen (q.v.).

MESSENIA: The western half of Lakedaimon in the Peloponnese; in spite of revolutions, held by Sparta from ca. 730 B.C. until her defeat by Thebes at Leuktra in 371 B.C.

MIKON: A famous Athenian painter of murals, who flourished between the Persian and Peloponnesian Wars.

MILESIAN: From Miletos, a city in Karia in Asia Minor, which had broken off its alliance with Athens in mid-412, following the Sicilian disaster.

MYRONIDES: Athenian general in the period between the Wars; his best-known victory was over the Boiotians at Oinophyta (456).

PAN: Rural Arkadian god of the flocks and woodlands; his cult at Athens was instituted by way of thanks for his help to the Athenians at the battle of Marathon.

PEISANDROS: Engineer of the oligarchic revolt which overthrew the Athenian constitution in May 411 and set up the Council of Four Hundred.

PERIKLEIDAS: The ambassador sent by Sparta to beg Athenian aid in putting down the Messenian revolt of 464.

PHORMION: Athenian admiral, noted for his victory over the Korinthians at Naupaktos in 429.

POSEIDON: Brother of Zeus and god of the sea. As god of the sea, he girdles the earth and has it in his power, as Poseidon the Earthshaker, to cause earthquakes. In still another manifestation, he is Poseidon Hippios, patron god of horses and horsemen.

PYLOS: Town of the southwestern coast of Messenia whose capture by Athens, along with the neighboring island of Sphakteria, in 425–24, became a *cause célèbre* of the Peloponnesian War, and remained a thorn in Sparta's side until they retook it in 409.

SALAMIS: An island in the Saronic Gulf, between Megara and Attika. Subject to Athens, it is divided from the shore by a narrow strait, site of the famous sea battle of 480 which saw the defeat of Xerxes' Persians by Themistokles' Athenians.

SAMOS: A large Aegean island lying off the coast of Ionia. At the beginning of 411, the effective headquarters of the Athenian forces, who had just aided a democratic revolution there. Other Athenians, especially Peisandros, were already fomenting an oligarchic counterrevolution.

SICILY: Scene of Athens' most disastrous undertaking during the war, the Sicilian Expedition of 415-413, which ended in the annihilation of the Athenian forces.

SKYTHIANS: Barbarians who lived in the region northeast of Thrace. Skythian archers were imported to Athens for use as police.

SPARTA: Capital city of Lakonia, principal opponent of Athens during the Peloponnesian War.

TAŸGETOS: A high mountain in central Lakedaimon that separates Lakonia from Messenia.

TELAMON: Legendary king of Salamis; father of Aias.

THASIAN: From Thasos, a volcanic island in the northern Aegean, celebrated for the dark, fragrant wine produced by its vineyards.

THEBES: The principal city of Boiotia; during the Peloponnesian War an ally of Sparta.

THEOGENES: An Athenian braggart, member of the war party.

THESSALY: A large district in northern Greece.

THRACE: The eastern half of the Balkan peninsula.

TIMON: The famous Athenian misanthrope, a contemporary of Aristophanes; a legend during his own lifetime.

ZAKYNTHOS: A large island in the Ionian Sea, south of Kephallenia and west of Elis; during the Peloponnesian War, an ally of Athens.

ZEUS: Chief god of the Olympian pantheon; son of Kronos, brother of Poseidon, father of Athene. As supreme ruler of the world, he is armed with thunder and lightning and creates storms and tempests.

Plautus
THE MENAECHMUS TWINS

IT IS DIFFICULT to reconstruct the dramatic world of Plautus (250–184 B.C.). He was born in what is now Italy, but his plays all imitate Greek New Comedy originals, which are unfortunately lost. Plautus is above all a popular entertainer, who drives his points home without any attention to subtlety or shading. His characters tend to be stock types. Unlike Aristophanes and Old Comedy, Plautus writes about the comic problems and frustrations of ordinary life. His stage settings anchor his plays in daily routine: meals; domestic quarrels; vain pursuits after women; an excessive interest in money and material advantage. *The Menaechmus Twins* opens with the stage picture that will serve for the entire play: *"A street in Epidamnus. Two houses front on it: stage left Menaechmus; stage right Lovey's."* These are both substantial and comfortable upper-middle-class houses. There is no hint of fantasy and illusion as there is in Aristophanes.

The use of twins tends to distract us from problems of human identity and to throw the entire weight of the action on identification rather than identity. There is no doubt that the twins are mirror images of each other, since everyone takes the one Menaechmus for the other. Plautus, however, very explicitly distinguished the twins from each other in temperament: *"Menaechmus of Epidamnus is gay, generous, and fun loving; his brother is shrewd, calculating, and cynical."* There is a great deal of stupidity built into the play, so that it is virtually impossible for either of the twins—or for anyone else—to figure out that if everyone is calling the wrong Menaechmus by the right name, then the long-lost twin brothers must have been found. The obvious conclusion is violently rejected by all. This is the way that farce is built so solidly on foundations that strain credulity.

There is a point at which Menaechmus of Syracuse begins to enjoy his new situation, and he is converted from nay-saying to yea-saying. It is not only that he is *"shrewd, calculating, and cynical,"* but also that he wants to have some fun in Epidamnus. In the course of the play he seems to change characteristics with

105

his *"gay, generous, and fun loving"* brother. With Lovey, Menaechmus of Syracuse stops struggling and decides to yield to her blandishments: "I'm going to say yes to whatever she says: maybe I can get myself some free entertainment." In going along with the game, Menaechmus of Syracuse joins the world of comedy, and he is fittingly wined, dined, and wenched by a perfect stranger—not only that but gifts are heaped upon him.

Once Menaechmus of Syracuse agrees to go along with the mad reality that surrounds him, he also begins to enjoy himself and to indulge in the pleasures of his new status. All the good things that are showered upon him create a mood of comic euphoria. To the mythical dress and gold bracelet he claims he has given Lovey he adds, *"after a few seconds of highly histrionic deep thought,"* a pair of armlets. The maid catches him short: "You never gave her any armlets," and Menaechmus is forced to forgo the extravagance of fantasy generosity in which he has been indulging himself.

It is easy to understand, therefore, why the recognition scene between the two brothers proceeds so slowly and so disappointingly. Neither brother is too eager to welcome the other, and even though they are staring at each other for the entire scene, they demand proofs of identification that even the most scrupulous bank would not require of a total stranger. It is clear that they have no intention of throwing themselves into each other's arms. The servant Messenio is needed to urge them on in what presents itself as farcical obstinacy. Messenio's enthusiasm is matched by the brothers' reluctance, as in the following exchange:

MESSENIO (*excitedly*): He's your image! He couldn't be more like you.

MENAECHMUS OF SYRACUSE (*following Messenio's gaze*): By god, you know, when I think about what I look like, he *does* resemble me.

The audience solidly supports Messenio and is puzzled by Menaechmus' circumspect manner. Mistaken identity is such a rich comic device that it is allowably difficult to make it disappear.

Madness, too, in farce is enjoyable for its own sake as are all forms of eccentricity and irrationality. Menaechmus of Syracuse has a wonderful scene impersonating a madman who hears the voices of the gods directing his action:

That's a big order, Apollo. Now I'm to get a team of fierce

wild horses, harness them to a chariot, and mount it so I can trample down this stinking, toothless, broken-down lion, eh?

But the wife's enfeebled and ancient father does more than hold his own as he brandishes his stick menacingly. Madness, or the assumption of madness, is exceedingly common in farce as an equivalent of the total inexplicability of the events occurring on stage. Madness seems like a reasonable explanation for the comic mayhem we see before us.

The parasite, Sponge, is a standard figure of Plautine comedy. He is like the comic servant, go-between, and manipulator in other plays. He is a factotum, a toady, a flatterer, a scrounger, and a man who lives by his wits. He does odd jobs and is a yea-sayer and messenger boy in return for his meals; he is what we would call a freeloader. Sponge puts a rhapsodic emphasis on food, or at least the anticipation of food; comedy rarely deals in the actual satisfaction of appetites. As a kind of second chorus, the parasite opens the play with visions of Menaechmus' bounty:

> This Menaechmus is a man who doesn't just feed a man; he bloats the belly for you, he restores you to life . . . he overloads the tables, he piles up the plates like pyramids; you have to stand on your chair if you want something from on top.

Sponge is, of course, doomed for disappointment, since he is so dependent on the good mood of Menaechmus of Epidamnus. He is the one (to use an appropriate pun) who turns the tables by informing on his benefactor, although the affair with Lovey seems almost like a public event.

A word about Lionel Casson's slangy, musical-comedy translation. In the spirit of *A Funny Thing Happened on the Way to the Forum* and *The Boys from Syracuse*, two Broadway farces based on Plautus, Casson represents his author as a popular entertainer: "Plautus, in a very real sense, faced the same problems as a writer for Broadway today." The comedy is broad and energetic. Plautus is the father of what we now know as situation comedy—soap opera in its most extreme form. The situations from ordinary life are deliberately heated up and complicated so that the comedy arises from extravagance and wildness. The audience is genially pushed right over the edge of probability where it can wallow in wonderfully improbable mistakes and coincidences. Daily life in Plautus is deceptively tricky, unreliable, and unpredictable. We await the crazy idea, supposition, assumption, or course of action that will energize the farce.

THE MENAECHMUS TWINS

TRANSLATED BY LIONEL CASSON

CHARACTERS

SPONGE (PENICULUS), *hanger-on of Menaechmus of Epidamnus, who makes his way by scrounging from him and other well-to-do people* freeloader, in his 30's

MENAECHMUS OF EPIDAMNUS, *a well-to-do young married man, resident in Epidamnus*

LOVEY (EROTIUM), *a courtesan with whom Menaechmus of Epidamnus has been having an affair*

ROLL (CYLINDRUS), *her cook (slave)*

MENAECHMUS OF SYRACUSE, *twin brother of Menaechmus of Epidamnus, resident in Syracuse*

MESSENIO, *his servant (slave)*

MAID OF LOVEY *(slave)*

WIFE OF MENAECHMUS OF EPIDAMNUS

FATHER-IN-LAW OF MENAECHMUS OF EPIDAMNUS

A DOCTOR

DECIO, *servant of Menaechmus's wife*

SERVANTS

SCENE

A street in Epidamnus. Two houses front on it: stage left Menaechmus', stage right Lovey's. The exit on stage left leads downtown, that on stage right to the waterfront. The time is noon or a little after.

PROLOGUE

(The actor assigned to deliver the prologue enters, walks downstage, and addresses the audience.)

PROLOGUE: First and foremost, ladies and gentlemen, health and happiness to all of—me. And to you, too. I have Plautus here for you—not in my hands, on my tongue. Please be kind enough to take him—with your ears. Now, here's the plot. Pay attention, I'll make it as brief as I can.

Every comic playwright invariably tells you that the action of his piece takes place entirely at Athens; this is to give it that Greek touch. Well, I'm telling you the action takes place where the story says it does and nowhere else. The plot, as a matter of fact, *is* Greekish. Not Athensish, though; Sicilyish. But all this is so much preamble. Now I'll pour out your portion of plot for you. Not by the quart, not by the gallon, by the tankload. That's how big-hearted a plot-teller I am.

A certain man, a merchant, lived at Syracuse. His wife presented him with twin sons, two boys so alike that no one could tell them apart, neither the woman who nursed them, nor the mother who bore them. I got this from someone who'd seen them—I don't want you to get the idea I saw them myself; I never did.

Well, when the boys were seven years old, their father filled a fine freighter full of freight and put one twin aboard to take with him on a business trip to Tarentum. The other he left home with the mother. As it turned out, they arrived at Tarentum during a holiday, and—the usual thing during holidays—a lot of people had come to town, and son and sire got separated in the crowd.   merchant from Epidamnus happened to be on the spot; he picked the boy up and carried him off to Epidamnus. At the lad's loss, alas, the love of life left the father; a few days later, there at Tarentum, he died of a broken heart.

A message about all this—that the boy had been carried off

and the father had died at Tarentum—was brought back to Syracuse to the grandfather. When he heard the news, he changed the name of the boy who'd been left at home. The old man was so fond of the kidnaped twin that he transferred this one's name to his brother: he called the twin still left Menaechmus, the same name as the other had. (It was the old man's name too—I remember it so well because I heard it so often when his creditors dunned him.) To keep you from getting mixed up later I'm telling you now, in advance, that both twins have the same name.

Now, in order for me to make the whole story crystal clear for you, I have to retrace my steps and get back to Epidamnus. Any of you got some business you want me to take care of for you at Epidamnus? Step up, say the word, give me your orders. But don't forget the wherewithal for taking care of them. Anyone who doesn't give me some cash is wasting his time— and anyone who does is wasting a lot more. But now I'm really going back to where I started, and I'll stay put in one place.

The man from Epidamnus, the one I told you about a few seconds ago who carried off the other twin, had no children of his own—except his moneybags. He adopted the boy he had kidnaped, made him his son, found him a wife with a good dowry, and left him his whole estate when he died. You see, the old fellow happened to be going out to his country place one day after a heavy rain; a short way out of town he began fording a stream that was sweeping along, the sweeping current swept him off his feet the way he had once swept off that boy, and away to hell and gone he went.

So a handsome fortune dropped into his adopted son's lap. He—I mean the twin who was carried off—lives here (*pointing*). Now, the other, the one who lives in Syracuse, will arrive just today, along with a servant; he's searching for his twin brother. This (*gesturing toward the backdrop*) is Epidamnus—but only so long as our play is on the boards; when some other play goes on, it'll be some other city. It changes just the way the actors do—one day they're pimps, next day paupers; next youngsters, next oldsters; next beggars, kings, scroungers, cheats. . . .

ACT I

(Enter Sponge [Peniculus, literally "brush"], stage left, a man in his thirties with a protruding paunch and a general down-at-the-heels look. He is a parasitus, *"freeloader," the character, standard in ancient comedy, who, to fill his belly, runs errands and acts as general flunky and yes-man to anyone willing to issue an invitation to a meal. He walks downstage and addresses the audience.)*

SPONGE: The boys call me Sponge. Because, when I eat, I wipe the table clean.

It's stupid to put chains on prisoners or shackles on runaway slaves, at least to my way of thinking. This misery on top of all their others just makes the poor devils more set than ever on breaking out—and breaking the peace. Prisoners get out of the chains somehow or other, and slaves saw through the shackle or smash the pin with a rock. No, bolts and bars are the bunk. If you really want to keep someone from running away, chain him with dishes and glasses. Belay him by the beak to a groaning board. You give him all he wants to eat and drink daily and, so help me, he'll never run away, not even if he's up for hanging. Holding on to him is a cinch once you chain him with *that* kind of chain. And belly bonds are so firm and flexible—the more you stretch them, the tighter they get.

For example, I'm on my way to Menaechmus' house here (*pointing*). I sentenced myself to his jail years back: I'm going now of my own free will so he can put the irons on me. This Menaechmus is a man who doesn't just feed a man; he bloats the belly for you, he restores you to life—you won't find a finer physician. He's a fellow like this: he's as big an eater as they come himself, so every meal he serves looks like a thanksgiving day banquet: he overloads the tables, he piles up the plates like pyramids; you have to stand on your chair if you want something from on top. But it's been quite a while since my last invitation. I've had to be homebound with all

111

that's dear to me—you see, whatever I eat that I pay for is dear, very dear. And there's this: right now all that's so dear to me has broken ranks and deserted the table. So (*pointing again to Menaechmus' house*) I'm paying him a visit. Wait— the door's opening. There's Menaechmus himself; he's coming out.

(*Sponge moves off to the side. The door opens and Menaechmus of Epidamnus stomps out. He is a good-looking man in his middle twenties, whose grooming, clothes, and air all smack of a substantial income. His manifest irascibility is unusual: normally he is gay, an inveterate jokester, and always out for a good time. He is wearing a coat which he clutches tightly about him. He turns and addresses his wife who is visible in the doorway.*)

SONG

MENAECHMUS OF EPIDAMNUS (*angrily*):

If you weren't so stupid and sour,
Such a mean-tempered bitch, such a shrew,
What you see gives your husband a pain,
You'd make sure would give *you* a pain too.
From this moment henceforth,
You just try this once more,
And, a divorce in your hand,
You go darken Dad's door.

Every time that I want to go out
I get called, I get grabbed, I get grilled:
"Where are you going to go?"
"Why are you going outside?"
"What are you going to do?"
"What are you going to get?"
"What have you got in your hand?"
"What were you doing downtown?"

Why, the way I declare every act of my life,
It's a customs official I wed, not a wife!
Oh, you're spoiled, and I did it myself. Listen, you—
I'll explain here and now what I'm planning to do.

I've filled your every need:
The clothes you've on your back,
Your servants, food, and cash—
There's nothing that you lack.

> If you only had some sense,
> You'd watch what you're about.
> You'd let your husband be,
> And cut the snooping out.

And what's more, so your snooping's not lost
And the time you put in not a waste,
I'll be off to go find me a girl
Who can join me for dinner someplace.

SPONGE (*to the audience, in anguish*):

He pretends to be hard on his wife—
But it's *me* that he's giving the knife!
Eating out! Do you know who he'll hurt?
It's yours truly he'll hurt, not his wife.

MENAECHMUS OF EPIDAMNUS (*to himself, wonderingly, as his wife disappears inside*):
Well, I finally gave her what for—
And I drove the old bitch from the door!

(*To the audience, triumphantly*)

What's happened to the husbands who've been keeping mistresses?
What's holding up their plaudits and their cheers for what I've done?
They *all* owe me a medal for the fight I fought and won!

(*Throws his coat open to reveal a woman's dress he has on over his clothes*)

I stole this dress from her just now—I'll bring it to my girl.
Now *that's* the way to operate—outfox a foxy guard!
A beautiful piece of work it was, a feat to shout about,
A lovely piece of work it was, superbly carried out.

(*Losing his jubilation suddenly as realization dawns*)

I snitch from the bitch at *my* expense—and my downfall gets it all.

(*Cheering up again*)

But the enemy's camp's been looted, and we've safely made our haul!

SPONGE (*calling as Menaechmus starts marching toward Lovey's door*): Hey, mister, any share in that swag for me?

MENAECHMUS OF EPIDAMNUS (*stopping and closing his coat, but not turning around; to himself*): Ambushed! I'm lost!

SPONGE: Saved, you mean. Don't be afraid.

MENAECHMUS OF EPIDAMNUS (*still not turning*): Who is it?

SPONGE: Me.

MENAECHMUS OF EPIDAMNUS (*turning*): Hi, friend-in-need and Johnny-on-the-spot.

SPONGE: Hi.

MENAECHMUS OF EPIDAMNUS: What are you doing these days?

SPONGE (*grabbing Menaechmus' hand and pumping it*): I'm shaking the hand of my guardian angel.

MENAECHMUS OF EPIDAMNUS: You couldn't have timed it better to meet me.

SPONGE: I'm always like that—I know Johnny-on-the-spotitude down to the last dotitude.

MENAECHMUS OF EPIDAMNUS: You want to see a brilliant piece of work?

SPONGE (*smacking his lips*): Who cooked it? One look at the leftovers and I can tell in a minute if he slipped up anywhere.

MENAECHMUS OF EPIDAMNUS: Tell me, have you ever seen those famous pictures they hang on walls? The eagle carrying off Ganymede or Venus with Adonis?

SPONGE (*testily*): Lots of times. But what have those pictures got to do with me?

MENAECHMUS OF EPIDAMNUS (*throwing open his coat to reveal the dress*): See this? Do I look like one?

SPONGE (*staring*): What have you got on there, anyway?

MENAECHMUS OF EPIDAMNUS (*slyly*): Tell me I'm the nicest guy you know.

SPONGE (*suspiciously*): Where do we eat?

MENAECHMUS OF EPIDAMNUS (*pretending to be annoyed*): First tell me what I told you to.

SPONGE: All right, all right. You're the nicest guy I know.

MENAECHMUS OF EPIDAMNUS (*as before*): How about adding something on your own, please?

SPONGE (*grudgingly*): And the most fun to be with.

MENAECHMUS OF EPIDAMNUS: Go on.

SPONGE (*exploding*): God damn it, no going on till I know what for. You're on the outs with your wife, so I'm watching my step with you.

MENAECHMUS OF EPIDAMNUS (*sensing his teasing has gone far enough, gaily and conspiratorially*): Let's you and I, without letting my wife know a thing, kill off this day—

SPONGE (*interrupting*): Well, all right! That's something like! How soon shall I start the funeral? The day's already half dead, all the way down to the waist.

MENAECHMUS OF EPIDAMNUS (*with a great show of patience*): Interrupt me, and you just hold things up for yourself.

SPONGE (*hurriedly*): Menaechmus, poke my eye out if I utter another word. Orders from you excepted, of course.

MENAECHMUS OF EPIDAMNUS (*tiptoeing away from his house with anxious glances over his shoulder at the door*): Come on over here. Away from that door.

SPONGE (*following*): Sure.

MENAECHMUS OF EPIDAMNUS (*tiptoeing farther, with more glances*): Even more.

SPONGE (*following*): All right.

MENAECHMUS OF EPIDAMNUS (*now far enough away to give up tiptoeing—but still glancing*): Come on, step along. Farther from that lion's den.

SPONGE: I swear, if you ask me, you'd make a wonderful jockey.

MENAECHMUS OF EPIDAMNUS: Why?

SPONGE: The way you look behind every second to make sure your wife's not catching up.

MENAECHMUS OF EPIDAMNUS: I want to ask you a question.

SPONGE: Me? The answer's Yes, if you want yes; No, if you want no.

MENAECHMUS OF EPIDAMNUS: If you smelled something, could you tell from the smell—

SPONGE (*with one type of smell in mind, interrupting*): Better than a board of prophets.

MENAECHMUS OF EPIDAMNUS: All right, then, try this dress I have. What do you smell? (*He hands Sponge part of the skirt, Sponge sniffs, then jerks his nose away*) What did you do that for?

SPONGE: You've got to smell a woman's dress at the top. Down there there's an odor that never washes out, and it's death on the nose.

MENAECHMUS OF EPIDAMNUS (*moving the upper part toward him*): Smell here then. (*Laughing as Sponge sniffs gingerly*) You do a wonderful job of wrinkling up your nose.

SPONGE: I had good reason.

MENAECHMUS OF EPIDAMNUS: Well? What does it smell from? Tell me.

SPONGE: Loot, lechery—and lunch.

MENAECHMUS OF EPIDAMNUS (*clapping him on the back and leading him toward Lovey's door*): Right you are. Now it goes right to my lady friend Lovey here. And I'll have her fix up a lunch for me, you, and her.

SPONGE (*smacking his lips*): Fine!

MENAECHMUS OF EPIDAMNUS (*gaily*): We'll pass the bottle from now till the crack of dawn tomorrow.

SPONGE (*as before*): Fine! Now you're talking. Should I knock on the door?

MENAECHMUS OF EPIDAMNUS: Knock away. (*As Sponge races up to Lovey's door and raises a fist to deliver a lusty bang*) No, wait!

SPONGE (*bitterly*): You just passed that bottle back a mile.

MENAECHMUS OF EPIDAMNUS: Try a tiny tap.

SPONGE: What are you scared of? That the door's made of bone china? (*Turns to knock.*)

MENAECHMUS OF EPIDAMNUS (*excitedly*): Wait! Wait, for god's sake! See? She's coming out. Look how the sun grows gray 'gainst the glory of that gorgeous figure!

(*The door opens and Lovey* [Erotium, *literally "little love"*] *comes out, a good-looking girl in a brassy sort of way, flashily dressed and heavily made up.*)

LOVEY: Menaechmus, darling! How nice to see you!

SPONGE: How about me?

LOVEY (*witheringly*): You don't count.

SPONGE (*unruffled*): I do so. I'm in this man's army too. Rear guard.

MENAECHMUS OF EPIDAMNUS (*seeing a chance to tease her, slyly*): Orders from headquarters, Lovey: invite Sponge and me to your house today. For a duel.

LOVEY: All right. (*Throwing a baleful look at Sponge*) Just for today.

MENAECHMUS OF EPIDAMNUS (*as before*): A duel of drinks to the death. Whichever's the better man with the bottle becomes your bodyguard. You be referee, you decide which you'll sleep with tonight. (*Abruptly dropping his teasing as he notices her begin to sulk*) Honey, one look at you and, oh, do I hate that wife of mine!

LOVEY (*not yet mollified—and catching sight of the dress, frigidly*): In the meantime, you can't even keep from wearing her clothes. What is this, anyway?

MENAECHMUS OF EPIDAMNUS (*throwing his coat open, gaily*): Embezzled from her to embellish you, my flower.

LOVEY (*magically thawed out*): You always win out over all the other men who run after me. You have such winning ways.

SPONGE (*aside*): That's a mistress for you: nothing but sweet talk so long as she sees something to get her hands on. If you really loved him, you'd be kissing his mouth off this minute.

MENAECHMUS OF EPIDAMNUS (*taking off his coat*): Sponge, hold this. I want to carry out the dedication ceremony I scheduled.

SPONGE: Hand it over. (*Taking the coat and eying Menaechmus in the dress*) Since you're in costume, how about favoring us with a bit of ballet later?

MENAECHMUS OF EPIDAMNUS: Ballet? Me? Are you in your right mind?

SPONGE: You mean are *you* in your right mind. All right, if no ballet, get out of costume.

MENAECHMUS OF EPIDAMNUS (*taking the dress off and handing it to Lovey*): I took an awful chance stealing this today. Riskier, if you ask me, than when Hercules helped himself to Hippolyta's girdle. It's all for you—because you're the only person in the whole world who's really nice to me.

LOVEY: What a lovely thought! That's the way all nice lovers should think.

SPONGE (*aside*): You mean if they're hell-bent to get to the poorhouse.

MENAECHMUS OF EPIDAMNUS (*to Lovey*): I paid a thousand dollars last year for that dress you have there. Got it for my wife.

SPONGE (*aside*): Using your own figures, that works out to a thousand dollars down the drain.

MENAECHMUS OF EPIDAMNUS (*to Lovey*): You know what I'd like you to do?

LOVEY: I know one thing: I'll do whatever you like.

MENAECHMUS OF EPIDAMNUS: Then have your cook prepare lunch for the three of us. Send him to the market for some gourmetetitious shopping. Have him bring back the pig family: the Duke of Pork, Lord Bacon, the little Trotters, and any other relatives. Things that, served roasted, reduce me to ravenousness. Right away, eh?

LOVEY: But of course!

MENAECHMUS OF EPIDAMNUS: Sponge and I are on our way downtown but we'll be back in a few minutes. We can have drinks while the things are on the fire.

LOVEY: Come back whenever you like. Everything will be ready.

MENAECHMUS OF EPIDAMNUS: Just hurry it up. (*Turning and striding off, stage left; to Sponge*) Follow me.

SPONGE (*running after him*): I'm not only following you, I'm not letting you out of my sight. Today is the one day I wouldn't lose you for all the treasures of heaven!

(*As Menaechmus and Sponge leave, Lovey walks to the door of her house.*)

LOVEY (*calling through the door to her maids inside*): Tell Roll, the cook, to come out here right away. (*A second later, Roll [Cylindrus], a roly-poly cook, races out and stands attentively in front of her.*) You'll need a shopping basket and some money. Here's fifteen dollars.

ROLL: Yes, ma'am.

LOVEY: Go do the marketing. Get just enough for three—not a bit more and not a bit less.

ROLL: What people are you having?

LOVEY: Menaechmus, his parasite, and myself.

ROLL (*thoughtfully*): That makes ten—a parasite can do for eight. Easily.

LOVEY: Now you know who'll be there; you take care of the rest.

ROLL (*importantly*): Right. Consider lunch cooked. Tell your guests to go in and sit down. (*Races off, stage left.*)

LOVEY (*calling after him*): Come right back!

ROLL (*over his shoulder*): Be back in a flash.

(*Roll dashes off, Lovey enters her house, and the stage is now empty.*)

ACT II

(Enter, stage right, Menaechmus of Syracuse and his servant Messenio carrying a satchel; behind them, loaded down with luggage, is a pair of rowers from the skiff that brought them ashore. These two move off to the side of the stage and put their burdens down.

In appearance Menaechmus of Syracuse is identical with his twin. But there the likeness ends. Menaechmus of Epidamnus is gay, generous, and fun loving; his brother is shrewd, calculating, and cynical. Messenio, about the same age as his master, is the long-faced type who worries easily and takes himself very seriously.)

MENAECHMUS OF SYRACUSE: Messenio, if you ask me, the greatest joy a sailor can have is to sight land from the open sea.

MESSENIO *(pointedly)*: I'll be honest with you: it's even greater when the land you come near and see is your homeland. Will you please tell me why we're here in Epidamnus? Are we going to do like sea water and go around every island there is?

MENAECHMUS OF SYRACUSE *(grimly)*: We're here to look for my brother. My twin brother.

MESSENIO *(exasperated)*: When are we going to put an end to looking for that man? We've been at it six years! Austria, Spain, France, Jugoslavia, Sicily, every part of Italy near salt water, up and down the Adriatic—we've made the rounds of all of them. Believe me, if you were looking for a needle, and it was anywhere to be found, you'd have found it long ago. We're looking for the dead among the living. Because, if he was alive to be found, you'd have found him long ago.

MENAECHMUS OF SYRACUSE *(as before)*: Then I'm looking for someone who can prove it, someone who'll tell me he knows for certain my brother is dead. Once I hear that, I'll never look for him again. But until I do, so long as I live, I'll never stop, I know how much he means to me.

MESSENIO (*grumbling*): You're looking for hens' teeth. Why don't we turn around and go home? Or maybe you and I are going to write a travel book?

MENAECHMUS OF SYRACUSE (*sharply*): You do what you're told, eat what you're given, and stay out of trouble! Don't annoy me now; we're doing things my way, not yours.

MESSENIO (*aside*): Ho-ho! That's telling me who's the slave around here. Couldn't have put things plainer with fewer words. But I can't hold this in, I've got to speak up. (*To Menaechmus*) Listen, Menaechmus. I've been looking over our finances. So help me, we're traveling with a summer-weight wallet. If you want my opinion, either you head for home, or you'll be mourning your long-lost money while you look for your long-lost brother. Let me tell you what kind of people live in these parts. The hardest drinkers and worst rakes are right here in Epidamnus. Besides, the town's full of crooks and swindlers. And they say the prostitutes here have a smoother line of talk than anywhere else in the world. That's why this place is called Epidamnus: nobody stays here without a damned lot of damage.

MENAECHMUS OF SYRACUSE (*unperturbed*): I'll keep my eyes open. You just hand over the wallet.

MESSENIO (*suspiciously*): What do you want with it?

MENAECHMUS OF SYRACUSE: After what you've been telling me, I'm scared to leave it with you.

MESSENIO: Scared of what?

MENAECHMUS OF SYRACUSE: That you'll do me a damned lot of damage in Epidamnus. You're a big man with the women, Messenio, and I'm a man with a big temper, the explosive type. If I keep the money, I avoid trouble both ways: you don't lose your head and I don't lose my temper.

MESSENIO (*handing over the wallet*): Here it is. You keep it. Glad to have you take over.

(*Enter Roll, stage left, lugging a loaded shopping basket.*)

ROLL (*to himself*): No trouble at all with the shopping. I got just what I wanted. I'll serve the diners a delicious dinner. Hey—who's that I see there? Menaechmus! Heaven help my poor back! The guests already at the door before I'm even back from the market! Well, I'll say hello. (*Walking up to Menaechmus*) Good afternoon, Menaechmus.

MENAECHMUS OF SYRACUSE (*surprised but cordial*): Good afternoon to you—whoever you are.

ROLL (*taken aback*): Whoever I am? You don't know who I am?

MENAECHMUS OF SYRACUSE: Of course not.

ROLL (*deciding to overlook the exchange as just another of Menaechmus' jokes*): Where are the rest of the guests?

MENAECHMUS OF SYRACUSE: Guests? What guests are you looking for?

ROLL: That parasite of yours.

MENAECHMUS OF SYRACUSE (*blankly*): Parasite of mine? (*To Messenio, sotto voce*) The man's daft.

MESSENIO (*sotto voce to Menaechmus*): Didn't I tell you the place was full of swindlers?

MENAECHMUS OF SYRACUSE: Now, mister, who is this parasite you're looking for?

ROLL: Sponge.

MESSENIO (*digging into the satchel he is carrying*): Got it safe right here in the satchel. See?

ROLL (*apologetically*): Menaechmus, you're too early. Lunch isn't ready. I just got back from the shopping.

MENAECHMUS OF SYRACUSE (*with exaggerated concern*): Tell me, mister, what were fresh fish selling for today?

ROLL: Dollar apiece.

MENAECHMUS OF SYRACUSE: Here's a dollar. Buy some for yourself; it's on me. The food'll do your brains good. Because there's one thing I'm dead sure of: you're out of your senses, whoever you are. Otherwise why would you make such a nuisance of yourself to a total stranger?

ROLL (*smiling indulgently*): You don't know *me?* You don't know Roll?

MENAECHMUS OF SYRACUSE (*testily*): I don't care if you're roll or loaf. Go to the devil! I don't know you, and, what's more, I don't want to!

ROLL (*with an I'll-play-along-with-your-little-joke smile*): Your name's Menaechmus, isn't it?

MENAECHMUS OF SYRACUSE (*anger giving way to curiosity*): To the best of my knowledge. And when you call me "Menaechmus" you talk sense. Where do you know me from, anyway?

ROLL (*chuckling*): You're carrying on an affair with my owner Lovey (*gesturing toward the house*), and you have to ask *me* where I know you from?

MENAECHMUS (*tartly*): I'm not carrying on any affairs, and I haven't the slightest idea who you are.

ROLL (*as before*): You don't know who *I* am? Me? Your glass-filler all the times you come over to our house for drinks?

MESSENIO (*to the world at large*): Damn! Here I am without a thing to split that skull of his in half!

MENAECHMUS OF SYRACUSE: You my glass-filler? When I've never set foot in Epidamnus, never set eyes on the place in my life till today?

ROLL: You mean you deny it?

MENAECHMUS OF SYRACUSE: I certainly do deny it!

ROLL (*pointing to the house of Menaechmus of Epidamnus*): You mean to say you don't live in that house there?

MENAECHMUS OF SYRACUSE (*roaring*): To hell with any and every-one who lives in that house there!

ROLL (*to the audience, smiling*): Swearing at himself. *He's* the one who's daft. (*To Menaechmus*) Listen, Menaechmus.

MENAECHMUS OF SYRACUSE (*sourly*): What do you want?

ROLL: You know that dollar you offered to give me a minute ago? Take my advice and use it to buy fish for your own brains. You swore at your own self just now, you certainly can't be in your right mind.

MENAECHMUS OF SYRACUSE: God! Talk, talk, talk! He's getting on my nerves!

ROLL (*to the audience*): He always kids around with me like this. He's a real card—when his wife's not around. (*To Menaechmus*) I say, Menaechmus. (*As Menaechmus stubbornly stands with his back to him*) I say there, Menaechmus! (*Menaechmus throws up his hands in despair and turns around. Roll holds out the basket.*) Take a look. You think I bought enough for you, your parasite, and your lady? Or should I go back for more?

MENAECHMUS OF SYRACUSE (*wearily*): What lady? What parasite are you talking about?

MESSENIO (*to Roll, truculently*): What's the matter? Something on your conscience that's driving you out of your mind? Is that why you're making a nuisance of yourself to this man?

ROLL (*resentfully*): What are *you* butting in for? I don't know you. I'm talking to this man here. Him I know.

MESSENIO: There's one thing I know: you're stark-raving mad, you are.

ROLL (*pointedly ignoring Messenio; to Menaechmus, reassuringly*): I'll have everything cooked in a minute. You won't have to wait. So please don't go too far from the house. (*Turning to go*) Anything I can do for you before I go in?

MENAECHMUS OF SYRACUSE (*stalking away*): Yes. Go to hell.

ROLL (*muttering*): No, damn it, you go—(*as Menaechmus whirls around*) and have a seat while I (*importantly*) expose all this to the flame's fiery fury. I'll go and tell my mistress you're here so she can invite you in and not leave you standing around outside. (*Goes into the house.*)

MENAECHMUS OF SYRACUSE (*to Messenio*): Has he gone? (*Hearing the door slam*) He's gone. So help me, now I know that what you said was no lie.

MESSENIO (*importantly*): You just watch your step. It's my theory that one of those prostitutes lives here. That's what that lunatic who just left said.

MENAECHMUS OF SYRACUSE (*puzzled*): What amazes me is how he knew my name.

MESSENIO (*with the air of an expert*): Nothing amazing about that. These girls have a system. They send their tricky little maids and houseboys down to the docks. Whenever a foreigner heads for a berth, they start asking the name and the home port. The next minute the girls are hanging around his neck and sticking to him like glue. And, if he once takes the bait, he goes home a goner. (*Pointing to Lovey's house*) Now, there's a privateer moored in this berth right here. My advice is, let's steer clear of her.

MENAECHMUS OF SYRACUSE: Good advice. Messenio, you're on your toes.

MESSENIO: I'll know I'm on my toes when I see you on your guard, not before.

MENAECHMUS OF SYRACUSE: Sh! Quiet a minute. I hear the door opening. Let's see who's coming out.

MESSENIO: I'll get rid of this in the meantime. (*Handing the satchel to one of the rower-porters*) Hey, oar-power, keep an eye on this, will you please?

(*Lovey appears in the doorway. She turns and addresses a maid who was about to close the door behind her.*)

SONG

LOVEY (*adjusting the door*):
> No, not closed. Just like this, open wide.
> Now go in and get going inside.
> See that everything's set in the room.
> Spread some cushions. And lots of perfume.

(*Turns and addresses the audience*)

> Sophistication—that's the way
> To bring a lover-boy to bay.
> Plus saying Yes—to men a curse,
> To girls a way to fill a purse.

(*Looks around and, at first, doesn't see Menaechmus*)

> Now, where's he gone? My cook reports
> He's standing by the door.
> Oh, there he is—my useful and
> Most profitable amour.
>
> He's lord and master in my house.
> He's earned the right to be,
> And so I let him. Now I'll go
> And let him talk to me.

(*Walks up to Menaechmus*)

> Sweetie-pie! You surprise me, you do,
> With this standing around outside here.
> Why, my door's open wider to you
> Than your own. This is *your* house, my dear.
>
> Not a thing that you asked to be done
> Have my servants forgotten, not one.
> They're all ready inside, honeybunch,
> They've made *just* what you ordered for lunch.

So, whenever you'd like to come in,
We can all take our seats and begin.

MENAECHMUS OF SYRACUSE (*to Messenio*): Who's this woman talking to?

LOVEY (*with a dazzling smile*): You, of course.

MENAECHMUS OF SYRACUSE: And just what have you, in the present or past, ever had to do with me?

LOVEY (*meltingly*): So much! And just because Cupid told me to pick you out of all the men in the world and make you the most important man in my life. And it's no more than you deserve. I can't tell you how happy you've made me, just you alone, by all the nice things you've done for me.

MENAECHMUS OF SYRACUSE (*sotto voce to Messenio*): Messenio, this woman's either drunk or daft. She treats a total stranger like a bosom friend.

MESSENIO (*sotto voce*): Didn't I tell you? That's the kind of thing that goes on around here. But this is just the leaves falling. Stay three days longer and see what you get then: a tree trunk on your head. That's what prostitutes here are like—gold diggers, every one of them. (*Tapping himself importantly on the chest*) You just let *me* talk to her. Hey, lady! (*As Lovey looks at him blankly*) Yes, you.

LOVEY: What is it?

MESSENIO: Where do you know this man from?

LOVEY (*with a that's-a-silly-question air*): Same place he's known me from, all these years. Epidamnus.

MESSENIO: Epidamnus? When he never set foot in the place till today?

LOVEY: Tee-hee! You make such funny jokes. (*Taking Menaechmus by the arm*) Menaechmus dear, why don't you come inside? It's much nicer in here.

MENAECHMUS OF SYRACUSE (*extricating himself; sotto voce to Messenio*): What the devil! This woman's called me by my right name. I don't get it. What's going on here?

MESSENIO (*sotto voce*): She got a whiff of that wallet you're carrying.

MENAECHMUS OF SYRACUSE (*sotto voce*): Darned good thing you warned me (*Handing over the wallet*) Here, you take it. Now I'll find out whether it's me or my money she's so passionate about.

LOVEY: Let's go in and have lunch.

MENAECHMUS OF SYRACUSE: It's awfully nice of you, but, thank you, I really can't.

LOVEY (*staring at him in amazement*): Then why did you tell me to make lunch for you a little while ago?

MENAECHMUS OF SYRACUSE: *I* told you to make lunch?

LOVEY: You certainly did. For you and that parasite of yours.

MENAECHMUS OF SYRACUSE (*peevishly*): Damn it all, what parasite? (*Sotto voce to Messenio*) This woman must be out of her mind.

LOVEY: Sponge.

MENAECHMUS OF SYRACUSE: Sponge? What sponge? For cleaning shoes?

LOVEY (*accustomed to Menaechmus' jokes, patiently*): The one who was here with you a little while ago, of course. When you brought me the dress you stole from your wife.

MENAECHMUS OF SYRACUSE (*clutching his head*): What's this? I brought you a dress I stole from my wife? Are you crazy? (*Sotto voce to Messenio*) She's dreaming; she sure goes to sleep like a horse—standing up.

LOVEY (*starting to sulk*): You always get such pleasure out of teasing me. Why do you say you didn't do what you definitely did do?

MENAECHMUS OF SYRACUSE (*slowly, emphasizing each word*): Now, will you kindly tell me just what I did do that I say I didn't do?

LOVEY: Give me one of your wife's dresses today.

MENAECHMUS OF SYRACUSE (*helplessly*): And I *still* say I didn't! Listen: I never had a wife, I don't have one now, and never, since the day I was born, have I set foot inside this city till this minute. I had lunch aboard ship, I came from there here, and I ran into you.

LOVEY (*tearfully*): Well! Oh, this is terrible, this will be the end of me! What ship are you talking about?

MENAECHMUS OF SYRACUSE (*glibly*): A wooden one. Been scraped, calked, and repaired time and again. More pine plugs patching the planks than pegs holding pelts at a furrier's.

LOVEY (*pleading*): Please, dear, no more games. Come inside with me now.

MENAECHMUS OF SYRACUSE: Lady, it's not me you want. It's some other man. I haven't the slightest idea who.

LOVEY (*with a let's-be-serious-now air*): I know perfectly well who you are. You're Menaechmus, your father's name was Moschus, and I've heard say you were born in Syracuse in Sicily. (*Like a schoolgirl reciting—and getting most of her lesson wrong*) The king of Syracuse was Agathocles, then Phint-something, then Etna, and now Hiero. Etna gave it to Hiero when he died.

MENAECHMUS OF SYRACUSE (*amazed—and amused; dryly*): Absolutely right, lady, every word.

MESSENIO (*sotto voce to Menaechmus*): By god, I bet she comes from there, and that's how she knows all about you.

MENAECHMUS OF SYRACUSE (*sotto voce*): Then I really don't think I can turn down her invitation.

MESSENIO (*sotto voce*): You do nothing of the sort! You go through that door, and you're through.

MENAECHMUS OF SYRACUSE (*sotto voce, peevishly*): Shut up, will you? Everything's going fine. I'm going to say yes to whatever she says: maybe I can get myself some free entertainment. (*To Lovey*) My dear girl, I knew what I was doing when I kept saying no to you up to now. I was afraid that fellow (*gesturing toward Messenio*) would tell my wife about the dress and our date. Since you'd like to go in now, let's.

LOVEY: You're not going to wait for your parasite?

MENAECHMUS OF SYRACUSE (*exploding*): No, I am *not* going to wait for my parasite, I don't give a damn about my parasite, and, if he shows up, I want him kept out.

LOVEY: It'll be a pleasure, believe me. (*Going up to him and stroking his cheek*) Menaechmus, do you know what I'd like you to do for me?

MENAECHMUS OF SYRACUSE: Just say the word.

LOVEY: I'd like you to take that dress you just gave me to the dressmaker and have her make some alterations and add some touches I want.

MENAECHMUS OF SYRACUSE (*enthusiastically*): By god, you're right! That way nobody'll recognize it, and my wife won't know you have it on if she sees you in the street.

LOVEY: Then remember to take it with you when you leave.

MENAECHMUS OF SYRACUSE: I sure will!

LOVEY: Let's go in.

MENAECHMUS OF SYRACUSE: I'll be right with you: I want to have a last word with this fellow here. (*Lovey goes into the house; he turns to Messenio.*) Hey, Messenio, come over here.

MESSENIO (*angrily*): What's going on? What do you have to do *this* for?

MENAECHMUS OF SYRACUSE: I have to. (*As Messenio opens his mouth*) I know all about it, you can save your breath.

MESSENIO (*bitterly*): That makes it even worse.

MENAECHMUS OF SYRACUSE (*triumphantly*): Initial operation proceeding according to plan. I'm practically looting the enemy camp. Now, get going as fast as you can and take these fellows (*gesturing toward the rower-porters*) to the hotel this minute. Be sure you come back for me before sundown.

MESSENIO (*pleading*): Menaechmus, listen, you don't know these girls.

MENAECHMUS OF SYRACUSE (*sharply*): Enough talk. If I do anything stupid it'll be my neck, not yours. The stupid one's this woman. She doesn't have a brain in her head. From what I saw just now, there's rich pickings in here for us. (*Goes into the house.*)

MESSENIO (*calling after him*): Good lord, are you really going in? (*Shaking his head, to himself*) He's a dead duck. The privateer has our rowboat in tow and is hauling it straight to hell and gone. But I'm the one without a brain in my head for thinking I can run my master. He bought me to listen to what he says, not order him around. (*To the rower-porters*) Follow me. I have orders to get back here in time, and I don't want to be late.

(*Messenio and his men file out, stage right. The stage is now empty.*)

ACT III

(Enter Sponge, stage left, in a mad hurry. The sight of Lovey's closed door brings him to an abrupt halt. He claps a hand to his brow, then turns and walks downstage to address the audience.)

SPONGE: I'm over thirty now, and never have I ever in all those years pulled a more damned fool stunt than the one I pulled today: there was this town meeting, and *I* had to dive in and come up right in the middle of it. While I'm standing there with my mouth open, Menaechmus sneaks off on me. I'll bet he's gone to his girl friend. Perfectly willing to leave me behind, too!

(Paces up and down a few times, shaking his head bitterly. Then, in a rage) Damn, damn, damn the fellow who first figured out town meetings! All they do is keep a busy man away from his business. Why don't people pick a panel of men of leisure for this kind of thing? Hold a roll call at each meeting and whoever doesn't answer gets fined on the spot. There are plenty of persons around who need only one meal a day; they don't have business hours to keep because they don't go after dinner invitations or give them out. They're the ones to fuss with town meetings and town elections. If that's how things were run, I wouldn't have lost my lunch today. He sure wanted me along, didn't he? I'll go in, anyway. There's still hope of leftovers to soothe my soul. *(He is about to go up to the door when it suddenly swings open and Menaechmus of Syracuse appears, standing on the threshold with a garland, a little askew, on his head; he is holding the dress and listening to Lovey who is chattering at him from inside. Sponge quickly backs off into a corner.)* What's this I see? Menaechmus—and he's leaving, garland and all! The table's been cleared! I sure came in time—in time to walk him home. Well, I'll watch what his game is, and then I'll go and have a word with him.

130

MENAECHMUS OF SYRACUSE (*To Lovey inside*): Take it easy, will you! I'll have it back to you today in plenty of time, altered and trimmed to perfection. (*Slyly*) Believe me, you'll say it's not your dress; you won't know it any more.

SPONGE (*to the audience*): He's bringing the dress to the dressmaker. The dining's done, the drinks are down—and Sponge spent the lunch hour outside. God damn it, I'm not the man I think I am if I don't get even with him for this, but really even. You just watch. I'll give it to him, I will.

MENAECHMUS OF SYRACUSE (*closing the door and walking downstage; to the audience, jubilantly*): Good god, no one ever expected less—and got more blessings from heaven in one day than me. I dined, I wined, I wenched, and (*holding up the dress*) made off with this to which, from this moment on, she hereby forfeits all right, title, and interest.

SPONGE (*straining his ears, to the audience*): I can't make out what he's saying from back here. Is that full-belly talking about me and my right title and interest?

MENAECHMUS OF SYRACUSE (*to the audience*): She said I stole it from my wife and gave it to her. I saw she was mistaking me for someone else, so I promptly played it as if she and I were having a hot and heavy affair and began to yes her; I agreed right down the line to everything she said. Well, to make a long story short, I never had it so good for so little.

SPONGE (*clenching his fists, to the audience*): I'm going up to him. I'm itching to give him the works. (*Leaves his corner and strides belligerently toward Menaechmus.*)

MENAECHMUS OF SYRACUSE (*to the audience*): Someone coming up to me. Wonder who it is?

SPONGE (*roaring*): Well! You featherweight, you filth, you slime, you disgrace to the human race, you double-crossing good-for-nothing! What did I ever do to you that you had to ruin my life? You sure gave me the slip downtown a little while ago! You killed off the day all right—and held the funeral feast without me. Me who was coheir under the will! Where do you come off to do a thing like that!

MENAECHMUS OF SYRACUSE (*too pleased with life to lose his temper*): Mister, will you please tell me what business you and I have that gives you the right to use language like that to a stranger here, someone you never saw in your life? You hand me that talk and I'll hand you something you won't like.

SPONGE (*dancing with rage*): God damn it, you already have! I know god damned well you have!

MENAECHMUS OF SYRACUSE (*amused and curious*): What's your name, mister?

SPONGE (*as before*): Still making jokes, eh? As if you don't know my name!

MENAECHMUS OF SYRACUSE: So help me, so far as I know, I never heard of you or saw you till this minute. But I know one thing for sure: whoever you are, you'd better behave yourself and stop bothering me.

SPONGE (*taken aback for a minute*): Menaechmus! Wake up!

MENAECHMUS OF SYRACUSE (*genially*): Believe me, to the best of my knowledge, I am awake.

SPONGE: You don't know me?

MENAECHMUS OF SYRACUSE (*as before*): If I did, I wouldn't say I didn't.

SPONGE (*incredulously*): You don't know your own parasite?

MENAECHMUS OF SYRACUSE: Mister, it looks to me as if you've got bats in your belfry.

SPONGE (*shaken, but not convinced*): Tell me this: didn't you steal that dress there from your wife today and give it to Lovey?

MENAECHMUS OF SYRACUSE: Good god, no! I don't have a wife, I never gave anything to any Lovey, and I never stole any dress. Are you in your right mind?

SPONGE (*aside, groaning*): A dead loss, the whole affair. (*To Menaechmus*) But you came out of your house wearing the dress! I saw you myself!

MENAECHMUS OF SYRACUSE (*exploding*): Damn you! You think everybody's a pervert just because you are? I was wearing this dress? Is that what you're telling me?

SPONGE: I most certainly am.

MENAECHMUS OF SYRACUSE: Now you go straight to the one place fit for you! No—get yourself to the lunatic asylum; you're stark-raving mad.

SPONGE (*venomously*): God damn it, there's one thing nobody in the world is going to stop me from doing: I'm telling the whole story, exactly what happened, to your wife this minute. All these insults are going to boomerang back on your own head. Believe you me, you'll pay for eating that whole lunch yourself. (*Dashes into the house of Menaechmus of Epidamnus.*)

MENAECHMUS OF SYRACUSE (*throwing his arms wide, to the audience*): What's going on here? Must everyone I lay eyes on play games with me this way? Wait—I hear the door.

(*The door of Lovey's house opens, and one of her maids comes out holding a bracelet. She walks over to Menaechmus and, as he looks on blankly, hands it to him.*)

MAID: Menaechmus, Lovey says would you please do her a big favor and drop this at the jeweler's on your way? She wants you to give him an ounce of gold and have him make the whole bracelet over.

MENAECHMUS OF SYRACUSE (*with alacrity*): Tell her I'll not only take care of this but anything else she wants taken care of. Anything at all. (*He takes the piece and examines it absorbedly.*)

MAID (*watching him curiously, in surprise*): Don't you know what bracelet it is?

MENAECHMUS OF SYRACUSE: Frankly no—except that it's gold.

MAID: It's the one you told us you stole from your wife's jewel box when nobody was looking.

MENAECHMUS OF SYRACUSE (*forgetting himself, in high dudgeon*): I never did anything of the kind!

MAID: You mean you don't remember it? Well, if that's the case, you give it right back!

MENAECHMUS OF SYRACUSE (*after a few seconds of highly histrionic deep thought*): Wait a second. No, I *do* remember it. Of course—this is the one I gave her. Oh, and there's something else: where are the armlets I gave her at the same time?

MAID (*puzzled*): You never gave her any armlets.

MENAECHMUS OF SYRACUSE (*quickly*): Right you are. This was all I gave her.

MAID: Shall I tell her you'll take care of it?

MENAECHMUS OF SYRACUSE: By all means, tell her. I'll take care of it, all right. I'll see she gets it back the same time she gets the dress back.

MAID (*going up to him and stroking his cheek*): Menaechmus dear, will you do me a favor too? Will you have some earrings made for me? Drop earrings, please; ten grams of gold in each. (*Meaningfully*) It'll make me *so* glad to see you every time you come to the house.

MENAECHMUS OF SYRACUSE: Sure. (*With elaborate carelessness*) Just give me the gold. I'll pay for the labor myself.

MAID: Please, you pay for the gold, too. I'll make it up to you afterward.

MENAECHMUS OF SYRACUSE: No, you pay for the gold. I'll make it up to *you* afterward. Double.

MAID: I don't have the money.

MENAECHMUS OF SYRACUSE (*with a great air of magnanimity*): Well, any time you get it, you just let me have it.

MAID (*turning to go*): I'm going in now. Anything I can do for you?

MENAECHMUS OF SYRACUSE: Yes. Tell her I'll see to both things— (*sotto voce, to the audience*) that they get sold as quickly as possible for whatever they'll bring. (*As the maid starts walking toward the door*) Has she gone in yet? (*Hearing a slam*) Ah, she's in, the door's closed. (*Jubilantly*) The lord loves me! I've had a helping hand from heaven! (*Suddenly looks about warily*) But why hang around when I have the time and chance to get away from this (*jerking his thumb at Lovey's house*) pimping parlor here? Menaechmus! Get a move on, hit the road, forward march! I'll take off this garland and toss it to the left here (*doing so*). Then, if anyone tries to follow me, he'll think I went that way. Now I'll go and see if I can find my servant. I want to let him know all the blessings from heaven I've had.

(*He races off, stage right. The stage is now empty.*)

ACT IV

(The door of Menaechmus' house flies open and his wife bursts out, shrieking, with Sponge at her heels.)

WIFE: Am I supposed to put up with a marriage like this? Look the other way while that husband of mine sneaks off everything in the house and hands it all over to his lady friend?

SPONGE *(looking around uneasily)*: Not so loud, please! I'll see to it you catch him red-handed right now. Just follow me. *(Starting to walk off, stage left)* He was on his way to the dressmaker with that dress he stole from you today. Had a garland on his head and was dead drunk. *(Noticing the garland Menaechmus of Syracuse had thrown down)* Hey, look! The garland he had on! I wasn't lying to you, was I? There you are. That's the way he went if you want to follow his trail. *(Looking toward the wings, stage left)* Well, look at that! He's coming back. Perfect! *(Peering hard)* But he doesn't have the dress!

WIFE *(grimly)*: What should I do to him this time?

SPONGE: Same as usual: lace into him. That's what I'd vote for. *(Pulling her off to the side)* Let's go over here. Then jump on him from ambush.

(Enter Menaechmus of Epidamnus, hot, tired, and in a foul temper. He walks downstage and addresses the audience.)

SONG

MENAECHMUS OF EPIDAMNUS:
What a custom we have! Bothersome, bad,
Stupid, silly, senseless, mad!
And practiced most by our leading lights:
They all adore,
They're passionate for
A flock of fawning satellites.

Whether good or bad never bothers them:
The fawner's funds they're bothered about.
How people regard his character—
      They leave that out.

Is he good as gold but rather poor?
      He's a bum.
Is he worthless but has lots of gold?
      The best they come!

A patron goes wild with worry and care
      Because of his charges' acts.
They know no truth or law or justice;
      They deny undeniable facts;

They're vicious, avaricious crooks
      Forever up for trial—
Through usury and perjury
      They've made their pile.

In summary, civil, or criminal court,
Whenever a case of theirs comes up,
      We patrons come up too—
Of course: we have to take the stand
      And defend what the dastards do.

   *(Pauses, shakes his head despondently, then continues
bitterly.)*

      That's what *I* had to do just today.
      One of mine simply held me at bay.
      I couldn't do what I wished, nor with whom,
      For he hung and he clung; it was doom.
   I went up on the stand and I entered a plea
   On behalf of this creature's chicanery.

   I proposed the most twisted and tortuous terms;
      Here I'd skim, there go on for a while.
   I was arguing to settle the case out of court;
      What does *he* do? Insist on a trial!

There were three solid citizens who'd witnessed each crime—
Most open-and-shut case since the beginning of time!

      He ruined this day for me.
      God damn that stupid clown!
      And god damn me as well!
      For setting foot downtown.

I told her to make me lunch;
She's expecting me, I know.
A perfect day set up—
And I had to ruin it so!

I left as soon as I could
And hurried back uptown.
She'll be sore at me, I'm sure—
But that dress will calm her down,
The one I sneaked today from my wife
And handed to Lovey, the light of my life!

SPONGE (*sotto voce to the wife, triumphantly*): Well, what do you say?

WIFE (*sotto voce*): That I'm the miserable wife of a miserable husband.

SPONGE (*sotto voce*): You can hear what he's saying, can't you?

WIFE (*sotto voce, grimly*): I can hear, all right.

MENAECHMUS OF EPIDAMNUS (*to the audience, gesturing toward Lovey's door*): Now why don't I be smart and go right inside here where I can have myself a good time?

SPONGE (*springing out of his corner, shouting*): Wait! You're going to have a bad one, instead.

WIFE (*following him, shrieking*): You'll pay me and with interest, you burglar.

SPONGE (*gleefully*): That's giving it to him!

WIFE: So you thought you could commit all these crimes and get away with it, eh?

MENAECHMUS OF EPIDAMNUS (*all innocence*): My dear wife, what are you talking about?

WIFE (*witheringly*): You ask *me*?

MENAECHMUS OF EPIDAMNUS (*acting puzzled, and gesturing toward Sponge*): Should I ask him? (*Walks toward her as if to put an arm about her.*)

WIFE: Don't you dare touch me!

SPONGE (*to the wife*): Keep at him!

MENAECHMUS OF EPIDAMNUS (*switching from puzzlement back to innocence*): What are you so mad at me for?

WIFE (*grimly*): You ought to know.

SPONGE: He knows, all right, but he's pretending he doesn't, the dirty rat!

MENAECHMUS OF EPIDAMNUS (*to his wife, as before*): What *is* this all about?

WIFE: That dress—

MENAECHMUS OF EPIDAMNUS (*quickly*): Dress?

WIFE: Yes, dress. Which a certain person— (*Menaechmus begins to shake. She observes him with grim satisfaction.*) What are you so scared about?

MENAECHMUS OF EPIDAMNUS (*with a sickly attempt at nonchalance*): Me? Nothing. Nothing at all.

SPONGE (*to Menaechmus, sneering*): With one exception—dress distress. (*As Menaechmus looks at him startled and then begins to pass frantic nods and winks*) So you *would* eat lunch behind my back, would you? (*To the wife*) Keep at him!

MENAECHMUS OF EPIDAMNUS (*sotto voce to Sponge*): Shut up, will you!

SPONGE (*answering Menaechmus' stage whisper in ringing tones*): I most certainly will *not* shut up. (*To the wife*) He's making signs to me not to speak.

MENAECHMUS OF EPIDAMNUS: Me? I most certainly am not! I'm not winking, I'm not nodding, I'm not doing anything of the kind.

SPONGE (*to the wife, shaking his head incredulously*): Of all the nerve! He actually denies what you can see with your own eyes!

MENAECHMUS OF EPIDAMNUS (*to the wife, solemnly*): My dear wife, I swear to you by all that's holy, I did *not* make any signs to (*jerking his head contemptuously in Sponge's direction*) that there. Now are you satisfied?

SPONGE: All right, she believes you about that there; now get back to the point.

MENAECHMUS OF EPIDAMNUS (*with angelic innocence*): Get back where?

SPONGE: Get back to that dressmaker, *I* say. Go ahead. And bring back the dress.

MENAECHMUS OF EPIDAMNUS (*as before*): What dress are you talking about?

SPONGE: It's time for me to stop doing the talking. This lady is forgetting her duty.

WIFE (*responding promptly to the cue*): Oh, I'm a poor, unhappy woman!

MENAECHMUS OF EPIDAMNUS (*going over to her, solicitously*): Why are you so unhappy, dear? Please tell me. Has one of the servants done something wrong? Are the maids or the houseboys answering you back? (*Switching from solicitousness to righteous indignation*) You just let me know about it. They'll pay for it, they will!

WIFE (*witheringly*): Nonsense!

MENAECHMUS OF EPIDAMNUS (*tenderly, to himself—but aloud*): She's so out of sorts. This distresses me.

WIFE (*as before*): Nonsense!

MENAECHMUS OF EPIDAMNUS (*nodding with sympathetic understanding*): Yes, you must be angry at one of the servants.

WIFE (*as before*): Nonsense!

MENAECHMUS OF EPIDAMNUS (*chuckling, as if what he's going to say is a great joke*): You can't be angry at *me*, at any rate.

WIFE (*grimly*): Now you're making sense.

MENAECHMUS OF EPIDAMNUS: *I* certainly haven't done anything wrong.

WIFE: Hah! Back to nonsense again.

MENAECHMUS OF EPIDAMNUS (*going up and putting his arm about her*): My dear, *please* tell me what's troubling you so much.

SPONGE (*to the wife, sneering*): Your little bunny's buttering you up.

MENAECHMUS OF EPIDAMNUS (*over his shoulder to Sponge, exasperated*): Can't you lay off me? Who's talking to you?

WIFE (*suddenly screaming*): Take your hands off me! (*Menaechmus leaps back as if stunned.*)

SPONGE (*to the wife*): That's giving it to him! (*To Menaechmus*) So you'll hurry off to eat lunch without me, will you? And then get drunk and walk out the door with a garland on your head and make fun of me, eh?

(Menaechmus grabs Sponge and yanks him over to the side.)

MENAECHMUS OF EPIDAMNUS (*sotto voce*): So help me, I not only haven't eaten lunch, I haven't set foot inside that house today!

SPONGE (*sotto voce*): You mean you deny it?

MENAECHMUS OF EPIDAMNUS (*sotto voce*): Of course I deny it.

SPONGE (*sotto voce*): What a nerve! You mean to say I didn't see you a little while ago standing in front of the door there with a garland on your head? When you said I had bats in the belfry and that you didn't know me and that you were a stranger here?

MENAECHMUS OF EPIDAMNUS (*sotto voce, blankly*): How could I? I just this minute came back home after you and I got separated.

SPONGE (*sotto voce, sneering*): Oh, I know your type. Didn't think I could get even with you, did you? I told the whole story to your wife, that's what I did!

MENAECHMUS OF EPIDAMNUS (*sotto voce, anxiously*): What did you tell her?

SPONGE (*sotto voce, blandly*): I don't know. Ask the lady herself.

(Menaechmus turns on his heel and hurries to where his wife is standing.)

MENAECHMUS OF EPIDAMNUS (*nervously*): My dear wife, what's going on here? What sort of story did this fellow hand you? What is it? Why don't you answer me? Why don't you tell me what's the matter?

WIFE (*witheringly*): As if you don't know! (*Slowly, emphasizing each word*) A dress was stolen from me.

MENAECHMUS OF EPIDAMNUS (*with wide-eyed innocence*): A dress was stolen from you?

WIFE (*as before*): Do you have to ask?

MENAECHMUS OF EPIDAMNUS (*as before*): If I knew, I certainly wouldn't ask.

SPONGE: Damn you! What a faker! But you can't cover up any longer—she knows the whole story; I told it to her myself down to the last detail.

MENAECHMUS OF EPIDAMNUS (*as before*): What story?

WIFE (*grimly*): Since you have such an unmitigated gall and refuse to confess of your own free will, listen and listen hard. Believe you me, you'll find out what I'm mad about and what this fellow told me. (*Looking him straight in the eye*) A dress was stolen from me.

MENAECHMUS OF EPIDAMNUS (*with histrionic astonishment*): A dress was stolen from me?

SPONGE (*to the wife*): Look at that! The dirty rat's trying to fool you! (*To Menaechmus*) Stolen from *her*, not you. Damn it all, if it had been stolen from *you*, then it really would be lost.

MENAECHMUS OF EPIDAMNUS (*to Sponge, savagely*): You keep out of this. (*To his wife*) Now, what were you saying, dear?

WIFE (*tight-lipped*): I was saying that one of my dresses disappeared from the house.

MENAECHMUS OF EPIDAMNUS: Who could have stolen it?

WIFE (*meaningfully*): I should think the man who made off with it knows the answer to that one.

MENAECHMUS OF EPIDAMNUS: Who is he?

WIFE: Someone named Menaechmus.

MENAECHMUS OF EPIDAMNUS (*thundering*): God in heaven, the man's a criminal! Who is this Menaechmus?

WIFE: I'll tell you: *you*.

MENAECHMUS OF EPIDAMNUS: Me?

WIFE: You.

(They stand in silence for a few seconds, eying one another.)

MENAECHMUS OF EPIDAMNUS (*blustering*): Who says so?

WIFE: I do.

SPONGE: So do I. And I also say you gave it to your lady friend Lovey here.

MENAECHMUS OF EPIDAMNUS: *I* gave it?

WIFE: Yes, you. You yourself.

SPONGE: What do you want us to do? Bring an owl here to keep saying "yoo yoo" to you? We're getting hoarse, the both of us.

MENAECHMUS OF EPIDAMNUS (*solemnly, one hand on heart, the other raised*): My dear wife, I swear to you by all that's holy, I didn't give it. Does that satisfy you?

SPONGE: And, damn it all, we take the same oath that you're lying!

(*Menaechmus looks from one to the other. They glower back. He quails visibly.*)

MENAECHMUS OF EPIDAMNUS (*feebly*): Well, you see, I didn't *give* it away, I sort of lent it out.

WIFE (*exploding*): Good god in heaven! *I* don't lend out your coats or suits, do I? If there's any lending to do, the wife will see to her things, and the husband to his. Now you get that dress back into this house, do you hear?

MENAECHMUS OF EPIDAMNUS (*meekly*): I'll see you get it back.

WIFE (*grimly*): And my opinion is, you'd better. Because you don't enter this house unless that dress is with you. I'm going in now. (*Turns her back on him and stalks off toward the door.*)

SPONGE (*calling after her, alarmed*): Don't I get anything for all I've done for you?

WIFE (*pausing at the threshold, contemptuously*): I'll do the same for you when something's stolen from your house. (*Slams the door behind her.*)

SPONGE (*to the audience, horror-stricken*): My god! That means never—I don't have anything to steal! Husband, wife—to hell with the both of you! I'm off downtown in a hurry—one thing I know for sure: I've worn out my welcome with this household! (*Scuttles off, stage left.*)

MENAECHMUS OF EPIDAMNUS (*to the audience, gaily*): My wife thinks she's giving me a bad time by shutting me out. As if I don't have another place to go into, lots better. (*Addressing the closed door*) You don't like me, eh? (*With a mock sigh*) I'll just have to put up with it. But Lovey here likes me. She's not going to shut me out, she's going to shut me in. (*Turning back to the audience*) I'll go see her and ask her to return the dress I just gave her. I'll buy her another one, even better. (*Walking up to Lovey's door and knocking*) Hey! Anybody minding this door? Open up, someone, and call Lovey out here!

LOVEY (*from inside*): Who wants me?

MENAECHMUS OF EPIDAMNUS: Someone who'd sooner see his own self hurt than hurt you.

LOVEY (*opening the door*): Menaechmus! Darling! What are you standing outside for? Come on in. (*Turns to go inside.*)

MENAECHMUS OF EPIDAMNUS (*seriously*): No, wait. You don't know what I've come for.

LOVEY (*walking up to him and stroking his cheek*): Sure I do. So you can have your fun with me.

MENAECHMUS OF EPIDAMNUS (*as before*): Damn it all, it's not that. Would you please do me a big favor and give me back that dress I just gave you? My wife's found out everything, she knows exactly what happened. I'll buy you another that costs twice as much, anyone you like.

LOVEY (*staring at him blankly*): But I just gave it to you a few minutes ago to take to the dressmaker! Along with that bracelet you were to take to the jeweler so he could make it over.

MENAECHMUS OF EPIDAMNUS (*staring at her blankly*): What's that? You gave *me* the dress and a bracelet? Oh, no. You never did. Figure it out. Right after I gave it to you, I went downtown, I came back from there just a few minutes ago, and this is the first I've seen of you since.

LOVEY (*stepping back and eying him frigidly*): *I* see what your game is. I trusted you with the dress, and now you're looking for a way to do me out of it.

MENAECHMUS OF EPIDAMNUS (*earnestly*): I swear I'm not asking for it to do you out of it. I tell you my wife knows everything!

LOVEY (*building up a head of feminine steam*): *I* didn't ask you to give it to me. *You* brought it to me of your own free will. You gave it as a gift, and now you want it back. Well, *I* don't mind. Take it. Keep it. Let your wife wear it, wear it yourself, lock it up in a closet, for all I care. But don't you fool yourself: you're not setting foot inside this door from now on. After all I've done for you, you'll treat me like dirt under your feet, will you? Unless you come with cash in your hands, you're wasting your time, you'll get nothing out of me. Find some other girl to treat like—like a fool under your feet!

MENAECHMUS OF EPIDAMNUS: Don't carry on so, please! (*As she turns her back on him and flounces inside*) Hey, wait, I tell you! Come on back! Stop, won't you? Please, do me a favor, and come back! (*She slams the door behind her. Menaechmus turns despondently to the audience*) She's gone in and shut the door. I'm the shuttest-out man there is: my wife, my mistress—nobody believes a thing I say. Well, I'll go and talk things over with my friends and see what they think I ought to do.

(Menaechmus leaves, stage left. The stage is now empty.)

ACT V

(Menaechmus of Syracuse enters, stage right, back from his search for Messenio along the waterfront. At the same moment, the door of Menaechmus of Epidamnus' house opens, and the wife comes out.)

MENAECHMUS OF SYRACUSE *(to himself, disgustedly)*: That was a stupid stunt I pulled a little while ago, to trust the wallet with all our money to Messenio. If you ask me, he's made himself at home in some dive somewhere.

WIFE *(to herself)*: I'll keep an eye out for that husband of mine. See how soon he comes back. *(Noticing Menaechmus of Syracuse)* Well! There he is! And the day's saved—he's bringing back my dress.

MENAECHMUS OF SYRACUSE *(to himself, testily)*: I wonder where that Messenio would be wandering about now?

WIFE *(to herself)*: I'll go up to him and give him the welcome he deserves. *(Striding up to Menaechmus)* Aren't you ashamed to show yourself in front of me with that dress, you criminal!

MENAECHMUS OF SYRACUSE *(startled)*: What's the matter, madam? What's all the agitation about?

WIFE *(shrieking)*: The nerve of him! How dare you talk to me! How dare you utter a single solitary word in my presence!

MENAECHMUS OF SYRACUSE *(in astonishment)*: Will you please tell me what I did that I'm not allowed to utter a word?

WIFE *(as before)*: What a question! The unmitigated gall of this man!

MENAECHMUS OF SYRACUSE *(tartly)*: Madam, do you happen to know why the Greeks called Hecuba a bitch?

WIFE *(huffily)*: No, I don't.

MENAECHMUS OF SYRACUSE *(as before)*: Because she used to do

145

exactly what you're doing now. Everyone she laid eyes on,
she loaded with insults. And so they began to call her The
Bitch—and she deserved it.

WIFE (*after staring at him blankly for a few seconds, unable to
believe her ears*): I *will* not put up with this criminal behavior!
I'd sooner spend the rest of my days a divorcée than put up
with this absolutely criminal behavior of yours!

MENAECHMUS OF SYRACUSE (*shrugging*): What difference does it
make to me whether you put up with your marriage or walk out
on your husband? Is it the custom around here for people to
talk nonsense to every stranger who comes to town?

WIFE (*as before*): Talk nonsense? Well! I tell you I can't stand
this one second longer. I'll die a divorcée rather than put up
with the likes of you.

MENAECHMUS OF SYRACUSE (*as before*): Die a divorcée or live till
doomsday. Believe me, it makes no difference to me.

WIFE: A minute ago you were insisting you hadn't stolen it and
now you're holding it right in front of my eyes. Aren't you
ashamed of yourself?

MENAECHMUS OF SYRACUSE (*finally needled into an angry retort*):
Good god, woman, you certainly have a nerve! You're a bad
one, you are! How dare you say I stole from you what another
woman gave me to have trimmed and altered for her?

WIFE (*throwing up her hands*): So help me, you know what I'm
going to do? I'm going to call my father right here and now
and tell him about every one of your crimes. (*Calling*) Decio!
(*A scared houseboy scurries out and listens breathlessly.*) Go
get my father and bring him right here; tell him he must come.
(*Decio dashes off, stage left*). In a few minutes the whole
world will know all about these crimes of yours.

MENAECHMUS OF SYRACUSE: Are you in your right mind? What
crimes of mine?

WIFE: That you stole dresses and jewelry from your own wife and
carried them off to your lady friend. Is it the truth or isn't it?

MENAECHMUS OF SYRACUSE (*helplessly*): Please, lady, if you know
of any tranquilizer I can take to help me put up with your
tantrums, for god's sake, lead me to it! I haven't the vaguest
idea of who you think I am. I know you about as well as I
know the man in the moon.

WIFE (*pointing toward the wings, stage left*): You can make fun
of me, all right, but, believe me, you're not going to make fun
of *him*. There's my father coming this way. Turn around and
look. I suppose you don't know him.

MENAECHMUS OF SYRACUSE (*his gaze following her finger*): About
as well as I know the old man of the mountain. You know
when I saw him before? The same day I saw you.

WIFE: You deny that you know me? You deny that you know my
father?

MENAECHMUS OF SYRACUSE (*airily*): And the same goes for your
grandfather, if you want to add him.

WIFE (*disgustedly*): Ugh! Just what I'd expect from you!

(*Menaechmus moves away, stage right, and stands moodily,
looking off into the wings trying to catch the first glimpse of
Messenio. A wizened graybeard emerges from the wings, stage
left, leaning heavily on a stick; he makes his way at a snail's
pace across the stage.*)

SONG

FATHER (*stopping to address the audience*):
> As fast as these old legs can go—
> When duty calls I can't say no—
> I'll step, I'll stride, I'll speed, I'll run.
> I'm well aware this is no fun:
> The spryness has gone out of me,
> I'm buried deep in senility,
> My body's hard to haul along,
> I've lost the strength I had when young.
>
> In getting old you don't do well;
> It's bad stuff, age. Do well? It's hell!
> Its coming brings a load of grief—
> But, to tell it all, I can't be brief.

(*Totters on a few more steps, then stops abruptly and shakes
his head worriedly*)

> Now here's the thing that's on my mind
>   And worries me to the core:
> What brought my daughter so suddenly
>   To call me to her door?
> What does she want? She doesn't say!
>   What is it she's called me for?

(*Goes on for a few more steps, then halts again*)

I'm sure I know what it's all about:
A fight with her husband has broken out.
It's bound to happen to every shrew
Who feels her dowry entitles her to
A husband whose sole aim in life
Is to fetch and carry for his wife.

(A few more steps, then another stop and more worried headshakings)

Yet the men are not exactly pure.
And there's just so much a wife can endure.
A daughter doesn't call her dad
Unless the insult's pretty bad,
Or else the squabbling got too rough.
Whatever it is, I'll know soon enough.

(Turns and catches sight, finally, of his daughter and Menaechmus)

There she is before the door.
There's her husband, looking sore.
Just what I thought—a brawl once more.

FATHER *(to himself)*: I'll have a word with her.

WIFE *(to herself)*: I'll go up to him. *(Walking up to her father)* Papa! I'm *so* glad to see you!

FATHER: Glad to see you too. Well, here I am; any glad tidings? Were things glad around here when you sent for me? What are you looking so black for? *(Pointing to Menaechmus still watching out moodily for Messenio)* And what's he standing off over there in a huff for? You two have had a skirmish about something, all right. Well, speak up. Who's to blame? And make it short—no long lectures.

WIFE: *I* haven't done a thing wrong. Let me put your mind at ease about that first, Papa. It's simply that I can't go on living here, it's impossible, I can't stand it. So please take me away from here.

FATHER *(wearily)*: What's the trouble this time?

WIFE: Papa, he's making a fool of me.

FATHER: Who is?

WIFE: That man you trusted me to. That husband of mine.

FATHER *(throwing up his hands)*: I knew it! Another squabble.

(*Peevishly*) How many times have I expressly warned you to watch out about coming to me with your complaints. Both of you.

WIFE (*plaintively*): Watch out about *that?* How can I, Papa!

FATHER (*snappishly*): What a question! You can if you want to. How many times have I pointed out to you that you *must* give in to your husband and not keep checking on what he does and where he goes and how he spends his time.

WIFE (*expostulating*): But, Papa, he's passionately in love with that prostitute who lives next door!

FATHER: Very sensible of him. And, believe me, all this effort of yours will simply make him more passionate.

WIFE (*sulking*): He goes there for drinks too.

FATHER (*angrily*): If he likes to have a drink there—or anywhere— what's he supposed to do? Not go just to please you? You do have a devil of a nerve! By the same token you ought to stop him from accepting invitations to eat out or from bringing dinner guests to the house. If you think husbands are such slaves, why don't you hand him some wool, sit him down with the maids, and have him do a daily stint of spinning?

WIFE (*with heavy sarcasm*): Naturally, it wasn't *me* I brought you here to defend, but my husband. You take the stand for *me*—and plead *his* case!

FATHER (*sharply*): If he's done anything wrong, I'll go after him lots harder than I've gone after you. Since he keeps you in money and clothes, gives you maids, and pays for the household, the best thing you can do, my lady, is to start getting some sense.

WIFE (*in desperation*): But he steals my jewelry and dresses right out of my closets, he robs me, he carries off my things behind my back and brings them to those whores of his!

FATHER: If he does that, he's to be blamed. But if he doesn't, *you're* to be blamed for blaming a blameless man.

WIFE: Papa, he's got the dress and bracelet that he gave her with him right now. I found out all about it, so he's bringing them back.

FATHER (*shaking his head perplexedly, to himself*): I'll find out all about this right now. I'll go up and have a word with him.

(*Tottering over to Menaechmus, who is still looking impatiently, stage right, for Messenio*) Tell me, Menaechmus, what have you two been—er—discussing? What are you looking so black about? What are you standing off here in a huff for?

MENAECHMUS OF SYRACUSE: My dear sir, I don't know who you are or what your name is, but I swear to you by god almighty and—

FATHER (*interrupting in astonishment*): Swear? What in the world about?

MENAECHMUS OF SYRACUSE (*holding up the dress*): This woman claims I stole this out of her house and made off with it. She's crazy. I swear I never did a thing wrong to her. (*Solemnly*) So help me, may I become more miserable than the most miserable specimen of humanity alive if I ever set foot in the house where she lives.

FATHER: Listen, you madman, if you take an oath like that, if you say you never set foot in your own house, you're stark-raving mad.

MENAECHMUS OF SYRACUSE (*pointing to Menaechmus of Epidamnus' house*): My dear sir, are you telling me that I live in that house?

FATHER: Do you deny it?

MENAECHMUS OF SYRACUSE: I most certainly do deny it.

FATHER: No, you must certainly can't deny it. (*Suddenly struck by a thought*) Unless you moved out last night. (*Turning to the wife*) Daughter, come over here. What's this? You two haven't moved out of here?

WIFE: Now, just where or why would we be moving?

FATHER: Good god, *I* don't know.

WIFE (*disgustedly*): It's so obvious. He's pulling your leg. Don't you get it?

FATHER (*turning back to Menaechmus, sharply*): All right, Menaechmus, enough jokes. Now get to the point.

MENAECHMUS OF SYRACUSE (*finally losing his patience*): Please, what do you want with me? Where do you come from? Who are you? What have I got to do with you or this woman here who's pestering the life out of me?

WIFE (*fearfully, to her father*): Look! His eyes are green! He's turning green around his temples and his forehead! Look at the glitter in his eyes!

MENAECHMUS OF SYRACUSE (*to the audience*): They say I'm insane. Well, in that case, the best thing for me to do is act the part and scare them away.

(*Menaechmus proceeds forthwith to put on a garish performance.*)

WIFE (*as before*): Look at the way he's throwing his arms around! Look at the faces he's making! Papa! What should I do!

FATHER (*taking her by the arm and tottering off with her*): Come over here, daughter. As far away from him as we can get.

MENAECHMUS OF SYRACUSE (*pretending to be calling to the God of Wine*): Yoho! Yoho! Bacchus! Where away in what wood do you call me for the hunt? I hear you—but I can't leave these parts. They've got their eyes on me—on my left that mad bitch and, behind, that old stink-goat who's perjured himself plenty of times in his day to the ruination of innocent men.

FATHER: You go to hell!

MENAECHMUS OF SYRACUSE (*listening attentively as if to an unseen voice, and nodding briskly*): Ah! Orders from the Oracle of Apollo for me to burn her eyes out with blazing brands.

WIFE: Papa! This will be the end of me! He says he's going to burn my eyes out!

MENAECHMUS OF SYRACUSE (*aside, chuckling*): They say *I'm* crazy. Damn it all, they're the ones who're crazy.

FATHER: Psst! Daughter!

WIFE: What is it? What are we going to do?

FATHER: Why don't I call the servants out here? I'll go get some to carry him in the house and tie him up before he causes any more commotion.

MENAECHMUS OF SYRACUSE (*aside*): Stuck! If I don't come up with some scheme first, they're going to haul me into the house. (*Resumes his elaborate listening and nodding to celestial commands.*) Yes, Apollo: I'm not to spare the socks on the jaw unless she gets the hell out of my sight. I will carry out your orders, Apollo. (*Advances menacingly toward the wife.*)

FATHER (*frantically*): Run home as fast as you can or he'll beat you to a pulp!

WIFE (*making for the door*): I am! Papa dear, please, please keep an eye on him and don't let him get away. (*To herself*) Oh, this is terrible! The things I have to listen to! (*Rushes into the house and slams the door behind her.*)

MENAECHMUS OF SYRACUSE (*aside*): Not bad at all, the way I got rid of her. Now for this Titan here—a Titan with the shakes, a bearded, benighted one begat by the Holy Swan. (*Starts listening and nodding again.*) So your orders are to grab that stick he's holding and make pulp of his arms, legs, bones, and joints?

FATHER (*raising his stick*): You lay a hand on me or come any closer, and you're in for trouble!

MENAECHMUS OF SYRACUSE (*as before*): I will carry out your orders, Apollo: I'm to take an ax and chip off every scrap of flesh this old boy has until I'm down to the bone.

FATHER (*aside*): I've got to watch out and take care of myself now. These threats of his have me worried: he might hurt me.

(*Menaechmus advances, brandishing an imaginary ax, but the old man, instead of running, whirls his stick menacingly, and Menaechmus stops short before that formidable instrument. Forced to take another tack, he resumes his listening and nodding act.*)

MENAECHMUS OF SYRACUSE: That's a big order, Apollo. Now I'm to get a team of fierce wild horses, harness them to a chariot, and mount it so I can trample down this stinking, toothless, broken-down lion, eh? (*Launches into an elaborate dumb show.*) Now I'm in the chariot, I'm holding the reins, the whip's in my hand. (*Mimicking the manner of grand opera*) Come, my steeds! Let the clatter of your hoofs ring out! Bend the nimble knee in headlong haste!

FATHER (*grimly*): Threatening me with a team of horses, eh?

(*Menaechmus gallops madly about, then, full tilt, makes for the old man, who holds his ground gamely, swinging his stick. Just before getting within range, Menaechmus prudently swerves aside, pulls up, and readies himself for another try.*)

MENAECHMUS OF SYRACUSE: Ah, Apollo, the orders arc to make a second charge and wipe out this one who insists on standing his ground, eh? (*Charges down on the old man but the stick, whistling through the air, brings Menaechmus to an abrupt halt. He throws his head back and staggers backward as if irresistibly dragged against his will.*) What's this? Someone has me by the hair and is hauling me from my car! Who is it? Apollo! He's changing your direct orders!

FATHER (*shaking his head dolefully, to the audience*): Dear, oh dear! These fits are such terrible things! Heaven help us! This fellow, for instance, was perfectly sane a minute ago and now he's completely out of his mind. And it came on him so suddenly and with such force! I'll go get a doctor as quick as I can. (*Rushes out, stage left.*)

MENAECHMUS OF SYRACUSE (*to himself, in surprise*): Have they really gone? That pair who made a sane man insane? What am I waiting for? I should be off for the ship while the coast is clear. (*Walking downstage and addressing the audience*) Please, all of you, if the old fellow comes back, don't show him which street I took to get out of here.

(*Menaechmus of Syracuse dashes off, stage right. A second later the father re-enters, stage left, followed by a self-important little man who struts along majestically.*)

FATHER (*to the audience, grumbling*): My seat hurts from sitting and my eyes from watching while I waited for the doctor to finish his rounds. Finally the pain-in-the-neck tore himself away from his patients and came back. "Aesculapius fractured a leg and Apollo an arm, and I was mending the breaks," he tells me. I wonder what I'm bringing, a doctor or a repairman? Look at that walk! (*Under his breath*) Shake a leg, you ant!

DOCTOR (*in his professional manner*): What did you say his trouble is? Please describe it to me. Is it hallucinations or delirium? I'd like to know. Is he in a coma? Does he have water on the brain?

FATHER (*testily*): Listen, that's just the reason I brought you here. To give *me* the answers—and to cure him.

DOCTOR (*airily*): Nothing easier. He'll be a well man, I give you my word.

FATHER: I want you to be careful to take good care of him.

DOCTOR: Listen, I'll heave sixty sighs an hour for him. That's how careful I'll be to take good care of him.

FATHER: (*pointing toward the wings, stage left*): Look, there's your patient. Let's watch what he does.

(*The two back off to an unobtrusive spot. As they do, Menaechmus of Epidamnus trudges in despondently. Without noticing them, he walks downstage and addresses the audience.*)

MENAECHMUS OF EPIDAMNUS: God! What a day this one's been! Everything's gone against me. I thought I had kept what I did a secret—and my parasite spills the whole story, leaving me scared to death and in disgrace. That Ulysses of mine! The trouble he stirred up for his lord and master! (*Shaking his fist so hard his mantle slips from his shoulder*) As sure as I'm alive, I'll see to it he and his life part company. (*Snorting*) Now that's stupid of me, to call it *his* life. It's *mine:* he's stayed alive eating my food and at my expense. All right then, I'll make him part company with his soul. And that whore was every bit as bad. What else can you expect from a whore? Because I ask for the dress, so I can bring it back to my wife, she tells me she's already given it to me! Lord, oh lord, what a miserable life I lead!

FATHER (*sotto voce to the doctor*): You hear what he's saying?

DOCTOR (*sotto voce, with a knowing air*): Claim's he's miserable.

FATHER (*sotto voce*): I wish you'd talk with him.

DOCTOR (*walking up to Menaechmus*): Good afternoon, Menaechmus. Will you please tell me why you have to leave your arm bare? Don't you realize the harm this can do to a man in your condition?

MENAECHMUS OF EPIDAMNUS (*glaring*): Oh, go hang yourself.

FATHER (*sotto voce to the doctor, anxiously*): Notice anything?

DOCTOR (*sotto voce to the father*): Lord, yes! (*Shaking his head*) Even an acre of hellebore[1] couldn't cure this case. (*Turning back to Menaechmus*) I say, Menaechmus—

MENAECHMUS OF EPIDAMNUS (*impatiently*): What do you want?

DOCTOR (*assuming his professional manner*): Answer my questions, please. Do you drink white or red wine?

MENAECHMUS OF EPIDAMNUS: Why don't you go straight to hell?

---

[1] The standard ancient remedy for insanity.

DOCTOR (*sotto voce to the father, chuckling mournfully*): Beginning to show the initial symptoms of a seizure.

MENAECHMUS OF EPIDAMNUS (*disgustedly*): Why don't you ask me whether my diet includes purple or red or yellow bread? Or birds with scales? Or fish with feathers?

FATHER (*sotto voce to the doctor, urgently*): Good god! You hear him talk? He's delirious! What are you waiting for? Quick, give him some medicine before he goes completely insane!

DOCTOR (*sotto voce, pontifically*): Not yet. I still have some questions to ask.

FATHER (*to himself, between his teeth*): Your nonsense will be the death of me!

DOCTOR (*to Menaechmus*): Tell me this: do your eyes at times become fixed and staring?

MENAECHMUS OF EPIDAMNUS: What's that? You damned fool! What do you think I am, a lobster?

DOCTOR (*ignoring the outburst and nodding knowingly*): Now tell me this: does your stomach ever growl, so far as you've noticed?

MENAECHMUS OF EPIDAMNUS: After meals, no; when I'm hungry, yes.

DOCTOR (*sotto voce to the father, puzzled*): So help me, there's nothing insane about that answer! (*Turning back to Menaechmus*) Do you sleep through the night? Do you have trouble falling asleep when you go to bed?

MENAECHMUS OF EPIDAMNUS: When my bills are paid, I sleep through. (*Suddenly losing his patience*) You and your questions! God damn you to hell!

DOCTOR (*sotto voce to the father, nodding knowingly*): The start of a fit of insanity. Did you hear what he said? Watch out for him!

FATHER (*sotto voce to the doctor*): Oh no. To hear him talk now, he's Nestor himself compared with what he was before. After all, just a few minutes ago he was calling his wife a mad bitch.

MENAECHMUS OF EPIDAMNUS (*overhearing this, roaring*): What did I call her?

FATHER: I was saying that, in a fit of insanity—

MENAECHMUS OF EPIDAMNUS (*interrupting, as before*): Insanity? Me?

FATHER (*angrily*): Yes, you. And you threatened to trample me down with a four-horse chariot. I saw you do it with my own eyes. I can prove you did it.

MENAECHMUS OF EPIDAMNUS (*snorting*): Oh, sure. And I can prove you stole the holy halo from god almighty. And that you were packed off to prison for it. And that after they let you out, you were tarred and feathered. And what's more, I can prove you killed your father and sold your mother. What do you say? Don't I swap insult for insult just like someone who's sane?

FATHER (*to the doctor, pleading*): For god's sake, please, doctor, hurry and do whatever you're going to do! Don't you see the man's losing his mind?

DOCTOR: Do you know the best thing to do? Have him brought to my clinic.

FATHER (*doubtfully*): You really think so?

DOCTOR (*heartily*): Of course. I'll be able to treat him there just the way I want.

FATHER: Well, as you wish.

DOCTOR (*to Menaechmus, cheerily*): I'll dose you with hellebore for about three weeks.

MENAECHMUS OF EPIDAMNUS: And I'll string you up and dose you with a whip for four. (*Stomps away angrily out of earshot.*)

DOCTOR (*to the father*): Go get some men to carry him.

FATHER: How many will we need?

DOCTOR: Considering the symptoms I've observed, four would be the minimum.

FATHER: I'll have them here right away. Doctor, you keep an eye on him.

DOCTOR (*hastily*): Oh no. I've got to get back to make ready whatever—er—has to be made ready. (*Airily, as he prudently hustles off, stage left*) You just have your servants bring him to me.

FATHER: I'll see to it. He'll be there.

DOCTOR (*as he disappears into the wings*): I'm off now.

FATHER (*as he limps off resignedly at his top speed after the doctor*): Good-by.

MENAECHMUS OF EPIDAMNUS (*to the audience*): My father-in-law's left; the doctor's left; I'm alone. God almighty, what's going on? What are these men saying I'm crazy for? Why, I haven't had a sick day since the day I was born. Me insane? I don't even start fights or get into arguments! And I'm sane enough to think everyone else is sane and to recognize people and talk with them. If they can make the mistake of saying I'm crazy, maybe they're the ones who are crazy!

(*Paces up and down a moment in silence. Then, shaking his head despondently*) Now what do I do? I want to go home but my wife won't let me. (*Gesturing toward Lovey's house*) And no one's going to let me in *there*. Oh, the whole thing's a mess! I'll stay right where I am. I suppose when it gets dark I'll be allowed to go inside. (*Sits down gloomily in front of the door of his house.*)

(*Enter Messenio, stage right. He walks downstage and addresses the audience.*)

SONG

You know what marks the servant who's good,
The kind that'll watch, take care, arrange,
And plan for a master's livelihood?
It's taking as good—or better—care
When the master is out as when he's there.

If a slave's more concerned for his belly than back,
And his gullet than shins, then his brain's out of whack.

He must not forget that masters pay
The good-for-nothings in just one way:
    With shackles, whip, and mill,
    Hunger, fatigue, and chill;
The wage of no work and all play.

So to hell with bad acting, I'll be good, I've decided,
Since I hellishly hate to get hurt or get hided.
    I can stomach the curses and cries—
    It's the beatings and blows I despise.
And I'm many times happier having for lunch
    The bread that's been browned

From what others have ground
Than grinding myself for all others to munch.

> So I see that orders get obeyed
> With speed and skill and no fuss made.
> The system works out well for me:
> > Others are free to test
> > What seems for them the best,
> But *I'll* be as I have to be.

Be a Johnny-on-the-spot when the master commands—
If I only can keep this one worry in mind,
Not a fault will he ever be able to find.

But the day's soon to come when my worrying's done,
When he'll pay me the freedom I've worked for and won.
> So till then I'll behave
> Like a dutiful slave,
> And I'll practice my knack
> Of being kind to my back!

(He turns and walks briskly toward Lovey's door.)

Well, I settled the bags and the servants in the hotel as he ordered, and now I've come to get him. I'll knock on the door so he knows I'm here. Let's see if I can spring him safe and sound from this sink of iniquity. I'm afraid, though, I may be too late; the battle may be all over.

(Enter, stage left, the father with four husky slaves at his heels.)

FATHER *(to the slaves)*: I'm warning you: in the name of all that's holy, make sure you use your head when you carry out my orders, the ones I gave you before and am giving you now. Unless you don't give a damn for your shins and ribs, you'll pick up that man there *(pointing to Menaechmus of Epidamnus)* and carry him to the clinic. And none of you are to pay the slightest attention to any threats he makes. Well, why are you standing there? What are you waiting for? You should have had him up on your shoulders and on his way by now! I'm off to the doctor's; I'll be waiting when you get there.

(The old man hurries off, stage left. The four huskies make for Menaechmus, who looks up as they gallop toward him.)

MENAECHMUS OF EPIDAMNUS *(to himself)*: This looks bad! What's going on here? God knows why, but these men are running toward me! (*To the men as they draw near*) What do you want? What are you after? (*Frantically*) Why are you surrounding me? (*With a rush they grab him and swing him onto their shoulders.*) Where are you taking me? Where am I going? Help! Murder! Save me, citizens of Epidamnus! (*To his abductors*) Let go of me!

MESSENIO (*whirling about at the commotion*): Good god in heaven, what's this I see? Some strangers carrying off my master! This is an outrage!

MENAECHMUS OF EPIDAMNUS (*despairingly*): Doesn't anyone have the heart to help me?

MESSENIO (*calling*): I do, master, the heart of a hero! (*Orating at the top of his lungs, as he races to the rescue*) People of Epidamnus! This is a foul, a criminal act! In a city street, in broad daylight, in peacetime, to kidnap my poor master, a gentleman on a visit to your town! (*Tearing into the abductors*) Let go of him!

MENAECHMUS OF EPIDAMNUS: Whoever you are, for god's sake, stand by me! Don't let them get away with this flagrant miscarriage of justice!

MESSENIO (*shouting, as he flails away*): They won't. I'll stand by you. I'll help you. I'll defend you to the death. I won't let them kill you—better I get killed myself! Master, for god's sake, the one there that's got you by the shoulder—gouge his eye out! These three here, why, I'll plow their jaws and plant my fists there. (*To his opponents*) Kidnap him, will you? You'll pay for it and pay plenty! Let go of him!

MENAECHMUS OF EPIDAMNUS (*triumphantly*): I got him by the eye!

MESSENIO: Tear it out of the socket! (*To his adversaries*) Criminals! Kidnapers! Bandits!

THE SLAVES (*shouting*): Don't kill us! Please!

MESSENIO (*snarling*): Then let go!

MENAECHMUS OF EPIDAMNUS (*to his abductors*): What do you mean by laying hands on me! (*To Messenio*) Sock 'em on the jaw!

MESSENIO (*as his three opponents break and run*): On your way! Go to hell, the bunch of you! (*Rushes over and lands a haymaker on Menaechmus' opponent*) And here's this from me! A bonus for being the last one out of here. (*To Menaechmus, smugly, as the four scamper off, stage left*) Well, I rearranged the geography of their faces to suit my taste. Believe me, master, I came to the rescue just in time.

MENAECHMUS OF EPIDAMNUS (*fervently*): I don't know who you are, mister, but god's blessings on you forever. If it hadn't been for you, I wouldn't have lived to see the sun go down today.

MESSENIO (*promptly*): Then if you want to do right by me, damn it all, you'll set me free.

MENAECHMUS OF EPIDAMNUS: Set you free? Me?

MESSENIO: Sure, master. I just saved your life, didn't I?

MENAECHMUS OF EPIDAMNUS: What are you talking about? Mister, you're making a mistake.

MESSENIO: Me making a mistake? What do you mean?

MENAECHMUS OF EPIDAMNUS: I give you my solemn oath, I'm not your master.

MESSENIO (*taking this as a cruel joke, bitterly*): Don't give me that!

MENAECHMUS OF EPIDAMNUS (*earnestly*): I'm not lying to you. (*Ruefully*) No servant of mine ever did as much for me as you have.

MESSENIO (*as before*): All right. If you say I'm not your slave, why don't you let me go free?

MENAECHMUS OF EPIDAMNUS (*smiling*): If it's up to me, by all means. Be a free man. Go where you like.

MESSENIO (*unable to believe his ears*): You mean it? It's official?

MENAECHMUS OF EPIDAMNUS (*as before*): If I have any official rights over you, it certainly is.

MESSENIO (*ecstatically*): Hail, my patron! (*Menaechmus winces at the title, remembering the experience in that capacity that cost him his lunch. Messenio launches into an imaginary dialogue with his fellow slaves*) "Well, well, Messenio, so you're a free man. Congratulations!" "Thank you, thank you all." (*Turning back to Menaechmus, earnestly*) Patron, I want you to keep ordering me around the same as when I was your servant. I'll live with you, and, when you go back home, I'll go with you.

MENAECHMUS OF EPIDAMNUS (*aside, wincing again*): Not a chance!

MESSENIO: I'll go back to the hotel now and get the bags and the money for you. The wallet with our cash is safe under lock and key in my satchel. I'll bring it to you right now.

MENAECHMUS OF EPIDAMNUS (*promptly*): You do that. And hurry.

MESSENIO (*over his shoulder as he rushes off, stage right*): You'll get it back just as it was when you gave it to me. Wait for me here.

MENAECHMUS OF EPIDAMNUS (*to the audience, shaking his head in bewilderment*): Amazing, the amazing things that have happened to me! People tell me I'm not me and lock me out of the house. Then this fellow, (*grinning*) the one I just now emancipated, comes along, claims he's my slave, and tells me he's going to bring me a wallet full of cash. If he actually does, I'll tell him he's a free man and he's to leave me and go wherever he likes; I don't want him asking for the money back when he gets his sanity back. My father-in-law and the doctor say *I'm* mad. It's all a mystery to me. I must be dreaming the whole business. Well, I'll pay a call on this whore here, even if she is sore at me. Maybe I can get her to give back the dress so I can bring it home.

(*He enters Lovey's house. A second later Menaechmus of Syracuse and Messenio enter, stage right, deep in conversation.*)

MENAECHMUS OF SYRACUSE (*angrily*): I sent you off with orders to come back here for me. Where do you get the nerve to tell me I saw you anywhere since?

MESSENIO (*frantically*): Just a minute ago I rescued you, right in front of this house, from four men who were carrying you off on their shoulders. You were hollering to heaven and earth for help, and I ran up and by fighting hard made them let you go. And, because I saved your life that way, you set me free. (*Bitterly*) And then, when I said I was going for the money and the bags, you ran ahead and got there first just so you could deny everything you did!

MENAECHMUS OF SYRACUSE (*incredulously*): I set you free?

MESSENIO: You certainly did.

MENAECHMUS OF SYRACUSE (*grimly*): I'll tell you what I certainly did: made up my mind to be a slave myself before I ever set you free. (*Starts stalking off, stage right.*)

(The door of Lovey's house opens, and Menaechmus of Epidamnus stomps out. He turns and talks to Lovey and her maid inside.)

MENAECHMUS OF EPIDAMNUS *(through the doorway, excitedly)*: Listen, you bitches, you can cross your heart and swear all you want but, damn it all, that's not going to change things: I did *not* walk off with that bracelet and dress.

(Messenio glances over his shoulder at the sound of the voice—and does a double take.)

MESSENIO: Good god in heaven! What's this I see?

MENAECHMUS OF SYRACUSE *(sourly, and without stopping)*: What?

MESSENIO: Your reflection!

MENAECHMUS OF SYRACUSE *(stopping)*: What are you talking about?

MESSENIO *(excitedly)*: He's your image! He couldn't be more like you.

MENAECHMUS OF SYRACUSE *(following Messenio's gaze)*: By god, you know, when I think about what I look like, he *does* resemble me.

MENAECHMUS OF EPIDAMNUS *(turning from the door and noticing Messenio)*: Hello there, my savior, whoever you are.

MESSENIO *(to Menaechmus of Epidamnus, tensely)*: Mister, would you please do me a favor and tell me your name, if you don't mind?

MENAECHMUS OF EPIDAMNUS *(earnestly)*: I mind any favors you ask for? I should say not. That isn't the treatment you deserve from me! The name's Menaechmus—

MENAECHMUS OF SYRACUSE *(interrupting)*: Hell, no! That's my name!

MENAECHMUS OF EPIDAMNUS *(ignoring him)*: —and I was born at Syracuse in Sicily.

MENAECHMUS OF SYRACUSE *(resentfully)*: That's *my* city and country.

MENAECHMUS OF EPIDAMNUS *(looking at him for the first time)*: What's that you say?

MENAECHMUS OF SYRACUSE *(glowering)*: Nothing but the truth.

MESSENIO *(stares at the two in utter puzzlement. Then, to himself, uncertainly, pointing to Menaechmus of Epidamnus)*: This must be the one I know; *he's* my master. I thought I was (*pointing to Menaechmus of Syracuse*) his servant, but I'm really (*pointing to Menaechmus of Epidamnus*) his. (*Addressing Menaechmus of Epidamnus*) I thought he was you; (*guiltily*) matter of fact, I gave him quite a bit of trouble. (*To Menaechmus of Syracuse*) Please forgive me if I said anything to you that sounded stupid. I didn't mean to.

MENAECHMUS OF SYRACUSE (*in astonishment*): Are you crazy? You sound it. You and I came off the ship together today. Don't you remember?

MESSENIO (*astonished in his turn*): You're absolutely right. *You're* my master. (*To Menaechmus of Epidamnus, apologetically*) You'd better find yourself another servant. (*To Menaechmus of Syracuse*) Hello. (*To Menaechmus of Epidamnus*) Good-by. Take my word— (*pointing to Menaechmus of Syracuse*) this man is Menaechmus.

MENAECHMUS OF EPIDAMNUS: No. *I* am.

MENAECHMUS OF SYRACUSE (*to Menaechmus of Epidamnus*): What sort of nonsense is this? You're Menaechmus?

MENAECHMUS OF EPIDAMNUS: That's what I said. Son of Moschus.

MENAECHMUS OF SYRACUSE (*bewildered*): The son of my father? You?

MENAECHMUS OF EPIDAMNUS (*smiling*): No, mister, of *mine*. I have no intention of adopting your father or stealing him from you.

MESSENIO (*to the audience, in great excitement*): Something just dawned on me! A hope that no one could have hoped for! God in heaven, make it come true! I tell you, unless my mind is going back on me, these two are the twin brothers! After all, they both give the same father and fatherland. I've got to have a word with my master in private (*Calling out*) Menaechmus!

MENAECHMUS OF EPIDAMNUS ⎱
                                              ⎰ What do you want?
MENAECHMUS OF SYRACUSE ⎰

MESSENIO: I don't want you both! Which one of you was on the ship with me?

MENAECHMUS OF EPIDAMNUS: Not I.

MENAECHMUS OF SYRACUSE: I.

MESSENIO: Then you're the one I want. Step over here, will you?

(Messenio walks a few steps off to the side, and Menaechmus of Syracuse joins him.)

MENAECHMUS OF SYRACUSE: Here I am. What's up?

MESSENIO (*sotto voce, excitedly*): That man there is either a swindler or your twin brother! I've never seen two people more alike. Believe me, you two are more like each other than one drop of water or one drop of milk to another. Besides, he gives the same names as you for father and fatherland. We'd better go up to him and ask him some questions.

MENAECHMUS OF SYRACUSE (*catching Messenio's excitement*): That's a darned good idea! Thanks very much. But, please, do me a favor: you do it. (*As they walk back toward Menaechmus of Epidamnus*) Messenio, you're a free man if you can find out he's my brother.

MESSENIO (*fervently*): I hope I can.

MENAECHMUS OF SYRACUSE: I hope so too.

MESSENIO (*to Menaechmus of Epidamnus, drawing himself up self-importantly, like a judge questioning a party to a case*): Harrumph! (*As Menaechmus of Epidamnus looks at him inquiringly*) You stated, as I remember, that your name was Menaechmus.

MENAECHMUS OF EPIDAMNUS: That's right.

MESSENIO (*gesturing toward Menaechmus of Syracuse*): This man's name is Menaechmus too. You stated you were born at Syracuse in Sicily; he was born there. You stated your father's name was Moschus; so was his. Now you can both help me—and yourselves at the same time.

MENAECHMUS OF EPIDAMNUS: Anything you want from me, the answer's yes; you've earned it. I'm a free man, but I'm at your service just as if you'd bought and paid for me.

MESSENIO (*solemnly*): My hope is that the two of you will discover you are twin brothers, born the same day to the same mother and the same father.

MENAECHMUS OF EPIDAMNUS (*wistfully*): What you're talking about is a miracle. Ah, if you could only do what you hope to!

MESSENIO (*determinedly*): I can. But now let's start. Answer my questions, both of you.

MENAECHMUS OF EPIDAMNUS (*promptly*): Ask away. I'll tell you everything I know.

MESSENIO: Is your name Menaechmus?

MENAECHMUS OF EPIDAMNUS: It is.

MESSENIO (*to Menaechmus of Syracuse*): And yours too?

MENAECHMUS OF SYRACUSE: Yes.

MESSENIO (*to Menaechmus of Epidamnus*): And you say your father's name was Moschus?

MENAECHMUS OF EPIDAMNUS: I do.

MENAECHMUS OF SYRACUSE: So do I. (*Receives a lordly look of disapproval from Messenio for anticipating the question.*)

MESSENIO (*to Menaechmus of Epidamnus*): And you were born at Syracuse?

MENAECHMUS OF EPIDAMNUS: Absolutely.

MESSENIO (*to Menaechmus of Syracuse*): What about you?

MENAECHMUS OF SYRACUSE: You know I was.

MESSENIO: So far everything agrees perfectly. We'll go on; your attention please. (*To Menaechmus of Epidamnus*) Tell me, what is your earliest recollection of your homeland?

MENAECHMUS OF EPIDAMNUS (*holding his forehead and closing his eyes as he struggles to remember*): Going off to Tarentum with my father on a business trip. Then wandering off in the crowd and being carried away.

MENAECHMUS OF SYRACUSE (*exclaiming involuntarily*): God in heaven! Help me now!

MESSENIO (*with the voice of authority*): What's the meaning of this shouting? Can't you keep quiet! (*To Menaechmus of Epidamnus*) How old were you when your father took you from your fatherland?

MENAECHMUS OF EPIDAMNUS: Seven. I remember because I was just beginning to lose my baby teeth. (*Sadly*) I never saw my father again.

MESSENIO: Answer this: how many sons were there in your family?

MENAECHMUS OF EPIDAMNUS: As best as I can remember, two.

MESSENIO: Which was the older, you or your brother?

MENAECHMUS OF EPIDAMNUS: We were the same age.

MESSENIO: How is that possible?

MENAECHMUS OF EPIDAMNUS: We were twins.

MENAECHMUS OF SYRACUSE (*exclaiming fervently*): Heaven has come to my rescue!

MESSENIO (*icily*): If you're going to interrupt, I'm not going to say another word!

MENAECHMUS OF SYRACUSE (*meekly*): No, no—I won't say another word.

MESSENIO (*to Menaechmus of Epidamnus*): Tell me: did you both have the same name?

MENAECHMUS OF EPIDAMNUS: Oh, no. You see, I was called Menaechmus, as now, but his name was Sosicles.

MENAECHMUS OF SYRACUSE (*to himself, wildly excited*): For me the case is proved. I can't hold back, I've got to take him in my arms. (*Taking his hands*) Welcome, my brother, my twin brother! I'm Sosicles!

MENAECHMUS OF EPIDAMNUS (*gently disengaging his hands; uncertainly*): If that's so, how come you got the name Menaechmus?

MENAECHMUS OF SYRACUSE: When the news came about you and about father's death, grandfather changed it: he gave me yours instead.

MENAECHMUS OF EPIDAMNUS: I guess it could have happened that way. But answer this question.

MENAECHMUS OF SYRACUSE (*eagerly*): What is it?

MENAECHMUS OF EPIDAMNUS (*intently*): What was our mother's name?

MENAECHMUS OF SYRACUSE: Teuximarcha.

MENAECHMUS OF EPIDAMNUS (*rushing to embrace him*): Right! Welcome to you, my brother! I never expected to see you again, and now, after so many years, I have you before me.

MENAECHMUS OF SYRACUSE: And welcome to you, my brother. I searched and searched for you right up to this moment, and now, after so many trials and tribulations, I have the joy of having found you.

MESSENIO (*to Menaechmus of Syracuse, a light dawning*): That explains it! That girl called you by your brother's name. I'm sure she thought it was he she was inviting in to lunch, not you.

MENAECHMUS OF EPIDAMNUS (*smiling broadly*): As a matter of fact, I had told her to prepare lunch for me today. My wife wasn't to know a thing about it. I sneaked a dress of hers out of the house and gave it to the girl.

MENAECHMUS OF SYRACUSE (*holding up the dress*): You mean the one I have here?

MENAECHMUS OF EPIDAMNUS (*astonished*): That's it! How did it ever get to you?

MENAECHMUS OF SYRACUSE (*laughing*): That girl who carried me off to give me lunch insisted I had given it to her. The wench wined me and dined me in style and then went to bed with me. I made off with the dress and this bracelet (*holding it up.*)

MENAECHMUS OF EPIDAMNUS: Believe me, I'm delighted to hear something nice happened to you because of me. When she invited you in, she thought it was me, you know.

MESSENIO (*breaking in, anxiously*): There's nothing to stop you now, is there, from giving me my freedom the way you promised?

MENAECHMUS OF EPIDAMNUS: A perfectly proper and fair request, my brother. Do it for my sake.

MENAECHMUS OF SYRACUSE: Messenio, you're a free man.

MENAECHMUS OF EPIDAMNUS (*his eyes twinkling, mimicking the exact tone of voice Messenio had used a few moments ago*): Well, well, Messenio, so you're a free man. Congratulations!

MESSENIO (*meaningfully, holding out his hand, palm upward*): But I could use a better beginning to make sure I stay free.

MENAECHMUS OF SYRACUSE (*pointedly ignoring the hand and the remark*): Now that things have turned out just the way we wanted, my brother, let's both of us go back to our homeland.

MENAECHMUS OF EPIDAMNUS: Brother, I'll do whatever you wish. I can hold an auction and sell whatever I own around here. (*Leading him toward the door of his house*) But let's go inside for now.

MENAECHMUS OF SYRACUSE: Yes, let's.

MESSENIO (*who had been listening avidly to the last exhange*): Do you know what favor I'd like to ask?

MENAECHMUS OF EPIDAMNUS: What?

MESSENIO (*eagerly*): Let me run the auction.

MENAECHMUS OF EPIDAMNUS: It's all yours.

MESSENIO (*rubbing his hands delightedly*): Then how about my announcing right now that an auction will take place?

MENAECHMUS OF EPIDAMNUS: All right. Make it a week from today. (*The two brothers enter the house.*)

MESSENIO (*to the audience, in an auctioneer's chant*): Hear ye, hear ye! Selling at auction, one week from today, rain or shine, the property of Menaechmus. For sale: slaves, household effects, farm land, and buildings. All items to go for whatever they'll bring, and all payments strictly cash. Sale includes one wife—if anyone will bid. (*Leaning forward in a confidential tone*) If you ask me, the whole auction won't net fifty cents.

(*Straightening up, in ringing tones*) And now, ladies and gentlemen, good-by. Your loudest applause, please!

William Shakespeare
THE COMEDY OF ERRORS

The Comedy of Errors, a very early comedy (*c.* 1591), is Shakespeare's first and only attempt to imitate Plautus. The play is based on *The Menaechmus Twins,* but Shakespeare doubles the twins—both masters and servants—and complicates the rather simple and straightforward plot of Plautus. Shakespeare also introduces romantic elements that are foreign to Plautus's more prosaic temperament. The play opens like a tragedy with the old father Egeon condemned to death; at the end he is not only rescued but also restored to his long-lost wife, Emilia, who is conveniently an abbess at Ephesus. Shakespeare takes the theme of shipwreck and the separated twins more seriously than Plautus, as if the twins needed each other to complete their own being. This has overtones of Plato's *Symposium,* a popular Renaissance treatise applied to the lover's seeking of the other who will fulfill his or her essence. Antipholus of Syracuse's lyric and melancholy speech is unthinkable in Plautus:

> I to the world am like a drop of water
> That in the ocean seeks another drop,
> Who, falling there to find his fellow forth,
> Unseen, inquisitive, confounds himself. (I.ii.35–38)

The marriage debate between Adriana and her sister Luciana, in its serious exposition of feminist issues, is also foreign to Plautine farce.

Shakespeare mollifies the hard farce he found in Plautus and makes his play sweeter and more romantic than his source. In this he is influenced by Italian Renaissance notions of "supposes" and "errors" rather than simply mistaken identity. "Supposes" are suppositions of the mind and "errors" are wanderings of thought (from the Latin sense of *errare,* meaning to go astray or to lose oneself). *The Comedy of Errors* is a comedy about illusions rather than mistakes in perception. The characters are constantly speaking about dreams, witchcraft, magic, and fairyland. Shakespeare's characters seem less aware of everyday reality than do Plautus's, and Antipholus of Syracuse surrenders himself up to the willing suspension of disbelief with deliberation and self-awareness:

> To me she speaks, she moves me for her theme;
> What, was I married to her in my dream?
> Or sleep I now, and think I hear all this?
> What error drives our eyes and ears amiss?
> Until I know this sure uncertainty,
> I'll entertain the offered fallacy. (II.ii.182–87)

Like the true comic protagonist, Antipholus goes along with what he knows to be an "error" and a "fallacy." For a mere question of identity he cannot resist all the good things that are being thrust upon him.

Beatings in farce have a way of resolving what would otherwise be difficult metaphysical issues. The masters usually beat the servants with a bladder filled with dried peas or with a slapstick, a noisy device that still survives among circus clowns. These are loud blows that do not hurt; in other words, symbolic blows, thus fulfilling the requirement that in farce everything be insulated from physical pain or suffering. The beatings relieve the masters' frustration at the sea of errors in which they seem to be foundering. It is a simple solution to a complex problem. Thus, when Dromio of Syracuse reminds his master of actions that apply to the other Antipholus, the real Antipholus of Syracuse can only find an outlet to irrationality in blows:

> Yea, dost thou jeer, and flout me in the teeth?
> Think'st thou, I jest? Hold, take thou that! And that!
>
> (II.ii.22–23)

Dromio can obviously not beat his master; his only weapon is wit: "Hold, sir, for God's sake! Now your jest is earnest."

The material world plays an unduly large role in farce, and the play cannot end until all property is restored to its rightful owners. Mistaken identity is thus combined with mistaken ownership, as the resolution of all the difficulties also includes a vigorous session of lost and found. The courtesan, for example, pursues the diamond ring she has foolishly given to Antipholus, who now appears to be mad. In her concluding soliloquy in IV. iii, she schemes to tell Antipholus' wife how her mad husband rushed into her house and made off with her ring, "For forty ducats is too much to lose" (IV.iii.98). And so, by a kind of animation, the gold chain, the bag of money, and the rope's end earnestly seek out their rightful owners. When all the properties are finally returned, then the duke too is willing to forget about Egeon's ransom and free him from his sentence of death.

The resolution of the farce stresses the happy ending. All problems disappear in the general merrymaking and goodwill that closes the play, and no elaborate explanations are needed for the errors that mixed up everyone's perception. Errors reflect the role of fortune in human life; our word *happy* is derived from the innate conviction that "hap," or chance, always ultimately works out for the best. The wonder of the brothers who discover each other, the wives who find their husbands again, the parents reunited after long separation, the twin servants brought face-to-face are all romantic affirmations of the notion that all's well that ends well. Never to be put off with mere appearances, Adriana exclaims, "I see two husbands, or mine eyes deceive me" (V.i. 332), and Dromio of Ephesus looks upon his twin as a mirror: "I see by you I am a sweet-faced youth" (V.i.419). The final couplet of the play celebrates the democratic equality of twinship:

We came into the world like brother and brother;
And now let's go hand in hand, not one before another.
(V.i.426–27)

The classic comic ending is not only one of clarification—nothing at all has been learned—but rather one of positive assertion: despite appearances to the contrary, everything will work out well in the end.

Unlike Plautus, Shakespeare develops a real love interest in *The Comedy of Errors,* which is a farce that has affinities with later romantic comedies such as *As You Like It* and *Twelfth Night.* It is as if Shakespeare was not comfortable with the hard, clear lines of traditional farce and wanted to do something more. When Antipholus of Syracuse woos Luciana, the sister of his twin brother's wife, he speaks with the authentic amorous involvement of an Orlando or an Orsino:

O, train me not, sweet mermaid, with thy note,
To drown me in thy sister's flood of tears.
Sing, siren, for thyself, and I will dote;
Spread o'er the silver waves thy golden hairs;
And as a bed I'll take them, and there lie. . . .
(III.ii.45–49)

Antipholus is wandering, an errant knight, "Smoth'red in errors" (I.ii.35), which make him especially vulnerable to the charms of love. If anything is possible and all of reality is profoundly illusory, then it is not at all surprising to fall in love at first sight. In this way the acceptance of "errors" and "supposes" breaks down complacency and prepares the way for love.

CHARACTERS

SOLINUS, *Duke of Ephesus*
EGEON, *a merchant of Syracuse*
ANTIPHOLUS OF EPHESUS ⎱ *twin brothers, and sons of Egeon*
ANTIPHOLUS OF SYRACUSE ⎰ *and Emilia*
DROMIO OF EPHESUS ⎱ *twin brothers, and bondmen to the*
DROMIO OF SYRACUSE ⎰ *two Antipholuses*
BALTHASAR
ANGELO, *a goldsmith*
A MERCHANT, *friend to Antipholus of Syracuse*
ANOTHER MERCHANT, *to whom Angelo is in debt*
DOCTOR PINCH, *a schoolmaster*
EMILIA, *an Abbess at Ephesus, wife of Egeon*
ADRIANA, *wife of Antipholus of Ephesus*
LUCIANA, *her sister*
LUCE, *or* NELL, *kitchen maid to Adriana*
COURTESAN
JAILER, HEADSMAN, OFFICERS, AND OTHER ATTENDANTS

Scene: Ephesus

THE COMEDY OF ERRORS

ACT I

Scene I. *A public place.*

Enter the Duke of Ephesus, with [Egeon] the Merchant of Syracusa, Jailer, and other Attendants.

EGEON: Proceed, Solinus, to procure my fall,
And by the doom of death end woes and all.

DUKE: Merchant of Syracusa, plead no more;
I am not partial to infringe our laws.
5   The enmity and discord which of late
Sprung from the rancorous outrage of your Duke
To merchants, our well-dealing countrymen,
Who, wanting guilders to redeem their lives,
Have sealed his rigorous statutes with their bloods,
10   Excludes all pity from our threat'ning looks.
For, since the mortal and intestine jars[1]
'Twixt thy seditious countrymen and us,
It hath in solemn synods been decreed,
Both by the Syracusians and ourselves,
15   To admit no traffic to our adverse towns.
Nay more; if any born at Ephesus
Be seen at Syracusian marts and fairs;
Again, if any Syracusian born
Come to the bay of Ephesus, he dies,
20   His goods confiscate to the Duke's dispose,
Unless a thousand marks be levièd
To quit the penalty and to ransom him.
Thy substance, valued at the highest rate,
Cannot amount unto a hundred marks;
25   Therefore by law thou art condemned to die.

[1]conflicts

EGEON. Yet this my comfort: when your words are done,
My woes end likewise with the evening sun.

DUKE. Well, Syracusian, say, in brief, the cause
Why thou departed'st from thy native home,
And for what cause thou cam'st to Ephesus.   30

EGEON: A heavier task could not have been imposed
Than I to speak my griefs unspeakable;
Yet, that the world may witness that my end
Was wrought by nature, not by vile offense,
I'll utter what my sorrow gives me leave.   35
In Syracusa was I born, and wed
Unto a woman happy but for me,
And by me, had not our hap been bad.
With her I lived in joy, our wealth increased
By prosperous voyages I often made   40
To Epidamnum, till my factor's[1] death
And the great care of goods at random left
Drew me from kind embracements of my spouse;
From whom my absence was not six months old,
Before herself—almost at fainting under   45
The pleasing punishment that women bear—
Had made provision for her following me,
And soon and safe arrivèd where I was.
There had she not been long, but she became
A joyful mother of two goodly sons;   50
And, which was strange, the one so like the other,
As could not be distinguished but by names.
That very hour, and in the self-same inn,
A mean[2] woman was deliverèd
Of such a burden male, twins both alike.   55
Those, for their parents were exceeding poor,
I bought, and brought up to attend my sons.
My wife, not meanly proud of two such boys,
Made daily motions for our home return.
Unwilling I agreed; alas, too soon   60
We came aboard.
A league from Epidamnum had we sailed
Before the always wind-obeying deep
Gave any tragic instance of our harm.
But longer did we not retain much hope;   65
For what obscurèd light the heavens did grant

[1]business agent [2]poor, humble

Did but convey unto our fearful minds
A doubtful[1] warrant of immediate death,
Which, though myself would gladly have embraced,
70   Yet the incessant weepings of my wife,
Weeping before for what she saw must come,
And piteous plainings of the pretty babes,
That mourned for fashion, ignorant what to fear,
Forced me to seek delays for them and me.
75   And this it was—for other means was none:
The sailors sought for safety by our boat,
And left the ship, then sinking-ripe, to us.
My wife, more careful for the latter-born,
Had fast'ned him unto a small spare mast,
80   Such as seafaring men provide for storms;
To him one of the other twins was bound,
Whilst I had been like heedful of the other.
The children thus disposed, my wife and I,
Fixing our eyes on whom our care was fixed,
85   Fast'ned ourselves at either end the mast:
And floating straight, obedient to the stream,
Was carried towards Corinth, as we thought.
At length the sun, gazing upon the earth,
Dispersed those vapors that offended us,
90   And, by the benefit of his wishèd light,
The seas waxed calm, and we discoverèd
Two ships from far, making amain[2] to us:
Of Corinth that, of Epidaurus this.
But ere they came—O, let me say no more!
95   Gather the sequel by that went before.

DUKE: Nay, forward, old man; do not break off so,
For we may pity, though not pardon thee.

EGEON: O, had the gods done so, I had not now
Worthily termed them merciless to us.
100 For, ere the ships could meet by twice five leagues,
We were encount'red by a mighty rock,
Which being violently borne upon,
Our helpful ship was splitted in the midst;
So that, in this unjust divorce of us,
105 Fortune had left to both of us alike
What to delight in, what to sorrow for.
Her part, poor soul, seeming as burdenèd

[1]fearful   [2]at full speed

With lesser weight, but not with lesser woe,
Was carried with more speed before the wind;
And in our sight they three were taken up   *110*
By fishermen of Corinth, as we thought.
At length another ship had seized on us,
And, knowing whom it was their hap to save,
Gave healthful welcome to their shipwracked guests,
And would have reft[1] the fishers of their prey,   *115*
Had not their bark been very slow of sail;
And therefore homeward did they bend their course.
Thus have you heard me severed from my bliss,
That by misfortunes was my life prolonged
To tell sad stories of my own mishaps.   *120*

DUKE: And, for the sake of them thou sorrowest for,
Do me the favor to dilate[2] at full
What have befall'n of them and thee till now.

EGEON: My youngest boy, and yet my eldest care,
At eighteen years became inquisitive   *125*
After his brother, and importuned me
That his attendant—so his case was like,
Reft of his brother, but retained his name—
Might bear him company in the quest of him;
Whom whilst I labored of a love[3] to see,   *130*
I hazarded the loss of whom I loved.
Five summers have I spent in farthest Greece,
Roaming clean through the bounds of Asia,
And coasting homeward, came to Ephesus,
Hopeless to find, yet loath to leave unsought   *135*
Or that or any place that harbors men.
But here must end the story of my life;
And happy were I in my timely death,
Could all my travels warrant me they live.

DUKE: Hapless Egeon, whom the fates have marked   *140*
To bear the extremity of dire mishap!
Now trust me, were it not against our laws,
Against my crown, my oath, my dignity,
Which princes, would they, may not disannul,
My soul should sue as advocate for thee.   *145*
But though thou art adjudgèd to the death,
And passèd sentence may not be recalled
But to our honor's great disparagement,

[1]bereft, robbed   [2]expatiate   [3]from love

Yet will I favor thee in what I can;
150   Therefore, merchant, I'll limit thee this day
To seek thy health by beneficial help.
Try all the friends thou hast in Ephesus—
Beg thou, or borrow, to make up the sum,
And live; if no, then thou art doomed to die.
155   Jailer, take him to thy custody.

JAILER: I will, my lord.

EGEON: Hopeless and helpless doth Egeon wend,
But to procrastinate his lifeless end.   *Exeunt.*

Scene II. *The Marketplace.*

*Enter Antipholus [of Syracuse], a Merchant,
and Dromio [of Syracuse].*

MERCHANT: Therefore, give out you are of Epidamnum,
Lest that your goods too soon be confiscate.
This very day a Syracusian merchant
Is apprehended for arrival here,
5   And not being able to buy out his life,
According to the statute of the town,
Dies ere the weary sun set in the west.
There is your money that I had to keep.

S. ANTIPHOLUS: Go bear it to the Centaur, where we host,[1]
10   And stay there, Dromio, till I come to thee;
Within this hour it will be dinnertime;
Till that, I'll view the manners of the town,
Peruse the traders, gaze upon the buildings,
And then return and sleep within mine inn;
15   For with long travel I am stiff and weary.
Get thee away.

S. DROMIO: Many a man would take you at your word,
And go indeed, having so good a mean.
                                        Exit Dromio.

S. ANTIPHOLUS: A trusty villain,[2] sir, that very oft,
20   When I am dull with care and melancholy,

---

[1]lodge (at the Centaur)   [2]servant

Lightens my humor with his merry jests.
What, will you walk with me about the town,
And then go to my inn and dine with me?

MERCHANT: I am invited, sir, to certain merchants,
Of whom I hope to make much benefit.   25
I crave your pardon; soon at five o'clock,
Please you, I'll meet with you upon the Mart,
And afterward consort you[1] till bedtime.
My present business calls me from you now.

S. ANTIPHOLUS: Farewell till then. I will go lose myself,   30
And wander up and down to view the city.

MERCHANT: Sir, I commend you to your own content.

Exit.

S. ANTIPHOLUS: He that commends me to mine own content
Commends me to the thing I cannot get.
I to the world am like a drop of water   35
That in the ocean seeks another drop,
Who, falling there to find his fellow forth,
Unseen, inquisitive, confounds himself.
So I, to find a mother and a brother,
In quest of them, unhappy,[2] lose myself.   40

Enter Dromio of Ephesus.

Here comes the almanac of my true date.
What now? How chance thou art·returned so soon?

E. DROMIO: Returned so soon! Rather approached too late.
The capon burns, the pig falls from the spit;
The clock hath strucken twelve upon the bell;   45
My mistress made it one upon my cheek.
She is so hot because the meat is cold;
The meat is cold because you come not home;
You come not home because you have no stomach;[3]
You have no stomach, having broke your fast.   50
But we, that know what 'tis to fast and pray,
Are penitent for your default today.

S. ANTIPHOLUS: Stop in your wind, sir; tell me this, I pray:
Where have you left the money that I gave you?

E. DROMIO: O, sixpence, that I had o' Wednesday last,   55

---

[1]keep you company   [2]unlucky   [3]appetite

To pay the saddler for my mistress' crupper?
The saddler had it, sir, I kept it not.

S. ANTIPHOLUS: I am not in a sportive humor now.
Tell me, and dally not, where is the money?
60 We being strangers here, how dar'st thou trust
So great a charge from thine own custody?

E. DROMIO: I pray you, jest, sir, as you sit at dinner.
I from my mistress come to you in post;[1]
If I return, I shall not be post[2] indeed,
65 For she will scour your fault upon my pate.
Methinks your maw,[3] like mine, should be your clock,
And strike you home without a messenger.

S. ANTIPHOLUS: Come, Dromio, come, these jests are out
of season;
Reserve them till a merrier hour than this.
70 Where is the gold I gave in charge to thee?

E. DROMIO: To me, sir? Why, you gave no gold to me.

S. ANTIPHOLUS: Come on, sir knave, have done your foolishness,
And tell me how thou hast disposed thy charge.

E. DROMIO: My charge was but to fetch you from the Mart
75 Home to your house, the Phoenix, sir, to dinner.
My mistress and her sister stays for you.

S. ANTIPHOLUS: Now, as I am a Christian, answer me,
In what safe place you have bestowed my money;
Or I shall break that merry sconce[4] of yours
80 That stands on tricks when I am undisposed.
Where is the thousand marks thou hadst of me?

E. DROMIO: I have some marks of yours upon my pate,
Some of my mistress' marks upon my shoulders,
But not a thousand marks between you both.
85 If I should pay your worship those again,
Perchance you will not bear them patiently.

S. ANTIPHOLUS: Thy mistress' marks? What mistress, slave,
hast thou?

E. DROMIO: Your worship's wife, my mistress at the Phoenix;
She that doth fast till you come home to dinner,
90 And prays that you will hie you home to dinner.

---

[1]haste [2]beaten [3]stomach [4]head

S. ANTIPHOLUS: What, wilt thou flout me thus unto my face,
Being forbid? There, take you that, sir knave.

[Beats him.]

E. DROMIO: What mean you, sir? For God's sake, hold your
hands!
Nay, and[1] you will not, sir, I'll take my heels.

Exit Domio E.

S. ANTIPHOLUS: Upon my life, by some device or other,   *95*
The villain is o'er-raught[2] of all my money.
They say this town is full of cozenage:[3]
As nimble jugglers that deceive the eye,
Dark-working sorcerers that change the mind,
Soul-killing witches that deform the body,   *100*
Disguisèd cheaters, prating mountebanks,
And many suchlike liberties of sin.
If it prove so, I will be gone the sooner.
I'll to the Centaur, to go seek this slave.
I greatly fear my money is not safe.   *Exit.*   *105*

---

[1]if   [2]overreached, cheated out of   [3]cheating

ACT II

Scene I. *The house of Antipholus of Ephesus.*

Enter Adriana, wife to Antipholus [of Ephesus], with Luciana,
her sister.

ADRIANA: Neither my husband nor the slave returned,
That in such haste I sent to seek his master.
Sure, Luciana, it is two o'clock.

LUCIANA: Perhaps some merchant hath invited him,
5   And from the Mart he's somewhere gone to dinner.
Good sister, let us dine, and never fret;
A man is master of his liberty.
Time is their master, and when they see time,
They'll go or come; if so, be patient, sister.

10   ADRIANA: Why should their liberty than ours be more?

LUCIANA: Because their business still lies out o' door.

ADRIANA: Look when I serve him so, he takes it ill.

LUCIANA: O, know he is the bridle of your will.

ADRIANA: There's none but asses will be bridled so.

15   LUCIANA: Why, headstrong liberty is lashed with woe.
There's nothing situate under heaven's eye
But hath his bound, in earth, in sea, in sky.
The beasts, the fishes, and the wingèd fowls
Are their males' subjects, and at their controls;
20   Man, more divine, the master of all these,
Lord of the wide world and wild wat'ry seas,
Indued with intellectual sense and souls,
Of more preeminence than fish and fowls,
Are masters to their females, and their lords;
25   Then let your will attend on their accords.

ADRIANA: This servitude makes you to keep unwed.

LUCIANA: Not this, but troubles of the marriage bed.

ADRIANA: But, were you wedded, you would bear some sway.[1]

LUCIANA: Ere I learn love, I'll practice to obey.

ADRIANA: How if your husband start some other where?   *30*

LUCIANA: Till he come home again, I would forbear.

ADRIANA: Patience unmoved! no marvel though she pause;
They can be meek that have no other cause.
A wretched soul, bruised with adversity,
We bid be quiet when we hear it cry;   *35*
But were we burd'ned with like weight of pain,
As much or more we should ourselves complain:
So thou, that hast no unkind mate to grieve thee,
With urging helpless patience would relieve me;
But, if thou live to see like right bereft,   *40*
This fool-begged patience in thee will be left.

LUCIANA: Well, I will marry one day, but to try.
Here comes your man, now is your husband nigh.

Enter Dromio of Ephesus.

ADRIANA: Say, is your tardy master now at hand?

E. DROMIO: Nay, he's at two hands with me, and that my two   *45*
ears can witness.

ADRIANA: Say, didst thou speak with him? Know'st thou his
mind?

E. DROMIO: Ay, ay, he told his mind upon mine ear.
Beshrew his hand, I scarce could understand it.

LUCIANA: Spake he so doubtfully, thou couldst not feel his   *50*
meaning?

E. DROMIO: Nay, he struck so plainly, I could too well feel
his blows; and withal so doubtfully, that I could scarce
understand[2] them.

ADRIANA: But say, I prithee, is he coming home?   *55*
It seems he hath great care to please his wife.

E. DROMIO: Why, mistress, sure my master is horn-mad.

ADRIANA: Horn-mad, thou villain!

[1]command   [2]pun on "stand under" or withstand

E. DROMIO: I mean not cuckold-mad,
But sure he is stark mad.

60   When I desired him to come home to dinner,
He asked me for a thousand marks in gold.
" 'Tis dinnertime," quoth I. "My gold!" quoth he.
"Your meat doth burn," quoth I. "My gold!" quoth he.
"Will you come?" quoth I. "My gold!" quoth he.

65   "Where is the thousand marks I gave thee, villain?"
"The pig," quoth I, "is burned." "My gold!" quoth he.
"My mistress, sir—" quoth I. "Hang up thy mistress!
I know not thy mistress, out on[1] thy mistress!"

LUCIANA: Quoth who?

70 E. DROMIO: Quoth my master.
"I know," quoth he, "no house, no wife, no mistress."
So that my errand due unto my tongue,
I thank him, I bare home upon my shoulders;
For, in conclusion, he did beat me there.

75 ADRIANA: Go back again, thou slave, and fetch him home.

E. DROMIO: Go back again, and be new beaten home?
For God's sake, send some other messenger.

ADRIANA: Back, slave, or I will break thy pate across.

E. DROMIO: And he will bless that cross with other beating;

80   Between you, I shall have a holy head.

ADRIANA: Hence, prating peasant! Fetch thy master home.

E. DROMIO. Am I so round[2] with you, as you with me,
That like a football you do spurn me thus?
You spurn me hence, and he will spurn me hither;

85   If I last in this service, you must case me in leather.
                                    [Exit.]

LUCIANA: Fie, how impatience lowereth[3] in your face!

ADRIANA: His company must do his minions grace,
Whilst I at home starve for a merry look:
Hath homely age th' alluring beauty took

90   From my poor cheek? Then he hath wasted it.
Are my discourses dull? Barren my wit?
If voluble and sharp discourse be marred,
Unkindness blunts it more than marble hard.

[1]to hell with   [2]plainspoken   [3]frowns

Do their gay vestments his affections bait?[1]
That's not my fault; he's master of my state.   *95*
What ruins are in me that can be found,
By him not ruined? Then is he the ground
Of my defeatures.[2] My decayèd fair[3]
A sunny look of his would soon repair.
But, too unruly deer, he breaks the pale,   *100*
And feeds from home; poor I am but his stale.[4]

LUCIANA: Self-harming jealousy! fie, beat it hence.

ADRIANA: Unfeeling fools can with such wrongs dispense.
I know his eye doth homage otherwhere,
Or else what lets[5] it but he would be here?   *105*
Sister, you know he promised me a chain.
Would that alone, alone he would detain,
So he would keep fair quarter with his bed!
I see the jewel best enamelèd
Will lose his beauty; yet the gold bides still   *110*
That others touch, and often touching will
Wear gold, and no man that hath a name
But falsehood and corruption doth it shame.
Since that my beauty cannot please his eye,
I'll weep what's left away, and weeping die.   *115*

LUCIANA: How many fond fools serve mad jealousy!
                              Exit [with Adriana].

Scene II. *The Marketplace.*

Enter Antipholus [of Syracuse].

S. ANTIPHOLUS: The gold I gave to Dromio is laid up
Safe at the Centaur, and the heedful slave
Is wand'red forth, in care to seek me out,
By computation and mine host's report.
I could not speak with Dromio since at first   *5*
I sent him from the Mart! See, here he comes.

Enter Dromio of Syracuse.

How now, sir, is your merry humor altered?
As you love strokes, so jest with me again.

---

[1]entrap [2]ugliness [3]fairness, beauty [4]dupe [5]prevents

You know no Centaur? You received no gold?
10 Your mistress sent to have me home to dinner?
My house was at the Phoenix? Wast thou mad,
That thus so madly thou didst answer me?

S. DROMIO: What answer, sir? When spake I such a word?

S. ANTIPHOLUS: Even now, even here, not half an hour since.

15 S. DROMIO: I did not see you since you sent me hence,
Home to the Centaur, with the gold you gave me.

S. ANTIPHOLUS: Villain, thou didst deny the gold's receipt,
And told'st me of a mistress, and a dinner;
For which, I hope, thou felt'st I was displeased.

20 S. DROMIO: I am glad to see you in this merry vein.
What means this jest? I pray you, master, tell me.

S. ANTIPHOLUS: Yea, dost thou jeer, and flout me in the teeth?[1]
Think'st thou, I jest? Hold, take thou that! And that!
                                                            Beats Dromio.

S. DROMIO: Hold, sir, for God's sake! Now your jest is earnest.
25 Upon what bargain do you give it me?

S. ANTIPHOLUS: Because that I familiarly sometimes
Do use you for my fool and chat with you,
Your sauciness will jest upon my love,
And make a common of my serious hours.
30 When the sun shines, let foolish gnats make sport;
But creep in crannies, when he hides his beams.
If you will jest with me, know my aspect,
And fashion your demeanor to my looks,
Or I will beat this method in your sconce.

35 S. DROMIO: Sconce, call you it? So you would leave battering,
I had rather have it a head. And you use these blows long,
I must get a sconce for my head, and ensconce it too, or
else I shall seek my wit in my shoulders. But, I pray, sir,
why am I beaten?

40 S. ANTIPHOLUS: Dost thou not know?

S. DROMIO: Nothing, sir, but that I am beaten.

S. ANTIPHOLUS: Shall I tell you why?

[1]to my face

S. DROMIO: Ay, sir, and wherefore; for they say every why hath a wherefore.

S. ANTIPHOLUS: Why, first for flouting me, and then wherefore,   45
For urging it the second time to me.

S. DROMIO: Was there ever any man thus beaten out of season,
When in the why and the wherefore is neither rhyme nor reason?
Well, sir, I thank you.

S. ANTIPHOLUS: Thank me, sir, for what?

S. DROMIO: Marry,[1] sir, for this something that you gave   50
me for nothing.

S. ANTIPHOLUS: I'll make you amends next, to give you nothing for something. But say, sir, is it dinnertime?

S. DROMIO: No, sir. I think the meat wants that I have.   55

S. ANTIPHOLUS: In good time, sir. What's that?

S. DROMIO: Basting.

S. ANTIPHOLUS: Well, sir, then 'twill be dry.

S. DROMIO: If it be, sir, I pray you eat none of it.

S. ANTIPHOLUS: Your reason?   60

S. DROMIO: Lest it make you choleric and purchase me another dry basting.

S. ANTIPHOLUS: Well, sir, learn to jest in good time; there's a time for all things.

S. DROMIO: I durst have denied that, before you were so   65
choleric.

S. ANTIPHOLUS: By what rule, sir?

S. DROMIO: Marry, sir, by a rule as plain as the plain bald pate of Father Time himself.

S. ANTIPHOLUS: Let's hear it.   70

S. DROMIO: There's no time for a man to recover his hair that grows bald by nature.

[1]mild oath, "by the Virgin Mary"

S. ANTIPHOLUS: May he not do it by fine and recovery?[1]

75 S. DROMIO: Yes, to pay a fine for a periwig and recover the lost hair of another man.

S. ANTIPHOLUS: Why is Time such a niggard of hair, being, as it is, so plentiful an excrement?[2]

80 S. DROMIO: Because it is a blessing that he bestows on beasts: and what he hath scanted men in hair, he hath given them in wit.

S. ANTIPHOLUS: Why, but there's many a man hath more hair than wit.

85 S. DROMIO: Not a man of those but he hath the wit to lose his hair.

S. ANTIPHOLUS: Why, thou didst conclude hairy men plain dealers without wit.

S. DROMIO: The plainer dealer, the sooner lost; yet he loseth it in a kind of jollity.

90 S. ANTIPHOLUS: For what reason?

S. DROMIO: For two; and sound ones too.

S. ANTIPHOLUS: Nay, not sound, I pray you.

S. DROMIO: Sure ones, then.

S. ANTIPHOLUS: Nay, not sure, in a thing falsing.[3]

95 S. DROMIO: Certain ones, then.

S. ANTIPHOLUS: Name them.

S. DROMIO: The one, to save the money that he spends in tiring;[4] the other, that at dinner they should not drop in his porridge.

100 S. ANTIPHOLUS: You would all this time have proved there is no time for all things.

S. DROMIO: Marry, and did, sir: namely, e'en no time to recover hair lost by nature.

S. ANTIPHOLUS: But your reason was not substantial why there
105 is no time to recover.

S. DROMIO: Thus I mend it: Time himself is bald, and

---

[1] a legal process   [2] outgrowth   [3] that is false, deceptive   [4] hairdressing

therefore, to the world's end, will have bald fol-
lowers.

S. ANTIPHOLUS: I knew 'twould be a bald conclusion.

Enter Adriana and Luciana.

But soft, who wafts us yonder?   *110*

ADRIANA: Ay, ay, Antipholus, look strange[1] and frown;
Some other mistress hath thy sweet aspects.
I am not Adriana, nor thy wife.
The time was once when thou unurged wouldst vow
That never words were music to thine ear,   .   *115*
That never object pleasing in thine eye,
That never touch well welcome to thy hand,
That never meat sweet-savored in thy taste,
Unless I spake or looked or touched or carved to thee.
How comes it now, my husband, O how comes it,   *120*
That thou art then estrangèd from thyself?
Thyself I call it, being strange to me,
That, undividable, incorporate,
Am better than thy dear self's better part.
Ah, do not tear away thyself from me;   *125*
For know, my love, as easy mayst thou fall[2]
A drop of water in the breaking gulf,
And take unmingled thence that drop again
Without addition or diminishing
As take from me thyself, and not me too.   *130*
How dearly would it touch thee to the quick,
Shouldst thou but hear I was licentious,
And that this body, consecrate to thee,
By ruffian lust should be contaminate!
Wouldst thou not spit at me, and spurn at me,   *135*
And hurl the name of husband in my face,
And tear the stained skin off my harlot brow,
And from my false hand cut the wedding ring,
And break it with a deep-divorcing vow?
I know thou canst, and therefore see thou do it.   *140*
I am possessed with an adulterate blot.
My blood is mingled with the crime of lust;
For, if we two be one, and thou play false,
I do digest the poison of thy flesh,
Being strumpeted by thy contagion.   *145*

---

[1]odd, distant   [2]let fall

Keep then fair league and truce with thy true bed,
I live distained,[1] thou undishonorèd.

S. ANTIPHOLUS: Plead you to me, fair dame? I know you not.
In Ephesus I am but two hours old,
150   As strange unto your town as to your talk;
Who, every word by all my wit being scanned,
Wants wit in all one word to understand.

LUCIANA: Fie, brother, how the world is changed with you.
When were you wont to use my sister thus?
155   She sent for you by Dromio home to dinner.

S. ANTIPHOLUS: By Dromio?

S. DROMIO: By me?

ADRIANA: By thee, and this thou didst return from him:
That he did buffet thee, and in his blows
160   Denied my house for his, me for his wife.

S. ANTIPHOLUS: Did you converse, sir, with this gentlewoman?
What is the course and drift of your compact?[2]

S. DROMIO: I, sir? I never saw her till this time.

S. ANTIPHOLUS: Villain, thou liest; for even her very words
165   Didst thou deliver to me on the Mart.

S. DROMIO: I never spake with her in all my life.

S. ANTIPHOLUS: How can she thus then call us by our names,
Unless it be by inspiration?

ADRIANA: How ill agrees it with your gravity
170   To counterfeit thus grossly with your slave,
Abetting him to thwart me in my mood!
Be it my wrong you are from me exempt,[3]
But wrong not that wrong with a more contempt.
Come, I will fasten on this sleeve of thine:
175   Thou art an elm, my husband, I a vine,
Whose weakness, married to thy stronger state,
Makes me with thy strength to communicate.
If aught possess thee from me, it is dross,
Usurping ivy, briar, or idle[4] moss,
180   Who, all for want of pruning, with intrusion
Infect thy sap and live on thy confusion.[5]

---

[1]pure, unstained   [2]connection   [3]estranged   [4]worthless   [5]ruin

S. ANTIPHOLUS: [*Aside*] To me she speaks, she moves[1] me
  for her theme;
What, was I married to her in my dream?
Or sleep I now, and think I hear all this?
What error drives our eyes and ears amiss?   185
Until I know this sure uncertainty,
I'll entertain the offered fallacy.

LUCIANA: Dromio, go bid the servants spread for dinner.

S. DROMIO: O, for my beads![2] I cross me for a sinner.
This is the fairy land. O spite of spites!   190
We talk with goblins, owls, and sprites;
If we obey them not, this will ensue:
They'll suck our breath, or pinch us black and blue.

LUCIANA: Why prat'st thou to thyself and answer'st not?
Dromio, thou drone, thou snail, thou slug, thou
  sot.   195

S. DROMIO: I am transformèd, master, am not I?

S. ANTIPHOLUS: I think thou art in mind, and so am I.

S. DROMIO: Nay, master, both in mind and in my shape.

S. ANTIPHOLUS: Thou hast thine own form.

S. DROMIO: No, I am an ape.[3]

LUCIANA: If thou art changed to aught, 'tis to an ass.   200

S. DROMIO: 'Tis true, she rides me and I long for grass.
'Tis so, I am an ass; else it could never be
  But I should know her as well as she knows me.

ADRIANA: Come, come, no longer will I be a fool,
To put the finger in the eye and weep,   205
Whilst man and master laughs my woes to scorn.
Come, sir, to dinner. Dromio, keep the gate.
Husband, I'll dine above with you today,
And shrive[4] you of a thousand idle pranks.
Sirrah, if any ask you for your master,   210
Say he dines forth,[5] and let no creature enter.
Come, sister. Dromio, play the porter well.

S. ANTIPHOLUS: [*Aside*] Am I in earth, in heaven, or in hell?
Sleeping or waking, mad or well-advised?
Known unto these, and to myself disguised?   215

[1]takes up [2]rosary beads [3]mimic [4]absolve [5]away from home

I'll say as they say, and persever so,
And in this mist at all adventures[1] go.

S. DROMIO: Master, shall I be porter at the gate?

ADRIANA: Ay, and let none enter, lest I break your pate.

220   LUCIANA: Come, come, Antipholus, we dine too late.

[Exeunt.]

---

[1]chances

ACT III

Scene I. *Before the house of Antipholus of Ephesus.*

Enter Antipholus of Ephesus, his man Dromio,
Angelo the Goldsmith, and Balthasar the Merchant.

E. ANTIPHOLUS: Good Signor Angelo, you must excuse us all;
My wife is shrewish when I keep not hours.
Say that I lingered with you at your shop
To see the making of her carcanet,[1]
And that tomorrow you will bring it home.   5
But here's a villain that would face me down
He met me on the Mart, and that I beat him,
And charged him with a thousand marks in gold,
And that I did deny my wife and house.
Thou drunkard, thou, what didst thou mean by this?   10

E. DROMIO: Say what you will, sir, but I know what I know—
That you beat me at the Mart, I have your hand[2] to show;
If the skin were parchment and the blows you gave were ink,
Your own handwriting would tell you what I think.

E. ANTIPHOLUS: I think thou art an ass.

E. DROMIO: Marry, so it doth appear   15
By the wrongs I suffer and the blows I bear.
I should kick, being kicked, and being at that pass,
You would keep from my heels and beware of an ass.

E. ANTIPHOLUS: You're sad,[3] Signor Balthasar; pray God, our
    cheer
May answer my good will and your good welcome here.   20

BALTHASAR: I hold your dainties cheap, sir, and your welcome
    dear.

E. ANTIPHOLUS: O, Signor Balthasar, either at flesh or fish,
A tableful of welcome makes scarce one dainty dish.

[1]necklace [2]play on handwriting [3]serious

193

BALTHASAR: Good meat, sir, is common; that every churl[1] affords.

E. ANTIPHOLUS: And welcome more common, for that's nothing
25   but words.

BALTHASAR: Small cheer and great welcome makes a merry feast.

E. ANTIPHOLUS: Ay, to a niggardly host and more sparing guest.
But though my cates[2] be mean, take them in good part;
Better cheer may you have, but not with better heart.
30 But soft, my door is locked; go, bid them let us in.

E. DROMIO: Maud, Bridget, Marian, Cicely, Gillian, Ginn!

S. DROMIO *[Within]:* Mome,[3] malt-horse, capon, coxcomb, idiot, patch![4]
Either get thee from the door or sit down at the hatch.
Dost thou conjure for wenches, that thou call'st for such store,
35 When one is one too many? Go, get thee from the door.

E. DROMIO: What patch is made our porter? My master stays in the street.

S. DROMIO: Let him walk from whence he came, lest he catch cold on's feet.

E. ANTIPHOLUS: Who talks within there? Ho, open the door!

S. DROMIO: Right, sir, I'll tell you when, and you'll tell me wherefore.

E. ANTIPHOLUS: Wherefore? For my dinner; I have not
40   dined today.

S. DROMIO: Nor today here you must not; come again when you may.

E. ANTIPHOLUS: What art thou that keep'st me out from the house I owe?[5]

S. DROMIO: The porter for this time, sir, and my name is Dromio.

E. DROMIO: O villain, thou hast stol'n both mine office and my name.

---

[1]low fellow [2]dainties (food) [3]dolt [4]fool, jester [5]own

The one ne'er got me credit, the other mickle[1] blame.   *45*
If thou hadst been Dromio today in my place,
Thou wouldst have changed thy face for a name, or thy
      name for an ass.

Enter Luce [above].

LUCE: What a coil[2] is there, Dromio? Who are those at the
      gate?

E. DROMIO: Let my master in, Luce.

LUCE: Faith, no, he comes too late.
And so tell your master.

E. DROMIO: O Lord, I must laugh!   *50*
Have at you with a proverb: "Shall I set in my staff?"

LUCE: Have at you with another: that's "When? Can you
      tell?"

S. DROMIO: If thy name be called Luce—Luce, thou hast
      answered him well.

E. ANTIPHOLUS: Do you hear, you minion?[3] You'll let us
      in, I trow?

LUCE: I thought to have asked you.

S. DROMIO: And you said no.   *55*

E. DROMIO: So, come help! Well struck! There was blow
      for blow.

E. ANTIPHOLUS: Thou baggage, let me in.

LUCE: Can you tell for whose sake?

E. DROMIO: Master, knock the door hard.

LUCE: Let him knock till it ache.

E. ANTIPHOLUS: You'll cry for this, minion, if I beat the door
      down.

LUCE: What needs all that, and a pair of stocks[4] in the
      town?
                                                          60

Enter Adriana [above].

ADRIANA: Who is that at the door that keeps all this
      noise?

---

[1]much [2]commotion [3]darling, hussy [4]punishment in which the feet were
locked up

S. DROMIO: By my troth, your town is troubled with unruly boys.

E. ANTIPHOLUS: Are you there, wife? You might have come before.

ADRIANA: Your wife, sir knave! Go, get you from the door.   *[Exit with Luce.]*

65 E. DROMIO: If you went in pain, master, this knave would go sore.

ANGELO: Here is neither cheer, sir, nor welcome; we would fain have either.

BALTHASAR: In debating which was best, we shall part with neither.

E. DROMIO: They stand at the door, master. Bid them welcome hither.

E. ANTIPHOLUS: There is something in the wind, that we cannot get in.

70 E. DROMIO: You would say so, master, if your garments were thin.
Your cake here is warm within; you stand here in the cold.
It would make a man mad as a buck to be so bought and sold.

E. ANTIPHOLUS: Go, fetch me something. I'll break ope the gate.

S. DROMIO: Break any breaking here, and I'll break your knave's pate.

E. DROMIO: A man may break[1] a word with you, sir, and
75 words are but wind;
Ay, and break it in your face, so he break it not behind.

S. DROMIO: It seems thou want'st breaking.[2] Out upon thee, hind![3]

E. DROMIO: Here's too much "out upon thee." I pray thee, let me in.

S. DROMIO: Ay, when fowls have no feathers, and fish have no fin.

E. ANTIPHOLUS: Well, I'll break in. Go borrow me a
80 crow.[4]

[1]exchange   [2]beating   [3]base, menial   [4]crowbar

E. DROMIO: A crow without feather? Master, mean you so?
   For a fish without a fin, there's a fowl without a feather.
   If a crow help us in, sirrah, we'll pluck a crow together.

E. ANTIPHOLUS: Go, get thee gone, fetch me an iron crow.

BALTHASAR: Have patience, sir, O, let it not be so!   85
   Herein you war against your reputation,
   And draw within the compass of suspect
   Th' unviolated honor of your wife.
   Once this—your long experience of her wisdom,
   Her sober virtue, years, and modesty,   90
   Plead on her part some cause to you unknown;
   And doubt not, sir, but she will well excuse
   Why at this time the doors are made against you.
   Be ruled by me, depart in patience,
   And let us to the Tiger all to dinner.   95
   And, about evening, come yourself alone,
   To know the reason of this strange restraint.
   If by strong hand you offer to break in,
   Now in the stirring passage of the day,
   A vulgar comment will be made of it;   100
   And that supposèd by the common rout
   Against your yet ungallèd estimation,
   That may with foul intrusion enter in
   And dwell upon your grave when you are dead;
   For slander lives upon succession,   105
   For ever housed where it gets possession.

E. ANTIPHOLUS: You have prevailed. I will depart in quiet,
   And, in despite of mirth, mean to be merry.
   I know a wench of excellent discourse,
   Pretty and witty; wild and yet, too, gentle;   110
   There will we dine: this woman that I mean,
   My wife—but, I protest, without desert—
   Hath oftentimes upbraided me withal.
   To her will we to dinner. *[To Angelo]* Get you home,
   And fetch the chain; by this, I know, 'tis made;   115
   Bring it, I pray you, to the Porpentine,
   For there's the house. That chain will I bestow—
   Be it for nothing but to spite my wife—
   Upon mine hostess there. Good sir, make haste.
   Since mine own doors refuse to entertain me,   120
   I'll knock elsewhere, to see if they'll disdain me.

ANGELO: I'll meet you at that place some hour hence.

E. ANTIPHOLUS: Do so. This jest shall cost me some expense.
Exeunt.

Scene II. *Before the house of Antipholus of Ephesus.*

Enter Luciana, with Antipholus of Syracuse

LUCIANA: And may it be that you have quite forgot
A husband's office? Shall, Antipholus,
Even in the spring of love thy love-springs[1] rot?
Shall love, in building, grow so ruinous?
5   If you did wed my sister for her wealth,
Then for her wealth's sake use her with more kindness;
Or, if you like elsewhere, do it by stealth,
Muffle your false love with some show of blindness.
Let not my sister read it in your eye;
10   Be not thy tongue thy own shame's orator;
Look sweet, speak fair, become[2] disloyalty;
Apparel vice like virtue's harbinger.
Bear a fair presence, though your heart be tainted,
Teach sin the carriage of a holy saint,
15   Be secret-false: what need she be acquainted?
What simple thief brags of his own attaint?[3]
'Tis double wrong to truant[4] with your bed
And let her read it in thy looks at board.
Shame hath a bastard fame, well managèd;
20   Ill deeds is doubled with an evil word.
Alas, poor women! Make us but believe,
Being compact of credit, that you love us;
Though others have the arm, show us the sleeve:
We in your motion turn, and you may move us.
25   Then, gentle brother, get you in again;
Comfort my sister, cheer her, call her wife;
'Tis holy sport, to be a little vain,
When the sweet breath of flattery conquers strife.

S. ANTIPHOLUS: Sweet mistress, what your name is else, I
know not;
Nor by what wonder you do hit of[5] mine;   30
Less in your knowledge and your grace you show not
Than our earth's wonder, more than earth divine.

---

[1]young growths of love [2]make it becoming [3]disgrace [4]play the truant [5]guess at

Teach me, dear creature, how to think and speak:
Lay open to my earthy-gross conceit,[1]
Smoth'red in errors, feeble, shallow, weak,   35
The folded[2] meaning of your words' deceit.
Against my soul's pure truth why labor you
To make it wander in an unknown field?
Are you a god? Would you create me new?
Transform me, then, and to your pow'r I'll yield.   40
But if that I am I, then well I know
Your weeping sister is no wife of mine,
Nor to her bed no homage do I owe;
Far more, far more, to you do I decline.[3]
O, train[4] me not, sweet mermaid, with thy note,   45
To drown me in thy sister's flood of tears.
Sing, siren, for thyself, and I will dote;
Spread o'er the silver waves thy golden hairs;
And as a bed I'll take thee, and there lie,
And, in that glorious supposition, think   50
He gains by death that hath such means to die.
Let Love, being light, be drownèd if she sink!

LUCIANA: What, are you mad, that you do reason so?

S. ANTIPHOLUS: Not mad, but mated[5]—how, I do not
  know.

LUCIANA: It is a fault that springeth from your eye.   55

S. ANTIPHOLUS: For gazing on your beams, fair sun, being
  by.

LUCIANA: Gaze where you should, and that will clear your
  sight.

S. ANTIPHOLUS: As good to wink,[6] sweet love, as look on
  night.

LUCIANA: Why call you me love? Call my sister so.

S. ANTIPHOLUS: Thy sister's sister.

LUCIANA: That's my sister.

S. ANTIPHOLUS: No,   60
  It is thyself, mine own self's better part,
  Mine eye's clear eye, my dear heart's dearer heart;

[1]conception [2]hidden [3]incline [4]tempt [5]confounded [6]shut one's eyes

My food, my fortune, and my sweet hope's aim;
My sole earth's heaven, and my heaven's claim.

65 LUCIANA: All this my sister is, or else should be.

S. ANTIPHOLUS: Call thyself sister, sweet, for I am thee;
Thee will I love, and with thee lead my life;
Thou hast no husband yet, nor I no wife.
Give me thy hand.

LUCIANA: O, soft, sir, hold you still
70 I'll fetch my sister, to get her good will.   *Exit.*

Enter Dromio of Syracuse.

S. ANTIPHOLUS: Why, how now, Dromio! Where run'st thou
so fast?

S. DROMIO: Do you know me, sir? Am I Dromio? Am I
your man? Am I myself?

75 S. ANTIPHOLUS: Thou art Dromio, thou art my man, thou
art thyself.

S. DROMIO: I am an ass; I am a woman's man, and besides
myself.

S. ANTIPHOLUS: What woman's man? And how besides
80 thyself?

S. DROMIO: Marry, sir, besides myself, I am due to a
woman: one that claims me, one that haunts me, one
that will have me.

S. ANTIPHOLUS: What claim lays she to thee?

85 S. DROMIO: Marry, sir, such claim as you would lay to
your horse; and she would have me as a beast—not
that, I being a beast, she would have me, but that
she, being a very beastly creature, lays claim to
me.

90 S. ANTIPHOLUS: What is she?

S. DROMIO: A very reverend body; ay, such a one as a
man may not speak of without he say "sir-reverence."[1]
I have but lean luck in the match, and yet she is a
wondrous fat marriage.

95 S. ANTIPHOLUS: How dost thou mean a fat marriage?

[1] I beg your pardon.

S. DROMIO: Marry, sir, she's the kitchen-wench, and all grease; and I know not what use to put her to, but to make a lamp of her, and run from her by her own light. I warrant her rags and the tallow in them will burn a Poland winter. If she lives till doomsday, she'll burn a week 100 longer than the whole world.

S. ANTIPHOLUS: What complexion is she of?

S. DROMIO: Swart, like my shoe, but her face nothing like so clean kept; for why? She sweats; a man may 105 go over-shoes in the grime of it.

S. ANTIPHOLUS: That's a fault that water will mend.

S. DROMIO: No, sir, 'tis in grain;[1] Noah's flood could not do it.

S. ANTIPHOLUS: What's her name? 110

S. DROMIO: Nell, sir; but her name and three quarters—that's an ell[2] and three quarters—will not measure her from hip to hip.

S. ANTIPHOLUS: Then she bears some breadth?

S. DROMIO: No longer from head to foot than from hip 115 to hip. She is spherical, like a globe. I could find out countries in her.

S. ANTIPHOLUS: In what part of her body stands Ireland?

S. DROMIO: Marry, sir, in her buttocks; I found it out 120 by the bogs.

S. ANTIPHOLUS: Where Scotland?

S. DROMIO: I found it by the barrenness, hard in the palm of the hand.

S. ANTIPHOLUS: Where France? 125

S. DROMIO: In her forehead, armed and reverted,[3] making war against her heir.

S. ANTIPHOLUS: Where England?

S. DROMIO: I looked for the chalky cliffs,[4] but I could find no whiteness in them. But I guess, it stood in her 130

[1]indelible [2]45 inches [3]revolted [4]teeth

chin, by the salt rheum[1] that ran between France and it.

S. ANTIPHOLUS: Where Spain?

S. DROMIO: Faith, I saw it not; but I felt it hot in her
135   breath.

S. ANTIPHOLUS: Where America, the Indies?

S. DROMIO: O, sir, upon her nose, all o'er embellished with rubies, carbuncles, sapphires, declining[2] their rich aspect
140   to the hot breath of Spain, who sent whole armadoes of carracks[3] to be ballast[4] at her nose.

S. ANTIPHOLUS: Where stood Belgia, the Netherlands?[5]

S. DROMIO: O, sir, I did not look so low. To conclude, this drudge, or diviner, laid claim to me, called me Dromio,
145   swore I was assured to her, told me what privy marks I had about me, as the mark of my shoulder, the mole in my neck, the great wart on my left arm, that I, amazed, ran from her as a witch.
And, I think, if my breast had not been made of faith,
150   and my heart of steel,
She had transformed me to a curtal dog,[6] and made me turn i' th' wheel.[7]

S. ANTIPHOLUS: Go, hie thee presently, post to the road,[8]
And if the wind blow any way from shore,
I will not harbor in this town tonight.
155   If any bark put forth, come to the Mart,
Where I will walk till thou return to me.
If everyone knows us, and we know none,
'Tis time, I think, to trudge, pack, and begone.

S. DROMIO: As from a bear a man would run for life,
160   So fly I from her that would be my wife.   *Exit.*

S. ANTIPHOLUS: There's none but witches do inhabit here,
And therefore 'tis high time that I were hence.
She that doth call me husband, even my soul
Doth for a wife abhor. But her fair sister,
165   Possessed with such a gentle sovereign grace,

---

[1]moisture from nose   [2]bending   [3]large ships   [4]freighted   [5]The Low Countries (with sexual innuendo)   [6]dog with docked tail   [7]kitchen spit   [8]harbor

Of such enchanting presence and discourse,
Hath almost made me traitor to myself.
But, lest myself be guilty to[1] self-wrong,
I'll stop mine ears against the mermaid's song.

Enter Angelo with the chain.

ANGELO: Master Antipholus—

S. ANTIPHOLUS: Ay, that's my name.   *170*

ANGELO: I know it well, sir. Lo, here's the chain.
  I thought to have ta'en you at the Porpentine.
  The chain unfinished made me stay thus long.

S. ANTIPHOLUS: What is your will that I shall do with
  this?

ANGELO: What please yourself, sir; I have made it for
  you.   *175*

S. ANTIPHOLUS: Made it for me, sir? I bespoke[2] it not.

ANGELO: Not once, nor twice, but twenty times you
  have.
  Go home with it and please your wife withal,
  And soon at suppertime I'll visit you,
  And then receive my money for the chain.   *180*

S. ANTIPHOLUS: I pray you, sir, receive the money now,
  For fear you ne'er see chain nor money more.

ANGELO: You are a merry man, sir. Fare you well.   *Exit.*

S. ANTIPHOLUS: What I should think of this, I cannot
  tell:
  But this I think, there's no man is so vain[3]   *185*
  That would refuse so fair an offered chain.
  I see a man here needs not live by shifts,
  When in the streets he meets such golden gifts.
  I'll to the Mart, and there for Dromio stay;
  If any ship put out, then straight away.   *Exit.*   *190*

[1]of [2]ordered [3]foolish

ACT IV

Scene I. The Marketplace.

*Enter a Merchant, [Angelo the] Goldsmith, and
an Officer.*

MERCHANT: You know since Pentecost the sum is due,
And since I have not much importuned you,
Nor now I had not, but that I am bound
To Persia, and want guilders for my voyage;
5   Therefore make present satisfaction,
Or I'll attach[1] you by this officer.

ANGELO: Even just the sum that I do owe to you
Is growing to me by Antipholus,
And in the instant that I met with you
10   He had of me a chain. At five o'clock
I shall receive the money for the same.
Pleaseth you, walk with me down to his house;
I will discharge my bond, and thank you too.

*Enter Antipholus of Ephesus, [and] Dromio
[of Ephesus] from the Courtesan's.*

OFFICER: That labor may you save. See where he comes.

E. ANTIPHOLUS. While I go to the goldsmith's house, go
15   thou
And buy a rope's end; that will I bestow
Among my wife and her confederates,
For locking me out of my doors by day.
But soft, I see the goldsmith; get thee gone,
20   Buy thou a rope, and bring it home to me.

E. DROMIO: I buy a thousand pound a year! I buy a
rope!   *Exit Dromio.*

204

E. ANTIPHOLUS: A man is well holp[1] up that trusts to
  you!
I promisèd your presence and the chain,
But neither chain nor goldsmith came to me.
Belike you thought our love would last too long,   25
If it were chained together, and therefore came not.

ANGELO: Saving your merry humor, here's the note
How much your chain weighs to the utmost carat,
The fineness of the gold and chargeful fashion—
Which doth amount to three odd ducats more   30
Than I stand debted to this gentleman.
I pray you, see him presently discharged,
For he is bound to sea, and stays but for it.

E. ANTIPHOLUS: I am not furnished with the present
  money.
Besides, I have some business in the town.   35
Good signor, take the stranger to my house,
And with you take the chain, and bid my wife
Disburse the sum on the receipt thereof.
Perchance I will be there as soon as you.

ANGELO: Then you will bring the chain to her yourself?   40

E. ANTIPHOLUS: No, bear it with you, lest I come not time
  enough.[2]

ANGELO: Well, sir, I will. Have you the chain about
  you?

E. ANTIPHOLUS: And if I have not, sir, I hope you have,
Or else you may return without your money.

ANGELO: Nay, come, I pray you, sir, give me the chain: 45
Both wind and tide stays for this gentleman,
And I, too blame,[3] have held him here too long.

E. ANTIPHOLUS: Good Lord, you use this dalliance to excuse
Your breach of promise to the Porpentine.
I should have chid you for not bringing it,   50
But, like a shrew,[4] you first begin to brawl.

MERCHANT: The hour steals on; I pray you, sir, dispatch.

ANGELO: You hear how he importunes me—the chain!

---

[1]helped   [2]in good time   [3]blameworthy   [4]cold

E. ANTIPHOLUS: Why, give it to my wife, and fetch your
    money.

ANGELO: Come, come, you know, I gave it you even
55   now;
    Either send the chain or send me by some token.

E. ANTIPHOLUS: Fie, now you run this humor out of breath.
    Come, where's the chain? I pray you, let me see it.

MERCHANT: My business cannot brook this dalliance.
60   Good sir, say whe'er[1] you'll answer me or no:
    If not, I'll leave him to the officer.

E. ANTIPHOLUS: I answer you! What should I answer you?

ANGELO: The money that you owe me for the chain.

E. ANTIPHOLUS: I owe you none till I receive the chain.

65   ANGELO: You know I gave it you half an hour since.

E. ANTIPHOLUS: You gave me none; you wrong me much to
    say so.

ANGELO: You wrong me more, sir, in denying it.
    Consider how it stands upon my credit.

MERCHANT: Well, officer, arrest him at my suit.

70   OFFICER: I do,
    And charge you in the Duke's name to obey me.

ANGELO: This touches me in reputation.
    Either consent to pay this sum for me,
    Or I attach you by this officer.

75   E. ANTIPHOLUS: Consent to pay thee that I never had!
    Arrest me, foolish fellow, if thou dar'st.

ANGELO: Here is thy fee; arrest him, officer.
    I would not spare my brother in this case,
    If he should scorn me so apparently.

80   OFFICER: I do arrest you, sir; you hear the suit.

E. ANTIPHOLUS: I do obey thee, till I give thee bail.
    But, sirrah, you shall buy this sport as dear
    As all the metal in your shop will answer.

ANGELO: Sir, sir, I shall have law in Ephesus,
85   To your notorious shame, I doubt it not.

---

[1]whether

Enter Dromio of Syracuse from the Bay.

S. DROMIO: Master, there's a bark of Epidamnum,
That stays but till her owner comes aboard,
And then she bears away. Our fraughtage,[1] sir,
I have conveyed aboard, and I have bought
The oil, the balsamum, and aqua-vitae.   90
The ship is in her trim,[2] the merry wind
Blows fair from land; they stay for nought at all
But for their owner, master, and yourself.

E. ANTIPHOLUS: How now! a madman? Why, thou peevish
      sheep,
What ship of Epidamnum stays for me?   95

S. DROMIO: A ship you sent me to, to hire waftage.[3]

E. ANTIPHOLUS: Thou drunken slave, I sent thee for a
      rope,
And told thee to what purpose and what end.

S. DROMIO: You sent me for a rope's end as soon.
You sent me to the bay, sir, for a bark.   100

E. ANTIPHOLUS: I will debate this matter at more leisure,
And teach your ears to list[4] me with more heed.
To Adriana, villain, hie thee straight;
Give her this key, and tell her, in the desk
That's covered o'er with Turkish tapestry   105
There is a purse of ducats; let her send it.
Tell her I am arrested in the street,
And that shall bail me. Hie thee, slave, begone.
On, officer, to prison till it come.
                              Exeunt [all but Dromio].

S. DROMIO: To Adriana—that is where we dined,   110
Where Dowsabel did claim me for her husband.
She is too big, I hope, for me to compass.
Thither I must, although against my will;
For servants must their masters' minds fulfill.
                                        Exit.

[1]cargo   [2]ready to depart   [3]passage   [4]listen to

Scene II. *The house of Antipholus of Ephesus*.

Enter Adriana and Luciana.

ADRIANA: Ah, Luciana, did he tempt thee so?
Mightst thou perceive austerely in his eye,
That he did plead in earnest, yea or no?
Looked he or red or pale, or sad or merrily?
5   What observation mad'st thou in this case
Of his heart's meteors tilting[1] in his face?

LUCIANA: First, he denied you had in him no right.

ADRIANA: He meant he did me none; the more my spite.

LUCIANA: Then swore he that he was a stranger here.

10   ADRIANA: And true he swore, though yet forsworn he were.

LUCIANA: Then pleaded I for you.

ADRIANA: And what said he?

LUCIANA: That love I begged for you he begged of me.

ADRIANA: With what persuasion did he tempt thy love?

LUCIANA: With words that in an honest suit might move.
15   First he did praise my beauty, then my speech.

ADRIANA, Didst speak him fair?[2]

LUCIANA: Have patience, I beseech.

ADRIANA: I cannot, nor I will not, hold me still.
My tongue, though not my heart, shall have his[3] will.
He is deformèd, crookèd, old and sere,
20   Ill-faced, worse bodied, shapeless everywhere:
Vicious, ungentle, foolish, blunt, unkind,
Stigmatical in making,[4] worse in mind.

LUCIANA: Who would be jealous then of such a one?
No evil lost is wailed when it is gone.

25   ADRIANA: Ah, but I think him better than I say;
And yet would herein others' eyes were worse.
Far from her nest the lapwing cries away;

---

[1]thrusting, fighting   [2]give him good words   [3]its   [4]deformed in looks

My heart prays for him, though my tongue do curse.

Enter Dromio of Syracuse.

S. DROMIO: Here, go—the desk, the purse! Sweet, now,
  make haste.

LUCIANA: How hast thou lost thy breath?

S. DROMIO: By running fast.   *30*

ADRIANA: Where is thy master, Dromio? Is he well?

S. DROMIO: No, he's in Tartar limbo,[1] worse than hell:
  A devil in an everlasting garment hath him;
  One whose hard heart is buttoned up with steel:
  A fiend, a fairy, pitiless and rough: *35*
  A wolf, nay worse, a fellow all in buff:[2]
  A back-friend,[3] a shoulder-clapper,[4] one that countermands
  The passages of alleys, creeks,[5] and narrow lands;
  A hound that runs counter,[6] and yet draws dry-foot[7] well;
  One that, before the judgment, carries poor souls to hell.   *40*

ADRIANA: Why, man, what is the matter?

S. DROMIO: I do not know the matter, he is 'rested on the
  case.

ADRIANA: What, is he arrested? Tell me, at whose suit.

S. DROMIO: I know not at whose suit he is arrested well;
  But is in a suit of buff which 'rested him, that can I tell.   *45*
  Will you send him, Mistress Redemption, the money in
  his desk?

ADRIANA: Go fetch it, sister. This I wonder at,
                                Exit Luciana.
  Thus he, unknown to me, should be in debt.
  Tell me, was he arrested on a band?[8]

S. DROMIO: Not on a band, but on a stronger thing: *50*
  A chain, a chain! Do you not hear it ring?

ADRIANA: What, the chain?

S. DROMIO: No, no, the bell; 'tis time
  that I were gone.
  It was two ere I left him, and now the clock strikes one.

---

[1]prison (Tartarus was hell)   [2]leather (the arresting officer's uniform)   [3]false friend
[4]bailiff   [5]narrow passages   [6]contrary   [7]hunts by the scent of the foot   [8]bond

ADRIANA: The hours come back! That did I never hear.

S. DROMIO: O yes. If any hour meet a sergeant, 'a[1] turns
55   back for very fear.

ADRIANA: As if time were in debt! How fondly dost thou
    reason!

S. DROMIO: Time is a very bankrupt, and owes more than
    he's worth to season.
    Nay, he's a thief too: have you not heard men say,
    That time comes stealing on by night and day?
60   If 'a be in debt and theft, and a sergeant in the way,
    Hath he not reason to turn back an hour in a day?

Enter Luciana.

ADRIANA: Go, Dromio. There's the money, bear it straight,
    And bring thy master home immediately.
    Come, sister. I am pressed down with conceit:[2]
65   Conceit, my comfort and my injury.

Exit [with Luciana and Dromio].

Scene III. *The Marketplace.*

Enter Antipholus of Syracuse.

S. ANTIPHOLUS: There's not a man I meet but doth salute
    me
    As if I were their well-acquainted friend;
    And everyone doth call me by my name.
    Some tender money to me, some invite me;
5   Some other[3] give me thanks for kindnesses;
    Some offer me commodities to buy.
    Even now a tailor called me in his shop
    And showed me silks that he had bought for me,
    And therewithal took measure of my body.
10   Sure, these are but imaginary wiles,
    And Lapland sorcerers inhabit here.

Enter Dromio of Syracuse.

S. DROMIO: Master, here's the gold you sent me for.

---

[1] it (colloquial contraction)   [2] imagination   [3] others

What, have you got the picture of old Adam new-
appareled?

S. ANTIPHOLUS: What gold is this? What Adam dost thou   *15*
mean?

S. DROMIO: Not that Adam that kept the paradise, but that
Adam that keeps the prison; he that goes in the calf's skin
that was killed for the Prodigal; he that came behind
you, sir, like an evil angel, and bid you forsake your   *20*
liberty.

S. ANTIPHOLUS: I understand thee not.

S. DROMIO: No? Why, 'tis a plain case: he that went, like
a bass-viol, in a case of leather; the man, sir, that,
when gentlemen are tired gives them a sob[1] and 'rests   *25*
them; he, sir, that takes pity on decayed men, and
gives them suits of durance:[2] he that sets up his rest[3]
to do more exploits with his mace than a morris-
pike.

S. ANTIPHOLUS: What, thou mean'st an officer?   *30*

S. DROMIO: Ay, sir, the sergeant of the band: he that
brings any man to answer it that breaks his band;[4] one
that thinks a man always going to bed, and says, "God
give you good rest!"

S. ANTIPHOLUS: Well, sir, there rest in your foolery.   *35*
Is there any ships puts forth tonight? May we be
gone?

S. DROMIO: Why, sir, I brought you word an hour since
that the bark[5] *Expedition* put forth tonight, and then
were you hind'red by the sergeant to tarry for the hoy[6]   *40*
Delay. Here are the angels that you sent for to deliver
you.

S. ANTIPHOLUS: The fellow is distract, and so am I,
And here we wander in illusions.
Some blessèd power deliver us from hence!   *45*

Enter a Courtesan.

COURTESAN: Well met, well met, Master Antipholus.
I see, sir, you have found the goldsmith now.
Is that the chain you promised me today?

---

[1]a rest period for a horse [2]strong suits (with puns) [3]stakes all [4]bond [5]ship
[6]small coasting vessel

S. ANTIPHOLUS: Satan, avoid![1] I charge thee, tempt me not!

50 S. DROMIO: Master, is this Mistress Satan?

S. ANTIPHOLUS: It is the devil.

S. DROMIO: Nay, she is worse, she is the devil's dam;[2] and here she comes in the habit[3] of a light wench, and thereof comes that the wenches say, "God
55 damn me." That's as much to say, "God make me a light wench." It is written, they appear to men like angels of light. Light is an effect of fire, and fire will burn: ergo,[4] light wenches will burn. Come not near her.

60 COURTESAN: Your man and you are marvelous merry, sir. Will you go with me? We'll mend[5] our dinner here.

S. DROMIO: Master, if you do, expect spoon-meat,[6] or bespeak a long spoon.

S. ANTIPHOLUS: Why, Dromio?

65 S. DROMIO: Marry, he must have a long spoon that must eat with the devil.

S. ANTIPHOLUS: Avoid, then, fiend! What tell'st thou me of
    supping?
Thou art, as you are all, a sorceress.
I conjure thee to leave me and be gone.

70 COURTESAN: Give me the ring of mine you had at dinner,
Or, for my diamond, the chain you promised,
And I'll be gone, sir, and not trouble you.

S. DROMIO: Some devils ask but the parings of one's nail,
A rush, a hair, a drop of blood, a pin,
75 A nut, a cherry-stone;
But she, more covetous, would have a chain.
Master, be wise; and if you give it her,
The devil will shake her chain, and fright us with it.

COURTESAN: I pray you, sir, my ring, or else the chain.
80   I hope you do not mean to cheat me so!

---

[1]be gone [2]mother [3]dress [4]therefore [5]finish [6]soft food (that can be eaten with a spoon)

S. ANTIPHOLUS: Avaunt, thou witch! Come, Dromio, let us
    go.

S. DROMIO: Fly pride, says the peacock. Mistress, that
    you know.   *Exit [with Antipholus].*

COURTESAN: Now, out of doubt, Antipholus is mad,
    Else would he never so demean himself.
    A ring he hath of mine worth forty ducats,   85
    And for the same he promised me a chain;
    Both one and other he denies me now.
    The reason that I gather he is mad,
    Besides this present instance of his rage,
    Is a mad tale he told today at dinner,   90
    Of his own doors being shut against his entrance.
    Belike his wife, acquainted with his fits,
    On purpose shut the doors against his way.
    My way is now to hie home to his house,
    And tell his wife that, being lunatic,   95
    He rushed into my house and took perforce
    My ring away. This course I fittest choose,
    For forty ducats is too much to lose.   *[Exit.]*

Scene IV. *The Marketplace.*

Enter Antipholus of Ephesus with a Jailer.

E. ANTIPHOLUS: Fear me not, man, I will not break away.
    I'll give thee, ere I leave thee, so much money,
    To warrant[1] thee, as I am 'rested for.
    My wife is in a wayward mood today,
    And will not lightly trust the messenger   5
    That I should be attached[2] in Ephesus;
    I tell you, 'twill sound harshly in her ears.

Enter Dromio of Ephesus, with a rope's end.

    Here comes my man, I think he brings the money.
    How now, sir! Have you that I sent you for?

E. DROMIO: Here's that, I warrant you, will pay them all.   10

E. ANTIPHOLUS: But where's the money?

---

[1]secure   [2]arrested

E. DROMIO: Why, sir, I gave the money for the rope.

E. ANTIPHOLUS: Five hundred ducats, villain, for a rope?

E. DROMIO: I'll serve you, sir, five hundred at the rate.

15   E. ANTIPHOLUS: To what end did I bid thee hie thee home?

E. DROMIO: To a rope's end, sir, and to that end am I returned.

E. ANTIPHOLUS: And to that end, sir, I will welcome you.   *[Beats Dromio.]*

OFFICER: Good sir, be patient.

E. DROMIO: Nay, 'tis for me to be patient; I am in ad-
20   versity.

OFFICER: Good now, hold thy tongue.

E. DROMIO: Nay, rather persuade him to hold his hands.

E. ANTIPHOLUS: Thou whoreson,[1] senseless villain!

25   E. DROMIO: I would I were senseless, sir, that I might not feel your blows.

E. ANTIPHOLUS: Thou art sensible in nothing but blows, and so is an ass.

E. DROMIO: I am an ass, indeed; you may prove it by
30   my long ears. I have served him from the hour of my nativity to this instant, and have nothing at his hands for my service but blows. When I am cold, he heats me with beating; when I am warm, he cools me with beating. I am waked with it when I
35   sleep, raised with it when I sit, driven out of doors with it when I go from home, welcomed home with it when I return; nay, I bear it on my shoulders, as a beggar wont[2] her brat; and, I think, when he hath lamed me, I shall beg with it from door to
40   door.

*Enter Adriana, Luciana, Courtesan, and a
Schoolmaster called Pinch.*

E. ANTIPHOLUS: Come, go along; my wife is coming yonder.

---

[1]foolish fellow   [2]does

E. DROMIO: Mistress, *"respice finem,"* respect your end; or
rather, the prophecy like the parrot, "beware the rope's
end."

E. ANTIPHOLUS: Wilt thou still talk?   *Beats Dromio.*   *45*

COURTESAN: How say you now? Is not your husband mad?

ADRIANA: His incivility confirms no less.
Good Doctor Pinch, you are a conjurer;[1]
Establish him in his true sense again,
And I will please you what you will demand.   *50*

LUCIANA: Alas, how fiery and how sharp he looks!

COURTESAN: Mark how he trembles in his ecstasy![2]

PINCH: Give me your hand, and let me feel your pulse.
                              [*Antipholus strikes him.*]

E. ANTIPHOLUS: There is my hand, and let it feel your ear!

PINCH: I charge thee, Satan, housed within this man,   *55*
To yield possession to my holy prayers,
And to thy state of darkness hie thee straight;
I conjure thee by all the saints in heaven.

E. ANTIPHOLUS: Peace, doting wizard, peace; I am not mad.

ADRIANA: O, that thou wert not, poor distressèd soul!   *60*

E. ANTIPHOLUS: You minion,[3] you, are these your customers?
Did this companion with the saffron[4] face
Revel and feast it at my house today,
Whilst upon me the guilty doors were shut,
And I denied to enter in my house?   *65*

ADRIANA: O, husband, God doth know you dined at home,
Where would you had remained until this time,
Free from these slanders and this open shame!

E. ANTIPHOLUS: Dined at home! Thou villain, what sayest
thou?

E. DROMIO: Sir, sooth to say, you did not dine at home.   *70*

E. ANTIPHOLUS: Were not my doors locked up, and I shut
out?

_____
[1]exorcist [2]mad fit [3]whore [4]yellow

E. DROMIO: Perdie,[1] your doors were locked, and you shut out.

E. ANTIPHOLUS: And did not she herself revile me there?

E. DROMIO: *Sans fable,*[2] she herself reviled you there.

E. ANTIPHOLUS: Did not her kitchen maid rail, taunt, and
75   scorn me?

E. DROMIO: Certes,[3] she did; the kitchen vestal scorned you.

E. ANTIPHOLUS: And did not I in rage depart from thence?

E. DROMIO: In verity, you did; my bones bears witness,
That since have felt the vigor of his rage.

80   ADRIANA: Is't good to soothe him in these contraries?

PINCH: It is no shame; the fellow finds his vein,
And yielding to him humors well his frenzy.

E. ANTIPHOLUS: Thou hast suborned the goldsmith to arrest me.

ADRIANA: Alas, I sent you money to redeem you,
85   By Dromio here, who came in haste for it.

E. DROMIO: Money by me? Heart and goodwill you might,
But, surely, master, not a rag of money.

E. ANTIPHOLUS: Went'st not thou to her for a purse of ducats?

ADRIANA: He came to me, and I delivered it.

90   LUCIANA: And I am witness with her that she did.

E. DROMIO: God and the rope-maker bear me witness
That I was sent for nothing but a rope.

PINCH: Mistress, both man and master is possessed;
I know it by their pale and deadly looks.
95   They must be bound, and laid in some dark room.

E. ANTIPHOLUS: Say, wherefore didst thou lock me forth[4]
today,
And why dost thou deny the bag of gold?

ADRIANA: I did not, gentle husband, lock thee forth.

E. DROMIO: And, gentle master, I received no gold;
100   But I confess, sir, that we were locked out.

ADRIANA: Dissembling villain, thou speak'st false in both.

E. ANTIPHOLUS: Dissembling harlot, thou art false in all,

---

[1]by God   [2]without lying   [3]certainly   [4]out

And art confederate with a damnèd pack
To make a loathsome abject scorn of me;
But with these nails I'll pluck out these false eyes   *105*
That would behold in me this shameful sport.

Enter three or four, and offer to bind him.
He strives.

ADRIANA: O, bind him, bind him, let him not come near me!

PINCH: More company! The fiend is strong within him.

LUCIANA: Ay me, poor man, how pale and wan he looks.

E. ANTIPHOLUS: What, will you murder me? Thou jailer,
thou,   *110*
I am thy prisoner; wilt thou suffer them
To make a rescue?

OFFICER: Masters, let him go.
He is my prisoner, and you shall not have him.

PINCH: Go, bind this man, for he is frantic too.

ADRIANA: What wilt thou do, thou peevish officer?   *115*
Hast thou delight to see a wretched man
Do outrage and displeasure to himself?

OFFICER: He is my prisoner; if I let him go,
The debt he owes will be required of me.

ADRIANA: I will discharge[1] thee ere I go from thee.   *120*
Bear me forthwith unto his creditor,
And, knowing how the debt grows, I will pay it.
Good master doctor, see him safe conveyed
Home to my house. O most unhappy[2] day!

E. ANTIPHOLUS: O most unhappy strumpet!   *125*

E. DROMIO: Master, I am here ent'red in bond for you.

E. ANTIPHOLUS: Out on thee, villain! Wherefore dost thou
mad me?

E. DROMIO: Will you be bound for nothing? Be mad, good
master;
Cry, "The devil!"

LUCIANA: God help, poor souls, how idly do they talk!   *130*

ADRIANA: Go bear him hence. Sister, go you with me.

Exeunt [Pinch and others with Antipholus of
Ephesus and Dromio of Ephesus]. Manet[3] Officer,
Adriana, Luciana, Courtesan.

[1]pay   [2]unfortunate   [3]remains on stage

Say now, whose suit is he arrested at?

OFFICER: One Angelo, a goldsmith, do you know him?

ADRIANA: I know the man. What is the sum he owes?

OFFICER: Two hundred ducats.

135 ADRIANA: Say, how grows it due?

OFFICER: Due for a chain your husband had of him.

ADRIANA: He did bespeak a chain for me, but had it not.

COURTESAN: Whenas your husband, all in rage, today
Came to my house, and took away my ring—
140 The ring I saw upon his finger now—
Straight after did I meet him with a chain.

ADRIANA: It may be so, but I did never see it.
Come, jailer, bring me where the goldsmith is;
I long to know the truth hereof at large.

*Enter Antipholus of Syracuse, with his rapier
drawn, and Dromio of Syracuse.*

145 LUCIANA: God for thy mercy, they are loose again.

ADRIANA: And come with naked swords. Let's call more help
To have them bound again.

OFFICER: Away, they'll kill us!

*Run all out. Exeunt omnes as fast as may be,
frighted.*

S. ANTIPHOLUS: I see these witches are afraid of swords.

S. DROMIO: She that would be your wife now ran from you.

S. ANTIPHOLUS: Come to the Centaur; fetch our stuff from
150 thence.
I long that we were safe and sound aboard.

S. DROMIO: Faith, stay here this night; they will surely
do us no harm. You saw they speak us fair, give us
gold. Methinks they are such a gentle nation that,
155 but for the mountain of mad flesh that claims marriage
of me, I could find in my heart to stay here still, and
turn witch.

S. ANTIPHOLUS: I will not stay tonight for all the town;
Therefore away, to get our stuff aboard.   *Exeunt.*

ACT V

Scene I. *A street before a Priory.*

Enter [Another] Merchant and [Angelo] the Goldsmith.

ANGELO: I am sorry, sir, that I have hind'red you;
But I protest he had the chain of me.
Though most dishonestly he doth deny it.

MERCHANT: How is the man esteemed here in the city?

ANGELO: Of very reverend reputation, sir,   5
Of credit infinite, highly beloved,
Second to none that lives here in the city.
His word might bear[1] my wealth at any time.

MERCHANT: Speak softly; yonder, as I think, he walks.

Enter Antipholus and Dromio of Syracuse again.

ANGELO: 'Tis so; and that self chain about his neck,   10
Which he forswore most monstrously to have.
Good sir, draw near to me; I'll speak to him.
Signor Antipholus, I wonder much
That you would put me to this shame and trouble,
And not without some scandal to yourself,   15
With circumstance and oaths so to deny
This chain which now you wear so openly.
Beside the charge[2] the shame, imprisonment,
You have done wrong to this my honest friend,
Who, but for staying on our controversy,   20
Had hoisted sail and put to sea today.
This chain you had of me, can you deny it?

S. ANTIPHOLUS: I think I had; I never did deny it.

MERCHANT: Yes, that you did, sir, and forswore it too.

S. ANTIPHOLUS: Who heard me to deny it or forswear it?   25

¹command ²expense

219

MERCHANT: These ears of mine, thou know'st, did hear thee.
Fie on thee, wretch! 'Tis pity that thou liv'st
To walk where any honest men resort.

S. ANTIPHOLUS: Thou art a villain to impeach[1] me thus.
30   I'll prove mine honor and mine honesty
Against thee presently, if thou dar'st stand.[2]

MERCHANT: I dare, and do defy thee for a villain!

*They draw. Enter Adriana, Luciana, Courtesan,
and others.*

ADRIANA: Hold, hurt him not, for God's sake! He is mad.
Some get within him,[3] take his sword away.
35   Bind Dromio too, and bear them to my house.

S. DROMIO: Run, master, run; for God's sake, take a house![4]
This is some priory. In, or we are spoiled.

Exeunt to the Priory.

Enter Lady Abbess.

ABBESS: Be quiet, people. Wherefore throng you hither?

ADRIANA: To fetch my poor distracted husband hence.
40   Let us come in, that we may bind him fast,
And bear him home for his recovery.

ANGELO: I knew he was not in his perfect wits.

MERCHANT: I am sorry now that I did draw on him.

ABBESS: How long hath this possession held the man?

45 ADRIANA: This week he hath been heavy, sour, sad,
And much different from the man he was;
But till this afternoon his passion
Ne'er brake into extremity of rage.

ABBESS: Hath he not lost much wealth by wrack of sea?
50   Buried some dear friend? Hath not else his eye
Strayed[5] his affection in unlawful love—
A sin prevailing much in youthful men,
Who give their eyes the liberty of gazing?
Which of these sorrows is he subject to?

55 ADRIANA: To none of these, except it be the last,
Namely, some love that drew him oft from home.

---

[1]accuse   [2]fight me   [3]inside his guard   [4]take shelter in a house   [5]led astray

ABBESS: You should for that have reprehended him.

ADRIANA: Why, so I did.

ABBESS: Ay, but not rough enough.

ADRIANA: As roughly as my modesty would let me.

ABBESS: Haply, in private.

ADRIANA: And in assemblies too.   60

ABBESS Ay, but not enough.

ADRIANA: It was the copy[1] of our conference.
  In bed he slept not for[2] my urging it;
  At board he fed not for my urging it;
  Alone, it was the subject of my theme: 65
  In company I often glancèd[3] it;
  Still did I tell him it was vile and bad.

ABBESS: And thereof came it that the man was mad.
  The venom clamors of a jealous woman
  Poisons more deadly than a mad dog's tooth.   70
  It seems his sleeps were hind'red by thy railing,
  And thereof comes it that his head is light.
  Thou say'st his meat was sauced with thy upbraidings;
  Unquiet meals make ill digestions;
  Thereof the raging fire of fever bred—   75
  And what's a fever but a fit of madness?
  Thou sayest his sports were hind'red by thy brawls;
  Sweet recreation barred, what doth ensue
  But moody and dull melancholy,
  Kinsman to grim and comfortless despair,   80
  And at her heels a huge infectious troop
  Of pale distemperatures and foes to life?
  In food, in sport, and life-preserving rest
  To be disturbed, would mad or man or beast.
  The consequence is, then, thy jealous fits   85
  Hath scared thy husband from the use of wits.

LUCIANA: She never reprehended him but mildly,
  When he demeaned himself rough, rude, and wildly.
  Why bear you these rebukes and answer not?

ADRIANA: She did betray me to my own reproof.   90
  Good people, enter and lay hold on him.

[1]theme   [2]because of   [3]touched on it lightly

ABBESS: No, not a creature enters in my house.

ADRIANA: Then, let your servants bring my husband forth.

ABBESS: Neither. He took this place for sanctuary,[1]
95 And it shall privilege him from your hands
Till I have brought him to his wits again,
Or lose my labor in assaying it.

ADRIANA: I will attend my husband, be his nurse,
Diet his sickness, for it is my office,
100 And will have no attorney but myself;
And therefore let me have him home with me.

ABBESS: Be patient, for I will not let him stir
Till I have used the approvèd means I have,
With wholesome syrups, drugs, and holy prayers,
105 To make of him a formal[2] man again.
It is a branch and parcel of mine oath,
A charitable duty of my order;
Therefore depart, and.leave him here with me.

ADRIANA: I will not hence, and leave my husband here;
110 And ill it doth beseem your holiness
To separate the husband and the wife.

ABBESS: Be quiet and depart, thou shalt not have him.
                                        [Exit.]

LUCIANA: Complain unto the Duke of this indignity.

ADRIANA: Come, go. I will fall prostrate at his feet,
115 And never rise until my tears and prayers
Have won his Grace to come in person hither,
And take perforce my husband from the Abbess.

MERCHANT: By this, I think, the dial points at five:
Anon, I'm sure, the Duke himself in person
120 Comes this way to the melancholy vale,
The place of death and sorry execution,
Behind the ditches of the abbey here.

ANGELO: Upon what cause?

MERCHANT: To see a reverend Syracusian merchant,
125 Who put unluckily into this bay
Against the laws and statutes of this town,
Beheaded publicly for his offense.

[1]protected asylum   [2]normal

ANGELO: See, where they come. We will behold his death.

LUCIANA: Kneel to the Duke before he pass the abbey.

*Enter the Duke of Ephesus and [Egeon] the Merchant
    of Syracuse, barehead, with the Heads-
        man and other Officers.*

DUKE: Yet once again proclaim it publicly,   *130*
   If any friend will pay the sum for him,
   He shall not die; so much we tender[1] him.

ADRIANA: Justice, most sacred Duke, against the Abbess!

DUKE: She is a virtuous and a reverend lady.
   It cannot be that she hath done thee wrong.   *135*

ADRIANA: May it please your Grace, Antipholus, my husband,
   Who I made lord of me and all I had
   At your important[2] letters, this ill day
   A most outrageous fit of madness took him:
   That desp'rately he hurried through the street,   *140*
   With him his bondman all as mad as he,
   Doing displeasure to the citizens
   By rushing in their houses, bearing thence
   Rings, jewels, anything his rage did like.
   Once did I get him bound, and sent him home,   *145*
   Whilst to take order for the wrongs I went,
   That here and there his fury had committed.
   Anon, I wot[3] not by what strong escape,·
   He broke from those that had the guard of him,
   And with his mad attendant and himself,   *150*
   Each one with ireful passion, with drawn swords,
   Met us again and, madly bent on us,
   Chased us away, till, raising of more aid,
   We came again to bind them. Then they fled
   Into this abbey, whither we pursued them;   *155*
   And here the Abbess shuts the gates on us,
   And will not suffer us to fetch him out,
   Nor send him forth that we may bear him hence.
   Therefore, most gracious Duke, with thy command,
   Let him be brought forth and borne hence for help.   *160*

DUKE: Long since thy husband served me in my wars;
   And I to thee engaged a prince's word,
   When thou didst make him master of thy bed,

[1]have regard for [2]importunate, pressing [3]know

To do him all the grace and good I could.
165 Go, some of you, knock at the abbey gate,
And bid the Lady Abbess come to me.
I will determine this before I stir.

Enter a Messenger.

MESSENGER: O mistress, mistress, shift and save yourself.
My master and his man are both broke loose,
170 Beaten the maids a-row,[1] and bound the doctor,
Whose beard they have singed off with brands of fire,
And ever as it blazed, they threw on him
Great pails of puddled mire to quench the hair.
My master preaches patience to him, and the while
175 His man with scissors nicks him like a fool;
And, sure, unless you send some present help,
Between them they will kill the conjurer.

ADRIANA: Peace, fool, thy master and his man are here,
And that is false thou dost report to us.

180 MESSENGER: Mistress, upon my life, I tell you true;
I have not breathed almost since I did see it.
He cries for you and vows, if he can take you,
To scorch your face and to disfigure you.

Cry within.

Hard, hark! I hear him, mistress. Fly, begone.

DUKE: Come, stand by me; fear nothing. Guard with hal-
185 berds![2]

ADRIANA: Ay me, it is my husband! Witness you,
That he is borne about invisible.
Even now we housed him in the abbey here,
And now he's there, past thought of human reason.

Enter Antipholus and Dromio of Ephesus.

E. ANTIPHOLUS: Justice, most gracious Duke! O, grant me
190 justice,
Even for the service that long since I did thee,
When I bestrid thee in the wars, and took
Deep scars to save thy life; even for the blood
That then I lost for thee, now grant me justice.

---

[1]one after the other [2]battle-ax on a pole

EGEON: Unless the fear of death doth make me dote,   *195*
  I see my son Antipholus and Dromio.

E. ANTIPHOLUS: Justice, sweet Prince, against that woman
    there!
  She whom thou gav'st to me to be my wife;
  That hath abusèd and dishonored me,
  Even in the strength and height of injury: *200*
  Beyond imagination is the wrong
  That she this day hath shameless thrown on me.

DUKE: Discover how, and thou shalt find me just.

E. ANTIPHOLUS: This day, great Duke, she shut the doors
    upon me,
  While she with harlots[1] feasted in my house.   *205*

DUKE: A grievous fault. Say, woman, didst thou so?

ADRIANA: No, my good lord. Myself, he, and my sister
  Today did dine together; so befall my soul
  As this is false he burdens me withal.

LUCIANA: Ne'er may I look on day, nor sleep on[2] night,   *210*
  But she tells to your Highness simple truth.

ANGELO: O perjured woman! They are both forsworn.
  In this the madman justly chargeth them.

E. ANTIPHOLUS: My liege, I am advisèd what I say,
  Neither disturbed with the effect of wine,   *215*
  Nor heady-rash, provoked with raging ire,
  Albeit my wrongs might make one wiser mad.
  This woman locked me out this day from dinner.
  That goldsmith there, were he not packed[3] with her,
  Could witness it; for he was with me then,   *220*
  Who parted with me to go fetch a chain,
  Promising to bring it to the Porpentine,
  Where Balthasar and I did dine together.
  Our dinner done, and he not coming thither,
  I went to seek him. In the street I met him,   *225*
  And in his company that gentleman.
  There did this perjured goldsmith swear me down
  That I this day of him received the chain,
  Which, God he knows, I saw not; for the which,
  He did arrest me with an officer.   *230*

[1]rascals   [2]at   [3]in a conspiracy with

I did obey, and sent my peasant[1] home
For certain ducats; he with none returned.
Then fairly I bespoke the officer
To go in person with me to my house.
235 By th' way we met
My wife, her sister, and a rabble more
Of vile confederates. Along with them
They brought one Pinch, a hungry lean-faced villain;
A mere anatomy,[2] a mountebank,
240 A threadbare juggler[3] and a fortune-teller,
A needy-hollow-eyed-sharp-looking wretch;
A living dead man. This pernicious slave,
Forsooth, took on him as a conjurer;
And, gazing in mine eyes, feeling my pulse,

245 And with no face, as 'twere, out-facing me,
Cries out, I was possessed. Then all together
They fell upon me, bound me, bore me thence,
And in a dark and dankish vault at home
There left me and my man, both bound together,
250 Till gnawing with my teeth my bonds in sunder,
I gained my freedom; and immediately
Ran hither to your Grace, whom I beseech
To give me ample satisfaction
For these deep shames and great indignities.

255 ANGELO: My lord, in truth, thus far I witness with him;
That he dined not at home, but was locked out.

DUKE: But had he such a chain of thee, or no?

ANGELO: He had, my lord, and when he ran in here
These people saw the chain about his neck.

260 MERCHANT: Besides, I will be sworn these ears of mine
Heard you confess you had the chain of him,
After you first forswore it on the Mart;
And, thereupon, I drew my sword on you;
And then you fled into this abbey here,
265 From whence, I think, you are come by miracle.

E. ANTIPHOLUS: I never came within these abbey walls,
Nor ever didst thou draw thy sword on me.
I never saw the chain, so help me Heaven!
And this is false you burden me withal.

---

[1]servant [2]absolute skeleton [3]sorcerer

DUKE: Why, what an intricate impeach[1] is this!   *270*
I think you all have drunk of Circe's cup.[2]
If here you housed him, here he would have been;
If he were mad, he would not plead so coldly.[3]
You say he dined at home, the goldsmith here
Denies that saying. Sirrah, what say you?   *275*

E. DROMIO: Sir, he dined with her there at the Porpentine.

COURTESAN: He did, and from my finger snatched that ring.

E. ANTIPHOLUS: 'Tis true, my liege, this ring I had of her.

DUKE: Saw'st thou him enter at the abbey here?

COURTESAN: As sure, my liege, as I do see your Grace.   *280*

DUKE: Why, this is strange. Go call the Abbess hither.
I think you are all mated,[4] or stark mad.

> *Exit One to the Abbey.*

EGEON: Most mighty Duke, vouchsafe me speak a word.
Haply I see a friend will save my life,
And pay the sum that may deliver me.   *285*

DUKE: Speak freely, Syracusian, what thou wilt.

EGEON: Is not your name, sir, called Antipholus?
And is not that your bondman Dromio?

E. DROMIO: Within this hour I was his bondman, sir,
But he, I thank him, gnawed in two my cords.   *290*
Now am I Dromio, and his man, unbound.

EGEON: I am sure you both of you remember me.

E. DROMIO: Ourselves we do remember, sir, by you;
For lately we were bound, as you are now.
You are not Pinch's patient, are you, sir?   *295*

EGEON: Why look you strange on me? You know me well.

E. ANTIPHOLUS: I never saw you in my life till now.

EGEON: O, grief hath changed me since you saw me last,
And careful[5] hours with time's deformèd hand
Have written strange defeatures[6] in my face.   *300*
But tell me yet, dost thou not know my voice?

---

[1]accusation [2]a drink that turns men into beasts [3]reasonably
[4]stupefied [5]full of care [6]disfigurements

E. ANTIPHOLUS: Neither.

EGEON: Dromio, nor thou?

E. DROMIO: No, trust me, sir, nor I.

EGEON: I am sure thou dost!

305 E. DROMIO: Ay, sir, but I am sure I do not; and whatsoever a man denies, you are now bound to believe
him.

EGEON: Not know my voice! O, time's extremity,
Hast thou so cracked and splitted my poor tongue
310 In seven short years, that here my only son
Knows not my feeble key of untuned cares?
Though now this grainèd[1] face of mine be hid
In sap-consuming winter's drizzled snow,
And all the conduits of my blood froze up,
315 Yet hath my night of life some memory;
My wasting lamps[2] some fading glimmer left;
My dull deaf ears a little use to hear.
All these old witnesses—I cannot err—
Tell me thou art my son Antipholus.

320 E. ANTIPHOLUS: I never saw my father in my life.

EGEON: But seven years since, in Syracusa, boy,
Thou know'st we parted; but perhaps, my son,
Thou sham'st to acknowledge me in misery.

325 E. ANTIPHOLUS: The Duke and all that know me in the city
Can witness with me that it is not so.
I ne'er saw Syracusa in my life.

DUKE: I tell thee, Syracusian, twenty years
Have I been patron to Antipholus,
330 During which time he ne'er saw Syracusa
I see thy age and dangers make thee dote.

*Enter the Abbess with Antipholus of Syracuse
and Dromio of Syracuse.*

ABBESS: Most mighty Duke, behold a man much
wronged.   *All gather to see them.*

ADRIANA: I see two husbands, or mine eyes deceive me.

DUKE: One of these men is genius[3] to the other;

---

[1]wrinkled [2]dimming eyes [3]attendant spirit

And so of these, which is the natural man,
And which the spirit? Who deciphers them?   *335*

S. DROMIO: I, sir, am Dromio; command him away.

E. DROMIO: I, sir, am Dromio; pray let me stay.

S. ANTIPHOLUS: Egeon art thou not, or else his ghost?

S. DROMIO: O, my old master! Who hath bound him here?

ABBESS: Whoever bound him, I will loose his bonds,   *340.*
And gain a husband by his liberty.
Speak, old Egeon, if thou beest the man
That hadst a wife once called Emilia,
That bore thee at a burden two fair sons!
O, if thou beest the same Egeon, speak;   *345*
And speak unto the same Emilia.

DUKE: *[Aside]* Why, here begins his morning story right:
These two Antipholus', these two so like,
And these two Dromios, one in semblance,
Besides her urging of her wrack at sea;   *350*
These are the parents to these children,
Which accidentally are met together.

EGEON: If I dream not, thou art Emilia.
If thou art she, tell me where is that son
That floated with thee on the fatal raft?   *355*

ABBESS: By men of Epidamnum, he and I
And the twin Dromio, all were taken up;
But by and by rude fishermen of Corinth
By force took Dromio and my son from them,
And me they left with those of Epidamnum.   *360*
What then became of them, I cannot tell;
I to[1] this fortune that you see me in.

DUKE: Antipholus, thou cam'st from Corinth first.

S. ANTIPHOLUS: No, sir, not I; I came from Syracuse.

DUKE: Stay, stand apart; I know not which is which.   *365*

E. ANTIPHOLUS: I came from Corinth, my most gracious lord.

E. DROMIO: And I with him.

---

[1] I arrived at

E. ANTIPHOLUS: Brought to this town by that most famous
    warrior,
Duke Menaphon, your most renownèd uncle.

370 ADRIANA: Which of you two did dine with me today?

S. ANTIPHOLUS: I, gentle mistress.

ADRIANA: And are not you my husband?

E. ANTIPHOLUS: No, I say nay to that.

S. ANTIPHOLUS: And so do I, yet did she call me so;
And this fair gentlewoman, her sister here,
375 Did call me brother. What I told you then
I hope I shall have leisure to make good,
If this be not a dream I see and hear.

ANGELO: That is the chain, sir, which you had of me.

S. ANTIPHOLUS: I think it be, sir; I deny it not.

380 E. ANTIPHOLUS: And you, sir, for this chain arrested me.

ANGELO: I think I did, sir. I deny it not.

ADRIANA: I sent you money, sir, to be your bail,
By Dromio; but I think he brought it not.

E. DROMIO: No, none by me.

385 S. ANTIPHOLUS: This purse of ducats I received from you,
And Dromio, my man, did bring them me.
I see we still did meet each other's man,
And I was ta'en for him, and he for me,
And thereupon these errors are arose.

390 E. ANTIPHOLUS: These ducats pawn I for my father here.

DUKE: It shall not need; thy father hath his life.

COURTESAN: Sir, I must have that diamond from you.

E. ANTIPHOLUS: There, take it, and much thanks for my good
    cheer.

ABBESS: Renownèd Duke, vouchsafe to take the pains
395 To go with us into the abbey here,
And hear at large discoursèd all our fortunes;
And all that are assembled in this place,
That by this sympathizèd[1] one day's error

---

[1]shared

Have suffered wrong, go, keep us company,
And we shall make full satisfaction.   *400*
Thirty-three years have I but gone in travail[1]
Of you, my sons, and till this present hour
My heavy burden ne'er delivered.
The Duke, my husband, and my children both,
And you the calendars of their nativity,   *405*
Go to a gossips'[2] feast, and joy with me
After so long grief such festivity.

DUKE: With all my heart I'll gossip[3] at this feast.
                    Exeunt [all except] the two Dromios
                              and two Brothers.

S. DROMIO: Master, shall I fetch your stuff from shipboard?

E. ANTIPHOLUS: Dromio, what stuff of mine hast thou embarked? *410*

S. DROMIO: Your goods that lay at host,[4] sir, in the Centaur.

S. ANTIPHOLUS: He speaks to me. I am your master, Dromio.
Come, go with us; we'll look to that anon.
Embrace thy brother there; rejoice with him.
                    Exit [with Antipholus of Ephesus].

S. DROMIO: There is a fat friend at your master's house,   *415*
That kitchened me[5] for you today at dinner;
She now shall be my sister, not my wife.

E. DROMIO: Methinks you are my glass, and not my brother;
I see by you I am a sweet-faced youth.
Will you walk in to see their gossiping?   *420*

S. DROMIO: Not I, sir, you are my elder.

E. DROMIO: That's a question; how shall we try it?

S. DROMIO: We'll draw cuts for the senior; till then, lead thou
first.

E. DROMIO: Nay, then, thus: *425*
We came into the world like brother and brother:
And now let's go hand in hand, not one before another.
                                        Exeunt.

FINIS

[1]childbirth [2]godparents' [3]rejoice [4]with the host [5]entertained me in the kitchen

Molière

THE MISANTHROPE

LIKE SHAKESPEARE, Molière was completely a man of the theater—not only an actor but also a playwright and a director of his theatrical company. He was born Jean-Baptiste Poquelin in Paris in 1622, but he assumed the name Molière for the stage. He managed to avoid his father's prosperous career as furniture dealer and upholsterer to the French court and took a law degree in 1641. The rest of his life was occupied with the theater, and he died, characteristically, in 1673, while playing the leading role in his own comedy, *The Imaginary Invalid*.

Without making any claims for his plays as autobiography, we can still discern Molière's preoccupations in his work. In *The Misanthrope*, Molière wrote the part of Alceste for himself, and the lovable-cantankerous hero is a figure close to the playwright's heart. Everyone wants to be Alceste's friend—that is his most pressing problem—and he runs into difficulties keeping people off. In 1662, Molière married Armande Béjart, an actress of twenty, who was the younger sister of his long-time theatrical collaborator, Madeleine Béjart. With Armande playing Célimène to Molière's Alceste, a performance of *The Misanthrope* had a certain gritty and ironic resemblance to real life.

We should not exaggerate the play's realism—the formality of the couplets are enough to put us off any notion of actual speech. Wit and eloquence predominate, and the play is arranged in a series of confrontations and debates. Both Alceste and Célimène are very theatrical persons: stubborn, extreme, and headstrong even to the point of caricature. So is the prude Arsinoé and all the foplings who flutter around Célimène: Acaste; Clitandre; and Oronte, who also, with his sonnet, has a ludicrously separate relation with Alceste. All of these character types lend themselves wonderfully well to satire. The only fully believable characters who might qualify as realistic are the moderate, controlled, and very well behaved *raisonneurs*: Philinte and Éliante, who end the play plighted to each other. We are glad that Éliante doesn't accept Alceste's second-best offer of marriage. He is better off ending the play in a sulk and threatening to abandon mankind. By the logic of comedy we wishfully believe that Alceste will eventually be cured of his intense misanthropy, which is so hostile to comic values. He needs his fellow human beings if only to rail at. Molière is following classical precedents in the stories of Timon of Athens (about whom Shakespeare wrote a play) and Diogenes in his tub.

The question most hotly debated about this play is whether Alceste is a comic or a tragic figure. The play does not end happily with marriage and festivity, as comedies are supposed to do. It is a bittersweet ending, yet if Alceste flees mankind into the wilderness, we nevertheless applaud Célimène's refusal to accompany him as his wife. She is too young to waste her life in sterile misanthropy. Alceste is petulant, melancholy, and depressed (the "atrabilious lover," as Molière's original subtitle called him), full of righteous indignation, sermonistic, an angry moralizer and absolutist but hardly tragic. In theatrical terms he is so irritating on stage that he forfeits the tragic stature to which he so strenuously lays claim. If Philinte is a Horatio, Alceste is certainly no Hamlet.

One of Célimène's functions in the play is to undercut Alceste's role of lover. He doth protest too much, in the sense that he is constantly asserting the depth and magnitude of his passion but never demonstrating it. Alceste makes it clear that he loves Célimène against his own better judgment, and his only hope for the future is to reform her so that she is more like him. In this thirst for educating his beloved and shaping her in his own image, Alceste totally ignores Célimène's considerable charms, eloquence, and wit. He would like her to be the proverbial *tabula rasa,* or blank sheet of paper, which he could fill up with his own inscriptions:

> Yes, I could wish that no one found you charming,
> That your predicament was quite alarming,
> That Heaven had given you nothing at your birth,
> Not rank, nor family, nor any worth,
> So that my heart, a gleaming sacrifice,
> Might compensate and might alone suffice;
> 'Twould be my pride and joy, all else above,
> To have you owe everything to my love. (1425–32)

Célimène rightly protests against this kind of servitude, and in this attitude she has, I believe, the entire sympathy of the audience.

Whether Célimène is a worthy choice for Alceste is another much-debated point. Philinte and Éliante obviously don't think her good enough for their hero-worshiped idol, and Arsinoé, as unlikely as it may seem, wants Alceste for herself. Molière goes to great lengths to show Célimène as very young, very frivolous, and very flirtatious, especially in the gossipy scenes with Clitandre and Acaste. She is somewhat unstable and does not know her own mind, but there is no doubt that she admires and loves Alceste despite his self-righteous wrath against her. I think the point of the play is that she understands Alceste with a wonderful acuity and would make an excellent wife on that score alone. She could humanize her husband, as all his many other admirers are afraid to do. All the while that Alceste is playing the superior pedagogue, the lucid, intelligent, and charming Célimène is teaching him how to be a lover. She is actually setting a higher standard for him than he is for her:

> Your jealous frenzies make you mad, I swear,
> And you do not deserve the love I bear.
> What makes you think that I would condescend,
> On your account, to brazen and pretend?
> And why, if my heart leaned another way,
> Shouldn't I quite sincerely have my say? (1391–96)

On stage we take this protest at violated integrity much more seriously than we tend to do in reading.

The dismay of the sincere and high-minded man at the folly and chicanery of the world is not properly tragic at all, especially when his antagonists are such lightweights as Oronte, Acaste, Clitandre, and the nameless courtiers who are winning their crooked lawsuits. Alceste is clearly overreacting to the world as a social entity, and he is particularly severe with his friends and lovers. It is absurd, right at the beginning of the play, for Alceste to speak of Philinte as having a "corrupted heart" (12). There is a good deal of moral affectation in Alceste. His critique of Oronte's banal sonnet is overkill at its worst. It is a performance in which Alceste vastly enjoys himself by playing the "atrabilious critic." Oronte may be a foolish fop, but he is surely right in feeling that he has been had. Think of how Molière must have felt about his own critics, whose reaction to *The Misanthrope* was at best lukewarm. Alceste has an extraordinary dramatic energy. If he is generally misguided and mistaken—too stiff for the world—he is grandly and splendidly off the mark. His comic vitality arises from the ways in which he is different from us and from his audience. His eloquent and biting moral indignation fulfills our fantasy of what it means to be a free spirit.

THE MISANTHROPE
TRANSLATED BY DONALD M. FRAME

CHARACTERS

ALCESTE, *in love with Célimène*
PHILINTE, *friend of Alceste*
ORONTE, *in love with Célimène*
CÉLIMÈNE, *beloved of Alceste*
ÉLIANTE, *cousin of Célimène*
ARSINOÉ, *a friend of Célimène*
ACASTE ⎱ *marquis*
CLITANDRE ⎰
BASQUE, *servant of Célimène*
An OFFICER *of the Tribunal of Marshals of France*
DU BOIS, *servant of Alceste*

The scene is a salon in Célimène's house in Paris.

ACT I

Scene 1. ALCESTE, PHILINTE

PHILINTE: Well then? What's wrong?

ALCESTE: I pray you, let me be.

PHILINTE: Won't you explain this sudden wrath to me?

ALCESTE: Leave me alone, I say; run off and hide.

PHILINTE: Without such anger you should hear my side.

ALCESTE: Not I. I *will* be angry. I *won't* hear.

PHILINTE: The reasons for your fits escape me clear;
And though we're friends, I feel I must insist . . .

ALCESTE: What? I, your friend? Just scratch me off your list.
Till now I have professed to be one, true;
But after what I have just seen in you,   *10*
I tell you flatly now that here we part;
I want no place in a corrupted heart.

PHILINTE: Then in your eyes, Alceste, I'm much to blame?

ALCESTE: You should go off and die for very shame;
There's no excuse for such an act as yours;
It's one that any decent man abhors.
I see you greet a man like a long-lost friend
And smother him in sweetness without end;
With protestations, offers, solemn vows,
You load the frenzy of your scrapes and bows;   *20*
When I ask later whom you cherish so,
Even his name, I find, you barely know.
As soon as he departs, your fervor dies,
And you tell *me* he's nothing in your eyes.
Good Lord! You play a base, unworthy role
By stooping to betray your very soul;
And if (which God forbid) I'd done the same,
I'd go right out and hang myself for shame.

237

PHILINTE: To me the case does not deserve the rope;
30   Pray you, allow me to retain the hope
        That I may exercise some leniency
        And need not hang myself from the nearest tree.

ALCESTE: With what bad grace this jesting comes from you!

PHILINTE: But seriously, what would you have me do?

ALCESTE: A man should be sincere, and nobly shrink
        From saying anything he does not think.

PHILINTE: But when a man embraces you, I find
        You simply have to pay him back in kind,
        Respond to his effusions as you may,
40   And try to meet offers and vows halfway.

ALCESTE: No, I cannot endure this fawning guile
        Employed by nearly all your men of style.
        There's nothing I so loathe as the gyrations
        Of all these great makers of protestations,
        These lavishers of frivolous embraces,
        These utterers of empty commonplaces,
        Who in civilities won't be outdone,
        And treat the good man and the fool as one.
        What joy is there in hearing pretty phrases
50   From one who loud and fulsome sings your praises,
        Vows friendship, love, esteem for evermore,
        Then runs to do the same to any boor?
        No, no; a soul that is well constituted
        Cares nothing for esteem so prostituted;
        Our vanity is satisfied too cheap
        With praise that lumps all men in one vast heap;
        Esteem, if it be real, means preference,
        And when bestowed on all it makes no sense.
        Since these new vices seem to you so fine,
60   Lord! You're not fit to be a friend of mine.
        I spurn the vast indulgence of a heart
        That will not set merit itself apart;
        No, singled out is what I want to be;
        The friend of man is not the man for me.

PHILINTE: But one who travels in society
        Must show some semblance of civility.

ALCESTE: No, I say; an example should be made
        Of hypocrites who ply this shameful trade.

A man should be a man, and let his speech
At every turn reveal his heart to each;   *70*
His own true self should speak; our sentiments
Should never hide beneath vain compliments.

PHILINTE: But utter frankness would, in many a case,
Become ridiculous and out of place.
We sometimes—no offense to your high zeal—
Should rather hide what in our heart we feel.
Would it be either fitting or discreet
To air our views of them to all we meet?
Dealing with someone we dislike or hate,
Must we always be sure to set him straight?   *80*

ALCESTE: Yes.

PHILINTE: What? Old Émilie you'd promptly tell
That she has passed the age to be a belle,
And that her makeup is a sorry jest?

ALCESTE: No doubt.

PHILINTE: Tell Dorilas that he's a pest,
That all his talk has wearied every ear
About his noble blood and brave career?

ALCESTE: Assuredly.

PHILINTE: You're joking.

ALCESTE: I am not,
I'll spare no one on this point, not one jot.
It hurts my eyes to see the things I've seen,
And court and town alike arouse my spleen.   *90*
Dark melancholy seizes me anew
Each time I watch men act the way they do;
Cowardly flattery is all I see,
Injustice, selfishness, fraud, treachery;
I've had my fill; it makes me mad; I plan
To clash head-on with the whole race of man.

PHILINTE: You overdo your philosophic bile;
I see your gloomy fits and have to smile.
We two are like the brothers in *The School
For Husbands*,[1] who, though reared by the same rule,   *100*
Yet . . .

ALCESTE: Heavens! spare us these inane charades.

[1]One of Molière's earlier comedies.

PHILINTE: No, really, you should drop your wild tirades.
　　　Your efforts will not change the world, you know,
　　　And inasmuch as frankness charms you so,
　　　I'll tell you, frankly, that this malady
　　　Is treated everywhere as comedy,
　　　And that your wrath against poor humankind
　　　Makes you ridiculous in many a mind.

ALCESTE: By heaven! so much the better! that's first-rate.
110　It's a good sign; my joy in it is great.
　　　All men are so abhorrent in my eyes
　　　That I'd be sorry if they thought me wise.

PHILINTE: Toward human nature you are very spiteful.

ALCESTE: I am; the hate I feel for it is frightful.

PHILINTE: Shall all poor mortals, then, without exception,
　　　Be lumped together in this mass aversion?
　　　Even today you still find now and then . . .

ALCESTE: No, it is general; I hate all men:
　　　For some are wholly bad in thought and deed;
120　The others, seeing this, pay little heed;
　　　For they are too indulgent and too nice
　　　To share the hate that virtue has for vice.
　　　Indulgence at its worst we clearly see
　　　Toward the base scoundrel who's at law with me:
　　　Right through his mask men see the traitor's face,
　　　And everywhere give him his proper place;
　　　His wheedling eyes, his soft and cozening tone,
　　　Fool only those to whom he is not known.
　　　That this knave rose, where he deserved to fall,
130　By shameful methods, is well known to all,
　　　And that his state, which thanks to these is lush,
　　　Makes merit murmur and makes virtue blush.
　　　Whatever notoriety he's won,
　　　Such honor lacks support from anyone;
　　　Call him a cheat, knave, curséd rogue to boot,
　　　Everyone will agree, no one refute.
　　　Yet everywhere his false smile seems to pay:
　　　Everywhere welcomed, hailed, he worms his way;
　　　And if by pulling strings he stands to gain
140　Some honor, decent men compete in vain.
　　　Good Lord! It fairly turns my blood to ice
　　　To see the way men temporize with vice,

And sometimes I've a strong desire to flee
To some deserted spot, from humans free.

PHILINTE: Let's fret less over morals, if we can,
And have some mercy on the state of man;
Let's look at it without too much austerity,
And try to view its faults without severity.
In this world virtue needs more tact than rigor;
Wisdom may be excessive in its vigor;   *150*
Perfected reason flees extremity,
And says: Be wise, but with sobriety.
The unbending virtue of the olden days
Clashes with modern times and modern ways;
Its stiff demands on mortals go too far;
We have to live with people as they are;
And the greatest folly of the human mind
Is undertaking to correct mankind.
Like you I note a hundred things a day
That might go better, done another way,   *160*
But notwithstanding all that comes in view,
Men do not find me full of wrath like you;
I take men as they are, with self-control;
To suffer what they do I train my soul,
And I think, whether court or town's the scene,
My calm's as philosophic as your spleen.

ALCESTE: But, sir, this calm, that is so quick to reason,
This calm, is it then never out of season?
If by a friend you find yourself betrayed,
If for your property a snare is laid,   *170*
If men besmirch your name with slanderous lies,
You'll see that and your temper will not rise?

PHILINTE: Why yes, I see these faults, which make you hot,
As vices portioned to the human lot;
In short, it's no more shock to my mind's eye
To see a man unjust, self-seeking, sly,
Than to see vultures hungry for their prey,
Monkeys malicious, wolves athirst to slay.

ALCESTE: Then I should be robbed, torn to bits, betrayed,
Without . . . ? Good Lord! I leave the rest unsaid;   *180*
Such reasoning is patently absurd.

PHILINTE: Less talk would help your cause, upon my word:
Outbursts against your foe are out of place;
You should give more attention to your case.

ALCESTE: I'll give it none. That's all there is to say.

PHILINTE: Then who will speak for you and pave the way?

ALCESTE: The justice of my cause will speak for me.

PHILINTE: Is there no judge that you will stoop to see?[1]

ALCESTE: No; don't you think my case is just and clear?

190 PHILINTE: True, but intrigue is what you have to fear,
And . . .

ALCESTE: No, I'll take no steps. I'll not give in;
I'm either right or wrong.

PHILINTE: Don't think you'll win.

ALCESTE: I shall not budge.

PHILINTE: Your enemy is strong,
And by collusion he . . .

ALCESTE: What then? He's wrong.

PHILINTE: You're making a mistake.

ALCESTE: All right; we'll see.

PHILINTE: But . . .

ALCESTE: Let me lose my case; that will please me.

PHILINTE: But after all . . .

ALCESTE: In this chicanery
I'll see if men have the effrontery,
And are sufficiently base, vile, perverse,
200 To wrong me in the sight of the universe.

PHILINTE: Oh, what a man!

ALCESTE: My case—despite the cost,
For the sheer beauty of it—I'd see lost.

PHILINTE: People would really laugh at you, you know,
Alceste, if they could hear you talking so.

ALCESTE: Too bad for those who laugh.

PHILINTE: Even this rigor
Which you require of all with so much vigor,

[1] It was normal practice in Molière's France for a litigant to visit his judge while his case was pending.

This rectitude that you make so much of,
Do you observe it in the one you love?
It still amazes me when I see you,
Who censor humankind the way you do,   *210*
And see in it so much that you abhor,
Find in it anyone you can adore;
And what astonishes me further yet
Is the strange choice on which your heart is set.
The candid Éliante finds you attractive,
Arisinoé the prude would like you active;
Meanwhile your unconcern with them is plain;
Instead you are bewitched by Célimène,
One whose sharp tongue and whose coquettish ways
Are just the things in fashion nowadays.   *220*
How is it that in her you tolerate
Failings which, found in others, rouse your hate?
Are they no longer faults in one so dear?
Are they unseen? Are others too severe?

ALCESTE: No, love for this young widow does not blind
My eyes to all the faults that others find,
And I, despite my ardor for her, am
The first to see them and the first to damn.
But still, for all of that, she has an art;
She finds and fills a soft spot in my heart;   *230*
I see her flaws and blame them all I will,
No matter what I do, I love her still;
Her grace remains too strong. My love, no doubt,
Will yet prevail and drive these vices out.

PHILINTE: If you do that, it will be no small coup.
You think she loves you, then?

ALCESTE: Indeed I do!
I'd not love her unless I thought she did.

PHILINTE: But if her fondness for you is not hid,
Why do your rivals cause you such concern?

ALCESTE: A smitten heart wants to possess in turn,   *240*
And all I've come here for is to reveal
To her all that my passion makes me feel.

PHILINTE: For my part, if mere wishes had a voice,
Her cousin Éliante would be my choice.
Her heart esteems you and is stanch and true;
She'd be a sounder, better match for you.

ALCESTE: You're right, my reason says so every day;
    But over love reason has little sway.

PHILINTE: Your loving hopes I fear that she may flout,
    And . . .

Scene 2. ORONTE, ALCESTE, PHILINTE

250 ORONTE: Éliante, I hear downstairs, is out,
    And likewise Célimène, with things to do,
    But since they told me that I might find you,
    I came to tell you frankly, anyway,
    That I esteem you more than tongue can say,
    And that I long have wished and now intend
    To ask you to accept me as a friend.
    Yes, yes, I would see merit have its due;
    In friendship's bond I would be joined with you.
    An ardent friend, as nobly born as I,
260 Can surely not be easily passed by.
                (To ALCESTE*)*
    For you, if you don't mind, my words are meant.

(At this point ALCESTE *is lost in thought and seems not to
    hear that* ORONTE *is speaking to him.)*

ALCESTE: Me, sir?

ORONTE: You. Are they something to resent?

ALCESTE: No, but your praise of me comes unexpected;
    Such high regard I never had suspected.

ORONTE: My great esteem should come as no surprise,
    And you can claim the like in all men's eyes.

ALCESTE: Sir . . .

ORONTE: Our whole State possesses nothing higher
    Than all your merit, which men so admire.

ALCESTE: Sir . . .

ORONTE: Yes, you are far worthier, say I,
270 Than all I see that others rate so high.

ALCESTE: Sir . . .

ORONTE: If I lie, may heaven strike me dead!

And, to confirm to you what I've just said,
Allow me, sir, a heart-to-heart embrace,
And in your friendship let me find a place.
Shake on it, if you please. Then it is mine,
Your friendship?

ALCESTE: Sir . . .

ORONTE: What? Then do you decline?

ALCESTE: Sir, most excessively you honor me;
   But friendship asks a bit more mystery,
   And surely we profane its name sublime
   By using it on all, and all the time.   280
   Upon enlightened choice this bond depends;
   We need to know each other to be friends,
   And we might prove to be so different
   That both of us might presently repent.

ORONTE: By heaven! That's wisely spoken on that score,
   And I esteem you for it all the more.
   Let us let time prepare friendship's fruition;
   But meanwhile I am at your disposition.
   If you need help at court for anything,
   You know I have some standing with the King.   290
   He listens to me, and in every way
   Treats me more decently than I can say.
   In short, consider me as all your own;
   And, since your brilliant mind is widely known,
   I've come to ask your judgment as a friend
   Upon a sonnet that I lately penned,
   And learn whether I ought to publish it.

ALCESTE: For such a judgment, sir, I'm hardly fit.
   So please excuse me.

ORONTE: Why?

ALCESTE: For this defect:
   I'm always more sincere than men expect.   300

ORONTE: Exactly what I ask; I could complain
   If, when I urged you to speak clear and plain,
   You then disguised your thought in what you said.

ALCESTE: Since you will have it so, sir, go ahead.

ORONTE: "Sonnet . . ." It is a sonnet. "Hope . . ."
   You see, A lady once aroused some hope in me.

"Hope . . ." This is nothing grandiose or sublime,
But just a soft, sweet, tender little rhyme.

(At each interruption he looks at ALCESTE.*)*

ALCESTE: We shall see.

ORONTE: "Hope . . ." The style may not appear
310   To you sufficiently easy and clear,
And you may think the choice of words is bad.

ALCESTE: We shall see, sir.

ORONTE: Moreover, let me add,
A quarter hour was all the time I spent.

ALCESTE: Come, sir; the time is hardly pertinent.

ORONTE: Hope does, 'tis true, some comfort bring,
And lulls awhile our aching pain;
But, Phyllis, 'tis an empty thing
When nothing follows in its train.

PHILINTE: That is a charming bit, and full of verve.

320   ALCESTE *(aside):* You call that charming? What! You have
the nerve?

ORONTE: My flame you once seemed to invite;
'Twas pity that you let it live,
And kept me languishing, poor wight,
When hope was all you had to give.

PHILINTE: Oh, in what gallant terms these things are put!

ALCESTE *(aside):* You wretched flatterer! Gallant, my foot!

ORONTE: Should an eternity to wait
Render my ardor desperate,
Then my decease shall end my pains.

330   Your fond concern you well may spare;
Fair Phyllis, it is still despair
When hope alone is what remains.

PHILINTE: That dying fall casts a seductive spell.

ALCESTE *(aside, to* PHILINTE*):* Poisoner, you and your fall
may go to hell.
I wish you'd taken one right on your nose.

PHILINTE: I've never heard verses as fine as those.

ALCESTE: Good Lord!

ORONTE: You flatter me; perhaps you're trying . . .

PHILINTE: I am not flattering.

ALCESTE *(aside):*   No, only lying.

ORONTE *(to* ALCESTE*):* But you, sir, you recall what we agreed;
Please be sincere. How do these verses read?   340

ALCESTE: Questions of talent, sir, are ticklish matters,
And we all yearn to hear the voice that flatters;
But when a man—no matter who—one day
Read me his verses, I made bold to say
A gentleman must have the will to fight
Our universal human itch to write,
That he must overcome his great temptations
To make a fuss about such recreations,
And that our eagerness for self-display
Can give us many a sorry role to play.   350

ORONTE: I think I gather what you're getting at:
That I am wrong to want . . .

ALCESTE: I don't say that.
But frigid writing palls, and can bring down—
So I told him—a worthy man's renown;
Though one had every other quality,
Our weakest points are what men choose to see.

ORONTE: Then with my sonnet, sir, do you find fault?

ALCESTE: I don't say that; but urging him to halt,
I pointed out to him how, time and again,
This thirst has spoiled extremely worthy men.   360

ORONTE: Am I like them? Don't I know how to rhyme?

ALCESTE: I don't say that. But, I said, take your time:
Have you some urgent need to versify
And see yourself in print? I ask you, why?
The authors of bad books we may forgive
Only when the poor wretches write to live.
Take my advice and overcome temptations,
Hide from the public all these occupations,
Against all urgings raise a stout defense,
And keep your good name as a man of sense;   370

Don't change it in some greedy printer's stall
For that of author ridiculed by all.
—That's what I tried to make this man perceive.

ORONTE: All right. I understand you, I believe.
About my sonnet, though: may I be told . . . ?

ALCESTE: Frankly, your sonnet should be pigeonholed.
The models you have used are poor and trite;
There's nothing natural in what you write.
What is this "lulls awhile our aching pain"?
380   This "nothing follows in its train"?
Or "kept me languishing, poor wight,
When hope was all you had to give"?
And "Phyllis, it is still despair
When hope alone is what remains"?
This mannered style, so dear to people's hearts,
From human nature and from truth departs;
It's purest affectation, verbal play,
And Nature never speaks in such a way.
Standards today are wretched, I maintain;
390   Our father's taste, though crude, was far more sane.
What men now prize gives me far less delight
Than this old song which I will now recite:
    If the king had given me
      Great Paris for my own,
    And had said the price must be
      To leave my love alone,
    I would tell the king Henri:
    Then take back your great Paris,[1]
    I prefer my love, hey ho,
400   I prefer my love.
The rhyme's not rich, the style is old and rough,
But don't you see this is far better stuff
Then all this trumpery that flouts good sense,
And that here passion speaks without pretense?
    If the king had given me
      Great Paris for my own,
    And had said the price must be
      To leave my love alone,
    I would tell the king Henri:
410   Then take back your great Paris,

[1]Pronounce Paree.

I prefer my love, hey ho,
I prefer my love.
    That's what a really loving heart might say.
        (To PHILINTE*)*
    Laugh on. Despite the wits who rule today,
    I rate this higher than the flowery show
    Of artificial gems, which please men so.

ORONTE: And *I* maintain my verse is very good.

ALCESTE: I'm sure that you have reasons why you should;
    But grant my reasons leave to disagree
    And not let yours impose themselves on me.   *420*

ORONTE: Enough for me that others rate it high.

ALCESTE: They have the art of feigning, sir; not I.

ORONTE: No doubt you think you've quite a share of wit?

ALCESTE: To praise your verse, I should need more of it.

ORONTE: I'll get along without your praise, I trust.

ALCESTE: I hope you're right, sir, for I fear you must.

ORONTE: I'd like to see you try, in your own way,
    On this same theme, to show what you could say.

ALCESTE: My verses might be just as bad, I own,
    But I'd be careful not to make them known.   *430*

ORONTE: Your talk is high and mighty, and your ways . . .

ALCESTE: Look elsewhere for a man to sing your praise.

ORONTE: My little man, don't take this tone with me.

ALCESTE: Big man, my tone is just what it should be.

PHILINTE *(stepping between them):* Come, gentlemen,
    enough! I pray you, no!

ORONTE: My fault, I do admit. And now I'll go.
    With all my heart, I am your servant, sir.

ALCESTE: And I, sir, am your humble servitor.

Scene 3. PHILINTE, ALCESTE

PHILINTE: Well, there you are! You see? By being candid,
440   Just note in what a nasty mess you've landed;
Oronte's desire for praise was obvious . . .

ALCESTE: Don't speak to me.

PHILINTE: But . . .

ALCESTE: Finis between us.

PHILINTE: You're too . . .

ALCESTE: Leave me.

PHILINTE: If . . .

ALCESTE: Not another
word.

PHILINTE: But what! . . .

ALCESTE: I'm deaf.

PHILINTE: But . . .

ALCESTE: More?

PHILINTE: This is
absurd.

ALCESTE: Good Lord! I've had enough. Be off with you.

PHILINTE: You don't mean that. Where you go, I go too.

ACT II

Scene 1. ALCESTE, CÉLIMÈNE

ALCESTE: Madame, shall I speak frankly and be brief?
　Your conduct gives me not a little grief;
　It rouses too much bile within my heart,
　And I can see that we shall have to part.　　　　　450
　I have to tell you this for conscience' sake:
　Sooner or later we must surely break.
　A thousand pledges to the contrary
　I might make, but I could not guarantee.

CÉLIMÈNE: Indeed, your wish to bring me home was kind,
　When scolding me was what you had in mind.

ALCESTE: I do not scold; but what is my dismay,
　Madame, that the first comer makes his way
　Into your heart? By suitors you're beset;
　And I cannot see this without regret.　　　　　460

CÉLIMÈNE: You blame me for my suitors, this I see.
　Can I prevent people from liking me?
　And when they try to visit me, no doubt
　I ought to take a stick and drive them out?

ALCESTE: A stick, Madame, is not what I suggest,
　Merely a heart less easily impressed.
　I know that everywhere you cast a spell;
　But those your eyes attract you greet too well;
　Your graciousness to all who yield their arms
　Completes the conquering action of your charms.　　　　　470
　The over-brilliant hopes that you arouse
　Surround you with these suitors and their vows;
　If only your complaisance were less vast,
　This sighing mob would disappear at last.
　But by what spell, Madame, if I may know,
　Does your Clitandre contrive to please you so?
　In worth and virtue is he so supreme
　That you should honor him with your esteem?

251

His little fingernail is very long:
480   Is that why your regard for him is strong?
Has his blond wig, which has such great effect
Upon society, won your respect?
Do you love him for the ruffles at his knees?
Or do his multitudinous ribbons please?
Is it the charm of his vast German breeches
That, while he plays the slave, your soul bewitches?
Is it his laugh and his falsetto voice
That make of him the suitor of your choice?

CÉLIMÈNE: To take offense at him is most unfair!
490   You know why I must handle him with care,
And that he's pledged his many friends' support
To help me when my lawsuit comes to court.

ALCESTE: Then lose your suit, as bravely as you can,
And do not humor that offensive man.

CÉLIMÈNE: Why, everyone excites your jealousy.

ALCESTE: You welcome everyone so charmingly.

CÉLIMÈNE: But this should reassure your anxious mind:
That all who seek, this same complaisance find;
And you would have more cause for discontent
500   If there were only one recipient.

ALCESTE: But I, Madame, whose jealousy you blame,
In what way is my treatment not the same?

CÉLIMÈNE: Knowing that you are loved sets you apart.

ALCESTE: How can I prove this to my burning heart?

CÉLIMÈNE: To say what I have said exacts a price;
I think such an avowal should suffice.

ALCESTE: But how can I be certain, even then,
You do not say the same to other men?

CÉLIMÈNE: My! That's a charming way to pay your court,
510   And that makes me appear a pretty sort!
Well then, to give you no more cause to sigh,
All I have said I here and now deny.
There's no deceiving to be fearful of
Except your own.

ALCESTE: Lord! And I'm still in love!
If I could just get back my heart, I'd bless

Heaven above for such rare happiness!
I do my best—and this I don't conceal—
To break the cruel attachment that I feel;
But I have toiled in vain, and now I know
That it is for my sins I love you so.   *520*

CÉLIMÈNE: It's true, your love for me is matched by none.

ALCESTE: Yes, on that score I'll challenge anyone.
My love is past belief, Madame; I say
No one has ever loved in such a way.

CÉLIMÈNE: Indeed, your way is novel, and your aim;
The only token of your love is blame;
Your ardor shows itself in angry speech,
And never was a love so quick to preach.

ALCESTE: It rests with you that this should pass away.
Let's call a halt to quarreling, I pray,   *530*
Speak out with open hearts, then, and begin . . .

Scene 2. CÉLIMÈNE, ALCESTE, BASQUE

CÉLIMÈNE: What is it?

BASQUE: It's Acaste.

CÉLIMÈNE: Well, show him in.

ALCESTE: What? Can one never talk to you alone?
Must you then always welcome everyone?
And can you not for just one moment bear
To have a caller told you are not there?

CÉLIMÈNE: You'd have me quarrel with him too, for sure?

ALCESTE: Some of your courtesies I can't endure.

CÉLIMÈNE: That man would bear a grudge for evermore,
If he knew I find the sight of him a bore.   *540*

ALCESTE: And why should this make you put on an act?

CÉLIMÈNE: Heavens! Influence is an important fact.
I don't know why, but people of his sort
Can talk loud and importantly at court.
They push their way into each interview;

They cannot help, but they can damage you;
And even if your other aid is stout,
Don't quarrel with these men who love to shout.

ALCESTE: No matter what the reason or the base,
550   You find cause to receive the human race;
And the precautions that you take, perforce . . .

Scene 3. BASQUE, ALCESTE, CÉLIMÈNE

BASQUE: Madame, here is Clitandre as well.

ALCESTE *(showing that he wants to leave):*
                        Of course.

CÉLIMÈNE: Where are you going?

ALCESTE: Leaving.

CÉLIMÈNE: Stay.

ALCESTE: What for?

CÉLIMÈNE: Stay here.

ALCESTE: I can't.

CÉLIMÈNE: I want you to.

ALCESTE: No more.
These conversations weary me past cure;
This is too much to ask me to endure.

CÉLIMÈNE: You shall remain, you shall.

ALCESTE: It cannot be.

CÉLIMÈNE: All right, then, go; it's quite all right with me.

Scene 4. ÉLIANTE, PHILINTE, ACASTE, CLITANDRE, ALCESTE, CÉLIMÈNE, BASQUE

ÉLIANTE: Here are the two marquis who've come to call.
Were they announced?

560 CÉLIMÈNE: Indeed. *(To* BASQUE*)* Bring chairs for all.
(To ALCESTE*)* You haven't left?

ALCESTE: No, Madame. I demand
   That you declare to all just where you stand.

CÉLIMÈNE: Oh, hush.

ALCESTE: You shall explain yourself today.

CÉLIMÈNE: You're mad.

ALCESTE: I am not. You shall say your say.

CÉLIMÈNE: Ah!

ALCESTE: You'll make up your mind.

CÉLIMÈNE: I think you're joking.

ALCESTE: No, you *shall* choose; this doubt is too provoking.

CLITANDRE: My word! I've just come from the King's levee,
   Where Cléonte played the fool for all to see.
   Has he no friend who could, with kindly tact,
   Teach him the rudiments of how to act?   570

CÉLIMÈNE: Indeed, in social life the man's a dunce;
   His manner startles every eye at once;
   And when you see him, later on, once more,
   You find him more fantastic than before.

ACASTE: Speaking of characters fantastical,
   I've just endured the greatest bore of all:
   Damon, the talker, kept me, by your leave,
   One hour in the hot sun without reprieve.

CÉLIMÈNE: Yes, his strange mania for reasoning
   Makes him talk on, and never say a thing: 580
   His discourse in obscurity abounds,
   And all you listen to is merely sounds.

ÉLIANTE *(To* PHILINTE*):* Not a bad opening. Soon the entire
      nation
   Will be in danger of annihilation.

CLITANDRE: Timante is quite a character, you know.

CÉLIMÈNE: The man of mystery from top to toe,
   Who gives you a distracted glance, aside,
   Does nothing, yet is always occupied.
   Grimaces lend importance to each word;
   His high portentousness makes him absurd;   590
   He interrupts your talk, in confidence,

To whisper a secret of no consequence;
At making trifles great he has no peer;
Even "Good day" he whispers in your ear.

ACASTE: Géralde, Madame?

CÉLIMÈNE: He tells a tedious tale.
All but great nobles are beyond the pale;
He mingles with those of the highest note,
And none but duke or princess will he quote.
He is obsessed with rank; his monologues
600   Are all of horses, carriages, and dogs;
He uses *tu* in speaking to the great,
And seems to think *Monsieur*[1] is out of date.

CLITANDRE: They say Bélise appreciates his merit.

CÉLIMÈNE: How dry she is in talk, and poor in spirit!
I find it torture to receive her call;
You labor to say anything at all,
And the sterility of her expression
At every moment kills the conversation.
In vain, her stupid silence to annul,
610   You try each commonplace, however dull:
Sunny or rainy weather, heat or frost
Are topics that you rapidly exhaust;
Meanwhile her visit, draining all your strength,
Drags on and on at terrifying length;
You ask the time, you yawn and yawn, but no:
She sits there like a log and will not go.

ACASTE: What of Adraste?

CÉLIMÈNE: Oh, what colossal pride!
His love of self has puffed him up inside,
At court he misses due consideration;
620   So railing at it is his occupation;
No post or benefice goes to anyone,
But that he thinks injustice has been done.

CLITANDRE: On young Cléon what will your verdict be?
He entertains the best society.

CÉLIMÈNE: He has a cook who is extremely able;
And what they come to visit is his table.

---

[1] *Tu*, literally "thou," is the "you" of familiarity or condescension. *Monsieur* means both "Mr." and "Sir."

ÉLIANTE: He serves you nothing but the finest food.

CÉLIMÈNE: He serves himself as well, and that's less good:
   His stupid person is a sorry dish
   That spoils the taste of fowl and roast and fish.   *630*

PHILINTE: Some think Damis, his uncle, rather fine.
   What do you say?

CÉLIMÈNE: He is a friend of mine.

PHILINTE: He seems a decent sort, I must admit.

CÉLIMÈNE: Yes, but he tries too hard to be a wit;
   He talks so stiltedly you always know
   That he's premeditating some *bon mot*.
   Since he has set his mind on being clever,
   He takes delight in nothing whatsoever;
   In all that's written he finds only flaws,
   And thinks that cleverness forbids applause,   *640*
   That criticism is a sign of learning,
   Enjoyment only for the undiscerning,
   And that to frown on any book that's new
   Places him high among the happy few;
   He looks on common talk with condescension
   As much too trivial for his attention;
   Folding his arms, from high above the rabble,
   He glances down with pity on our babble.

ACASTE: Damme, Madame, that is exactly true.

CLITANDRE: There's no one can portray a man like you.   *650*

ALCESTE: That's right, my courtly friends, be strong, spare
      none,
   Strike hard, and have your sport with everyone;
   Yet when one of these victims comes in sight,
   Your haste in meeting him is most polite,
   And with a kiss and offer of your hand,
   You demonstrate that you're at his command.

CLITANDRE: But why blame us? If what is said offends you,
   'Tis to Madame that your remonstrance sends you.

ALCESTE: By God, no! 'Tis to you; your fawning laughter
   Affords her wit just the applause she's after.   *660*
   Her bent for character assassination
   Feeds constantly upon your adulation;
   For satire she would have less appetite

Were it not always greeted with delight.
Thus flatterers deserve our main assaults
For leading humans into many faults.

PHILINTE: But why so eager to defend the name
Of those in whom you damn the things we blame?

CÉLIMÈNE: Don't you see, he must be opposed to you?
670 Would you have him accept the common view,
And not display, in every company,
His heaven-sent gift for being contrary?
The ideas of others he will not admit;
Always he must maintain the opposite;
He'd fear he was an ordinary human
If he agreed with any man—or woman.
For him contrariness offers such charms,
Against himself he often turns his arms;
And should another man his views defend,
680 He will combat them to the bitter end.

ALCESTE: The laughers are with you, Madame; you've won.
Go on and satirize me; have your fun.

PHILINTE: But it is also true you have a way
Of balking at whatever people say;
And that your spite, which you yourself avow,
Neither applause nor censure will allow.

ALCESTE: My God! That's because men are never right;
It always is the season for our spite;
I see them on all matters, in all ways,
690 Quick with rash censure and untimely praise.

CÉLIMÈNE: But . . .

ALCESTE: No, Madame, you *shall* learn, though it
      kill me,
With what distaste some of your pleasures fill me,
And that I find those persons much to blame
Who foster faults that damage your good name.

CLITANDRE: As for me, I don't know; but I aver
That up to now I've found no fault in her.

ACASTE: Her charms and grace are evident to me;
But any faults I fear I cannot see.

ALCESTE: I see them all; she knows the way I feel;
700 My disapproval I do not conceal.

Loving and flattering are worlds apart;
The least forgiving is the truest heart;
And I would send these soft suitors away,
Seeing they dote on everything I say,
And that their praise, complaisant to excess,
Encourages me in my foolishness.

CÉLIMÈNE: In short, if we're to leave it up to you,
All tenderness in love we must eschew;
And love can only find its true perfection
In railing at the objects of our affection.   *710*

ÉLIANTE: Love tends to find such laws somewhat austere,
And lovers always brag about their dear;
Their passion never sees a thing to blame,
And everything is lovely in their flame:
They find perfection in her every flaw,
And speak of her with euphemistic awe.
The pallid one's the whitest jasmine yet;
The frightful dark one is a sweet brunette;
The spindly girl is willowy and free;
The fat one bears herself with majesty;   *720*
The dowdy one, who's ill-endowed as well,
Becomes a careless and neglectful belle;
The giantess is a divinity;
The dwarf, a heavenly epitome;
With princesses the proud one can compete;
The tricky one has wit; the dull one's sweet;
The tireless talker's charmingly vivacious,
The mute girl modest, womanly, and gracious.
Thus every man who loves beyond compare
Loves even the defects of his lady fair.   *730*

ALCESTE: And *I*, for my part, claim . . .

CÉLIMÈNE: Let's end this talk
And step outside for just a little walk.
What? You are leaving, sirs?

CLITANDRE and ACASTE: No, Madame, no.

ALCESTE: You're certainly afraid that they may go.
Leave when you like, sirs; but I'm warning you,
I shall not leave this place until you do.

ACASTE: Unless Madame should be a little tired,
There's nowhere that my presence is required.

CLITANDRE: I must go later to the King's couchee,
740   But until then I am quite free today.

CÉLIMÈNE: You're joking, surely.

ALCESTE: No. I need to know
    Whether you wish for them, or me, to go.

Scene 5. BASQUE, ALCESTE, CÉLIMÈNE, ÉLIANTE,
               ACASTE, PHILINTE, CLITANDRE

BASQUE: Sir, there's a man to see you in the hall
    Who says his business will not wait at all.

ALCESTE: Tell him I have no business of such note.

BASQUE: He has a uniform, a great tailcoat
    With pleats and lots of gold.

CÉLIMÈNE: Please go and see,
    Or let him in.

ALCESTE (to the OFFICER):
                         What do you want with me?
    Come in, sir.

Scene 6. OFFICER, ALCESTE, CÉLIMÈNE, ÉLIANTE, ACASTE,
               PHILINTE, CLITANDRE

OFFICER: Sir, with you I crave a word.

750 ALCESTE: You may speak up, sir; let your news be heard.

OFFICER: The Marshals,[1] sir, have ordered me to say
    You must appear before them right away.

ALCESTE: Who, I, sir?

OFFICER: You yourself.

ALCESTE: What can they want?

PHILINTE: It's that ridiculous business with Oronte.

---

[1]The Tribunal of Marshals regulated quarrels among gentlemen. By this time dueling
was on the wane.

CÉLIMÈNE: How's that?

PHILINTE: They are about to take the sword
  Over some verse with which Alceste was bored.
  The Marshals want of course to quash the matter.

ALCESTE: They'll never force me to back down and flatter.

PHILINTE: You'll have to follow orders; come, let's go.

ALCESTE: What can they reconcile, I'd like to know?   760
  Shall I now, after everything that's passed,
  Be sentenced to admire his verse at last?
  I don't take back a single thing I said,
  I think they're bad.

PHILINTE: But with a calmer head . . .

ALCESTE: I won't back down; his verse is a disgrace.

PHILINTE: Intransigence like yours is out of place.
  Come on.

ALCESTE: I'll go; but I shall not unsay
  One thing I've said.

PHILINTE: Come, let's be on our way.

ALCESTE: Unless I have the King's express command
  To like these verses, I have made my stand.   770
  That they are bad, on this I'll never falter,
  And that their author well deserves the halter.
          (*To* CLITANDRE *and* ACASTE, *who laugh*)
  By God! Messieurs, I never really knew
  I was so funny.

CÉLIMÈNE: Come, be off with you.
  Go where you must.

ALCESTE: I go, Madame, but straight
  I shall return to settle our debate.

ACT III

Scene 1. CLITANDRE, ACASTE

CLITANDRE: You glow with satisfaction, dear Marquis:
You're free from worriment and full of glee.
But do you think you're seeing things aright
780   In taking such occasion for delight?

ACASTE: My word! When I regard myself, I find
No reason for despondency of mind,
I'm rich, I'm young, I'm of a family
With some pretention to nobility;
And through the rank that goes with my condition,
At court I can aspire to high position.
For courage, something we must all admire,
'Tis known I have been tested under fire,
And an affair of honor recently
790   Displayed my vigor and my bravery.
My wit is adequate, my taste discerning,
To judge and treat all subjects without learning;
When a new play is shown (which I adore),
To sit upon the stage, display my lore,
Determine its success, and stop the show
When any passage merits my "Bravo!"
I make a good appearance, rather chic;
I have fine teeth, an elegant physique.
And as for dress, all vanity aside,
800   My eminence can scarcely be denied.
I could not ask for more regard; I seem
To have the ladies' love, the King's esteem.
With all this, dear Marquis, I do believe
That no man anywhere has cause to grieve.

CLITANDRE: When elsewhere easy conquests meet your eyes,
Why linger here to utter useless sighs?

ACASTE: I? 'Pon my word, I'm not the sort to bear
A cool reception from a lady fair.

262

It is for vulgar men, uncouth in dress,
To burn for belles who will not acquiesce, 810
Pine at their feet, endure their cold disdain,
Seek some support from sighs and tears—in vain,
And strive to win by assiduity
What is denied their meager quality.
But men of my class are not made to yearn
For anyone, Marquis, without return.
However fair the girls, however nice,
I think, thank God, we too are worth our price;
If they would claim the heart of one like me,
They should in reason pay the proper fee; 820
And it would be no more than fair that they
Should meet our every overture halfway.

CLITANDRE: Then you are pleased, Marquis, with prospects
here?

ACASTE: They offer me, Marquis, good grounds for cheer.

CLITANDRE: Believe me, leave these fantasies behind;
Dear chap, your self-delusion makes you blind.

ACASTE: Of course, delusion makes me blind; ah, yes.

CLITANDRE: But what assures you of such happiness?

ACASTE: Delusion.

CLITANDRE:　　　　Have you grounds for confidence?

ACASTE: I'm blind.

CLITANDRE:　　　　What constitutes your evidence? 830

ACASTE: I tell you, I'm all wrong.

CLITANDRE:　　　　　　　　Well, have you, then,
Received some secret vow from Célimène?

ACASTE: No, I am badly treated.

CLITANDRE:　　　　　　　Tell me, please.

ACASTE: Nothing but snubs.

CLITANDRE:　　　　　A truce on pleasantries;
Tell me what makes you set your hopes so high.

ACASTE: Yours is the luck, and I can only sigh.
So great is her aversion for my ways
That I shall hang myself one of these days.

CLITANDRE: Come now, Marquis, to mend our rivalry,
840   Let us agree on one thing, you and me:
   If either one can show beyond a doubt
   That in her heart he has been singled out,
   The other shall admit defeat and yield,
   Leaving the victor master of the field.

ACASTE: My word! Your notion matches my intent;
   With all my heart and soul I do consent.
   But hush!

Scene 2. CÉLIMÈNE, ACASTE, CLITANDRE

CÉLIMÈNE: Still here?

CLITANDRE: Love will not let us go.

CÉLIMÈNE: I heard a carriage in the court below:
   Who is it?

CLITANDRE: I don't know.

Scene 3. BASQUE, CÉLIMÈNE, ACASTE, CLITANDRE

BASQUE: Arsinoé
   Is here, Madame.

850 CÉLIMÈNE: Why, what can bring her, pray?

BASQUE: She's now downstairs talking with Éliante.

CÉLIMÈNE: What can be on her mind? What can she want?

ACASTE: She plays the perfect prude where'er she goes;
   Her ardent zeal . . .

CÉLIMÈNE: Yes, yes, it's quite a pose:
   Her soul is worldly, and her fondest plan
   Is, by some miracle, to catch a man.
   She can see only with an envious eye
   The suitors someone else is courted by.
   Left all alone, but not the least resigned,
860   She rages at the world that is so blind.

She tries to hide, by acting like a prude,
Her obvious and frightful solitude.
Rather than find her feeble charms to blame,
She calls the power they lack a cause for shame.
A suitor, though, is what would please her best,
Especially if that suitor was Alceste.
His visits to me make her feel bereft,
And she pronounces this a kind of theft.
In jealous spite, which she can hardly bear,
She covertly attacks me everywhere.   *870*
In short, a sillier soul I never saw;
In her absurdity there's not a flaw.
And . . .

Scene 4. ARSINOÉ, CÉLIMÈNE.

CÉLIMÈNE: Ah! Madame! Why, what a nice surprise!
I've missed you so! I can't believe my eyes.

ARSINOÉ: There's something that I think I ought to say.

CÉLIMÈNE: Just seeing you makes this a perfect day.
                    (*Exit* ACASTE *and* CLITANDRE, *laughing.*)

ARSINOÉ: Their leaving now was apropos indeed.

CÉLIMÈNE: Shall we sit down?

ARSINOÉ: I do not see the need,
Madame. True friendship should be manifest
In subjects that concern our interest;   *880*
And since none matter more to you or me
Than those of honor and propriety,
I come to tell you something, as a friend,
On which your reputation may depend.
I spent the other day with virtuous folk,
And, as it happened, 'twas of you they spoke.
And there, Madame, the freedom of your ways
Had the misfortune not to meet with praise.
The many men from whom you seek applause,
The rumors your coquettish manners cause,   *890*
Found far more censors than they ever ought,
And harsher than I could have wished or thought.
On this, you can imagine where I stood;

I sprang to your defense—as best I could,
Excusing your behavior as well-meant,
And stating I would vouch for your intent.
But there are things, you know as well as I,
We can't excuse, however hard we try;
And so I had to grant the others' claim
900   That your behavior does not help your name,
That it affords you anything but glory,
And makes of you the butt of many a story,
And that your ways, if you amended them,
Might offer less occasion to condemn.
Not that I think you grant more than you ought:
Heaven preserve my mind from such a thought!
But people hanker so for signs of vice,
To live well for oneself does not suffice.
Madame, I think you have too wise a heart
910   Not to accept this counsel in good part,
And to suspect a motive in my breast
Other than fervor for your interest.

CÉLIMÈNE: Madame, do not misjudge my attitude:
Advice like yours is cause for gratitude;
Now let me show my deep appreciation
By counsel that concerns your reputation,
And since I see you show your amity
By telling me what people say of me,
I'll take your kind example as my cue,
920   And let you know the things they say of you.
I visited some friends the other day—
People of merit—and it chanced that they
Sought to define the art of living well.
On you, Madame, the conversation fell.
Your prudery, your ready indignation
Were not, alas! held up for admiration.
That affectation of a pious face,
Eternal talk of honor and of grace,
Your screams and airs of outraged innocence,
930   When a harmless word allows a doubtful sense,
The self-esteem that gratifies your mind,
The pitying eye you cast upon mankind,
Your frequent lessons, and the wrath you vent
On matters that are pure and innocent:
All this, to speak without equivocation,
Madame, gave rise to general condemnation.

"Why does she wear," they said, "this modest guise,
This pious mask which all the rest belies?
Though she would never miss a time to pray,
She beats her servants and withholds their pay.   *940*
In church she flaunts her zealous sense of duty,
Yet paints her face and strives to be a beauty.
She covers up the nude when it's in paint,
But of the thing itself makes no complaint."
Against them all I spoke right up for you,
Assuring them that none of this was true;
Still nothing would they do but criticize,
And they concluded that you would be wise
To leave the acts of others more alone,
And think a little more about your own;   *950*
That we should take an earnest look within
Before we censure other people's sin;
That only those whose lives approach perfection
Are licensed to administer correction;
And that we leave this better, even then,
To those whom Heaven has chosen among men.
Madame, you too have far too wise a heart
Not to accept this counsel in good part,
And to suspect a motive in my breast
Other than fervor for your interest.   *960*

ARSINOÉ: I know we run a risk when we exhort,
But I did not expect quite this retort;
And since, Madame, it is so very tart,
I see my frank advice has stung your heart.

CÉLIMÈNE: Why, not at all, Madame; if we were wise,
Such chance for mutual counsel we would prize;
And honesty would banish from our mind
The blindness toward oneself that plagues mankind.
So, if you wish it, we need never end
This helpful interchange from friend to friend,   *970*
And we can tell each other, *entre nous*,
All that you hear of me, and I of you.

ARSINOÉ: Why, nothing can be heard against your name,
Madame, and it is I whom people blame.

CÉLIMÈNE: Madame, we either praise or blame, in truth,
According to our taste and to our youth.
And thus there is one season for romance,
Another fitter for a prudish stance.

The latter may be suited to the time
980 When our attractiveness has passed its prime:
It helps to cover our pathetic lacks.
Some day I may well follow in your tracks:
Age brings all things; but who is in the mood,
Madame, at twenty, to become a prude?

ARSINOÉ: You flaunt a scant advantage there, in truth,
And preen yourself a lot about your youth.
If I am just a bit older than you,
This is no reason for such great ado;
And I confess, Madame, I do not know
990 What passion drives you to attack me so.

CÉLIMÈNE: And I, Madame, would like to know the reason
Why hunting me is never out of season.
Why do you blame me for your unsuccess?
And can I help it if men seek you less?
If I inspire so many men with love,
If I am offered daily proofs thereof,
Proofs that you wish might be addressed to you,
It's not my fault; there's nothing I can do:
The field is free, and I do not prevent
1000 Your charming menfolk to your heart's content.

ARSINOÉ: Come, do you think I envy you that crowd
Of suitors whose attentions make you proud,
And that it is so hard for us to tell
At what a price you hold them in your spell?
Would you have us believe, the way things go,
That it just your merit charms them so?
That it is with a proper love they burn,
And that they hope for nothing in return?
Vain explanations never do ring true,
1010 No one is fooled; and I know women who,
Though made for every mortal to adore,
Yet do not summon suitors to their door.
From this I think we safely may conclude
That such devotion springs from gratitude,
That no one courts us for our lovely eyes.
And that we pay a price for all their sighs.
So be a little less inclined to gloat
On conquests that deserve such little note;
Correct your disposition to be vain,
1020 And show your fellow humans less disdain.

If we were envious of such as you,
I rather think we could, as others do,
Let ourselves go; and then you soon would find
All can have suitors who are so inclined.

CÉLIMÈNE: Then help yourself, Madame, and we shall see
If you can lure them with this recipe;
And if . . .

ARSINOÉ: Madame, let's leave things as they are;
More talk would carry both of us too far;
I would have taken leave, as soon I will,
But that my carriage keeps me waiting still.   *1030*

CÉLIMÈNE: Madame, believe me, you are free to stay
As long as you like; please do not rush away;
But, lest more formal talk from me fatigue you,
Here's someone much more likely to intrigue you;
This gentleman, who comes just when he should,
Will entertain you better than I could.
Alceste, I have a letter I must send,
Or else I shall antagonize a friend.
Please stay here with Madame; I have no doubt
She'll graciously excuse my stepping out.   *1040*

Scene 5. ALCESTE, ARSINOÉ

ARSINOÉ: She wants the two of us to talk, you see,
While waiting till my carriage comes for me;
And she could show me no consideration
As nice as such a private conversation.
Truly, people whose merit is supreme
Attract unanimous love and esteem;
And by its charm your high distinction earns
The interest of my heart in your concerns.
I only wish the court would have the grace
To set ·your merit in its proper place: *1050*
You are ill-treated, and I swear it hurts
To see you fail to get your true deserts.

ALCESTE: Who, I, Madame? And what should be my claim?
What service to the state adorns my name?
What splendid thing have I achieved, in short,
To justify my preference at court?

ARSINOÉ: The court regards some with a kindly eye
Which their achievements hardly justify.
Merit requires a chance to meet some test;
1060 And yours, which is so plainly manifest,
Should . . .

ALCESTE: Heavens! forget my merit; be so kind.
How can the court keep such things on its mind?
It would be quite a task for it to scan
The merit that resides in every man.

ARSINOÉ: True merit is most difficult to hide;
Yours commands high esteem on every side;
And yesterday, in two distinguished places,
I heard important persons sing your praises.

ALCESTE: But undiscerning praise today is cheap,
1070 Madame, and lumps us all in one great heap:
With merit all are equally endowed;
Applause no longer makes us justly proud;
We toss bouquets in one another's face;
And in the news my valet has his place.

ARSINOÉ: I wish your quality was more in view,
And that a post at court appealed to you.
If you would show the slightest inclination,
Machinery would be in operation;
And I have influence to bring to bear
1080 To make your progress smooth beyond compare.

ALCESTE: And there, Madame, what role am I to play?
My character demands I stay away.
And Heaven did not make me of the sort
To get along contentedly at court;
I do not have the virtues that you need
To do your business there and to succeed.
Only in honesty can I compete,
I simply have no talent for deceit;
And anyone who can't equivocate
1090 Should leave the place before it is too late.
Away from court we lack support, no doubt,
And all the titles that are handed out;
But there is consolation for our soul:
We do not have to play a silly role,
Brook the rebuffs that all must undergo,
Admire the verse of Mr. So-and-So,

Burn incense at the shrine of Madam Blank,
And suffer every noble mountebank.

ARSINOÉ: All right; about the court I shall be mute;
But I am much distressed about your suit,   *1100*
And I could wish, if I may speak my mind,
To see your love more suitably assigned.
You certainly deserve a better fate,
And Célimène is not your proper mate.

ALCESTE: One thing, Madame, I do not comprehend:
Do you forget this lady is your friend?

ARSINOÉ: Yes; but my conscience has been grieved too long
At watching you endure so great a wrong;
Seeing you in this state, I am dismayed,
And you should know your passion is betrayed.   *1110*

ALCESTE: Your tender sentiments I now discover,
Madame: what welcome tidings for a lover!

ARSINOÉ: Yes, though she is my friend, I do declare
That she does not deserve your loving care,
And that her kindness to you is but show.

ALCESTE: Perhaps, Madame; the heart we cannot know;
But could you not in charity decline
To plant such a disloyal thought in mine?

ARSINOÉ: If you would rather look the other way,
There's no use talking, and I've said my say.   *1120*

ALCESTE: Whatever we are told in this domain,
Doubt is the thing that gives the greatest pain;
And I would rather not have information
Without the chance for clear verification.

ARSINOÉ: Enough said. Very well. To set things right,
On this score you shall have abundant light.
Yes, with your own eyes you shall clearly see:
All you need do is to come home with me;
Convincing proof I will provide you there
Of your betrayal by your lady fair;   *1130*
And if you're cured of your infatuation,
You might even be offered consolation.

ACT IV

Scene 1. ÉLIANTE, PHILINTE

PHILINTE: I've never seen such stubborn indignation,
Or such a difficult accommodation:
We could not budge the man, hard as we tried,
With all our arguments from every side,
Nor has a case of such a curious sort
Ever, I think, preoccupied this court.
"No, gentlemen," he said, "to this I cling:
I'll concede all, except for this one thing.
Why must he bridle and strike out so madly?
Is his honor at stake in writing badly?
Why must he twist my judgment for the worse?
Even a gentleman can write bad verse.
These things concern our honor not a whit.
That he's a gentleman I do admit,
A man of quality, merit, and heart,
All that you like—his authorship apart.
I'll praise his lavish get-up for its charms,
His skill at dancing, horsemanship, or arms,
But praise his verse? That takes a diplomat.
And if a man can't write better than that,
He should resist rhyming to his last breath—
At least, unless it's under pain of death."
In short, the best grace and accommodation
He found to cover up his irritation
Was to seek—thus—to put Oronte at ease:
"Sir, I regret that I'm so hard to please,
And for your sake I wish with all my heart
I'd thought your sonnet was a work of art."
After these words, they had the two embrace,
And hastily concluded the whole case.

ÉLIANTE: His actions are peculiar and extreme,
But, I admit, I hold him in esteem,

272

And the sincerity that is his pride
Has a heroic and a noble side.
It's an uncommon virtue in this day
Which I wish others had in the same way.

PHILINTE: The more I see the man, the more I wonder
At the impassioned spell his heart is under: *1170*
Considering what Heaven made him of,
I cannot think how he can fall in love;
And why he loves your cousin, I confess,
Is something I can fathom even less.

ÉLIANTE: This clearly shows that love, in human hearts,
Need not imply community of parts;
And theories of mutual admiration
In this case show themselves without foundation.

PHILINTE: But as you see it, is he loved in turn?

ÉLIANTE: That point is far from easy to discern.   *1180*
Whether she really loves him, who can tell?
She knows her own emotions none too well:
Sometimes she's been in love, and never knew it,
Or thought she was, when there was nothing to it.

PHILINTE: With this cousin of yours, I think he'll find
More sorrow than has ever crossed his mind;
And if he had this heart of mine, I swear,
He promptly would bestow his love elsewhere,
And, turning in a far better direction,
Would take advantage of your deep affection.   *1190*

ÉLIANTE: I am not ceremonious, I fear,
And on these points I like to be sincere:
His love for her causes me no distress;
With all my heart I wish her happiness;
And if the thing were up to me alone,
I'd let him have her for his very own.
But if in such a choice, as just might be,
His love should not be crowned by destiny,
If she should spurn him for some substitute,
I could be willing to receive his suit;   *1200*
And in this case I would not take offense
To know she had his earlier preference.

PHILINTE: And I do not begrudge him, for my part,
Madame, the feeling for him in your heart;

And he himself can tell you even more
Just how I have advised him on that score.
But if the bonds of marriage joined those two
So that he could not pay his court to you,
My hope would be that I might take his place
1210   And seek to sin some measure of your grace,
Happy if his poor judgment left you free,
And if that grace, Madame, might fall on me.

ÉLIANTE: Philinte, you're jesting.

PHILINTE: No indeed, Madame,
No one could be more earnest than I am,
And eagerly I wait upon the day
When I can tell you all I long to say.

Scene 2. ALCESTE, ÉLIANTE, PHILINTE

ALCESTE: Ah, Madame! You must help me gain redress
For an offense that cracks my steadfastness.

ÉLIANTE: What is it? What has made you so upset?

1220   ALCESTE: I've had . . . I cannot understand it yet;
And the collapse of the whole firmament
Could never crush me as has this event.
It's done . . . My love . . . There's nothing I can say.

ÉLIANTE: Try to regain your mind's composure, pray.

ALCESTE: Just Heaven! Must such graces be combined
With vices worthy of the meanest mind?

ÉLIANTE: But still, what . . . ?

ALCESTE: Everything is devastated;
I'm . . . I'm betrayed; why, I'm assassinated!
Yes, Célimène—can such things be believed?—
1230   Yes, Célimène's untrue, and I'm deceived.

ÉLIANTE: Have you strong reasons for this supposition?

PHILINTE: This might be just an ill-conceived suspicion.
Your jealous mind, an easy prey to snares . . .

ALCESTE: Good Lord, sir! Won't you mind your own affairs?

I've proof of her betrayal, all too clear,
In her own hand, right in my pocket, here.
Madame, a letter bearing Oronte's name
Has shown me my disfavor and her shame:
Oronte, whose suit I thought she viewed askance,
The one I feared the least of her gallants.   *1240*

PHILINTE: A letter often gives the wrong impression
And bears a false likeness to a confession.

ALCESTE: Once more, sir, if you please, leave me alone
And mind your business; let me mind my own.

ÉLIANTE: Alceste, control your temper; all this spite . . .

ALCESTE: Madame, this task belongs to you by right;
It is with you my heart now seeks relief
From the torment of overwhelming grief.
Avenge me on that cousin without shame
Who basely has betrayed so true a flame;   *1250*
Avenge me for what I trust your soul abhors.

ÉLIANTE: Avenge you? How?

ALCESTE: Madame, my heart is yours.
Take it, replace the faithless Célimène.
Oh, I'll have my revenge upon her then!
I want her punished by the deep emotion,
The heartfelt love, the assiduous devotion,
The eager duties and the service true
Which now my heart will sacrifice to you.

ÉLIANTE: Of course I sympathize with what you suffer,
And I do not disdain the heart you offer;   *1260*
But it may be the harm is not so great,
And you may drop your vengeance and your hate.
When it's a charming person does us wrong,
Our plans for vengeance do not linger long:
Whatever the offenses we resent,
A guilty loved one is soon innocent;
The harm we wish her has no aftermath;
And nothing passes like a lover's wrath.

ALCESTE: No, Madame, that is not the way I burn;
I'm breaking off with her; there's no return;   *1270*
Nothing could ever change what I project;
I'd be ashamed to view her with respect.
—Here she is. My blood boils at her approach;

Her turpitude deserves a sharp reproach;
I shall confound her utterly, and then
Bring you a heart quite free of Célimène.

Scene 3. CÉLIMÈNE, ALCESTE

ALCESTE: Great Heavens! Can I control my indignation?

CÉLIMÈNE: Oh dear! What has brought on your agitation?
What do you mean by these portentous sighs
1280   And by the somber passion in your eyes?

ALCESTE: Nothing can match, no, not the ugliest crimes,
The faithlessness you've shown these many times;
The worst that Fate, Hell, wrathful Heaven could do
Never made anything as bad as you.

CÉLIMÈNE: I marvel at these sweet amenities.

ALCESTE: No, no, this is no time for pleasantries.
You should be blushing; you have ample reason,
And I have certain tokens of your treason.
The cause of my distress is all too plain;
1290   My apprehensiveness was not in vain;
My doubts, which you thought odious and unsound,
Have led me to the ill my eyes have found;
My star, though you were skillful to pretend,
Warned me of what I had to apprehend.
But don't presume to make a fool of me
And hope to flout me with impunity.
I know that we cannot control desire,
That love's autonomy must be entire,
That force won't strike a heart's responsive chord,
1300   And that each soul is free to choose its lord.
So I would find no subject for complaint
If you had spoken frankly, without feint;
Had you spurned my advances from the first,
I'd have blamed fate and waited for the worst.
But thus to fan my hopes with false acclaim
Is faithless treachery, quite without shame,
Deserving the severest castigation;
And I can freely vent my indignation.

Yes, after such a slight, avoid my path:
I am beside myself with righteous wrath: *1310*
Pierced by the mortal blow with which you slay me,
My reason cannot make my sense obey me;
Ruled by the anger that I feel for you,
I cannot answer for what I may do.

CÉLIMÈNE: Come, please explain this latest of your fits.
Tell me, have you completely lost your wits?

ALCESTE: Yes, yes, I lost them at that fatal hour
When first I fell into your poisonous power,
And when I sought sincerity as well
In the false charms that caught me in their spell.   *1320*

CÉLIMÈNE: Pooh! Of what treachery can you complain?

ALCESTE: Oh, what duplicity! How well you feign!
But I have ready proof at my command.
Just look at this, and recognize your hand.
This note at least should leave you mortified;
Its evidence is not to be denied.

CÉLIMÈNE: Then *this* explains your mood, and all you've said?

ALCESTE: Can you behold this note, and not turn red?

CÉLIMÈNE: If I should blush, perhaps you'll state the reason?

ALCESTE: What? Are you adding shamelessness to treason?   *1330*
Do you disown it, as an unsigned note?

CÉLIMÈNE: But why disown a letter that I wrote?

ALCESTE: And you can look at it without dismay
Although its very style gives you away?

CÉLIMÈNE: You really are too patently absurd.

ALCESTE: Against this witness, who could take your word?
And how can you offend me so, and flaunt
Your clear infatuation with Oronte?

CÉLIMÈNE: Oronte! Who says he is the addressee?

ALCESTE: The persons who today gave it to me.   *1340*
But let's assume it's for some other swain;
Does that give me less reason to complain?
Will that make you less guilty in the end?

CÉLIMÈNE: But if it's written to a lady friend,
    Where is the guilt, and what's this all about?

ALCESTE: Oh! that's an artful dodge, a neat way out.
    I grant I'd not expected such deceit,
    And that just makes my certainty complete.
    How can you stoop to such a lame excuse?
1350   And do you really think me that obtuse?
    Come, come, let's see in just what way you'll try
    To lend support to such an obvious lie,
    And by what artifice you will pretend
    This ardent note was for a lady friend.
    Just tell me how you will explain away
    What I shall read . . .

CÉLIMÈNE: I do not choose to say.
    I don't concede to you or anyone
    The right to talk to me as you have done.

ALCESTE: Don't take offense; just tell me, if you please,
1360   How you can justify such terms as these.

CÉLIMÈNE: No, I'll do nothing of the kind, I swear.
    Think what you like of me; I just don't care.

ALCESTE: Please, show me how this letter could be meant
    For any woman, and I'll be content.

CÉLIMÈNE: No, no, it's for Oronte; you must be right;
    I welcome his attentions with delight;
    In all he says and does, he has a way;
    And I'll agree to anything you say.
    Make up your mind, let nothing interfere;
1370   But I have heard from you all I will hear.

ALCESTE: Heavens! How could such a cruel trick be invented?
    And has a heart ever been so tormented?
    I come to tax her with her perfidy,
    I'm the complainant—and she turns on me!
    My pain and my suspicions she provokes.
    She won't deny her guilt, but boasts and jokes!
    And yet my heart is still too weak and faint
    To break the chains that hold it in constraint
    And arm itself with generous disdain
1380   Against the object that it loves in vain!
    Ah, faithless girl, with what consummate skill
    You play upon my utter lack of will

And make capital of the vast excess
Of my ill-omened, fatal tenderness!
At least defend yourself for this offense
And drop this claim of guilt, this vain pretense;
Show me the innocence of what you wrote;
My fond heart will forget about the note.
Just try your best to seem faithful, and know
That I will try my best to think you so.   *1390*

CÉLIMÈNE: Your jealous frenzies make you mad, I swear,
And you do not deserve the love I bear.
What makes you think that I would condescend,
On your account, to brazen and pretend?
And why, if my heart leaned another way,
Shouldn't I quite sincerely have my say?
What? Can the way in which I've spoken out
About my feelings leave you any doubt?
Has that such weight against this guarantee?
Can you regard it and not outrage me?   *1400*
And since it's hard for women to confess
Their sentiments of love and tenderness,
Since honor bids us never to reveal
The force of any ardor we may feel,
A man for whom this hurdle is surmounted
Should know our word is not to be discounted.
Shouldn't he be ready to stake his life
On what costs us so much internal strife?
Come, such suspicions earn my indignation;
And you are not worth my consideration.   *1410*
I am a fool; I'm sorry this is true
And that I still have some regard for you;
I should look elsewhere, that is all too plain,
And give you proper reason to complain.

ALCESTE: Treacherous girl! How can I be so weak?
I cannot trust the sugared words you speak;
Yet fate enjoins—and follow it I must—
That my soul be abandoned to your trust;
Although you may betray me, even so
I must learn to what lengths your heart will go.   *1420*

CÉLIMÈNE: No, you don't love me in the proper fashion.

ALCESTE: Ah! Nothing can be likened to my passion.
My eagerness to prove it goes so far
That I could wish you worse off than you are.

Yes, I could wish that no one found you charming,
That your predicament was quite alarming,
That Heaven had given you nothing at your birth,
Not rank, nor family, nor any worth,
So that my heart, a gleaming sacrifice,
1430 Might compensate and might alone suffice;
'Twould be my pride and joy, all else above,
To have you owe everything to my love.

CÉLIMÈNE: You surely wish me well in your own way!
I hope to Heaven I never see the day . . .
But here's . . . Monsieur Du Bois. I do declare!

Scene 4. DU BOIS, CÉLIMÈNE, ALCESTE

ALCESTE: What does this outfit mean, this frightened air?
What's wrong?

DU BOIS: Sir . . .

ALCESTE: Well?

DU BOIS: I have strange things to tell.

ALCESTE: What are they?

DU BOIS: Our affairs aren't going well.

ALCESTE: What?

DU BOIS: Shall I speak?

ALCESTE: Yes, yes, speak up, and quick.

DU BOIS: Isn't that someone . . . ?

1440 ALCESTE: Oh! You'll make me sick.
Will you speak up?

DU BOIS: Monsieur, we must give ground.

ALCESTE: How's that?

DU BOIS: We must decamp without a sound.

ALCESTE: And why?

DU BOIS: I tell you, sir, we've got to fly.

ALCESTE: What for?

DU BOIS: We mustn't stop to say good-by.

ALCESTE: But for what reason? What's this all about?

DU BOIS: This reason, sir: we promptly must get out.

ALCESTE: Honestly, I will break your head in two,
   You knave, if that's the best that you can do.

DU BOIS: Sir, a black somber man, in face and dress,
   Came to our place—the kitchen door, no less—   *1450*
   And left a paper filled with such a scrawl
   You'd have to be a demon to read it all.
   It's all about your lawsuit, I've no doubt;
   But even Satan couldn't make it out.

ALCESTE: Well then? What of it? Just explain to me:
   Why should this paper mean we have to flee?

DU BOIS: A little later, sir, an hour or more,
   A man who's been to visit you before
   Came in great haste, and finding you not there,
   Gave me a message that I was to bear   *1460*
   (Knowing I'm the most dutiful of men),
   To tell you . . . Wait, what *is* his name again?

ALCESTE: What did he tell you, wretch? Forget his name.

DU BOIS: Well, he's a friend of yours; it's all the same.
   He told me you have got to get away,
   And you could be arrested if you stay.

ALCESTE: But why? Nothing specific? Think, man, think.

DU BOIS: No; but he did ask me for pen and ink,
   And wrote this note, in which I think you'll see
   The explanation of this mystery.   *1470*

ALCESTE: Well, give it to me.

CÉLIMÈNE: What's this all about?

ALCESTE: I don't know, but I hope soon to find out.
   Come on, you oaf, what are you waiting for?

DU BOIS (*after a long search*): My goodness, sir! I left it in
   your drawer.

ALCESTE: I don't know why I don't . . .

CÉLIMÈNE: No, that can wait;
    You'd better go and set this matter straight.

ALCESTE: It seems that fate, no matter what I do,
    Will never let me have a talk with you;
    But let me come again ere day is done,
1480 And I shall think for once my love has won.

ACT V

Scene 1. ALCESTE, PHILINTE

ALCESTE: No use. My mind is quite made up, I tell you.

PHILINTE: But must this blow, however hard, compel you . . . ?

ALCESTE: No, you may talk and argue all you can,
Nothing that you can say will change my plan:
On every side such wickedness I find
That I mean to withdraw from humankind.
What? Honor, virtue, probity, the laws
Impugn my enemy and plead my cause;
Everyone knows of my integrity;
I put my trust in right and equity;   *1490*
And yet the outcome leaves me destitute:
Justice is with me, and I lose my suit!
A man whose shame is written on his face
Perjures himself outright, and wins the case!
Good faith gives way before his treachery:
He cuts my throat, and puts the blame on me!
His artificial grimace is so strong
As to taint justice and turn right to wrong!
He gets a court decree to crown his sin,
And not content with having done me in,   *1500*
There's a revolting book in circulation,
A book subject to solemn condemnation,
Deserving to be banned by law—and he
Foully ascribes the authorship to me!
And thereupon Oronte, that evil cheat,
Nods his assent, and seconds the deceit!
Oronte, whose name at court shines bright and clear,
With whom I've always been frank and sincere,
Who comes to me to wheedle and coerce,
And make me comment on his wretched verse;   *1510*
And just because I answer in good sooth,
Refusing to betray him or the truth,

283

He attests a crime that never did exist
And sets me up as his antagonist!
I'll never have his pardon, count upon it,
For failing to appreciate his sonnet!
Lord! What a sordid and familiar story:
Men led to evil by their itch for glory!
Yes, this is the good faith, the virtuous zeal,
1520   The equity and honor they reveal!
Come, I've endured more than enough from men:
Let's flee this ugly wood, this robbers' den.
And since you men behave the way you do—
Like wolves—I bid my last farewell to you.

PHILINTE: I think your plan's a little premature,
And men are not all that depraved, I'm sure;
Your enemy's charges, it is manifest,
Have not availed to bring on your arrest.
His false report has burst like any bubble,
1530   And might well get him into serious trouble.

ALCESTE: He? He need have no fear at any time:
He has some sort of privilege for crime;
And far from hurting him, this added shame
Will only serve to magnify his name.

PHILINTE: At any rate, I think you will concede
His rumors have been given little heed:
You have no cause at all for worry there;
As for your lawsuit, which was most unfair,
A higher court will surely countermand
This verdict . . .

1540 ALCESTE: No; I mean to let it stand.
The wrong it does me is so manifest,
I won't appeal it; no, I'll let it rest.
It shows the right downtrodden and maligned,
And I want it exposed to all mankind
As a clear testimony and display
Of all the evil of the present day.
At twenty thousand francs the cost is high;
But for those twenty thousand francs I'll buy
The right to rail against man's wicked state
1550   And look upon it with undying hate.

PHILINTE: But still . . .

ALCESTE: But still, don't press me any more.

What can you tell me further on this score?
Do you mean to justify, right to my face,
The evil conduct of the human race?

PHILINTE: No, no, all that I'll readily concede:
The world is ruled by pure intrigue and greed;
Nothing but trickery prevails today,
And humans should be made some other way.
But should their disaffection for the right
Lead us to try to flee their very sight?   *1560*
These human flaws give us the satisfaction
Of testing our philosophy in action:
In such employment virtue can take pride;
And if goodness were found on every side,
If all men's hearts were docile, frank, and just,
Most of our virtues would but gather rust,
Since they can serve to help us calmly bear
The injustices that face us everywhere.
Just as a heart instinct with virtue can . . .

ALCESTE: Sir, you can talk as well as any man.   *1570*
Your stock of arguments is most profuse,
But now your eloquence is just no use.
Reason bids me retire for my own good:
My tongue will not obey me as it should;
I could not answer for what I might say,
And I'd have a new quarrel every day.
Don't argue, let me wait for Célimène:
I've got to try to talk with her again.
Whether she really loves me, I don't know;
And I must have her answer, yes or no.   *1580*

PHILINTE: Let's wait for her with Éliante upstairs.

ALCESTE: No, I am too oppressed with anxious cares.
Go on and see her; I'll sit here apart
In this dark corner with my gloomy heart.

PHILINTE: That's not good company for any man;
I'll ask Éliante to join us if she can.

Scene 2. ORONTE, CÉLIMÈNE, ALCESTE

ORONTE: Yes, Madame, it is for you to decide
Whether a bond between us shall be tied.
I must ask you to answer with precision:
1590   A lover will not stand for indecision.
If you're at all responsive to my flame,
You can reveal that to me without shame;
And as you know, the proof that I request
Is that you end the courtship of Alceste,
Sacrifice him, Madame, and promptly break
All your relations with him for my sake.

CÉLIMÈNE: But why do you attack him with such spirit,
When I've so often heard you praise his merit?

ORONTE: Madame, let's let such explanations be;
1600   The question is just how you feel toward me.
So kindly make your choice between us two,
And my decision will depend on you.

ALCESTE *(coming out of his corner):* Madame, the gentle-
man's request is just,
And I support it; yes, decide you must.
The same ardor, the same concern are mine;
My love can't do without some clearcut sign;
Matters have gone too far for more delay,
And now's the time for you to have your say.

ORONTE: Sir, I've no wish to be importunate
1610   And bother you, if you're so fortunate.

ALCESTE: Sir, I've no wish to have you share a part—
Even if this be jealous—of her heart.

ORONTE: If your love is more precious in her view . . .

ALCESTE: If she can have the slightest taste for you . . .

ORONTE: I swear I'll leave her to you there and then.

ALCESTE: I swear I'll never see her face again.

ORONTE: Madame, pray tell us what we've come to hear.

ALCESTE: Madame, you can speak freely, without fear.

ORONTE: All you need do is say how you're inclined.

ALCESTE: All you need do is to make up your mind.   *1620*

ORONTE: What? When we ask your choice, you seem put
   out?

ALCESTE: What? Your soul hesitates and seems in doubt?

CÉLIMÈNE: Good Lord! This urgency is out of place,
   And both of you show no more sense than grace.
   My mind's made up about this situation,
   And in my heart there is no hesitation;
   Between you two it is in no suspense,
   And I could well declare its preference.
   But I think it a painful indiscretion
   To utter such a face-to-face confession;   *1630*
   I think these words that are so hard to bear
   Should not be spoken when both men are there;
   I think our hearts betray our inclinations
   Without being forced to such harsh revelations,
   And that there are much gentler ways to use
   When we must tell a lover such bad news.

ORONTE: No, no, the truth! I have no cause to fear it.
   Come, please speak up.

ALCESTE: And I demand to hear it.
   There's nothing in your openness to scare us;
   Believe me, I've no wish to have you spare us.   *1640*
   You don't need everyone under your sway;
   Enough uncertainty, enough delay:
   Now is the time to answer our demand.
   If you decline, I shall know where I stand;
   Your silence will amount to an admission
   That will corroborate my worst suspicion.

ORONTE: I'm grateful for your indignation, sir;
   And what you say is what I say to her.

CÉLIMÈNE: Oh, how you weary me with this caprice!
   Can't you be fair, and let me have some peace?   *1650*
   Haven't I told you why I will not budge?
   But here comes Éliante: I'll let her judge.

Scene 3. ÉLIANTE, PHILINTE, CÉLIMÈNE, ORONTE,
ALCESTE

CÉLIMÈNE: Cousin, I find myself beset indeed
By these two men, who seem to have agreed.
With equal warmth they both insist, my dear,
That I should make my choice between them clear,
And, by a sentence uttered face to face,
That I make one of them give up the chase.
Has anyone ever behaved this way?

1660   ÉLIANTE: Don't seek my frank opinion on this, pray:
I'm not the one to ask, as you will find,
And I'm for people who will speak their mind.

ORONTE: Madame, you may defend yourself in vain.

ALCESTE: No use in being devious, that's plain.

ORONTE: You must speak up, you must, and end this doubt.

ALCESTE: Or if you won't, your silence will speak out.

ORONTE: One word from you, and there'll be no more scenes.

ALCESTE: And if you're silent, I'll know what that means.

Scene 4. ACASTE, CLITANDRE, ARSINOÉ, PHILINTE,
ÉLIANTE, ORONTE, CÉLIMÈNE, ALCESTE

ACASTE: Madame, with no offense, we two are here
1670   To try to get a little matter clear.

CLITANDRE: Your presence, sirs, is timely, I declare,
And you are both involved in this affair.

ARSINOÉ: Madame, my coming must be a surprise,
But these men would not have it otherwise:
They both came to me angry and aggrieved
Over an act too mean to be believed.
I think there is a goodness in your soul
That would not let you play so base a role:
My eyes belied their strongest evidence,
1680   My friendship overlooked our difference,

And so I came to keep them company
And see you overthrow this calumny.

ACASTE: Yes, Madame, let's see, with a peaceful mind,
What sort of explanation you can find.
You wrote Clitandre this note, now didn't you?

CLITANDRE: It was you wrote Acaste this billet-doux?

ACASTE: To you this handwriting is not obscure,
Messieurs, and her indulgence, I am sure,
Has made it known to every person here;
But this is something for you all to hear.   *1690*
(He reads)

"You're a strange man to condemn my sprightliness and reproach me with never being so happy as when I'm not with you. Nothing could be more unjust; and if you don't come very soon and ask my pardon for this offense, I shall never forgive you for it as long as I live. Our great lout of a Viscount . . ."

He *should* be here.

"Our great lout of a Viscount, whom you complain about first, is a man I never could fancy; and since I watched him for a good three-quarters of an hour spitting into a well to make circles in the water, I have never been able to think well of him. As for the little Marquis . . ."

"All vanity aside, gentlemen, that's me.

"As for the little Marquis, who held my hand so long yesterday, I don't know anything as insignificant as his whole person; and the only merit of his kind lies in his cloak and sword. As for the man with the green ribbons . . ."

(To ALCESTE): Your turn, sir.

"As for the man with the green ribbons, he sometimes amuses me with his bluntness and his surly grouchiness; but there are hundreds of times when I find him as tiresome as can be. And as for the man with the jacket . . ."

(To ORONTE): Here's your bundle.

"And as for the man wit the jacket, who has gone in for wit and wants to be an author in spite of everyone, I can't give myself the trouble to listen to what he says; and his prose wearies me as much as his poetry. So get it into your head that I don't always have as good a time as you think; that I miss you more than I could wish in all the parties that I'm dragged into; and that a marvelous seasoning for the pleasures we enjoy is the presence of the persons we love."

CLITANDRE. And now here I am.

(He reads)

"You're Clitandre, whom you mention, and who puts on such sweetish airs, is the last man I could be fond of. He is absurd to suppose he is loved; and so are you, to think you are not. To be reasonable, exchange your beliefs for his; and see me as muich as you can to help me endure the vexation of being beleaguered by him."

It's a fine character these portraits show,
Madame, and there's a name for it, you know.
Enough: we two shall everywhere impart
This glorious self-portrait of your heart.

ACASTE: I could well speak, I've ample provocation;
But you're not worthy of my indignation;
And there are nobler hearts, as you shall see,
Ready to comfort a *petit marquis*.

(Exit ACASTE *and* CLITANDRE*)*

ORONTE: What? You can tear me into shreds this way
1700   After the things I've seen you write and say!
And your false heart, which seems for love designed,
Offers itself in turn to all mankind!
Go to, I've been a dupe too much, too long;
I *should* be grateful that you've proved me wrong.
You give me back my heart, a welcome prize,
And in your loss of it my vengeance lies.

(To ALCESTE*)*

If I was in your way, I no longer am,
So pray conclude your business with Madame.

(Exit ORONTE*)*

ARSINOÉ: Really, that is the blackest action yet.
1710   I can't keep silent, I am too upset.
How can such treachery be justified?
I leave the other gentlemen aside;
But take a man of honor like Alceste,
Whose heart by your good fortune you possessed,
Who worshipped you beyond what tongue can say,
Should he have been . . . ?

ALCESTE: Madame, allow me, pray,
To guard my interest here; that's all I ask;
Don't charge yourself with this superfluous task.
My heart, though grateful for your vindication,
1720   Is in no state to pay its obligation;
And if—I have to tell you, for it's true—
I sought revenge, it would not be with you.

ARSINOÉ: Do you think, sir, that that was in my mind,
And that I look on you as such a find?
To tell the truth, I find you very vain
If that's the kind of thought you entertain.
To hanker for the leavings of Madame,
I'd have to be less choosy than I am.
Come down a peg, open your eyes, give heed:
I'm not the kind of person that you need;   1730
Keep sighing for her; she is quite a catch;
I can hardly wait to see so fine a match.

(Exit ARSINOÉ)

ALCESTE: Well! I have held my tongue, for all I see,
And let everyone speak ahead of me:
Have my feelings been long enough suppressed?
And may I now . . . ?

CÉLIMÈNE: Yes, tell me all the rest.
You've every reason to complain your fill
And reproach me for everything you will.
I'm wrong, I do confess; my consternation
Leads me to seek no vain extenuation.   1740
The others' wrath I treated with disdain,
But I agree, my crime toward you is plain;
I've earned your bitterness, lost your esteem;
I know full well how guilty I must seem,
That everything proclaims I have betrayed you,
And if you hate me, it's because I've made you.
Go ahead; I consent.

ALCESTE: Ah! traitress, how?
Can I conquer my passion even now?
And though I burn to hate you, as you say,
Do you think my heart is ready to obey?   1750
(To ÉLIANTE *and* PHILINTE)
See what unworthy tenderness can do;
Bear witness to my frailty, you two.
But this is not yet all, I must confess,
And you shall see me push it to excess,
Proving that those who call us wise are wrong,
And that mere human nature is too strong.
(To CÉLIMÈNE)
I'm willing to forget the things you've done;
My soul will find excuse for every one;
And I'll contrive to view your blackest crimes
As youthful foibles caused by evil times,   1760

Provided only that your heart agree
To flee human society with me,
And that you'll follow me without delay
To the seclusion where I've vowed to stay:
Only thus, in the minds of everyone,
Can you repair the harm your note has done,
And after a scene which noble hearts abhor,
Enable me to love you as before.

CÉLIMÈNE: What! *I* renounce the world before I'm old,
1770 And molder in some solitary hold?

ALCESTE: If your love matches mine and is as true,
Why should all other men matter to you?
Why can't I be sufficient to your need?

CÉLIMÈNE: At twenty, solitude is grim indeed.
I fear I lack the loftiness of soul
To undertake so difficult a role.
If marriage can fulfill your aspiration,
I think I could resolve on that relation,
And thus . . .

ALCESTE: No, never did I hate you so,
1780 And this refusal is the final blow.
Since this is something that you cannot do—
Find all in me, as I find all in you—
Go, I refuse you, and at last I sever
My most unworthy ties to you forever.
                (*Exit* CÉLIMÈNE. *To* ÉLIANTE)
Madame, your beauty is adorned with worth,
You only are sincere in all the earth;
For you my admiration is extreme.
But now please be content with my esteem;
Forgive me if the turmoil in my soul
1790 No longer lets me seek a suitor's role:
I feel unworthy, and that Heaven's plan
Did not create me for a married man;
That you deserve a hand better than mine,
And not the discard of a heart less fine,
And that . . .

ÉLIANTE: Follow this notion to the end;
I do not find myself without a friend;
And if I asked Philinte, I understand
He might be happy to accept my hand.

PHILINTE: Madame, if I could have you for my wife,
  I'd gladly sacrifice my blood, my life.   *1800*

ALCESTE: May both of you forever feel like this,
  And thus experience true wedded bliss!
  While I, betrayed, and overwhelmed with wrong,
  Leave an abyss where vices are too strong,
  And seek some solitary place on earth
  Where one is free to be a man of worth.

                                        (Exit ALCESTE*)*

PHILINTE *(To* ÉLIANTE*):* Come, Madame, let's do everything
    we can
  To thwart the aims of this unhappy man.

Nikolai Gogol
THE INSPECTOR GENERAL

NIKOLAI GOGOL (1809–1852) was a trenchant satirist of the pettiness, bureaucracy, and corruption of Czarist Russia in the earlier nineteenth century. He seems very modern in his ironic detachment from the events he describes, and there is little overt bitterness beneath a surface of foolish social conventions that mistake gestures for truths. In *The Inspector General* (1836) a small provincial town is self-deceived by its own cringing respect for authority and all the appearances of high station and power. Gogol is masterful in representing the fawning servility of the petty bureaucracy of his nameless town. They want to believe that the world is a very small and petty place; everything outside their town, and especially the Russian capital of St. Petersburg, is seen to be a mythical, fantasy-fulfilling place.

The inspection by the Inspector General becomes an analogue for evaluation, assessment, scrutiny, and self-knowledge, and this is what the town most fears. The commitment to illusion is also a commitment to comedy. Nothing can withstand the searching eye of the Inspector General, so everything must be cosmetically transformed to deceive the all-knowing Inspector General, who is the greatest impostor of all. The play turns almost entirely on the ironic confrontation of genial crooks and impostors. In the hospital, for example, the patients' nightgowns must be washed, neat little cards must be placed over their beds explaining, in Latin or German, the name of the disease, and, as the Mayor insists with such practical wisdom, "if any of them are dead, I want them taken out right away." The town to be inspected is the stage-set of farce because everything one could possibly see is an illusion. It is like Plautus' Epidamnum or Shakespeare's Ephesus, and we are immediately embarked on a comedy of errors.

Hlestakov is a wonderful comic figure who derives from the Braggart Soldier stereotype (Plautus' Miles Gloriosus and Shakespeare's Falstaff). In the tradition of comedy, the Braggart Soldier

294

is a splendid talker, a thoroughly expansive and heartwarming figure. That he is a coward rather than a military hero seems almost incidental to his grandly rhetorical posture; he is essentially an entertainer. Hlestakov hardly makes any pretensions to the august role that is thrust upon him. He is always quintessentially himself. There is an important visual irony in the fact that he is an entirely unheroic and unimposing figure; in fact he is a gawky and clownish young man. As Gogol describes him in his notes on the characters, he is "about 23, rather insignificant in appearance; dresses in the latest fashion. He would be considered frivolous in the government offices." In contrast, when the real Inspector General appears in that apocalyptic moment at the very end of the play, he is "*a tall, imperious figure in magnificent uniform, with glowering eyes and fierce mustache.*" He arouses "*cries of amazement and fear*" that remove the final, frozen tableau abruptly from the world of comedy. It is the moment of fear and trembling that comedy cannot cope with.

Hlestakov is a modern type of antihero. He is the confidence man who gets carried away with his own glorious fantasies. This is not exactly lying but more in the line of fabulation. Everything depends on a hyperbolic and imperious style. Gogol shrewdly describes Hlestakov as someone who "speaks and acts abruptly, without thinking, and cannot concentrate on one subject for long. . . . He is not a professional liar or impostor; he forgets he is telling lies and almost believes what he is saying. As he realizes he is believed, he becomes expansive, poetic, inspired."

In Hlestakov's drunken oration at the end of I.ii, he tells the gaping officials of the town exactly what they want to hear about the scintillating and corrupt world of St. Petersburg. Hlestakov is an insouciant and nonchalant artist, politician, and man about town. His fancy dress balls are lavishly decadent:

> The centerpiece, for example, is a watermelon made into a fountain, with bubbling watermelon juice! It sets me back seven hundred rubles. The soup comes straight from Paris by steamer in my own tureen.

In short, he fills to overflowing all the overheated wish fulfillments of his gross, greedy, and crude auditors. To students of comedy Hlestakov's magnificent peroration ends characteristically when "*He slips off his chair and sprawls on the floor.*" By the nice workings of dramatic irony, his drunken boorishness, so obvious to us, is invisible to his awestruck listeners.

The Mayor is always somewhat skeptical, but he cringes with

fear at the very idea of a higher authority. Hlestakov violates the Mayor's faith in the material world: "You should be able to tell if a man is important by his appearance." But Hlestakov is disturbing: "this miserable, skinny kid! How can anyone figure out who he is? With a military man, it's easy—when he puts on civilian clothes he looks like a fly with its wings clipped." The Mayor cannot deal with the affront to his own dignity that is involved in being mistaken. Thus comedy engages us in testing our objective correlatives; in the end everything turns out to be a fantasy or an illusion.

Gogol's satirical brilliance is devoted almost exclusively to exposing the pompousness, narrowness, and fatuity of the officials of his provincial town. They are fearful, passive, and unimaginative in the extreme, and slyly toadyish, too, as in the Postmaster's clever retort to the Mayor: "How do *I* feel? The important thing is—how do *you* feel?" No one has the audacity to question Hlestakov's pretensions. Actually everyone is so benighted that no one has the sophistication or intellectual capacity to see through Hlestakov's shallow boasting. This is the sort of town where everyone is awed by the fact that Hlestakov can be both bored and working on his novel, two clear indications of "aristocratic poise."

The most charmingly comic detail comes from the real estate twins, Bobchinski and Dobchinski, whom Gogol describes as "short, fat and inquisitive. . . . Both wear short waistcoats, and talk fast with constant gestures." They are both remarkably innocent and disingenuous. Note that in their joint interview with Hlestakov, they are the only ones who don't offer bribes even greater than those demanded. Hlestakov's idle request for a thousand rubles is answered quite adequately by Bobchinski's forty and Dobchinski's twenty-five. But Hlestakov offers the same solid value to them as he does to any of the big spenders. Bobchinski's request is modest in the extreme:

> I beg you, sir, when you return to St. Petersburg and tell all the notables there, all those councilors and admirals, about your visit, just say, "In that town, Your Excellency or Your Highness, in that very town lives Peter Ivanovich Bobchinski." That's all. Just say, "Peter Ivanovich Bobchinski lives there."

Hlestakov is always scrupulously obliging:

> Why not? And when I call on the Emperor, I'll slip it into

the conversation, "It's the town, Your Imperial Majesty, where Peter Ivanovich Bobchinski lives."

This is a convincing demonstration that comedy deals in word magic. Bobchinski's heartfelt wish is merely a verbal formula that will be spoken for posterity. It is grandiosely bathetic, but it is enough to stave off oblivion.

THE INSPECTOR GENERAL

TRANSLATED BY ROBERT SAFFRON

The Inspector General was first produced at St. Petersburg in April, 1836, during the reign of Czar Nicholas I. Despite the play's criticism of the regime's corruption, the Czar never ordered it to be censored or banned.

CHARACTERS

ANTON ANTONOVICH, *Mayor of a provincial town*
ANNA ANDREYEVNA, *his wife*
MARYA ANTONOVNA, *his daughter*
LUKA LUKICH HLOPOV, *Commissioner of Schools*
HIS WIFE
AMMOS FYODOROVICH LYAPKIN-TYAPKIN, *a Judge*
ARTEMI PHILIPOVICH ZEMLYANIKA, *Commissioner of Charities*
IVAN KUZMICH SHPYOKIN, *Postmaster*
IVAN ALEXANDROVICH HLESTAKOV, *a government clerk from*
   St. Petersburg
OSIP, *his servant*
DOBCHINSKI, *a landowner*
BOBCHINSKI, *a landowner*
HUBNER, *a doctor*
LYULYUKOV ⎫
RASTAKOVSKI ⎬ *former officials*
KAROBKIN ⎭
UKHAVYORTOV, *police superintendent*
SVISTUNOV ⎫
PUGOVKIN ⎬ *policemen*
DERZHIMORDA ⎭
ABDULIN, *a merchant*
LOCKSMITH'S WIFE
SERGEANT'S WIFE
MISHKA, *Mayor's servant*
WAITER *at the inn*
Other merchants, citizens, ladies and gentlemen of the town

The action of the play takes place in a provincial town in Russia, in the 1830s.

GOGOL'S NOTES ON THE CHARACTERS

THE MAYOR: An old-timer in government service who knows all the tricks. He has an air of dignified respectability but is not adverse to taking a gift. His coarse features and frequently uneducated language betray the lower-class man who has worked his way up; he shifts quickly from fear to joy and from servility to arrogance.

ANNA ANDREYEVNA: His wife, still tolerably young, is a small-town coquette, raised on romantic novels and the trivia of the household. She is most inquisitive and vain, and henpecks her husband whenever she can get away with it. She changes her costume four times during the play.

HLESTAKOV: A young man, about 23, rather insignificant in appearance; dresses in the latest fashion. He would be considered frivolous in the government offices. He speaks and acts abruptly, without thinking, and cannot concentrate on one subject for long. . . . He is not a professional liar or impostor; he forgets he is telling lies and almost believes what he is saying. As he realizes he is believed, he becomes expansive, poetic, inspired.

OSIP: His servant, middle-aged, keeps his head down in mock servility but lectures his master bluntly, even rudely. He is the cleverer of the two, a real rogue.

BOBCHINSKI AND DOBCHINSKI: Both are short, fat and inquisitive and look like twins. Both wear short waistcoats, and talk fast with constant gestures. DOBCHINSKI is taller and more practical; BOBCHINSKI is somewhat lightheaded.

LYAPKIN-TYAPKIN: The Judge has read five or six books and so considers himself something of a free-thinker. He is fond of philosophic discussion, carefully weighing each word. Speaks with a bass voice and prolonged drawl, clearing his voice beforehand like an old clock that buzzes before it strikes.

COMMISSIONER OF CHARITIES: Very fat, slow and awkward; still he's an intriguing rascal, obliging but officious.

POSTMASTER: An artless simpleton.

The other characters require no special explanation since their prototypes can be found almost anywhere.

The performers must pay special attention to the final scene. The last word spoken must strike them like an electric shock,

suddenly and simultaneously, and the entire group should fall
into a tableau at the same instant. The ladies' cry of astonishment must seem to come from one throat. The neglect of these
directions will ruin the entire effect.

ACT I

Scene I

A room in the MAYOR'S *house, stuffy and over-furnished in heavy furniture and bibelots of the period. The entrance, center, has double doors; other doors lead to back of house and a side room.*

It is a drowsy afternoon. The COMMISSIONER OF CHARITIES *and* HUBNER, *the doctor, are playing cards mechanically. One* POLICEMAN *is asleep in a chair and snoring; occasionally he moves his hand or twitches his nose to shake off a fly which continues to pester him. Another* POLICEMAN *is leaning against the center doorway. The* JUDGE *is staring vacantly at the ceiling of the room. The* COMMISSIONER OF SCHOOLS *has a large ledger in one hand and a sheaf of papers in the other; as he swiftly skims through the papers he checks off names in the ledger. Papers fall to the floor but he doesn't bother to pick them up.*

The center doors are pushed open and the MAYOR *enters, breathing heavily and obviously flustered. The* POLICEMAN *doesn't move. Nobody looks up. The* MAYOR *slaps a table heavily to get their attention. The* POLICEMAN *slowly, eyes still shut, shuffles to the door and leans against it to balance his partner on the other side.*

MAYOR: I've called you to my house, gentlemen, to warn you! An Inspector General is coming here!

JUDGE: What? An Inspector?

COMMISSIONER OF CHARITIES: An Inspector?

MAYOR: Yes, an Inspector from St. Petersburg. Incognito! With *secret* instructions!

JUDGE: What a despicable trick!

COMMISSIONER OF CHARITIES: Well, our district has escaped so far. Now it's our turn to catch hell.

301

COMMISSIONER OF SCHOOLS *(appalled)*: Good God! *Secret* instructions?

MAYOR: I knew this would happen, I knew it! All last night I had a dream about two monster rats! I've never seen anything like them—so huge and all *black!* They came into my room, sniffed around, then vanished.

JUDGE: Two *black* rats you say? But there is only one inspector. Possibly he has blacked up his face to hide—?

MAYOR *(ignoring him)*: I have a letter here from Andrei Chmikov. *(To* COMMISSIONER OF CHARITIES.*)* You know him . . . he's reliable. *(He reads.)* "My dear friend and benefactor . . ." *(He mutters through a few lines.)* ah, here it is—"an official has been sent out with instructions to inspect the entire province and especially your district. *(Points a finger significantly.)* I know from reliable sources that he will pretend to be just a private citizen. And so, since you're a sensible man and don't let any little graft slip through your fingers . . ." *(Looks up, irritably.)* People shouldn't send that kind of joke through the mails. *(Reading.)* "He might come any day—if he's not already there—and remember, he's incognito. My cousin has grown very fat and now he has trouble sticking his fiddle under his chin. . . ." Well, there you are. This is a real trap!

JUDGE: Extraordinary! Most extraordinary! There must be some hidden motive behind all this.

COMMISSIONER OF SCHOOLS: Of course! Why should *we* in particular be cursed with an Inspector?

MAYOR *(sighing)*: It's the heavy hand of God!

JUDGE: It is my opinion that this is a subtle political move. It means . . . let me think now . . . that Russia wants—yes, that's it! Russia is about to declare war! And the government has sent a secret agent to sniff out disloyalty here.

MAYOR: Oh, what a brain! What good could an enemy spy do here? We're not on the border—you could gallop for three years before you hit a border!

JUDGE: Disloyalty knows no borders! The government may be far away in St. Petersburg but its eyes are everywhere, watching, lurking. . . .

MAYOR *(disturbed)*: Maybe so, maybe so. Anyhow, gentlemen, I've warned you. I've taken steps to straighten out my office,

and you'd better do the same. *(To* COMMISSIONER OF CHARITIES.*)*
And especially you. I'll bet the first thing the Inspector wants
to see is the hospital. Better clean it up fast. Get the patients
into some presentable nightgowns. And scrub up the wretches
a little. I don't want them to look like they've been sleeping in
a blacksmith's shop.

COMMISSIONER OF CHARITIES *(irritably)*: All right, all right. I'll
have some nightgowns washed.

MAYOR: I can't even recognize any of those people. *(To* DOCTOR.*)*
You ought to have a little card over the bed, in Latin or German
or whatever language you doctors use, with the name of the
patient, his disease and so on. And if any of them are dead, I
want them taken out right away! *(*DOCTOR *doesn't answer.*
MAYOR *turns to* COMMISSIONER OF CHARITIES.*)* Another thing.
You have too damn many patients. The Inspector will say
that's bad management. You'll have to— *(Waves his hand.)*
lose some of them somehow.

COMMISSIONER OF CHARITIES: I assure you, we don't waste expensive medicines on those cases. We prefer nature's own reme-
dies. If they die, they die. If they live—we are proved right. . . .
Unfortunately, it's hard for the patients to explain their symptoms to the doctor.

MAYOR: Why?

COMMISSIONER OF CHARITIES: All he can speak is German.

(The DOCTOR *grunts unintelligibly. The* MAYOR *throws up his
hands.)*

MAYOR *(to* JUDGE*)*: And you, Ammos Fyodorovich, you ought
to spend a little more time in the Courthouse. Have you been in
the lobby lately? Some of your clever attendants are raising
geese there! And the goslings go poking their beaks under the
women's skirts. It's not respectable! And all those feathers
floating around! . . . *(Wearily.)* I was going to mention it to
you before but somehow I forgot.

JUDGE: Very well. I shall order the attendants to take the geese
over to my kitchen today. Would you like to come to dinner
tonight?

MAYOR: Not tonight! . . . And what about that relative of yours,
that assessor? He reeks of liquor, as though he's just come out

of a distillery—and he probably has. There must be some way to get rid of that stink.

JUDGE: He claims that's the way he has always smelled.

MAYOR: Tell him to cover it up with onions or garlic or something. Can't the Doctor give him some pills?

(The DOCTOR *grunts.)*

JUDGE *(shrugs)*: My cousin swears his nurse dropped him when he was a baby, and ever since he's smelled of vodka.

MAYOR: My God! I'm surrounded by idiots! That reminds me. I know no man is free of sin—God made him that way—but starting today no one is to accept any bribes! Is that clear? No one!

JUDGE: What do you mean by sin? There are small sins and there are great sins. I admit I take gifts, but what kind? Greyhound puppies. That's a small sin.

MAYOR: I don't care if it's a small puppy or a big dog, that's a sin.

JUDGE: Just a moment. Let us examine the evidence. Suppose the defendant receives a cloak, worth five hundred rubles, or your wife, say, gets a fancy shawl . . .

MAYOR *(angrily)*: Are you making *me* a defendant? You're a great one to be arguing about sin. You're an atheist! You've never been inside a church. At least I attend service every Sunday. When I hear you talking about Original Sin, it just makes my hair curl! God will punish you for this.

JUDGE: At least I thought it all out with my own brain—it's not dogma—

MAYOR: That's the trouble—everybody is *thinking* around here! *(He turns on the* COMMISSIONER OF SCHOOLS.*)* You better watch those teachers in your schools. I know a few of them have gone to the university and they're damned queer. That fat-faced one—I forget his name—why is he always screwing up his mug like this? *(He imitates a monster.)* Then he starts clawing at his necktie and scratching his chin. I don't care if he makes faces at the pupils—maybe they need it—but if he sticks out his tongue at the Inspector he may take it personally and there'll be hell to pay.

COMMISSIONER OF SCHOOLS *(a martyr)*: I've told him time and again. What can I do? I keep getting complaints from people about the revolutionary notions being planted in the children's heads.

MAYOR: That's all I need now—bomb-throwers in the schools! And what about that history teacher? He looks smart, all right, but when he starts lecturing he goes absolutely crazy! I heard him once. As long as he was on the Assyrians and the Babylonians, he was fine. But when he got to Alexander the Great—good God! He threw books around and smashed his chair on the floor, and broke it into little pieces. Alexander the Great is a hero, but does your madman have to break up the furniture to prove it? That's state property, and some day somebody will have to pay for it.

COMMISSIONER OF SCHOOLS *(resigned)*: I've spoken to him about the damages several times. All he says is—"In the cause of learning I will even sacrifice my life!"

MAYOR *(sighs)*: It's a strange law of heaven—your scholar is either a drunkard or an anarchist!

COMMISSIONER OF SCHOOLS *(fervently)*: God preserve us from the influence of books!

MAYOR *(suddenly remembering)*: God preserve us from this Inspector! He'll put his head in here suddenly: "Aha! so you're all together, my friends? And who's the Judge?" he'll say. "Lyapkin-Tyapkin." "Well, ship Lyapkin-Tyapkin away," he'll order. "And who is the Commissioner of Charities?" "Zemlyanika." "Take Zemlyanika, too!" That's what's so terrifying—we don't know when he'll pop in!

(At this instant, the POSTMASTER *rushes in, frightening all of them.)*

POSTMASTER: Am I too late? Who's coming? I heard something from Bobchinski at the post office.

MAYOR: *You're* the postmaster. What do you think about these reports?

POSTMASTER *(thinking hard)*: What do *I* think? Why, there'll be war with the Turks for sure.

JUDGE *(to the group)*: That is exactly what I said.

MAYOR: The Turks? It's *us* who're going to be shot at, not the Turks. I've got a letter that proves it.

POSTMASTER: Ah, good. Then we *won't* go to war with the Turks.

MAYOR *(restraining himself)*: What do you feel about all this?

POSTMASTER *(slyly)*: How do *I* feel? The important thing is—how do *you* feel?

MAYOR: I'm not afraid of anything . . . but those crafty shop-keepers bother me. I'm sure they've drawn up some complaints against me. God knows, if I've put pressure on them for contributions now and then, I've done it without any personal spite. I don't have any grudge against them. *(Takes* POSTMASTER *by the lapels and draws him aside.)* Listen, Ivan, couldn't you open every letter that comes into the post office— just a little? *(*POSTMASTER *is shocked.)* It's really a public service—to see if it has any lies about me. If it's all right, paste it up again.

POSTMASTER: *(amiably)*: Oh, you don't have to teach me *that* trick. I like to know what's going on in the world. And it sure is interesting, I tell you! Sometimes I come across a love letter with some hot little tidbits . . .

MAYOR: Have you read anything lately about an official from St. Petersburg?

POSTMASTER: No, but lots about Kostroma and Saratov. Too bad you don't get to read 'em, Mayor. Some great stuff there. I remember once an artillery lieutenant wrote to a friend about a dance. "I live in paradise," he writes. "Lots of music, girls— all well fortified. Let me tell you about the breastworks . . ." Oh, it would make your mouth water. I kept that letter—would you like to read it?

MAYOR: Not now . . . *(Wearily.)* If only I knew what that damned Inspector looks like! I expect the door to open and all of a sudden—

(The door flies open and BOBCHINSKI *and* DOBCHINSKI *tumble in, out of breath. The* MAYOR *chokes as if God is about to strike him dead.)*

BOBCHINSKI: What a fantastic thing just happened!

DOBCHINSKI: Incredible!

ALL: What is it? What happened?

DOBCHINSKI: Who would have expected it? We go into the inn—

BOBCHINSKI *(interrupting)*: Yes, he and I go into the inn—

DOBCHINSKI: All right, Peter Ivanovich, just let *me* tell it.

BOBCHINSKI: No, no. Let me—let me! . . . You don't know the first thing about telling a story—

DOBCHINSKI: Oh, you'll just get mixed up and won't remember anything.

BOBCHINSKI: Oh no, I won't! Now don't interrupt me, damn it! Please, gentlemen, tell Dobchinski to keep quiet!

MAYOR: Well, tell it, for God's sake. My heart's in my mouth. Sit down, gentlemen—take a chair. Here's one for you, Bobchinski. *(They all sit around* BOBCHINSKI *and* DOBCHINSKI.*)*

BOBCHINSKI *(to* MAYOR*)*: . . . As soon as I left you—after you got that letter that worried you so much—I ran right out. . . . Now, please stop trying to interrupt, Dobchinski. I know all the details, I assure you. . . . So, as I was saying, I ran out to see Karobkin. But since he wasn't home, I dashed off to find Rastakovski. And since *he* wasn't home either, I went to see the Postmaster to tell *him* of the news you'd received. Ah yes, and going on from there I ran into Dobchinski—

DOBCHINSKI *(breaking in)*: Near the stall, where they sell cakes—

BOBCHINSKI *(grimly)*: —near the stall where they sell cakes. Well, I meet Dobchinski and I say, "Have you heard the news our Mayor got?" But he had already heard it *(To* MAYOR.*)* from your housekeeper who'd been sent to Philip Antonovich Pachechuyev . . . only I can't remember why—

DOBCHINSKI: You see why I should tell it? *(Triumphantly.)* It was for a bottle of French brandy—

BOBCHINSKI: Oh yes, French brandy—will you stop butting in, Peter Ivanovich? Damn it!—So we both rush off to Pachechuyev's, but on the way Dobchinski says, "Let's stop at the inn. I haven't eaten anything since morning . . . there's such a rumbling inside me!" Yes sir, right in his belly—

JUDGE: Spare us the details!

BOBCHINSKI: "They've just delivered some fresh salmon at the inn," he says. "So we can have a nice snack." Well, we hadn't been inside the inn for a minute when in comes this young fellow—

DOBCHINSKI: Rather good-looking and well-dressed—

BOBCHINSKI *(firmly)*: *Plain*-looking and well-dressed, he walks into the room with such a look on his face—important!—and what style—and a really distinguished forehead, that I had a hunch. I say to Dobchinski, "Aha! There's *something going on here!*" Oh, yes! And Dobchinski calls over Vlas, the innkeeper, you know *(To* MAYOR.*)* three weeks ago his wife presented him with a baby—what a fine, active boy—when he grows older he'll be just like his dad and keep an inn—

MAYOR: We'll all grow old before you come to the point!

BOBCHINSKI: Well, we calls over Vlas, and Dobchinski asks him quietly, "Who," says he, "is that young fellow?" And Vlas answers, "That," says he, "is"—don't interrupt me, Peter Ivanovich! Please! Good God, you can't tell a story, you never could! You just can't speak clearly, you lisp! Yes you do! You've got one tooth in your mouth and that one whistles.

COMMISSIONER OF CHARITIES *(To* DOBCHINSKI*)*: Really? I never noticed that. Let's see—

MAYOR *(about to explode)*: For the love of God—go on!

BOBCHINSKI: Well, Vlas says, "That young fellow is an official" —yes, sir! "who has come from St. Petersburg. And his name," says he, "is Ivan Alexandrovich Hlestakov. And he's on his way," says he, "to the governor of Saratov, and he acts very strange—he's stayed here over two weeks, he doesn't leave the inn and he charges everything! He doesn't pay a single kopek!" When he told me that, it dawned on me at last! And I said to Peter Ivanovich, "Aha!—"

DOBCHINSKI: No, *I* said "Aha!"

BOBCHINSKI: Well, first *you* said it then *I* did. "Aha! Why does he hang around here when he's on the way to Saratov, huh?" Yes sir—that official is the *one!*

MAYOR *(exploding)*: *What* one?

BOBCHINSKI: The official you were warned about—the Inspector General!

MAYOR *(in a panic)*: What are you talking about? It *can't* be!

DOBCHINSKI: It *is!* He won't pay for anything and he doesn't stick his nose outside the inn. What else could he be but an Inspector?

BOBCHINSKI *(exultantly)*: It's him, it's him! Good God! It's him! He sees everything. He noticed that Dobchinski and I were eating salmon—all on account of Dobchinski's stomach, you know—and he snooped right into our plates like this *(Imitating the action.)* Oh, I choked!

MAYOR: May God have mercy on sinners like us! What room is he in?

DOBCHINSKI: Number five, first floor.

BOBCHINSKI *(eagerly)*: That's the same room where the officers had that brawl last year—

MAYOR: How long has he been there?

DOBCHINSKI: Two weeks or more. He came on St. Vasili's—

MAYOR: *Two weeks!* Holy father and saints, save us! He's had time to find out about the sergeant's wife who was flogged! And the prisoners haven't been fed! And people staggering drunk in the streets—and the streets full of filth! What a scandal! *(To* BOBCHINSKI.*)* You say he's a *young* fellow?

BOBCHINSKI: Well, about twenty-three or four.

MAYOR: It'll be easier to feel him out. It's tough when you've got a sly old buzzard to deal with, but a young fellow is more transparent. Now you men run and straighten out your departments, while I go around by myself—or with Dobchinski here—and have a little look *(With a wink.)* to see that visitors to our town are treated with proper consideration. *(He calls to one of the* POLICEMEN.*)* Svistunov!

SVISTUNOV: Yes, sir?

MAYOR: Run to your Superintendent—no, no. I'll need you here. Tell somebody to send him here on the double, and then you come right back. *(*SVISTUNOV *runs out.)*

COMMISSIONER OF CHARITIES *(to* JUDGE*)*: Let's go, let's go. All sorts of devilment may have broken out.

JUDGE: What are *you* afraid of? Cover the patients with some clean gowns and you're clear.

COMMISSIONER OF CHARITIES: Gowns, hell! I had orders from St. Petersburg to give the patients oatmeal porridge. And who snatched the oatmeal? *(He indicates the* MAYOR.*)* So I had to switch to cabbage. Now there's such a stink of cabbage in my corridors, you'd think you were drowning in a tub of borscht!

JUDGE: I don't worry. If the Inspector ever peeps into the pile of documents in my court, he'll be more confused than I am. I've been sitting on that bench for fifteen years and I've never opened a single statement of charges.

(The JUDGE, COMMISSIONER OF CHARITIES, COMMISSIONER OF SCHOOLS *and* POSTMASTER *go out. The* POLICEMAN *bumps violently into them as he dashes in.)*

MAYOR: Well, is the carriage ready?

SVISTUNOV: Yes, sir.

MAYOR: Go into the street—no, stop! go and bring . . . Where are the other men? Didn't I give orders for Prokhorov to come here? Where is he?

SVISTUNOV: Prokhorov is in the police station. He can't go on duty right now.

MAYOR: Why not?

SVISTUNOV: They carried him in this morning, dead drunk. His head's in a bucket of water, but he hasn't sobered up yet.

MAYOR *(tearing his hair)*: Oh, my God! Run to my room fast and get my new hat and sword! (POLICEMAN *runs out.) (To* DOBCHINSKI.*)* Let's be off.

BOBCHINSKI: And me? Me, too! Let me come along.

MAYOR: Oh no, Bobchinski. There's no room in the carriage.

BOBCHINSKI: I don't care. I'll run along behind the carriage. I just want to peep through the door, to see what that Inspector acts like.

*(*POLICEMAN *returns with ceremonial sword and hatbox.)*

MAYOR *(to* POLICEMAN *as he straps on the sword)*: Run and get the street cleaners together. Let each one take a—oh, look how this sword is rusted! That fatbelly shopkeeper Abdulin knows the Mayor's sword is all banged out of shape, but does he supply me with a new one? Oh, no! The stingy crook! *(To* POLICEMAN.*)* I want each of the cleaners to take hold of a street—damn, I mean a broom—and sweep all of the street that leads to the inn. Sweep it clean, do you hear? And you'd better watch out, too. I know your little tricks. You worm your way into my kitchen by fondling the cook, and slip silver spoons into your boots. And how about that shopkeeper

Chornyaiev, hm? He donated two yards of cloth for your uniform, but you stole the entire bolt. Watch yourself! Don't steal any more than your job entitles you to. Get out!

(POLICEMAN *runs out, just as* POLICE SUPERINTENDENT *rushes in. They collide.*)

MAYOR: Where in hell have you been? What kind of invisible Police Superintendent are you?

SUPERINTENDENT: I was just outside the door all the while.

MAYOR: Listen, Ukhavyortov. That spy is here from St. Petersburg. What arrangements have you made?

SUPERINTENDENT: Just as you ordered. I've dispatched the sweepers to clean the streets.

MAYOR: But where is Derzhimorda?

SUPERINTENDENT: Uh, he's driven off with the fire pump. . . .

MAYOR (*betrayed*): But you told me the wheel was broken?

SUPERINTENDENT: He had to see his poor old mother and father.

MAYOR: You idiot! What if there's a fire?

SUPERINTENDENT: Oh, his father is a blacksmith—he'll *fix* the wheel.

MAYOR: I'm surrounded by traitors! . . . Well, here's what you have to do. The police lieutenant—tell him to stand on the bridge. He's tall—that will make a good impression. Then that old fence, near the shoemaker's, I want you to tear it down and scatter the boards around and then put up a pole with a sign on it: NEW STREET UNDER CONSTRUCTION. The more destruction we have, the more it'll show we're building! The best thing would be to tear down the whole damn town! . . . Good God!—I forgot! That fence! There are about forty cartloads of rubbish dumped behind it. . . . What a filthy town this is! No matter where you put a fence or even a monument, somebody always collects rubbish and dumps it there! Where in hell do they find it all? . . . Listen, if the Inspector asks any of my officials if they're satisfied with conditions, they're to say, "Perfectly, your honor." And if anybody is *not* satisfied, I'll give him something to be dissatisfied about! (*Sighs wearily.*) Oh, I'm a sinner, a terrible sinner! (*Takes the hatbox instead of his hat.*) Heaven only grant that I get out of this trap, and I'll give a candle for a thank-offering such as our cathedral has never seen before. Every goddamn merchant in town will donate a hundred pounds of wax for that candle! . . . Oh, God, God! . . . Let's be off, Dobchinski. *(Puts on the hatbox instead of the hat.)*

SUPERINTENDENT: That's not your hat!

MAYOR *(throwing the box down)*: Damn it—I know *that*. . . . And another thing.—If the Inspector asks why the hospital chapel was never built—the money was appropriated five years ago—everybody has to say the building was started all right, but it burned down. Don't you remember? I drew up the report on the fire myself! . . . Come on, come on, Dobchinski. *(He rushes out, and runs back in again.)* And another thing—I don't want those soldiers running around in the streets half-dressed. Those rookies put on their jackets over their shirts, all right, but then they're too lazy to put on their pants! It looks sloppy, damn it!

(All go out. ANNA ANDREYEVNA *and* MARYA ANTONOVNA *hurry in from another door.)*

ANNA: Where are they, where are they? Oh, my goodness! *(Opening another door.)* Husband! Anton! Where are you? *(To* MARYA.*)* It's all your fault, fussing around—"I need a pin, I want a handkerchief!" *(Runs to window and yells out.)* Anton! Where are you going? Has he come—the Inspector? What does he look like? Does he have a mustache?

VOICE OF THE MAYOR: Later, dear—wait a while.

ANNA: What do you mean, wait? I want only one word out of you—is he a general or not? *(Disgusted.)* There you are—he's gone! Oh, he won't get away with *that!* (To MARYA*).* And *you!* Primping and chattering: "Mamma, dear, wait a minute while I pin my scarf: I'll be ready in a moment!" Moment my foot! It's all your fault we've missed this big news. Vanity, sheer vanity! You heard the Postmaster was here, so you had to preen in front of the mirror, and stare at yourself this way and that way. You really think he's sweet on you! Why, you silly girl, he smirks as soon as you turn your back.

MARYA: There's no need to go on screaming, Mamma. We'll get all the details in an hour or so.

ANNA: An *hour* or so! That's a *great* answer!—We'll know it all in a month, you mean. *(She leans out the window.)* Oh, Avdotya dear! . . . Have you heard anything about a stranger

in town, sweetie? . . . No? Well, that shows what a fool you
are. You should have asked. . . . What? They went off in a
hurry? Well, you should have run after the carriage! Go right
now, do you hear? Run and ask everybody you meet—but do
it discreetly—and find out all about him—what sort of eyes he
has, if they're black or what. And come back here right away,
you understand . . . sweetie? *(Aside.)* What a stupid moron!
. . . Hurry up, hurry up!

*(She continues shouting and they both stand at the window as
the scene ends.)*

Scene II

HLESTAKOV'S *tiny room at the inn, furnished with a broken-
down bed, table and chair. A satchel, empty bottles, books,
clothes brush are scattered around the room.*

OSIP *(lounging on his master's bed)*: I'm so hungry there's a
barrage in my belly like a whole battery of cannon! Two
months since we left St. Pete and I'm damned if I see how
we'll ever get back. He threw away all his cash on this trip,
that dumb dog, and now he's stuck here—with his tail between his legs. We had enough to take care of the fare, but oh
no! He has to put on a big show in every town, high-class
style. *(Imitating Hlestakov.)* "Oh, I say, Osip! Engage the
best lodgings they have. And order the most exquisite meal on
the menu. You know, I can't endure anything cheap or shoddy."
The boy's lost his head—he's only a pencil-pusher, fourteenth
rank, in the Civil Service. If they had a fifteenth, he'd be it.
And he picks up pals on the road, and he has to play cards—
and gets gypped, naturally. I'm sick of this crazy life. It was a
lot better in my hick town—not so much going on, but there's
a lot less to worry you. You lay around all day near the stove
and eat hot rolls. . . . Ah, but there's nothing like life in St.
Pete, that's a fact, and I can't kid myself. All you need is
money, and you live like a noble—theaters, dancing dogs, any
little thing you want. And everybody so polite. If you go to
the bazaar, the shopkeepers call you My Lord. . . . Then
some old officer's wife tries to pick you up, or a pretty
chambermaid gives you a wink. Oh, you gay dog! *(Smirks and
wags his head.)* If you're tired of walking, why, you rent a
carriage and ride around like a real gent. And if you don't feel

like paying—every house has an open door; you sneak in one and out the other so fast the devil himself couldn't grab you. Only trouble is, sometimes you eat first-class and sometimes you starve, like now. The old man sends him money—enough to get by—and what happens? He goes on a binge, and in a week I have to sell his new coat. Such beautiful English cloth! Every suit costs him a hundred and fifty rubles, and he lets it go for twenty. All because he never goes to his office! Instead of sticking to his job, he's out following women on the boulevards or he sneaks off to play cards. Oh, if your old man ever finds out! He'll lift your little shirt-tail and spank you so hard you wouldn't sit at a card table for a week. . . . Now the innkeeper says he won't let us have one bone to chew unless that dumb dog pays in advance—and what's going to happen if he *don't* pay? *(With a sigh.)* Oh, Christ, if I only had a little borscht! I'll bet everybody else in this dump is eating except me. . . . Oh, oh! He's coming. . . . *(He jumps off the bed just as* HLESTAKOV *comes in.)*

HLESTAKOV: Here, take these. *(Hands his hat and cane to* OSIP.*)* So you've been rolling around on my bed again?

OSIP: Me? Roll on your bed? What for?

HLESTAKOV: Stop lying. Look how it's all wrinkled.

OSIP: I've got two legs—I can stand on them. What do I need your bed for?

HLESTAKOV *(searching the room)*: Is there any tobacco left?

OSIP: Tobacco? You know you smoked it all four days ago!

HLESTAKOV *(pacing up and down, biting his lip, then loudly and peremptorily)*: Listen, Osip. Are you listening to me?

OSIP: What do you want?

HLESTAKOV *(less sure of himself)*: I want you to go down there . . .

OSIP: Down where?

HLESTAKOV *(almost pleading)*: Down to the dining room. . . . tell them, uh . . . we need some food. . . .

OSIP: Oh, no, I won't.

HLESTAKOV: What? You dare disobey me, you blockhead!

OSIP: You watch who you call a blockhead! . . . What's the

use? . . . if I go down there, they wouldn't serve you nothing. The boss says your food is cut off.

HLESTAKOV: He wouldn't dare say that!

OSIP: Is that so? He said, "I'm going to see the Mayor. This is the third week your master hasn't paid his bill. You're a couple of fakers, and what's more—your master is a good-for-nothing bum!" That's what he said.

HLESTAKOV: You don't have to look so happy about it!

OSIP: That's not all. He said, "Yah, I know that kind. They come around here, make themselves at home, run up a big bill and then I can't collect. I'm not kidding," he says. "I'm going to sign a complaint and have him thrown right into jail."

HLESTAKOV: Now stop talking like a fool. Just go and speak to the proprietor nicely—that foul-mouth pig!

OSIP: Maybe I oughtta call him and let *you* talk.

HLESTAKOV: I wouldn't talk to him! You go—you understand him. . . .

OSIP *(innocently)*: But I wouldn't know what to say.

HLESTAKOV: Oh, damn it! Call him—see if I care!

(OSIP *shuffles out.*)

HLESTAKOV: I'm starving to death! I'll just lie down and die. I took a little walk to take my mind off my appetite, but it's worse now. My stomach's full of flapping vultures! . . . That infantry captain in Penza certainly cleaned me out! Didn't take him more than fifteen minutes to pluck me like a chicken. I wish I could take him on again—with *my* cards. But I suppose I never will now. . . . What a beastly little town this is! They won't give you any food on credit. (*He whistles an incomprehensible tune.*) The innkeeper will never come. Nobody wants to climb all the way up here.

(OSIP *and a sullen* WAITER *enter.*)

WAITER: Boss wants to know what's on your mind.

HLESTAKOV: Ah, good day, my friend. And how are you? How's business? Doing nicely?

WAITER: Very nice.

HLESTAKOV: Plenty of guests?

WAITER: We got enough.

HLESTAKOV: Look here, my friend. My dinner hasn't been sent up yet, so would you please hurry it? I have an important engagement immediately after dinner.

WAITER: Boss says you don't get no more service. He was going to see the Mayor today with a complaint.

HLESTAKOV: A complaint? About *me?* Whatever for? . . . Now, my good fellow, if this dreadful service continues, I shall dissolve into a skeleton. I'm not joking any more with your boss. . . .

WAITER: He ain't jokin' either. Boss says, "No dinner till he coughs up for what he swallowed already."

HLESTAKOV: Tell him it's a matter of life or death! He seems to think that because he's a peasant who can go all day without food—everybody can. That sort of thinking will ruin his business.

(WAITER *shrugs and goes out with* OSIP)

HLESTAKOV: What a way to die—by slow starvation! I can feel the wings of the angel of death hovering over me! Wonder if I could pawn my pants? . . . No, I'd rather starve than come home without style. . . . I really ought to drive into St. Petersburg in an elegant hired rig, with the carriage lamps glowing and Osip behind, in livery. Oh, how the society belles will flutter with excitement! "Who's *that?* How handsome!" Then my footman goes up in his gold livery (*Draws himself up to imitate him.*) and announces, "Ivan Alexandrovich Hlestakov!" And then I glide up to the prettiest girl and murmur, "How charmed I am, my dear. *Charmant!*" (*Bows as if kissing a hand, then catches at his stomach.*) Oh, my God! I'm sick! I'm really going to die!

(OSIP *enters happily, followed by the* WAITER)

HLESTAKOV (*to* OSIP): I forbid you to be so damned cheerful!

OSIP: He got your dinner.

HLESTAKOV (*claps his hands and sits quickly in his chair*): Aha! Dinner! Dinner! Haha!

WAITER (*with plates and a napkin*): This is the last time the boss is feeding you.

HLESTAKOV: The boss? My good fellow, I spit on your boss! Now, what have you brought me?

WAITER: Soup and roast beef.

HLESTAKOV: Only two courses?

WAITER: That's all.

HLESTAKOV: I won't put up with it! What does he mean by this? It's not enough.

WAITER: Boss says it's too much.

HLESTAKOV: But there isn't even a sauce!

WAITER: That's right.

HLESTAKOV: No cutlets—no salmon?

WAITER: No pay—no salmon.

HLESTAKOV (*tastes the soup*): Do you call that chicken soup? They just poured lukewarm water in a pot and let a chicken walk through with boots on! Bring some other soup!

WAITER: All right, I'll take it away. Boss says, if you don't like it, you can lump it.

HLESTAKOV (*holding on to his plate*): If that's his attitude, I'll show him. I reject his insults! I'll eat this soup! And *you!* You may be a smart-aleck with other guests but don't try it on me. (*Swallowing soup hungrily.*) My God! what slop! Here are some feathers floating around! (*Comes across a tiny bit of chicken.*) Well, well!—a piece of chicken! That poor bird must have slipped. . . . Hand me the roast beef. There's some soup left, Osip. Possibly you can stomach it. (*Cuts the meat.*) Is *that* what you call roast beef?

WAITER: Yeh. What do you think it is?

HLESTAKOV: It's more like cold armor plate. (*Eats.*) Crooks and scoundrels! The slop they dish out! Why, one mouthful is enough to make my jaw ache. (*Picks his teeth with his finger.*) Can't get it out—it's like iron filings! (*Wipes mouth with napkin.*) What else do you have?

WAITER: That's all.

HLESTAKOV: There should have been some pastry! So this is how you fleece your guests! Robber!

(WAITER *removes the dishes and goes out, followed by* OSIP.)

HLESTAKOV: I swear, I feel as if I hadn't eaten at all: it only sharpened my appetite. If only I had a few kopeks I'd send out for a roll.

OSIP *(returning)*: The Mayor just showed up—I can't figure why—
and he's asking about you.

HLESTAKOV *(alarmed): What?* There you are! That louse of an
innkeeper has gone and turned me in! . . . What if they really
haul me off to jail? I'll go—but with elegant style . . . like a
French aristocrat, standing erect in the tumbril as he goes to
the guillotine? . . . Oh, no! I couldn't. I've already caught the
eye of a rich man's daughter—it would ruin the match. . . .
Who in hell does that innkeeper think he is? He's got a lot of
nerve treating me as if I were some shopkeeper or ditch-
digger. *(Draws himself up to his full height.)* I'll just stand up
to him and say, "How dare you try—"

(The door handle is rattled. HLESTAKOV *pales; his courage
collapses. The* MAYOR *and* DOBCHINSKI *enter, the* MAYOR *leading. The* MAYOR *fumbles with his hat and stares from* DOBCHINSKI
to HLESTAKOV, *afraid to begin.)*

MAYOR *(gathering his courage, stands at attention)*: I hope you
are well, sir.

HLESTAKOV *(bowing)*: How do you do, sir.

MAYOR: Excuse the intrusion . . .

HLESTAKOV: Oh, don't mention it . . .

MAYOR: It is my duty, as chief magistrate of this town, to take
proper measures to see that travelers and important persons
don't suffer any inconvenience . . .

HLESTAKOV *(warily at first but gathering confidence as he goes
along)*: Well, what was I to do? . . . It's not *my fault* . . . I
assure you, I am . . . going to pay . . . I'm about to receive a
remittance from home. (BOBCHINSKI *peeps in through open
door.) He's* the one to blame! He sends me beef as stiff as cast
iron! And the soup! I had to pour it out the window. . . . And
the tea is most peculiar—it stinks of fish. And the fish has the
consistency of tea! . . .

MAYOR *(nervously)*: I assure you it was not my fault! Our town
market receives the best beef. I'm sure I don't know where the
innkeeper gets his meat. But if anything's unsatisfactory, please
come with me and we'll find better quarters.

HLESTAKOV: Oh, no I won't! I know exactly what "better quarters" means. It's another word for jail! . . . And what right
have you? . . . How dare you? Why, I'm a government official from St. Petersburg. *(Defiantly.)* Yes, I am! I—I—

MAYOR (*aside*): Oh, my God! How angry he is! He knows everything! Those pig shopkeepers must have squealed!

HLESTAKOV (*aggressively, snaps his fingers*): That's for you and your whole gang! I will not go with you. I will go straight to the Prime Minister! (*Bangs fist on table.*) What do you say to that?

MAYOR (*quivering all over*): Take pity on me! I have a wife and small children! Don't ruin me!

HLESTAKOV: Do you expect me to go to Siberia just because you have a wife and small children? Oh, I like that—that's just lovely! (BOBCHINSKI *peeps in again, then disappears in terror.*) Oh no—thank you very much, but I will not budge!

MAYOR (*quaking*): It was just my inexperience—so help me! —just my inexperience . . . and inadequate funds. Judge for yourself—the salary I get is hardly enough for tea and sugar. And if I've taken any, ah . . . contributions, they were *tiny* ones—something for the table, or possibly a coat—a *short* coat. As for that sergeant's wife they say I had flogged—she was whoring without a permit. But it's all a lie anyhow—she never was flogged. My enemies made that up! They're just waiting to murder me in cold blood.

HLESTAKOV (*bewildered*): I don't know why you're rattling on about your enemies or your affair with that sergeant's widow. . . . But don't you dare try to flog *me!* I'll pay—I'll pay the bill. But at the moment I'm strapped for cash. Yes—that's the only reason I'm staying here—I find myself temporarily short of funds.

MAYOR (*aside, relieved*): What a sly operator! I don't know where to start working on him. Well, it won't hurt to make a wild stab. . . . (*Aloud.*) Ah, my friend, if you're so short of cash, allow me to help you out—immediately. It's . . . ah, my civic duty to assist gentlemen travelers.

HLESTAKOV (*eagerly*): Then lend me—oh, a pittance—just enough to settle with my host. I'll need two hundred rubles, more or less.

(*The* MAYOR *immediately presses a wad of bills into his hand.*)

MAYOR: Exactly two hundred. You don't even have to count it.

HLESTAKOV: I'm very obliged to you! I'll return it as soon as I arrive at my country house. . . . Just a case of stupidity on the part of my financial secretary. You are, indeed, a great gentleman. Everything's quite satisfactory now.

MAYOR (*aside*): Well, thank God, he took the money. I guess now it'll all be smoothed over . . . but maybe I was a little too eager to slip him four hundred instead of two. . . .

HLESTAKOV: Say, Osip! *(OSIP enters.)* Call the waiter. *(To MAYOR and DOBCHINSKI.)* But why are you still standing? Please, take a seat.

MAYOR: Oh, no . . . we'll just stand.

HLESTAKOV: Please, please be seated. I see now your utter generosity and sincerity. I must confess I thought when you first came in you intended to— *(To DOBCHINSKI.)* Take a chair—I insist!

(MAYOR and DOBCHINSKI finally sit down. BOBCHINSKI looks in at the door and listens.)

MAYOR *(aside)*: He wants to keep his incognito. All right. *(Aloud.)* I was just going around inspecting, with Peter Dobchinski— he's a landowner here—and we stopped at this inn to see how travelers are treated. I'm not like other mayors who don't pay attention to these important details. But aside from that, out of pure Christian charity, I want every human being to be well treated. And you see? . . . as a reward for doing good, I have the opportunity to make such a pleasant acquaintance!

HLESTAKOV: I'm delighted, too. Without your kind help, I must confess, I might have been trapped here for days. I hadn't the foggiest notion of how I would raise the cash.

MAYOR *(aside)*: Listen to that! Didn't know how he was going to pay! Ha! *(Aloud.)* May I ask where you are going from here?

HLESTAKOV: I am on my way to Saratov province, to my own estate.

MAYOR *(aside, with deep irony)*: To Saratov province! Oh, I'll bet you are! And he doesn't even blush. You have to keep a sharp eye on this fellow. *(Aloud.)* I'm sure you'll enjoy the trip. It's a most pleasant way to stretch your mind. You're traveling for your own amusement, I suppose?

HLESTAKOV: Oh no, it's my father's idea. The old man is mad because, so far, I haven't climbed very high in the civil service. He thinks that the minute you get to St. Petersburg, they hang a medal on you. I'd like to send *him* there, see how fast he gets shoved around in a government office.

MAYOR *(aside)*: Just listen to that fairy tale—and he has to drag in his old father, too. *(Aloud.)* May I ask, are you going to stay there for a while?

HLESTAKOV: I really don't know. You see, the old man is as stubborn as a chunk of wood. I intend to make it quite clear: "You can do as you please, Father, but I absolutely cannot live away from St. Petersburg!" Why should I receive a life sentence to rot away among the yokels? That's not *living*—my soul demands the civilized world.

MAYOR *(aside)*: This fellow is a virtuoso—he's the *liar's* liar! But he's sure to make a little slip. I'll just give him more rope. . . . *(To* HLESTAKOV.*)* You're right—my friend. What can any man with brains accomplish in a provincial town? You work and sweat for the good of your country, you lie awake at night *thinking*, and what reward do you get?—complete misunderstanding! *(Looks about the room.)* Rather damp here, isn't it?

HLESTAKOV: Yes, it is a shabby hole. And the bugs! I've never seen anything like them—they bite like dogs.

MAYOR: Oh, no! Tsk, tsk. What a way to treat a distinguished visitor! To welcome him with disgusting insects, that shouldn't even be alive! And I suppose this room is dark, too?

HLESTAKOV: The innkeeper has a quaint custom of refusing me candles. Now and then I want to read—or work on my novel— but, oh what a bore—it's dark as a well-hole.

MAYOR: I wonder if I could ask you—oh, no! I'm not worth it. . . .

HLESTAKOV: What do you mean?

MAYOR: No, no. I don't deserve the honor. . . .

HLESTAKOV: What honor?

MAYOR: I hope you won't think I'm being presumptuous but . . . I have a charming little room at home you might like . . . comfortable and full of light . . . but it's too great an honor. Don't be offended, sir—I only wanted to help. . . .

HLESTAKOV: Why, of course! I'll accept with pleasure. I know I'll be much more comfortable in a private home than in this pest house.

MAYOR: Oh, thank you, bless you! My wife will be delighted. It's a little failing I have—I always was hospitable, even when I was a child. Especially when my guest is so distinguished and civilized. And don't think I say this just to butter you up. Oh no—I don't have *that* vice. I welcome you from the bottom of my heart.

HLESTAKOV: Thank you so much. I hate two-faced people. I'm impressed with your plain speaking and generosity, and I assure you I don't expect much. All I ask is to be treated with consideration and . . . a bit of respect. Yes, that's all—a bit of respect.

(Enter the WAITER, escorted by OSIP. BOBCHINSKI peeps in again.)

WAITER: What d'you want?

HLESTAKOV: The bill.

WAITER: I gave you a bill.

HLESTAKOV: Oh, I can't remember your idiotic figures! Just tell me the total. *(Brings out the wad of bills the MAYOR gave him.)*

MAYOR: Don't let it upset you. *(To WAITER.)* Get out! The money will be sent to you.

HLESTAKOV: That's the way to handle 'em. Yes, you're quite right! *(He puts the bills back in his pocket. The WAITER goes out. BOBCHINSKI looks in again.)*

MAYOR: Would you like to inspect a few of our town's high spots? Such as the hospital?

HLESTAKOV: Hospital? What would I see there?

MAYOR: You'll see how we manage things . . . our smooth system.

HLESTAKOV: Oh, certainly, certainly . . . *(BOBCHINSKI puts his head in again.)*

MAYOR: Afterward you might like to look in at the town jail—

HLESTAKOV *(uneasy)*: The jail? Why go there?

MAYOR: To see how we take good care of criminals.

HLESTAKOV: No, let's just look into the hospital.

MAYOR: Whatever you wish. Do you prefer to ride in your carriage—or in mine?

HLESTAKOV: In yours, by all means.

MAYOR *(to DOBCHINSKI)*: I'm afraid there's no room for you.

DOBCHINSKI: Oh, I can squeeze in.

MAYOR (*aside to* DOBCHINSKI): Listen, I want you to run as fast as you can with a couple of notes—to the hospital and my wife. (*To* HLESTAKOV.) Do you mind if I send a word to my wife now, so that she can prepare to receive her honored guest?

HLESTAKOV: But why all this fuss? . . . There's the ink. I don't know about paper, though . . . (*Looks around room.*) How about this bill? (*Hands him the paper previously left by the* WAITER.)

MAYOR: That's just the thing! (*Talks to himself as he writes.*) We'll see how things go after lunch and a nice fat bottle or two. We'll have some local wine—not much to look at but it can roll a mule under the table. Then maybe I'll find out who he really is—and how much he knows.

(*He hands the notes to* DOBCHINSKI, *who runs to the door just as it suddenly breaks off its hinges.* BOBCHINSKI, *who has been eavesdropping behind it, falls on the floor atop the door, his arms outstretched. Cries of surprise.* BOBCHINSKI *slowly picks himself up.*)

HLESTAKOV: What's this? Are you hurt?

BOBCHINSKI: Oh, nothing, nothing, sir. Nothing to worry about— just a little crack on the nose. (*Smiles wanly.*) I'll run over to Doctor Hubner—he has some special plaster. I'll live.

MAYOR (*gesturing angrily to* BOBCHINSKI *as he talks to* HLESTAKOV): Oh, it doesn't matter, sir. If you're ready, let's be off. Your man can bring your bags over. (*To* OSIP.) Take everything over to my house—the Mayor's. Just ask anybody—they'll show you. (*He makes way for* HLESTAKOV.) After you, sir, after you. (*As soon as* HLESTAKOV *exits, he turns angrily on* BOBCHINSKI.) You muttonhead! Did you have to break down the door? What if you had landed on the Inspector? . . . Oh, God help me—I'm surrounded by assassins!

(*He pushes* BOBCHINSKI *out ahead of him.*)

Scene III

ANNA *and* MARYA *are standing at the window in the Mayor's house, in the same position as at the end of Scene I.*

ANNA: We've been waiting a whole hour, all because of your stupid vanity! You were all dressed but still you had to dawdle around. . . . Oh, dear! And what's become of Avdotya? I send her on an important mission and she's probably gossiping in the square. How exasperating! . . . Not a soul in sight. It looks as if the whole town has been hit by a plague.

MARYA: Now, now, Mamma. We'll know all about it in a minute or two. Avdotya *has* to come back. *(Looks out window and squeals.)* Oh, Mamma, Mamma! See! Someone is coming—way down there at the end of the street!

ANNA: Who's coming? Where? You're always seeing things! . . . Ah, yes . . . Now, who can it be? He's short—in a dress coat. How frustrating? Who the devil is it?

MARYA: It's Dobchinski, Mamma.

ANNA: Dobchinski? Another one of your wild visions! It certainly is *not* Dobchinski. *(Waves her handkerchief.)* I say there—you! Come here—quick.

MARYA: Mamma, it really *is* Dobchinski.

ANNA: Must you contradict me every time? I've told you, it is *not* Dobchinski!

MARYA: Mamma, can't you see? It *is* Dobchinski.

ANNA: Oh, so it is . . . but why did you have to argue about it? *(Shouts out the window.)* Hurry up! My, how slow you walk! Well, where are they? You can tell me from where you are. What? Has he been tough? Eh? . . . *(Moves away from the window, disgusted.)* What a pretentious creature! He won't say a word till he comes in! (DOBCHINSKI *runs in, breathless.*) Now, aren't you ashamed of yourself? I used to think you were the only one in the group who's a gentleman. Then they all dash off—and *you* after them. I've been marooned here for ages, without a soul to tell me what's going on! You've been just horrid. I was godmother to your little Ivan and Lisa, and this is the way you repay me!

DOBCHINSKI: I swear, dear lady. I ran so fast to pay my respects that I'm all out of breath. *(He takes a deep breath and bows formally.)* I have the honor to greet you, Marya Antonovna.

MARYA: Good afternoon to you, Peter Ivanovich.

ANNA: Tell me, tell me! What's happened?

DOBCHINSKI: Your husband sent this note.

ANNA: But what is he—a general?

DOBCHINSKI: Not quite—but just as important. What manners—what dignity!

ANNA: That's just what Chmikov's letter to my husband said.

DOBCHINSKI: Exactly. And, remember, Bobchinski and I were the first to spot him.

ANNA: Good for you. Now tell me about it.

DOBCHINSKI: I will . . . God help us, everything's smoothed out now. At first he was really rough with your husband. Believe me, madame, he was *angry*. He said the inn was shabby and he wouldn't go to your house, either, and then he swore he wouldn't go to Siberia for your husband. But when he found out how innocent your husband was, he changed his mind and then, thank God, everything went well. They're out inspecting the hospital now. . . . I have to admit your husband thought a secret complaint had been filed against him. I was a little scared myself.

ANNA: You're not an official. Why should you be scared?

DOBCHINSKI: That's how I am—sympathetic.

ANNA: Well, the most important thing is—what does he look like? Is he young or old?

DOBCHINSKI: Oh, young. Very young—about twenty-three. But he speaks like a mature man of the world. "All I ask," he says, "is to be treated with a little respect." *(Gesticulating.)* All this with a most aristocratic poise. "Now and then I like to read—or work on my novel, but oh, what a bore," he says, "my room is as dark as a well-hole!" (MARYA *gasps.)*

ANNA: But what does he *look* like—dark or fair?

DOBCHINSKI: Sort of in between. His eyes flash like a wild beast's—they made me jittery.

ANNA: Hm . . . let's see what Anton's note says. *(She reads.)* "I want you to know, dear, that I was in a tight hole, but relying on the mercy of God, two pickles on the side and a half portion of caviar—one ruble twenty-five kopeks—" *(Baffled.)* What the devil is he babbling about—God and pickles . . .?

DOBCHINSKI: Anton wrote it on the back of the waiter's bill.

ANNA: Lately he doesn't make sense, either. . . . *(Reads on.)* "But relying on the mercy of God . . . it's all right now. Get a room ready right away—the one with the gold wallpaper—for our distinguished guest. Don't bother to lay out anything extra for dinner; we'll have lunch at the hospital with Artemi Philippovich. But order some domestic wine. Tell Abdulin to send his best or I'll smash his whole cellar. I kiss your hand, my dear, and so on." Oh, my God! Not a minute to lose! *(She calls.)* Mishka!

DOBCHINSKI: *(runs to door and shouts).* Mishka! Hey, Mishka!

(The boy MISHKA shuffles in.)

ANNA: Now, listen. Run over to Abdulin's. Wait, I'll give you a note. *(Writes and talks at the same time.)* Give this note to the coachman; he's to run with it to Abdulin's and pick up the wine. Then you come right back and get the gold room ready for our guest. Put in a bed, washstand, and everything. And don't forget to sweep off the mattress.

DOBCHINSKI: Well, I'll run along and see how the inspection is coming.

ANNA: Yes, by all means. *(DOBCHINSKI goes out.)* Now, Marya, we have to figure out our ensembles. He's a young dandy from the capital; we don't want to look small-townish, God forbid. So you'd better put on your blue dress with the little flounces.

MARYA *(exasperated)*: Oh, no, Mamma! The *blue?* I hate it! Old Lady Lyapkin-Tyapkin wears blue, and so does Zemlyanika's daughter. I want to put on my light pink.

ANNA: Your light pink? You're just trying to start an argument again! You'll look much better in blue because I intend to wear my best shade—buttercup yellow.

MARYA: Oh, Mamma, buttercup doesn't do anything for you at all!

ANNA *(temper rising)*: My buttercup doesn't do anything?

MARYA: It won't be right. Your eyes would have to be very dark to go with buttercup.

ANNA: How do you like *that!* Do you mean to say my eyes are *not* dark? They're dark enough for all normal purposes! How can they help not being dark? When I tell fortunes with cards, don't I always draw the queen of *clubs?*

MARYA: I don't care. Your best color is the queen of *hearts*.

ANNA: Oh, pishtosh! I never was a queen of hearts! *(They go out, but she can still be heard offstage.)* Queen of hearts! Where do you get those stupid ideas? Certainly not from your mother. . . .

(As they go out, the door of side room opens and MISHKA *appears, sweeping the dust. He sweeps it right into the face of* OSIP *who enters at center, carrying bags on his head.)*

OSIP *(angrily)*: Where's this go?

MISHKA: Here, Pop—this way. *(But he doesn't help with bags.)*

OSIP: Don't call me Pop. Hold it—let me catch my breath. What a lousy life . . . on an empty stomach, every load feels like your own coffin.

MISHKA: Say, Pop—is the general coming soon?

OSIP: What general?

MISHKA: Your boss.

OSIP: My boss is a general? *(He bellows with laughter.)*

MISHKA: Ain't he a general?

OSIP: Oh, sure.

MISHKA: Is he higher or lower than Inspector General?

OSIP: He's both.

MISHKA: No wonder the old lady's raising hell today.

OSIP: I can see you're a real smart kid. How about slipping me something to eat?

MISHKA: For a bigshot like you, Pop, nothin's ready that's good enough. You wouldn't want the plain food. When your boss sits down at the table, they'll toss you a bone.

OSIP *(restraining himself)*: Just tell me what that plain food is.

MISHKA: Borscht, kasha and meat pies.

OSIP: I'll take the borscht, kasha and meat pies. Now give me a hand with the bags.

MISHKA *(blankly)*: Huh?

OSIP *(with a* HLESTAKOV *gesture)*: I'll take care of you later, my boy. *(They carry the bags into the side room.)*

(Both doors of the entrance are pushed open by the two POLICE-MEN. HLESTAKOV *enters. After him come the* MAYOR, COMMIS-

SIONER OF CHARITIES, COMMISSIONER OF SCHOOLS, *and* BOBCHINSKI *with a plaster on his nose. The* MAYOR *angrily indicates a scrap of paper on the floor to the* POLICEMEN. *They rush about to pick it up and bump into each other.)*

HLESTAKOV: Splendid institutions in this town. I'm charmed by the way you show strangers everything! In other places they didn't show me a single thing.

MAYOR: In other towns—if I may say so—the administrators and officials are only concerned with their own advancement. But here, I must admit, there is only one rule—to win the recognition of St. Petersburg by good order and vigilance.

HLESTAKOV: That was indeed a gourmet lunch. I'm afraid I may have overeaten a bit. Do you have a banquet like that every day?

MAYOR: Oh, no. It was in honor of our lovable guest.

HLESTAKOV: I certainly enjoyed that lunch. What does any man live for but to pluck the flowers of pleasure! . . . What was that fish called?

COMMISSIONER OF CHARITIES: *(stepping forward)*: Salted cod.

HLESTAKOV: It was exquisite! And where did we lunch—in the hospital?

COMMISSIONER OF CHARITIES: Exactly right, sir. In one of our sick rooms.

HLESTAKOV: Oh, of course. I remember—there were beds. But where were the patients? I didn't see many.

COMMISSIONER OF CHARITIES: Oh, about ten—no more. The rest have all recovered. You see, the hospital is so well organized it operates almost by itself. . . . It may seem incredible to you, sir, but ever since I became Commissioner, the sick recover like . . . flies. We carry the patients in and—as soon as they see the sick ward, they're well again.

MAYOR: And I'd like to point out what a nightmare job the Mayor has. Every problem that comes to him has so many ramifications, such as sanitation and repairs and street improvements. It's just one sewer after another . . . even a man of superhuman knowledge could get into the most hopeless snarl. But, God be thanked, everything here operates smoothly. Other mayors, I'm sure, are only lining their own pockets with graft. But, believe me, when I lie down to sleep, my only prayer is: "O Lord, my God, please grant that the Government will see my zeal and be satisfied!" They may not reward me—that's up to them, of course—but, my conscience is clear. When there's law and order all through the town, when the streets are swept spotless, and the jailbirds are safely locked up, when you can count the drunkards on one hand—what more can I ask? I don't want any medals. They are alluring, I'm sure, but to the upright man they are as dust!

COMMISSIONER OF CHARITIES *(aside)*: Listen to that old crook pour it on! It's a gift from heaven. . . .

HLESTAKOV *(awed)*: How true. I don't mind saying I also have a bent for philosophy. Sometimes it's in prose—and sometimes I toss off verses.

BOBCHINSKI *(to* DOBCHINSKI*)*: Did you hear that? How very well that was put.

DOBCHINSKI: What insight! Oh, you can see he's been to the university.

HLESTAKOV: Oh, I say—do you have any amusements here? Places where, for instance, one could relax with a spot of cards?

MAYOR *(aside)*: Ah, my little pigeon . . . I can see where you're aiming. . . . *(Aloud.)* Heaven forbid! Why, we've never heard of a card club here. I've never dealt a hand of cards in my life . . . I can't even stand to *look* at cards! Why, if I ever happen to see a king of diamonds or something like that—in someone's house—I'm overcome by such a feeling of disgust, I have to spit! *(Shudders.)* I remember one time, just to please the children, I built them a little house of cards. And, do you know what? All night those cursed images made me toss and groan in my sleep!

COMMISSIONER OF SCHOOLS *(aside)*: Why, that sharper took me for a hundred at faro yesterday!

HLESTAKOV: Oh, we mustn't sneer at cards—actually they're like a mathematics exercise.

*(*ANNA *and* MARYA *bustle in.)*

MAYOR: May I take the liberty of introducing my wife and daughter?

HLESTAKOV *(bowing to each)*: How fortunate I am, madame, to have this pleasure of meeting you.

ANNA: Meeting such a distinguished person is a far greater pleasure for *us*.

HLESTAKOV *(with a gallant gesture)*: Oh, no. I insist—the pleasure is much more mine.

ANNA: Oh, impossible, sir. You're just saying that to be gallant. It's my pleasure! Please, do sit down.

HLESTAKOV: To stand near you is happiness enough. However, if you insist, I will sit. What a lucky man I am to sit by your side!

ANNA: Oh, sir. I don't dare take that as anything more than big-city flattery. . . . I suppose you've found traveling quite unpleasant after the gay life of the capital?

HLESTAKOV: Terribly. After being accustomed, *comprenez-vous*, to high society, to find myself thrust into filthy inns, in the depths of barbarism . . . I must admit, if it weren't for the luck . . . *(Stares meaningfully at* ANNA.*)* which repays me for all that—

ANNA: How dreadfully unpleasant it must have been!

HLESTAKOV: Oh, but madame, right now I find it quite pleasant.

ANNA: Oh, sir, you do me too much honor. I don't deserve it.

HLESTAKOV: Why not? If I say it, you deserve it.

ANNA: Even if I only live in . . . barbarian country?

HLESTAKOV: Oh, the country has its own charm—hills and dales, you know. Of course, you simply can't compare it to St. Petersburg. Ah, Petersburg—what a life! You might think I'm just a minor cog there but, on the contrary—I'm on the friendliest terms with the chief of my department. Why, he slaps me on the back and says, "Come on, let's have lunch, my friend!" I look into the place only a few minutes now and then, just to give a few orders, "Do it this way—phrase it that way . . ." And then my clerk—what a mouse he is!—scribbles away for dear life. *(He imitates a pen scratching paper.)* Why, they even wanted to make me an assistant bureau chief—it's quite obvious I'm the fair-haired boy. And the porter runs after me on the stairs with a brush: "Oh, allow me, sir, to shine your boots." *(To* MAYOR.*)* But why do you stand, gentlemen? Please, sit down.

MAYOR: Oh, we don't rank that high—we'll stand.

COMMISSIONER OF CHARITIES: I'd feel better standing . . .

COMMISSIONER OF SCHOOLS: Oh, don't worry about us!

HLESTAKOV: No ceremony! I insist—sit down! *(They sit slowly.)* I don't like protocol. On the contrary, I always try to avoid stiff state functions. But it's impossible to hide oneself. Quite impossible. No matter where I go, they call out, "There goes

Ivan Alexandrovich!'' Once they even took me for the Commander in Chief. All the soldiers rushed out of the guardhouse and saluted! Yes, sir, one officer, whom I knew very well, said to me afterward, ''I could have sworn you were the Commander in Chief.''

ANNA: You don't say!

HLESTAKOV: I'm quite close to most of the pretty, up-and-coming actresses—you see, I write all sorts of sketches for the stage. I'm on the inner circle of the literary set. Why, Pushkin and I are old pals. I often say to him, ''Well, how's it going, Pushkin, old boy?'' Oh, he's a rare bird, that one.

ANNA: You *write*, too? How delightful! Do you write for the papers?

HLESTAKOV: Oh, I toss off some things for them, too. I write in so many fields . . . operas—*Marriage of Figaro . . . Robert the Devil . . . Norma*—and some others I've forgotten about. I somehow fell into it. I didn't want to fool around with the stage, but a manager I knew kept bothering me, ''Come on, write something for me, old boy!'' So I thought, ''Why not?'' I dashed off *Figaro* in one day. Or was it two? . . . Oh, I have a prolific flow of ideas. I also work under the name of Baron Brambeus for the Moscow *Telegraph*—

ANNA: So *you're* Brambeus!

HLESTAKOV: Of course. And you know that sensational novel, *The Frigate of Hope?* It came out under the pseudonym Marlinski. That was me—I mean, I. As for most of the top-rank poets—why, Smirdin, the publisher, pays me forty thousand a year to polish their stuff.

ANNA: Then *you* must have written *Yuri Miroslavski.*

HLESTAKOV: One of my minor efforts.

ANNA: I knew it right away!

MARYA: But Mamma, it says on the title page the author is Zagoskin.

ANNA: There you go again—trying to start an argument . . .

HLESTAKOV: That's true. There is a *Yuri Miroslavski* by a Zagoskin. He stole my title.

ANNA: I'm sure I read *yours.* What lovely writing.

HLESTAKOV: My salon is the most exquisite and famous in St. Petersburg. Everyone tries to crash it. Because of my cutting wit, I'm called . . . Ivan the Terrible! *(Suddenly, to the group.)* If any of you ever visit St. Petersburg, you must be sure to visit me. I insist on it . . . I give lavish fancy dress balls, too.

ANNA: I can imagine the good taste and magnificence!

HLESTAKOV: Really impossible to describe. The centerpiece, for example, is a watermelon made into a fountain, with bubbling watermelon juice! It sets me back seven hundred rubles. The soup comes straight from Paris by steamer in my own tureen. Oh, there's nothing in the world to compare with the aroma! I'm forced to go out in the social whirl every evening. And we have our whist club . . . the Foreign Minister . . . the French Ambassador . . . the German Ambassador, myself. Oh, it can be an exhausting bore. They insist on fighting duels with me because of their poor luck . . . and so the government has to put up with a constant flow of new ambassadors. . . . Most nights, it's all I can do to stagger home, and up four flights of stairs, and murmur, "Here, Mavrusha, take my coat before I expire!" Did I say fourth floor? I live on the first floor, of course. . . . You see, I'm still in a daze from my harsh travels. Why, that staircase alone cost me—it's simply priceless! It's studded with my coat of arms in precious stones. . . . And you really ought to see my waiting room: counts and princes jostling and hovering around there like bees. All you can hear is buzz, buzz, buzz. Why, once the Prime Minister was there! . . . *(The* MAYOR *and others rise out of their chairs, alarmed.)* Why, one time I took charge of an entire Department. That was an amusing story. The Director had gone off somewhere—disappeared—nobody knew where. Naturally, people began to whisper: how could his job be filled? Who would be the unlucky man? I say unlucky, because any number of generals tried it and flopped. It looked easy enough, but when they got right down to it, it was fiendishly complicated. The upshot was—I was the government's last resort. They had to come to *me.* Instantly the streets were choked with messengers, and messengers and more messengers! How's that for a crisis? "Ivan Alexandrovich," they begged me, "you must come and take over the Department!" I admit, I was a little hesitant. I went out to address them in my dressing gown, and I was all set to refuse, but then it occurred to me: what if the Emperor hears of this? And it won't look good on my service record, either. "Very well!" I said. "I'll *take* the job. I'll accept. But, remember—no nonsense from anybody! You'll have to be sharp! Sharp's my motto—sharp!" And that's the way it was. Every time I inspected the Department, it was like an earthquake: they all shivered and shook like aspen leaves. *(The* MAYOR *and others quake with terror.* HLESTAKOV *is transported by his own vehemence.)* Oh, I don't fool around with them, I tell you! I give those clowns hell! Even the Imperial Council is afraid of me. And why shouldn't they be? I am Ivan the Terrible! I don't attack any one man—I slash them all! I say, "Nobody can stop me! Nobody! I know my duty! I know my power!" My eyes are everywhere—*every*where! Every day I visit the Palace. Why, if I wanted it, they would make me a field marshal tomorrow— *(He slips off his chair and sprawls on the floor. The officials respectfully help him up.)*

MAYOR *(trembling all over)*: But your ex-ex— *(He chokes with fear.)*

HLESTAKOV *(sharply)*: What's the matter with you?

MAYOR: Your ex-ex—

HLESTAKOV: I can't understand a word you say. Don't talk nonsense.

MAYOR: Your Excellency . . . Your Highness. Wouldn't you like to take a little . . . rest? Your room is ready and—

HLESTAKOV: Rest? How dare you intimate I am drunk! *(He draws himself up erect.)* Your lunch, gentlemen, was excellent. I am delighted. *(He gives a stiff military salute.)* To salted cod! It was cod! Cod by God!

(He bows low to the ladies and collapses. But OSIP *is waiting right behind him, and catches him under the arms before he reaches the floor.)*

ALL *(in despair and surprise)*: Oh, heaven help us now! . . . Is he poisoned? . . . We are all destroyed! . . . Who got him drunk? . . . Anton! It's all Anton's doing! Anton made him sick. . . .

(All eyes turn to the MAYOR *and there is a moment of deathly silence.)*

MAYOR *(in anguish, shivering)*: I feel the cold wind of Siberia! . . . *(He sinks to his knees to pray.)*

A C T   I I

Scene I

The same scene, a few moments later. The MAYOR, HLESTAKOV *and* OSIP *have disappeared.*

BOBCHINSKI: I nearly fainted from fright!

DOBCHINSKI: Let's go quick and warn the Judge and Karobkin! Good afternoon, Anna Andreyevna!

BOBCHINSKI: Good afternoon, my dears! *(Both run out.)*

COMMISSIONER OF SCHOOLS *(to* COMMISSIONER OF CHARITIES*)*: I could smell disaster coming! This fellow not only reads books—he *writes* them! The first thing he'll do when he wakes up is write a report to St. Petersburg. *(Suddenly.)* And we're not even in dress uniform! Oh, God help us!

COMMISSIONER OF CHARITIES: Perhaps we should have a formal reception for him. If he sees us all in uniform he will realize we are not barbarians.

COMMISSIONER OF SCHOOLS: Ah, yes. I'd better go now and have my uniform repaired. The cursed mice have nibbled away the seat of my pants.

COMMISSIONER OF CHARITIES *(groaning)*: We may never survive tomorrow!

COMMISSIONER OF SCHOOLS *and* COMMISSIONER OF CHARITIES *(to* ANNA, *as they hurry out)*: Good day, madam!

ANNA *(to* MARYA*)*: What an utterly charming young man that Inspector is!

MARYA: How delightful!

ANNA: What refinement! You can see he's spent his entire life in society. That dignity and everything. . . . Oh, how elegant! I'm easy prey for young men like that—I'm afraid he's swept me off my feet. I'm sure I made a hit with *him*, too. You noticed how he kept staring at me all the time?

MARYA: Oh, Mamma dear. He was staring at *me!*

ANNA: There you go, arguing again! *When* did he look at you, for goodness sake? *Why* should he ever look at you?

MARYA: Really, Mamma, he gave me the eye all night. When he started to talk about literature he was practically *hypnotizing* me, and when he told how he played whist with the ambassadors, I felt his eyes going up and down—Oh! *(She almost swoons.)*

ANNA: Well, maybe he did turn to you once or twice, but that was only to make it look right. He must have thought, "I'd better throw her a glance, just to protect Anna!"

MAYOR *(tiptoes in from* HLESTAKOV'S *room):* Sh . . . sh . . .

ANNA: Well, well?

MAYOR: I'm worried—he really sopped up that wine. . . . If even half of what he claimed is true, we're in deep trouble. *(Thoughtfully.)* When a man is in his cups everything comes out. What's in his heart flies right to his tongue. . . . So he plays whist with ambassadors and hangs around the palace? . . . Damn it, the more I think about it—I feel as dizzy as if I were standing on top of a steeple—or *(Frightened.)* on a gallows and they were about to hang me.

ANNA: I didn't feel nervous at all. I merely saw in him an educated, polished, well-bred young man.

MAYOR: That's just like a woman! What could they do to you? —just flog you, that's all. But your poor husband—I may be sent away and never heard of again. And all the while you, my darling, treated this high official as if he was some old pal, another Dobchinski.

ANNA: You don't have to worry in that department. We know how to take care of him. *(Glances significantly at daughter.)*

MAYOR: Your kind of help I can only wish on my enemies! *(He opens door and calls off.)* Mishka, get those policemen— Svistunov and Dherzimorda. They're leaning on the gate. *(Closes door, pauses.)* What a mixed-up world this is! You should be able to tell if a man is important by his appearance. But no—this miserable, skinny kid! How can anyone figure out who he is? With a military man, it's easy—when he puts on civilian clothes he looks like a fly with its wings clipped. Well anyhow, before he passed out, he *looked* happy. . . .

(OSIP enters from HLESTAKOV'S *room. All run to him.)*

ANNA: Come over here, friend.

MAYOR: Ssh . . . Is he—is he still sleeping?

OSIP: Nah, he's stretching.

ANNA: Tell me. What's your name?

OSIP: Osip, ma'am.

MAYOR *(to wife and daughter)*: All right. That's enough now. *(To* OSIP*).* My dear friend, did they take good care of you in the kitchen?

OSIP: Yes, sir. I did all right. Thank you very much.

ANNA: Tell me, do a lot of counts and princes call on your master?

OSIP *(aside)*: Maybe if I say yes, I'll eat better. *(Aloud.)* Oh, yes, ma'am. Lots of counts come around. Counts . . . dukes . . . kings. . . .

MARYA: How handsome your master is!

ANNA: Tell me, please, how does he—?

MAYOR: You're only getting in my way with that fool talk. Now listen, my friend—

ANNA: But what is your master's rank?

OSIP: Oh, the regular rank . . .

MAYOR: Oh, good God! Must you rattle on with this stupid cross-examination? You don't make one point that could uncover anything. . . . Now, my good man. What is your master like? Strict, huh? Does he scold you, or beat you?

OSIP: Oh, yah. He likes everything in order. He wants everything just so.

MAYOR: You know, I like your face, Osip. I can see that you're a man I can trust. Now, what—

ANNA: Listen, Osip, what does your master wear in town—a dress uniform or—?

MAYOR: What a blabbermouth! I tell you, this is a matter of life and death. . . . *(To* OSIP*.)* Yes, sir. I like you a lot. I know an extra cup of tea on a trip is always welcome. And it's so cold now . . . how about a couple of rubles for tea?

OSIP *(taking the money)*: Yes, sir. Thank you kindly. God give you good health, you're a holy sight for a poor man's eyes.

MAYOR: It gives me great pleasure to help you. Now, my friend, what—?

ANNA:—color eyes does your master like best?

MARYA: Oh, Osip—your master has the most exciting little turned-up nose!

MAYOR: If you don't shut up, you'll have the reddest, turned-up bottom! (*To* OSIP.) Tell me, my good man where exactly does your master inspect—I mean, what pleases him most on his trips?

OSIP: Oh, he likes to see everything. Most of all, he likes to be glad-handed . . . you know, taken care of right.

MAYOR: Taken care of?

OSIP: Yah. I mean, I'm only a serf, see, but he makes sure I'm fixed up right. Let me tell you! We go some place, he says, "Well, Osip, how'd they take care of you?" And I comes right back with, "Oh, shabby, your excellency. Shabby." "Aha" he says. "Our host rates down at the bottom in my book. You remind me about that when we visit next time." And I thinks to myself, "God help that one!"

MAYOR: You speak right to the point. What I gave you before was for tea. Now here's something extra for cakes.

OSIP: Oh, you're too good, your highness. (*Pockets the money.*) I'll make sure I spend this drinking toasts to you.

ANNA: Come to me, Osip, and you'll get something more.

MARYA: Osip, dear, kiss your master for me!

(HLESTAKOV *is heard coughing in the next room.*)

MAYOR: Ssh! (*Walks on tiptoe; rest of scene is played in low voices.*) Good God, don't make a sound! (*To* ANNA.) That's enough. You can get out now.

ANNA: Let's go, Marya. I want to tell you something I noticed about our guest that I can only say in private. (*They go out.*)

MAYOR: Oh, they're at it again! You listen to them and you'd have to stop up your ears fast to keep from getting nauseous. (*To* OSIP.) Now that we're alone, my dear friend—

(*Enter* DERZHIMORDA *and* SVISTUNOV.)

MAYOR: Sssh! Damn bowlegged bears, stomping around! You sound like you're throwing a body into the police wagon! What in hell took you so long?

DERZHIMORDA: My orders was—

MAYOR: Sssh! *(Puts hand over his mouth.) My orders was!*—for God's sake! Do you have to bellow like a bull in heat? *(To* OSIP.*)* Now, my good man, you can go and freshen up . . . order anything you want—the house is yours. *(*OSIP *goes out.)* Now you two bums. You stand on the front steps and don't budge. Don't let any stranger in the house—especially no shopkeepers. If you just let one slip past, I'll flog your skin off! And remember, if anybody comes up with a complaint, or even *without* one—if he only looks like the kind who *might* complain—you kick him right out! Headfirst! Like this! *(He demonstrates.)* You understand? Now ssh! *(He sighs worriedly, exits on tiptoe, following the* POLICEMEN.*)*

Scene II

The MAYOR'*s house, the next morning.*
Enter cautiously, the JUDGE, *the* COMMISSIONER OF CHARITIES, *the* COMMISSIONER OF SCHOOLS, *the* POSTMASTER, DOBCHINSKI *and* BOBCHINSKI. *All are in full dress uniform. The scene is played in hushed voices.*

JUDGE *(arranging them in a semicircle)*: For God's sake, gentlemen, take your places quickly, and let's have some semblance of order! Good heavens, he knows everybody at the Court, and he bullies the Imperial Council! Line up with military precision. Chin up, pull your stomachs in! . . . Bobchinski, you stand there. Dobchinski—there! *(They run to their assigned places.)*

COMMISSIONER OF CHARITIES: Bud Judge, we certainly should try something *positive*.

JUDGE: Positive?

COMMISSIONER OF CHARITIES: You know, a little palm oil.

JUDGE: He's liable to kick up a storm. After all, he's a State official. I believe it might better take the form of a testimonial from the nobility and the gentry. Some sort of souvenir.

POSTMASTER: How about, say—there's some money arrived at the post office—and we don't know who it's for?

COMMISSIONER OF CHARITIES: These matters should be arranged more smoothly in a well-run town. What's a whole regiment doing here? We ought to approach him individually . . . and conduct our business in private, so that nobody knows anything about anything. That's how a well-organized community operates. Judge—you ought to go first.

JUDGE: It would be more correct if it were *you*. The illustrious visitor broke bread at *your* hospital.

COMMISSIONER OF CHARITIES: No. No! It should be Luka Lukich, the man who enlightens youth.

COMMISSIONER OF SCHOOLS: I can't, gentlemen. Really I can't. I've had an unfortunate education. If anyone a single degree in rank above me, addresses me—my tongue seems to be stuck in glue. No, gentlemen, I really must be excused.

COMMISSIONER OF CHARITIES: You see, the only one who can bring it off is you, Judge. Why, your every word sounds as if Cicero himself were talking.

JUDGE: Nonsense! Cicero indeed! Just because one now and then discourses on housedogs or greyhound puppies . . . ?

ALL (*surrounding him*): Not just dogs! . . . You could have made sense out of the Tower of Babel, too! . . . Oh, no, Judge. Don't desert us. . . . We need a great mind to lead us! . . . Don't abandon us, Lyapkin-Tyapkin!

JUDGE: Let go of me, gentlemen!

(HLESTAKOV *is heard stumbling about in his room; he coughs and mumbles.* ALL *rush to the center door, squeezing and pushing to get out.*)

BOBCHINSKI'S VOICE: Owh! Dobchinski, you're standing on my corn!

COMMISSIONER OF CHARITIES: I'm smothering, smothering! Give me air before I pass out!

(*More cries of despair and pain until they all push out. The room is empty for a moment.* HLESTAKOV *comes out, yawning and sleepy.*)

HLESTAKOV: I must have had a pretty long snooze. . . . What a lovely featherbed! . . . Oh, my tongue, it feels like the dragoons have been marching over it. . . . I *like* this kind of hospitality. . . . That Mayor's daughter, she's not bad at all. And his wife, I mustn't neglect her, either. This sort of life just suits me perfectly. . . .

JUDGE (*enters, his eyes turned up to heaven*): Oh, Lord, Lord! I know I've made some foolish statements about You before but, as one judge to another, You can't let me down. At least, stop my knees from knocking! *(Draws himself up and leans on his sword to steady himself.)* I have the honor to present myself: Judge of the District Court and College Assessor Lyapkin-Tyapkin.

HLESTAKOV: Do sit down. So, you are the judge here?

JUDGE *(sitting):* I was chosen for the position for three years by the nobility and gentry in 1816—and I've continued in that office ever since.

HLESTAKOV: I dare say, you find the position . . . profitable?

JUDGE: After nine years, I was decorated with the Order of St. Vladimir, Fourth Class, with a commendation from my superiors. *(Aside.)* This money is burning a hole through my hand!

HLESTAKOV: Well, I *like* the Vladimir. It has much more color than the Anna of the Third Class.

JUDGE *(thrusting his clenched fist forward, as if in pain; aside)*: Oh, good Lord! I feel as if I'm sitting on hot, burning coals!

HLESTAKOV: What have you got in your hand?

JUDGE *(shaken, dropping money on the floor)*: Oh, no-nothing, sir!

HLESTAKOV: Nothing? You've dropped some money.

JUDGE *(shaking all over)*: I?—impossible, sir! *(Aside.)* Oh, Lord! Now I'm in front of the judge. They've got the cart ready to take me to the hangman!

HLESTAKOV *(picking up the money)*: Why, so it is—it's money!

JUDGE: It's all over, now. I'm doomed, doomed!

HLESTAKOV: I wonder—could you *lend* me this?

JUDGE *(eagerly):* If you wish, sir, if you would condescend to . . . with the greatest of pleasure! *(Aside.)* Stand by me, Holy Mother!

HLESTAKOV: I'm a bit low in cash—spent it all on the road for one thing or another . . . However, I'll reimburse you as soon as I reach my estate.

JUDGE: Oh, don't give it a second thought. The honor of serving you is enough. . . . Indeed, though my powers are feeble, still with all zeal and loyalty . . . I shall endeavor to serve. . . . *(Rises and stands at attention, hands at his sides.)* I will not presume to disturb you further with my presence. . . . Will there be any orders?

HLESTAKOV: Orders? What kind of orders?

JUDGE: I mean, will you issue any orders for the District Court?

HLESTAKOV: Why? I have nothing to say to your Court. Now, thank you very much.

JUDGE *(bowing as he exits, aside)*: Now the town is ours again!

HLESTAKOV: Good man—a gentleman of the old school.

*(*POSTMASTER *enters in full regalia, sword in hand. He comes to attention.)*

POSTMASTER: I have the honor to present myself: Postmaster and Court Councilor Shpyokin.

HLESTAKOV: Welcome! How nice to have so many callers so early. Have a seat. . . . So, you've always lived here?

POSTMASTER: Yes, sir.

HLESTAKOV: You know, I like this little town. Of course, it's not overly populated—but what of it? It's not the capital. Eh— that's true, isn't it—it's *not* the capital?

POSTMASTER: That's true. Exactly.

HLESTAKOV: It's only in the capital that one finds the *bon ton*, and escapes the country clodhoppers. What do you think?

POSTMASTER: You're exactly right, sir.

HLESTAKOV: After all, what does a man want out of life? In my opinion, all one wants is to have people respect one, and sincerely like one. Isn't that so?

POSTMASTER: Absolutely. Exactly.

HLESTAKOV: I'm glad we think the same way. I suppose some people may consider me eccentric—but that's the way I am. *(Aside.)* I might as well put the touch on him, too. *(Aloud.)* A strange thing happened to me on the way into town—I spent my last kopek. Could you lend me three hundred rubles?

POSTMASTER: Of course! It will give me the greatest happiness. Here you are—take it, sir. Please . . . delighted to be of service.

HLESTAKOV: Thank you very much. You see, I have a dreadful

fear of cramping myself when I'm traveling—and anyhow, why the devil should I? Isn't that right?

POSTMASTER: Oh, exactly. Yes, sir! *(Rises and comes to attention, hand on sword.)* I won't presume to disturb you further with my presence. . . . Do you have any suggestions . . . random thoughts on the postal administration?

HLESTAKOV: Not a single one.

(POSTMASTER bows and exits.)

HLESTAKOV *(lighting a cigar)*: The Postmaster seems to be very obliging, too. That's the kind of man I like.

(There is a commotion offstage, and a voice is heard: "Go on, what are you afraid of?" A door is opened and the COMMISSIONER OF SCHOOLS *is pushed into the room.)*

COMMISSIONER OF SCHOOLS *(saluting frantically, his hand on his sword)*: I have the honor to present myself: Commissioner of Schools and Honorary Councilor Hlopov!

HLESTAKOV: Ah, how do you do. Have a seat. Take a chair. Will you have a cigar? *(Offers one to him.)*

COMMISSIONER OF SCHOOLS *(aside)*: I never thought of *that!* Should I take it?

HLESTAKOV: Take it, take it. It's not a bad brand. Of course, it's not what I'm accustomed to. In St. Petersburg I smoke only imported tobacco; when you inhale a puff you float up to heaven with the angels. Here's a match—light up. *(Gives him a match.* COMMISSIONER, *shaking all over, lights it).* You're lighting the wrong end.

COMMISSIONER OF SCHOOLS *(throws cigar down, spits. Aside)*: Damn it—my nervousness ruins me every time!

HLESTAKOV: I see you're not very fond of cigars. Well, I admit they're one of my weaknesses. Not the only one, though. I'm rather susceptible to the charm of the fair sex. What's your taste—brunette or blonde?

(COMMISSIONER OF SCHOOLS is stunned.)

HLESTAKOV: Come on, out with it—brunette or blonde?

COMMISSIONER OF SCHOOLS: I wouldn't dare have an opinion.

HLESTAKOV: Oh, now, don't weasel out of it that way. I'm interested in *your* taste.

COMMISSIONER OF SCHOOLS: I'm too shy, Your Nob . . . Excell . . . enity! *(Aside.)* My confounded tongue has betrayed me for sure!

HLESTAKOV: Too shy? Well, let me help you overcome that shyness . . . a funny thing happened to me on the way here. I ran out of cash. Could you lend me three hundred?

COMMISSIONER OF SCHOOLS *(aside, fumbling with his purse)*: Oh, oh! Do I have that much? . . . Ah, I do, I do! *(Takes out some bills and, trembling, hands them to* HLESTAKOV.*)*

HLESTAKOV: I'm deeply indebted to you.

COMMISSIONER OF SCHOOLS: I won't presume to disturb you further with my presence.

HLESTAKOV: Good-bye, then.

COMMISSIONER OF SCHOOLS *(sotto voce as he runs out)*: Thank heaven! He won't poke around the schools now.

(Enter the COMMISSIONER OF CHARITIES. *He stands at attention, his hand on his sword.)*

COMMISSIONER OF CHARITIES: I have the honor to present myself: Commissioner of Charities and Court Councilor Zemlyanika.

HLESTAKOV: How do you do. Won't you take a seat?

COMMISSIONER OF CHARITIES: I had the honor of personally conducting you through the charitable institutions in my charge.

HLESTAKOV: Ah, yes: Salted cod. You made an excellent impression. But I could have sworn you were . . . *shorter* yesterday.

COMMISSIONER OF CHARITIES *(agreeably)*: It's very possible. *(After a short silence.)* I spare no effort to perform my duties with zeal and dispatch. *(Draws his chair closer to* HLESTAKOV *and speaks confidentially.)* Now, this Postmaster. He does absolutely nothing. The Post Office is falling apart . . . letters are lost, packages break open mysteriously. It's something you should look into. As for the Judge, he hunts rabbits while the court is in session, and he kennels his dogs in the Courthouse! And his behavior in general—well, he's a friend of mine, but I must do this for the good of the country. There's a certain landowner around here—Dobchinski, you've possibly met him—well, as soon as Dobchinski goes out to collect his rent, the Judge hops into bed with his wife! I'll swear it on the Bible! The five children, all the way down to the youngest girl, look exactly like the Judge.

HLESTAKOV (*delighted*): Well, well! Who would have thought it!

COMMISSIONER OF CHARITIES: Then there's the Commissioner of Schools. I can't understand how the government ever appointed him. He's worse than an anarchist, and he poisons the minds of the youngsters with revolutionary doctrines I don't even understand myself. Would you like me to put all this down on paper?

HLESTAKOV: By all means. It'll be something amusing to read when I'm bored. . . . By the way, what is your name? I keep forgetting.

COMMISSIONER OF CHARITIES: Zemlyanika.

HLESTAKOV: Ah, of course. Zemlyanika.

COMMISSIONER OF CHARITIES: I will not presume to disturb you further with my presence, or take up the time which you devote to performing your duties . . . (*Bows, prepares to leave*).

HLESTAKOV (*accompanying him out*): Oh, I assure you, what you've told me was a great treat. (*Closes door, then remembers. He reopens door, yells out.*) Oh, I say there! What is your *first* name?

COMMISSIONER OF CHARITIES (*returning*): Artemi. Artemi Philipovich.

HLESTAKOV: Well, Artemi, somehow or other, I've lost all my money. This town is full of thieves. Do you happen to have four hundred to lend me?

COMMISSIONER OF CHARITIES: Why, yes, I believe I do. (*Gives packet of bills to him.*)

HLESTAKOV: My, that *is* lucky. Thank you, most sincerely.

(COMMISSIONER OF CHARITIES *goes out.*)

HLESTAKOV (*calling through door*): Next!

(BOBCHINSKI *and* DOBCHINSKI *stumble in.*)

BOBCHINSKI: I have the honor to present myself: Peter Ivanovich Bobchinski, a citizen of this town.

DOBCHINSKI: And I am Pyotr Ivanovich Dobchinski, landowner.

HLESTAKOV: Oh, yes. I've met you before—when you fell in. And how is your nose?

BOBCHINSKI: Quite well, thank you. It's swollen up nicely, don't you think? I'm very pleased with it.

HLESTAKOV: It's a lovely job. If only your money could double so quickly . . . *(Suddenly.)* By the way, do you have any of it on you?

DOBCHINSKI: Any of what?

HLESTAKOV: Money. Lend me a thousand.

BOBCHINSKI: A thousand? Good God, I don't have that much. Maybe you do, Pyotr?

DOBCHINSKI: I? Oh, no. I'm completely in hock to the damned shysters.

HLESTAKOV: Well, if not a thousand—say, a hundred rubles?

BOBCHINSKI *(rummaging through his pockets)*: You must have a hundred, Dobchinski? All I can find is forty.

DOBCHINSKI: I never carry more than twenty-five.

BOBCHINSKI: Why don't you take another look? I know you have a hole in your right pocket—some might have dropped through.

DOBCHINSKI *(firmly)*: I'm positive there's nothing in the hole.

BOBCHINSKI: Of course, there's nothing *there!* That's why it's called a hole. Maybe it dropped into your—lining—

HLESTAKOV: Never mind. I'll manage with sixty-five. It's quite all right. *(He takes the bills).* Good-bye.

DOBCHINSKI: I was going to ask you a favor in a very delicate matter—

HLESTAKOV: Well, what is it?

DOBCHINSKI: It's very, very delicate. My oldest son, you see, was born just a few days before I got married—

HLESTAKOV: Oh?

DOBCHINSKI: I don't think a few days, more or less, should matter, in the date of the registration. I want him to be called Dobchinski, just like me. I wouldn't trouble you, sir, but it would be a great pity since the boy has so many talents. He has so much promise. He's memorized entire poems by heart, and if he picks up a knife, he'll immediately carve a little toy droshky as quick as a magician. Bobchinski will testify to that.

BOBCHINSKI: The boy is a genius.

HLESTAKOV: Very well. Let him be called Dobchinski.

DOBCHINSKI: Don't I need some sort of . . . document?

HLESTAKOV: If I say he's a Dobchinski, he's a Dobchinski! By God, just let anybody try to question it! *(To* BOBCHINSKI *grandly.)* Don't you have something you'd like me to do for you?

BOBCHINSKI: Ah, yes. A very small favor.

HLESTAKOV: Certainly. What is it?

BOBCHINSKI: I beg you, sir, when you return to St. Petersburg and tell all the notables there, all those councilors and admirals, about your visit, just say, "In that town, Your Excellency or Your Highness, in that very town lives Peter Ivanovich Bobchinski." That's all. Just say, "Peter Ivanovich Bobchinski lives there."

HLESTAKOV: Why not? And when I call on the Emperor, I'll slip it into the conversation, "It's the town, Your Imperial Majesty, where Peter Ivanovich Bobchinski lives."

BOBCHINSKI: Oh, God bless you!

DOBCHINSKI and BOBCHINSKI *(together)*: And pardon us for giving you so much trouble with our presence.

HLESTAKOV: Not at all! It was a great pleasure. *(He conducts them out. Alone.)* I've really fallen into a barrel of butter! . . . What a bunch of idiots! . . . I think I'll write Tryapichkin about this. He scribbles for the St. Petersburg papers . . . this might give him a little comic inspiration. Hey, Osip! Bring some ink and paper!

OSIP *(putting his head in the door)*: Yes, sir.

HLESTAKOV: This ought to hit Tryapichkin right in the funny bone. He'd sell his own father for a joke. . . . First, let's add up the take: Three hundred from the Judge and three hundred from the Postmaster . . . Six . . . seven . . . eight hundred—what a greasy bill! . . . Eight hundred, nine hundred . . . Oh, my! It comes out to over a thousand . . . Now, where's that light-fingered captain? Just let me catch you now, with *my* cards! *(OSIP enters with inkwell and paper and pen.)* Well, you old windbag, you see how well they treat me? *(Begins to write.)*

OSIP: Yeh, thank God for that. Only, you know what . . . ?

HLESTAKOV: What?

OSIP: I think we better get the hell out of here. Fast!

HLESTAKOV *(writing)*: Nonsense! Why should I?

OSIP: You been having a high old time here for two days. All right. That's enough, ain't it? What do you want to hang around for? Spit on 'em! How do you know who's gonna show up here tomorrow and spill the beans? They've got fast horses here—they go like lightning.

HLESTAKOV: I've decided to accept a bit more of their hospitality. We might leave tomorrow.

OSIP: Tomorrow? Christ, we better get outta here right now! It's a big honor for you, and all that, but don't overdo it. They musta took you for somebody else, but your old man won't believe it—you'll catch hell for taking so long. . . . Since you're such a big shot, they'll give you the best horses. Come on, let's beat it.

HLESTAKOV *(still writing):* Very well then. But first take this letter and then get an order for post-horses. Tell the drivers I'll give them a ruble each if they bring horses that run like the Imperial Couriers'. And I want the drivers to sing for me, too. *(Continues writing.)* There. Tryapichkin ought to die laughing—

OSIP: I'll send it with this man here. I better pack up so's we don't lose any time.

HLESTAKOV: Very good. But bring me a candle.

OSIP *(goes off and is heard yelling):* Hey, you there! Get ready to run a letter to the post office. And tell 'em to send their best troika—a courier's troika, you understand?—and my boss don't pay. He travels at government expense. And tell 'em they better look alive, or my boss'll get mad. . . . Ah, wait a minute. The letter ain't ready yet.

HLESTAKOV *(goes on writing):* I wonder where he's living now . . . Post Office Street or Peas Street? He likes to change his room regularly—saves paying rent. I'll take a chance on Post Office Street. *(Folds the letter and addresses it.)*

*(*OSIP *brings the candle.* HLESTAKOV *seals the letter.)*

DERZHIMORDA'S VOICE *(offstage):* Where are you goin', Black Beard? I told you—orders is orders. Nobody goes in!

HLESTAKOV *(gives letter to* OSIP*):* There, send it out.

SHOPKEEPER'S VOICE: Come on, be a good fellow. . . . You can't stop us—we're here on business!

DERZHIMORDA: Get out, get out! He ain't receivin' nobody. He's sleepin'. *(The noise increases.)*

HLESTAKOV: What is it, Osip? What's that uproar?

OSIP *(looking out window):* Some shopkeepers want to come in, but the cop won't let 'em. They're wavin' papers—they must want to see you.

HLESTAKOV *(at window):* What do you want, my friends?

SHOPKEEPERS' VOICE: We throw ourselves at your mercy! Your Lordship, please receive our petition.

HLESTAKOV: Let them in! Let them all in, Osip. (OSIP *exits.* HLESTAKOV *accepts some petitions through the window; he turns them over and reads:)* "To His High Well-Born Illustrious Lord of Finance, from Abdulin the Merchant—'' damned if I know what this is all about! But what a title!

(The SHOPKEEPERS *push in, carrying sugar loaves and bottles of wine in a basket.)*

HLESTAKOV: Now, now, my friends. What is all this?

SHOPKEEPERS: We beg your indulgence!

HLESTAKOV: Well, tell me what you want?

SHOPKEEPERS: Save us from bankruptcy, Your Lordship! We are grievously and unjustly oppressed.

HLESTAKOV: By who—whom?

ABDULIN: The Mayor. It's all because of the Mayor of this town. You never saw such a Mayor! Who can describe the outrages he commits? He billets so many of his visiting relatives in our houses, we're bankrupt. We might as well end the misery by hanging ourselves! And if he doesn't like your looks, he grabs you by the beard and calls you a Mongolian dog! My God! as if we didn't pay him enough respect! We've never refused anything his wife or daughter might pick out to wear. But no, that's not enough for him! He'll see a piece of cloth, and he'll say, "Ah, my friend, that's a nice little piece of material. Just send it over to my house." And the piece can be 50 yards long.

HLESTAKOV: My, what sticky fingers!

A SHOPKEEPER: Yes, by God! Nobody can remember another mayor like this in the whole history of this town! Whenever we see him coming, we cover up everything in the shop. He'll take any kind of junk. I had some prunes laying around in a barrel seven years—even my helper-boy wouldn't eat them— but this Mayor stuffs a whole fistful into his pocket. He claims his name-day is the feast of St. Anthony, so you've got to bring him gifts. And then, next month, he decides St. Onufri's is another name-day of his, so you have to contribute again!

HLESTAKOV: Why, he's no better than a pirate!

ANOTHER SHOPKEEPER: That's right. But just you try to cross him, and he'll quarter a whole regiment of soldiers in your house. And if you bar the door to him, he'll say, "I won't subject you to corporal punishment or torture—that is forbidden by law." But, my dear fellow, it'll be worse than swallowing herring without water!

HLESTAKOV: What a hypocrite! He ought to be ashamed of himself.

ABDULIN: Your Lordship, if you can just remove him, we'll be able to breathe again. And please accept a little token of our hospitality—these sugar loaves and wine.

HLESTAKOV: Now, now! Don't even think of that. I never accept bribes. However, if you offered me a loan of, say, three hundred rubles, that would be an entirely different matter. I could accept that.

SHOPKEEPERS: Take it, noble lord! *(They produce bags of coins.)* But three hundred may not be enough. . . . Better have five hundred. Just help us!

HLESTAKOV: If you wish . . . as long as it's a loan, I can't refuse. I'll take it.

ABDULIN *(offering money on a silver tray)*: Please accept the tray, too.

HLESTAKOV: Why, yes. How thoughtful of you.

ANOTHER SHOPKEEPER: *(bowing)*: Take the sugar loaves, too.

HLESTAKOV: Oh, no. That would be an out-and-out bribe.

OSIP: Your Highness, please accept it. It'll make these gents feel better. And it can be mighty useful on the trip . . . *(To* SHOPKEEPERS*)* Give me the loaves and the basket—I hate waste. What's this? Rope? Let's have that, too—everything comes in handy on the road.

SHOPKEEPERS: Please grant us this favor, Your Lordship. If you don't come to our rescue, we just don't know which way to turn—

ABDULIN: We'll hang ourselves!

HLESTAKOV: Of course, I will. Of course. I'll do my best.

(THE SHOPKEEPERS *go out.*)

WOMAN'S VOICE (*off*): Don't you dare stop me, you bum! Don't shove me!

HLESTAKOV: Who's there? (*Goes to window.*) Well, what's the trouble, madam?

VOICES OF TWO WOMEN: Take pity on us, sir! Say that you'll listen to us!

HLESTAKOV (*at window*): Let them in.

(*Enter the* LOCKSMITH'S WIFE, *an old harridan, and* SERGEANT'S WIFE.)

LOCKSMITH'S WIFE (*bowing to the ground*): Have pity on me!

SERGEANT'S WIFE: Have pity on me, too!

HLESTAKOV: Who are you?

SERGEANT'S WIFE: I'm Sergeant Ivanov's wife.

LOCKSMITH'S WIFE: I live here, sir. I'm the locksmith's wife, Fevronya Pyetrova Pashlyopkina—

HLESTAKOV: One at a time! (*To* LOCKSMITH'S WIFE) What do you want?

LOCKSMITH'S WIFE: Beggin' your mercy, I want to complain against the Mayor! I hope the Lord curses him with every kind of disease he can dig up, so that crook and his children and his uncles and his aunts never have any luck in anything!

HLESTAKOV: Really? Why?

LOCKSMITH'S WIFE: Why, that grafter stuck my man into the army—and it ain't his turn yet! Besides, it's against the law because my man's *married!* To me!

HLESTAKOV: But how could the Mayor do that?

LOCKSMITH'S WIFE: He done it anyhow, the swindler. He just done it! I hope God blasts him good in this world *and* the next! And his aunt—if he *had* an aunt—let every kind of sickness shrivel her up! And his father—if he *had* a father and he's alive—let him rot to death, the rat! I hope he chokes forever and ever, that thief! They shoulda took the tailor's son, the drunk, but his family slipped the Mayor a big bribe. So he snatched Panteleyeva's son, but his old lady sent around three bolts of cloth to the Mayor's wife. So he picks on *me!* "What do you need a husband for?" he says. "He's no use to you." Well,

I'm the one that oughta know if he's any use or not! Then he says, "Your husband is a crook. It don't matter if he ain't stole nothin' yet, he sure will someday. So what's the difference if they take him now or next year?" What am I gonna do without my dear husband? You stinkin' Mayor! I hope not one of your family wakes up tomorrow to see God's blessed light. And your mother-in-law—if you *have* a mother-in-law—

HLESTAKOV: Now! now! That's enough! *(He dismisses her. To the other.)* Now, what do you have to complain about?

LOCKSMITH'S WIFE *(as she goes out)*: Don't forget me, little father. And bless you.

SERGEANT'S WIFE: I want justice from the Mayor!

HLESTAKOV: Well, what is it? Make it short.

SERGEANT'S WIFE: He had me flogged by mistake!

HLESTAKOV: How can that happen?

SERGEANT'S WIFE: Well, a couple of us girls was arguing in the marketplace, strictly a private thing. And the cops come up and grab me. I don't know why—and next thing I know, I can't sit down for two days.

HLESTAKOV: What do you expect me to do about it now?

SERGEANT'S WIFE: I know you can't take back the flogging. I just want him to pay me compensation. I took a terrible beating for nothing.

HLESTAKOV: You can go now—I'll take care of everything.

(Hands with petitions are thrust in through the window.)

What? They're still coming! *(Goes to window.)* No, no! I can't take care of any more. Impossible, impossible! *(Turning away from window.)* They certainly are pests, damn them! Don't let any more in, Osip.

OSIP *(calling out the window)*: Break it up! . . . Beat it, I said! That's all. Come back tomorrow.

(MARYA ANTONOVNA enters from another door.)

MARYA *(in mock surprise)*: Oh, dear me!

HLESTAKOV: Why are you so frightened, mademoiselle?

MARYA: Oh, I wasn't frightened.

HLESTAKOV *(strutting)*: Forgive me if I say so, my dear girl, but I'm quite pleased to think you have taken me for the kind of man who. . . . May I ask where you were going?

MARYA: Actually, I was not going anywhere.

HLESTAKOV: Well then, might I ask *why* you were not going anywhere.

MARYA: I wondered if Mamma was here. . . .

HLESTAKOV: I really would like to know why you were not going anywhere.

MARYA: Oh, I'm interrupting you. You were in the middle of important business.

HLESTAKOV *(the lady-killer)*: But just a glance from your eyes is more important to me than any business! . . . *You* could never interrupt me. On the contrary, just to see you gives me the greatest pleasure.

MARYA: Ah, you toss compliments around just like they do in the capital.

HLESTAKOV: That's the only proper way to address an entrancing creature such as you. Dare I offer you a chair? Alas, you should have not a chair but a throne!

MARYA: I really don't know . . . I ought to be going. . . .

(Takes seat.)

HLESTAKOV: What an enchanting scarf!

MARYA: Oh, now! You're making fun. You're just laughing at us small-towners.

HLESTAKOV: Oh, mademoiselle, how I wish I were that scarf, so that I could wrap myself around your lily neck!

MARYA: I really don't understand what you mean. . . . Isn't this unusual weather we're having?

HLESTAKOV: For your little lips, my dear, I would come running through the most unusual weather in the world!

MARYA: You do say the strangest things. . . . I was going to ask you to write some poetry in my souvenir album. You must know a lot of poems.

HLESTAKOV: For you, mademoiselle, I will compose an entirely original one. Just command me—what kind shall it be?

MARYA: I don't know . . . as long as it's new.

HLESTAKOV: Let me think a moment—my head is simply swarming with rhymes. Would you like this little thing I dashed off:

> Good night, good night, parting is such sweet sorrow,
> I shall say good night till it's tomorrow . . .

MARYA (*clutching him*): Oh, don't go! . . . How lovely that is!

HLESTAKOV: Well, I have others, even better. I just can't recall them now. . . . What does it matter? Instead of my verses, I give you my love! Ever since your first smile . . . (*Moves his chair closer.*)

MARYA: Love? I've never understood just what it is. . . . (*She moves her chair away.*)

HLESTAKOV: Why move your chair away? It's far better that we sit closer together.

MARYA (*moves farther away*): Why closer? It's better to sit farther!

HLESTAKOV (*moves toward her*): Why farther? It's better to sit closer.

MARYA: But why do you do that?

HLESTAKOV (*edging nearer*): So that I can only *seem* to be close to you. Actually, I am far, far away. . . .

MARYA (*mollified, looks out window*): What was that flying by? A magpie?

HLESTAKOV (*kisses her on the shoulder*): Just the wings of a bird. . . .

MARYA (*rises indignantly*): That was not a bird—that was you! . . . How bold!

HLESTAKOV (*holding her back*): Can you blame me, mademoiselle? I did it in the heat of love. Love for *you!*

MARYA: So you think I'm some kind of country . . . milkmaid!

(*Struggles to free herself.*)

HLESTAKOV (*still holding her*): I was driven mad by love, really. Just love! Marya Antonovna, don't be angry! I'm ready to get down on my knees to beg your pardon. (*Falls on his knees.*) You see? Now, will you pardon me?

(ANNA ANDREYEVNA *enters.*)

ANNA: My, what a position!

HLESTAKOV *(rising, exasperated)*: Doesn't anyone ever knock?

ANNA *(turning on her daughter)*: As for you, young lady, what is the meaning of this?

MARYA: Mamma, dear, I—

ANNA: Leave the room! Do you hear me? March right out of here and don't you dare show your face to me again. *(MARYA runs out in tears.)* Excuse me, sir, but I'm so shocked by all this . . .

HLESTAKOV *(aside)*: Well, this one isn't too bad-looking. . . . *(Throws himself at her feet.)* Madam, you see before you a man burning with love. For *you!*

ANNA: What are you doing on your knees again? Oh, get up, sir, get up. The floor's quite dirty.

HLESTAKOV: No, I insist. I will stay on my knees until I learn my fate. What will it be—life or death?

ANNA: Sir, I don't understand what you're talking about. If my eyes didn't deceive me, you were just now making a proposal to my daughter.

HLESTAKOV: No, I am in love with *you!* My life hangs on a thread! If you will not crown my eternal burning love, then I cannot endure existence on earth! While the flame licks at my heart, I beg for your hand!

ANNA: But, sir, I must mention that I am, so to speak . . . well, actually I *am* married!

HLESTAKOV: What does that matter? Love does not recognize such trifles. Didn't Karamazin say, "It's only the law that condemns"? We will fly away together, under the canopy of heaven. Your hand. I must have your hand—!

(Suddenly, MARYA *runs in.)*

MARYA: Papa wants you to— *(Finally realizes* HLESTAKOV *is on his knees again.)* My, what a position!

ANNA: Well, what do *you* want? Leaping around like a cat in a fit! What's so surprising about what you've seen? You act like a three-year-old, not at all like a girl of eighteen! Not at all! When will you ever learn good manners in front of a gentleman?

MARYA *(through her tears)*: Honest, Mamma dear, I didn't know—

ANNA: There's a constant draft blowing through your head!

HLESTAKOV (*seizing* MARYA'S *hand but talking to* ANNA): Do not oppose our happiness. Give your blessing to our eternal, burning love!

ANNA (*astounded*): So it's *her* you want—?

HLESTAKOV: Decide my fate—is it love or death?

ANNA (*recovering, to* MARYA): There now, you silly girl. Now you see it was all on your account that our guest had to fall on his knees. And then you suddenly barge in as if you'd gone crazy. It would serve you right if I refused permission—you're really not worth such good fortune.

(MAYOR *runs in, out of breath.*)

MAYOR: I'll never do it again, Your Excellency. Don't ruin me, don't destroy me!

HLESTAKOV: What's the matter with you?

MAYOR: So the shopkeepers have been complaining about me! I swear, on my honor, not half of what they say is true. *They* are the ones who cheat and rob the people. That sergeant's wife lied when she told you I flogged her. It's a damned, dirty lie, by God! She flogged herself!

HLESTAKOV: Oh, who cares about the sergeant's wife?

MAYOR: Don't you believe 'em—not for a minute. They're such liars . . . not even a baby would trust them.

ANNA: Anton, shut up! Ivan Alexandrovich has asked for our daughter's hand!

MAYOR: What's that? You're mad, woman! . . . Don't be alarmed, Your Excellency, she has a few screws loose in her head— takes after her mother.

HLESTAKOV: But I really do ask for her hand! I am in love! Madly!

MAYOR: I can't quite believe it. Your Excellency—?

ANNA: Not even when he *tells* you?

HLESTAKOV: I am not joking. I am madly in love with your daughter.

MAYOR: I just can't believe it—you must be joking, Excellency?

ANNA: You numskull! How many times does he have to say it?

MAYOR: No—it's incredible!

HLESTAKOV: You must give me your consent! I'm a desperate man—capable of anything. If I blow my brains out, you will be held responsible in court.

MAYOR: Court? Oh, my God! I am innocent, body and soul! Don't be angry, I beg you! Do whatever you want! My head is going round and round. . . .

ANNA: There now, give them your blessing.

(HLESTAKOV and MARYA come to him.)

MAYOR: May the Lord bless you—but I swear I'm innocent! *(HLESTAKOV kisses MARYA. The MARYOR at last realizes this is not some plot.)* What the devil! . . . They really are—! *(Rubs his eyes.)* They're really kissing each other—just as if they were engaged! Haha! What a barrel of luck! Well, I *am* blessed!

(OSIP enters.)

OSIP: The horses are here.

HLESTAKOV: I'll be out in a minute.

MAYOR: You're leaving?

HLESTAKOV: Of course.

MAYOR: But just when . . . after you condescended to . . . hint . . . I thought . . . at marriage?

HLESTAKOV: I'm only going for a day to pay my respects to my uncle—he's a rich old fellow. I'll be back tomorrow.

MAYOR: Then we certainly don't want to detain you. Take our blessings for a safe return.

HLESTAKOV: Thank you, thank you. I'll be right back. *(To MARYA.)* Good-bye, my love—no, I can't bear to say that!—au revoir, my dearest darling. *(Kisses her hand.)*

MAYOR: Do you need anything for the trip? You were good enough to say that you were a . . . little short of cash?

HLESTAKOV: Oh, no. It's quite all right . . . *(Reflects.)* But, since you do insist—

MAYOR: How much would you want?

HLESTAKOV: Well, you know, you've already lent me two hundred. Oh, no—it was actually four hundred—let's keep our accounts clear—so if you'd like to make it a nice easy-remembered sum, make it another four hundred.

MAYOR: Certainly! (*He takes the bills out of his purse.*) There, just as if I'd been thinking of you—brand-new bills!

HLESTAKOV (*examines bills*): Ah, so they are! That's wonderful. They say new bills mean new luck.

MAYOR: So they do, sir. Exactly right.

HLESTAKOV: Well, good-bye, Anton Antonovich. I am deeply grateful for your hospitality. I've never been so well treated—anywhere. Good-bye, Anna Andreyevna! Au revoir, Marya, my darling!

(*They start off.* OSIP *goes out.*)

HLESTAKOV: Farewell, Marya Antonovna, angel of my soul!

MAYOR (*looking out window*): What's that—you're riding in a broken-down post-carriage? Without springs?

HLESTAKOV: I prefer that. Springs bounce, they give me a headache.

DRIVER'S VOICE: Whoa, there!

MAYOR: Let's make it comfortable. A rug? Won't you let me give you a rug?

HLESTAKOV: Oh, it's a bother . . . still, if you like, let's have the rug.

MAYOR (*calling off*): Hey, Avdotya! Run to the closet and get the best rug—the Persian with the blue background. Hurry up!

DRIVER: Whoa, there! Ho!

HLESTAKOV: Good-bye, Anton Antonovich! (MAYOR *embraces him.*)

MAYOR: Good-bye, Your Excellency.

ANNA (*tearfully*): Au revoir, Ivan Alexandrovich!

HLESTAKOV: Au revoir, dear Mamma! (*He kisses her in a long embrace.* MAYOR *and* MARYA *stare perplexedly at each other.* HLESTAKOV *runs out, blowing kisses to the group.*)

MARYA: What a cute little nose!

OSIP'S VOICE: We've got the rug, Your Honor. Let's beat it!

DRIVER: Giddyap, my beauties!

(*Bells tinkle as the horses slowly trot away. The* WOMEN *wipe away a few furtive tears.*)

MAYOR *(roaring with pleasure)*: Well, Anna! How do you like that masterstroke, eh? Now admit it—never in your whole life did you ever dream of such a prize! Just a Mayor's wife but look what we hooked—an aristocrat! a holy terror, by Christ!

ANNA: *We?* It took *you* a long time to catch on.

MAYOR: I'll make it hot for all those bloodsuckers who were so free and easy with their petitions! *(Puts head out door.)* Hey, who's out there? *(The policeman* PUGOVKIN *enters.)* Call those shopkeepers in here! I'll give it to you hyenas! Squeal on *me*, will you? Just wait, you damned pack of traitors! I've been too easy on you before—now I'll really use the whip! *(To* POLICE-MAN.*)* Make a list of all those that complained—especially the scribblers with the goddamned petitions. And be sure to let 'em all know what an honor heaven has sent down for me, the Mayor! He's going to marry his daughter—not to a hayseed nobody—but to a gentleman, a man as big as anybody in the whole empire, a man who can fix everything—everything— everything! Yell that out so everybody can hear it—ring the bells! It's my hour of triumph and, so help me, Christ, I'm going to enjoy it! *(*POLICEMAN *goes out).* Now, Anna, we have to think about where we're going to live. Here or in St. Pete?

ANNA: Oh, St. Petersburg, of course. How could we remain here?

MAYOR: All right! St. Pete it is! Now we're really going straight to the top! Since he's such a pal of the ministers and hangs around the Court, he'll get me promoted fast. In no time at all, I ought to be right up there with the generals! How about that, Anna? How would I look as a general?

ANNA: Beautiful, just beautiful.

MAYOR: They'll hang a ribbon across my shoulder. Which do you like best—the red one for the Order of St. Anne or the blue for the White Eagle?

ANNA: Oh, I adore blue.

MAYOR: Well, the red one is pretty high, too! Do you know why everybody wants to be a general? When you travel anywhere, you have couriers and orderlies galloping ahead, ordering up horses, so nobody else can get them. And everybody has to wait for you—all the councilors and big shots! You dine with the governors and snub the mayors. *(Roars with laughter.)* That's what I call living, by Christ!

ANNA: Sure. Anything coarse like that makes you happy. But just remember, we'll have to change our whole way of living. You can't run around with that dog-loving Judge, chasing rabbits, or with slobs like Zemlyanika. Oh no! From now on, all our friends must be people of distinction—counts and society people. . . . Only I'm a little worried about you. You're liable to open your big mouth and let out some dirty word.

MAYOR: I can be just as clean-minded as you pretend to be. . . . You know, in St. Pete you can get all sorts of fresh fish—eels and smelts. My mouth's watering already!

ANNA: Is that all you can think about at a time like this—fish?

(The SHOPKEEPERS *file in, bowing very low.)*

MAYOR *(pleasantly)*: Ah, good afternoon, my little pigeons.

SHOPKEEPERS: Good health to you, Little Father.

MAYOR *(sweetly)*: How are you getting along? How's business? *(Roaring.)* So you thought you'd get rid of me, huh? You tea-guzzlers, you mother-peddlers! You would, would you! —you fatbelly skunks, you bloodsuckers, you beetle-headed pimps! *You* complain about blackmail! So you thought, here's a chance to toss our pal into jail! May the seven fiends and a witch grab you—

ANNA: Heavens—what language!

MAYOR *(impatiently)*: This is no time to be particular! *(To* SHOPKEEPERS*).* Don't you know the very official you complained to is now engaged to my daughter? I'll take care of you! . . . Why, you gyp the whole country! . . . You make a contract with the government and cheat it out of a hundred thousand with your rotten cloth. And then, if I ask you to contribute fifteen or twenty yards, you expect a monument in the square. If the government only knew all your thievery, they'd crack down so hard! . . . And how you stick your belly out so proud—"I'm a merchant, you can't touch me! I rank just as high as any gentleman," you say. Ha! A gentleman has an education, you apes! I'm sure you were all properly flogged at school, but it didn't help. What did you learn—the ABC's of swindling? While you're still kids, you may not know the Lord's Prayer, but goddamn it, you sure know how to mix the sand in with the pepper. And then, when your belly swells out and your purse swells up, don't you put on the airs! Just because you drink up sixteen samovars a day, that makes you gentlemen? Those fancy airs really stink! Phew! I can't stand you!

SHOPKEEPERS *(bowing low)*: We are all guilty, Anton Antonovich. We are guilty. Forgive us.

MAYOR: You complained about *me!* Who closed his eyes when you built that bridge and charged twenty thousand for less than a hundred rubles' worth of lumber? It was *me*—you flea-infested goat's-beard!

ABDULIN: God knows, we are guilty. But it's not our fault—the devil tempted us. We'll never complain again. Tell us what the fine will be . . . but don't be mad at us.

MAYOR *(roaring)*: Don't be mad! If you were in my position, you'd stick me feet-first into the mud and drive me in with a sledge-hammer!

SHOPKEEPERS *(prostrating themselves)*: Spare us, Anton Antonovich!

MAYOR *(waves his hand condescendingly)*: All right, I'm not spiteful. There will be no fine. Just stay in line. . . . And remember, I'm not giving my daughter to any ordinary small-town yokel. So the presents better be appropriate. And no dried fish! . . . You may go now, gentlemen, and God be with you. *(The SHOPKEEPERS exit gratefully through center door. The JUDGE, COMMISSIONER OF CHARITIES and, afterward, RATAKOVSKI come in through another.)*

JUDGE *(as he enters)*: What's this I hear, Anton Antonovich? An extraordinary piece of good fortune has come your way?

COMMISSIONER OF CHARITIES: I have the honor to congratulate you on your great good fortune. *(Kisses ANNA'S hand.)* Anna Andreyevna! *(Kisses MARYA'S.)* Marya Antonovna!

RATAKOVSKI *(entering)*: Congratulations, Anton! God grant you long life, and the same to the bridal couple. May they bless you with grandchildren and great-grandchildren and many others. Anna Andreyevna! *(Kisses her hand.)* Marya Antonovna! *(Kisses her hand.)*

(KAROBKIN and his wife enter with LYULYUKOV.)

KAROBKIN: I have the honor to congratulate Anton Antonovich! Anna Andreyevna! . . . Marya Antonovna! *(Kisses their hands.)*

KAROBKIN'S WIFE: I heartily congratulate you, Anton Antonovich, on your good fortune!

LYULYUKOV: I have the honor to congratulate you, Anna Andreyevna! *(He kisses her hand, and turns to the audience to smack his lips with gusto.)* Marya Antonovna! I have the honor. *(Goes through the same business.)*

(A number of visitors, who have entered before, now shake ANNA'S *hand and then* MARYA'S, *exclaiming "Anna Andrey-evna!" and "Marya Antonovna!"* BOBCHINSKI *and* DOBCHINSKI *rush in.)*

BOBCHINSKI: I have the honor to congratulate you . . .

DOBCHINSKI: Anton Antonovich, I have the honor to congratulate you!

BOBCHINSKI: . . . on this happy occasion.

DOBCHINSKI: Anna Andreyevna!

BOBCHINSKI: Anna Andreyevna!

(They both try to kiss her hand and bump foreheads.)

DOBCHINSKI: Marya Antonovna! *(Kisses her hand.)* I have the honor to congratulate you. May you enjoy the best of all happiness, and dress in cloth of gold and eat all kinds of beautifully-spiced soups. . . .

BOBCHINSKI *(interrupting)*: Marya Antonovna, I have the honor to congratulate you. May God bring you all sorts of wealth and gold pieces and a baby boy as tiny as this—*(Measures with hand.)* Just big enough to sit in the palm of your hand. Yes! And may the little darling cry with joy all the time! *(He mimics a happy cry.)* Wah, wah, wah!

(Enter COMMISSIONER OF SCHOOLS *and his* WIFE.*)*

COMMISSIONER OF SCHOOLS: I have the honor—

HIS WIFE *(running ahead of him)*: I congratulate you, Anna Andreyevna! *(They kiss each other.)* I am so delighted, really I am! When they told me of the engagement, I was so carried away I couldn't talk. All I could do was cry. I cried and cried—I really sobbed! Then Lukanchik says, "What are you sobbing for, Nastenka?" And I say, "How should I know?" but the tears keep flowing like a river! *(She cries.)*

MAYOR: Please sit down, everybody! Mishka, bring some more chairs. *(The visitors take seats.)*

(The POLICE SUPERINTENDENT *enters.)*

SUPERINTENDENT: I have the honor to congratulate you, your honor.

MAYOR: Thanks, thanks. Please be seated, gentlemen. *(They sit.)*

JUDGE: Now tell us, how it all happened. Give us the complete history of the case.

MAYOR: It was very unusual—he condescended to make the proposal himself.

ANNA: In a most respectful and dignified way. He put it so sweetly: "You have simply made a conquest of me, Anna Andreyevna!"

MARYA: Mamma, now really! That's what he said to *me!*

ANNA: Oh, no doubt he meant it for you, too. Did I say not?

MAYOR: And how he frightened us! "If you refuse me," he screamed, "I'll shoot myself! I'll blow my brains out!"

VISITORS *(ad lib)*: Goodness! . . . You don't say!

JUDGE: That's evidence of strong character!

KAROBKIN: May I ask where our distinguished guest is now?

MAYOR: He has gone away for the day on very important business—

ANNA: To see an uncle and ask for his blessing.

MAYOR: Yes, to ask for his blessing, but tomorrow— *(He sneezes; everyone choruses "Bless you!")* Thanks. As I said, he'll be back again to—*(Sneezes again; again a chorus of "Bless you!" During this, the following voices are heard:)*

SUPERINTENDENT OF POLICE: Good health, your honor.

BOBCHINSKI: A sack of gold pieces and a hundred years!

DOBCHINSKI: May the Lord stretch it to a thousand.

COMMISSIONER OF CHARITIES *(aside)*: I hope you go straight to hell!

KAROBKIN'S WIFE *(aside)*: Drop dead!

MAYOR: Thank you all, and the same to you!

ANNA: We intend to move to St. Petersburg . . . The air here is too . . . too rural! And my husband—he'll be promoted to general.

MAYOR: Yes, gentlemen. I have a consuming ambition to be a general.

JUDGE *(nodding)*: A great voyage demands a great ship.

COMMISSIONER OF CHARITIES: It's the least you deserve for your unselfish service.

JUDGE *(aside)*: Why, a general's uniform fits him like a saddle fits a cow. Now, my friend, that's going too far.

COMMISSIONER OF CHARITIES *(aside)*: General? Well, I'll be goddamned! But he's stupid enough to make it. *(To* MAYOR.*)* When you're a general, don't forget us!

JUDGE: And if any little opening appears, one in which you'll need a talented administrator, don't hesitate—

MAYOR; Of course, of course.

ANNA: There you go again, handing out promises. How can you weigh yourself down with so many obligations?

MAYOR: Promises never hurt anybody.

ANNA: But you can't go on, tying yourself up with nobodies!

KAROBKIN'S WIFE *(aside)*: Did you hear what she called us?

LADY VISITOR: Oh, I *know* her! Just let her have a seat at the table and she'll put her big feet up on it!

*(*POSTMASTER *runs in, out of breath, waving an opened letter.)*

POSTMASTER: Say, here's a funny thing! That man we took for the Inspector—he's not an Inspector!

ALL: What! Not an Inspector?

POSTMASTER: No Inspector at all. I found it out from the letter.

MAYOR *(outraged)*: What? What do you mean? What letter?

POSTMASTER: From the letter he wrote. They bring me a letter to send off. I look at the address and I see "Post Office Street." You could have knocked me over with a stamp! I figures, he's found out something in the Post Office, and he's turning me in. So I take the letter and . . . and open it . . .

MAYOR *(outraged)*: How *could* you?

POSTMASTER: I don't know—some little voice inside kept saying, "Go ahead, open it!" And then a voice came in the other ear, "Stop before you're ruined!" And then back came the other voice, "Open it just a little. . . ." So I broke the seal— Oh, my veins were on fire. But after I read it, they froze, by God! They froze!

MAYOR: How dare you open the letter of such an important official?

POSTMASTER: That's what's so funny. He isn't important or official!

MAYOR: You idiot! Don't you know he's going to marry my

daughter? I'm going to be a general! I'll ship you straight to Siberia!

POSTMASTER: Ech! That Siberia is a long way off. . . . Let me read you this letter.

ALL: Yes, read it! Hurry up!

POSTMASTER *(reading with great difficulty)*: ". . . just to let you know hastily, my dear Tryapichkin, all my adventures. On the way here, an infantry captain had cleaned me out completely, so the keeper of the local flea-bag wanted to throw me into jail. Then all of a sudden—due to my St. Petersburg clothes and aristocratic manner—the entire town assumed I was an Inspector General! At the moment, I am living in style at the Mayor's mansion. It's really open house. I'm flirting madly with the mayor's wife *and* daughter. I can't decide which to start on first. I think the old lady would be more grateful. . . . And everybody lends me as much money as I ask for! They're a ridiculous bunch—feel free to use them in any comic sketches you may want to write. First, there's the Mayor. He's stupid as a mule—"

MAYOR: Impossible! That can't be in there!

POSTMASTER *(showing the line)*: Read it yourself!

MAYOR *(reading)*: . . . "stupid as a mule." *You* wrote it!

POSTMASTER: Me? I'm lucky I can *read!*

COMMISSIONER OF CHARITIES *(impatiently)*: All right, read!

COMMISSIONER OF SCHOOLS: Read it, read it!

POSTMASTER *(resuming)*: . . . . "The Mayor. He's stupid as a mule—"

MAYOR: Damn it! Do you have to keep repeating it?

POSTMASTER *(continues)*: . . . . hmmmmm . . . hmmmmm . . . "as a mule. The Postmaster is a pretty good fellow" . . . hmmmmm . . . hmmmmm . . .

MAYOR: Well, what does it say?

POSTMASTER: Something dirty about me.

MAYOR: Damn it, if you can read dirty things about me, you can read them about yourself!

COMMISSIONER OF CHARITIES: Let me try. *(Puts on his spectacles and reads.*) The Postmaster is like our porter Mikheyev—drinks like a fish.''

POSTMASTER *(to the group.)* Why, the lousy brat ought to be flogged!

COMMISSIONER OF CHARITIES *(continuing)*: "The Charity Commissioner . . . eh . . . hmmm . . . hmmm . . . *(hesitates.)*

KAROBKIN: What are you stopping for?

COMMISSIONER OF CHARITIES: I can't decipher the writing.

KAROBKIN: Let me try. I have perfect eyesight. *(Grabs for letter.* COMMISSIONER *holds it back.)*

COMMISSIONER OF CHARITIES: It's easier to read farther on . . .

MAYOR: Read it all! If one person can be insulted, everybody can be insulted!

KAROBKIN *(reading)*: "The Charity Commissioner, Zemlyanika, is a regular pig in a skull-cap—"

COMMISSIONER OF CHARITIES *(appealing to the group)*: That's supposed to be witty? Who ever saw a pig in a skull-cap?

KAROBKIN *(continues)*: "The Commissioner of Schools stinks of onions . . ."

COMMISSIONER OF SCHOOLS *(to others)*: So help me, no onion has ever touched my lips!

KAROBKIN: ". . . the Judge—"

JUDGE *(quickly)*: I think this letter is irrelevant. What's the point of reading all that rubbish?

COMMISSIONER OF SCHOOLS, CHARITIES *and* POSTMASTER *(together)*: Get on with it . . . Read it through!

KAROBKIN: . . . "Lyapkin-Tyapkin is really *mauvais ton.* *(He pronounces it moves tun, then stops, puzzled.)* That must be some dirty French word.

JUDGE: Devil knows what it means! If it means *swindler*— I'll take him to court!

KAROBKIN *(reading on)*: "Au revoir my dear Tryapichkin. It's such a bore to live as I do—marooned, without sustenance for the intellect" . . .

MAYOR *(in panic)*: He's cut my throat! I'm assassinated—dead!

After him, I say! Catch him! *(Staring wildly.)* Holy Christ! All I can see are pigs' snouts! I'm surrounded by pigs' snouts!

POSTMASTER: How are ya gonna catch him? I told the stable to give him the best troika and horses! God must be laughing at us!

KAROBKIN'S WIFE *(delighted)*: What a mess! I've never heard of anything as awful as this!

JUDGE *(dazed)*: Not only that—he borrowed three hundred from me!

COMMISSIONER OF CHARITIES: And three hundred from *me*.

POSTMASTER *(groaning)*: And me, too.

BOBCHINSKI: And Dobchinski and I were taken for sixty-five— *in bills!*

MAYOR *(beating himself on the forehead)*: How could I *do* it? I must be senile! My brains have turned to mush! Thirty years in the government—not one shopkeeper or contractor could ever gyp me! I outsmarted one slick crook after another! Three governors—themselves the greatest grafters in the empire!—could never find a shred of evidence against me! And now, this simpering little punk! *(He chokes up with wrath.)*

ANNA *(soothingly)*: Oh, it can't be. He's engaged to Machenka! . . .

MAYOR *(furiously)*: Engaged! Your stupidity has even infected me! *(In desperation.)* Look at me, world! All of Christendom— look at me, see how the Mayor's made an ass of himself! Featherbrain! Butter-fingers! *(Shakes fist at himself).* Oh, you hayseed! Taking a brat, a kid in diapers, for a gentleman of rank! And I'm sure some pen-pusher, some paper-stainer will go and put him in a play! He won't spare your rank or profession and everybody will roar and clap their hands! It's driving me mad! . . . Who are you laughing at? Laugh at yourself! *(Stamps on the ground ferociously).* That's what I'd do to the whole pack of scribblers! Ugh, you damned liberals— devil's bastards! I'd scrag you all—grind you to powder! You'd make a great dish for the foul fiend! *(Shakes his fist and grinds his heel into the floor. After a pause.)* I'd better pull myself together. It's true, who God will punish he first drives mad. . . . But that little fathead didn't even *look* like an Inspector! Who was it first said he's the Inspector, huh? Tell me!

COMMISSIONER OF CHARITIES: Our wits were befogged—it was the devil who did it.

JUDGE: Who started the whole idea? Why, there they are—those two enterprising connivers—Dobchinski and Bobchinski!

BOBCHINSKI: I swear it never occurred to me—

DOBCHINSKI: I *hated* even to think of it—

COMMISSIONER OF SCHOOLS: They ran like mad from the inn— (*Mimicking them.*) "He's here! He doesn't pay any money!" What a rare, stinking bird you discovered!

MAYOR: Sure it was you—you snooping old biddies, you goddamned lousy liars! All you do is run around town and stick your pigs' snouts into everything, you blabbermouths—

JUDGE: You cursed Mongolian idiots!

COMMISSIONER OF SCHOOLS: Filthy sausage-heads!

COMMISSIONER OF CHARITIES: Fat-nose dribblers!

MAYOR: Scandal-farters!

(ALL *crowd around them threateningly.*)

BOBCHINSKI: By heaven, it wasn't *me!* It was Dobchinski!

DOBCHINSKI: Oh, now, Peter! You certainly were first—

BOBCHINSKI: Don't blame me! *You* began it!

(A POLICEMAN *enters.*)

POLICEMAN (*loudly, slowly like a court chamberlain*): Gentlemen! On orders of the Emperor, the Inspector-General has arrived!

(*In stalks a tall, imperious figure in magnificent uniform, with glowering eyes and fierce mustache. From the group come simultaneous cries of amazement and fear.* ALL *freeze into position.*)

TABLEAU

(*The* MAYOR *stands at center, stiff as a post, arms outstretched as if begging for mercy, his head bent back. At his right are his angry wife and daughter, turning on him. Beyond them the* POSTMASTER *is turned out to audience with a question on his lips; behind him is the* COMMISSIONER OF SCHOOLS, *completely innocent. At the outer edge of the scene are three lady visitors, sneering at the* MAYOR *and his family. On* MAYOR'S *left is* ZEMLYANIKA, *his head slightly to one side as if eavesdropping. Behind him the* JUDGE *shrugs, lips pursed, his shoulders bent low, as if to say, "Here comes the hangman!" Next to him is* KAROBKIN, *winking at the audience and gesturing contemptuously at the* MAYOR. *Outside the group,* BOBCHINSKI *and* DOBCHINSKI *stare at each other, open-mouthed. All guests stand motionless as statues. They maintain positions for a minute or so.*)

THE CURTAIN FALLS

Georges Feydeau
A FITTING CONFUSION

THE FRENCH WRITER of farces, Georges Feydeau (1862–1921), is very much in the tradition of Plautus. He wrote for popular audiences and was tremendously successful. His farces are not in any way literary or intellectual, but they are enormously ingenious and complex. He is a master of plot construction down to the most unexpected detail, and his plays are consistently energetic and vigorous. Like Plautus, his comedy depends much more on frustration than on fulfillment. Except for the happy ending, we are constantly titillated by itches and lusts that are curiously misdirected or blocked. Feydeau's characters are wonderfully articulate, and they manage to flow together or disturb each other's comfortable spaces in a pattern of crazy crossings and coincidences. In Feydeau's world it seems as if everybody knows—or was once the lover of or married to—everybody else, and all are destined to meet in the same place at the same time. Feydeau was a master of acceleration and snowballing.

A Fitting Confusion (1886), Norman R. Shapiro's punning adaptation and translation of *Tailleur pour Dames*, was Feydeau's first full-length play. Balthasar Moulineaux is a fashionable society doctor, whose medical furnishings and paraphernalia are plainly visible. Like Molière, Feydeau indulges in satire on medical jargon, which is a form of professional mumbo-jumbo and mystification. When Dr. Moulineaux is in a tight spot about his philandering, he usually offers medical explanations. With infinite resourcefulness he tells his wife Yvonne why he had two women in his arms: "A fascinating case of comparative physiology! . . . I was only there as an expert, a specialist. . . . You see, two similar subjects, Yvonne . . . one perfectly normal . . . and the other, a rare example of . . . of . . . of congenital neuroendocrinological pathology. With complications! Lots and lots of fascinating complications! Fainting spells . . . Amnesia . . ." There is no reason why the doctor shouldn't love his beautiful, young wife of six months—he does indeed have great affection for her—but he loves the game of flirtation and seduction even more. He is fascinated by the erotic charms of the illicit.

He is also fascinated by the power of words to create reality. Thus his inventiveness is almost completely verbal. His constantly interrupted seduction scene with Madame Dartagnan is excessively theatrical in its script. Moulineaux is determined to speak as the conventional lover of boulevard comedy, and when he is distracted by the constant comings and goings in his place of assignation, he lapses into the kind of babble that even his highly romantic (but "plutonic") Suzanne is aware of:

SUZANNE: I just had to come! *(Naively.)* That was good of me, wasn't it? Aren't you pleased that I did?

MOULINEAUX *(abstractedly)*: Dear, sweet Suzanne!

SUZANNE *(waiting for an answer)*: Aren't you, Balthasar?

MOULINEAUX *(aside, preoccupied)*: Just knowing he's downstairs . . . Damn! That spoils everything!

SUZANNE: Balthasar?

MOULINEAUX *(aside)*: I wish she didn't tell me. . . . Talk about putting a damper on things! *(Aloud, mechanically.)* Ah! Dear, sweet Suzanne!

SUZANNE *(with a smile)*: You said that, dearest.

This is a seduction that will never, of course, be consummated, which emphasizes its febrile, rhetorical quality, but Moulineaux seems fully committed to the gestures and lexicon of philandering. He is not so vulgar as to make his erotic flourishes depend on mere success or failure. Success, in fact, is unthinkable in a Feydeau comedy.

Feydeau's women are radically different from his men, and the war between the sexes is the most basic force driving the plot. Like Shaw, Feydeau creates women who may seem naive and childlike in worldly matters but who are nevertheless strangely wise, manipulative, and inscrutable, and who usually triumph over the men with effortless certainty. Madame Aigreville, the doctor's mother-in-law, is typical of Feydeau's overtly aggressive and controlling females. She rules her daughter's life and would like to keep her son-in-law in check. She is a flirtatious harpy who schemes to install herself in Moulineaux's household, and she stirs up domestic discord for her own benefit: "Lucky for her [Yvonne, her daughter] I'm here! If not, they would have kissed and made up by now. . . ." Yvonne is doll-like, naive, and good-tempered, but she demands from her husband a full measure of flattering cajolery. She impresses us as totally mindless, as does Moulineaux's would-be mistress, Suzanne, whose kittenish flirtation is never destined to lead anywhere—and certainly not to bed.

Mimi La Flamme, otherwise known as Mathilde de Sainte-Vinaigrette, has a triple status in the play: she is Dartagnan's mistress; she is the former mistress of Moulineaux (alias Baba); and she is also the long-lost wife of Bassinet. She is the archetypal *femme de monde* (or *demi-monde*) who keeps reappearing in Feydeau's comedies and who represents a French type in the upper-middle-class society of the late nineteenth and early twentieth centuries. Mimi/Mathilde is the most status-conscious of all the characters, and she reminds everyone, especially the men, of that solid bourgeois respectability from which they are trying so desperately to flee. Feydeau's attitude to women is strikingly ambivalent, if not occasionally misogynistic. He fears the secret power that women have over men and their capacity, through sex, to destroy—or at least to infantalize—their lovers. *A Fitting Confusion* is a relatively early play (1886); Feydeau's comic anxiety about women will become much more acute in his later work.

For all his extraordinary inventiveness and originality, Feydeau still relies on traditional comic types, many of whom have their roots in Plautus. In this play Etienne is the clever servant who is like Plautus' slaves and parasites. His authority extends far beyond his humble function in the play, and he freely offers his master advice and commiserates with him. He is a plot manipulator, but he seems to do many things for his own pleasure rather than for that of his superiors. There is some question whether he or any of the servants in Feydeau or Plautus really acknowledge the existence of any superiors. Etienne certainly considers Moulineaux extremely stupid, gauche, inept, and vulgar. That doesn't seem to block his genuine affection for him. He tolerates and indulges the doctor's irrationality as one would that of a child.

The classic bore is brilliantly represented by Bassinet, and he is a character who will reappear over and over again in Feydeau's work, since boredom may be the most formidable enemy of the men about town who are determined, at all costs, to pursue their pleasure. Bassinet is fantastically persistent; it is almost impossible to get rid of him. Even his long-escaped wife Mimi cannot ultimately shake him off, but through amazing coincidences, is forcibly reunited with him. Boredom is always tenacious—that is why it is so maddeningly intolerable in polite society. No one will allow Bassinet to complete his story about his dressmaker tenant who ran off with a young gigolo. But Bassinet can take an infinite amount of insult without being ruffled. That is another characteristic of bores: they are remarkably thick-skinned. There is no getting rid of them through any offense to their presumed sensitivity. Feydeau works a double irony in having Bassinet constantly commenting on the oppressiveness of others: "Some people are born pests. . . . You can never get rid of them." The ultimate irony of *A Fitting Confusion* is that Moulineaux ends the play in the style of Bassinet with a shaggy-dog story that no one will allow him to finish.

A FITTING CONFUSION

TRANSLATED BY NORMAN R. SHAPIRO

CHARACTERS

BASSINET — *friend*
MOULINEAUX — *husband*
DARTAGNAN
ETIENNE — ~~wife~~ *maid*
MADAME AIGREVILLE — *mother*
SUZANNE
MIMI
YVONNE — ~~maid~~ *wife*
MADAME D'HERBLAY
LILY

ACT I

(The living room in Dr. Moulineaux's apartment. In the rear wall, center, a double door leading to the hall. Near the door, a small table. Down right, the door to Yvonne's bedroom; down left, the door to Moulineaux's. Up right and left, two more doors. Left of center, a desk and armchair. The desk is covered with books, papers, medical instruments, etc. Down right, an end table, flanked by two chairs. On the table, a small bell. Down left, a chaise longue. Other furniture, pictures, medical accessories, etc. ad libitum.*)*

(At rise, the set is in semi-darkness, indicating that it is still early in the morning. ETIENNE *enters, up left, carrying a feather duster, broom, bucket, etc., and yawning sleepily.)*

ETIENNE *(putting down his equipment and partially opening the double door to air out the room)*: There! *(Rubbing his eyes, yawning.)* Aaah! Of all times to have to get up! First thing in the morning! Did you ever see . . . ? Just when you finally feel like sleeping . . . Really, it's all backwards. We do it all wrong. We should wait until we have to get up to go to bed. It would make more sense . . . *(Yawning.)* Aaah! Talk about being tired! *(He gives an even more energetic yawn.)* Aaaaaah! *(Shaking his head.)* One more like that and I'll never get it shut! I must be coming down with something. It's the liver, that's what it is. Mine, I mean. Not cook's . . . *(Yawning.)* I'll have to ask monsieur. That's one good thing about working for a doctor. When you're sick, you don't get a bill to make you sicker! And for someone like me . . . *(Shaking his head.)* Talk about being sick . . . Really . . . Monsieur says I've got a bad case of "terminal inertia" . . . Whatever that is . . . Something about my *limp* glands . . . Anyway, I save a bundle. Of course, it was even better before . . . *(Yawning.)* Six months ago . . . Before he went and got married . . . But I shouldn't complain. Madame is very nice . . . As wives go, that is . . . And as long as there has to be one . . . *(Yawning.)*

373

I suppose we could have done a lot worse, monsieur and me! Well, time to wake him up . . . *(Moving down left, he stops at the door and shakes his head.)* Did you ever see . . . ? *(Pointing down right, then down left.)* His room . . . Her room . . . Why bother to get married? I mean, if you're not even going to . . . *(With a shrug.)* I guess I'll just never understand these society people! *(Knocking on the door, calling.)* Monsieur! Monsieur! *(After a pause.)* Hmm! Fast asleep! I'd better go in. *(He opens the door and stands at the threshold.)* Monsieur! *(Gaping.)* What? *(He disappears offstage for a few seconds, still speaking.)* Monsieur? Monsieur? *(Reappearing.)* And his bed isn't even slept in! *(With a sudden realization, shocked.)* Oh! Don't tell me. No! I don't believe it! No, no! Not monsieur! Someone else, maybe, but . . . No! Not monsieur! *(Looking across to the door, down right.)* And his wife . . . So trusting, poor thing . . . Did you ever see . . . ?

YVONNE'S VOICE: Etienne?

ETIENNE: Oh, my! Speak of the devil . . .

(YVONNE enters, down right.)

YVONNE: Ah, there you are!

ETIENNE *(moving upstage)*: Madame?

YVONNE: Is monsieur out of bed?

ETIENNE *(flustered)*: Yes. Yes, he . . . No! I mean . . . Yes . . . That is . . .

YVONNE: What are you talking about, Etienne? Yes? No? What on earth is the matter with you?

ETIENNE: The matter, madame? With me?

YVONNE: Yes! I ask you a perfectly simple question . . .

(She crosses toward the door, down left.)

ETIENNE *(quickly blocking her path)*: No, no! Madame shouldn't . . .

YVONNE *(surprised)*: I what?

ETIENNE: It's monsieur . . . He's . . . He's . . . *(At a loss.)* He's sick!

YVONNE: Sick? My husband?

ETIENNE: Well . . .

YVONNE: Then I have to . . . *(Trying to get past him.)* Let me . . . If he's sick, for goodness' sake . . .

ETIENNE *(correcting himself)*: Maybe not sick, exactly . . . Not very, I mean . . .

YVONNE: But you said . . .

ETIENNE: And besides, it's . . . it's . . . *(Struggling to find an excuse.)* It's full of dust in there! I've been sweeping. And . . . and the windows are wide-open. Madame will catch cold!

YVONNE: Sweeping, Etienne? When monsieur is sick in bed? Really, what's got into you?

(She pushes her way past him and into the room, down left.)

ETIENNE: But madame . . . *(To the audience.)* Oh, my! He's done for now! *(With a shrug.)* Well, he can't say I didn't try . . .

YVONNE'S VOICE: Oh! That . . . That . . .

(She reappears.)

YVONNE: That beast! That . . . that philanderer! *(Crossing right.)* That . . . That . . . *(Confronting* ETIENNE, *sarcastically.)* Well, Etienne! Very nice! Congratulations!

ETIENNE *(playing innocent)*: Madame?

YVONNE: "Sick," my foot!

ETIENNE: But I was only—

YVONNE: Monsieur would be proud of you! You're worth every sou he pays you, I'm sure!

ETIENNE: I was only trying to spare madame . . .

YVONNE: Yes, of course! How can I ever thank you? *(At the door, down right.)* Oh! Six months, and already he . . . Oh!

(She storms out.)

ETIENNE: Poor thing! I don't blame her. Did you ever see . . . ? It's a shame, that's what it is. Well, he'll never hear the end of it! And it will serve him right if you ask me! *(A knocking is heard offstage.)* Now how on earth . . . ? At eight in the morning. *(More persistent knocking.)* Who's there?

MOULINEAUX'S VOICE *(in a loud whisper)*: Open the door, for heaven's sake!

ETIENNE *(to the audience)*: It's about time!

(He exits, upstage, ostensibly to open the outer door.)

ETIENNE'S VOICE: Sorry, monsieur, I—

MOULINEAUX'S VOICE: Yes, yes . . . Never mind.

(MOULINEAUX enters in bedraggled evening clothes, looking very much the worse for wear, with ETIENNE at his heels.)

MOULINEAUX *(softly)*: Just let me get to my room . . .

ETIENNE *(ingenuously)*: Has monsieur been out all evening?

MOULINEAUX *(at the door, down left)*: Shhh! Not so loud!

ETIENNE: Sorry! *(Repeating, in a whisper.)* Has monsieur been out all evening?

MOULINEAUX: What does it look like? My wife doesn't know, does she?

ETIENNE: I'm afraid she has a strong suspicion, monsieur. She was here just a moment ago, and . . .

MOULINEAUX: Damn!

ETIENNE: And none too pleased, I might add. (MOULINEAUX *begins pacing nervously.)* Not that I blame her, if monsieur doesn't mind my saying . . .

MOULINEAUX: Not that you . . . What business is it—

ETIENNE: Tsk tsk tsk! If monsieur would take a friend's advice. A good friend . . .

MOULINEAUX: What? Who, damn it?

ETIENNE *(modestly)*: Me, monsieur.

MOULINEAUX: I beg your pardon! I'll thank you to remember your . . . Oh, never mind! *(Pacing again.)* Good God, what a night! I should have had my head examined! A place like that! And then, to have to sleep on that bench! *(He sneezes.)* I'll be lucky if I don't come down with pneumonia! The Folies Exotiques indeed!

ETIENNE: Ah? Monsieur spent the night at the Folies Exotiques?

MOULINEAUX: Yes. No! I mean . . . Please, Etienne, it's none of your concern.

ETIENNE: One look and anyone can tell that he's been out all night. Doing heaven knows what . . .

MOULINEAUX *(losing patience)*: Really, that's quite enough! Go about your business, and leave me to mine!

ETIENNE: Very good, monsieur. I'm going. *(Shaking his head.)* Tsk tsk tsk! And at his age . . . Did you ever see . . . ?

(He picks up his equipment and exits, up center.)

MOULINEAUX: Just what I need! A little folk wisdom from *(Emphasizing.)* my *friend*! Oh, that place! Never again, believe me! *(He sneezes.)* Never! And it's not as if it was my idea, damn it! But Madame Dartagnan . . . Suzanne . . . That gorgeous creature! That . . . that vixen! That . . . *(Sighing.)* Ah! I'm putty in her hands! Those sweet little hands. You'd think I should know better! "Never have a beautiful woman for a patient!" That's what they used to tell us. "Especially if she's married. And has a husband. You'll be playing with fire!" How right they were! Only they should have added: "And be sure to stay away from the ones who love the Folies Exotiques and who tell you to meet them there. Under the clock. At two in the morning. And to wait for them." And wait, and wait, and wait! She might as well have told me: "Till hell freezes over!" So there I was, standing under that damn clock, like an idiot. Two. Two-fifteen. Two-thirty. By three, when I see that I don't see her . . . that she's nowhere to be seen . . . Well, you can imagine. I was fit to be tied. Not to mention that I could hardly keep my eyes open. So I came straight back here. "At least I'll get a good night's sleep," I told myself. Just one little problem. I get to the door, and . . . no key! I left it in my pants. My other ones. Before I got dressed. Dressed up, I mean. *(Sardonically.)* For my big night with Madame Dartagnan. Well, now what? Here I am, locked out of my own apartment. I can't very well ring the bell or I'll wake Yvonne. I'd pick the lock if I had anything to pick it with. And if I knew how . . . So the only thing to do is to get some sleep and wait until it's light. On that damn bench downstairs. *(He sits down at his desk.)* Oh! If you never slept on a bench, you don't know what you're missing! I ache all over. *(He sneezes.)* And cold? You can't imagine! *(Picking up a pad and pen from the desk.)* Maybe I should write myself a prescription. *(He pauses.)* On second thought, not if I want to get better!

(YVONNE *enters, down right.*)

YVONNE: Well, look who's here!

MOULINEAUX *(startled)*: Yvonne! I—

YVONNE *(interrupting, sarcastically)*: What a nice surprise! Of all people . . .

MOULINEAUX: You . . . I . . . Did you sleep well, my love? I must say, you're up early.

YVONNE: And so are you, my sweet!

MOULINEAUX *(embarrassed, trying to be natural)*: Me? Not really. No earlier than usual.

YVONNE: Oh?

MOULINEAUX: Well, maybe a little. Nothing like getting a nice early start. Especially when you have a lot of work to do.

YVONNE *(confronting him, point-blank)*: Where did you spend the night?

MOULINEAUX *(with a start)*: What?

YVONNE: I said, "Where did you spend the night?"

MOULINEAUX: I . . . I heard you. Where did I spend . . . You mean . . . *(With a nervous little laugh.)* You mean, you don't remember?

YVONNE *(curtly)*: Remember what?

MOULINEAUX *(stalling for time)*: What . . . What I told you . . . Yesterday, when I left. I . . . I did tell you, didn't I? Just before I went out the door . . . Remember? *(Pointing upstage.)* You were standing there . . . and I was there . . . and I told you about . . . About Bassinet, remember? Poor Bassinet. I said: "I'm going to be with Monsieur Bassinet. He's sick. Terribly sick, and . . . and . . ."

YVONNE: And you spent the night with him.

MOULINEAUX: Exactly! I had to . . . You have no idea how sick he is, poor devil!

YVONNE *(sarcastically)*: Really?

MOULINEAUX: It was my duty, Yvonne! A doctor's first duty is to care for his patients. Even if it means sitting up with them all night.

YVONNE: Of course! In evening clothes?

MOULINEAUX *(beginning to babble)*: Yes, in . . . in . . . in . . . No, not always, but . . . Look, I'll explain. Bassinet is very sick.

YVONNE: Yes, you said that.

MOULINEAUX: He's . . . He's at death's door. The least little shock could kill him, but . . . But he has no idea. And, naturally, we want to keep it from him. So . . . So a few of us . . . a few of my colleagues and myself . . . Well, we decided to have our consultation, but to make believe it was a party. Everything very fancy. Evening clothes and all that. So he wouldn't suspect. A little dancing. You know. A little dancing, a little singing. *(He does a little dance, singing to the tune of "Sur le Pont d'Avignon.")*

> Cholera, cholera,
> If you get it, you'll regret it.
> Cholera, cholera,
> Sorry, friend, but that's the end.
> La la la, la la la . . .

Really, it worked like a charm. He never suspected a thing.

YVONNE *(hypocritcally)*: How clever!

MOULINEAUX: Well, sometimes we doctors have to tell a white lie.

YVONNE: Yes, don't you . . . ? Your duty to your patients, after all.

MOULINEAUX: Exactly!

YVONNE: Especially a patient like Bassinet, who's at death's door . . .

MOULINEAUX *(relieved at having apparently convinced her, with conviction)*: Especially . . .

(ETIENNE appears at the double door, up center.)

ETIENNE *(announcing)*: Monsieur Bassinet.

(BASSINET enters in hat and coat as ETIENNE exits.)

BASSINET *(to MOULINEAUX)*: Good morning, monsieur.

MOULINEAUX *(under his breath)*: Good God!

BASSINET *(noticing YVONNE, nodding)*: Madame . . .

MOULINEAUX (*moving quickly to join* BASSINET *in front of the double door, in a whisper*): Shhh! Don't say a word! You're sick! You're sick!

BASSINET (*confused*): I'm what?

YVONNE (*with exaggerated affability*): So nice to see you, Monsieur Bassinet! I hope you're well?

BASSINET (*jovially*): Thank you, madame! You can see for yourself—

MOULINEAUX (*quickly interrupting*): How sick he is! You can see how sick . . . (*To* YVONNE.) Just look . . . Death's door . . . (*To* BASSINET, *in a whisper.*) Will you please keep quiet! You're sick, I'm telling you . . .

BASSINET (*to* MOULINEAUX): But why . . .

YVONNE (*to* BASSINET): I must say, monsieur, you look quite healthy . . .

BASSINET (*to* YVONNE): Thank you, madame!

MOULINEAUX (*to* YVONNE): But he's not! (*To* BASSINET.) You're not!

BASSINET (*to* MOULINEAUX): I'm not?

YVONNE: And he says he feels so well!

MOULINEAUX: He says . . . He says . . . What does he know? Is he a doctor? I'm telling you, he's at death's door!

BASSINET (*with a start*): I am?

MOULINEAUX (*to* BASSINET): Yes, yes, yes! (*To* YVONNE.): Just look at him! (*To* BASSINET.) Only we've been trying to keep it from you. The least little shock could kill you! (*Aside.*) Too bad! Better him than me!

(*He moves upstage.*)

BASSINET: My God! What did he say?

YVONNE (*to* BASSINET): Why yes, monsieur! Tsk tsk tsk! Didn't you know? (*Pointedly.*) That's why my husband spent all night with you.

MOULINEAUX (*aside*): Ayyy!

BASSINET (*to* YVONNE): He did? When?

YVONNE: Why . . . Just last night . . . With all those other doctors . . . The party . . . The singing, the dancing . . .

MOULINEAUX (*frantically, to* BASSINET): Of course! Don't tell me you don't remember! Or . . . Or . . . Or maybe you never noticed! (*To* YVONNE.) Can't you see he's delirious? (*To* BASSINET, *in a whisper, face-to-face.*) Will you please shut up! All you do is put your foot in your mouth!

   (*He crosses up right.*)

BASSINET: What? (*Aside.*) If you ask me, he's the sick one! (*Tapping his temple with his forefinger.*) Sick in the head!

YVONNE (*moving toward* BASSINET): Well now, Monsieur Bassinet. You be sure to take good care of yourself, won't you! Even if if you are the picture of health. (*Glaring at* MOULINEAUX.) For a man at death's door!

BASSINEȚ: But . . .

YVONNE: Then again, there's no telling. You could linger for days.

BASSINET: But I—

MOULINEAUX (*with a casual wave*): Oh, weeks! Months! Years!

YVONNE: Yes, I'm sure.

BASSINET: But—

MOULINEAUX: Some people linger all their lives! It's possible . . .

YVONNE (*to* MOULINEAUX): At death's door?

BASSINET: But I—

MOULINEAUX (*to* YVONNE): Yes . . . It's . . . It's what we doctors call "chronic."

YVONNE: And so seldom fatal.

BASSINET: But . . . But . . .

MOULINEAUX: Right! Only when they die . . .

YVONNE (*to* MOULINEAUX): My! How interesting!

BASSINET (*to* MOULINEAUX): Monsieur . . . ?

YVONNE (*aside*): He's not fooling me for one minute! I know what he's up to. (*Crossing up right.*) Just wait until I tell Mamma about this!

(She exits.)

MOULINEAUX *(to* BASSINET, *furious)*: You . . . You, you . . . Oh! Have you any idea what you . . . You and your big mouth! Can't you take a little hint, for heaven's sake?

BASSINET: A little . . . When you keep telling me I'm dying . . . What kind of a—

MOULINEAUX: Of course I did! And you . . . You kept denying it! You wouldn't shut up! Anybody else would have understood. But you . . .

BASSINET: Understood? Understood what?

MOULINEAUX: What's going on, goddammit!

BASSINET: But I don't have the slightest—

MOULINEAUX: If I tell you you're at death's door, you should stay put! I've got my reasons. But, no! You've got to argue.

BASSINET: Please, I—

MOULINEAUX: Besides, who asked you to stick your nose in my business?

BASSINET *(taken aback)*: I beg your pardon? Stick my—

MOULINEAUX: And at a time like this! Today of all days! If you had any common sense, you wouldn't have come here in the first place.

BASSINET *(beginning to grow indignant)*: Really, monsieur—

MOULINEAUX *(angrily)*: A child would know better than to come to someone's home the morning after a gala at the Folies Exotiques. Especially when they told their wife they were with you the night before. Taking care of you. Because you were so sick . . .

BASSINET: The Folies . . . *(Suddenly comprehending)*. Oh! You mean, you told madame . . . She thinks that you . . . That I . . . Oh! Well, why didn't you say so? I had no idea . . .

MOULINEAUX: No idea, no idea! You have to spell everything out for some people!

BASSINET: Well, you can hardly expect me to—

MOULINEAUX: All right, never mind! The damage is done! *(Brusquely.)* What is it? What do you want?

BASSINET: Monsieur?

MOULINEAUX *(sarcastically)*: To what do I owe the pleasure?

BASSINET: You mean, why am I here?

MOULINEAUX: So to speak . . .

BASSINET: Well, I'll tell you.

MOULINEAUX: Please do!

BASSINET: As one friend to another. After all, what's the good of being friends if we can't do a little favor now and then? Don't you agree?

MOULINEAUX: I'm sure . . .

BASSINET: That's why I'm here.

MOULINEAUX (*aside*): Now that's more like it! (*To* BASSINET.) Well, I never refuse a favor!

BASSINET: No, monsieur. That's why I came to ask you. I knew you wouldn't say no.

MOULINEAUX: Why *you* came to ask *me* . . . ?

BASSINET: And I'll be terribly grateful, believe me.

MOULINEAUX (*realizing that he has misunderstood.*) Aha . . . I see . . . (*Aside.*) I should have known. (*Passing his hand in front of his eyes.*) You'll have to forgive me, monsieur. I'm rather tired this morning. I haven't had a wink of sleep.

BASSINET: Oh, I'm sorry.

MOULINEAUX: I had to spend the night on the bench, downstairs. And if you ever slept on a bench . . .

BASSINET: Me? Hardly, monsieur.

MOULINEAUX: Well, if you had, you'd know what I mean! I'm really not myself.

   (*He sits down on one of the chairs by the end table, down right.*)

BASSINET: Quite all right, monsieur. I understand.

   (*He sits down on the other chair, next to him.*)

MOULINEAUX: Besides, my mother-in-law is coming in from the country this afternoon, for heaven knows how long, and . . . Well, what more do I have to say?

BASSINET (*nodding*): Indeed . . . Indeed . . .

MOULINEAUX *(aside)*: Now to get rid of him. *(He rings the little bell on the end table.)* If you don't mind, monsieur, I'll just be a moment.

BASSINET: Please . . .

(ETIENNE appears at the double door.)

ETIENNE: Monsieur rang?

MOULINEAUX *(getting up)*: Ah, Etienne . . . *(Joining him at the door and speaking ·in a whisper, indicating BASSINET with a subtle nod.)* I want that pest out of here in five minutes, understand?

ETIENNE *(whispering)*: Yes, monsieur. The usual?

MOULINEAUX *(whispering)*: The usual. The calling card. Any one you can find. Someone who has to see me immediately. You know . . .

ETIENNE *(whispering)*: Monsieur can count on me.

MOULINEAUX *(aloud, pretending)*: And be sure everything is ready when madame's mother arrives.

ETIENNE *(aloud)*: Very good, monsieur.

(He exits.)

MOULINEAUX *(returning down right, sitting, to BASSINET)*: Now then, you were saying . . . something about a favor.

BASSINET: Yes. I don't know if you recall, but last year my uncle died.

MOULINEAUX: Oh, tsk tsk tsk! I'm sorry to hear it.

BASSINET: No need to be, monsieur. I inherited a small fortune.

MOULINEAUX: You did? Congratulations!

BASSINET: Yes. And I used it to buy a house. Around the corner. On Rue de Milan. Number seventy.

MOULINEAUX *(feigning great interest)*: Aha. Aha . . .

BASSINET: The only trouble is, I'm having a devil of a time renting the apartments.

MOULINEAUX *(nodding sympathetically)*: Well . . .

BASSINET *(standing up)*: So I thought, if I came to you, maybe you wouldn't mind . . . Since you see so many patients . . .

Well, I thought maybe you could help me try to rent one or two . . .

(*He takes a packet of prospectuses from his pocket.*)

MOULINEAUX (*jumping to his feet*): What?

BASSINET (*handing him a prospectus*): See? All the information . . .

MOULINEAUX (*furious*): Help you try to . . . You mean to stand there and tell me you had the nerve . . .

BASSINET: But—

MOULINEAUX: . . . to come here . . .

BASSINET: But monsieur—

MOULINEAUX: . . . to burst in on me, first thing in the morning . . .

BASSINET: Please! Let me—

MOULINEAUX: . . . to complicate my life, just for . . . for . . . (*He brandishes the prospectus.*) for your apartments?

(*He puts the prospectus into his pocket.*)

BASSINET: But don't you understand? It can help you too!

MOULINEAUX: Of all the . . .

BASSINET: My apartments are unhealthy! They're . . . they're cold and damp. They have drafts. They'll do wonders for your practice!

MOULINEAUX: They'll do . . . (*Losing his temper.*) You can't be serious! If you think for one moment that I'm going to recommend your damn unhealthy apartments to anyone . . .

(*He crosses left.*)

BASSINET (*following him*): Only some of them. Really! Not all of them are that bad!

MOULINEAUX: I don't care! Some of them . . . All of them . . .

BASSINET (*insistent*): Take One B, for example. It's a beauty! And all furnished! It's a steal at the price.

MOULINEAUX: I'm sure!

BASSINET: A dressmaker used to rent it, but she ran off without paying. It's really quite a story if you want a good laugh. You see, she was a dressmaker, I told you, but one day—

MOULINEAUX *(interrupting)*: Excuse me, but I'm not interested! I don't give a damn about your story or your apartment! And I couldn't care less about your dressmaker, understand?

BASSINET: My . . . ? Oh, no, not *my* dressmaker, monsieur. *(Chuckling)* Why would I have—

MOULINEAUX: Whatever!

BASSINET: She was only my tenant.

MOULINEAUX: Yes. Well, what am I supposed to do with her?

BASSINET: You? Why, nothing. But if you could help me rent her apartment . . .

MOULINEAUX *(losing patience)*: Look! That's enough about your apartment! You really picked a fine time. *(Crossing up right.)* As if I didn't have enough to worry about . . . *(Pointing to the door, up right.)* You saw, just now . . . My wife . . . Thanks to you!

BASSINET *(with a note of bitterness)*: Ah, monsieur . . . Don't complain. At least you have one. All of us aren't so lucky. *(Sighing.)* Take me . . . I lost mine.

MOULINEAUX *(absentmindedly, nodding)*: Fine! Fine!

BASSINET *(startled)*: "Fine"? What's so fine about it?

MOULINEAUX *(correcting, himself)*: Sorry! I meant: "Shame! What a shame!" *(Shaking his head.)* Tsk tsk tsk!

(He moves left.)

BASSINET *(dramatically)*: Yes. Life can be so cruel, monsieur! One minute I have a beautiful, lovely wife, and the next minute she's taken from me.

MOULINEAUX *(surprised)*: That quick? By what? Apoplexy?

BASSINET: No, monsieur. By a soldier. I left them sitting on a park bench one morning. In the Tuileries. To go get a cigar. When I came back, they were gone. That's the last I ever saw of her!

MOULINEAUX *(unconvincingly)*: What a shame! Tsk tsk tsk!

BASSINET *(sighing)*: Oh, well.

(The door bell rings.)

MOULINEAUX *(aside)*: Ah, Etienne. Thank heavens!

(He moves up toward the double door as ETIENNE *appears carrying a little tray with a calling card.)*

ETIENNE: Excuse me, monsieur, but there's a gentleman . . . *(Handing him the card, whispering.)* It was the only one I could find, monsieur *(Aloud.)* He says he has to see monsieur immediately. Urgent business.

MOULINEAUX: Aha! *(With a broad wink to* ETIENNE, *back turned to* BASSINET.) Of course, Etienne . . . of course. *(To* BASSINET.) I'm sorry, Monsieur Bassinet. You'll have to excuse me. *(Holding up the calling card.)* This fellow's a terrible nuisance, but I really have no choice. I'm afraid I'll have to see him.

BASSINET: Certainly. I understand.

MOULINEAUX *(trying to urge him out the double door)*: So please . . . You will excuse me . . .

BASSINET *(not budging)*: Believe me, I know the type.

MOULINEAUX: Yes, I imagine.

BASSINET: Some people are born pests. *(MOULINEAUX casts a meaningful glance at* ETIENNE.) You can never get rid of them. *(Sitting down on the chaise longue, down left, to* ETIENNE.) Show him in, young man!

MOULINEAUX: What?   a pest

BASSINET *(to* MOULINEAUX): If he sees that you have a guest, maybe he'll take the hint and leave.

MOULINEAUX *(aside)*: Incredible! *(Aloud.)* But I'm sure it's a personal matter.

BASSINET: It is?

MOULINEAUX *(moving over to the chaise longue, waving the calling card in* BASSINET'S *face)*: I'm sure that Monsieur . . . Monsieur . . . *(He tries unsuccessfully to catch a glimpse of the name on the card.)* I mean, I'm sure he wants to speak to me in private!

BASSINET: Oh. Well, if you think so . . . *(Grabbing the card out of* MOULINEAUX'S *hand.)* Monsieur Who? by the way . . .

MOULINEAUX *(recoiling)*: I beg your—

BASSINET *(reading)*: Chevassus? Why didn't you say so? Of all people! Old Chevassus! He's one of my dearest friends!

MOULINEAUX (*with a start*): He is?

BASSINET: I'll just say hello, and then I'll be on my way.

MOULINEAUX (*abashed*): But . . . No! No! You can't! (*Grabbing the card back.*) It's . . . it's not him! It's . . . it's his father!

BASSINET (*laughing*): His . . . Don't be silly! Chevassus? He doesn't have one. He never did!

MOULINEAUX: But . . . but . . .

BASSINET (*reflecting on his last remark*): That is . . . I suppose he did, but . . .

MOULINEAUX: I mean, his uncle!

BASSINET (*hardly listening*): But long ago, and . . .

MOULINEAUX: It's his uncle. (*Babbling.*) His brother's father . . . His . . . His father's son. His . . . his uncle!

BASSINET: Oh? His uncle?

MOULINEAUX: Yes! Yes! And I'm sure he'd rather not let anyone know he's here.

BASSINET: Aha.

MOULINEAUX: So please . . . (*He pulls him up bodily from the chaise longue.*) If you don't mind . . . Etienne will show you out. (*To* ETIENNE.) Etienne, monsieur is leaving.

ETIENNE (*still at the double door*): Very good, monsieur.

(BASSINET *begins to move toward the door, but once there he stops.*)

BASSINET: Look . . . (*Moving to the door, up left.*) Why don't I just wait in here until he leaves? That will save me the trouble of coming back tomorrow.

(*He exits.* MOULINEAUX *hands on hips, agape, watches in disbelief as he shuts the door behind him.*)

ETIENNE: Not meaning to contradict, but I believe monsieur is staying.

MOULINEAUX: Yes. It would seem . . . (*With a shrug.*) Well, let him! He'll have a good long wait in there.

(BASSINET *opens the door and pokes his head out.*)

BASSINET (*to* MOULINEAUX): I say . . .

MOULINEAUX: Now what?

BASSINET: I was just thinking. I can help you get rid of him, monsieur, if you like. It's a trick I use sometimes. I'll ring the bell and send in my card. You can tell him there's somebody who wants to see you. Some pest! See what I mean?

MOULINEAUX: Oh, I do. I do. But it really won't be . . . (BASSINET *pulls his head back and shuts the door without waiting for* MOULINEAUX'S *answer.*) . . . necessary, thank you! I said . . . (*Letting himself fall into the armchair by the desk, shaking his head with a sigh.*) Some days, Etienne! Some days . . .

ETIENNE: Yes, monsieur.

MOULINEAUX: Isn't that idiot ever going to leave?

ETIENNE: Begging monsieur's pardon, but I should think that, as a doctor . . . Well . . .

MOULINEAUX (*hardly listening*): Damn nuisance!

ETIENNE: If I had the right to poison people, like monsieur . . .

MOULINEAUX (*getting up, yawning*): Good God, what a morning! It never rains but it pours! I can't keep my eyes open.

ETIENNE: Perhaps monsieur should get some rest. (*Rather ironically*). After all he's been through . . .

MOULINEAUX: My sentiments exactly! (*He goes over to the chaise longue.*) What I need is a nap. (*He lies down and stretches out.*) A nice long nap. See that I'm not disturbed.

ETIENNE: Certainly, monsieur. (*He starts to leave, up center, as* MOULINEAUX *already begins to snore, but stops at the door.*) Does monsieur want me to wake him?

MOULINEAUX (*rousing himself*): Hmm? What?

ETIENNE: I asked monsieur if he wants me to come and wake him.

MOULINEAUX: Yes. Tomorrow. Next week. Only not if I'm sleeping.

ETIENNE (*nodding*): Aha. Of course.

(*He exits as* MOULINEAUX *falls asleep and begins to snore again. After a few moments the door bell rings, followed by the sounds of general commotion offstage.*)

MADAME AIGREVILLE'S VOICE: I'm here, loves. I'm here!

ETIENNE'S VOICE: But . . . but . . .

(MADAME AIGREVILLE *bursts in, up center, closely followed by an anxious* ETIENNE. *She is carrying an overnight bag.*)

MADAME AIGREVILLE (*laying the bag down on the table by the double door*): Yvonne! Moulineaux!

ETIENNE (*trying to quiet her*): But madame, monsieur is—

MOULINEAUX (*waking with a start*) ⎫
⎬ (*Together*) ⎫ What in the name of—
MADAME AIGREVILLE ⎭ ⎬ I'm here!

ETIENNE (*to* MOULINEAUX): Monsieur, it's madame . . .

MOULINEAUX (*jumping up*): Already? . . . I mean . . .

MADAME AIGREVILLE (*to* ETIENNE): Go call my daughter . . .

MOULINEAUX (*to* MADAME AIGREVILLE): Mother! . . . How nice! . . .

ETIENNE (*at the door, up right, calling*): Madame . . . Madame . . .

   (*He exits.*)

MOULINEAUX (*to* MADAME AIGREVILLE): How nice to see you!

ETIENNE'S VOICE: It's madame's mother, madame . . .

MADAME AIGREVILLE: I'm early!

MOULINEAUX: Yes, yes. I see . . .

   (YVONNE *appears at the door, up right, and runs to greet* MADAME AIGREVILLE, *center stage.*)

YVONNE: Mamma!

MADAME ALGREVILLE: Yvonne, precious! I'm here! I'm here!

YVONNE: Let me look at you, Mamma!

   (*She gives her a kiss.*)

MOULINEAUX (*aside, rubbing his eyes*): Damn! It's not a bad dream . . .

MADAME AIGREVILLE (*going over to the chaise longue, to* MOULI-NEAUX, *holding out her cheek*): Moulineaux, you naughty boy! Aren't you going to give Mother a nice big kiss too?

MOULINEAUX: Of course I am. As soon as I get over the surprise . . . the joy . . .

MADAME AIGREVILLE: Why, thank you.

MOULINEAUX: The pleasure of waking up suddenly and finding you here . . . One minute, no mother-in-law, next minute, there she is. *(Aside.)* Hovering like a harpie! *(Aloud, to* MADAME AIGREVILLE.*)* It takes a moment to adjust, to calm the nerves.

MADAME AIGREVILLE: You sweet thing!

MOULINEAUX: Besides, I want to be wide-awake. I want to savor the moment to the fullest.

MADAME AIGREVILLE *(on whom the irony is lost, throwing her arms around his neck)*: Moulineaux, you're a gem!

(She gives him a resounding kiss.)

YVONNE *(to* MADAME AIGREVILLE, *curtly)*: Yes, isn't he!

MOULINEAUX: I agree. A little tired, but a gem.

MADAME AIGREVILLE *(to* YVONNE*)*: You're such a lucky girl, Yvonne.

(While MADAME AIGREVILLE'S *back is turned,* MOULINEAUX *wipes his mouth surreptitiously on his sleeve.)*

MOULINEAUX *(with mock sincerity)*: Mother!

MADAME AIGREVILLE *(glancing back and forth at them, with a sob in her voice)*: So lucky, so lucky. I'm so happy to be here. And to see you both so . . . so happy.

YVONNE *(aside)*: Ha!

MADAME AIGREVILLE: So lucky.

MOULINEAUX *(to* MADAME AIGREVILLE*)*: And we're so happy, Mother, to see you so happy. And so lucky that you could come. So lucky . . .

MADAME AIGREVILLE: Ah! Marriage agrees with you both, I can tell! *(Scrutinizing.)* Though, now that I look at you . . . *(To* MOULINEAUX.*)* Have you lost weight, son? You look a little thin, poor dear.

MOULINEAUX: Well, perhaps a little.

MADAME AIGREVILLE *(to* YVONNE, *ingenuously)*: Of course, you make up for him. So it all evens out!

YVONNE: Mother!

MADAME AIGREVILLE *(to* MOULINEAUX*)*: But tell me, son, why are you all dressed up? You look as if you're going to a funeral.

MOULINEAUX: Why, it's for you, Mother.

MADAME AIGREVILLE: What?

MOULINEAUX: I mean, in your honor.

YVONNE: He means, he's been up all night, Mother. That's what he means!

MADAME AIGREVILLE *(to* MOULINEAUX*)*: You have?

MOULINEAUX: That is . . .

YVONNE *(pointedly)*: With a very sick patient.

MADAME AIGREVILLE: Tsk tsk tsk! Poor thing.

MOULINEAUX *(misunderstanding)*: Thank you.

MADAME AIGREVILLE: What? No, no. Your patient.

MOULINEAUX: Oh.

YVONNE: Yes. Very, very sick. For months now he's had only a few days to live.

MADAME AIGREVILLE: Tsk tsk tsk!

YVONNE: And last night monsieur simply had to be at his bedside.

MADAME AIGREVILLE: Of course! *(To* MOULINEAUX.*)* You doctors . . . so noble . . . so selfless.

MOULINEAUX *(modestly)*: Well . . .

YVONNE *(aside, to* MOULINEAUX*)*: So faithful . . .

MADAME AIGREVILLE: And you have to be out every night, Moulineaux?

MOULINEAUX: Every night? *(Absentmindedly.)* No, no. But when there are parties, galas . . . *(Catching himself and coughing to cover his* faux pas.*)* Sick parties . . . Patients . . . So many sick parties to care for. *(Coughing.)* Galore! Sick parties galore!

MADAME AIGREVILLE: Do you have a cold, son?

MOULINEAUX *(clearing his throat)*: Just a little. My throat . . .

MADAME AIGREVILLE: And your wife isn't making you a nice hot camomile? *(To* YVONNE.*)* Really, love, you should!

YVONNE (*very dryly, beginning to let her pique show through*):
Oh, I wouldn't worry, Mamma! I'm sure monsieur can take
care of himself! The way he takes care of all those sick
parties!

MADAME AIGREVILLE: Now, now . . .

YVONNE: With the very latest treatments! With singing and dancing and . . .

MADAME AIGREVILLE: My goodness, Yvonne, you sound like an
old *passcrotch* this morning!

YVONNE: I what?

MOULINEAUX (*correcting*): Crosspatch. (*To* YVONNE) Crosspatch. (*To*
MADAME AIGREVILLE.) Yes, doesn't she! I was just telling her . . .

MADAME AIGREVILLE (*to* YVONNE): What's the trouble, precious?
Is something the matter?

YVONNE: The matter? (*Pointing to* MOULINEAUX.) Ask him!

MADAME AIGREVILLE (*to* MOULINEAUX): Is something wrong, son?
Are you having a little spat?

MOULINEAUX: Wrong, Mother? (*Ingenuously.*) Why, no. Some
people just get up on the wrong side of the bed.

YVONNE (*giving tit for tat, angrily*): And some people don't get
up on any side at all!

MADAME AIGREVILLE: Now, now. Temper, temper. Is that any
way for two newlyweds to behave?

MOULINEAUX: But, really . . .

MADAME AIGREVILLE: Well, Mother is here now, and she's going to
patch up our little lovers' quarrel. That's what mothers-in-law
are for!

MOULINEAUX (*aside*): Talk about the cure being worse than the
disease!

   (ETIENNE *appears at the door, up left, carrying a calling card
on a little tray.*)

ETIENNE: Monsieur . . .

MOULINEAUX: Yes, Etienne? What is it?

ETIENNE (*joining him, down left, in a whisper*): It's that gentleman, monsieur. He asked me to give monsieur his card.

MOULINEAUX (*reading the card, aside*): Bassinet! Oh, for heaven's sake! No, not him again! (*To* ETIENNE, *aloud.*) Tell him I can't give him an appointment for at least a month.

MADAME AIGREVILLE: What is it, son?

MOULINEAUX: Nothing. No one important. Just one of my patients. (*Aside.*) And he's pushing mine to the limit!

MADAME AIGREVILLE: But if he's sick . . . If he needs you . . .

MOULINEAUX: He can wait!

YVONNE (*with a wry smile*): So noble . . . so selfless . . .

MOULINEAUX (*to* ETIENNE): Go tell him, Etienne.

ETIENNE: Very good, monsieur.

(*He goes to leave, up left.*)

MOULINEAUX (*stopping him*): Oh, and while you're there . . . my dressing gown. (*Pointing down left.*) You know where I keep it?

ETIENNE: Certainly, monsieur.

MOULINEAUX: Good. No hurry, but next time you come in here, I'd like you to have it.

ETIENNE: Excuse me. Did I hear . . . ? Monsieur would like me to . . .

MOULINEAUX: To have it. My dressing gown.

ETIENNE: Oh, thank you, monsieur! Monsieur is much too kind!

(*He exits, down left.*)

MOULINEAUX (*puzzled, aside*): I am? Now what did he mean by that?

(*Suddenly* BASSINET *opens the door, up left, and pokes his head out.*)

BASSINET: I say . . . you haven't forgotten me, I hope!

MOULINEAUX: You? (*Rushing up left and vigorously pushing him out.*) Get out of here!

(*He slams the door in* BASSINET'S *face.*)

MADAME AIGREVILLE (*surprised*): What on earth? (*To* MOULINEAUX.) Who is that person?

MOULINEAUX: Nobody! A . . . a patient.

YVONNE *(wryly)*: One of those sick, sick parties, Mamma!

MADAME AIGREVILLE *(to* MOULINEAUX*)*: But . . . then why don't you let him in?

MOULINEAUX *(categorically)*: Impossible! He's contagious!

MADAME AIGREVILLE: Him?

MOULINEAUX: And when I say "contagious" . . . *(With a shudder.)* Brr! Deadly! Deadly!

YVONNE: Why, yes! He's at death's door!

MADAME AIGREVILLE: That man?

MOULINEAUX: That's right!

MADAME AIGREVILLE: He is?

YVONNE: Couldn't you tell?

MOULINEAUX: At death's door!

MADAME AIGREVILLE: But he looks so . . . so healthy.

YVONNE *(glaring at* MOULINEAUX*)*: Yes, doesn't he!

MOULINEAUX *(aside)*: Touché!

MADAME AIGREVILLE *(aside)*: No, there's someting going on. If I could talk with Yvonne alone . . . *(To* MOULINEAUX.*)* Excuse me, son, but would you mind terribly if my daughter and I had a little chat. In private . . .

MOULINEAUX: Mind? Not in the slightest. Not when she's in one of her moods! Take your time.

   (He exits, down left.)

MADAME AIGREVILLE *(leading* YVONNE *to the chairs, down right)*: Now, then, precious . . . you can't fool Mamma. Come, tell me about it.

   (They sit down.)

YVONNE: Oh, Mamma. It's . . . it's . . . *(Breaking out in sobs.)* It's a scandal!

MADAME AIGREVILLE: Oh, my! That bad?

YVONNE: Worse! Much worse. He . . . Moulineaux . . . He didn't come home . . .

MADAME AIGREVILLE: He didn't? When?

YVONNE: Last night.

MADAME AIGREVILLE: Last . . . *(Suddenly understanding.)* Oh, you mean . . . to sleep . . .

YVONNE: That's right.

MADAME AIGREVILLE: Last night?

YVONNE *(standing up)*: And who knows how many other nights before that? How would I ever know?

MADAME AIGREVILLE: How? How, indeed! I should think it would be obvious! Especially in bed, if you don't mind my saying . . .

YVONNE *(innocently)*: In bed?

MADAME AIGREVILLE: Really, Yvonne! Some things are too hard for a husband to hide!

YVONNE: But . . .

MADAME AIGREVILLE *(half in jest)*: You do have a bed, don't you?

YVONNE: Of course I do.

MADAME AIGREVILLE: You? And Moulineaux?

YVONNE: Oh, yes. He has one too!

MADAME AIGREVILLE *(surprised)*: "Too"? But . . . Where do you people sleep?

YVONNE: Well . . . *(Pointing down right.)* There . . . and . . . *(Pointing down left.)* And there . . .

MADAME AIGREVILLE: What? You mean . . . After only six months . . . ?

YVONNE *(sheepishly)*: Oh, it didn't even take that long, Mamma.

MADAME AIGREVILLE: Well, precious, there's your problem!

YVONNE *(naively)*: It is?

MADAME AIGREVILLE: I mean, how can a woman know where her man is sleeping, unless they sleep together? It's elementary.

YVONNE: Well, I suppose.

MADAME AIGREVILLE: Married or not, it's only logical, love.

(Suddenly the door, up left, opens, and BASSINET *appears, carrying his hat and coat.)*

BASSINET: Oh, pardon me. I thought—

(He moves downstage.)

MADAME AIGREVILLE *(jumping up)*: You! *(To* YVONNE*)* It's him! *(Waving him off as she takes refuge behind the chairs.)* Get away! Get away!

BASSINET *(to* YVONNE*)*: I wanted to see the doctor.

YVONNE: Yes, I'm sure! To trump up more lies, I suppose!

BASSINET: What? No . . . I . . . *(Taking a few steps, to* MADAME AIGREVILLE.*)* Madame, is the doctor—

MADAME AIGREVILLE *(recoiling)*: Get away, I told you! Go to bed! Go to bed!

BASSINET *(moving close to her)*: But, madame, I'm not tired!

MADAME AIGREVILLE *(moving around the chairs, trying desperately to avoid him)*: I don't care! Go to bed! When you're sick, you go to bed!

BASSINET: Sick? *(Aside.)* What's the matter with these people? *(To* MADAME AIGREVILLE, *trying to approach her.)* Then you'll tell him . . . ? You'll tell the doctor . . . ?

MADAME AIGREVILLE *(waving him off)*: Yes! Anything you say!

BASSINET *(catching her hand, about to bring it to his lips, with a little bow)*: Thank you, madame. *Enchanté.* I'm sure . . .

MADAME AIGREVILLE *(horrified, pulling her hand away with a shriek)*: Ayyy! Don't touch me! Get away! Get away! Go infect someone else!

*(*BASSINET *gives a shrug toward the audience as* MADAME AIGREVILLE *frantically wipes her hand on her clothing.)*

BASSINET *(to* MADAME AIGREVILLE, *bowing)*: Madame . . . *(To* YVONNE.*)* Madame . . . *(Aside.)* They're crazy! Every one of them!

(He bows his way back to the door, up left, and exits.)

MADAME AIGREVILLE *(still wiping)*: I wish my son-in-law would leave his patients at home, like every other doctor! The idea! *(To* YVONNE.*)* All right now. What's this talk about your husband? You say he's been gallivanting?

YVONNE: Yes, Mamma! I'm sure of it!

(She begins sobbing again.)

MADAME AIGREVILLE: Now, now, now. Tell me about it. First of all, who is she?

YVONNE: "She," Mamma? Who?

MADAME AIGREVILLE: Who? Why, the other woman! Who else? When a man doesn't come home at night, he's not sleeping in the park!

YVONNE *(sighing)*: No, I don't suppose . . .

MADAME AIGREVILLE: Have you found anything? You know . . . a key, an earring . . .

YVONNE: Well . . . *(Pulling a lady's glove from her bosom.)* Just this. I found it yesterday in his coat. When I was going through his pockets . . .

MADAME AIGREVILLE *(taking it from her)*: Hmm! A lady's glove! That's a start! And anything in his papers? Any letters?

YVONNE: Oh, Mamma! I wouldn't look through his papers!

MADAME AIGREVILLE: You wouldn't? Come now, precious! How else are you supposed to find out what's in them? Wives do it all the time.

(MOULINEAUX *appears at the door, down left.)*

MOULINEAUX: Well, still having our little chat?

MADAME AIGREVILLE *(to* YVONNE*)*: I'll take care of this, love. Let me talk to him alone.

YVONNE: Yes, Mamma.

(She stalks off, down right, without giving MOULINEAUX *a look.)*

MOULINEAUX *(aside)*: I hope the old battle-ax has cooled her off a little!

MADAME AIGREVILLE *(sharply)*: Monsieur!

MOULINEAUX *(aside)*: Uh-oh. I guess not. *(To* MADAME AIGREVILLE, *sweetly, joining her center stage.)* Mother?

MADAME AIGREVILLE: I won't beat around the bush! *(Holding up the glove, which she has been holding behind her back.)* Does this look familiar?

MOULINEAUX: That? Oh, thank you. I've been looking all over—

(He reaches for the glove.)

MADAME AIGREVILLE *(slapping his hand with it)*: Not so fast, monsieur! Whose is it?

MOULINEAUX *(ingenuously)*: Whose is what?

MADAME AIGREVILLE: This, monsieur!

MOULINEAUX *(as innocently as possible)*: Why, it's mine. Whose do you think?

MADAME AIGREVILLE: Yours? A glove this size?

MOULINEAUX: Yes, it's . . . it's the latest thing for rheumatism. Does wonders for the circulation. Tightens the nerves. Massages the joints. It's . . . it's . . .

MADAME AIGREVILLE *(finishing his sentence)*: It's a lady's glove, monsieur.

MOULINEAUX *(objecting)*: A lady's . . . Oh, no! *(With a little forced laugh.)* It might look like a lady's, but that's only because it shrank. In the rain. It got all wet.

MADAME AIGREVILLE *(pulling the glove lengthwise)*: And the length, monsieur? Have you ever seen a man with fingers this long? *(Sarcastically.)* Even one whose nerves need tightening . . . and whose joints need massaging!

MOULINEAUX: Exactly! It . . . it shrank in the width and . . . and got longer in the length. The rain always does that. The moisture. Something in the molecules... . .

MADAME AIGREVILLE *(nodding, ironically)*: I'm sure . . .

MOULINEAUX: Stand out in the rain for a day or two. You'll see.

(He mimes the phenomenon of a body going from fat to thin and short to tall.)

MADAME AIGREVILLE: Very interesting, thank you. *(Holding up the glove.)* Especially since it's marked size six and a half.

MOULINEAUX *(confidently)*: Nine and a half! Nine! You've got it upside down.

MADAME AIGREVILLE *(losing patience, hands on hips)*: That's enough, monsieur! What kind of fool do you take me for? Really!

MOULINEAUX *(aside)*: Any kind. I'm not fussy.

MADAME AIGREVILLE *(growing angry)*: Do you want to know the truth? *(Not waiting for an answer.)* I'll tell you. You're a cad! An absolute cad, monsieur! And you don't deserve a wife like my Yvonne, you . . . you lecher!

MOULINEAUX *(taken aback)*: What?

MADAME AIGREVILLE: Yes! I said it and I'm glad! You're a lecher, monsieur! A depraved, degenerate lecher.

MOULINEAUX: I beg your—

MADAME AIGREVILLE: Who stays out all night, Heaven only knows where! And who comes home with women's gloves in your pocket.

MOULINEAUX *(correcting)*: One glove. One . . .

MADAME AIGREVILLE *(emphasizing)*: *Women's* gloves, monsieur!

MOULINEAUX: But I told you, the moisture . . .

MADAME AIGREVILLE *(menacing)*: Now just you listen to me! If you're cheating on my daughter . . . if you dare . . . I'm warning you! You'll have me to answer to! And don't you forget it!

MOULINEAUX *(recoiling)*: I? Me? Cheating?

MADAME AIGREVILLE *(pressing her attack)*: I'll thank you to remember you're a married man, monsieur!

MOULINEAUX *(aside)*: You're welcome!

MADAME AIGREVILLE: And you've sworn to be faithful . . .

MOULINEAUX: *(beginning to resist)*: To her, damn it! Not to you!

MADAME AIGREVILLE: The law says a wife is supposed to follow her husband. Well, let me tell you, my friend, we'll follow you! We'll follow you to the ends of the earth if we have to!

MOULINEAUX: "We"? "We" who? The law says "the wife." It doesn't say anything about her mother, goddammit!

MADAME AIGREVILLE: Well, whose fault is that? It should!

MOULINEAUX: Of course! I guess they just forgot!

MADAME AIGREVILLE: What kind of a heartless creature are you? To want to separate a mother from her daughter . . . From her own flesh and blood . . .

MOULINEAUX *(at a loss for words)*: "What kind of a . . ."

MADAME AIGREVILLE: Heartless! Simply heartless!

MOULINEAUX: Oh . . . *(Exploding.)* Go to blazes!

MADAME AIGREVILLE *(startled)*: What? What did you say?

MOULINEAUX: You heard me! I've had enough of your nagging!

MADAME AIGREVILLE: Monsieur! I never—

MOULINEAUX: I'll do what I please! I don't have to answer to you.

MADAME AIGREVILLE: How dare—

MOULINEAUX: Or to anyone else, thank you! And I don't have to let you stand there and rip me to pieces.

MADAME AIGREVILLE: That's right! Tell me to leave!

MOULINEAUX *(furious)*: You can do what you like!

MADAME AIGREVILLE: I never . . . *(To the audience.)* And then they blame the mother-in-law! *(To* MOULINEAUX, *coldly.)* I'm beginning to feel very unwelcome, monsieur!

(She moves upstage.)

MOULINEAUX *(aside)*: Beginning! *(To* MADAME AIGREVILLE, *following her.)* What do you expect? When you keep butting in . . .

MADAME AIGREVILLE: Go ahead, monsieur! Tell me to leave, why don't you? *(Dramatically.)* Throw me out of my own daughter's house! Go ahead!

MOULINEAUX: Oh . . .

MADAME AIGREVILLE: Well, you won't have to tell me twice, monsieur!

MOULINEAUX *(about to lose his temper)*: You . . . Good God! Let me out of here before I . . . *(Resisting the urge to strangle her.)* Oh! That woman! *(Turning to leave, aside.)* She could give the Lord himself an ulcer!

(He storms out, down left.)

MADAME AIGREVILLE *(gradually regaining her composure)*: All the same . . . every one of them . . . Just like my Wenceslas and my poor saint of a mother! Before he went and died, that is. Well, I know when I'm not wanted! Nothing on earth could keep me here. Not even for one night! Even if I have to go sleep in the street!

(The door, up left, opens, and BASSINET *appears, still carrying his hat and coat.)*

BASSINET *(looking around, aside)*: Where in the name of . . . How much longer . . .

MADAME AIGREVILLE *(without noticing him)*: In the meantime I'd better try to find myself an apartment.

BASSINET *(overhearing)*: What? Did I hear you say you were looking for an apartment, madame?

MADAME AIGREVILLE: I . . . *(Turning and seeing him.)* Oh! You!

(She takes refuge behind the desk.)

BASSINET *(aside)*: Again? What on earth . . . ? *(To* MADAME AIGREVILLE, *chasing her around the desk)*. Listen . . . Stop . . .

MADAME AIGREVILLE: Get away! Get away!

BASSINET: Please . . . I've got just what you're looking for. You can move in right away. And it's furnished, madame. Furnished. A lovely little apartment.

MADAME AIGREVILLE *(stopping, interested)*: Oh?

BASSINET: Yes. Just a stone's throw. Seventy Rue de Milan. One B.

(He holds out a prospectus. She pulls back, obviously unwilling to touch him. Finally he hits on the expedient of passing it to her on the crown of his hat.)

MADAME AIGREVILLE *(holding it gingerly)*: And . . . and you say you live there, monsieur?

BASSINET: Me? *(Laughing.)* No, no, no! A dressmaker used to, but it's really quite a story, if you want a good laugh. You see—

MADAME AIGREVILLE *(cutting him off)*: Yes, that's fine. And it's safe? No health problems . . . no germs, no drafts?

BASSINET: Safe, madame? To live there, you mean?

MADAME AIGREVILLE: Of course, to live there. What else—

BASSINET: Because sometimes people rent by the night, madame. You know . . . *(With a broad wink.)* To bring their friends.

MADAME AIGREVILLE *(shocked)*: What?

BASSINET *(realizing his* faux pas*)*: But I'm sure that's not what you had in mind.

MADAME AIGREVILLE: Indeed!

BASSINET: Well, anyway, madame. No germs, no drafts. It's as safe as an apartment can be.

MADAME AIGREVILLE *(nodding)*: Aha.

(*During the ensuing exchange she gradually moves up left, followed at a distance by* BASSINET.)

BASSINET *(aside)*: As long as you don't catch something terrible! *(To* MADAME AIGREVILLE.*)* No problems, madame.

MADAME AIGREVILLE: Well . . .

BASSINET *(with a shrug, aside)*: What do I care? A total stranger!

MADAME AIGREVILLE: If you're sure . . .

BASSINET *(aside)*: And besides, it's for Moulineaux. *(To* MADAME AIGREVILLE.*)* Madame?

MADAME AIGREVILLE: Absolutely sure . . .

BASSINET *(aside)*: I'll be taking her off his hands. *(To* MADAME AIGREVILLE.*)* Of course, madame! Of course! *(Aside.)* What are friends for, after all?

MADAME AIGREVILLE *(up left)*: Very well! I'll have a look at it.

BASSINET *(rubbing his hands)*: And you'll love it, believe me!

(*The door, down left, opens, and* MOULINEAUX *enters.*)

MOULINEAUX *(talking to himself)*: Where the devil is that Etienne with my dressing gown?

MADAME AIGREVILLE *(to* BASSINET*)*: Excuse me, monsieur. *(Loud enough for* MOULINEAUX *to hear).* It's getting a little crowded!

BASSINET *(looking around, naively)*: It is?

MADAME AIGREVILLE *(to* BASSINET*)*: We'll discuss the matter later.

(*She crosses down right, nose in the air, without deigning to glance at* MOULINEAUX, *and strides out the door into* YVONNE'S *room.*)

MOULINEAUX *(watching her leave)*: No change, I see!

BASSINET *(to* MOULINEAUX*)*: I say, monsieur, if you want to get the old bag off your hands . . .

MOULINEAUX: Ah, Bassinet! Just the man I was looking for!

BASSINET *(surprised)*: I am? But I thought . . .

MOULINEAUX: You know your apartment? One B? The dressmaker . . .

BASSINER: Yes.

MOULINEAUX: Well, I've been thinking. I'm going to rent it from you.

BASSINET: You are? *(Aside)*: Drat! Maybe I should auction it off to the highest bidder!

MOULINEAUX: Because . . . well, I suppose I can tell you. I'm sure you'll be discreet.

BASSINET: Discretion itself, monsieur.

MOULINEAUX *(confidentially)*: You see, I need a little place to . . . to . . .

BASSINET: To bring a friend!

MOULINEAUX: Exactly! But all very platonic. At least, it is so far. You see, she's a married woman. A patient of mine. I've been treating her for years.

BASSINET: Tsk tsk tsk! Is she sick?

MOULINEAUX: Not anymore. She was.

BASSINET: With what?

MOULINEAUX: Chronic good health. I cured her.

BASSINET: Ah! And what does her husband have to say about all this?

MOULINEAUX *(laughing)*: Her husband? Who knows? Who cares? I've never even met him. *(Taking* BASSINET'S *prospectus from his pocket.)* Now tell me. How much are you asking?

BASSINET *(pointing to the prospectus)*: Just what it says: two hundred fifty francs.

MOULINEAUX: A year? You're right, it's a steal! I'll take it!

BASSINET: Excuse me, monsieur. A month. Two hundred fifty a month.

MOULINEAUX *(jovially)*: What? Raising my rent already?

(He gives a little chuckle. BASSINET *joins in.)*

BASSINET: Of course, if that's too expensive, you can rent it by the hour. . . .

MOULINEAUX: No, no. By the month will be fine! I'll take it!

BASSINET (*unable to believe his ears*): You will? When?

MOULINEAUX: Today. Right away. As soon as I can have it.

BASSINET: Today? Well, I don't know. It's not quite ready. I mean, everything is rather helter-skelter and topsy-turvy. All the dressmaker's things. She left in such a hurry!

MOULINEAUX: Yes.

BASSINET: It's really quite a story. You see, she had a—

MOULINEAUX (*cutting him off*): Yes, yes. Later. You'll tell me about it tomorrow. Right now all I want is the key.

BASSINET: But I told you, it's not ready.

MOULINEAUX: No problem. I'll make do.

BASSINET: Well, if you're sure . . .

(ETINNE *appears at the door, up center, wearing* MOULINEAUX'S *dressing gown.*)

ETIENNE (*announcing*): Madame Dartagnan, monsieur. For her consultation.

MOULINEAUX: Ah! (*To* BASSINET.) Look, if you don't mind . . .

BASSINET: Another pest, monsieur? If you want, I can ring the bell and send in my—

MOULINEAUX (*pushing him toward the door, up left*): No, no! That won't be necessary! You go in here and . . . and write up the lease. That's it. Write up the lease.

BASSINET: Aha! Good idea!

(MOULINEAUX *pushes him out the door.*)

MOULINEAUX (*to* ETIENNE): Tell madame. (*Noticing his dressing gown.*) Etienne! My dressing gown! Just what do you think you're—

ETIENNE: But monsieur said . . . He told me: "I'd like you to have it, Etienne." And very generous of monsieur!

MOULINEAUX: What? *With* you, damn it! Not *on* you!

ETIENNE (*sheepishly*): Oh, I see. . . .

MOULINEAUX: Of all the . . .

(The door, up center, opens, and SUZANNE *enters quickly.)*

SUZANNE *(to* MOULINEAUX*):* Monsieur . . .

MOULINEAUX: Ah, madame. I was just . . . *(To* ETIENNE.*)* You can go now, Etienne.

ETIENNE: Very good, monsieur. *(Aside, shaking his head.)* Did you ever see . . . ? I was sure he told me . . .

(He exits, up center.)

MOULINEAUX *(to* SUZANNE, *as soon as* ETIENNE *has closed the door):* Suzanne!

SUZANNE: Balthasar!

MOULINEAUX *(cajoling):* You naughty thing, you! "Meet me under the clock!" I could still be waiting!

SUZANNE: I know, dearest! I'm so terribly sorry. Can you ever forgive me?

MOULINEAUX: Well, maybe. *(Suggestively.)* That depends . . .

SUZANNE: I was sure that my husband would be going off, as usual. And then I would be free . . . and we , . . you and I . . . *(With a passionate sigh.)* Balthasar!

MOULINEAUX: Suzanne!

SUZANNE: But, no. He stayed and stayed and stayed. He simply didn't budge! The whole night long! I couldn't get rid of him!

MOULINEAUX: I suspected it must be something . . .

SUZANNE: In fact, the man hasn't let me out of his sight for days. He acts that way sometimes. It's almost as if he didn't trust me.

MOULINEAUX: No! You? Suzanne . . .

SUZANNE: In fact, he's downstairs at this very moment, waiting. He wanted to come up with me, but I told him I didn't think he should . . . to the doctor's, after all.

MOULINEAUX: Of course not! It's not ethical! It just isn't done.

SUZANNE: No. That's what I told him.

MOULINEAUX: And a good thing you did. *(Aside.)* You should never meet the husband. It's bad for the conscience! *(Aloud, gazing romantically into her eyes.)* Ah, Suzanne . . .

(He takes her by the hand and leads her down right to the chairs.)

SUZANNE: Ah, Balthasar, Balthasar, Balthasar! What are we doing? It's madness, I tell you! I shouldn't be here! I shouldn't . . .

MOULINEAUX: Yes, you should! Of course, you should!

SUZANNE: But . . . *(Sighing.)* It's too late to turn back. Tell me it's too late.

MOULINEAUX: That's right! It's too late. Come.

(He holds out one of the chairs for her.)

SUZANNE: It's just that . . . this is the first time I've ever . . . *(Sitting down.)* The very first . . . really. Because I never—

MOULINEAUX *(sitting down next to her.)* I know, I know. And that's why . . . Ah, Suzanne! I can't tell you the thrill, the bliss, the . . . *(Waxing lyrical.)* The ecstasy! To know that I'm the first . . .

SUZANNE: Ah, Balthasar!

MOULINEAUX *(coming back to earth)*: But still, we can't take chances.

SUZANNE: Dearest?

MOULINEAUX: We can't go on meeting like this. Not here. A visit to the doctor is a wonderful excuse, but it can't last forever.

SUZANNE: But . . .

MOULINEAUX: People will notice. They'll begin to talk.

SUZANNE: Of course. I never thought . . .

MOULINEAUX: And it won't take them long to discover the truth! That . . . that this is no everyday doctor and patient, but . . . *(Waxing poetic again.)* but two passionate hearts, two noble souls yearning to be one and to soar off together to the giddying realm of love!

SUZANNE: Oh, Balthasar! You're so right! It's all bound to come out.

MOULINEAUX: That is, unless we're careful.

SUZANNE: But how? What can we do?

MOULINEAUX: Well, I was thinking. There's no reason why we

can't keep meeting. As long it's in some—how shall I say?
—some neutral arena . . .

SUZANNE: Oh, no! Not an arena! I'd much rather a nice little
apartment . . . like in the novels.

MOULINEAUX: Exactly! And I've got one!

SUZANNE: You have?

MOULINEAUX: Yes! And it's perfect! Just around the corner. On
Rue de Milan. Number seventy. A cozy little furnished apartment. Just the two of us. And we can have it anytime. Today
if you like . . .

SUZANNE *(having second thoughts)*: Well, I don't know. An
apartment . . . I'm not sure, Balthasar!

MOULINEAUX: But what's the difference? Here or there? It's just
so much safer. No prying eyes, no wagging tongues . . .

SUZANNE: Yes, I suppose you're right. *(Deciding resolutely.)*
Well, why not!

MOULINEAUX *(jubilant)*: That's what I say! Why not!

SUZANNE: As long as it's all still *plutonic,* you understand.

MOULINEAUX: "Plu . . ." *(Hypocritically.)* Certainly! What do you
take me for, Suzanne!

SUZANNE: Because I'd never cheat on my husband, Balthasar!

MOULINEAUX: You'd never . . . Heaven forbid, my dear lady!
The thought never entered my mind!

SUZANNE: I should hope not.

MOULINEAUX: No, no. Strictly "plutonic." I give you my word.

SUZANNE *(standing up)*: Then it's settled. In an hour. Seventy
Rue de Milan.

MOULINEAUX: One B.

SUZANNE: One B.

MOULINEAUX *(standing up)*: In an hour!

SUZANNE: An hour! *(Moving upstage.)* Oh, Balthasar! What must
you think of me? You must think I'm perfectly awful!

MOULINEAUX: Me?

SUZANNE: But, really, this is the first time I've ever . . . The very first. Really . . .

MOULINEAUX: I know, I know. *(Aside, as* SUZANNE *reaches the double door.)* That was easier than I expected! These society ladies . . .

SUZANNE: Well, I'd better be going. My husband will be wondering . . .

MOULINEAUX *(joining her, taking her hand)*: If you must, you must. But it's only au revoir.

(Just as he is about to bring her hand to his lips, the door opens and ETIENNE *appears, still in the dressing gown.)*

ETIENNE: A gentleman who says he's Monsieur Dartagnan, monsieur . . .

(He moves down right.)

MOULINEAUX *(moving left)*: ⎫   ⎫ Who? But I don't want to see—

               (Together)

SUZANNE *(pulling away)* ⎭   ⎭ My husband? Good heavens!

*(*DARTAGNAN *enters, up center, coat in hand.)*

DARTAGNAN: Good morning. *(To* SUZANNE.*)* Ah, Suzanne . . .

SUZANNE: Anatole! I was just leaving.

DARTAGNAN *(casually)*: Fine! I'll join you in a moment. After I've had a quick word or two with the doctor. *(To* MOULINEAUX, *noticing him in evening clothes and mistaking him for a butler, handing him his coat.)* Thank you, my good man. *(*MOULINEAUX *stands staring at him blankly for a moment.)* That will be all. *(Waving him off.)* If you don't mind. This is a private conversation. *(To* ETIENNE, *holding out his hand.)* Doctor Moulineaux! What a pleasure . . . After all these years . . .

ETIENNE *(startled, shaking his head)*: Monsieur . . .

*(*MOULINEAUX'S *jaw drops in disbelief.)*

SUZANNE *(to* DARTAGNAN*)*: But . . . but . . . Anatole . . .

MOULINEAUX *(in a whisper, to* SUZANNE*)*: Shhh! Never mind! It's better . . .

(He pushes her out the double door, then crosses down left and exits.)

DARTAGNAN *(to* ETIENNE*)*: Well, now that we're alone, I thought, since I was so close . . . I'm sure it's probably nothing, but it seemed like a good time. You see, I've been getting these nosebleeds recently, and my feet fall asleep.

ETIENNE *(nodding)*: Aha. Very interesting. At the same time?

DARTAGNAN: Well, not always.

ETIENNE: Have you tried holding your breath and counting to ten?

DARTAGNAN: No. No . . .

ETIENNE: Or putting your head in a sack?

DARTAGNAN: My head . . . *(Objecting feebly.)* But . . . but I thought those were for hiccoughs.

ETIENNE: Right. Right. I meant, a key.

DARTAGNAN: Monsieur?

ETIENNE: A key . . . You press it against the back of your neck . . .

DARTAGNAN: Aha.

ETIENNE: A dining room key.

DARTAGNAN: Does it have to be the dining room? Won't the front door do as well?

ETIENNE: No, no! The dining room. Then you pinch your nose shut and stick your head in a basin of water. For an hour and a half.

DARTAGNAN: What? An hour and a . . . but . . . how on earth do I breathe?

ETIENNE: Through your mouth.

DARTAGNAN: My mouth? Under water?

ETIENNE: It cures nosebleeds, monsieur.

DARTAGNAN: Yes. And anything else! I . . . I think I'd rather not . . .

ETIENNE: It's up to you.

DARTAGNAN: Maybe if you looked at my tongue. Can we sit down?

(They sit down on the chairs, down right. DARTAGNAN *sticks his tongue out.)*

ETIENNE: Aha!

DARTAGNAN: How is it?

ETIENNE: Well, for one thing, mine is longer. See?

(He sticks his tongue out.)

DARTAGNAN: What?

ETIENNE: And besides, yours is round at the end, but mine is pointed. (*He sticks it out again.*) And I can curl mine up . . . like this. (*He illustrates.*) Can you?

DARTAGNAN: I beg your . . . Really! What kind of a doctor are you?

ETIENNE: No kind at all, monsieur.

DARTAGNAN (*jumping up*): What?

ETIENNE (*standing up*): But I may as well be. I'm his butler.

DARTAGNAN: His butler! Then why are you standing here talking to me, for goodness' sake?

ETIENNE: Oh, I don't mind, monsieur. I'll talk to anyone.

DARTAGNAN (*not listening to him, aside*): Then who the devil did I give my coat to just now?

(*He moves up center, scratching his head. As he reaches the double door,* MOULINEAUX *enters, down left, in his frock coat. At the same moment* BASSINET *enters, up left, still carrying his hat and coat, and with a sheet of paper in hand.*)

MOULINEAUX (*talking to himself*): There! All ready.

BASSINET (*to* MOULINEAUX): Ah, monsieur . . .

MOULINEAUX: You . . .

BASSINET (*waving the paper at him*): The lease, monsieur! The lease!

MOULINEAUX (*taking it*): Yes. Thank you. That's fine.

BASSINET: By the way, I still haven't told you the story . . . about the dressmaker, I mean. You see, she—

MOULINEAUX (*avoiding him*): Not now. I'm in a hurry. A date with destiny, my friend!

(*He strides quickly to the door, up center.*)

BASSINET: But it's really very funny. If you want a good laugh . . .

DARTAGNAN (*stopping* MOULINEAUX *before he reaches the door*): Ah, doctor! You must excuse me.

MOULINEAUX (*aside*): Oh, my! Him too! (*To* DARTAGNAN.) Doctor? Doctor? Who's a doctor?

(*He bolts out.*)

DARTAGNAN *(as* MOULINEAUX *slams the door)*: Oh, pardon me. I thought . . . *(Aside.)* A patient, I suppose. *(Catching sight of* BASSINET, *who is standing, left, back turned, brushing his hat.)* Ah! Then that must be the doctor. *(To* BASSINET, *joining him.)* Pardon, me monsieur. It was a foolish mistake. I hope you'll excuse me.

BASSINET *(turning around)*: Me, monsieur?

DARTAGNAN: Yes. My coat. Before . . . Your patient . . . *(Confused.)* Whoever . . . I thought . . . My mistake . . .

BASSINET *(without the slightest idea what he is talking about)*: Aha. Don't mention it. *(Returning to his* idée fixe.*)* I say, if you'd like to hear a really funny story . . .

DARTAGNAN: Monsieur?

BASSINET: It's about my tenant, the dressmaker. That is, she was . . . My tenant, I mean. Because one day—

DARTAGNAN *(to* BASSINET, *who has followed him to the door, up center)*: Yes, I'm sure. But if you don't mind . . . *(Freeing himself.)* Another time . . . *(With a little bow.)* Monsieur . . .

   (He exits.)

BASSINET *(calling after him as he leaves)*: Wait! I haven't finished. *(As the door closes.)* Hmm! He must be in a hurry. *(Noticing* ETIENNE, *still standing by his chair, who has been watching the proceedings with a smirk.)* Ah! The butler. *(To* ETIENNE.*)* I say, my good man, I have a terribly funny story . . .

ETIENNE *(suddenly serious)*: Excuse me, monsieur, but they want me in the pantry.

BASSINET *(ignoring his objections, making him sit down next to him, right)*: You see, it's about my tenant. The dressmaker. The one who ran away in the middle of the night. *(Laughing to himself.)* Really, it's just too funny. *(While* BASSINET *is reveling in his story,* ETIENNE *takes advantage of his inattention to get up and slip out the upstage door.)* Anyway, she had this young gigolo who used to . . . *(Suddenly, noticing that he is all alone, he gets up and looks around the room for* ETIENNE.*)* Now where did he go, I wonder? *(To the audience.)* Well, as I was saying, the dressmaker had this gigolo . . .

   (The orchestra cuts him off, despite his efforts to shout above it. And the curtain falls in his face.)

                    CURTAIN

ACT II

(The apartment on Rue de Milan. In the rear wall, center, a door leading to the hall, opening in. The door is open, and the landing can be glimpsed outside. On each side of the door, a chair. Up right, a dressmaker's wicker mannequin covered with a lady's gown. Up right, a door. Down right and left, a workbench with appropriate articles strewn in disorder: boxes, swatches of cloth, patterns, scissors, pad and pencil, etc. Near the workbench, right, a chair; left, a sofa. The whole apartment is in obvious disarray.)

(At rise, the set is empty. After a few moments MOULINEAUX *appears at the door, up center.)*

MOULINEAUX *(talking to himself)*: One B. One B. Ah, here we are! *(He enters, tries to push the door shut, but finds that it won't close.)* Hmm! Broken! Very nice! Problems already! *(Tinkering with the doorknob.)* I mustn't forget to tell Bassinet. *(Turning around quickly, he finds himself face-to-face with the mannequin and instinctively gives a little bow.)* Madame . . . *(Realizing his mistake.)* Oh . . . *(With a little laugh.)* Of course. The dressmaker. His famous dressmaker. *(Looking around, surveying the disorder.)* And all this. Well, it's going to take a little work. But once I put everything in order . . . *(Nodding.)* Not bad. Not bad at all. *(Continuing his inspection, after a pause.)* Ah, Moulineaux, you cad! You bounder! Her mother is right! You ought to be ashamed! With a nice little wife . . . It's hard not to feel guilty. *(Caressing the back of the sofa.)* And I do! I do! Guilty, guilty, guilty! I just don't let it bother me, that's all.

(While he is talking, SUZANNE *appears at the open door, in hat and coat, carrying a muff.)*

SUZANNE *(poking her head in tentatively)*: Balthasar?

MOULINEAUX: Suzanne!

SUZANNE: Am I early?

MOULINEAUX *(going to meet her)*: Come in! Come in!

SUZANNE: Well . . .

(She enters cautiously, lays her muff down on one of the chairs up center, and tries unsuccessfully to shut the door behind her.)

MOULINEAUX: Oh, don't mind that. It's broken. Here, let me . . . *(He takes the other chair and props it against the door.)* There!

SUZANNE: Are you sure it's safe, dearest? What if somebody comes in?

MOULINEAUX *(taking her by the hand and leading her downstage)*: Why should anyone come in? It's as safe as can be!

SUZANNE: Because . . . What we're doing, Balthasar . . . It's so wrong. So wrong . . . *(Almost as an afterthought.)* Especially if anyone saw me . . .

MOULINEAUX *(aside)*: Especially! *(To* SUZANNE.*)* Believe me, Suzanne, we couldn't be more alone. *(At the sofa.)* Come, sit down.

(He takes both her hands in his and sits down.)

SUZANNE *(resisting)*: But . . .

MOULINEAUX: Why, Suzanne, you're trembling.

SUZANNE *(still standing)*: I know. It's . . . it's only because this is all so new. My first . . . adventure!

MOULINEAUX: I know, I know.

SUZANNE: Like a soldier at the front!

MOULINEAUX: Well . . .

SUZANNE: That's what my husband always says. Even the bravest soldiers are afraid the first time.

MOULINEAUX *(still trying to urge her onto the sofa)*: Yes.

SUZANNE: And he should know. He was in the Army. The Quartermaster Reserves.

MOULINEAUX: Yes. He speaks from experience. *(Urging.)* Come, take off your hat.

SUZANNE (*pulling away*): Oh, no! Good heavens! I can only stay a minute!

MOULINEAUX: What?

SUZANNE: Anatole is downstairs. If he ever came up . . .

MOULINEAUX (*jumping up*): Who?

SUZANNE: Anatole . . . my husband. He insisted on coming with me.

MOULINEAUX (*unable to believe his ears*): You . . . you mean, you told him?

SUZANNE (*hesitating*): Well . . . that is . . . yes and no.

MOULINEAUX: "Yes and . . ." But you shouldn't have! No one does. That's . . . that's not the way it's done.

SUZANNE: But I had to tell him something! You know how he's been acting lately.

MOULINEAUX: I know, but still—

SUZANNE: So I told him . . . I told him I was going to my tailor's.

MOULINEAUX (*with a relieved little laugh*): Your what?

SUZANNE: For a fitting. I remembered what you said. About a dressmaker that used to live here.

MOULINEAUX: Quick thinking! (*With a sigh.*) Thank heavens!

SUZANNE: After all, I certainly didn't want him tagging along.

MOULINEAUX: Hardly!

SUZANNE: But I couldn't very well say no, or he'd begin to suspect. Besides, after last night . . . Making you wait and wait the way I did . . . Well, I didn't have the heart. I just had to come! (*Naively.*) That was good of me, wasn't it? Aren't you pleased that I did?

MOULINEAUX (*abstractedly*): Dear, sweet Suzanne!

SUZANNE (*waiting for an answer*): Aren't you, Balthasar?

MOULINEAUX (*aside, preoccupied*): Just knowing he's downstairs . . . damn! That spoils everything!

SUZANNE: Balthasar?

MOULINEAUX (*aside*): I wish she didn't tell me. Talk about putting

a damper on things! *(Aloud, mechanically.)* Ah! Dear, sweet
Suzanne!

SUZANNE *(with a smile)*: You said that, dearest.

MOULINEAUX: I did? Said what?

SUZANNE: What you just said . . .

MOULINEAUX: Oh, did I, Suzanne? Dear, sweet Suzanne.

SUZANNE: Again? Really, Balthasar. Is something bothering you?

MOULINEAUX *(aside)*: I don't know what I'm saying! *(Aloud.)*
Bothering me?

SUZANNE *(growing serious)*: Oh, I know. Don't pretend. You
don't have to tell me. You think I'm perfectly dreadful, don't
you?

MOULINEAUX: Me?

SUZANNE: Coming here this way. That's it, isn't it?

MOULINEAUX: No! That's not it at all. Of course not, Suzanne.
Dear—

SUZANNE *(interrupting)*: Sweet Suzanne! Yes, yes. But really,
you shouldn't! Because I never . . . Believe me, it's the very
first time.

MOULINEAUX: I know. I'm sure. *(Aside.)* Like trying to make
love under Damocles' sword! *(Aloud.)* I know, Suzanne. I
know.

SUZANNE: And you don't think I'm just too dreadful for words?

MOULINEAUX: No, no, no.

SUZANNE: And you're pleased that I came?

MOULINEAUX *(unconvincingly)*: Pleased? That isn't the word! I'm
delighted. Ecstatic! *(Aside.)* Two hundred fifty francs a month
to stand here and babble!

SUZANNE: But you seem so cold. I thought, when I came here—

MOULINEAUX: Me? Cold? How can you say that when . . . when
all I want . . . *(Trying to sound passionate.)* is . . . is to spend
the rest of my life at your feet?

SUZANNE *(with a pout.)* Oh, that's easy to say . . .

MOULINEAUX: But I mean it, Suzanne! I do! I do! Look!

(He falls to his knees in front of her. At that moment the door, up center, flies open, knocking over the chair, and DARTAGNAN *appears.)*

DARTAGNAN: Oh, my! Clumsy, clumsy.

(He picks up the chair and replaces it by the door.)

MOULINEAUX *(still kneeling, petrified, aside)*: My God! Anatole! *(Aloud, to* DARTAGNAN, *standing up.)* No, no! You can't come in! It's closed!

DARTAGNAN *(entering, looking at the open door)*: Closed?

MOULINEAUX *(trying not to panic)*: I mean, come in! Please! Come right in!

DARTAGNAN: Thank you, monsieur . . . I have . . .

MOULINEAUX: Please! Make yourself at home!

DARTAGNAN: It's not much fun waiting down there all alone.

MOULINEAUX *(trying to sound natural)*: Of course! I can imagine.

DARTAGNAN: So I said to myself: "I'm sure they won't mind if I drop in and say hello."

MOULINEAUX: Not at all! Good idea!

DARTAGNAN: "As long as I'm not a bother." *(As agreeably as possible.)* So please, just go right ahead and make believe I'm not here.

MOULINEAUX *(aside)*: God willing!

DARTAGNAN: After all, you have your work.

MOULINEAUX: Yes. My work.

(He goes over to the workbench, right, and pretends to busy himself with cloths, patterns, etc.)

DARTAGNAN: You were taking madame's measurements. Please don't let me interrupt.

MOULINEAUX: Her measurements?

SUZANNE *(jumping in, to* DARTAGNAN*)*: That's right. He just finished my waist.

MOULINEAUX: Yes, I . . . Yes, yes. Precisely . . . Her waist. *(Pretending to write some figures on a notepad.)* "Waist . . . one hundred and four."

SUZANNE ⎫ *(together)* ⎧ What?
DARTAGNAN ⎭　　　　　 ⎩ How much?

MOULINEAUX: One hundred—

SUZANNE *(scandalized)*: Fifty-two, monsieur! And not one centimeter more!

DARTAGNAN *(laughing)*: I daresay . . .

MOULINEAUX *(covering his* faux pas*)*: Centimeter? Oh, if you want it in centimeters . . . Well . . . *(Calculating.)* That's right. Fifty-two. Exactly. Nowadays the best designers measure in half centimeters, but if you prefer . . .

DARTAGNAN: Oh? Half?

MOULINEAUX: Yes. All the great couturiers, monsieur.

DARTAGNAN: Interesting. I didn't know.

MOULINEAUX *(as if it were perfectly logical)*: That way everything comes out double.

DARTAGNAN *(chuckling)*: Except the bill, I hope!

MOULINEAUX: No. That's usually triple. That's how you can tell us from the—if you'll pardon the expression, monsieur—from the nobodies in the field.

DARTAGNAN: Indeed.

MOULINEAUX: And, anyway, it was just a rough estimate. It's not easy without a tape. Not even for an expert. With an eye like mine . . . *(Looking around the workbench for a tape.)* You don't happen to have one, monsieur?

DARTAGNAN: A tape? *(Laughing.)* No, I can't say I do! But surely you must have one.

MOULINEAUX: One? I have dozens! Only not here, that's all. They're all in my shop. My shops . . . My huge workshops . . .

DARTAGNAN: Aha. *(Aside.)* Odd chap, this tailor! *(To* MOULINEAUX.*)* You know, I must say, Monsieur . . . Monsieur . . . *(Pausing, trying to recall his name.)* Sorry. What was your name again?

SUZANNE *(trying unsuccessfully to save the day)*: It's Monsieur . . . Monsieur . . .

MOULINEAUX: Monsieur . . . you know . . . you know.

DARTAGNAN: Yuno? Is that Italian?

MOULINEAUX: Ital— No, no. I mean, yes. That is, sometimes. *Sì, sì!* Sometimes . . .

DARTAGNAN: I must say, Monsieur . . . *(Correcting.)* Signor Yuno, you look terribly familiar. Have we met?

MOULINEAUX *(turning his back, trying his best to hide his face)*: Met? Us? You and Me? *(Aside.)* Oh, my. *(To* DARTAGNAN.*)* No! Impossible!

DARTAGNAN: But . . .

MOULINEAUX: I . . . I never go out! Never, monsieur! Never!

DARTAGNAN *(suddenly remembering)*: I know! The doctor's. Doctor Moulineaux. This morning . . . Madame's doctor . . .

MOULINEAUX *(with a casual gesture)*: Oh, him . . .

DARTAGNAN: Do you go to him too?

MOULINEAUX *(as offhand as possible)*: Well, once in a while . . . I don't make it a habit.

DARTAGNAN: You're smart! They say he's a quack!

MOULINEAUX *(indignantly)*: That's not true! Not . . . *(Realizing that he is about to give himself away.)* Not Moulineaux, not my doctor. . . .

DARTAGNAN: Well, that's what they tell me. *(Nodding to* SUZANNE.*)* Needless to say, madame doesn't think so! She's been going to him for years.

MOULINEAUX: Oh?

DARTAGNAN: Though I can't imagine why. *(*SUZANNE *and* MOULINEAUX *exchange glances in spite of themselves.)* At any rate, signore, if that's not where I met you . . .

MOULINEAUX: No, no. I'm sure!

DARTAGNAN: Now then . . . *(He takes the chair near the workbench, right, and places it in front of* MOULINEAUX.*)* You and my wife. *(Sitting down.)* Tell me, what are you doing?

MOULINEAUX *(agape)*: What . . . What are we . . . ? Monsieur . . . ?

DARTAGNAN: What kind of a gown are you making for her?

MOULINEAUX: What kind of a . . . *(Recovering.)* Yes, yes. *(Correcting.)* Sì sì . . . Her gown . . .

DARTAGNAN: Yes. What did you have in mind?

MOULINEAUX: Oh, believe me! A creation!

DARTAGNAN: I'm sure. And what will it look like?

MOULINEAUX: Well, it's going to be a . . . *(Spouting the first terms that come to mind.)* . . . a dirndl, monsieur. With a lovely pleated bodice. All in Chantilly lace. And a full-flaring skirt with ruffles, monsieur. Lots and lots of ruffles. And a bustle with ostrich plumes and a black sable trim.

DARTAGNAN *(impressed)*: Sable?

MOULINEAUX: Only on the legs!

DARTAGNAN: Legs? What legs?

MOULINEAUX: Under the petticoat! Don't worry, you can't see them.

DARTAGNAN: Good heavens! What a novel combination, I must say! Ostrich plumes . . . black sable.

MOULINEAUX *(perspiring)*: Yes! *Sì!* It's an inspiration.

DARTAGNAN *(to* SUZANNE*)*: Not too risqué, my love, I hope. *(To* MOULINEAUX.*)* May I have a peek at the model?

MOULINEAUX: The . . . the model? Of the gown?

DARTAGNAN: Yes. The design. You have one, don't you?

MOULINEAUX: One? I have dozens! But they're all in my shops. The designs are in my shops.

DARTAGNAN: Ah . . . along with the tapes . . .

MOULINEAUX *(ignoring his remark)*: Under lock and key! Competition, you know. It's such a cutthroat business! My competitors would kill for just one look.

DARTAGNAN: My goodness! You mean, we can't choose the one we like?

MOULINEAUX: Yes! Of course! Who's stopping you? You can choose all you want! You just can't look at them, that's all. *(Aside.)* Good God! Won't he leave?

(LILY *appears at the open door and knocks.)*

LILY *(entering without waiting for an answer)*: The door was open. *(Coming down left, nodding to each in turn.)* Monsieur, monsieur, madame.

MOULINEAUX *(aside)*: Oh, my! Now what?

(There is a brief moment of uncomfortable silence while every-one looks quizzically at one another.)

LILY *(to* MOULINEAUX*)*: Excuse me, but . . . Madame Durand?

MOULINEAUX: What?

LILY: Madame Durand?

MOULINEAUX: No, Doc . . . *(Quickly correcting himself.)* Signor Yuno. *(Pointing to* SUZANNE, *still by the sofa.)* Madame Dartagnan. *(Pointing to* DARTAGNAN, *still sitting, right.)* Monsieur . . .

LILY *(with a little cursty)*: Delighted! *(To* MOULINEAUX.*)* No. I mean, where is she?

MOULINEAUX: Where is who?

LILY: Madame Durand. Isn't she here?

(There is another brief silence, during which MOULINEAUX, *at a loss, looks back and forth at* SUZANNE *and* DARTAGNAN.*)*

MOULINEAUX *(blankly)*: Oh! Madame Durand. No . . . no. She's away.

LILY: Too bad! I wanted to see her about my bill.

MOULINEAUX *(nodding, echoing)*: About your bill . . .

LILY: Yes. For her dress. That is, mine. But she made it.

MOULINEAUX *(suddenly comprehending)*: Oh, you mean Madame Durand! The dressmaker. *That* Madame Durand!

LILY: That's right.

DARTAGNAN *(to* MOULINEAUX*)*: Don't you know her, signore?

MOULINEAUX: Know her? Madame Durand? Certainly I know her! Why shouldn't I know her? Dear, dear Madame Durand! She's my partner. *(Aside.)* Bassinet should have warned me she had customers, damn it! Just what I need!

LILY *(to* MOULINEAUX*)*: Well, as long as you're her partner . . . I'm Mademoiselle Leluxe. Mademoiselle Lily Leluxe.

MOULINEAUX *(nodding)*: Aha. If you say so.

LILY: And I'd like you to do something about my bill, monsieur. It's really much too high.

MOULINEAUX: You're right! With pleasure! I couldn't agree more.

LILY: Oh?

MOULINEAUX *(writing on the notepad, aside)*: What do I care? If it gets rid of her . . . No skin off my nose.

LILY *(holding out the bill)*: You see? Three hundred forty francs.

MOULINEAUX: Tsk tsk tsk! Too high! Much too high! *(With a look toward DARTAGNAN.)* Just what I was saying to Madame Durand . . .

LILY: Only chintz, after all. Two pieces of chintz.

MOULINEAUX: Yes. *Sì, sì.* You were the one with the double chintz. I remember.

LILY: And for chintz . . . I mean, it's not like satin or silk.

MOULINEAUX: No, no. You're right. *(To DARTAGNAN.)* She's absolutely right! *(To SUZANNE.)* Three hundred forty francs for chintz! Tsk tsk tsk! *(To LILY.)* Now then, what did you have in mind? How much would you like us to take off, mademoiselle?

LILY *(startled)*: How much would I . . .

MOULINEAUX: Whatever you say.

LILY: Well, I think three hundred is more than enough, don't you?

MOULINEAUX *(as agreeably as possible)*: Absolutely! Very fair. *(Figuring on the notepad.)* Three hundred from three hundred and forty . . . that leaves forty, mademoiselle. Forty francs. *(Changing the bill.)* There! Will that be satisfactory?

LILY *(about to correct him)*: Forty? But monsieur, you . . . I think there's a mistake.

MOULINEAUX: No, no. That's fine. "The customer is always right!" That's our motto, mademoiselle.

LILY *(not knowing what to say)*: Yes, I . . . it's . . . But monsieur, it's really much more. So much more than I—

MOULINEAUX *(interrupting)*: Then let's say thirty-five, for round figures! And because you're such a good customer! *(Changing the bill again.)* Thirty-five!

LILY *(moving upstage)*: Well, that certainly is fair.

DARTAGNAN *(aside, laughing)*: Damn thieves, if you ask me!

LILY (*to* MOULINEAUX): I must say, it's a pleasure doing business with you, monsieur . . . Monsieur . . .

SUZANNE (*quickly, afraid that* MOULINEAUX *might put his foot in his mouth*): Yuno! Signor Yuno!

LILY: Signor Yuno . . .

MOULINEAUX: Yes. Likewise.

LILY: I'll be on my way.

MOULINEAUX: *Sì, sì.* So nice of you to come by.

LILY (*at the door, up center*): Au revoir, monsieur. I'll be sure to come again.

MOULINEAUX (*under his breath*): Please! Don't bother!

LILY: Especially when Madame Durand is away.

   (*She nods at the company and exits.*)

DARTAGNAN (*standing up, taking out his watch*): My, my! One-thirty! I'd better be going too. (*Aside.*) My little Mathilde will be furious if I'm not right on time. (*To* MOULINEAUX.) Well, signore, I'm leaving madame in your capable hands.

MOULINEAUX: *Sì, sì.*

DARTAGNAN: I'm sure you know how to take care of her needs. (SUZANNE *and* MOULINEAUX *exchange subtle glances.*) Outdo yourself, my friend! No holds barred, as they say. But nothing too vulgar, you understand. Especially around the hips and . . . and—if I may say—the bosom . . .

MOULINEAUX: Yes, especially.

DARTAGNAN (*going over to* SUZANNE): Remember, my love. Shapely but not too risqué.

SUZANNE: No. No.

DARTAGNAN (*shaking* MOULINEAUX'S *hand*): A pleasure meeting you, signore. (*Going to the door, up center.*) How do you say? *Arrivederci!* Bye-bye!

   (*He exits. As soon as the door closes* MOULINEAUX *makes a dash, stands one of the chairs against it, and falls on it in a heap, obviously worn-out by the experience.*)

MOULINEAUX (*heaving a sigh of relief*): At last! I thought he'd never leave!

SUZANNE (*moving upstage, fanning herself with a handkerchief*): Oh! Balthasar! This is terrible! What now? Never in all my life . . .

MOULINEAUX: I know, I know.

SUZANNE: But what are you going to do?

MOULINEAUX: Do? Me? (*Determined.*) Get out of here, that's what I'm going to do! You can bet that this is the last time I ever get caught with . . . with my gown down!

SUZANNE: No, no! You can't! You can't leave, Balthasar! You mustn't.

MOULINEAUX: And why not? You don't expect me to put up with more like—

SUZANNE (*interrupting*): But Anatole, my husband . . .

MOULINEAUX: Just give me one good reason.

SUZANNE: He thinks you're my tailor! If he comes back and doesn't find you, he'll suspect . . . He'll know. He'll know that you and I . . . that we . . . Oh, Balthasar! With his temper he'll kill you!

MOULINEAUX: He will? (*Backing down.*) Hmm . . . all right, that's a good enough reason. You may have a point. (*Prostrate on the chair.*) Good God! What a lovely mess we've got ourselves into!

SUZANNE (*wringing her hands, up right*): I knew it! I just knew it was madness! I just knew! I never should have come here. Because—

MOULINEAUX: I know. It's the first time.

(*At that moment the door, up center, flies open, knocking over the chair and sending* MOULINEAUX *sprawling on the floor to the sofa as* BASSINET *appears.*)

SUZANNE (*stifling a little shriek, taking refuge behind the mannequin, up right*): Oh!

BASSINET (*entering*): I say . . . (*He stumbles over the chair.*) Ayyy!

MOULINEAUX (*licking his wounds*): You! Can't you even come in like any normal human being?

BASSINET *(limping down left, rubbing his knee)*: Drat it all! Who asked you to sit against the door, monsieur! Really!

MOULINEAUX *(painfully getting to his feet)*: And who asked you to rent me an apartment with a door that doesn't lock! Heaven only knows what else doesn't work! Just look at this place.

BASSINET: But I told you, monsieur. You wanted it right away.

MOULINEAUX: Yes, yes, yes.

BASSINET: I said it would take time to put things in order. After the dressmaker . . . But you said, "No, no, I'll make do!" You insisted . . .

MOULINEAUX: But a lock, for goodness! sake! A door you can shut! Is that too much to ask? It's like living in the street! Every idiot and his brother can just barge right in!

(He paces up and down.)

BASSINET: But who would do a thing like that, monsieur?

MOULINEAUX: You, that's who! Who else! *(Sarcastically.)* Now all we need is your brother!

BASSINET: My brother, monsieur! But I don't have a—

MOULINEAUX *(down center)*: Never mind! Just get it fixed!

BASSINET *(moving left)*: Certainly, monsieur. As soon as I can find the locksmith. You see, I had to break the lock myself a few days ago. To get in. When the dressmaker left in such a hurry. You remember. *(Laughing.)* When that gigolo of hers went and—

MOULINEAUX *(cutting him off)*: Really, I'm not interested! I just want a door that locks! I don't care about her gigolo!

BASSINET: Oh . . . Sorry, I thought . . . Well, the locksmith came to fix it the very same day, monsieur. Only first he said he had to go have lunch, and I haven't seen him since. But I'm sure he'll come back.

MOULINEAUX: Yes. Next month!

BASSINET *(moving up left)*: Anyway, aside from the minor inconveniences . . . Is everything going . . . *(With a broad wink.)* . . . according to plan?

MOULINEAUX: Excuse me, Monsieur Bassinet. *(Pointing to* SU-

ZANNE, *still cowering by the mannequin.)* But, as you can see, I'm not alone.

BASSINET *(finally catching sight of* SUZANNE*)*: Oh. Pardon me. I didn't notice. *(To* SUZANNE, *with a little bow.)* Madame . . . Please don't go. You're not interrupting. *(With a little laugh.)* Monsieur and I have no secrets!

MOULINEAUX: You're much too kind!

BASSINET *(coming down and settling in on the sofa, to* MOULINEAUX*)*: In fact, I was just going to tell you—

MOULINEAUX: Later! Later! *(Aside.)* Damn leech! That's all I needed!

(There is a knock at the door, up center, and MADAME D'HER-BLAY *appears.)*

MADAME D'HERBLAY *(entering, looking around timidly)*: Oh, excuse me. I was looking for Madame Durand.

MOULINEAUX: Another one?

SUZANNE *(hands on hips)*: Oh!

MOULINEAUX: That's the limit!

(He begins pacing up and down.)

MADAME D'HERBLAY: I . . . I came about my dickie.

MOULINEAUX *(gruffly)*: Who?

MADAME D'HERBLAY: My dickie . . . My blouse . . . I wanted Madame Durand to—

MOULINEAUX: Yes, but not today! Try next month. Next year.

MADAME D'HERBLAY: But my dickie, monsieur.

MOULINEAUX *(losing patience, upstage)*: Your dickie can go hang!

MADAME D'HERBLAY *(offended but still timid)*: Well! See if I bother to pay!

MOULINEAUX *(giving tit for tat)*: Well! See if I bother to give a damn!

MADAME D'HERBLAY *(turning to leave)*: Oh! It's a wonder they have any customers here at all! Oh!

(She exits, up center.)

MOULINEAUX: Good riddance!

SUZANNE (*in a whisper, to* MOULINEAUX, *pointing to* BASSINET, *still blithely sitting on the sofa*): Now what about him?

MOULINEAUX: Just leave him to me! (*He moves down to the sofa.*) Monsieur Bassinet . . .

BASSINET: Ah! There you are! As I was saying . . .

MOULINEAUX (*trying in vain to interrupt*): Monsieur . . .

BASSINET: I was just about to tell you . . . You'll never guess what happened . . .

MOULINEAUX: Monsieur . . .

BASSINET: I still haven't gotten over it. Can you imagine! Of all things, monsieur! I thought I found my wife!

MOULINEAUX: Yes, yes. But monsieur . . .

BASSINET: After all these years! You remember, I told you. The Tuileries . . . The soldier . . .

MOULINEAUX: Yes.

BASSINET: Well, believe it or not, someone told me about a Madame Bassinet on Rue de Seine. So, naturally, I went over.

MOULINEAUX: Excuse me, monsieur, but . . . (*Pointing to* SUZANNE.) Madame and I . . .

BASSINET (*naively*): Oh, she's not bothering me. I don't mind.

MOULINEAUX: You don't—

BASSINET (*continuing*): Anyway, when I got there and knocked on the door, you'll never guess . . .

MOULINEAUX: No.

BASSINET: She opened it, monsieur. And there she was. A total stranger!

MOULINEAUX: Monsieur . . .

BASSINET: She wasn't my wife at all! So, naturally, I excused myself. "Pardon me," I told her, "I expected to find a lady, not you." Well, it must have been something in the way I said it! Because, really . . .

MOULINEAUX: I'm sure . . .

(All of a sudden MADAME AIGREVILLE *appears at the door, up center.)*

MADAME AIGREVILLE *(just outside)*: One B. One B. This must be it.

(She enters.)

BASSINET *(still absorbed in his story, to* MOULINEAUX*)*: You have no idea . . .

MOULINEAUX *(turning and catching sight of* MADAME AIGREVILLE, *suppressing a scream)*: Ayyy! *(Aside.)* What's she doing here?

SUZANNE *(furious)*: Another one?

BASSINET *(noticing* MADAME AIGREVILLE, *getting up, turning to her)*: Oh, madame . . .

SUZANNE *(aside)*: Really, this is simply too much!

MADAME AIGREVILLE *(to* BASSINET*)*: Ah, you! I've come to look at your apartment.

MOULINEAUX *(trying to remain inconspicuous, aside)*: What?

BASSINET *(to* MADAME AIGREVILLE*)*: You. Oh, I'm terribly sorry, madame. It's already rented.

MADAME AIGREVILLE: It is? But you told me . . . I thought you said . . . *(Suddenly turning and finding herself face-to-face with* MOULINEAUX.*)* Moulineaux! What on earth . . .

MOULINEAUX *(as casually as possible)*: Hello, Mother!

MADAME AIGREVILLE: What are you doing here?

MOULINEAUX: What a nice surprise!

MADAME AIGREVILLE *(sharply)*: I asked you a question! What are you doing here, monsieur?

MOULINEAUX: Me?

MADAME AIGREVILLE: I'm warning you . . . *(With a look at* SU-ZANNE, *still up right, pointedly)*: I'm quite prepared to believe the worst!

MOULINEAUX *(innocently)*: Worst what, Mother, dear?

MADAME AIGREVILLE: I'll ask you once again, monsieur! What are you doing here?

MOULINEAUX *(as naturally as possible)*: Why . . . visiting

a patient. I'm here for a consultation. Why else would I be here?

MADAME AIGREVILLE *(distressed at his logical answer)*: What?

MOULINEAUX *(to* SUZANNE*)*: Isn't that so, madame? You are my patient, aren't you?

SUZANNE *(picking up the hint)*: Of course, doctor! And so good of you to come. *(Affecting a little cough.)* In my condition . . .

MADAME AIGREVILLE *(embarrassed, to* SUZANNE*)*: Why certainly, madame! I never doubted for a moment . . .

SUZANNE *(to* MADAME AIGREVILLE*)*: He's so obliging. Such a saint . . .

MADAME AIGREVILLE: Indeed . . .

SUZANNE *(to* MADAME AIGREVILLE, *very properly, playing her role to the hilt)*: Tell me, madame. To what do I owe the honor. Is there something I can do for you?

MADAME AIGREVILLE *(still very embarrassed)*: Do? Well, that is . . . I . . . You see, I was making the rounds of the neighborhood—

SUZANNE: Of course! For the poor! How noble, madame! How utterly noble!

MADAME AIGREVILLE *(taken aback)*: What?

SUZANNE: Please! No one can say that I don't support our widows and orphans! *(She takes a coin from her muff, on the chair by the door, and strides down to* MADAME AIGREVILLE.*)* Here! Will five francs do?

(She presses the coin into MADAME AIGREVILLE'S *palm.)*

MADAME AIGREVILLE *(shocked)*: Five francs, madame? But—

SUZANNE: Unless that's not enough . . .

MOULINEAUX *(to* MADAME AIGREVILLE, *feigning shock)*: Aren't you ashamed of yourself? To go begging from door to door . . .

BASSINET *(shaking his head, scornfully)*: Tsk tsk tsk!

MADAME AIGREVILLE: But I'm not doing anything of the kind!

MOULINEAUX: Tsk tsk tsk!

MADAME AIGREVILLE *(to* SUZANNE*)*: Here! I don't want your money! *(She gives it to* MOULINEAUX, *to pass it to* SUZANNE.*)* I'm not taking a collection! I'm looking for an apartment!

*(*MOULINEAUX *mechanically pockets the coin.)*

SUZANNE *(to* MADAME AIGREVILLE*)*: Oh! I do beg your pardon, madame! No offense! *(To* MOULINEAUX, *having caught his maneuver, holding out her hand.)* If you please . . .

MOULINEAUX *(giving her the coin)*: Sorry. I wasn't thinking.

SUZANNE *(with affected aplomb, to* MOULINEAUX*)*: Well, doctor, aren't you going to introduce us?

MOULINEAUX *(aghast)*: Intro— *(To* SUZANNE*)*: You want me to . . . ? *(She nods.)* Why, certainly! Excuse me! Where are my manners? *(Introducing, with an acid note in his voice.)* Madame Aigreville . . . my mother-in-law . . . *(Almost voluptuously.)* Madame Dartagnan . . . Madame Suzanne Dartagnan.

MADAME AIGREVILLE: Delighted!

SUZANNE: The pleasure is all mine!

MADAME AIGREVILLE *(nodding toward* BASSINET*)*: And this is Monsieur Dartagnan, I take it! *(To* BASSINET.*)* Not our famous Musketeer, monsieur?

(The others gasp in disbelief.)

BASSINET: Our what?

MADAME AIGREVILLE *(naively)*: I mean, one wouldn't think so to look at you . . .

SUZANNE *(to* MADAME AIGREVILLE*)*: Monsieur is just a friend, madame.

MADAME AIGREVILLE: Oh . . .

MOULINEAUX *(quickly, clearing his throat)*: Pardon the anachronism! *(To* MADAME AIGREVILLE.*)* Really, you should know better!

MADAME AIGREVILLE *(not quite comprehending, embarrassed)*: Oh? Did I say something? Sorry. *(Changing the subject, to* SUZANNE.*)* So, you've put yourself into my son-in-law's hands, I see.

SUZANNE: Yes. Quite. *(Quickly, to avert suspicion.)* My husband too.

MADAME AIGREVILLE: Aha.

SUZANNE: Especially my husband.

MADAME AIGREVILLE: Oh? Is he ill, my dear?

SUZANNE: Well.

MOULINEAUX *(jumping into the breach)*: Yes! Impetigo!

MADAME AIGREVILLE: Please?

MOULINEAUX: Impetigo! Impetigo! An eczematose impetigo. With subcutaneous inflammation . . . and . . . and epidermal suppuration.

MADAME AIGREVILLE: Oh, my heavens!

MOULINEAUX: And desquamation! Desquamation!

MADAME AIGREVILLE: Poor man! What does it come from?

MOULINEAUX *(babbling)*: From . . . from . . . from childbirth. Complications . . .

MADAME AIGREVILLE: What? Him?

MOULINEAUX *(pointing to* SUZANNE*)*: Her! Her!

SUZANNE: Me?

MADAME AIGREVILLE *(to* SUZANNE*)*: Oh, you have a child, my dear?

| MOULINEAUX | *(together)* | Yes! |
| SUZANNE | | No! *(Realizing she is committing a* faux pas.*)* That is . . . |

MOULINEAUX: Almost . . . She thought . . . I thought . . . We thought . . .

MADAME AIGREVILLE: And Monsieur Dartagnan?

MOULINEAUX: He . . . he thought so too! He thought she was going to . . . But . . . But then, when she didn't . . . Well, you know . . . Nerves! Nerves! Skin rash . . . Hives . . . Eczema . . . Impetigo!

MADAME AIGREVILLE: Oh, my! Poor thing!

MOULINEAUX: The whole business! Classic case! Very stubborn!

MADAME AIGREVILLE: How sad.

MOULINEAUX: Yes, very. And now, Mother, if you don't mind, I'd like to get on with my consultation.

(SUZANNE, *taking the hint, gives a few little coughs.*)

MADAME AIGREVILLE: Of course. How thoughtless of me. I'll be
on my way.

(She goes to leave, up center.)

MOULINEAUX *(accompanying her, aside)*: Not a minute too soon!

MADAME AIGREVILLE *(aside)*: If Yvonne comes, she just won't
find me, that's all.

MOULINEAUX *(holding the door open for her)*: Au revoir, Mother,
dear!

MADAME AIGREVILLE: Don't "Mother dear" me, you cad! I'm not
forgetting a thing! *(Very proper.)* But I do know how to
behave in front of strangers!

MOULINEAUX *(very affable)*: Yes. I'll try to remember to invite
some for you.

MADAME AIGREVILLE *(to* SUZANNE*)*: Madame . . .

SUZANNE: Madame . . .

(Suddenly MOULINEAUX, *still at the open door, see* DARTAGNAN
coming up the stairs.)

MOULINEAUX *(with a start)*: Oh, no! Dartagnan! *(Rushing to join*
SUZANNE, *in a whisper.)* Your husband! He's back!

SUZANNE *(petrified)*: What? Good heavens!

(She grabs her muff and makes a hasty exit, up right.)

MADAME AIGREVILLE: What?

MOULINEAUX *(trying to push* MADAME AIGREVILLE *out the door, up
right)*: You too! You too!

MADAME AIGREVILLE *(dumbfounded)*: But . . . What is it? What
are you—

MOULINEAUX: Don't ask questions! Just get in there!

(He succeeds in pushing her out, despite her protestations.)

BASSINET *(who has been looking on, caught up in the sudden
excitement, automatically following* MOULINEAUX *to the door)*:
I say . . . Should I come too, monsieur!

MOULINEAUX *(half out the door)*: You . . . No, no! You stay!
You tell him . . . If he asks for a Monsieur Yuno . . . Signor
Yuno . . . He thinks that's my name . . .

BASSINET *(puzzled)*: Signor?

MOULINEAUX: Just tell him I'm busy! Tell him anything you like! I'm . . . I'm in conference . . . with the . . . the queen of Greenland! Anything! But for God's sake, get rid of him!

(He slams the door in BASSINET'S *face.)*

BASSINET: Of course, monsieur! *(Coming down center.)* Some pest, I suppose. I know the type. *(Hands on hips, puzzled.)* Signor? *(Tapping his temple with his forefinger.)* I think our friend the doctor needs . . . a doctor!

(DARTAGNAN appears at the open door.)

DARTAGNAN *(entering)*: Hello! It's me again, monsieur. *(Laying his hat on one of the chairs by the door.)* Signore . . . *(Looking around.)* Oh . . . Pardon me, I thought . . . Where's Signor Yuno? Isn't he in?

BASSINET *(facing the audience, back to* DARTAGNAN*)*: No. That is, yes. But he's busy.

DARTAGNAN *(recognizing him)*: Ah! Our friend the doctor . . .

BASSINET *(turning around, misunderstanding)*: That's right. Our friend. Oh, you know. *(Aside.)* Then what's all this "Signor Yuno"? *(To* DARTAGNAN.*)* I'm sorry. He's very busy.

DARTAGNAN *(coming down, joining him)*: Our dear friend the doctor . . .

BASSINET *(echoing mechanically)*: Yes. Our dear friend the doctor.

DARTAGNAN: What a small world, monsieur! You never know where you're going to meet a familiar face, now, do you?

BASSINET *(trying to be agreeable)*: Quite. Quite.

DARTAGNAN: Then again, I don't know why I should be surprised. You and Signor Yuno, after all . . .

BASSINET: Monsieur?

DARTAGNAN: You do see him, I mean . . .

BASSINET: Yes.

DARTAGNAN: In fact, he was just telling me, not half an hour ago . . .

BASSINET: He was?

DARTAGNAN: He's a patient, isn't he?

BASSINET *(misunderstanding)*: Impatient? Well, as a matter of fact, sometimes . . . not always . . . *(Aside.)* Curious question!

DARTAGNAN *(trying to be funny)*: No. Only when he's sick!

BASSINET: Yes, only . . . Oh, you noticed . . . Yes, I daresay . . .

DARTAGNAN: Tell me, what seems to be his problem exactly?

BASSINET *(unconsciously unbuttoning* DARTAGNAN'S *coat as he talks)*: Well, frankly, monsieur, if you ask me, I think . . . *(Confidentially.)* I think he's got a bat loose in the belfry, as they say.

DARTAGNAN *(rebuttoning his coat)*: I rather had the same impression myself. Just a layman's opinion. But if you say so too . . . Well . . .

BASSINET *(unbuttoning again)*: Yes. Lately he's been behaving rather strangely. Little things, mind you. Nothing serious, but still . . .

DARTAGNAN *(rebuttoning)*: Yes. And I assume you've suggested that he do something for it? Hydrotherapy. Cold showers.

BASSINET *(beginning to unbutton again)*: Oh, I don't know that I would want to take the liberty . . .

DARTAGNAN *(pulling away, rebuttoning)*: Please! Thank you. It's not necessary.

BASSINET: Though, just between you and me . . . *(Flicking a speck of lint from* DARTAGNAN'S *collar.)* It wouldn't hurt him to take a shower!

DARTAGNAN *(backing away)*: Yes. I'm sure.

BASSINET *(repeating his maneuver)*: But that's his business.

DARTAGNAN *(backing away, deciding to change the subject)*: You know, as long as we're standing here chatting . . . I wonder if you would mind . . .

BASSINET *(repeating it again)*: Monsieur?

DARTAGNAN *(stepping to one side)*: It's not that I'm looking for free advice, understand. It's just that . . . Well, ordinarily I'm rather hot-blooded by nature.

BASSINET (*grasping* DARTAGNAN'S *lapels and arranging them, hardly listening*): Yes. Yes, that's nice.

DARTAGNAN (*stepping to the other side*): But lately I've been having problems. Circulation, monsieur. Nosebleeds, mainly.

BASSINET: Aha.

DARTAGNAN: And my feet keep falling asleep.

BASSINET (*still arranging his lapels*): Yes. Yes, that's too bad.

DARTAGNAN: In fact . . . (*In semi-desperation, taking off his coat and draping it over his arm.*) I was mentioning it to your butler . . .

BASSINET: Oh? (*At a loss what to do with his hands, finally folding his arms on his chest.*) You know my butler?

DARTAGNAN: Well . . . That is, we've met . . .

BASSINET: Which one? Joseph or Baptiste?

DARTAGNAN: I'm afraid I couldn't tell you. All I know is that he gave me some rather unusual suggestions.

BASSINET: And massage, monsieur? Did he tell you to try massage? That's what always works for me.

DARTAGNAN: I've tried it, but I'm afraid it hasn't done much good.

BASSINET: Well, maybe you don't know how. You see, the way I do it . . . First you find yourself a good masseur. Big and strong. The stronger the better. Then you have him take off his clothes and lie down on the table, and you massage him as hard as you can for an hour. If that doesn't get your blood moving, I'll eat my hat!

DARTAGNAN: Aha. You're right. I was doing it all wrong. Thank you, monsieur. I'll try it.

BASSINET: Don't mention it. My pleasure . . .

(*There is a brief pause as* DARTAGNAN, *remembering the purpose of his visit, looks at his watch with an impatient sigh.*)

DARTAGNAN: And you say Signor Yuno is too busy to see me?

BASSINET: Oh, much too busy! He's in conference with Her Majesty!

DARTAGNAN: Who?

BASSINET: The green of Queenland!

DARTAGNAN: What?

BASSINET: The green . . . *(Correcting.)* The queen, I mean . . . The queen of Greenland, monsieur!

DARTAGNAN *(impressed)*: He is? With a queen? My, my, my! A real queen?

BASSINET: Yes, monsieur. Of Greenland . . .

DARTAGNAN *(with a gesture of admiration)*: Pfff! Talk about high fashion! You can't get much higher! He must be the best in the business! *(Aside.)* Who would ever think . . . ? A queen . . .

BASSINET: So if you would like to come back . . . Maybe another time.

DARTAGNAN: No, no. I don't think so. You see, I wanted to tell him to expect a visit from a . . . *(Clearing his throat.)* a certain young friend of mine . . . Madame de Sainte-Vinaigrette . . .

BASSINET *(nodding)*: Aha.

DARTAGNAN: The dear child is simply queen with . . . *(Correcting.)* simply green with envy. She's dying to know where my wife has her gowns made. A whim . . . You know . . .

BASSINET *(nodding)*: Some women . . .

>   *(He reaches over and flicks off a speck of lint from* DAR-TAGNAN'S *coat, draped over his arm.)*

DARTAGNAN: So I thought it would be better if I . . . Well, if I came here first, just in case. To see if my wife was still here, that is. With Signor Yuno . . .

BASSINET: Aha.

DARTAGNAN *(confidentially)*: I'm not especially anxious for madame to meet the child. She might not understand, you understand . . .

BASSINET: I understand.

DARTAGNAN: Some women . . .

BASSINET: I say, monsieur, you mean . . . *(Flicking off another speck.)* That lovely lady just now was your wife? The one who was here a few moments ago with . . . with Signor Yuno?

DARTAGNAN: Why, yes.

BASSINET: And you let her go out all alone, monsieur? In Paris?

DARTAGNAN: Oh, heaven forbid! I'd never . . . I brought her here myself!

BASSINET *(with a sardonic smile)*: Aha. Well, in that case . . .

DARTAGNAN *(looking at his watch again)*: Tell me, do you think Signor Yuno will be much longer?

BASSINET: Who can say, monsieur? With a queen, after all . . .

(*He goes to flick off another speck, but* DARTAGNAN *turns aside suddenly at the sound of* MADAME AIGREVILLE'S *voice.*)

MADAME AIGREVILLE'S VOICE: No, no, no! I'm telling you, I've got an appointment!

BASSINET *(aside)*: The mother-in-law!

MADAME AIGREVILLE'S VOICE: I'm not staying another minute!

BASSINET *(aside)*: Here's my chance to rent Three A . . .

DARTAGNAN: Good heavens!

SUZANNE'S VOICE: But . . .

BASSINET *(aside)*: I'll go wait for her in the hall.

MOULINEAUX'S VOICE: But . . .

(BASSINET *exits quickly, up center, unseen by* DARTAGNAN, *who is still looking inquisitively up right.*)

MADAME AIGREVILLE'S VOICE: No, no, no!

DARTAGNAN: My goodness, doctor. What do you suppose . . . ? *(Turning left, finding* BASSINET *gone.)* Doctor? Now where on earth . . . ? Odd chap, this Doctor Moulineaux, I must say!

(*He moves up center and retrieves his hat from the chair as* MADAME AIGREVILLE *enters, up right.*)

MADAME AIGREVILLE: The very idea . . . Trying to keep me here . . .

DARTAGNAN *(looking up, aside)*: Ah! That must be . . . *(To* MADAME AIGREVILLE.*)* Your Queenship . . .

(*He bows with a little flourish of his hat, then stands at attention with the hat over his heart.*)

MADAME AIGREVILLE: Now who . . . *(Nodding politely.)* Monsieur . . .

DARTAGNAN *(with more flourishes)*: Your Highness! Your Majesty!

MADAME AIGREVILLE *(surprised)*: My what?

DARTAGNAN *(with a deep bow)*: I bow before your gracious presence!

MADAME AIGREVILLE *(coquettishly)*: Why, thank you, I'm sure! How terribly sweet! And to whom do I have the honor, monsieur . . . ?

DARTAGNAN *(bowing)*: Monsieur Dartagnan. Monsieur Anatole Dartagnan.

MADAME AIGREVILLE: Oh, then you must be . . . I've met your charming wife, monsieur.

DARTAGNAN *(bowing)*: The pleasure is all ours, Your Grace . . .

MADAME AIGREVILLE *(without transition)*: Tell me, how is your impetigo?

DARTAGNAN *(uncomprehending)*: Excuse me?

MADAME AIGREVILLE: Your impetigo, monsieur. You have one, I understand.

DARTAGNAN: I do? *(Aside.)* I didn't know.

MADAME AIGREVILLE: Yes. *(Trying to be sympathetic.)* I imagine that when it itches, it must drive you crazy!

DARTAGNAN *(quizzically)*: When it itches? My . . .

MADAME AIGREVILLE: You know, monsieur. Your rash. Your eczema.

DARTAGNAN: My . . . *(As deferentially as possible.)* I beg your pardon! What rash? What eczema?

MADAME AIGREVILLE: Yours, monsieur. *(Aside.)* Oh, my! He's sensitive, poor thing! I shouldn't have . . .

DARTAGNAN: Excuse me, but I don't know what makes you think . . .

(He moves left, examining his hands.)

MADAME AIGREVILLE *(aside)*: Another blunder! *(To* DARTAGNAN.*)*

No, no! My mistake! Please, pardon the . . . the . . . (*Trying to remember the word.*) the anachronism, monsieur.

DARTAGNAN (*aside*): Anachronism? (*To* MADAME AIGREVILLE, *still very obsequious.*) Not at all, I assure you.

MADAME AIGREVILLE: Thank you! You're too kind.

DARTAGNAN (*aside*): Hmm! Maybe it means something else in Greenlandish.

MADAME AIGREVILLE (*at the door, up center, ready to leave*): Well, if you'll excuse me. It's a pleasure to meet madame's husband, monsieur. Perhaps we'll meet again. (DARTAGNAN *bows with a flourish.*) Monsieur . . .

   (*She exits.*)

DARTAGNAN (*with a gesture of admiration*): Pfff! Who would ever think . . . ? A queen! You would never know, to look at her. She seems so . . . ordinary. (*Catching sight of* MOULINEAUX, *who appears at the door, up right.*) Ah! Signor Yuno . . . I've been waiting.

   (*He comes down right, looking at his watch.*)

MOULINEAUX (*aside*): Still here, damn it? (*To* SUZANNE, *pushing her back into the room as she appears momentarily at his heels.*) No! Not yet!

   (*He pulls the door shut quickly.*)

DARTAGNAN (*turning to look*): What?

MOULINEAUX (*innocently*): Hmm? What's that, monsieur?

DARTAGNAN: Oh, I thought you said something.

MOULINEAUX: Me, monsieur? No.

DARTAGNAN (*joining him*): Tell me, signore. My wife . . . has she left?

MOULINEAUX: Oh, long ago! Long ago! She said if you came back, to tell you she's at the Louvre. In case you want to look for her.

DARTAGNAN (*taking his arm and leading him down center*): Not at all, my friend. Quite the contrary! This is just fine. You see . . . (*Confidentially.*) There's a lady ·. . . a certain young friend of mine . . . and I expect she'll be coming here to meet me any moment.

MOULINEAUX: Here, did you say? You told her to meet you here? *(Aside.)* The nerve of some people!

DARTAGNAN: So, you can understand. I'd just as soon not have her run into madame.

MOULINEAUX: Aha. I see! You mean, a little—how shall I say?—affair?

DARTAGNAN *(laughing)*: Oh, little! Very little! Hardly worth mentioning. But still, there's no need for my wife. You understand. You're Italian.

MOULINEAUX: Oh, yes! *Sì, sì!* After all, she might . . . Well, an eye for an eye . . .

DARTAGNAN *(with conviction)*: My wife? No, no! Impossible!

MOULINEAUX *(sardonically)*: Aha. I'm glad to hear it.

DARTAGNAN: Some wives, of course. But mine! No. Never!

MOULINEAUX *(echoing)*: Never!

DARTAGNAN: Believe me, I know what I'm talking about.

MOULINEAUX: I'm sure.

DARTAGNAN: If there's one thing I know, it's married women, my friend. I've had more affairs with them . . . more than you can count! I know all their tricks! I'm not one of your blind husbands, like so many of them.

MOULINEAUX: Aha.

DARTAGNAN *(laughing)*: I knew one. Would you believe it? Every time his wife would come to meet me, the old fool would bring her to my place himself!

MOULINEAUX: No!

DARTAGNAN: Yes! She would tell him she was going up to have her fortune told! Well, guess who was the fortune-teller!

MOULINEAUX *(with affected naïveté)*: You, monsieur?

DARTAGNAN *(laughing)*: Exactly! In the meantime the idiot would be downstairs, waiting.

(He doubles up with laughter.)

MOULINEAUX *(joining in)*: No! *(Slapping him on the back.)* Downstairs?

DARTAGNAN: The stupidity of some people, monsieur! It's unbelievable!

MOULINEAUX *(with forced guffaws)*: Yes, isn't it.

(After a few moments of hilarity the laughter gradually subsides.)

DARTAGNAN: Besides, my wife would never . . . she knows me too well. She knows what I would do the minute I caught her cheating!

MOULINEAUX *(anxiously)*: You mean . . . A duel, monsieur?

DARTAGNAN: Heavens, no! That's too dangerous. *(*MOULINEAUX *heaves a sigh of relief.)* I would just kill the man, that's all. No questions asked.

MOULINEAUX: What?

DARTAGNAN: Bang, bang, bang! Between the eyes! Whenever I saw him . . .

MOULINEAUX *(aside, with a shudder)*: Good God!

DARTAGNAN: I'd teach him not to trifle with Anatole Dartagnan!

MOULINEAUX: You . . . Yes, I daresay . . .

DARTAGNAN *(changing the subject)*: But why are we talking about such things, my friend? That's hardly what I came here to tell you.

MOULINEAUX: Hardly.

DARTAGNAN: I've got good news for you!

MOULINEAUX *(apprehensively)*: For me?

DARTAGNAN: My friend . . . The young lady. She wants you, Signor Yuno.

MOULINEAUX *(with a start)*: What?

DARTAGNAN: As her tailor . . .

MOULINEAUX *(recoiling)*: Her tailor? But . . . what for?

DARTAGNAN: What for? What do you think? She wants you to make her a gown.

MOULINEAUX: She . . . *(Aside.)* Oh, my! *(To* DARTAGNAN, *sarcastically.)* Now there's a brilliant idea!

DARTAGNAN *(missing his sarcasm)*: Why, thank you.

MOULINEAUX *(forgetting himself)*: No, no! Thank *you!* You think that's all I've got to do? Make gowns? What about my patients, monsieur? My patients.

(He bites his lip, suddenly realizing his faux pas.*)*

DARTAGNAN *(taken aback)*: But . . . Take as long as you like, Signor Yuno! She's in no hurry.

MOULINEAUX *(trying to cover it over)*: She . . . Yes . . . Quite right . . .

DARTAGNAN *(rather piqued)*: Really! What kind of a business do you run? Complaining that you have too many customers! I never . . .

MOULINEAUX: No, no. I didn't mean—

DARTAGNAN *(more and more worked up)*: Just because crowned heads beat a path to your door!

MOULINEAUX: Crowned—

DARTAGNAN: Either you're a tailor or you're not! Now which is it?

MOULINEAUX *(moving far right)*: But, of course, I'm a tailor! What else would I be? *(Aside.)* If not, it's bang, bang, bang!

(Just then MADAME D'HERBLAY *appears, up center.)*

MADAME D'HERBLAY *(at the door, timidly, to* MOULINEAUX*)*: Ah, monsieur. There you are.

MOULINEAUX *(turning)*: Who . . .

MADAME D'HERBLAY: I hope you'll excuse me for disturbing you again. I know how busy you must be.

MOULINEAUX: Ah, madame . . .

(During their exchange DARTAGNAN *goes over to the sofa and sits down.)*

MADAME D'HERBLAY: But I was hoping, perhaps, that you might have time for my blouse.

MOULINEAUX *(seizing the occasion to prove himself to* DARTAGNAN*)*: Yes! Of course! Your . . . Your *ducky* . . .

MADAME D'HERBLAY: My . . . ?

MOULINEAUX *(as pleasant as he can be)*: Please, come in. Come right in. *(To* DARTAGNAN.*)* If I'm a tailor, indeed!

MADAME D'HERBLAY *(still apologetic)*: If you're sure I'm not disturbing you . . .

MOULINEAUX: Disturbing me, madame? A client like you? The very idea!

MADAME D'HERBLAY *(moving down, reluctantly)*: Why, thank you, monsieur. *(To* DARTAGNAN, *noticing him on the sofa.)* Oh! I hope I'm not interrupting . . .

DARTAGNAN *(with a wave)*: Please . . . Please . . .

MADAME D'HERBLAY: Well, if you're sure . . . *(Taking off her coat and showing* MOULINEAUX *her blouse.)* You see? It really doesn't fit. See all the tucks and gathers?

MOULINEAUX *(scrutinizing very professionally)*: Yes . . . Yes . . . The tucks and gathers . . .

MADAME D'HERBLAY: It's simply too big, monsieur. You must have cut it on the bias.

MOULINEAUX: Yes. Obviously. *(To* DARTAGNAN.*)* On the bias . . .

MADAME D'HERBLAY: I think you're simply going to have to cut it again.

MOULINEAUX *(terrified)*: I am?

MADAME D'HERBLAY: And as soon as possible, if it's not asking too much.

MOULINEAUX: Cut it?

MADAME D'HERBLAY: Why, yes. Don't you think so?

MOULINEAUX: Certainly, madame! I couldn't agree more. *(Aside, under his breath.)* Cut it, she says. *(He picks up a pair of shears from one of the workbenches.)* Cut it . . .

(He returns to MADAME D'HERBLAY, *brandishing the shears.)*

MADAME D'HERBLAY *(recoiling)*: Good heavens . . .

MOULINEAUX *(about to cut into the blouse)*: Hold still, will you! How can I—

MADAME D'HERBLAY *(squirming)*: Monsieur! What are you—

MOULINEAUX: Well, make up your mind! Do you want me to cut it or don't you?

MADAME D'HERBLAY: Yes! Of course! But not right now. My goodness . . .

MOULINEAUX: Oh, I thought. . . . *(To* DARTAGNAN.*)* "As soon as possible," she said . . .

MADAME D'HERBLAY: As long as you see what has to be done. You can send someone around to pick it up, if you would.

(She puts on her coat and gets ready to leave.)

MOULINEAUX *(mechanically opening and closing the shears)*: Yes . . . Yes . . .

MADAME D'HERBLAY *(stopping at the door, up center)*: Oh, by the way, monsieur . . . I've moved.

MOULINEAUX: Aha.

MADAME D'HERBLAY: That is, I'm still at the same address. Only one floor up.

MOULINEAUX *(echoing)*: One floor up . . .

MADAME D'HERBLAY: You won't forget . . .

MOULINEAUX: No, no . . .

MADAME D'HERBLAY: And thank you so much for taking the time . . .

MOULINEAUX: Oh, don't mention it! My pleasure.

MADAME D'HERBLAY *(nodding)*: Monsieur . . . *(Nodding to* DARTAGNAN.*)* Monsieur . . .

(She exits. MOULINEAUX *stands for a moment, staring blankly, still playing absentmindedly with the shears.)*

DARTAGNAN *(watching him, laughing, aside)*: My, my! He looks as if he's seen a ghost! Odd chap, I must say! *(Getting up, to* MOULINEAUX.*)* You know, maybe a nice cold shower would help.

MOULINEAUX *(rousing himself)*: Maybe what?

DARTAGNAN: A nice cold shower. I think you should take one.

MOULINEAUX *(dumbfounded)*: You think . . .

DARTAGNAN: It would do you a world of good, you know. And that's not just my opinion.

MOULINEAUX: Oh? Who else, may I ask . . .

DARTAGNAN: Moulineaux!

MOULINEAUX *(looking at him as if he were out of his mind)*: Moulineaux?

DARTAGNAN: Yes. Doctor Moulineaux. We were chatting just now.

MOULINEAUX: You were? Just now?

DARTAGNAN: Yes.

MOULINEAUX: My friend, you must be sick!

DARTAGNAN *(laughing)*: Why? Just because I talk to a doctor? Come now! We happened to meet . . .

MOULINEAUX *(nodding)*: Aha. You and Moulineaux. Balthasar Moulineaux.

DARTAGNAN: Yes.

MOULINEAUX *(moving down right)*: That's the best one yet!

(While they have been talking, MIMI *has appeared at the open door.)*

MIMI *(entering, carrying a little dog under her arm, to* DARTAGNAN*)*: Ah, Anatole.

DARTAGNAN *(rushing to greet her)*: Mathilde, chérie . . .

MOULINEAUX *(glancing up right, aside)*: Damn! And his wife is still in there!

DARTAGNAN *(leading* MIMI *downstage)*: Come. Let me introduce you. Signor Yunó, Madame de Sainte-Vinaigrette. *(To* MOULINEAUX.*)* The friend I was telling you about . . .

MOULINEAUX *(turning)*: Delighted, I'm . . . *(Thunderstruck, aside.)* No! Mimi! Mimi Laflamme!

MIMI *(holding out her hand)*: Monsieur . . . *(Suddenly recognizing him, pulling her hand away, aside.)* Baba . . . Baba . . . It can't be!

MOULINEAUX *(aside)*: I don't believe it! *(Taking her hand back and kissing it.)* Madame . . .

MIMI *(aside)*: Baba! Baba le Distingué! Of all people!

DARTAGNAN *(to* MOULINEAUX*)*: I'm sure you'll find her worthy of your talents, signore. Madame de Sainte-Vinaigrette is from one of the oldest and finest families of the Boulévard Saint-Germain!

MOULINEAUX *(nodding)*: How nice.

MIMI *(aside)*: And he's recognized me! Damnation! I'd better have a long talk with him and in a hurry! *(To* DARTAGNAN, *holding up the dog.)* Look, Anatole! See how Bijou's little ears are twitching!

DARTAGNAN: Chérie!

MIMI: Mamma's precious wants to go bye-bye. Be an absolute dear and take him out, won't you? A few times around the block should be enough. Five or six . . .

DARTAGNAN *(scandalized)*: Your dog? Certainly not!

MIMI *(with a frown)*: I beg your pardon? Perhaps you didn't hear me.

DARTAGNAN *(humbled)*: Certainly, Mathilde. Good idea! Right away. *(Taking the dog, aside.)* The things I won't do for that woman! It's humiliating!

(He exits up center. MIMI *follows him to the door to watch him leave.)*

MIMI *(when she is sure that he is gone, coming down, joining* MOULINEAUX*)*: Baba le Distingué! Is it really you?

MOULINEAUX: Mimi Laflamme!

(They shake hands warmly.)

MIMI: What a nice surprise! Small world, isn't it!

MOULINEAUX: I should say!

MIMI: And so far from the Latin Quarter . . .

MOULINEAUX: Yes. Those wonderful days when we . . . You and I . . . All of us . . .

MIMI: Yes. Those were the days.

MOULINEAUX: Me, studying my medicine and you . . . you . . . *(With a shrug.)* Whatever . . .

MIMI: And that famous diploma, Baba? Did you ever get it?

MOULINEAUX *(hands in pockets, trying to appear casual)*: Well, I . . . Can't you tell?

MIMI: And so now you're a tailor!

MOULINEAUX *(after a moment of reflection)*: That is . . . Once you learn to be a surgeon . . . *(He snaps his fingers.)* It's so simple! Besides, it's so much more chic.

MIMI: Oh?

MOULINEAUX: Yes. Any doctor can be a . . . a doctor! But to be a tailor too.

MIMI *(laughing)*: Ha! You haven't changed a bit! Same old Baba le Distingué!

MOULINEAUX: Shhh! Please. *(With an anxious glance, up right.)* Not so loud!

MIMI: Oh, I'm sorry. Is someone sick?

MOULINEAUX: No . . . no . . . But still . . . No need to keep screaming "Baba le Distingué." Times have changed.

MIMI: But not you!

MOULINEAUX *(fatuously)*: Well, maybe I'm still "distingué." I suppose. But no more "Baba." It was all right for a student, but I've come a long way.

MIMI: But what else can I call you? That's the only name I ever knew.

MOULINEAUX: It was short for "Balthasar."

MIMI: No! Balthasar what?

MOULINEAUX *(without thinking)*: Balthasar Mouli— *(Catching himself just in time.)* Yuno!

MIMI: Mouliyuno? *(Laughing.)* What a name!

MOULINEAUX: No, no! Yuno! Just plain Yuno!

MIMI: Oh, I thought you said . . .

MOULINEAUX: Balthasar Yuno!

MIMI: Are you Italian?

MOULINEAUX: Just a little . . .

MIMI *(crossing left in front of him, with a rather affected gait)*: Well, Balthasar, if you're not Baba le Distingué anymore, I'm not Mimi Laflamme, either.

MOULINEAUX: So I gather.

MIMI: I'm Madame de Sainte-Vinaigrette.

MOULINEAUX: Yes. Mathilde, if I'm not mistaken . . .

MIMI: That's right . . .

MOULINEAUX: You mean, you settled down?

MIMI *(sitting on the sofa, seductively)*: Well, let's say "settled in." First of all, I got married.

MOULINEAUX: You?

MIMI: Yes. An absolute idiot!

MOULINEAUX *(aside)*: I never would have guessed!

MIMI: Then, once I was a wife, instead of just a . . . Well, after two days of honeymoon, I left him. For a general . . .

MOULINEAUX: Damn! Not bad! A general? They don't grow on trees! Where the devil did you find him?

MIMI: On a park bench in the Tuileries. One morning, while my imbecile of a husband went to buy some cigarettes . . .

MOULINEAUX *(with a quizzical tilt of the head)*: Oh? Funny. Someone else told me a story just like that. Only with him it was a cigar.

   (All of a sudden there is a noise of breaking glass from the room, up right.)

MIMI *(jumping)*: Oh!

MOULINEAUX *(aside)*: Good God! *(Looking in the direction of the noise.)* I almost forgot about her! She's getting impatient and taking it out on the furniture!

MIMI: What was that?

MOULINEAUX *(innocently)*: What was what?

MIMI: Do you have some kind of an animal in here?

MOULINEAUX: Do I . . . *(Quickly.)* Yes! As a matter of fact . . . a . . . a . . . an ostrich. From Africa.

MIMI: A real one?

MOULINEAUX: Yes. I . . . I need it for the plumes.

MIMI *(getting up)*: Oh, please, Baba. Balthasar . . . May I see it?

MOULINEAUX: Impossible! It . . . it's wild! It hates people!

MIMI *(insisting)*: I don't mind! Please! I'd love to—

MOULINEAUX: Dumb bird! Dumb bird! *(Quickly changing the subject.)* That reminds me. Your husband . . . Have you ever seen him since?

MIMI: Oh, thanks just the same! Never would be too soon! He served his purpose! He made me a lady, if you see what I mean.

MOULINEAUX: Yes.

MIMI: From there it was just a skip and a jump to become a real somebody!

MOULINEAUX *(nodding)*: Madame de . . .

MIMI: De Sainte-Vinaigrette! Exactly! *(There is another crash.)* Damnation! Are you sure your ostrich is all right?

MOULINEAUX: Fine, thank you! *(Mechanically.)* And you? *(Realizing the absurdity of his remark.)* I . . . I mean . . . Wait here. I'm going to go ask her.

MIMI: The ostrich? A lot of good that's going to do you!

(The door, up right, flies open, and SUZANNE *comes storming in.)*

SUZANNE *(furious, coming down right)*: Oh! I never . . . How much longer . . . ?

MOULINEAUX *(jumping at the intrusion)*: Suzanne!

SUZANNE ⎫ *(together)* ⎧ What do you take me for?
MOULINEAUX ⎭   ⎩ Please . . . please . . .

SUZANNE *(catching sight of* MIMI*)*: What? Another woman? Oh! Now it's all so clear!

MOULINEAUX: Suzanne!

SUZANNE *(to* MOULINEAUX, *pacing up and down)*: Now I see what you've been up to. Why you've kept me stuck away . . .

MIMI *(to* MOULINEAUX*)*: Who is that person?

MOULINEAUX *(to* MIMI*)*: She . . . nobody! My bookkeeper . . .

SUZANNE *(still pacing)*: Oh! I never . . .

MOULINEAUX (*to* MIMI): Very sick, poor thing! Nerves! A mental case. (*To* SUZANNE, *as she passes on her way downstage.*) Please, Suzanne, I can explain . . .

MIMI: Tsk tsk tsk!

SUZANNE (*still pacing and fuming*): Of all the cheating, scheming . . .

MOULINEAUX (*to* SUZANNE, *on her way upstage*): Please! If you'll only listen . . .

SUZANNE (*stopping abruptly in her tracks*): To what? To your lies?

MOULINEAUX: No.

SUZANNE: Why didn't you just come right out and admit . . . ?

MOULINEAUX: But . . .

SUZANNE: . . . that you came here to be with your mistress!

MIMI (*with a start*): } (*together*) { His what?

MOULINEAUX } { But Suzanne . . . Dear, sweet Suzanne . . .

MIMI (*to* SUZANNE): I beg your pardon! Nerves or not, just what do you take me for?

MOULINEAUX } (*together*) { Please . . .

SUZANNE } { What, indeed!

MIMI (*to* SUZANNE, *continuing*): I came here for a fitting!

(*Both women stand confronting each other, separated only by an increasingly frantic* MOULINEAUX.)

SUZANNE (*to* MIMI): Oh, yes! Tell me . . . I know that story. (*To* MOULINEAUX.) Don't I, monsieur!

MOULINEAUX } (*together*) { But . . . But . . .

MIMI } { Yes! I'm sure you do!

MOULINEAUX: Please, ladies . . .

SUZANNE (*to* MOULINEAUX): You have your nerve, monsieur, I must say!

MIMI (*to* MOULINEAUX, *caustically*): My friend, when a gentleman is his bookkeeper's lover . . .

MOULINEAUX: His what?

MIMI: . . . he owes it to his clients not to let her insult them!

SUZANNE: Bookkeeper? What bookkeeper?

MIMI: Even mental cases!

MOULINEAUX *(exploding)*: Now just one minute! *(To* MIMI.*)* What do you mean, her lover?

SUZANNE: What is she talking about? Who's a bookkeeper?

MOULINEAUX *(to* SUZANNE*)*: Nothing, damn it! Nothing! She's not talking to you!

MIMI: We Sainte-Vinaigrettes . . . *de* Sainte-Vinaigrettes . . . aren't accustomed to being insulted!

MOULINEAUX: Please, Mimi. She didn't mean it.

MIMI: If I say I came here for a fitting . . .

SUZANNE *(to* MOULINEAUX*)*: Who says I didn't mean it?

MIMI: . . . then I came here for a fitting!

MOULINEAUX *(to* SUZANNE*)*: She did! Really! That's all.

SUZANNE: Oh, I'm sure.

MIMI *(to* SUZANNE*)*: And the proof is that I came here with my husband, madame!

MOULINEAUX *(aside)*: Oh, my . . .

SUZANNE *(with a sarcastic little laugh)*: Yes! Of course you did! Your husband! And where is the gentleman, may I ask?

MIMI: Out walking my dog, if it's any business of yours! He'll be back any moment!

MOULINEAUX *(moving left, aghast)*: Oh, my, my, my! Oh, my . . .

MIMI *(pricking up her ears)*: In fact, I hear him now.

   (She moves up center to the door.)

SUZANNE: No doubt, madame!

   *(*DARTAGNAN *appears at the door with the dog under his arm.)*

MIMI *(to* DARTAGNAN*)*: Come in! Come in! Let everyone see you! Madame here doesn't believe who you are!

DARTAGNAN *(entering)*: I . . . Who? I . . . *(Turning and seeing* SUZANNE, *with a start.)* My wife!

SUZANNE *(with a scream)*: My husband!

MOULINEAUX *(clapping his hands together in despair)*: Boom![1]

SUZANNE: You . . . oh!

DARTAGNAN: Suzanne!

SUZANNE: You won't get away with this!

DARTAGNAN: Suzanne . . . Suzanne . . .

SUZANNE: I'll make you pay, you . . . you wretch!

  (She stalks out, up center.)

DARTAGNAN *(following her)*: But, Suzanne . . . *(To* MIMI, *thrusting the dog into her hands.)* Here! Take your damn dog! *(At the door.)* Suzanne . . .

MIMI: But, Anatole . . .

DARTAGNAN: Go to blazes!

  (He runs out in hot pursuit.)

MIMI *(holding the dog)*: "Go to . . ." Oh! The nerve of that man! After all I've . . . *(Fanning herself.)* Oh . . . My . . . Oh . . . I'm going to faint.

  (She falls in a heap.)

MOULINEAUX *(frantic, catching her with his right arm and the dog with his left)*: No! Please . . . Of all times . . . Mimi, please. Don't . . . don't do this to me.

  (At that moment YVONNE *appears outside the open door.)*

YVONNE: One B. *(Entering, calling.)* Mamma?

MOULINEAUX *(petrified)*: Good God!

YVONNE: Mamma? Are you still here?

MOULINEAUX *(turning, finding himself face-to-face with* YVONNE*)*: Yvonne!

YVONNE *(agape)*: You . . . Here? *(Noticing* MIMI*)* Oh! And with a woman in your arms!

[1]Author's note: From here to the end of the act the pace must be frenetic and uninterrupted.

MOULINEAUX (*desperately trying to explain*): Yvonne, please, it's not—

YVONNE: Well! I've seen quite enough!

MOULINEAUX: But it's not what you—

YVONNE: And I'll thank you never to darken my door again!

(*She strides out, up center.*)

MOULINEAUX (*trying to follow her as best he can*): But . . . wait! Let me explain! (*Obviously encumbered by his two charges, looking for a way to dispose of them.*) Goddammit! Of all times . . .

(*Just then* BASSINET *appears at the open door and pokes his head in.*)

BASSINET: I say . . .

MOULINEAUX: You . . . Quick! Come here!

BASSINET (*entering*): Monsieur, the locksmith—

MOULINEAUX (*shoving* MIMI *and the dog in his face*): Here! Take these! (*At the door.*) Yvonne! Wait! Yvonne!

(*He runs out.*)

BASSINET (*watching him streak off*): But, monsieur . . . who the devil . . . (*Looking at* MIMI.) What? (*Stupefied.*) It can't be. Mimi! You've come back!

(*He plants a huge kiss on her cheek.*)

MIMI (*coming to*): Where . . . Where am I? Who . . . (*Recognizing* BASSINET.) My husband! Damnation!

(*She gives his face a resounding slap and frees herself.* BASSINET, *agape, collapses onto the sofa, dropping the dog as* MIMI *runs out the open door.*)

BASSINET (*rubbing his cheek, watching her go*): But it's me, Mimi! Mimi! It's me. . . .

CURTAIN

ACT III

(The scene is the same as in Act I.)

(At rise, the stage is empty. After a few moments the door bell rings. There is a brief pause.)

ETIENNE'S VOICE *(offstage)*: Never mind, monsieur. It's nothing.

MOULINEAUX *(entering, down left, obviously anxious, muttering)*: I wonder if it's . . . *(Calling.)* Etienne! Etienne!

ETIENNE *(entering, up center)*: Monsieur?

MOULINEAUX: Who was that? Who rang?

ETIENNE *(with a shrug)*: Oh, it's nothing, monsieur. Nothing at all.

(He turns to leave.)

MOULINEAUX: "Nothing"? What do you mean, "nothing"? Someone rang. Who was it?

ETIENNE *(at the double door)*: Only one of monsieur's patients, monsieur. For a treatment. He asked if monsieur was in, and when I said that he was . . .

MOULINEAUX: You didn't! I thought I told you, Etienne . . .

ETIENNE: No matter. He said he felt fine all of a sudden, and he left.

MOULINEAUX *(under his breath)*: Idiot! *(Carping.)* Yes, well . . . Next time somebody comes, and it's nobody, that's what you tell me: "It's nobody, monsieur." Not "it's nothing." Understand?

ETIENNE: I didn't think it made much difference, monsieur.

MOULINEAUX: Not to you, but it does to me.

ETIENNE: Yes, monsieur.

MOULINEAUX (*annoyed*): That's fine. You can go now.

(*He moves right, obviously out of sorts and deep in thought.* ETIENNE *watches him for a moment.*)

ETIENNE (*shaking his head sympathetically, aside*): Did you ever see? Tsk tsk tsk. (*To* MOULINEAUX.) If monsieur doesn't mind my saying . . .

MOULINEAUX (*looking up*): Hmm?

ETIENNE: I can understand how monsieur must feel and how concerned he is. No offense, but if only he had taken my advice . . .

MOULINEAUX: Etienne . . .

ETIENNE: About the gala, I mean.

MOULINEAUX: Etienne, I'll thank you . . .

ETIENNE: I told monsieur no good would come of it! (MOULINEAUX, *hands on hips, looks at him in disbelief.*) Besides, there are ways of doing things, and there are ways . . . As long as we're going to do them, at least we should do them right!

MOULINEAUX: Are you quite through?

ETIENNE: Not quite, monsieur.

MOULINEAUX (*sarcastically, nodding*): Oh, please! Don't let me interrupt.

ETIENNE: No. Monsieur should have told me what he intended to do. "Etienne," he should have said, "I'm going to the gala at the Folies Exotiques." I would have taken the trouble to sleep in monsieur's bed. For appearances' sake . . .

MOULINEAUX (*unable to contain himself*): My bed?

ETIENNE: Oh, I don't mind. Monsieur is quite clean. (MOULINEAUX *shakes his head.*) And, anyway, I would have changed the bedclothes before . . .

MOULINEAUX: Perhaps even after.

ETIENNE: And madame would never know.

MOULINEAUX (*sighing*): Ah, yes! Madame. Wherever she is . . .

ETIENNE (*sadly*): We were wondering the same thing in the pantry, monsieur.

MOULINEAUX: It's almost a whole day since . . . *(Dramatically.)* since she left my bed and board . . .

ETIENNE: So to speak! *(Aside.)* Board, yes. *(Gesturing down left and right toward their separate rooms, still aside.)* But bed . . . ? Tsk tsk tsk.

MOULINEAUX: Almost twenty-four hours . . .

ETIENNE: I know I express the sentiments of all the help, monsieur, when I say that I hope this matter can be resolved.

MOULINEAUX: Thank you, Etienne.

ETIENNE: . . . and that monsieur will do his best. If only for me, monsieur.

MOULINEAUX: For you?

ETIENNE *(on the verge of tears)*: It's the first time I've ever gone through something like this, monsieur. The first time.

MOULINEAUX *(aside)*: Where have I heard that before!

ETIENNE: Believe me . . . The very first time . . .

MOULINEAUX: I know, I know.

ETIENNE: All my previous employers were faithful to their wives.

MOULINEAUX: Aha.

ETIENNE: To a fault. They never subjected me to such emotions, monsieur. And I'm terribly sensitive . . . *(Sniffling.)* As I think monsieur can see . . .

(The door bell rings.)

MOULINEAUX *(looking up)*: Etienne!

ETIENNE: Monsieur?

MOULINEAUX: The bell . . .

ETIENNE *(in the same tone of voice)*: Oh, it's nothing, I'm sure.

MOULINEAUX: Again? "Nothing"?

ETIENNE: Whoever it is, monsieur, they can't come in until I open the door.

MOULINEAUX: Precisely! That's why I'm asking you . . . Will you please . . .

ETIENNE: Monsieur will do his best, then? For my sake?

MOULINEAUX: Yes, yes, yes! Just go see who that is!

ETIENNE: Thank you, monsieur. *(He holds out his hand, but, seeing that* MOULINEAUX *doesn't reciprocate, shakes it in space.)* Thank you. Much obliged . . .

MOULINEAUX *(crossing left)*: And don't forget this time! I'm not at home for anyone. Except madame, that is.

ETIENNE: Anyone, monsieur?

MOULINEAUX: Anyone, Etienne! I don't care if it's the pope!

(He exits, down left. ETIENNE *exits, up center.)*

ETIENNE'S VOICE: No, I'm sorry, monsieur. I'm sorry. He's not at home.

*(*DARTAGNAN *enters, up center, with* ETIENNE *at his heels.)*

DARTAGNAN *(at the door)*: But, my good man, the concierge distinctly told me that he was.

ETIENNE: And monsieur himself distinctly told me to say that he wasn't! I should think he would know better than the concierge, monsieur!

DARTAGNAN: Very well. He's not in. Now please go tell him that Monsieur Dartagnan would like to see him. It's urgent!

ETIENNE: Excuse me, but he told me: "I don't care if it's the pope!" And I'm afraid you're not even—

DARTAGNAN: No. But I've still got to see him. On account of my wife.

ETIENNE: And he's not seeing anyone, monsieur. On account of his!

DARTAGNAN: Really? Why is that?

ETIENNE *(self-importantly)*: I'm sorry, monsieur, but some things are confidential! Family matters . . . For the master and the help . . .

DARTAGNAN: Oh?

ETIENNE: Not for outsiders. They can say what they like, but at least I can keep a secret! *(Categorically.)* Wild horses, monsieur! Wild horses!

DARTAGNAN: Beg pardon?

ETIENNE: They wouldn't make me talk, monsieur. Not family matters . . . You could even try to trick me . . .

DARTAGNAN: Me? Perish the thought!

ETIENNE: But you'd never worm it out of me! You could come here and stand right in front of me, and say: "Etienne, my good man, is it true what I hear? That things have been all at sixes and sevens? That monsieur went to the gala the other night and didn't come home?"

DARTAGNAN *(with a chuckle, aside)*: No!

ETIENNE *(continuing)*: "And madame, Etienne, is it true that no one knows where she is? That she hasn't been home all night and that monsieur is worried sick?"

DARTAGNAN *(aside)*: Of all things . . .

ETIENNE: Well, I'm sorry, monsieur. But it just wouldn't work! Wild horses . . .

DARTAGNAN *(nodding)*: Wild horses . . .

ETIENNE: I'd look you straight in the eye, and I'd say: "I don't know what you're talking about! Sorry!"

DARTAGNAN *(shaking his head)*: Admirable. Admirable.

ETIENNE: Thank you, monsieur. But that's just how I am when it comes to family matters.

DARTAGNAN: Yes, I understand. *(After a pause, offhand.)* Etienne, my good man, tell me, is it true what I hear? That madame hasn't been home all night and that monsieur is worried sick?

ETIENNE *(surprised)*: What? How did you know?

DARTAGNAN: Someone told me.

ETIENNE: The nerve! You just can't trust some people with a secret! Did you ever see . . . ?

DARTAGNAN: I know what the poor chap is going through, believe me! My wife didn't come home last night either, I'm afraid.

ETIENNE: No, monsieur! Yours too?

DARTAGNAN: And after what happened yesterday, I'm not surprised! I haven't seen hide nor hair . . .

ETIENNE: Tsk tsk tsk! It sounds like an epidemic, monsieur!

DARTAGNAN: Not that I really blame her, I suppose. Goodness me, what a scene! *(Moving down left.)* But I'm sure it won't last. She'll come to her senses.

ETIENNE: Yes, monsieur. I hope so.

DARTAGNAN: Anyway, that's why I have to see the doctor. This is about the time she comes for her daily treatment, so I thought . . . I thought if I came and waited . . .

ETIENNE: Maybe so, monsieur. But she won't see him, either. Not today. Not even if she's the pope! "Nobody!" he said. Order are orders. At least, until madame comes back home, where she belongs . . .

DARTAGNAN: Yes, but, my good man . . .

(The door bell rings.)

ETIENNE: Ah! Excuse me, monsieur. That might just be . . .

(He exits, up center.)

DARTAGNAN *(crossing right)*: No. No two ways about it. I've got to see her and make amends. Even if it means . . . *(Taking a picture from his pocket.)* . . . giving up Mathilde forever.

(He kisses the picture, sighing, as ETIENNE *enters, up center, excitedly.)*

ETIENNE: It is, monsieur! It's the ladies! I think you'd better leave.

DARTAGNAN *(putting the picture back in his pocket)*: What ladies?

ETIENNE: Madame Moulineaux and her mother, monsieur.

DARTAGNAN: His wife? Lucky devil! I wish I could say the same!

*(*MADAME AIGREVILLE *storms in, up center, followed by* YVONNE.*)*

MADAME AIGREVILLE *(to* ETIENNE, *commandingly)*: Go tell him I'm here, young man!

DARTAGNAN *(surprised, aside)*: Good heavens! The queen!

MADAME AIGREVILLE *(to* ETIENNE*)*: Immediately, understand?

ETIENNE: Very good, Madame Aigreville. Right away.

DARTAGNAN *(still down left, overhearing, aside)*: Madame who?

ETIENNE *(turning to leave)*: Ah! I know monsieur will be pleased
. . . very pleased . . .

DARTAGNAN *(aside)*: But I thought . . .

(ETIENNE *exits, down left.*)

MADAME AIGREVILLE *(as he leaves)*: That remains to be seen!

(She comes down right and takes an authoritative stance.
YVONNE *hangs back, up right.)*

DARTAGNAN *(puzzled, tentatively approaching* MADAME AIGREVILLE*)*:
Pardon me, madame, but do I understand correctly that you're
not . . .

MADAME AIGREVILLE: Monsieur?

DARTAGNAN: . . . that you're not the queen of Greenland?

MADAME AIGREVILLE *(agape)*: The what? *(With a little laugh.)* Me?
I hardly think so!

DARTAGNAN: But, madame, you're the image . . .

MADAME AIGREVILLE: I am?

DARTAGNAN *(emphasizing)*: Spitting . . . spitting . . .

MADAME AIGREVILLE *(putting her hand to her mouth)*: Oh, I
beg—

DARTAGNAN: Two peas in a pod! You're sure you're not the
queen?

MADAME AIGREVILLE: Really, monsieur! I think I would know!
(Aside.) His eczema must be spreading . . . to his head!

DARTAGNAN: Sorry, my mistake. *(Trying to make a graceful exit.)*
Well, if you'll excuse me, madame, I'm sure you have things
to discuss with the doctor.

MADAME AIGREVILLE: To say the least!

DARTAGNAN: So I'll be on my way.

MADAME AIGREVILLE: Yes.

DARTAGNAN *(with a little bow)*: Your High— *(Correcting.)* Madame . . .

MADAME AIGREVILLE *(nodding)*: Monsieur . . .

DARTAGNAN *(moving up center, with a bow to* YVONNE*)*: And

Madame Moulineaux . . . a pleasure, I assure you. *(As* YVONNE *gives a little noncommittal nod, aside.)* Oh! Pretty. Pretty.

(He exits, leaving the double door ajar.)

MADAME AIGREVILLE *(to* YVONNE*):* Now down to business, precious!

YVONNE: Yes, Mamma.

MADAME AIGREVILLE: And you won't forget what I told you. You'll be firm.

YVONNE: Oh, indeed I will, Mamma! Indeed I will!

(The door, down left, opens and MOULINEAUX *hurries in.)*

MOULINEAUX *(spying* YVONNE, *up right):* Yvonne! At last! *(Rushing to join her, arms outstretched, sighing.)* Ah! You don't know how worried—

MADAME AIGREVILLE *(quickly moving up to intercept him, planting herself in front of* YVONNE*):* Oh, no, monsieur! Back!

MOULINEAUX *(stopping in his tracks):* What?

MADAME AIGREVILLE: Not another step, I'm warning you!

MOULINEAUX: But . . .

MADAME AIGREVILLE: That's not what we're here for!

MOULINEAUX *(trying to talk around her, to* YVONNE*):* But, Yvonne. I can explain.

MADAME AIGREVILLE: Perhaps you thought you could get away with your seamy little escapade.

MOULINEAUX *(trying to object):* My seamy . . . But it wasn't . . .

MADAME AIGREVILLE: Well, if so, you forgot about me, my good man! You forgot that your wife has a mother!

MOULINEAUX *(aside):* No such luck!

MADAME AIGREVILLE: And a mother who knows her duty, my friend! *(Very businesslike.)* Now then, monsieur. You're my daughter's husband, much though I might regret it . . .

MOULINEAUX: Much obliged!

MADAME AIGREVILLE: Her spouse in the eyes of the law. *(To* YVONNE.*)* Alas! *(To* MOULINEAUX.*)* And I have no choice but to bring her back . . .

MOULINEAUX (*suddenly softening*): Oh, at least you're being reasonable.

MADAME AIGREVILLE: . . . to live with you under the *conjungle* roof.

MOULINEAUX: The . . . well, now, that's more like it!

(*He makes a move toward* YVONNE.)

MADAME AIGREVILLE (*menacing*): Back! Back! I said, not another step! Monsieur!

MOULINEAUX: But . . .

MADAME AIGREVILLE: I'm afraid you haven't quite grasped the situation.

MOULINEAUX: You just said . . .

MADAME AIGREVILLE: We've given it a good deal of thought, my daughter and I . . .

MOULINEAUX: If she listened to you, God help us!

MADAME AIGREVILLE: . . . and we've decided that from now on, you'll be husband and wife in name only.

MOULINEAUX (*with a sarcastic laugh, to the audience*): She listened! (*To* MADAME AIGREVILLE, *hands on hips.*) Just like that!

MADAME AIGREVILLE: First I thought I would take her back home, monsieur. With me. That's why we spent last night at the Hotel Royal.

MOULINEAUX (*beginning to pace up and down*): Yes! While I was worried sick!

MADAME AIGREVILLE (*casually*): They'll be sending you the bill.

MOULINEAUX: No doubt!

MADAME AIGREVILLE: But people do talk, monsieur. Tongues wag and fingers point. And I won't have my daughter subjected to hoos and boots.

MOULINEAUX: To what?

MADAME AIGREVILLE: To public ridicule, my friend. To hoos and . . . (*Correcting.*) Boos . . . To boos and hoots.

MOULINEAUX: I see. And so?

MADAME AIGREVILLE: And so we've decided that she will continue to live here.

MOULINEAUX: Yes. Under the "conjungle" roof.

MADAME AIGREVILLE: Exactly! But only for appearances! I hope that's clear, monsieur!

MOULINEAUX: Yes, thank you! Quite clear! *(Down left, aside.)* We'll work things out ourselves once the old witch goes home! *(To* MADAME AIGREVILLE.*)* Fine, then. It's settled! That's that!

MADAME AIGREVILLE: And just to be sure, I'm going to live here with her.

MOULINEAUX *(with a start)*: What?

MADAME AIGREVILLE: . . . to look after her and protect her! *(To* YVONNE.*)* Isn't that right, precious?

YVONNE *(unenthusiastically)*: Yes, Mamma.

MOULINEAUX *(furious, aside)*: "Conjungle" is right, damn it! Meddling old gorilla!

MADAME AIGREVILLE *(to* MOULINEAUX*)*: But don't go getting any ideas, monsieur. We're going to divide the apartment in half.

MOULINEAUX: Oh, we are, are we?

MADAME AIGREVILLE *(moving center, pointing left)*: The men's side for you. *(Pointing right.)* The women's side for us.

MOULINEAUX *(almost good-naturedly, with a wave of the hand)*: Aha! And this?

MADAME AIGREVILLE: No man's land.

MOULINEAUX: Or no woman's, if you'd rather.

MADAME AIGREVILLE *(ignoring his witticism)*: And that, monsieur, is how I intend to bring peace and tranquillity to my daughter's unfortunate marriage.

MOULINEAUX *(beginning to seethe)*: Unfortunate. Uh . . . *(Pacing, trying to control himself, but finally exploding.)* Now let me tell you something! It's crazy! You're crazy, if you want to know. Divide the apartment. What have I done to deserve this? *(To* YVONNE.*)* What, Yvonne? Tell me.

(He continues pacing.)

YVONNE: Me?

MADAME AIGREVILLE *(by her side, up right)*: Don't answer him, precious! He's trying to trick you!

MOULINEAUX *(down left, sharply)*: Will you let her speak, damn it!

MADAME AIGREVILLE: I'll thank you to keep a civil tongue in your head!

YVONNE *(to MOULINEAUX, approaching him)*: Really, monsieur! Do you have the nerve . . . the gall . . . to ask me what you've done?

MOULINEAUX: But, Yvonne . . .

MADAME AIGREVILLE *(to YVONNE)*: He does! He has the gall. He has . . .

MOULINEAUX *(shouting up right, to MADAME AIGREVILLE, furious)*: You . . . It's my gall, damn it! No one's asking you, you old—

YVONNE: Please, monsieur! *(Very proper.)* Remember that you're talking to my mother!

MOULINEAUX *(trying to calm down)*: Yes. All right, for your sake. *(He takes a deep breath.)* Now, tell me . . .

YVONNE: I think it's quite obvious. I catch you at the dressmaker's with your mistress in your arms.

MOULINEAUX *(objecting quickly)*: But not mine! Not mine!

YVONNE *(with a smirk)*: Not your arms?

MOULINEAUX: Not my mistress!

YVONNE: Oh? Then who was she, monsieur?

MOULINEAUX: Just . . . some woman . . .

YVONNE: Yes. Some woman you just happened to take in your arms . . .

MOULINEAUX: Yes. No! I mean . . . I didn't take her! Someone put her there. *(He mimes the action.)* Like that!

YVONNE: Of course! I'm sure they did. That's why you were hugging her!

MOULINEAUX: But I wasn't . . .

YVONNE: Please, monsieur! I've got eyes! I can see! She was fainting, and you were hugging her.

MOULINEAUX *(jumping in)*: There! There! You admit it! She was sick! That proves it!

YVONNE: Proves what? That you chase skirts, monsieur! Fainting or not!

MADAME AIGREVILLE *(still up right, to* MOULINEAUX*)*: And you tell me they're your patients!

MOULINEAUX: No, no. *(To* MADAME AIGREVILLE.*)* That's another one. Please! Don't confuse the issue! *(Moving toward her.)* The patient you met is Madame Dartagnan, Monsieur Dartagnan's wife. This one . . .

MADAME AIGREVILLE *(sharply)*: Yes? Whose is she?

MOULINEAUX *(quickly, without thinking)*: Dartagnan's.

MADAME AIGREVILLE: Oh, I see! He has two!

MOULINEAUX: Yes.

MADAME AIGREVILLE: How nice! He's a bigamist!

MOULINEAUX: He's . . . no, no! That's not what I . . . *(To* YVONNE.*)* Really, Yvonne, that's not . . . *(To* MADAME AIGREVILLE.*)* You keep getting everything all . . . *(Growing angry.)* Can't you mind your own business? It's no concern of yours!

MADAME AIGREVILLE: Indeed! I think my daughter's happiness—

MOULINEAUX: All you can do is meddle! You come here out of a clear blue sky, and all of a sudden . . .

YVONNE *(to* MOULINEAUX*)*: Please . . .

MOULINEAUX: Meddle, meddle, meddle!

MADAME AIGREVILLE: Oh, yes! Now it's my fault! Tell me I'm the unfaithful husband who sleeps heaven knows where!

YVONNE *(to* MADAME AIGREVILLE*)*: Mamma, please.

MADAME AIGREVILLE *(pressing her attack, to* MOULINEAUX*)*: Tell me I'm the philanderer . . . the . . . the *bauchee.*

MOULINEAUX: The what?

MADAME AIGREVILLE: The *adulterator!* Go ahead, monsieur! Tell me!

MOULINEAUX *(furious)*: Tell you? No, damn it! I have nothing to tell you! Nothing! Nothing! Not a thing!

MADAME AIGREVILLE *(simply, as if proving her assertion)*: Aha!

MOULINEAUX *(pointing to* YVONNE*)*: I'm married to her! She's my wife, not you! *(He turns aside and crosses himself.)* If I have anything to say, I'm going to say it to my wife! And in private, thank you!

MADAME AIGREVILLE: Oh, no! I suppose you think I'm going to leave you alone with her? Let her fall into your clutches?

MOULINEAUX *(exasperated)*: My clutches? What clutches? I'm her husband, remember? If I want to have a word with my own wife . . . alone . . . I think I have the right! Don't you?

MADAME AIGREVILLE *(categorically)*: No, monsieur! I don't!

MOULINEAUX *(repressing a cry of rage)*: Oh!

(He makes a move toward her, as if about to lunge at her throat, but controls himself, striding nervously up left and then down right.)

YVONNE *(to* MADAME AIGREVILLE*)*: I don't mind, Mamma. Let him! I'll listen to whatever monsieur has to say. *(Very proper.)* After all, I wouldn't want to give him any reason to criticize.

MADAME AIGREVILLE: But I know you. You're so trusting, so naive. He'll wrap you around his little finger! I don't think . . .

MOULINEAUX *(to* YVONNE, *sarcastically dramatic)*: Yes! You'll fall into my clutches!

YVONNE *(to* MADAME AIGREVILLE, *pointedly ignoring him)*: Don't worry, Mamma. I'll be careful.

MADAME AIGREVILLE: Well . . . all right, if you're absolutely sure. *(Turning toward* MOULINEAUX.*)* At least some of us try to be reasonable, monsieur! *(To* YVONNE.*)* Don't forget, precious. Be firm!

YVONNE: Yes, Mamma.

MADAME AIGREVILLE *(aside)*: Lucky for her I'm here! If not, they would have kissed and made up by now. *(Crossing to the door, up right, stopping, casting a look of disdain over her shoulder at* MOULINEAUX, *still down right.)* Hmmph!

(She exits. YVONNE *moves left, by the chaise longue, turning*

her back to MOULINEAUX, *arms folded, gazing into the distance in an attitude of indifference. There is a brief moment of uncomfortable silence.* MOULINEAUX *finally gets up his courage and walks slowly and deliberately over to her.)*

MOULINEAUX *(very calmly):* Yvonne . . .

YVONNE *(coldly, without turning to look at him):* I'm listening, monsieur.

MOULINEAUX: Please try to forget about your mother for a minute. Forget you even have one! *(Quickly, realizing that the remark might be misinterpreted.)* I mean . . . Not that you have one, but . . . but some of the things she says . . . *(There is another uncomfortable silence.)* You see . . . *(Floundering, hoping for an inspiration.)* That woman, Yvonne . . . Dartagnan and his wife . . . That woman in my arms . . . The two of them, that is . . . Well, that's Dartagnan's business, not mine, Yvonne. *(Waiting for a reaction.)* Yvonne?

YVONNE *(still with her back turned):* Go on, monsieur.

MOULINEAUX: Yes, you see, it's . . . it's . . . *(Suddenly inspired.)* It's a scientific study! Very confidential! A fascinating case of comparative physiology! I was only there as an expert, a specialist.

YVONNE: Oh?

MOULINEAUX: You see, two similar subjects, Yvonne. One perfectly normal and the other, a rare example of . . . of . . . of congenital neuro-endocrinological pathology. With complications! Lots and lots of fascinating complications! Fainting spells. Amnesia.

YVONNE *(finally turning around):* And that's all? Really?

MOULINEAUX *(delighted at his apparent success):* Really! I'd try to explain it if I thought it would help, but . . . *(With a wave.)* You know . . . Years and years of school. All terribly scientific. But as long as you understand what I was doing there, Yvonne. And what I wasn't doing . . .

YVONNE: Well . . .

MOULINEAUX: And that it was only an experiment. And that it's over and done with.

YVONNE: Yes! That's what you say.

(MADAME AIGREVILLE *suddenly pokes her head out the door,
up right.*)

MADAME AIGREVILLE: Are you finished?

MOULINEAUX *(growling)*: You . . . No, goddammit! We'll send
you a telegram!

MADAME AIGREVILLE *(to* YVONNE*)*: Don't you believe a word he
says, precious!

(*She pulls her head back and slams the door.*)

MOULINEAUX *(furious, aside)*: Old battle-ax! And just when I was
going so strong! *(Suddenly, changing his tone, to* YVONNE,
very gently.) Don't listen to her. What I'm telling you is true.
You know I wouldn't lie. *(Aside.)* Just bend the truth a little,
to save a few reputations!

YVONNE *(weakening)*: Oh. If only I thought I could believe you!
But it's hard . . .

MOULINEAUX *(pressing his advantage)*: Try! Try, Yvonne! Try!

YVONNE: I would so like to feel that I could trust you again.

MOULINEAUX: You can! You can!

YVONNE *(sighing)*: No! I'm afraid I can't! *(Matter-of-fact.)* You
men are all liars.

MOULINEAUX: How can you say that? Who ever told you . . .

YVONNE: Mamma . . .

MOULINEAUX *(with a bitter smile)*: Of course! Mamma! I should
have guessed! *(Fuming.)* Mamma, Mamma! Dear, sweet, lovable Mamma!

YVONNE *(eager to have an excuse to believe him)*: I suppose, if
you swore . . .

MOULINEAUX: Me? Swear? Damn! I never—

YVONNE: No, I mean, if you swore that what you're telling me is
true . . .

MOULINEAUX: Oh. "Swore." You mean . . . *(Holding up his
right hand.)* "I swear . . ."? That kind of "swore"?

YVONNE: Yes. Just to convince Mamma. I'm sure it would . . .

MOULINEAUX *(sarcastically agreeable)*: Why, certainly! Why not?

Anything for Mamma! *(Raising his left hand, and with his right behind his back, crossing his fingers.)* I swear it's the truth, the whole truth . . . *(Wagging his crossed fingers.)* . . . and nothing but the truth! So help me!

YVONNE: Oh, thank you, Balthasar!

MOULINEAUX *(aside)*: My pleasure.

YVONNE: And that woman in your arms? You swear she was a stranger?

MOULINEAUX *(categorically)*: I swear she was a stranger. *(As if continuing the oath, aside.)* Until the first time I met her . . . *(To* YVONNE.*)* And if I ever see her again, may everything your mother says about me be true! There! Now do you forgive me?

YVONNE *(coquettishly)*: Well, almost . . . not yet.

MOULINEAUX: But . . .

YVONNE: When Mamma leaves, Balthasar, that's when I'll forgive you.

MOULINEAUX: And can't I even have a little kiss while I wait?

   (He purses his lips invitingly. Just then, DARTAGNAN *appears at the double door, still ajar, unseen by the others.)*

YVONNE *(with a little laugh)*: Oh, I suppose. If you insist . . .

   (They embrace and kiss.)

DARTAGNAN *(watching, thunderstruck, aside)*: Good heavens! Signor Yuno and the doctor's wife! Lovers?

   (He stands at the threshold in uncomfortable silence, watching and listening.)

MOULINEAUX: Yvonne! Angel!

YVONNE *(cajoling)*: And you promise me you're going to behave from now on? Not like the other night when I didn't know where you were?

MOULINEAUX: I promise!

YVONNE: Instead of coming here and sleeping where you belong, you naughty thing!

DARTAGNAN *(shocked, aside)*: Oh, my!

MOULINEAUX: You'll never have any more fault to find, believe me!

YVONNE: Oh. The only fault I find is that . . . *(With a pout.)* . . . you don't love your wife enough.

MOULINEAUX *(playing along)*: And you don't love your husband enough, either! That's your trouble!

DARTAGNAN *(aside)*: Now that's a novel complaint! *(Clearing his throat, pretending not to notice them.)* Anyone here? *(Coming down right without closing the door.)* Anyone at home? *(To* MOULINEAUX.*)* Ah, signore . . .

MOULINEAUX *(flustered, aside)*: Dartagnan! Goddamn! He'll put his foot in it for sure! *(To* DARTAGNAN, *joining him right.)* Why, monsieur, what a surprise! *(Introducing.)* Monsieur Dartagnan . . . Madame . . . Madame Moulineaux . . .

DARTAGNAN: Yes, yes. I've had the pleasure. Not ten minutes ago. *(Aside, to* MOULINEAUX, *with a little laugh and a nudge.)* Sly devil! Congratulations!

MOULINEAUX: What?

DARTAGNAN: And everything else is going well, too, I hope?

MOULINEAUX *(on edge)*: Fine. Fine.

DARTAGNAN: And our little project? My wife's gown is progressing?

MOULINEAUX *(trying to be offhand)*: Oh, you know . . .

DARTAGNAN: Our famous dirndl with the ruffles and the ostrich plumes . . .

MOULINEAUX *(taking him by the arm and almost dragging him up right, abruptly)*: How nice to see you again, monsieur! Have you seen any good plays lately? *(Without waiting for a reply.)* Neither have I! But nowadays, don't you know . . . What a shame you can't stay . . .

(He tries to escort him to the double door, but DARTAGNAN *resists.)*

DARTAGNAN *(moving right)*: But, signore . . .

YVONNE *(still down left)*: Balthasar?

MOULINEAUX *(rushing to her side)*: Yes. Yes, Yvonne dearest?

YVONNE: What does he mean? What gown is he talking about?

MOULINEAUX: Gown? *(Casually.)* Oh, that. *(Whispering.)* For his wife. It's . . . it's for her rheumatism, poor thing! But, please, it's strictly confidential. She's terribly sensitive.

(They continue their exchange in whispers.)

YVONNE: Rheumatism?

MOULINEAUX: Yes. It's . . . it's like a glove. Only bigger. Tight. Nice and tight. And electromagnetic! Massages the joints.

YVONNE *(growing suspicious)*: With ruffles? And ostrich plumes?

MOULINEAUX: Well, in case company comes . . .

YVONNE: Balthasar . . .

MOULINEAUX: Now, now, Yvonne. You said you were going to trust me.

(He gives her a little peck on the lips.)

DARTAGNAN *(aside)*: My goodness! And with an audience?

MOULINEAUX: And I'm going to hold you to it! *(Aloud.)* You know you're the only woman I've ever loved.

DARTAGNAN *(aside)*: I never!

MOULINEAUX: . . . and the only one I ever will.

(He gives her another peck.)

DARTAGNAN *(aside):* Have they no shame?

YVONNE *(to* MOULINEAUX*)*: Well, I'm not sure.

(While they are thus engaged BASSINET *appears at the open double door and stands for a moment, silently, at the threshold, watching.)*

DARTAGNAN *(up right, catching sight of him, aside)*: Good heavens! Her husband! The doctor!

(He pulls out his handkerchief and waves it frantically at MOULINEAUX, *trying to get his attention.)*

MOULINEAUX *(back turned to him, not noticing, to* YVONNE*)*: But I love you, I tell you. I love you! I love you!

DARTAGNAN *(still trying to signal, in a loud whisper)*: Signore! Signore!

BASSINET *(at the threshold, smiling)*: That's sweet!

DARTAGNAN: Signor Yuno!

(Noticing that BASSINET *is looking at him quizzically, he pretends to be fanning himself with the handkerchief while nodding*

a greeting to BASSINET, *who proceeds to pull out his handker-chief and do likewise. The two continue to wave and nod during the following exchange.)*

MOULINEAUX *(tenderly)*: I love you, Yvonne!

(He puts his arms around her and attempts to give her a kiss.)

YVONNE *(resisting)*: Please! Not in public!

MOULINEAUX: Why? I'm not ashamed. I want everyone to know. Ah, Yvonne . . .

(He locks her in a long, passionate embrace.)

DARTAGNAN *(aside)*: Really! There's a limit! Even for an Italian. *(Looking, not without scorn, at* BASSINET, *who continues smiling, nodding, and waving his handkerchief, intermittently—aside.)* And that one just stands there! What kind of a man is he?

BASSINET *(clearing his throat)*: Ahem . . . Ahem . . .

(He strides down left, toward MOULINEAUX, *who is still kissing* YVONNE.)*

DARTAGNAN *(aside)*: Well! Finally . . .

BASSINET *(tapping him on the shoulder)*: I say, monsieur . . .

DARTAGNAN *(aside)*: Oh, my! There's going to be a scene!

BASSINET *(to* MOULINEAUX*)*: I'm here, you know.

DARTAGNAN *(aside)*: He'll kill him! And who can blame him!

MOULINEAUX *(without turning around, still embracing* YVONNE, *grumbling to* BASSINET*)*: That's nice. So what?

BASSINET *(good-naturedly)*: Well, I . . . Aren't you even going to say hello, monsieur?

DARTAGNAN *(aside)*: What?

MOULINEAUX *(turning around, impatiently)*: Hello! All right?

BASSINET *(with a little wave)*: Hello there.

MOULINEAUX: Hello! Hello! *(Under his breath.)* Damn pest!

DARTAGNAN *(dumbfounded)*: I don't believe it! *(To* MOULINEAUX.*)* Signore! Really, signore! If you don't mind my saying . . .

YVONNE *(aside)*: "Signore"? *(To* MOULINEAUX, *puzzled.)* Is he speaking to you, Balthasar?

MOULINEAUX *(on edge)*: Yes, he . . . *(Aside, to* YVONNE.*)* He's learning Italian, and . . . and he likes to use it every chance he gets.

YVONNE: Oh. *(Crossing up right, to a perplexed* DARTAGNAN.*) Com'è bella la lingua italiana, non è vero?*

MOULINEAUX *(aside)*: Good God!

YVONNE *(continuing)*: *Mi piacerebbe molto parlare con Lei, se vuole . . .*

DARTAGNAN *(with a blank look)*: Madame?

MOULINEAUX *(aside)*: If he opens his mouth, I'm done for!

YVONNE *(continuing)*: *Le piacerebbe, signore?*

MOULINEAUX *(pushing* BASSINET *out of his way, rushing up right and grabbing* YVONNE *by the arm)*: Quick! Didn't you hear your mother calling?

YVONNE *(resisting)*: *Mia madre? (Correcting.)* My mother?

MOULINEAUX: Come! You know how she gets when we keep her waiting.

YVONNE: But . . .

(He whisks her off, and they exit up right. There is a moment of silence, during which DARTAGNAN *and* BASSINET *eye each other, back and forth. Finally* BASSINET *points up right with a little laugh.)*

BASSINET: Now where are they off to in such a hurry?

DARTAGNAN: Where indeed!

BASSINET *(still laughing)*: Our two little lovebirds . . .

DARTAGNAN *(forcing a laugh)*: Yes. Our two . . . *(Aside.)* Incredible! He accepts it! Just like that!

BASSINET: I think they're sweet!

DARTAGNAN: Oh, very . . . *(Aside.)* My heavens! Is he deaf? Is he blind?

BASSINET *(still laughing)*: You know, I'm afraid we interrupted them!

DARTAGNAN: I daresay! And that doesn't bother you, monsieur?

BASSINET: Well . . . of course, I hate to spoil their fun. But . . . *C'est la vie!*

DARTAGNAN *(echoing, incredulous)*: *C'est la vie!* *(Aside.)* What is this world coming to!

BASSINET *(with a touch of exhibitionism)*: *Che sarà sarà!*

DARTAGNAN: I'm sure. *(Aside.)* No sense of morality. No notion of right and wrong. Simply incredible! *(Unable to contain himself, to* BASSINET, *approaching him.)* I . . . Excuse me, my friend, I . . . I know it's none of my business . . .

BASSINET *(joining him, center)*: Monsieur?

DARTAGNAN: Heaven knows I'm no prude! But I simply don't understand how . . . Your wife, monsieur . . . Your wife . . .

BASSINET *(taken aback, aside)*: My wife *(To* DARTAGNAN.) Yes, monsieur? What about her?

DARTAGNAN: That is . . . How do you let her . . . I mean, if she were mine . . . I should think you would be more careful, more . . . discerning, more . . . more . . . more concerned, to say the least!

BASSINET: My wife, monsieur? *(Aside.)* What brought that on, I wonder? *(Aloud.)* My goodness! Give me a chance, drat it all! I've only just found her! I haven't seen her for years!

DARTAGNAN *(surprised)*: You haven't?

BASSINET: No. Not until yesterday. We still hardly know each other.

DARTAGNAN *(aside)*: So I see! *(Aloud.)* Oh, I didn't realize.

BASSINET *(aside)*: Why my wife, all of a sudden? *(Aloud.)* Yes. Ever since she ran away, I've been looking—

DARTAGNAN: Ran away? With the tailor?

BASSINET: A tailor? No, no. With a soldier.

DARTAGNAN: Hmm! Soldiers too! *(Aside.)* Brazen hussy!

BASSINET: It's a fascinating story. *(Sensing an audience.)* You see, we were sitting in the Tuileries one morning, and I went—

DARTAGNAN *(cutting him off)*: And you say you just found her again yesterday?

BASSINET: Believe it or not! After all these years! Like a bolt from the blue! Isn't it always the way? When you least expect it . . .

DARTAGNAN *(politely)*: Yes. Always the way.

BASSINET: And you'll never guess . . . when I found her . . . you'll never guess whose arms she was in, monsieur!

DARTAGNAN *(cynically)*: Let me try. Our own Signor Yuno!

BASSINET: Signor Yuno! *(Surprised.)* How did you know?

DARTAGNAN *(chuckling)*: How did I know? You know . . . I know Signor Yuno. *(Aside.)* He takes it all in stride, I must say!

BASSINET: Yes. In fact, when she saw me, she was so overcome that she slapped my face with joy! I was never so happy.

DARTAGNAN: I'm sure. *(Aside.)* Slap-happy!

BASSINET: After all these years . . . And now she's back where she belongs! *(Aside, to the audience.)* Won't Moulineaux be surprised when she comes here to meet him!

(MOULINEAUX *enters, up right.)*

MOULINEAUX *(under his breath)*: There! A few choice words to Mamma. "I swear this. I swear that." And everything is fine! *(To* BASSINET.) Ah, my friend. I'm sorry if I was a little abrupt just now.

BASSINET: Not at all! Not at all! I understand perfectly.

DARTAGNAN *(to* MOULINEAUX*)*: Excuse me, signore, but . . .

MOULINEAUX *(to* DARTAGNAN*)*: Still here? I thought you left.

DARTAGNAN *(taking him aside, far right, confidentially)*: If you don't mind, I'd like a word with you. It's terribly important.

MOULINEAUX: Oh?

(BASSINET, *naively, moves over to join them, listening.)*

DARTAGNAN *(annoyed, to* BASSINET*)*: I beg your pardon.

BASSINET *(ingenuously)*: Please! Don't mind me . . .

DARTAGNAN *(with an embarrassed little laugh)*: It's . . . it's personal, monsieur.

BASSINET *(nodding)*: Aha.

(He goes over to the desk, left, sits down, and begins thumbing aimlessly through a book during the ensuing dialogue.)

DARTAGNAN *(to* MOULINEAUX, *softly)*: I can tell you, signore, because I'm sure you'll understand. After all, you know women.

MOULINEAUX *(uneasy)*: Sì. Sì.

DARTAGNAN: . . . and especially my wife!

MOULINEAUX *(objecting)*: Well, just her measurements.

DARTAGNAN: You see, this is the time she usually comes to see Dr. Moulineaux, and I thought if I waited . . . Since I haven't seen her since yesterday—

MOULINEAUX *(agape)*: God in heaven!

DARTAGNAN *(misinterpreting his reaction for sympathy)*: I know. That's what I say too! But I'm afraid it doesn't help! The only thing for me to do now is to see her and . . . and make up some story or other. Something that will let me explain away Mathilde.

MOULINEAUX: Oh, by all means . . . *(Aside.)* By why here, damn it!

DARTAGNAN *(musing)*: Something logical and not too hard to believe. Something simple, like . . . like . . . *(Suddenly inspired.)* I've got it! Oh! That's a perfect idea!

MOULINEAUX *(aside)*: Congratulations!

DARTAGNAN: Can I count on you, signore?

MOULINEAUX: Can you . . . ?

DARTAGNAN: To help me?

MOULINEAUX: I suppose.

DARTAGNAN *(delighted)*: Fine! Then why don't I tell her that Mathilde is your mistress? You have nothing to lose.

MOULINEAUX: Why don't you . . . *(Horrified.)* No! No, thank you! Thank you just the same!

DARTAGNAN: But . . .

MOULINEAUX: Not in a million years! *(Aside.)* The icing on the cake!

DARTAGNAN: Why not? She's the only one I'll tell. Just my wife.

MOULINEAUX: That's one wife too many!

DARTAGNAN *(pleading)*: But, signore. Signor Yuno. Please! Please! You're my only hope!

MOULINEAUX: No, no, no, I tell you! It's insane! I . . . I can't . . .

DARTAGNAN: But . . .

MOULINEAUX *(forgetting himself momentarily)*: Madame Moulineaux would be . . . *(Clapping his hand to his mouth.)* I mean . . .

DARTAGNAN: She would? Why? *(With a glance toward* BASSINET.*)* It's not as if you were her husband, after all. Besides, she doesn't have to know!

MOULINEAUX: No! No! Absolutely not! Ask someone else!

DARTAGNAN *(desperately)*: But who?

(BASSINET, *still sitting at the desk, casually flipping pages, begins to hum a little tune.)*

MOULINEAUX: Anyone! I don't care! *(Pointing to* BASSINET.*)* Him! Him, for instance!

DARTAGNAN *(with an air of disgusted disbelief)*: Him? *(Aside.)* His mistress's husband?

MOULINEAUX: Why not? He's as good as any! What difference can it make?

DARTAGNAN *(shocked)*: Oh, maybe not to him! And Madame Moulineaux?

MOULINEAUX *(ingenuously)*: Yes? What about her?

DARTAGNAN: Well, I thought . . . I just thought . . . *(Aside.)* Good heavens! These people are utterly depraved! *(To* MOULINEAUX.*)* If you think it's all right . . .

MOULINEAUX: Of course, it is! Why not?

DARTAGNAN *(resisting)*: I don't know. *(Aside.)* And a doctor, too.

(BASSINET, *still humming, throws the book down on the desk and stands up.)*

BASSINET: I say . . . Have you two finished?

(He moves toward them.)

MOULINEAUX *(to* BASSINET*)*: Monsieur . . . my friend has something to ask you.

(He moves off left, discreetly.)

BASSINET *(happy to be included in the conversation)*: Oh? Something I can do?

DARTAGNAN: Yes, monsieur. *(Taking him by the arm and leading him down right.)* A favor. A very big favor.

BASSINET: Me?

DARTAGNAN: Immense . . . monumental . . .

BASSINET *(embarrassed)*: I . . . I'd really like to help, but . . . it's the end of the month, and . . . and . . .

DARTAGNAN *(reassuring him)*: Please! It won't cost you a thing.

BASSINET: Oh, well, then . . .

DARTAGNAN: You see, I've had something of a spat with my wife. She caught me with my mistress!

BASSINET *(with a silly little laugh)*: My, my! That wasn't very bright!

DARTAGNAN *(forcing a laugh)*: It was stupid!

BASSINET: Well, I didn't want to say . . .

DARTAGNAN: Yes, and she'll be here any minute. But I don't have to tell you, I'm sure. And what I would like you to do is . . . It's really very simple. *(Very matter-of-fact.)* I'd appreciate it if you would tell her that Madame de Sainte-Vinaigrette is your mistress.

BASSINET: Aha. That's the favor, monsieur?

DARTAGNAN: Yes.

BASSINET *(noncommittally)*: Very interesting idea.

DARTAGNAN: Then you'll do it?

BASSINET *(turning on his heel)*: But, impossible!

DARTAGNAN: But, monsieur! Please! Please! You're my only hope!

MOULINEAUX *(aside)*: Ha!

BASSINET: Out of the question!

MOULINEAUX *(rushing over to BASSINET, down right, in a whisper)*: Say yes! He has a lot of clients who need apartments!

BASSINET (*to* MOULINEAUX): He does? (*To* DARTAGNAN, *suddenly.*) I accept!

(MOULINEAUX *retreats, up left.*)

DARTAGNAN (*to* BASSINET): You mean, you will?

BASSINET: As long as I don't have to get involved, monsieur.

DARTAGNAN: Absolutely!

BASSINET (*jovially*): And as long as she's pretty . . .

DARTAGNAN: Oh, very!

BASSINET: And a good sense of humor . . .

DARTAGNAN: I should say!

BASSINET (*laughing*): Not a prude . . .

DARTAGNAN (*laughing*): Oh, hardly!

BASSINET (*laughing suggestively*): Likes to have a good time . . . (*Giving him a meaningful poke.*) If you know what I mean . . .

DARTAGNAN (*laughing*): Loves to, monsieur. Loves to. (*Taking the picture from his pocket.*) Look, here's her picture. (*Holding it out to* BASSINET.) In fact, you can show it to my wife. That will help convince her.

(ETIENNE *appears suddenly at the double door before* BASSINET *has a chance to look.*)

ETIENNE (*announcing*): Madame Dartagnan!

DARTAGNAN (*excited*): Ah! Already? Shhh! Here she is! (*Stuffing the photo into* BASSINET'S *coat pocket.*) Here! Hide this! Quick! Hide it. (*Aside.*) Not a second too soon!

(SUZANNE *enters, and* ETIENNE *exits.*)

MOULINEAUX (*nodding*): Good morning, madame.

DARTAGNAN (*timidly*): Hello, Suzanne.

SUZANNE (*to* DARTAGNAN, *scornfully*): You, monsieur? Here? (*To* MOULINEAUX.) Excuse me. I'll be going.

DARTAGNAN: Suzanne! Please! Listen! I'm innocent! I can prove it!

SUZANNE (*to* DARTAGNAN): You'll have your chance, monsieur. In court!

(She turns to leave but stops.)

DARTAGNAN: In court? Don't say that, Suzanne! Please! If you'll only listen . . . It's all a terrible mistake. A misunderstanding . . .

SUZANNE *(with a withering glance)*: Ha! I understand perfectly!

DARTAGNAN: That woman . . . I . . . I don't even know her! I never laid eyes on her.

SUZANNE: Of course!

DARTAGNAN: And if you don't believe me . . . *(Pointing to BAS-SINET.)* Ask him! She's his . . . *(To BASSINET.)* Isn't she, monsieur?

BASSINET *(without much conviction)*: Why, yes. Yes, yes.

DARTAGNAN *(to SUZANNE)*: You see?

BASSINET *(continuing)*: Yes.

SUZANNE *(to DARTAGNAN, sharply)*: Balderdash, monsieur!

DARTAGNAN: "Balder—" But I'm telling you . . .

MOULINEAUX *(to SUZANNE)*: Tsk tsk tsk! Heartless, madame.

DARTAGNAN *(to SUZANNE)*: You're making a mistake. *(Pointing to BASSINET.)* She's his, I tell you! *(Aside, to BASSINET.)* The picture! The picture!

BASSINET *(fishing in his pocket)*: Ah . . .

(He moves off, left, as ETIENNE appears at the double door.)

ETIENNE *(announcing)*: Madame . . .

(Before he has a chance to give her name, MIMI enters. ETIENNE shrugs and exits, closing the double door behind him.)

BASSINET *(looking up, going to meet her)*: Oh, there you are! Come in! Come in!

SUZANNE *(aside)*: Her! Anatole's mistress!

BASSINET *(bringing MIMI down right, about to introduce her to DARTAGNAN)*: Monsieur, I'd like you to meet my—

DARTAGNAN *(looking up from his preoccupation)*: Oh no!

(He rushes out, crossing down left.)

BASSINET *(watching, surprised)*: What . . . ? *(Bringing MIMI left, to MOULINEAUX.)* Doctor Moulineaux, let me introduce my—

MOULINEAUX (*suddenly recognizing her*): Good God! Her? Here?

(*He rushes out, crossing down right.*)

BASSINET: What's the matter?

MIMI (*annoyed*): Not very polite, are they?

BASSINET: I say . . . (*Moving upstage, about to introduce her to* SUZANNE.) Madame, I'd like you to meet—

SUZANNE (*curtly*): You needn't bother!

(*She strides out, up left.*)

MIMI: Again?

BASSINET: Maybe something they ate . . .

(*The door, up right, opens and* YVONNE *enters.*)

BASSINET (*noticing her*): Ah, madame. (*Bringing* MIMI *up to meet her.*) I'd like to introduce you—

YVONNE (*recognizing* MIMI): You! (*To* BASSINET, *sharply.*) Really, monsieur! Enough is enough!

(*She turns on her heel and exits, up right.*)

MIMI (*furious*): Damnation! Who do they think they are?

BASSINET (*offhand*): Oh . . . They do it to me all the time.

MIMI: And you let them?

BASSINET (*halfheartedly*): Well, no. That is . . . Just a moment . . . I'm sure . . .

(*He goes to the door, up right, and knocks. In the meantime* MOULINEAUX *has poked his head out the door, down right, and, not seeing* BASSINET, *thinks that* MIMI *is alone.*)

MOULINEAUX (*rushing to join her, center*): Are you out of your mind? Coming here like this?

MIMI: What . . . ?

MOULINEAUX: To my home, for God's sake!

MIMI: But, Baba, I'm with my husband! What's the harm?

MOULINEAUX: Your what? Who? Where?

MIMI (*pointing up right*): Him! There!

MOULINEAUX (*shouting*): Bassinet?

MIMI: Since yesterday. He found me . . .

BASSINET *(turning around at the sound of his name)*: Ah, monsieur . . . *(Coming down to join them.)* I'd like to introduce you—

MOULINEAUX *(laughing)*: Him? That's a good one!

(He doubles up with laughter as MIMI *moves down left.)*

BASSINET: What's so funny monsieur? What's the joke?

MOULINEAUX: Nothing! Nothing! You wouldn't understand!

(During the previous exchange DARTAGNAN *has peeked out the door, down left. Seeing* MIMI, *he looks around to make sure that* SUZANNE *isn't there, and enters.)*

DARTAGNAN *(to* MIMI, *in a frantic whisper)*: Please, Mathilde! Will you get out of here! My wife, for heaven's sake. My wife . . .

MIMI *(losing patience, moving far right)*: Damnation! I've had enough! They can all go hang!

BASSINET *(coming down left, to* DARTAGNAN*)*: Why all the whispering, monsieur?

(At that moment, YVONNE *and* MADAME AIGREVILLE *enter, up right, and* SUZANNE, *up left, simultaneously.)*

YVONNE *(with* MADAME AIGREVILLE *at her side, to* MOULINEAUX*)*: This is the last straw! You're a cad, monsieur!

MADAME AIGREVILLE *(echoing)*: A cad!

MOULINEAUX *(innocently)*: But . . . But . . .

YVONNE: It's not bad enough that you go chasing every skirt in Paris.

MOULINEAUX: But . . . But . . .

YVONNE: But to bring them here. Here, to my home, monsieur.

MADAME AIGREVILLE *(echoing)*: Her home!

MOULINEAUX: But who . . . Who? Who?

YVONNE: Who? Who? *(Pointing to* MIMI.*)* Her, that's who!

MIMI: Me? Me?

MADAME AIGREVILLE *(pointing to* SUZANNE, *still at the door, up left)*: No! Her!

SUZANNE: "Her" who? Who? Me?

(*She comes downstage, between* MOULINEAUX *and* DARTAGNAN, *resulting in the following disposition, right to left:* MIMI, MA-DAME AIGREVILLE, YVONNE, MOULINEAUX, DARTAGNAN, BASSINET.)

MOULINEAUX (*at his wit's end*): But you don't understand!

DARTAGNAN (*to* MADAME AIGREVILLE): I beg your pardon, but . . . (*With a gesture toward* SUZANNE.) Madame is my wife!

BASSINET (*pointing to* MIMI): And madame is mine! I'll thank you to remember—

MADAME AIGREVILLE (*looking at* YVONNE) ⎫   ⎫ She is?

YVONNE (*looking at* MOULINEAUX)   ⎬ (*together*) ⎬ She is?

SUZANNE (*looking at* DARTAGNAN)   ⎬   ⎬ She is?

DARTAGNAN (*looking at* BASSINET)   ⎭   ⎭ She is?

BASSINET: Why, yes.

DARTAGNAN (*looking at* YVONNE, *aside*): Then who on earth . . . ?

MADAME AIGREVILLE (*looking at* MIMI)   ⎫   ⎫ His wife?

YVONNE (*looking at* MADAME AIGREVILLE) ⎬ (*together*) ⎬ His wife?

SUZANNE (*looking at* MOULINEAUX)   ⎭   ⎭ His wife?

BASSINET: I've been trying to introduce you . . .

DARTAGNAN (*aside*): Oh, my! The picture . . .

BASSINET: . . . only nobody would listen . . .

DARTAGNAN (*to* SUZANNE, *taking her by the arm and whisking her up left*): You see? I told you. You didn't believe me. (*Coming back down left, holding out his hand, to* BASSINET, *in a whisper.*) Monsieur . . . Please, the picture . . .

BASSINET: Oh, yes. Of course.

(*He takes it out of his pocket and is about to look at it.*)

DARTAGNAN (*trying to stop him*): No, no! Don't look! (*He tries to take it from him, but* BASSINET *eludes his grasp.*) No! Please!

(*There is a moment of give-and-take before* BASSINET *finally succeeds in looking at the picture.*)

BASSINET (*surprised*): I say!

DARTAGNAN *(between his teeth, aside)*: That does it!

BASSINET: If I didn't know better . . . *(To* DARTAGNAN, *showing him the picture.)* It's the image of my wife, monsieur. Don't you think?

DARTAGNAN *(pretending to scrutinize it, offhand)*: Your . . . No . . . No . . . *(Touching his nose.)* Too big. *(Touching his chin.)* Too big.

BASSINET: But . . . *(To* MOULINEAUX.*)* Monsieur . . . *(Showing it to him.)* Don't you think this looks like my wife?

MOULINEAUX: Like your . . . No . . . No . . . *(Touching his chin.)* Too small. *(Touching his nose.)* Too small.

BASSINET *(to* MIMI, *showing her the picture)*: I say . . . Don't you think . . . Look . . .

MIMI *(pretending to be offended)*: That? Really, Perceval! Is that what you think I look like?

BASSINET *(studying the picture)*: Well, now that you mention it . . . no. I guess not.

SUZANNE *(coming down to* DARTAGNAN, *pointing to* MIMI*)*: You mean, that woman . . . she really is his wife?

DARTAGNAN: Of course! I've been trying to tell you.

SUZANNE: Oh! Anatole, dearest! I . . . What can I say?

DARTAGNAN *(with a noble gesture)*: Please! Please! I forgive you.

YVONNE *(swallowing her pride, to* MOULINEAUX*)*: And can you forgive me?

DARTAGNAN *(puzzled, aside)*: For what? Being his mistress?

MOULINEAUX *(to* YVONNE*)*: Do you have to ask, Yvonne?

MADAME AIGREVILLE *(aside)*: Lucky for them I was here to make peace!

YVONNE: Oh, Balthasar! What a dear, faithful, wonderful husband you are!

MOULINEAUX: Ayyy!

DARTAGNAN *(with a start)*: Husband?

MOULINEAUX: That is . . .

DARTAGNAN: But . . . Dr. Moulineaux? *(To* BASSINET.*)* Doctor . . . ?

BASSINET: Not me, monsieur. *(Pointing to* MOULINEAUX.*)* Him!

MOULINEAUX *(aside)*: Swine!

BASSINET: He's the doctor.

DARTAGNAN: He is? But . . . Signor Yuno . . . ?

YVONNE: Yuno?

MADAME AIGREVILLE: Yuno?

MIMI: Yuno?

DARTAGNAN *(to* MOULINEAUX*)*: But I thought you were a tailor.

MOULINEAUX *(covering up, before* YVONNE *and* MADAME AIGREVILLE *grow suspicious, speaking as fast as he can)*: Italian, monsieur? Italian? Me, Italian? Well, I did have an aunt once who married an Italian, and . . . It's really a funny story, if you'd like a good laugh! You see, she had a young gigolo, this aunt of mine. . . .

BASSINET: She did?

MOULINEAUX: And one day he went out and he bought her a parrot. And . . .

(The others shout him down with appropriate cries: "Never mind!"; "We're not interested!"; "Who cares!"; etc.; as the curtain falls.)

CURTAIN

Bernard Shaw

CANDIDA

THE EARLY CAREER of George Bernard Shaw (1856–1950) was enormously varied and versatile. When he came to London from Dublin in 1876, he worked as a novelist, a journalist, a Fabian Socialist orator, a book reviewer, and a critic of art, music, and theater. He became a playwright in the early 1890s, more or less as a by-product of his other activities.

Candida (1895) is a domestic comedy, a genre in which Shaw showed a special genius. Into the happy household of the Reverend James Mavor Morell and his wife Candida comes the aristocratic and waiflike poet, Eugene Marchbanks, who is "*a strange, shy youth of eighteen.*" Although a foolishly petulant, unmanly, and romantic youth, he exposes the complacency and smugness of Morell's marriage. The play is like Ibsen's *A Doll's House* (1879) with a comic twist. Candida is no Nora about to slam the door on her artificial existence, but Morell has many resemblances to the well-fed and successful husband, Torvald, utterly self-satisfied and uncomprehending to the end, as Shaw points out in a letter to the *Evening Standard* of November 30, 1944: *Candida* is "a counterblast to Ibsen's *Doll House*, showing that in the real typical doll's house it is the man who is the doll." Morell and Torvald are exemplars of male privilege and female overprotection.

At the heart of the comedy is Candida, who is introduced to us with her characteristic expression: "*an amused maternal indulgence.*" She is clearly a superior being, and her indulgence is needed for the folly of others, especially men. She is skillful at manipulating her own limited, domestic world; as Shaw puts it, she is "*cunning in the affections.*" Her basic function is to reveal, as gently and as indulgently as possible, the truth about themselves to her husband, to the young poet, and also to her father. Morell seems to understand nothing about the real world, and he is content to spout clerical and moralistic platitudes at moments of high crisis. That is what gives Marchbanks such a clear edge in exposing the clergyman's inadequacies.

Candida is constantly aware of how obtuse her husband really is, and that it is her role to point out to him that marriage depends on love and not on a handful of high-minded Christian principles: "Put your trust in my love for you, James; for if that went, I should care very little for your sermons: mere phrases that you cheat yourself and others with every day." Candida and Marchbanks share in the certainty that feelings are more important than language. In this respect Morell is trapped by his own oratorical self-sufficiency. He is too articulate to distrust the medium in which he has been so brilliantly attractive. Shaw, the infallibly witty and eloquent man of words, seems to be self-consciously poking fun at himself through Morell.

Candida is rightly offended by her husband's inability to speak to her as an individual, a private person rather than an audience. As Morell presses his jealous rivalry with Marchbanks—a conflict that he would have done better to ignore—his tone grows less and less adequate for the occasion. There is good Shavian comedy in the painful bromides of Morell by which he tries to answer Marchbanks's taunts: "I have nothing to tell her, except (*Here his voice deepens to a measured and mournful tenderness*) that she is my greatest treasure on earth—if she is really mine." Candida is stung with the ridiculous posturing of her husband's "mellow" style, and she is tempted to agree with Marchbanks against her intuitive judgment. She speaks "*coldly*," offended by Morell's "*yielding to his orator's instinct and treating her as if she were the audience in the Guild of St. Matthew.*" A bit later in this scene we learn from the stage direction that her heart is "*hardened by his rhetoric in spite of the sincere feeling behind it.*" Since Shaw's elaborate commentaries in italics are messages to actors (and readers) that will disappear in performance, he seems to be demanding from his actors a degree of intelligence and skill that are remarkable. At the same moment that Candida recognizes her husband's "*sincere feeling*," we are also told that she is "*hardened by his rhetoric*," presumably his professional, impersonal, and insincere speech. It is left to the actor to convey this paradoxical doubleness of Candida's emotions.

Shaw's Candida—and many of his other female characters—have the freedom and self-assertion that George Meredith in his *Essay on Comedy* (1877) claimed as an essential ingredient of all comedy. Candida easily masters both her husband and Marchbanks and establishes her own identity outside the narrow possessiveness of both lovers. When she is forced to choose between them, she startles them with the possibility that she is also free to choose neither. As Marchbanks puts it, "Morell: you dont

understand. She means that she belongs to herself." To belong
to oneself is one of the basic characteristics of the comic hero: he
or she cannot be manipulated. Is Candida a feminist? The term is
not fully relevant to Shaw but by choosing the "weaker,"
Candida loudly asserts her superiority to her husband. She is the
nurturer of his illusions of maleness and dominance:

> Where there is money to give, he gives it: when there is
> money to refuse, I refuse it. I build a castle of comfort and
> indulgence and love for him, and stand sentinel always to
> keep little vulgar cares out. I make him master here, though
> he does not know it and could not tell you a moment ago how
> it came to be so.

Candida rules with love and indulgence, although the histrionic
antics of Morell and Marchbanks drive her to the outer limits of
her patience.

Marchbanks the poet and arch-romantic is a Shavian eccentric
brilliantly portrayed in his nest of contradictions. Besides being a
ridiculous, sniveling adolescent, he is also an infallible truth-
speaker and exploder of cant. Although Shaw identifies himself
temperamentally with Morell, Marchbanks—and Candida, too—
they are mouthpieces for Shavian ideas and Shavian satire of the
domestic verities. The poet rightly despises Morell's vanity and
empty phrase-making, but he is harshly abstracted from all human values. His assault on everyone in the play in the name of
poetry and truth is, of course, insufferable. When he lectures
Prossy, Morell's secretary, on the nature of love, he is at his
most absurd: "All the love in the world is longing to speak; only
it dare not, because it is shy! shy! shy! That is the world's
tragedy." Marchbanks's sensitivity is rather bathetic when he
complains about seeing "the affection I am longing for given to
dogs and cats and pet birds, because they come and ask for it."
This is not very useful advice for Prossy.

But Shaw never completely makes up his mind about Marchbanks. Candida takes him seriously, although she does fall asleep
when he reads his poetry. Candida seems to be worried about
him and especially about how his poetic soul may be tarnished
by contact with the real world. Her maternal indulgence is
touching and in no way comic, but the fact that Morell takes the
poet so literally as a potent rival in love is comic in the classic
sense. Marchbanks is a kind of braggart in love, and his inflated
rhetoric is not meant to be convincing. Both Morell and
Marchbanks are put out of their humor—their silly self-importance

and self-preoccupation—by the end of the play. Morell is finally told the truth about his "weakness," and Marchbanks is driven out into the night. But Shaw does not let him go without teasing us with a mysterious and unanswerable question. In the final tableau Morell and Candida, newly restored to each other, embrace: *"But they do not know the secret in the poet's heart."* How do the actors convey this stage direction to the audience? Clearly Shaw does not want his readers to leave without a powerful romantic assertion on behalf of the poet. Since this play is unusual in the Shaw canon in not having a preface, we may never learn the secret that is throbbing in the poet's unsatisfied heart—certainly not from Shaw himself.

CANDIDA

ACT I

(A fine morning in October 1894 in the north east quarter of
London, a vast district miles away from the London of Mayfair
and St James's, and much less narrow, squalid, fetid and airless
in its slums. It is strong in unfashionable middle class life:
wide-streeted; myriad-populated; well served with ugly iron
urinals, Radical clubs, and tram lines carrying a perpetual
stream of yellow cars; enjoying in its main thoroughfares the
luxury of grass-grown "front gardens" untrodden by the foot of
man save as to the path from the gate to the hall doors blighted
by a callously endured monotony of miles and miles of unlovely
brick houses, black iron railings, stony pavements, slated roofs,
and respectably ill dressed or disreputably worse dressed people, quite accustomed to the place, and mostly plodding
uninterestedly about somebody else's work. The little energy and
eagerness that crop up shew themselves in cockney cupidity and
business "push." Even the policemen and the chapels are not
infrequent enough to break the monotony. The sun is shining
cheerfully: there is no fog; and though the smoke effectually
prevents anything, whether faces and hands or bricks and mortar, from looking fresh and clean, it is not hanging heavily
enough to trouble a Londoner.

This desert of unattractiveness has its oasis. Near the outer
end of the Hackney Road is a park of 217 acres, fenced in, not
by railings, but by a wooden paling, and containing plenty of
greensward, trees, a lake for bathers, flower beds which are
triumphs of the admired cockney art of carpet gardening, and a
sandpit, originally imported from the seaside for the delight of
children, but speedily deserted on its becoming a natural vermin
preserve for all the petty fauna of Kingsland, Hackney, and
Hoxton. A bandstand, an unfurnished forum for religious, anti-
religious, and political orators, cricket pitches, a gymnasium,
and an old fashioned stone kiosk are among its attractions.
Wherever the prospect is bounded by trees or rising green
grounds, it is a pleasant place. Where the ground stretches flat

to the grey palings, with bricks and mortar, sky signs, crowded chimneys and smoke beyond, the prospect makes it desolate and sordid.

The best view of Victoria Park is commanded by the front window of St Dominic's Parsonage, from which not a brick is visible. The parsonage is semi-detached, with a front garden and a porch. Visitors go up the flight of steps to the porch: tradespeople and members of the family go down by a door under the steps to the basement, with a breakfast room, used for all meals, in front, and the kitchen at the back. Upstairs, on the level of the hall door, is the drawingroom, with its large plate glass window looking out on the park. In this, the only sitting room that can be spared from the children and the family meals, the parson, the Reverend James Mavor Morell, does his work. He is sitting in a strong round backed revolving chair at the end of a long table, which stands across the window, so that he can cheer himself with a view of the park over his left shoulder. At the opposite end of the table, adjoining it, is a little table only half as wide as the other, with a typewriter on it. His typist is sitting at this machine, with her back to the window. The large table is littered with pamphlets, journals, letters, nests of drawers, an office diary, postage scales and the like. A spare chair for visitors having business with the parson is in the middle, turned to his end. Within reach of his hand is a stationery case, and a photograph in a frame. The wall behind him is fitted with bookshelves, on which an adept eye can measure the parson's casuistry and divinity by Maurice's Theological Essays and a complete set of Browning's poems, and the reformer's politics by a yellow backed Progress and Poverty, Fabian Essays, A Dream of John Ball, Marx's Capital, and half a dozen other literary landmarks in Socialism. Facing him on the other side of the room, near the typewriter, is the door. Further down opposite the fireplace, a bookcase stands on a cellaret, with a sofa near it. There is a generous fire burning; and the hearth, with a comfortable armchair and a black japanned flower-painted coal scuttle at one side, a miniature chair for children on the other, a varnished wooden mantelpiece, with neatly moulded shelves, tiny bits of mirror let into the panels, a travelling clock in a leather case (the inevitable wedding present), and on the wall above a large autotype of the chief figure in Titian's Assumption of the Virgin, is very inviting. Altogether the room is the room of a good housekeeper, vanquished, as far as the table is concerned, by an untidy man, but elsewhere mistress of the situation. The furniture, in its ornamental aspect, betrays the style of the *advertized "drawingroom suite" of the pushing suburban furniture dealer; but there is nothing useless or pretentious in the room, money being too scarce in the house of an east end parson to be wasted on snobbish trimmings.*

The Reverend James Mavor Morell is a Christian Socialist clergyman of the Church of England, and an active member of the Guild of St Matthew and the Christian Social Union. A vigorous, genial, popular man of forty, robust and goodlooking, full of energy, with pleasant, hearty, considerate manners, and a sound unaffected voice, which he uses with the clean athletic articulation of a practised orator, and with a wide range and perfect command of expression. He is a first rate clergyman, able to say what he likes to whom he likes, to lecture people without setting himself up against them, to impose his authority on them without humiliating them, and, on occasion, to interfere in their business without impertinence. His well-spring of enthusiasm and sympathetic emotion has never run dry for a moment: he still eats and sleeps heartily enough to win the daily battle between exhaustion and recuperation triumphantly. Withal, a great baby, pardonably vain of his powers and unconsciously pleased with himself. He has a healthy complexion: good forehead, with the brows somewhat blunt, and the eyes bright and eager, mouth resolute but not particularly well cut, and a substantial nose, with the mobile spreading nostrils of the dramatic orator, void, like all his features, of subtlety.

The typist, Miss Proserpine Garnett, is a brisk little woman of about 30, of the lower middle class, neatly but cheaply dressed in a black merino skirt and a blouse, notably pert and quick of speech, and not very civil in her manner, but sensitive and affectionate. She is clattering away busily at her machine whilst Morell opens the last of his morning's letters. He realizes its contents with a comic groan of despair.)

PROSERPINE: Another lecture?

MORELL: Yes. The Hoxton Freedom Group want me to address them on Sunday morning. (*He lays great emphasis on Sunday, this being the unreasonable part of the business.*) What are they?

PROSERPINE: Communist Anarchists, I think.

MORELL: Just like Anarchists not to know that they cant have a parson on Sunday! Tell them to come to church if they want to hear me: it will do them good. Say I can come on Mondays and Thursdays only. Have you the diary there?

PROSERPINE (*taking up the diary*): Yes.

MORELL: Have I any lecture on for next Monday?

PROSERPINE (*referring to the diary*): Tower Hamlets Radical Club.

MORELL: Well, Thursday then?

PROSERPINE: English Land Restoration League.

MORELL: What next?

PROSERPINE: Guild of St Matthew on Monday. Independent Labor Party, Greenwich Branch, on Thursday. Monday, Social-Democratic Federation, Mile End Branch. Thursday, first Confirmation class. (*Impatiently.*) Oh, I'd better tell them you cant come. Theyre only half a dozen ignorant and conceited costermongers without five shillings between them.

MORELL (*amused*): Ah, but you see theyre near relatives of mine.

PROSERPINE (*staring at him*): Relatives of yours!

MORELL: Yes: we have the same father—in Heaven.

PROSERPINE (*relieved*): Oh, is that all?

MORELL (*with a sadness which is a luxury to a man whose voice expresses it so finely*): Ah, you dont believe it. Everybody says it: nobody believes it: nobody. (*Briskly, getting back to business.*) Well, well! Come, Miss Proserpine: cant you find a date for the costers? what about the 25th? That was vacant the day before yesterday.

PROSERPINE (*referring to diary*): Engaged. The Fabian Society.

MORELL: Bother the Fabian Society! Is the 28th gone too?

PROSERPINE: City dinner. Youre invited to dine with the Founders' Company.

MORELL: Thatll do: I'll go to the Hoxton Group of Freedom instead. (*She enters the engagement in silence, with implacable disparagement of the Hoxton Anarchists in every line of her face. Morell bursts open the cover of a copy of The Church Reformer, which has come by post, and glances through Mr Stewart Headlam's leader and the Guild of St Matthew news. These proceedings are presently enlivened by the appearance of Morell's curate, the Reverend Alexander Mill, a young gentleman gathered by Morell from the nearest University settlement, whither he had come from Oxford to give the*

*east end of London the benefit of his university training. He is
a conceitedly well intentioned, enthusiastic, immature novice,
with nothing positively unbearable about him except a habit of
speaking with his lips carefully closed a full half inch from
each corner for the sake of a finicking articulation and a set of
university vowels, this being his chief means so far of bringing
his Oxford refinement [as he calls his habits] to bear on
Hackney vulgarity. Morell, whom he has won over by a
doglike devotion, looks up indulgently from The Church Reformer, and remarks)* Well, Lexy? Late again, as usual!

LEXY: I'm afraid so. I wish I could get up in the morning.

MORELL *(exulting in his own energy)*: Ha! Ha! *(Whimsically.)*
Watch and pray. Lexy: watch and pray.

LEXY: I know. *(Rising wittily to the occasion.)* But how can I
watch and pray when I am asleep? Isnt that so, Miss Prossy?
(He makes for the warmth of the fire.)

PROSERPINE *(sharply)*: Miss Garnett, if you please.

LEXY: I beg your pardon. Miss Garnett.

PROSERPINE: Youve got to do all the work today.

LEXY *(on the hearth)*: Why?

PROSERPINE: Never mind why. It will do you good to earn your
supper before you eat it, for once in a way, as I do. Come!
dont dawdle. You should have been off on your rounds half an
hour ago.

LEXY *(perplexed)*: Is she in earnest, Morell?

MORELL *(in the highest spirits; his eyes dancing)*: Yes. *I* am
going to dawdle today.

LEXY: You! You dont know how.

MORELL *(rising)*: Ha! ha! Dont I? I'm going to have this morning
all to myself. My wife's coming back; she's due here at 11.45.

LEXY *(surprised)*: Coming back already! with the children? I
thought they were to stay to the end of the month.

MORELL: So they are: she's only coming up for two days, to get
some flannel things for Jimmy, and to see how we're getting
on without her.

LEXY *(anxiously)*: But, my dear Morell, if what Jimmy and
Fluffy had was scarlatina, do you think it wise—

MORELL: Scarlatina! Rubbish! It was German measles. I brought it into the house myself from the Pycroft Street school. A parson is like a doctor, my boy: he must face infection as a soldier must face bullets. (*He claps Lexy manfully on the shoulders.*) Catch the measles if you can, Lexy: she'll nurse you; and what a piece of luck that will be for you! Eh?

LEXY (*smiling uneasily*): It's so hard to understand you about Mrs Morell—

MORELL (*tenderly*): Ah, my boy, get married; get married to a good woman; and then you'll understand. Thats a foretaste of what will be best in the Kingdom of Heaven we are trying to establish on earth. That will cure you of dawdling. An honest man feels that he must pay Heaven for every hour of happiness with a good spell of hard unselfish work to make others happy. We have no more right to consume happiness without producing it than to consume wealth without producing it. Get a wife like my Candida; and youll always be in arrear with your repayment. (*He pats Lexy affectionately and moves to leave the room.*)

LEXY: Oh, wait a bit: I forgot. (*Morell halts and turns with the door knob in his hand.*) Your father-in-law is coming round to see you.

(*Morell, surprised and not pleased, shuts the door again, with a complete change of manner.*)

MORELL: Mr Burgess?

LEXY: Yes. I passed him in the park, arguing with somebody. He asked me to let you know that he was coming.

MORELL (*half incredulous*): But he hasnt called here for three years. Are you sure, Lexy? Youre not joking, are you?

LEXY (*earnestly*): No, sir, really.

MORELL (*thoughtfully*): Hm! Time for him to take another look at Candida before she grows out of his knowledge. (*He resigns himself to the inevitable, and goes out.*)

(*Lexy looks after him with beaming worship. Miss Garnett, not being able to shake Lexy, relieves her feelings by worrying the typewriter.*)

LEXY: What a good man! What a thorough loving soul he is! (*He takes Morell's place at the table, making himself very comfortable as he takes out a cigaret.*)

PROSERPINE *(impatiently, pulling the letter she has been working at off the typewriter and folding it)*: Oh, a man ought to be able to be fond of his wife without making a fool of himself about her.

LEXY *(shocked)*: Oh, Miss Prossy!

PROSERPINE *(snatching at the stationery case for an envelope, in which she encloses the letter as she speaks)*: Candida here, and Candida there, and Candida everywhere! *(She licks the envelope.)* It's enough to drive anyone out of their senses *(Thumping the envelope to make it stick.)* to hear a woman raved about in that absurd manner merely because she's got good hair and a tolerable figure.

LEXY *(with reproachful gravity)*: I think her extremely beautiful, Miss Garnett. *(He takes the photograph up; looks at it; and adds, with even greater impressiveness)* extremely beautiful. How fine her eyes are!

PROSERPINE: Her eyes are not a bit better than mine: now! *(He puts down the photograph and stares austerely at her)*. And you know very well you think me dowdy and second rate enough.

LEXY *(rising majestically)*: Heaven forbid that I should think of any of God's creatures in such a way! *(He moves stiffly away from her across the room to the neighborhood of the bookcase.)*

PROSERPINE *(sarcastically)*: Thank you. Thats very nice and comforting.

LEXY *(saddened by her depravity)*: I had no idea you had any feeling against Mrs Morell.

PROSERPINE *(indignantly)*: I have no feeling against her. She's very nice, very good-hearted: I'm very fond of her, and can appreciate her real qualities far better than any man can. *(He shakes his head sadly. She rises and comes at him with intense pepperiness.)* You dont believe me? You think I'm jealous? Oh, what a knowledge of the human heart you have, Mr Lexy Mill! How well you know the weaknesses of Woman, dont you? It must be so nice to be a man and have a fine penetrating intellect instead of mere emotions like us, and to know that the reason we dont share your amorous delusions is that we're all jealous of one another! *(She abandons him with a toss of her shoulders, and crosses to the fire to warm her hands.)*

LEXY: Ah, if you women only had the same clue to Man's strength that you have to his weakness, Miss Prossy, there would be no Woman Question.

PROSERPINE (*over her shoulder, as she stoops, holding her hands to the blaze*): Where did you hear Morell say that? You didnt invent it yourself: youre not clever enough.

LEXY: That's quite true, I am not ashamed of owing him that, as I owe him so many other spiritual truths. He said it at the annual conference of the Women's Liberal Federation. Allow me to add that though they didnt appreciate it, I, a mere man, did. (*He turns to the bookcase again, hoping that this may leave her crushed.*)

PROSERPINE (*putting her hair straight at a panel of mirror in the mantelpiece*): Well, when you talk to me, give me your own ideas, such as they are, and not his. You never cut a poorer figure than when you are trying to imitate him.

LEXY (*stung*): I try to follow his example, not to imitate him.

PROSERPINE (*coming at him again on her way back to her work*): Yes, you do: you i m i t a t e him. Why do you tuck your umbrella under your left arm instead of carrying it in your hand like anyone else? Why do you walk with your chin stuck out before you, hurrying along with that eager look in your eyes? you! who never get up before half past nine in the morning. Why do you say "knoaledge" in church, though you always say "knolledge" in private conversation! Bah! do you think I dont know? (*She goes back to the typewriter*). Here! come and set about your work: weve wasted enough time for one morning. Here's a copy of the diary for today. (*She hands him a memorandum.*)

LEXY (*deeply offended*): Thank you. (*He takes it and stands at the table with his back to her, reading it. She begins to transcribe her shorthand notes on the typewriter without troubling herself about his feelings.*)

(*The door opens; and Mr Burgess enters unannounced. He is a man of sixty, made coarse and sordid by the compulsory selfishness of petty commerce, and later on softened into sluggish bumptiousness by overfeeding and commercial success. A vulgar ignorant guzzling man, offensive and contemptuous to people whose labor is cheap, respectful to wealth and rank, and quite sincere and without rancor or envy in both*) *attitudes. The world has offered him no decently paid work except that of a sweater; and he has become, in consequence, somewhat hoggish. But he has no suspicion of this himself, and honestly regards his commercial prosperity as the inevitable and socially wholesome triumph of the ability, industry, shrewdness, and experience in business of a man who in private is easygoing, affectionate, and humorously convivial to a fault. Corporeally he is podgy, with a snoutish nose in the centre of a flat square face, a dust colored beard with a patch of grey in the centre under his chin, and small watery blue eyes with a plaintively sentimental expression, which he transfers easily to his voice by his habit of pompously intoning his sentences.)*

BURGESS *(stopping on the threshold, and looking round)*: They told me Mr Morell was here.

PROSERPINE *(rising)*: I'll fetch him for you.

BURGESS *(staring disappointedly at her)*: Youre not the same young lady as hused to typewrite for him?

PROSERPINE: No.

BURGESS *(grumbling on his way to the hearth-rug)*: No: she was young-er. *(Miss Garnett stares at him; then goes out, slamming the door.)* Startin on your rounds, Mr Mill?

LEXY *(folding his memorandum and pocketing it)*: Yes: I must be off presently.

BURGESS *(momentously)*: Dont let me detain you, Mr. Mill. What I come about is p r i v a t e between me and Mr Morell.

LEXY *(huffily)*: I have no intention of intruding, I am sure, Mr Burgess. Good morning.

BURGESS *(patronizingly)*: Oh, good morning to you.

(Morell returns as Lexy is making for the door.)

MORELL *(to Lexy)*: Off to work?

LEXY: Yes, sir.

MORELL: Take my silk handkerchief and wrap your throat up. Theres a cold wind. Away with you.

(Lexy, more than consoled for Burgess's rudeness, brightens up and goes out.)

BURGESS: Spoilin your korates as usu'l, James. Good mornin. When I pay a man, an' 'is livin depens on me, I keep him in 'is place.

MORELL *(rather shortly)*: I always keep my curates in their places as my helpers and comrades. If you get as much work out of your clerks and warehousemen as I do out of my curates, you must be getting rich pretty fast. Will you take your old chair.

(He points with curt authority to the armchair beside the fireplace; then takes the spare chair from the table and sits down at an unfamiliar distance from his visitor.)

BURGESS *(without moving)*: Just the same as hever, James!

MORELL: When you last called—it was about three years ago, I think—you said the same thing a little more frankly. Your exact words then were "Just as big a fool as ever, James!"

BURGESS *(soothingly)*: Well, praps I did; but *(with conciliatory cheerfulness)* I meant no hoffence by it. A clorgyman is privileged to be a bit of a fool, you know: it's ony becomin in 'is profession that he should. Anyhow, I come here, not to rake up hold differences, but to let bygones be bygones. *(Suddenly becoming very solemn, and approaching Morell.)* James: three years ago, you done me a hil turn. You done me hout of a contrac: as when I gev you arsh words in my natral disappointment, you turned my daughrter again me. Well, Ive come to hact the part of a Kerischin. *(Offering his hand.)* I forgive you, James.

MORELL *(starting up)*: Confound your impudence!

BURGESS *(retreating, with almost lachrymose deprecation of this treatment)*: Is that becomin language for a clorgyman, James? And you so particlar, too!

MORELL *(hotly)*: No, sir: it is not becoming language for a clergyman. I used the wrong word. I should have said damn your impudence: thats what St Paul or any honest priest would have said to you. Do you think I have forgotten that tender of yours for the contract to supply clothing to the workhouse?

BURGESS *(in a paroxysm of public spirit)*: I hacted in the hinterest of the ratepayers, James. It was the lowest tender: you carnt deny that.

MORELL: Yes, the lowest, because you paid worse wages than any other employer—starvation wages—aye, worse than starvation

wages—to the women who made the clothing. Your wages
would have driven them to the streets to keep body and soul
together. *(Getting angrier and angrier.)* Those women were
my parishioners. I shamed the Guardians out of accepting your
tender: I shamed the ratepayers out of letting them do it: I
shamed everybody but you. *(Boiling over.)* How dare you, sir,
come here and offer to forgive me, and talk about your
daughter, and—

BURGESS: Heasy, James! heasy! heasy! Dont git hinto a fluster
about nothink. Ive howned I was wrong.

MORELL: Have you? I didn't hear you.

BURGESS: Of course I did. I hown it now. Come: I harsk your
pardon for the letter I wrote you. Is that enough?

MORELL *(snapping his fingers)*: Thats nothing. Have you raised
the wages?

BURGESS *(triumphantly)*: Yes.

MORELL: What!

BURGESS *(unctuously)*: Ive turned a moddle hemployer. I dont
hemploy no women now: theyre all sacked; and the work is
done by machinery. Not a man 'as less than sixpence a *h*our;
and the skilled ands gits the Trade Union rate. *(Proudly.)*
What ave you to say to me now?

MORELL *(overwhelmed)*: Is it possible! Well, theres more joy in
heaven over one sinner that repenteth! *(Going to Burgess with
an explosion of apologetic cordiality.)* My dear Burgess: how
splendid of you! I most heartily beg your pardon for my hard
thoughts. *(Grasping his hand.)* And now, dont you feel the
better for the change? Come! confess! youre happier. You look
happier.

BURGESS *(ruefully)*: Well, praps I do. I spose I must, since you
notice it. At all events, I git my contrax assepted by the
County Council. *(Savagely.)* They dussent ave nothink to do
with me unless I paid fair wages: curse em for a parcel o
meddlin fools!

MORELL *(dropping his hand, utterly discouraged)*: So that was
why you raised the wages! *(He sits down moodily.)*

BURGESS *(severely, in spreading, mounting tones)*: Woy hclsc
should I do it? What does it lead to but drink and huppishness

in workin men? *(He seats himself magisterially in the easy chair.)* It's hall very well for you, James: it gits you hinto the papers and makes a great man of you; but you never think of the arm you do, puttin money into the pockets of workin men that they dunno ow to spend, and takin it from people that might be makin a good huse on it.

MORELL *(with a heavy sigh, speaking with cold politeness)*: What is your business with me this morning? I shall not pretend to believe that you are here merely out of family sentiment.

BURGESS *(obstinately)*: Yes I ham: just family sentiment and nothink helse.

MORELL *(with weary calm)*: I dont believe you.

BURGESS *(rising threateningly)*: Dont say that to me again, James Mavor Morell.

MORELL *(unmoved)*: I'll say it just as often as may be necessary to convince you that it's true. I dont believe you.

BURGESS *(collapsing into an abyss of wounded feeling)*: Oh, well, if youre detormined to be hunfriendly, I spose I'd better go. *(He moves reluctantly towards the door. Morell makes no sign. He lingers.)* I didnt hexpect to find a hunforgivin spirit in you, James. *(Morell still not responding, he takes a few more reluctant steps doorwards. Then he comes back, whining.)* We huseter git on well enough, spite of our different hopinions. Woy are you so changed to me? I give you my word I come here in peeorr [pure] frenliness, not wishin to be hon bad terms with my hown daughrter's usban. Come, James: be a Kerischin, and shake ands. *(He puts his hand sentimentally on Morell's shoulder.)*

MORELL *(looking up at him thoughtfully)*: Look here, Burgess. Do you want to be as welcome here as you were before you lost that contract?

BURGESS: I do, James. I do—honest.

MORELL: Then why dont you behave as you did then?

BURGESS *(cautiously removing his hand)*: Ow d'y'mean?

MORELL: I'll tell you. You thought me a young fool then.

BURGESS *(coaxingly)*: No I didnt, James. I—

MORELL *(cutting him short)*: Yes, you did. And I thought you an old scoundrel.

BURGESS (*most vehemently deprecating this gross self-accusation on Morell's part*): No you didnt, James. Now you do yourself a hinjustice.

MORELL: Yes I did. Well, that did not prevent our getting on very well together. God made you what I call a scoundrel as He made me what you call a fool. (*The effect of this observation on Burgess is to remove the keystone of his moral arch. He becomes bodily weak, and, with his eyes fixed on Morell in a helpless stare, puts out his hand apprehensively to balance himself, as if the floor had suddenly sloped under him. Morell proceeds, in the same tone of quiet conviction.*) It was not for me to quarrel with His handiwork in the one case more than in the other. So long as you come here honestly as a self-respecting, thorough, convinced, scoundrel, justifying your scoundrelism and proud of it, you are welcome. But (*And now Morell's tone becomes formidable; and he rises and strikes the back of the chair for a greater emphasis.*) I wont have you here snivelling about being a model employer and a converted man when youre only an apostate with your coat turned for the sake of a County Council contract. (*He nods at him to enforce the point; then goes to the hearth-rug, where he takes up a comfortably commanding position with his back to the fire, and continues.*) No: I like a man to be true to himself, even in wickedness. Come now: either take your hat and go; or else sit down and give me a good scoundrelly reason for wanting to be friends with me. (*Burgess, whose emotions have subsided sufficiently to be expressed by a dazed grin, is relieved by this concrete proposition. He ponders it for a moment, and then, slowly and very modestly sits down in the chair Morell has just left.*) That's right. Now out with it.

BURGESS (*chuckling in spite of himself*): Well, you orr a queer bird, James, and no mistake. But (*almost enthusiastically*) one carnt elp likin you: besides, as I said afore, of course one dont take hall a clorgyman says seriously, or the world couldnt go on. Could it now? (*He composes himself for a graver discourse, and, turning his eyes on Morell, proceeds with dull seriousness.*) Well, I dont mind tellin you, since it's your wish we should be free with one another, that I did think you a bit of a fool once; but I'm beginnin to think that praps I was be'ind the times a bit.

MORELL (*exultant*): Aha! Youre finding that out at last, are you?

BURGESS (*portentously*): Yes: times 'as changed mor'n I could a believed. Five yorr [year] ago, no sensible man would a thought o takin hup with your hidears. I hused to wonder you was let preach at all. Why, I know a clorgyman what 'as bin kep hout of his job for yorrs by the Bishop o London, although the pore feller's not a bit more religious than you are. But today, if hennyone was to horffer to bet me a thousan poun that youll hend by being a bishop yourself, I dussen take the bet. *(Very impressively.)* You and your crew are gittin hinfluential: I can see that. Theyll ave to give you somethink someday, if it's honly to stop your mouth. You ad the right instinc arter all, James: the line you took is the payin line in the long run for a man o your sort.

MORELL *(offering his hand with thorough decision)*: Shake hands, Burgess. Now youre talking honestly. I dont think they'll make me a bishop; but if they do, I'll introduce you to the biggest jobbers I can get to come to my dinner parties.

BURGESS *(who has risen with a sheepish grin and accepted the hand of friendship)*: You will ave your joke, James. Our quarrel's made up now, ain it?

A WOMAN'S VOICE: Say yes, James.

(Startled, they turn quickly and find that Candida has just come in, and is looking at them with an amused maternal indulgence which is her characteristic expression. She is a woman of 33, well built, well nourished, likely, one guesses, to become matronly later on, but now quite at her best, with the double charm of youth and motherhood. Her ways are those of a woman who has found that she can always manage people by engaging their affection, and who does so frankly and instinctively without the smallest scruple. So far, she is like any other pretty woman who is just clever enough to make the most of her sexual attractions for trivially selfish ends; but Candida's serene brow, courageous eyes, and well set mouth and chin signify largeness of mind and dignity of character to ennoble her cunning in the affections. A wise-hearted observer, looking at her, would at once guess that whoever had placed the Virgin of the Assumption over her hearth did so because he fancied some spiritual resemblance between them, and yet would not suspect either her husband or herself of any such idea, or indeed of any concern with the art of Titian.

(Just now she is in bonnet and mantle, carrying a strapped rug with her umbrella stuck through it, a handbag, and a supply of illustrated papers.)

MORELL *(shocked at his remissness)*: Candida! Why— *(He looks at his watch, and is horrified to find it so late.)* My darling! *(Hurrying to her and seizing the rug strap, pouring forth his remorseful regrets all the time.)* I intended to meet you at the train. I let the time slip. *(Flinging the rug on the sofa.)* I was so engrossed by—*(returning to her)*—I forgot—oh! *(He embraces her with penitent emotion.)*

BURGESS *(a little shamefaced and doubtful of his reception)*: How orr you, Candy? *(She, still in Morell's arms, offers him her cheek, which he kisses.)* James and me is come to a nunnerstannin. A honorable unnerstannin. Ain we, James?

MORELL *(impteuously)*: Oh bother your understanding! youve kept me late for Candida. *(With compassionate fervor.)* My poor love: how did you manage about the luggage? How

CANDIDA *(stopping him and disengaging herself)*: There! there! there! I wasnt alone. Eugene has been down with us; and we travelled together.

MORELL *(pleased)*: Eugene!

CANDIDA: Yes: he's struggling with my luggage, poor boy. Go out, dear, at once; or he'll pay for the cab; and I dont want that. *(Morell hurries out. Candida puts down her handbag; then takes off her mantle and bonnet and puts them on the sofa with the rug, chatting meanwhile.)* Well, papa: how are you getting on at home?

BURGESS: The ouse aint worth livin in since you left it, Candy. I wish youd come round and give the gurl a talkin to. Who's this Eugene thats come with you?

CANDIDA: Oh, Eugene's one of James's discoveries. He found him sleeping on the Embankment last June. Havnt you noticed our new picture? *(Pointing to the Virgin.)* He gave us that.

BURGESS *(incredulously)*: Garn! D'you mean to tell me—your hown father!—that cab touts or such like, orf the Embankment, buys pictures like that? *(Severely.)* Dont deceive me, Candy: it's a 'Igh Church picture; and James chose it hisself.

CANDIDA: Guess again. Eugene isnt a cab tout.

BURGESS: Then what is he? *(Sarcastically.)* A nobleman, I spose.

CANDIDA *(nodding delightedly)*: Yes. His uncle's a peer! A real live earl.

BURGESS (*not daring to believe such good news*): No!

CANDIDA: Yes. He had a seven day bill for £55 in his pocket when James found him on the Embankment. He thought he couldnt get any money for it until the seven days were up; and he was too shy to ask for credit. Oh, he's a dear boy! We are very fond of him.

BURGESS (*pretending to belittle the aristocracy, but with his eyes gleaming*): Hm! I thort you wouldnt git a hearl's nevvy visitin in Victawriar Pawrk unless he were a bit of a flat. (*Looking again at the picture.*) Of course I dont old with that picture, Candy; but still it's a 'igh class fust rate work of ort: I can see that. Be sure you hintrodooce me to im, Candy. (*He looks at his watch anxiously.*) I can ony stay about two minutes.

(*Morell comes back with Eugene, whom Burgess contemplates moist-eyed with enthusiasm. He is a strange, shy youth of eighteen, slight, effeminate, with a delicate childish voice, and a hunted tormented expression and shrinking manner that shew the painful sensitiveness of very swift and acute apprehensiveness in youth, before the character has grown to its full strength. Miserably irresolute, he does not know where to stand or what to do. He is afraid of Burgess, and would run away into solitude if he dared; but the very intensity with which he feels a perfectly commonplace position comes from excessive nervous force; and his nostrils, mouth, and eyes betray a fiercely petulant wilfulness, as to the bent of which his brow, already lined with pity, is reassuring. He is so uncommon as to be almost unearthly; and to prosaic people there is something noxious in this unearthliness, just as to poetic people there is something angelic in it. His dress is anarchic. He wears an old blue serge jacket, unbuttoned, over a woollen lawn tennis shirt, with a silk handkerchief for a cravat, trousers matching the jacket, and brown canvas shoes. In these garments he has apparently lain in the heather and waded through the waters; and there is no evidence of his having ever brushed them.*)

(*As he catches sight of a stranger on entering, he stops, and edges along the wall on the opposite side of the room.*)

MORELL (*as he enters*): Come along: you can spare us quarter of an hour at all events. This is my father-in-law. Mr Burgess—Mr Marchbanks.

MARCHBANKS (*nervously backing against the bookcase*): Glad to meet you, sir.

BURGESS (*crossing to him with great heartiness, whilst Morell joins Candida at the fire*): Glad to meet y o u, I'm shore, Mr Morchbanks. (*Forcing him to shake hands.*) Ow do you find yoreself this weather? Ope you aint lettin James put no foolish ideas into your ed?

MARCHBANKS: Foolish ideas? Oh, you mean Socialism? No.

BURGESS: Thats right. (*Again looking at his watch.*) Well, I must go now: theres no elp for it. Yore not comin my way, orr you, Mr Morchbanks?

MARCHBANKS: Which way is that?

BURGESS: Victawriar Pawrk Station. Theres a city train at 12.25.

MORELL: Nonsense. Eugene will stay to lunch with us, I expect.

MARCHBANKS (*anxiously excusing himself*): No—I—I—

BURGESS: Well, well, I shornt press you: I bet youd rather lunch with Candy. Some night, I ope, youll come and dine with me at my club, the Freeman Founders in Nortn Folgit. Come: say you will!

MARCHBANKS: Thank you, Mr Burgess. Where is Norton Folgate? Down in Surrey, isnt it?

(*Burgess, inexpressibly tickled, begins to splutter with laughter.*)

CANDIDA (*coming to the rescue*): Youll lose your train, papa, if you dont go at once. Come back in the afternoon and tell Mr Marchbanks where to find the club.

BURGESS (*roaring with glee*): Down in Surrey! Har, har! thats not a bad one. Well, I never met a man as didnt know Nortn Folgit afore. (*Abashed at his own noisiness.*) Goodbye, Mr Morchbanks: I know yore too ighbred to take my pleasantry in bad part. (*He again offers his hand.*)

MARCHBANKS (*taking it with a nervous jerk*): Not at all.

BURGESS: Bye, bye, Candy. I'll look in again later on. So long, James.

MORELL: Must you go?

BURGESS: Dont stir. (*He goes out with unabated heartiness.*)

MORELL: Oh, I'll see you off. (*He follows him.*)

(Eugene stares after them apprehensively, holding his breath until Burgess disappears.)

CANDIDA *(laughing)*: Well, Eugene? *(He turns with a start, and comes eagerly towards her, but stops irresolutely as he meets her amused look.)* What do you think of my father?

MARCHBANKS: I—I hardly know him yet. He seems to be a very nice old gentleman.

CANDIDA *(with gentle irony)*: And youll go to the Freeman Founders to dine with him, wont you?

MARCHBANKS *(miserably, taking it quite seriously)*: Yes, if it will please you.

CANDIDA *(touched)*: Do you know, you are a very nice boy, Eugene, with all your queerness. If you had laughed at my father I shouldn't have minded; but I like you ever so much better for being nice to him.

MARCHBANKS: Ought I to have laughed? I noticed that he said something funny; but I am so ill at ease with strangers; and I never can see a joke. I'm very sorry. *(He sits down on the sofa, his elbows on his knees and his temples between his fists with an expression of hopeless suffering.)*

CANDIDA *(bustling him goodnaturedly)*: Oh come! You great baby, you! You are worse than usual this morning. Why were you so melancholy as we came along in the cab?

MARCHBANKS: Oh, that was nothing. I was wondering how much I ought to give the cabman. I know it's utterly silly; but you dont know how dreadful such things are to me—how I shrink from having to deal with strange people. *(Quickly and reassuringly.)* But it's all right. He beamed all over and touched his hat when Morell gave him two shillings. I was on the point of offering him ten.

(Morell comes back with a few letters and newspapers which have come by the midday post.)

CANDIDA: Oh, James dear, he was going to give the cabman ten shillings! ten shillings for a three minutes drive! Oh dear!

MORELL *(at the table, glancing through the letters)*: Never mind her, Marchbanks. The overpaying instinct is a generous one: better than the underpaying instinct, and not so common.

MARCHBANKS *(relapsing into dejection)*: No: cowardice, incompetence. Mrs Morell's quite right.

CANDIDA: Of course she is. *(She takes up her handbag.)* And now I must leave you to James for the present. I suppose you are too much of a poet to know the state a woman finds her house in when she's been away for three weeks. Give me my rug. *(Eugene takes the strapped rug from the couch, and gives it to her. She takes it in her left hand, having the bag in her right.)* Now hang my cloak across my arm. *(He obeys.)* Now my hat. *(He puts it into the hand which has the bag.)* Now open the door for me. *(He hurries before her and opens the door.)* Thanks. *(She goes out; and Marchbanks shuts the door.)*

MORELL *(still busy at the table)*: Youll stay to lunch, Marchbanks, of course.

MARCHBANKS *(scared)*: I mustnt. *(He glances quickly at Morell, but at once avoids his frank look, and adds, with obvious disingenuousness.)* I mean I cant.

MORELL: You mean you wont.

MARCHBANKS *(earnestly)*: No: I should like to, indeed. Thank you very much. But—but—

MORELL: But—but—but—but—Bosh! If youd like to stay, stay. If youre shy, go and take a turn in the park and write poetry until half past one; and then come in and have a good feed.

MARCHBANKS: Thank you, I should like that very much. But I really musnt. The truth is, Mrs Morell told me not to. She said she didnt think youd ask me to stay to lunch, but that I was to remember, if you did, that you didnt really want me to. *(Plaintively.)* She said I'd understand; but I dont. Please dont tell her I told you.

MORELL *(drolly)*: Oh, is that all? Wont my suggestion that you should take a turn in the park meet the difficulty?

MARCHBANKS: How?

MORELL *(exploding good-humoredly)*: Why, you duffer— *(But this boisterousness jars himself as well as Eugene. He checks himself.)* No: I wont put it in that way. *(He comes to Eugene with affectionate seriousness.)* My dear lad: in a happy marriage like ours, there is something very sacred in the return of the wife to her home. (*Marchbanks looks quickly at him, half anticipating his meaning.*) An old friend or a truly noble and sympathetic soul is not in the way on such occasions; but a chance visitor is. (*The hunted horrorstricken expression comes out with sudden vividness in Eugene's face as he understands. Morell, occupied with his own thoughts, goes on without noticing this.*) Candida thought I would rather not have you here; but she was wrong. I'm very fond of you, my boy; and I should like you to see for yourself what a happy thing it is to be married as I am.

MARCHBANKS: Happy! Your marriage! You think that! You believe that!

MORELL (*buoyantly*): I know it, my lad. Larochefoucauld said that there are convenient marriages but no delightful ones. You dont know the comfort of seeing through and through a thundering liar and rotten cynic like that fellow. Ha! ha! Now, off with you to the park, and write your poem. Half past one, sharp, mind: we never wait for anybody.

MARCHBANKS (*wildly*): No: stop: you shant. I'll force it into the light.

MORELL (*puzzled*): Eh? Force what?

MARCHBANKS: I must speak to you. There is something that must be settled between us.

MORELL (*with a whimsical glance at his watch*): Now?

MARCHBANKS (*passionately*): Now. Before you leave this room. (*He retreats a few steps, and stands as if to bar Morell's way to the door.*)

MORELL (*without moving, and gravely, perceiving now that there is something serious the matter*): I'm not going to leave it, my dear boy: I thought you were. (*Eugene, baffled by his firm tone, turns his back on him, writhing with anger. Morell goes to him and puts his hand on his shoulder strongly and kindly, disregarding his attempt to shake it off.*) Come: sit down quietly; and tell me what it is. And remember: we are friends, and need not fear that either of us will be anything but patient and kind to the other, whatever we may have to say.

MARCHBANKS (*twisting himself round on him*): Oh, I am not forgetting myself: I am only (*covering his face desperately with his hands*) full of horror. (*Then, dropping his hands, and thrusting his face forward fiercely at Morell, he goes on threateningly.)* You shall see whether this is a time for patience and kindness. *(Morell, firm as a rock, looks indulgently at him.)* Dont look at me in that self-complacent way. You think yourself stronger than I am; but I shall stagger you if you have a heart in your breast.

MORELL *(powerfully confident)*: Stagger me, my boy. Out with it.

MARCHBANKS: First—

MORELL: First?

MARCHBANKS: I love your wife.

(Morell recoils, and, after staring at him for a moment in utter amazement, bursts into uncontrollable laughter. Eugene is taken aback, but not disconcerted; and he soon becomes indignant and contemptuous.)

MORELL *(sitting down to have his laugh out)*: Why, my dear child, of course you do. Everybody loves her: they can't help it. I like it. But *(looking up whimsically at him)* I say, Eugene: do you think yours is a case to be talked about? Youre under twenty: she's over thirty. Doesnt it look rather too like a case of calf love?

MARCHBANKS *(vehemently)*: You dare say that of her! You think that way of the love she inspires! It is an insult to her!

MORELL *(rising quickly, in an altered tone)*: To her! Eugene: take care. I have been patient. I hope to remain patient. But there are some things I wont allow. Dont force me to shew you the indulgence I should shew to a child. Be a man.

MARCHBANKS *(with a gesture as if sweeping something behind him)*: Oh, let us put aside all that cant. It horrifies me when I think of the doses of it she has had to endure in all the weary years during which you have selfishly and blindly sacrificed her to minister to your self-sufficiency—you *(turning on him)* who have not one thought—one sense—in common with her.

MORELL *(philosophically)*: She seems to bear it pretty well. *(Looking him straight in the face.)* Eugene, my boy: you are making a fool of yourself—a very great fool of yourself. Theres a piece of wholesome plain speaking for you.

MARCHBANKS: Oh, do you think I dont know all that? Do you think that the things people make fools of themselves about are any less real and true than the things they behave sensibly about? (*Morell's gaze wavers for the first time. He instinctively averts his face and stands listening, startled and thoughtful.*) They are more true: they are the only things that are true. You are very calm and sensible and moderate with me because you can see that I am a fool about your wife; just as no doubt that old man who was here just now is very wise over your socialism, because he sees that you are a fool about it. (*Morell's perplexity deepens markedly. Eugene follows up his advantage, plying him fiercely with questions.*) Does that prove you wrong? Does your complacent superiority to me prove that *I* am wrong?

MORELL (*turning on Eugene, who stands his ground*): Marchbanks: some devil is putting these words into your mouth. It is easy—terribly easy—to shake a man's faith in himself. To take advantage of that to break a man's spirit is devil's work. Take care of what you are doing. Take care.

MARCHBANKS (*ruthlessly*): I know. I'm doing it on purpose. I told you I should stagger you.

(*They confront one another threateningly for a moment. Then Morell recovers his dignity.*)

MORELL (*with noble tenderness*): Eugene: listen to me. Some day, I hope and trust, you will be a happy man like me. (*Eugene chafes intolerantly, repudiating the worth of his happiness. Morell, deeply insulted, controls himself with fine forbearance, and continues steadily with great artistic beauty of delivery.*) You will be married; and you will be working with all your might and valor to make every spot on earth as happy as your own home. You will be one of the makers of the Kingdom of Heaven on earth; and—who knows?—you may be a master builder where I am only a humble journeyman; for dont think, my boy, that I cannot see in you, young as you are, promise of higher powers than I can ever pretend to. I well know that it is in the poet that the holy spirit of man—the god within him—is most godlike. It should make you tremble to think of that—to think that the heavy burthen and great gift of a poet may be laid upon you.

MARCHBANKS (*unimpressed and remorseless, his boyish crudity of assertion telling sharply against Morell's oratory*): It does not make me tremble. It is the want of it in others that makes me tremble.

MORELL (*redoubling his force of style under the stimulus of his genuine feeling and Eugene's obduracy*): Then help to kindle it in them—in m e—not to extinguish it. In the future, when you are as happy as I am, I will be your true brother in the faith. I will help you to believe that God has given us a world that nothing but our own folly keeps from being a paradise. I will help you to believe that every stroke of your work is sowing happiness for the great harvest that all—even the humblest—shall one day reap. And last, but trust me, not least, I will help you to believe that your wife loves you and is happy in her home. We need such help, Marchbanks: we need it greatly and always. There are so many things to make us doubt, if once we let our understanding be troubled. Even at home, we sit as if in camp, encompassed by a hostile army of doubts. Will you play the traitor and let them in on me?

MARCHBANKS *(looking round wildly)*: Is it like this for her here always? A woman, with a great soul, craving for reality, truth, freedom; and being fed on metaphors, sermons, stale perorations, mere rhetoric. Do you think a woman's soul can live on your talent for preaching?

MORELL *(stung)*: Marchbanks: you make it hard for me to control myself. My talent is like yours insofar as it has any real worth at all. It is the gift of finding words for divine truth.

MARCHBANKS *(impetuously)*: It's the gift of the gab, nothing more and nothing less. What has your knack of fine talking to do with the truth, any more than playing the organ has? Ive never been in your church; but Ive been to your political meetings; and Ive seen you do whats called rousing the meeting to enthusiasm: that is, you excited them until they behaved exactly as if they were drunk. And their wives looked on and saw what fools they were. Oh, it's an old story: youll find it in the Bible. I imagine King David, in his fits of enthusiasm, was very like you. *(Stabbing him with the words.)* "But his wife despised him in her heart."

MORELL *(wrathfully)*: Leave my house. Do you hear? *(He advances on him threateningly.)*

MARCHBANKS *(shrinking back against the couch)*: Let me alone. Dont touch me. *(Morell grasps him powerfully by the lappell of his coat; he cowers down on the sofa and screams passionately.)* Stop, Morell: if you strike me, I'll kill myself: I wont bear it. *(Almost in hysterics.)* Let me go. Take your hand away.

MORELL *(with slow emphatic scorn)*: You little snivelling, cowardly whelp. *(He releases him.)* Go, before you frighten your-self into a fit.

MARCHBANKS *(on the sofa, gasping, but relieved by the withdrawal of Morell's hand)*: I'm not afraid of you; it's you who are afraid of me.

MORELL *(quietly, as he stands over him)*: It looks like it, doesnt it?

MARCHBANKS *(with petulant vehemence)*: Yes, it does. *(Morell turns away contemptuously. Eugene scrambles to his feet and follows him.)* You think because I shrink from being brutally handled—because *(with tears in his voice)* I can do nothing but cry with rage when I am met with violence—because I cant lift a heavy trunk down from the top of a cab like you—because I can't fight you for your wife as a drunken navvy would: all that makes you think I'm afraid of you. But youre wrong. If I havnt got what you call British pluck, I havnt British cowardice either: I'm not afraid of a clergyman's ideas. I'll fight your ideas. I'll rescue her from your slavery to them. I'll pit my own ideas against them. You are driving me out of the house because you darent let her choose between your ideas and mine. You are afraid to let me see her again. *(Morell, angered, turns suddenly on him. He flies to the door in involuntary dread.)* Let me alone, I say. I'm going.

MORELL *(with cold scorn)*: Wait a moment: I am not going to touch you: dont be afraid. When my wife comes back she will want to know why you have gone. And when she finds that you are never going to cross our threshold again, she will want to have that explained too. Now I dont wish to distress her by telling her that you have behaved like a blackguard.

MARCHBANKS *(coming back with renewed vehemence)*: You shall. You must. If you give any explanation but the true one, you are a liar and a coward. Tell her what I said; and how you were strong and manly, and shook me as a terrier shakes a rat; and how I shrank and was terrified; and how you called me a snivelling little whelp and put me out of the house. If you dont tell her, I will: I'll write it to her.

MORELL *(puzzled)*: Why do you want her to know this?

MARCHBANKS *(with lyric rapture)*: Because she will understand me, and know that I understand her. If you keep back one word of it from her—if you are not ready to lay the truth at her feet as I am—then you will know to the end of your days that she really belongs to me and not to you. Goodbye. *(Going.)*

MORELL *(terribly disquieted)*: Stop: I will not tell her.

MARCHBANKS *(turning near the door)*: Either the truth or a lie you m u s t tell her, if I go.

MORELL *(temporizing)*: Marchbanks: it is sometimes justifiable—

MARCHBANKS *(cutting him short)*: I know: to lie. It will be useless. Goodbye, Mr Clergyman.

(As he turns to the door, it opens and Candida enters in her housekeeping dress.)

CANDIDA: Are you going, Eugene? *(Looking more observantly at him.)* Well, dear me, just look at you, going out into the street in that state! You a r e a poet, certainly. Look at him, James! *(She takes him by the coat, and brings him forward, shewing him to Morell.)* Look at his collar! look at his tie! look at his hair! One would think somebody had been throttling you. *(Eugene instinctively tries to look at Morell: but she pulls him back.)* Here! Stand still. *(She buttons his collar; ties his neckerchief in a bow; and arranges his hair.)* There! Now you look so nice that I think youd better stay to lunch after all, though I told you you mustnt. It will be ready in half an hour. *(She puts a final touch to the bow. He kisses her hand.)* Dont be silly.

MARCHBANKS: I want to stay, of course; unless the reverend gentleman your husband has anything to advance to the contrary.

CANDIDA: Shall he stay, James, if he promises to be a good boy and help me to lay the table?

MORELL *(shortly)*: Oh yes, certainly: he had better. *(He goes to the table and pretends to busy himself with his papers there.)*

MARCHBANKS *(offering his arm to Candida)*: Come and lay the table. *(She takes it. They go to the door together. As they pass out he adds)* I am the happiest of mortals.

MORELL: So was I—an hour ago.

ACT II

(The same day later in the afternoon. The same room. The chair for visitors has been replaced at the table. Marchbanks, alone and idle, is trying to find out how the typewriter works. Hearing someone at the door, he steals guiltily away to the window and pretends to be absorbed in the view. Miss Garnett, carrying the notebook in which she takes down Morell's letters in shorthand from his dictation, sits down at the typewriter and sets to work transcribing them, much too busy to notice Eugene. When she begins the second line she stops and stares at the machine. Something wrong evidently.)

PROSERPINE: Bother! Youve been meddling with my typewriter, Mr Marchbanks; and theres not the least use in your trying to look as if you hadnt.

MARCHBANKS *(timidly)*: I'm very sorry, Miss Garnett. I only tried to make it write. *(Plaintively.)* But it wouldnt.

PROSERPINE: Well, youve altered the spacing.

MARCHBANKS *(earnestly)*: I assure you I didn't. I didnt indeed. I only turned a little wheel. It gave a sort of click.

PROSERPINE: Oh, now I understand. *(She restores the spacing, talking volubly all the time.)* I suppose you thought it was a sort of barrel-organ. Nothing to do but turn the handle, and it would write a beautiful love letter for you straight off, eh?

MARCHBANKS *(seriously)*: I suppose a machine could be made to write love letters. Theyre all the same, arnt they?

PROSERPINE *(somewhat indignantly: any such discussion, except by way of pleasantry, being outside her code of manners)*: How do I know? Why do you ask me?

MARCHBANKS: I beg your pardon. I thought clever people—people who can do business and write letters and that sort of thing—always had to have love affairs to keep them from going mad.

515

PROSERPINE (*rising, outraged*): Mr Marchbanks! *(She looks severely at him, and marches majestically to the bookcase.)*

MARCHBANKS (*approaching her humbly*): I hope I havnt offended you. Perhaps I shouldnt have alluded to your love affairs.

PROSERPINE (*plucking a blue book from the shelf and turning sharply on him*): I havnt any love affairs. How dare you say such a thing? The idea! *(She tucks the book under her arm, and is flouncing back to her machine when he addresses her with awakened interest and sympathy.)*

MARCHBANKS: Really! Oh, then you are shy, like me.

PROSERPINE: Certainly I am not shy. What do you mean?

MARCHBANKS (*secretly*): You must be: that is the reason there are so few love affairs in the world. We all go about longing for love: it is the first need of our natures, the first prayer of our hearts; but we dare not utter our longing: we are too shy. *(Very earnestly.)* Oh, Miss Garnett, what would you not give to be without fear, without shame—

PROSERPINE (*scandalized*): Well, upon my word!

MARCHBANKS (*with petulant impatience*): Ah, dont say those stupid things to me: they dont deceive me: what use are they? Why are you afraid to be your real self with me? I am just like you.

PROSERPINE: Like me! Pray are you flattering me or flattering yourself? I dont feel quite sure which. *(She again tries to get back to her work.)*

MARCHBANKS (*stopping her mysteriously*): Hush! I go about in search of love; and I find it in unmeasured stores in the bosoms of others. But when I try to ask for it, this horrible shyness strangles me; and I stand dumb, or worse than dumb, saying meaningless things: foolish lies. And I see the affection I am longing for given to dogs and cats and pet birds, because they come and ask for it. *(Almost whispering.)* It must be asked for: it is like a ghost: it cannot speak unless it is first spoken to. *(At his usual pitch, but with deep melancholy.)* All the love in the world is longing to speak; only it dare not, because it is shy! shy! shy! That is the world's tragedy. *(With a deep sigh he sits in the visitors' chair and buries his face in his hands.)*

PROSERPINE (*amazed, but keeping her wits about her: her point of honor in encounters with strange young men)*: Wicked people get over that shyness occasionally, dont they?

MARCHBANKS *(scrambling up almost fiercely)*: Wicked people means people who have no love: therefore they have no shame. They have the power to ask love because they dont need it: they have the power to offer it because they have none to give. *(He collapses into his seat, and adds, mournfully)* But we, who have love, and long to mingle it with the love of others: we cannot utter a word. *(Timidly.)* You find that, dont you?

PROSERPINE: Look here: if you dont stop talking like this, I'll leave the room, Mr Marchbanks: I really will. It's not proper.

(She resumes her seat at the typewriter, opening the blue book and preparing to copy a passage from it.)

MARCHBANKS *(hopelessly)*: Nothing thats worth saying is proper. *(He rises, and wanders about the room in his lost way.)* I cant understand you, Miss Garnett. What am I to talk about?

PROSERPINE *(snubbing him)*: Talk about indifferent things. Talk about the weather.

MARCHBANKS: Would you talk about indifferent things if a child were by, crying bitterly with hunger?

PROSERPINE: I suppose not.

MARCHBANKS: Well: *I* cant talk about indifferent things with my heart crying out bitterly in i t s hunger.

PROSERPINE: Then hold your tongue.

MARCHBANKS: Yes: that is what it always comes to. We hold our tongues. Does that stop the cry of your heart? for it does cry: doesnt it? It must, if you have a heart.

PROSERPINE *(suddenly rising with her hand pressed on her heart)*: Oh, it's no use trying to work while you talk like that. *(She leaves her little table and sits on the sofa. Her feelings are keenly stirred.)* It's no business of yours whether my heart cries or not; but I have a mind to tell you, for all that.

MARCHBANKS: You neednt. I know already that it must.

PROSERPINE: But mind! if you ever say I said so, I'll deny it.

MARCHBANKS *(compassionately)*: Yes, I know. And so you havnt the courage to tell him?

PROSERPINE (*bouncing up*): H i m! Who?

MARCHBANKS: Whoever he is. The man you love. It might be anybody. The curate, Mr Mill, perhaps.

PROSERPINE (*with disdain*): Mr Mill!!! A fine man to break my heart about, indeed! I'd rather have y o u than Mr Mill.

MARCHBANKS (*recoiling*): No, really: I'm very sorry; but you mustnt think of that. I—

PROSERPINE (*testily, going to the fireplace and standing at it with her back to him*): Oh, dont be frightened: it's not you. It's not any one particular person.

MARCHBANKS: I know. You feel that you could love anybody that offered—

PROSERPINE (*turning, exasperated*): Anybody that offered! No, I do not. What do you take me for?

MARCHBANKS (*discouraged*): No use. You wont make me r e a l answers: only those things that everybody says. (*He strays to the sofa and sits down disconsolately.*)

PROSERPINE (*nettled at what she takes to be a disparagement of her manners by an aristocrat*): Oh well, if you want original conversation, youd better go and talk to yourself.

MARCHBANKS: That is what all poets do: they talk to themselves out loud; and the world overhears them. But it's horribly lonely not to hear someone else talk sometimes.

PROSERPINE: Wait until Mr Morell comes. H e ' l l talk to you. (*Marchbanks shudders.*) Oh, you neednt make wry faces over him: he can talk better than you. (*With temper.*) He'd talk your little head off. (*She is going back angrily to her place, when he, suddenly enlightened, springs up and stops her.*)

MARCHBANKS: Ah! I understand now.

PROSERPINE (*reddening*): What do you understand?

MARCHBANKS: Your secret. Tell me: is it really and truly possible for a woman to love him?

PROSERPINE (*as if this were beyond all bounds*): Well!!

MARCHBANKS (*passionately*): No: answer me. I want to know: I must know. *I* cant understand it. I can see nothing in him but words, pious resolutions, what people call goodness. You cant love that.

PROSERPINE (*attempting to snub him by an air of cool propriety*): I simply dont know what youre talking about. I dont understand you.

MARCHBANKS (*vehemently*): You do. You lie.

PROSERPINE: Oh!

MARCHBANKS: You do understand; and you know. (*Determined to have an answer.*) It is possible for a woman to love him?

PROSERPINE (*looking him straight in the face*): Yes. (*He covers his face with his hands.*) Whatever is the matter with you! (*He takes down his hands. Frightened at the tragic mask presented to her, she hurries past him at the utmost possible distance, keeping her eyes on his face until he turns from her and goes to the child's chair beside the hearth, where he sits in the deepest dejection. As she approaches the door, it opens and Burgess enters. Seeing him, she ejaculates.*) Praise heaven! here's somebody. (*and feels safe enough to resume her place at her table. She puts a fresh sheet of paper into the typewriter as Burgess crosses to Eugene.*)

BURGESS (*bent on taking care of the distinguished visitor*): Well: so this is the way they leave you to yoreself, Mr Morchbanks. Ive come to keep you company. (*Marchbanks looks up at him in consternation, which is quite lost on him.*) James is receivin a deppitation in the dinin room; and Candy is hupstairs heducating of a young stitcher gurl she's hinterested in. (*Condolingly.*) You must find it lonesome here with no one but the typist to talk to. (*He pulls round the easy chair, and sits down.*)

PROSERPINE (*highly incensed*): He'll be all right now that he has the advantage of your polished conversation: thats one comfort, anyhow. (*She begins to typewrite with clattering asperity.*)

BURGESS (*amazed at her audacity*): Hi was not addressin myself to you, young woman, that I'm awerr of.

PROSERPINE: Did you ever see worse manners, Mr Marchbanks?

BURGESS (*with pompous severity*): Mr Morchbanks is a gentleman, and knows his place, which is more than some people do.

PROSERPINE (*fretfully*): It's well you and I are not ladies and gentlemen: I'd talk to you pretty straight if Mr Marchbanks wasnt here. *(She pulls the letter out of the machine so crossly that it tears.)* There! now I've spoiled this letter! have to be done all over again! Oh, I cant contain myself: silly old fathead!

BURGESS *(rising, breathless with indignation)*: Ho! I'm a silly ole fat'ead, am I? Ho, indeed! *(Gasping.)* Hall right, my gurl! Hall right. You just wait till I tell that to your hemployer. Youll see. I'll teach you: see if I dont.

PROSERPINE *(conscious of having gone too far)*: I—

BURGESS *(cutting her short)*: No: youve done it now. No huse a-talking to me. I'll let you know who I am. *(Proserpine shifts her paper carriage with a defiant bang, and disdainfully goes on with her work.)* Dont you take no notice of her, Mr Morchbanks. She's beneath it. *(He loftily sits down again.)*

MARCHBANKS *(miserably nervous and disconcerted)*: Hadnt we better change the subject? I—I don't think Miss Garnett meant anything.

PROSERPINE *(with intense conviction)*: Oh, didnt I though, j u s t!

BURGESS: I wouldnt demean myself to take notice on her.

(An electric bell rings twice.)

PROSERPINE *(gathering up her note-book and papers)*: Thats for me. *(She hurries out.)*

BURGESS *(calling after her)*: Oh, we can spare you. *(Somewhat relieved by the triumph of having the last word, and yet half inclined to try to improve on it, he looks after her for a moment; then subsides to his seat by Eugene, and addresses him very confidentially.)* Now we're alone, Mr Morchbanks, let me give you a friendly int that I wouldnt give to heverybody. Ow long ave you known my son-in-law James ere?

MARCHBANKS: I dont know. I never can remember dates. A few months, perhaps.

BURGESS: Ever notice hennythink queer about him?

MARCHBANKS: I dont think so.

BURGESS *(impressively)*: No more you wouldnt. Thats the danger on it. Well, he's mad.

MARCHBANKS: Mad!

BURGESS: Mad as a Morch 'are. You take notice on him and youll see.

MARCHBANKS *(uneasily)*: But surely that is only because his opinions—

BURGESS *(touching him on the knee with his forefinger, and pressing it to hold his attention)*: Thats the same what I hused to think, Mr Morchbanks. Hi thought long enough that it was ony his opinions; though, mind you, hopinions becomes vurry serious things when people takes to hactin on em as e does. But thats not what I go on. *(He looks round to make sure that they are alone, and bends over to Eugene's ear.)* What do you think he sez to me this mornin in this very room?

MARCHBANKS: What?

BURGESS: He sez to me—this is as sure as we're settin here now—he sez "I'm a fool," he sez; "and yore a scounderl." Me a scounderl, mind you! And then shook ands with me on it, as if it was to my credit! Do you mean to tell me as that man's sane?

MORELL *(outside, calling to Proserpine as he opens the door)*: Get all their names and addresses, Miss Garnett.

PROSERPINE *(in the distance)*: Yes, Mr Morell.

(Morell comes in, with the deputation's documents in his hands.)

BURGESS *(aside to Marchbanks)*: Yorr he is. Just you keep your heye on im and see. *(Rising momentously)*: I'm sorry, James, to ave to make a complaint to you. I dont want to do it; but I feel I oughter, as a matter o right and dooty.

MORELL: Whats the matter?

BURGESS: Mr Morchbanks will bear me hout: he was a witness. *(Very solemnly.)* Yore young woman so far forgot herself as to call me a silly old fat'ead.

MORELL *(with tremendous heartiness)*: Oh, now, isnt that e x a c t l y like Prossy? She's so frank: she cant contain herself! Poor Prossy! Ha! ha!

BURGESS *(trembling with rage)*: And do you hexpec me to put up with it from the like of er?

MORELL: Pooh, nonsense! you cant take any notice of it. Never mind. *(He goes to the cellaret and puts the papers into one of the drawers.)*

BURGESS: Oh, Hi dont mind. Hi'm above it. But is it r i g h t ? thats what I want to know. Is it right?

MORELL: Thats a question for the Church, not for the laity. Has it done you any harm? thats the question for you, eh? Of course it hasnt. Think no more of it. *(He dismisses the subject by going to his place at the table and setting to work at his correspondence.)*

BURGESS *(aside to Marchbanks)*: What did I tell you? Mad as a atter. *(He goes to the table and asks, with the sickly civility of a hungry man)* When's dinner, James?

MORELL: Not for a couple of hours yet.

BURGESS *(with plaintive resignation)*: Gimme a nice book to read over the fire, will you, James: thur's a good chap.

MORELL: What sort of book? A good one?

BURGESS *(with almost a yell of remonstrance)*: Nah-oo! Summat pleasant, just to pass the time. *(Morell takes an illustrated paper from the table and offers it. He accepts it humbly.)* Thank yer, James. *(He goes back to the big chair at the fire, and sits there at his ease, reading.)*

MORELL *(as he writes)*: Candida will come to entertain you presently. She has got rid of her pupil. She is filling the lamps.

MARCHBANKS *(starting up in the wildest consternation)*: But that will soil her hands. I cant bear that, Morell: it's a shame. I'll go and fill them. *(He makes for the door.)*

MORELL: Youd better not. *(Marchbanks stops irresolutely.)* She'd only set you to clean my boots, to save me the trouble of doing it myself in the morning.

BURGESS *(with grave disapproval)*: Dont you keep a servant now, James?

MORELL: Yes: but she isnt a slave; and the house looks as if I kept three. That means that everyone has to lend a hand. It's not a bad plan: Prossy and I can talk business after breakfast while we're washing up. Washing up's no trouble when there are two people to do it.

MARCHBANKS (*tormentedly*): Do you think every woman is as coarse-grained as Miss Garnett?

BURGESS (*emphatically*): Thats quite right, Mr Morchbanks: thats q u i t e right. She is corse-grained.

MORELL (*quietly and significantly*): Marchbanks!

MARCHBANKS: Yes?

MORELL: How many servants does your father keep?

MARCHBANKS (*pettishly*): Oh, I dont know. (*He moves to the sofa, as if to get as far as possible from Morell's questioning, and sits down in great agony of spirit, thinking of the paraffin.*)

MORELL (*very gravely*): So many that you dont know! (*More aggressively.*) When theres anything coarse-grained to be done, you just ring the bell and throw it on to somebody else, eh?

MARCHBANKS: Oh, dont torture me. You dont even ring the bell. But your wife's beautiful fingers are dabbling in parrafin oil while you sit here comfortably preaching about it: everlasting preaching! preaching! words! words! words!

BURGESS (*intensely appreciating this retort*): Har, har! Devil a better! (*Radiantly.*) Ad you there, James, straight.

(*Candida comes in, all aproned, with a reading lamp trimmed, filled, and ready for lighting. She places it on the table near Morell, ready for use.*)

CANDIDA (*brushing her finger tips together with a slight twitch of her nose*): If you stay with us, Eugene, I think I will hand over the lamps to you.

MARCHBANKS: I will stay on condition that you hand over all the rough work to me.

CANDIDA: Thats very gallant; but I think I should like to see how you do it first. (*Turning to Morell.*) James: youve not been looking after the house properly.

MORELL: What have I done—or not done—my love?

CANDIDA (*with serious vexation*): My own particular pet scrubbing brush has been used for blackleading. (*A heart-breaking wail bursts from Marchbanks. Burgess looks round, amazed. Candida. hurries to the sofa.*) Whats the matter? Are you ill, Eugene?

MARCHBANKS: No: not ill. Only horror! horror! horror! *(He bows his head on his hands.)*

BURGESS *(shocked)*: What! Got the orrors, Mr Morchbanks! Oh, thats bad, at your age. You must leave it off grajally.

CANDIDA *(reassured)*: Nonsense, papa! It's only poetic horror, isnt it, Eugene? *(Petting him.)*

BURGESS *(abashed)*: Oh, poetic orror is it? I beg your pordon, I'm shore. *(He turns to the fire again, deprecating his hasty conclusion.)*

CANDIDA: What is it, Eugene? the scrubbing brush? *(He shudders.)* Well, there! never mind. *(She sits down beside him.)* Wouldnt you like to present me with a nice new one, with an ivory back inlaid with mother-of-pearl?

MARCHBANKS *(softly and musically, but sadly and longingly)*: No, not a scrubbing brush, but a boat: a tiny shallop to sail away in, far from the world, where the marble floors are washed by the rain and dried by the sun; where the south wind dusts the beautiful green and purple carpets. Or a chariot! to carry us up into the sky, where the lamps are stars, and dont need to be filled with paraffin oil every day.

MORELL *(harshly)*: And where there is nothing to do but to be idle, selfish, and useless.

CANDIDA *(jarred)*: Oh James! how could you spoil it all?

MARCHBANKS *(firing up)*: Yes, to be idle, selfish, and useless: that is, to be beautiful and free and happy: hasnt every man desired that with all his soul for the woman he loves? Thats my ideal: whats yours, and that of all the dreadful people who live in these hideous rows of houses? Sermons and scrubbing brushes! With you to preach the sermon and your wife to scrub.

CANDIDA *(quaintly)*: He cleans the boots, Eugene. You will have to clean them to-morrow for saying that about him.

MARCHBANKS: Oh, dont talk about boots! Your feet should be beautiful on the mountains.

CANDIDA: My feet would not be beautiful on the Hackney Road without boots.

BURGESS *(scandalized)*: Come, Candy! dont be vulgar. Mr

Morchbanks aint accustomed to it. Youre givin him the orrors again. I mean the poetic ones.

(Morell is silent. Apparently he is busy with his letters: really he is puzzling with misgiving over his new and alarming experience that the surer he is of his moral thrusts, the more swiftly and effectively Eugene parries them. To find himself beginning to fear a man whom he does not respect afflicts him bitterly.

Miss Garnett comes in with a telegram.)

PROSERPINE *(handing the telegram to Morell)*: Reply paid. The boy's waiting. *(To Candida, coming back to her machine and sitting down.)* Maria is ready for you now in the kitchen, Mrs Morell. *(Candida rises.)* The onions have come.

MARCHBANKS *(convulsively)*: Onions!

CANDIDA: Yes, onions. Not even Spanish ones: nasty little red onions. You shall help me to slice them. Come along.

(She catches him by the wrist and runs out, pulling him after her. Burgess rises in consternation, and stands aghast on the hearth-rug, staring after them.)

BURGESS: Candy didnt oughter andle a hearl's nevvy like that. It's goin too fur with it. Lookee ere, James: do e often git taken queer like that?

MORELL *(shortly, writing a telegram)*: I dont know.

BURGESS *(sentimentally)*: He talks very pretty. I awlus had a turn for a bity of poetry. Candy takes arter me that-a-way. Huseter make me tell er fairy stories when she was only a little kiddy not that igh. *(Indicating a stature of two feet or thereabouts.)*

MORELL *(preoccupied)*: Ah, indeed. *(He blots the telegram and goes out.)*

PROSERPINE: Used you to make the fairy stories up out of your own head?

(Burgess, not deigning to reply, strikes an attitude of the haughtiest disdain on the hearth-rug.)

PROSERPINE *(calmly)*: I should never have supposed you had it in you. By the way, I'd better warn you, since youve taken such a fancy to M: Marchbanks. He's mad.

BURGESS: Mad! What! Im too!!

PROSERPINE: Mad as a March hare. He did frighten me, I can tell you, just before you came in that time. Havnt you noticed the queer things he says?

BURGESS: So thats what the poetic orrors means. Blame me if it didnt come into my ed once or twyst that he was a bit horff is chump! (*He crosses the room to the door, lifting up his voice as he goes.*) Well, this is a pretty sort of asylum for a man to be in, with no one but you to take care of him!

PROSERPINE (*as he passes her*): Yes, what a dreadful thing it would be if anything happened to y o u!

BURGESS (*loftily*): Dont you haddress no remorks to me. Tell your hemployer that Ive gone into the gorden for a smoke.

PROSERPINE (*mocking*): Oh!

(*Before Burgess can retort, Morell comes back.*)

BURGESS (*sentimentally*): Goin for a turn in the gording to smoke, James.

MORELL (*brusquely*): Oh, all right, all right. (*Burgess goes out pathetically in the character of a weary old man. Morell stands at the table, turning over his papers, and adding, across to Proserpine, half humorously, half absently*) Well, Miss Prossy, why have you been calling my father-in-law names?

PROSERPINE (*blushing fiery red, and looking quickly up at him, half scared, half reproachful*): I— (*She bursts into tears.*)

MORELL (*with tender gaiety, leaning across the table towards her, and consoling her*): Oh, come! come! come! Never mind, Pross: he is a silly old fathead, isnt he?

(*With an explosive sob, she makes a dash at the door, and vanishes, banging it. Morell, shaking his head resignedly, sighs, and goes wearily to his chair, where he sits down and sets to work, looking old and careworn.*
(*Candida comes in. She has finished her household work and taken off the apron. She at once notices his dejected appearance, and posts herself quietly at the visitors' chair, looking down at him attentively. She says nothing.*)

MORELL (*looking up, but with his pen raised ready to resume his work*): Well? Where is Eugene?

CANDIDA: Washing his hands in the scullery under the tap. He will make an excellent cook if he can only get over his dread of Maria.

MORELL *(shortly)*: Ha! No doubt. *(He begins writing again.)*

CANDIDA *(going nearer, and putting her hand down softly on his to stop him as she says)*: Come here, dear. Let me look at you. *(He drops his pen and yields himself to her disposal. She makes him rise, and brings him a little away from the table, looking at him critically all the time.)* Turn your face to the light. *(She places him facing the window.)* My boy is not looking well. Has he been overworking?

MORELL: Nothing more than usual.

CANDIDA: He looks very pale, and grey, and wrinkled, and old. *(His melancholy deepens: and she attacks it with wilful gaiety.)* Here: *(pulling him towards the easy chair)* youve done enough writing for today. Leave Prossy to finish it. Come and talk to me.

MORELL: But—

CANDIDA *(insisting)*: Yes, I must be talked to. *(She makes him sit down, and seats herself on the carpet beside his knee.)* Now *(patting his hand)* youre beginning to look better already. Why must you go out every night lecturing and talking? I hardly have one evening a week with you. Of course what you say is all very true; but it does no good: they dont mind what you say to them one little bit. They think they agree with you; but whats the use of their agreeing with you if they go and do just the opposite of what you tell them the moment your back is turned? Look at our congregation at St Dominic's! Why do they come to hear you talking about Christianity every Sunday? Why, just because theyve been so full of business and money-making for six days that they want to forget all about it and have a rest on the seventh; so that they can go back fresh and make money harder than ever! You positively help them at it instead of hindering them.

MORELL *(with energetic seriousness)*: You know very well, Candida, that I often blow them up soundly for that. And if there is nothing in their churchgoing but rest and diversion, why dont they try something more amusing? more self-indulgent? There must be some good in the fact that they prefer St Dominic's to worse places on Sundays.

CANDIDA: Oh, the worse places arnt open; and even if they were, they darent be seen going to them. Besides, James dear, you preach so splendidly that it's as good as a play for them. Why do you think the women are so enthusiastic?

MORELL (*shocked*): Candida!

CANDIDA: Oh, *I* know. You silly boy: you think it's your Socialism and your religion; but if it were that, theyd do what you tell them instead of only coming to look at you. They all have Prossy's complaint.

MORELL: Prossy's complaint! What do you mean, Candida?

CANDIDA: Yes, Prossy, and all the other secretaries you ever had. Why does Prossy condescend to wash up the things, and to peel potatoes and abase herself in all manner of ways for six shillings a week less than she used to get in a city office? She's in love with you, James: thats the reason. Theyre all in love with you. And you are in love with preaching because you do it so beautifully. And you think it's all enthusiasm for the kingdom of Heaven on earth; and so do they. You dear silly!

MORELL: Candida: what dreadful! what soul-destroying cynicism! Are you jesting? Or—can it be?—are you jealous?

CANDIDA (*with curious thoughtfulness*): Yes, I feel a little jealous sometimes.

MORELL (*incredulously*): Of Prossy?

CANDIDA (*laughing*): No, no, no, no. Not jealous of anybody. Jealous for somebody else, who is not loved as he ought to be.

MORELL: Me?

CANDIDA: You! Why, youre spoiled with love and worship: you get far more than is good for you. No: I mean Eugene.

MORELL (*startled*): Eugene!

CANDIDA: It seems unfair that all the love should go to you, and none to him; although he needs it so much more than you do. (*A convulsive movement shakes him in spite of himself.*) Whats the matter? Am I worrying you?

MORELL (*hastily*): Not at all. (*Looking at her with troubled intensity.*) You know that I have perfect confidence in you, Candida.

CANDIDA: You vain thing! Are you so sure of your irresistible attractions?

MORELL: Candida: you are shocking me. I never thought of my attractions. I thought of your goodness, of your purity. That is what I confide in.

CANDIDA: What a nasty uncomfortable thing to say to me! Oh, you a r e a clergyman, James: a thorough clergyman!

MORELL (*turning away from her, heart-stricken*): So Eugene says.

CANDIDA (*with lively interest, leaning over to him with her arms on his knee*): Eugene's always right. He's a wonderful boy: I have grown fonder and fonder of him all the time I was away. Do you know, James, that though he has not the least suspicion of it himself, he is ready to fall madly in love with me?

MORELL (*grimly*): Oh, he has no suspicion of it himself, hasnt he?

CANDIDA: Not a bit. (*She takes her arms from his knee, and turns thoughtfully, sinking into a more restful attitude with her hands in her lap.*) Some day he will know: when he is grown up and experienced, like you. And he will know that I must have known. I wonder what he will think of me then.

MORELL: No evil, Candida. I hope and trust, no evil.

CANDIDA (*dubiously*): That will depend.

MORELL (*bewildered*): Depend!

CANDIDA (*looking at him*): Yes: it will depend on what happens to him. (*He looks vacantly at her.*) Dont you see? It will depend on how he comes to learn what love really is. I mean on the sort of woman who will teach it to him.

MORELL (*quite at a loss*): Yes. No. I dont know what you mean.

CANDIDA (*explaining*): If he learns it from a good woman, then it will be all right: he will forgive me.

MORELL: Forgive?

CANDIDA: But suppose he learns it from a bad woman, as so many men do, especially poetic men, who imagine all women are angels! Suppose he only discovers the value of love when he has thrown it away and degraded himself in his ignorance! Will he forgive me then, do you think?

MORELL: Forgive you for what?

CANDIDA (*realizing how stupid he is, and a little disappointed, though quite tenderly so*): Dont you understand? (*He shakes his head. She turns to him again, so as to explain with the fondest intimacy.)* I mean, will he forgive me for not teaching him myself? For abandoning him to the bad women for the sake of my goodness, of my purity, as you call it? Ah, James, how little you understand me, to talk of your confidence in my goodness and purity! I would give them both to poor Eugene as willingly as I would give my shawl to a beggar dying of cold, if there were nothing else to restrain me. Put your trust in my love for you, James; for if that went, I should care very little for your sermons: mere phrases that you cheat yourself and others with every day. *(She is about to rise.)*

MORELL: H i s words!

CANDIDA *(checking herself quickly in the act of getting up)*: Whose words?

MORELL: Eugene's.

CANDIDA *(delighted)*: He is always right. He understands you; he understands me; he understands Prossy; and you, darling, you understand nothing. *(She laughs, and kisses him to console him. He recoils as if stabbed, and springs up.)*

MORELL: How can you bear to do that when—Oh, Candida *(with anguish in his voice)* I had rather you had plunged a grappling iron into my heart than given me that kiss.

CANDIDA *(amazed)*: My dear: whats the matter?

MORELL *(frantically waving her off)*: Dont touch me.

CANDIDA: James!!!

(They are interrupted by the entrance of Marchbanks with Burgess, who stop near the door, staring.)

MARCHBANKS: Is anything the matter?

MORELL *(deadly white, putting an iron constraint on himself)*: Nothing but this: that either you were right this morning, or Candida is mad.

BURGESS *(in loudest protest)*: What! Candy mad too! Oh, come! come! come! *(He crosses the room to the fireplace, protesting as he goes, and knocks the ashes out of his pipe on the bars.)*

(Morell sits down at his table desperately, leaning forward to hide his face, and interlacing his fingers rigidly to keep them steady.)

CANDIDA (*to Morell, relieved and laughing*): Oh, youre only shocked! Is that all? How conventional all you unconventional people are! (*She sits gaily on the arm of the chair.*)

BURGESS: Come: be'ave yourself, Candy. Whatll Mr Morchbanks think of you?

CANDIDA: This comes of James teaching me to think for myself, and never to hold back out of fear of what other people may think of me. It works beautifully as long as I think the same things as he does. But now! because I have just thought something different! look at him! Just look! (*She points to Morell, greatly amused.*)

(*Eugene looks, and instantly presses his hand on his heart, as if some pain had shot through it. He sits down on the sofa like a man witnessing a tragedy.*)

BURGESS (*on the hearth rug*): Well, James, you certnly haint as himpressive lookin as usu'l.

MORELL (*with a laugh which is half a sob*): I suppose not. I beg all your pardons: I was not conscious of making a fuss. (*Pulling himself together.*) Well, well, well, well, well! (*He sets to work on his papers again with resolute cheerfulness.*)

CANDIDA (*going to the sofa and sitting beside Marchbanks, still in a bantering humor*): Well, Eugene: why are you so sad? Did the onions make you cry?

MARCHBANKS (*aside to her*): It is your cruelty. I hate cruelty. It is a horrible thing to see one person make another suffer.

CANDIDA (*petting him ironically*): Poor boy! I have been cruel? Did I make it slice nasty little red onions?

MARCHBANKS (*earnestly*): Oh, stop, stop: I dont mean myself. You have made him suffer frightfully. I feel his pain in my own heart. I know that it is not your fault: it is something that must happen; but dont make light of it. I shudder when you torture him and laugh.

CANDIDA (*incredulously*): *I* torture James! Nonsense, Eugene: how you exaggerate! silly! (*She rises and goes to the table, a little troubled.*) Dont work any more, dear. Come and talk to us.

MORELL (*affectionately but bitterly*): Ah no: *I* cant talk. I can only preach.

CANDIDA *(caressing his hand)*: Well, come and preach.

BURGESS *(strongly remonstrating)*: Aw no, Candy. Ang it all!

(Lexy Mill comes in, anxious and important.)

LEXY *(hastening to shake hands with Candida)*: How do you do, Mrs Morell? So glad to see you back again.

CANDIDA: Thank you, Lexy. You know Eugene, dont you?

LEXY: Oh yes. How do you do, Marchbanks?

MARCHBANKS: Quite well, thanks.

LEXY *(to Morell)*: Ive just come from the Guild of St Matthew. They are in the greatest consternation about your telegram.

CANDIDA: What did you telegraph about, James?

LEXY *(to Candida)*: He was to have spoken for them tonight. Theyve taken the large hall in Mare Street and spent a lot of money on posters. Morell's telegram was to say he couldnt come. It came on them like a thunderbolt.

CANDIDA *(surprised, and beginning to suspect something wrong)*: Given up an engagement to speak!

BURGESS: Fust time in his life, I'll bet. Aint it, Candy?

LEXY *(to Morell)*: They decided to send an urgent telegram to you asking whether you could not change your mind. Have you received it?

MORELL *(with restrained impatience)*: Yes, yes: I got it.

LEXY: It was reply paid.

MORELL: Yes, I know. I answered it. I cant go.

CANDIDA: But why, James?

MORELL *(almost fiercely)*: Because I dont choose. These people forget that I am a man: they think I am a talking machine to be turned on for their pleasure every evening of my life. May I not have one night at home, with my wife, and my friends?

(They are all amazed at this outburst, except Eugene. His expression remains unchanged.)

CANDIDA: Oh, James, you mustnt mind what I said about that. And if you dont go youll have an attack of bad conscience tomorrow.

LEXY (*intimidated, but urgent*): I know, of course, that they make the most unreasonable demands on you. But they have been telegraphing all over the place for another speaker; and they can get nobody but the President of the Agnostic League.

MORELL (*promptly*): Well, an excellent man. What better do they want?

LEXY: But he always insists so powerfully on the divorce of Socialism from Christianity. He will undo all the good we have been doing. Of course you know best; but— (*He shrugs his shoulders and wanders to the hearth beside Burgess.*)

CANDIDA (*coaxingly*): Oh, d o go, James. We'll all go.

BURGESS (*grumblingly*): Look ere, Candy! I say! Lets stay at home by the fire, comfortable. He wont need to be more'n a couple-o-hour away.

CANDIDA: Youll be just as comfortable at the meeting. We'll all sit on the platform and be great people.

MARCHBANKS (*terrified*): Oh please dont let us go on the platform. No: everyone will stare at us: I couldnt. I'll sit at the back of the room.

CANDIDA: Dont be afraid. Theyll be too busy looking at James to notice you.

MORELL: Prossy's complaint, Candida! Eh?

CANDIDA (*gaily*): Yes: Prossy's complaint.

BURGESS (*mystified*): Prossy's complaint! What are you talkin about, James?

MORELL (*not heeding him, rises; goes to the door; and holds it open, calling in a commanding tone*): Miss Garnett.

PROSERPINE (*in the distance*): Yes, Mr Morell. Coming.

(*They all wait, except Burgess, who turns stealthily to Lexy.*)

BURGESS: Listen ere, Mr Mill. Whats Prossy's complaint? Whats wrong with er?

LEXY (*confidentially*): Well, I dont exactly know; but she spoke very strangely to me this morning. I'm afraid she's a little out of her mind sometimes.

BURGESS (*overwhelmed*): Why, it must be catchin! Four in the same ouse!

PROSERPINE *(appearing on the threshold)*: What is it, Mr Morell?

MORELL: Telegraph to the Guild of St Matthew that I am coming.

PROSERPINE *(surprised)*: Dont they expect you?

MORELL *(peremptorily)*: Do as I tell you.

(*Proserpine, frightened, sits down at her typewriter, and obeys. Morell, now unaccountably resolute and forceful, goes across to Burgess. Candida watches his movements with growing wonder and misgiving.*)

MORELL: Burgess: you dont want to come.

BURGESS: Oh, dont put it like that, James. It's òny that it aint Sunday, you know.

MORELL: I'm sorry. I thought you might like to be introduced to the chairman. He's on the Works Committee of the County Council, and has some influence in the matter of contracts. *(Burgess wakes up at once.)* Youll come?

BURGESS *(with enthusiasm)*: Cawrse I'll come, James. Aint it awlus a pleasure to ear you!

MORELL *(turning to Prossy)*: I shall want you to take some notes at the meeting, Miss Garnett, if you have no other engagement. *(She nods, afraid to speak.)* You are coming, Lexy, I suppose?

LEXY: Certainly.

CANDIDA: We're all coming, James.

MORELL: No: you are not coming; and Eugene is not coming. You will stay here and entertain him—to celebrate your return home. *(Eugene rises, breathless.)*

CANDIDA: But, James—

MORELL *(authoritatively)*: I insist. You do not want to come; and he does not want to come. *(Candida is about to protest.)* Oh, dont concern yourselves: I shall have plenty of people without you: your chairs will be wanted by unconverted people who have never heard me before.

CANDIDA *(troubled)*: Eugene: wouldn't you like to come?

MORELL: I should be afraid to let myself go before Eugene: he is so critical of sermons. *(Looking at him.)* He knows I am afraid of him: he told me as much this morning. Well, I shall shew him how much afraid I am by leaving him here in your custody, Candida.

MARCHBANKS (*to himself, with vivid feeling*): Thats brave. Thats beautiful.

CANDIDA (*with anxious misgiving*): But—but— Is anything the matter, James? (*Greatly troubled.*) I cant understand—

MORELL (*taking her tenderly in his arms and kissing her on the forehead*): Ah, I thought it was *I* who couldnt understand, dear.

ACT III

(Past ten in the evening. The curtains are drawn, and the lamps lighted. The typewriter is in its case: the large table has been cleared and tidied: everything indicates that the day's work is over.

(Candida and Marchbanks are sitting by the fire. The reading lamp is on the mantelshelf above Marchbanks, who is in the small chair, reading aloud. A little pile of manuscripts and a couple of volumes of poetry are on the carpet beside him. Candida is in the easy chair. The poker, a light brass one, is upright in her hand. Leaning back and looking intently at the point of it, with her feet stretched towards the blaze, she is in a waking dream, miles away from the surroundings and completely oblivious of Eugene.)

MARCHBANKS *(breaking off in his recitation)*: Every poet that ever lived has put that thought into a sonnet. He must: he cant help it. *(He looks to her for assent, and notices her absorption in the poker.)* Havnt you been listening? *(No response.)* Mrs Morell!

CANDIDA *(starting)*: Eh?

MARCHBANKS: Havnt you been listening?

CANDIDA *(with a guilty excess of politeness)*: Oh yes. It's very nice. Go on, Eugene. I'm longing to hear what happens to the angel.

MARCHBANKS *(letting the manuscript drop from his hand to the floor)*: I beg your pardon for boring you.

CANDIDA: But you are not boring me, I assure you. P l e a s e go on. Do, Eugene.

MARCHBANKS: I finished the poem about the angel quarter of an hour ago. Ive read you several things since.

CANDIDA (*remorsefully*): I'm so sorry, Eugene. I think the poker must have hypnotized me. (*She puts it down.*)

MARCHBANKS: It made me horribly uneasy.

CANDIDA: Why didnt you tell me? I'd have put it down at once.

MARCHBANKS: I was afraid of making you uneasy too. It looked as if it were a weapon. If I were a hero of old I should have laid my drawn sword between us. If Morell had come in he would have thought you had taken up the poker because there was no sword between us.

CANDIDA (*wondering*): What? (*With a puzzled glance at him.*) I cant quite follow that. Those sonnets of yours have perfectly addled me. Why should there be a sword between us?

MARCHBANKS (*evasively*): Oh, never mind. (*He stoops to pick up the manuscript*).

CANDIDA: Put that down again. Eugene. There are limits to my appetite for poetry: even your poetry. Youve been reading to me for more than two hours, ever since James went out. I want to talk.

MARCHBANKS (*rising, scared*): No: I mustnt talk. (*He looks round him in his lost way, and adds, suddenly*) I think I'll go out and take a walk in the park. (*He makes for the door*).

CANDIDA: Nonsense: it's closed long ago. Come and sit down on the hearth-rug, and talk moonshine as you usually do. I want to be amused. Dont you want to?

MARCHBANKS (*half in terror, half enraptured*): Yes.

CANDIDA: Then come along. (*She moves her chair back a little to make room.*)

(*He hesitates; then timidly stretches himself on the hearth-rug, face upwards, and throws back his head across her knees, looking up at her.*)

MARCHBANKS: Oh, Ive been so miserable all the evening, because I was doing right. Now I'm doing wrong; and I'm happy.

CANDIDA (*tenderly amused at him*): Yes: I'm sure you feel a great grown-up wicked deceiver. Quite proud of yourself, arnt you?

MARCHBANKS (*raising his head quickly and turning a little to look round at her*): Take care. I'm ever so much older than you, if you only knew. (*He turns quite over on his knees, with his hands clasped and his arms on her lap, and speaks with growing impulse, his blood beginning to stir.)* May I say some wicked things to you?

CANDIDA *(without the least fear or coldness, and with perfect respect for his passion, but with a touch of her wise-hearted maternal humor)*: No. But you may say anything you really and truly feel. Anything at all, no matter what it is. I am not afraid, so long as it is your real self that speaks, and not a mere attitude: a gallant attitude, or a wicked attitude, or even a poetic attitude. I put you on your honor and truth. Now say whatever you want to.

MARCHBANKS *(the eager expression vanishing utterly from his lips and nostrils as his eyes light up with pathetic spirituality)*: Oh, now I cant say anything: all the words I know belong to some attitude or other—all except one.

CANDIDA: What one is that?

MARCHBANKS *(softly, losing himself in the music of the name)*: Candida, Candida, Candida, Candida, Candida. I must say that now, because you have put me on my honor and truth; and I never think or feel Mrs Morell: it is always Candida.

CANDIDA: Of course. And what have you to say to Candida?

MARCHBANKS: Nothing but to repeat your name a thousand times. Dont you feel that every time is a prayer to you?

CANDIDA: Doesnt it make you happy to be able to pray?

MARCHBANKS: Yes, very happy.

CANDIDA: Well, that happiness is the answer to your prayer. Do you want anything more?

MARCHBANKS: No: I have come into Heaven, where want is unknown.

(Morell comes in. He halts on the threshold, and takes in the scene at a glance.)

MORELL *(grave and self-contained)*: I hope I dont disturb you.

(Candida starts up violently, but without the smallest embarrassment, laughing at herself. Eugene, capsized by her sudden movement, recovers himself without rising, and sits on the rug hugging his ankles, also quite unembarrassed.)

CANDIDA: Oh, James, how you startled me! I was so taken up

with Eugene that I didnt hear your latchkey. How did the meeting go off? Did you speak well?

MORELL: I have never spoken better in my life.

CANDIDA: That was first rate! How much was the collection?

MORELL: I forgot to ask.

CANDIDA (*to Eugene*): He must have spoken splendidly, or he would never have forgotten that. (*To Morell.*) Where are all the others?

MORELL: They left long before I could get away: I thought I should never escape. I believe they are having supper somewhere.

CANDIDA (*in her domestic business tone*): Oh; in that case, Maria may go to bed. I'll tell her. (*She goes out to the kitchen.*)

MORELL (*looking sternly down at Marchbanks*): Well?

MARCHBANKS (*squatting cross-legged on the hearth-rug, and actually at ease with Morell—even impishly humorous*): Well?

MORELL: Have you anything to tell me?

MARCHBANKS: Only that I have been making a fool of myself here in private whilst you have been making a fool of yourself in public.

MORELL: Hardly in the same way, I think.

MARCHBANKS (*scrambling up—eagerly*): The very, very, very same way. I have been playing the good man just like you. When you began your heroics about leaving me here with Candida—

MORELL (*involuntarily*): Candida?

MARCHBANKS: Oh, yes. Ive got that far. Heroics are infectious: I caught the disease from you. I swore not to say a word in your absense that I would not have said a month ago in your presence.

MORELL: Did you keep your oath?

MARCHBANKS (*suddenly perching himself grotesquely on the easy chair*): I was ass enough to keep it until about ten minutes ago. Up to that moment I went on desperately reading to her—reading my own poems—anybody's poems—to stave off a conversation. I was standing outside the gate of Heaven, and refusing to go in. Oh, you can't think how heroic it was, and how uncomfortable! Then—

MORELL *(steadily controlling his suspense)*: Then?

MARCHBANKS *(prosaically slipping down into a quite ordinary attitude in the chair)*: Then she couldnt bear being read to any longer.

MORELL: And you approached the gate of Heaven at last?

MARCHBANKS: Yes.

MORELL: Well? *(Fiercely.)* Speak, man: have you no feeling for me?

MARCHBANKS *(softly and musically)*: Then she became an angel; and there was a flaming sword that turned every way, so that I couldnt go in; for I saw that that gate was really the gate to Hell.

MORELL *(triumphantly)*: She repulsed you!

MARCHBANKS *(rising in wild scorn)*: No, you fool: if she had done that I should never have seen that I was in Heaven already. Repulsed me! You think that would have saved me —virtuous indignation! Oh, you are not worthy to live in the same world with her. *(He turns away contemptuously to the other side of the room.)*

MORELL *(who has watched him quietly without changing his place)*: Do you think you make yourself more worthy by reviling me, Eugene?

MARCHBANKS: Here endeth the thousand and first lesson, Morell: I dont think much of your preaching after all: I believe I could do it better myself. The man I want to meet is the man that Candida married.

MORELL: The man that—? Do you mean me?

MARCHBANKS: I don't mean the Reverend James Mavor Morell, moralist and windbag. I mean the real man that the Reverend James must have hidden somewhere inside his black coat—the man that Candida loved. You cant make a woman like Candida love you by merely buttoning your collar at the back instead of in front.

MORELL *(boldly and steadily)*: When Candida promised to marry me, I was the same moralist and windbag that you now see. I wore my black coat; and my collar was buttoned behind instead of in front. Do you think she would have loved me any the better for being insincere in my profession?

MARCHBANKS (*on the sofa, hugging his ankles*): Oh, she forgave you, just as she forgives me for being a coward, and a weakling, and what you call a snivelling little whelp and all the rest of it. (*Dreamily.*) A woman like that has divine insight: she loves our souls, and not our follies and vanities and illusions, nor our collars and coats, nor any other of the rags and tatters we are rolled up in. (*He reflects on this for an instant: then turns intently to question Morell.*) What I want to know is how you got past the flaming sword that stopped me.

MORELL: Perhaps because I was not interrupted at the end of ten minutes.

MARCHBANKS (*taken aback*): W h a t!

MORELL: Man can climb to the highest summits; but he cannot dwell there long.

MARCHBANKS (*springing up*): It's false: there can he dwell for ever, and there only. It's in the other moments that he can find no rest, no sense of the silent glory of life. Where would you have me spend my moments, if not on the summits?

MORELL: In the scullery, slicing onions and filling lamps.

MARCHBANKS: Or in the pulpit, scrubbing cheap earthenware souls?

MORELL: Yes, that too. It was there that I earned my golden moment, and the right, in that moment, to ask her to love me. *I* did not take the moment on credit; nor did I use it to steal another man's happiness.

MARCHBANKS (*rather disgustedly, trotting back towards the fireplace*): I have no doubt you conducted the transaction as honestly as if you were buying a pound of cheese. (*He stops on the brink of the hearth-rug, and adds, thoughtfully, to himself, with his back turned to Morell*) I could only go to her as a beggar.

MORELL (*staring*): A beggar dying of cold! asking for her shawl!

MARCHBANKS (*turning, surprised*): Thank you for touching up my poetry. Yes, if you like: a beggar dying of cold, asking for her shawl.

MORELL (*excitedly*): And she refused. Shall I tell you why she refused? I c a n tell you, on her own authority. It was because of—

MARCHBANKS: She didnt refuse.

MORELL: Not!

MARCHBANKS:; She offered me all I chose to ask for: her shawl, her wings, the wreath of stars on her head, the lilies in her hand, the crescent moon beneath her feet—

MORELL *(seizing him)*: Out with the truth, man: my wife is my wife: I want no more of your poetic fripperies. I know well that if I have lost her love and you have gained it, no law will bind her.

MARCHBANKS *(quaintly, without fear or resistance)*: Catch me by the shirt collar, Morell: she will arrange it for me afterwards as she did this morning. *(With quiet rapture.)* I shall feel her hands touch me.

MORELL: You young imp, do you know how dangerous it is to say that to me? Or *(with a sudden misgiving)* has something made you brave?

MARCHBANKS: I'm not afraid now. I disliked you before: that was why I shrank from your touch. But I saw today—when she tortured you—that you love her. Since then I have been your friend: you may strangle me if you like.

MORELL *(releasing him)*: Eugene: if that is not a heartless lie—if you have a spark of human feeling left in you—will you tell me what has happened during my absence?

MARCHBANK: What happened! Why, the flaming sword—*(Morell stamps with impatience.)* Well, in plain prose, I loved her so exquisitely that I wanted nothing more than the happiness of being in such love. And before I had time to come down from the highest summits, you came in.

MORELL *(suffering deeply)*: So it is still unsettled. Still the misery of doubt.

MARCHBANKS: Misery! I am the happiest of men. I desire nothing now but her happiness. *(In a passion of sentiment.)* Oh, Morell, let us both give her up. Why should she have to choose between a wretched little nervous disease like me, and a pig-headed parson like you? Let us go on a pilgrimage, you to the east and I to the west, in search of a worthy lover for her: some beautiful archangel with purple wings—

MORELL: Some fiddlestick! Oh, if she is mad enough to leave me for you, who will protect her? who will help her? who will work for her? who will be a father to her children? *(He sits down distractedly on the sofa, with his elbows on his knees and his head propped on his clenched fists.)*

MARCHBANKS *(snapping his fingers wildly)*: She does not ask those silly questions. It is she who wants somebody to protect, to help, to work for: somebody to give her children to protect, to help and to work for. Some grown up man who has become as a little child again. Oh, you fool, you fool, you triple fool! I am the man, Morell: I am the man. *(He dances about excitedly, crying.)* You dont understand what a woman is. Send for her, Morell: send for her and let her choose between— *(The door opens and Candida enters. He stops as if petrified.)*

CANDIDA *(amazed, on the threshold)*: What on earth are you at, Eugene?

MARCHBANKS *(oddly)*: James and I are having a preaching match; and he is getting the worst of it.

(Candida looks quickly round at Morell. Seeing that he is distressed, she hurries down to him, greatly vexed.)

CANDIDA: You have been annoying him. Now I wont have it, Eugene: do you hear? *(She puts her hand on Morell's shoulder, and quite forgets her wifely tact in her anger.)* My boy shall not be worried: I will protect him.

MORELL *(rising proudly)*: Protect!

CANDIDA *(not heeding him: to Eugene)*: What have you been saying?

MARCHBANKS *(appalled)*: Nothing. I—

CANDIDA: Eugene! Nothing?

MARCHBANKS *(piteously)*: I mean—I—I'm very sorry. I wont do it again: indeed I wont. I'll let him alone.

MORELL *(indignantly, with an aggressive movement towards Eugene)*: Let me alone! You young—

CANDIDA *(stopping him)*: Sh!—no: let me deal with him, James.

MARCHBANKS: Oh, youre not angry with me, are you?

CANDIDA *(severely)*: Yes I am: very angry. I have a good mind to pack you out of the house.

MORELL *(taken aback by Candida's vigor, and by no means relishing the position of being rescued by her from another man)*: Gently, Candida, gently. I am able to take care of myself.

CANDIDA *(petting him)*: Yes, dear: of course you are. But you mustnt be annoyed and made miserable.

MARCHBANKS *(almost in tears, turning to the door)*: I'll go.

CANDIDA: Oh, you neednt go: I cant turn you out at this time of night. *(Vehemently.)* Shame on you! For shame!

MARCHBANKS *(desperately)*: But what have I done?

CANDIDA: I know what you have done: as well as if I had been here all the time. Oh, it was unworthy! You are like a child: you cannot hold your tongue.

MARCHBANKS: I would die ten times over sooner than give you a moment's pain.

CANDIDA *(with infinite contempt for this puerility)*: Much good your dying would do me!

MORELL: Candida, my dear: this altercation is hardly quite seemly. It is a matter between two men; and I am the right person to settle it.

CANDIDA: Two m e n ! Do you call that a man! *(To Eugene.)* You bad boy!

MARCHBANKS *(gathering a whimsically affectionate courage from the scolding)*: If I am to be scolded like a boy, I must make a boy's excuse. He began it. And he's bigger than I am.

CANDIDA *(losing confidence a little as her concern for Morell's dignity takes the alarm)*: That cant be true. *(To Morell.)* You didnt begin it, James, did you?

MORELL *(contemptuously)*: No.

MARCHBANKS *(indignant)*: Oh!

MORELL *(to Eugene)*: You began it: this morning. *(Candida, instantly connecting this with his mysterious allusion in the afternoon to something told him by Eugene in the morning, looks at him with quick suspicion. Morell proceeds, with the emphasis of offended superiority.)* But your other point is true. I am certainly the bigger of the two, and, I hope, the stronger, Candida. So you had better leave the matter in my hands.

CANDIDA (*again soothing him*): Yes, dear; but— (*Troubled.*) I dont understand about this morning.

MORELL (*gently snubbing her.*) You need not understand, my dear.

CANDIDA: But, James, I —(*The street bell rings.*) Oh bother! Here they all come. (*She goes out to let them in.*)

MARCHBANKS (*running to Morell*): Oh, Morell, isnt it dreadful? She's angry with us: she hates me. What shall I do?

MORELL (*with quaint desperation, walking up and down the middle of the room*): Eugene: my head is spinning round. I shall begin to laugh presently.

MARCHBANKS (*following him anxiously*): No, no: she'll think Ive thrown you into hysterics. Dont laugh.

(*Boisterous voices and laughter are heard approaching. Lexy Mill, his eyes sparkling, and his bearing denoting unwonted elevation of spirit, enters with Burgess, who is greasy and self-complacent, but has all his wits about him. Miss Garnett, with her smartest hat and jacket on, follows them; but though her eyes are brighter than before, she is evidently a prey to misgiving. She places herself with her back to her typewriting table, with one hand on it to steady herself, passing the other across her forehead as if she were a little tired and giddy. Marchbanks relapses into shyness and edges away into the corner near the window, where Morell's books are.*)

LEXY (*exhilarated*): Morell: I m u s t congratulate you. (*Grasping his hand.*) What a noble, splendid, inspired address you gave us! You surpassed yourself.

BURGESS: So you did, James. It fair kep me awake to the lars' word. Didnt it, Miss Gornett?

PROSERPINE (*worriedly*): Oh, I wasnt minding you: I was trying to make notes. (*She takes out her notebook, and looks at her stenography, which nearly makes her cry.*)

MORELL: Did I go too fast, Pross?

PROSERPINE: Much too fast. You know I cant do more than ninety words a minute. (*She relieves her feelings by throwing her note-book angrily beside her machine, ready for use next morning.*)

MORELL (*soothingly*): Oh well, well, never mind, never mind, never mind. Have you all had supper?

LEXY: Mr Burgess has been kind enough to give us a really splendid supper at the Belgrave.

BURGESS (*with effusive magnanimity*): Dont mention it, Mr Mill. (*Modestly.*) Youre arty welcome to my little treat.

PROSERPINE: We had champagne. I never tasted it before. I feel quite giddy.

MORELL (*surprised*): A champagne supper! That was very handsome. Was it my eloquence that produced all this extravagance?

LEXY (*rhetorically*): Your eloquence, and Mr Burgess's goodness of heart. (*With a fresh burst of exhilaration.*) And what a very fine fellow the chairman is, Morell! He came to supper with us.

MORELL (*with long drawn significance, looking at Burgess*): O-o-o-h! the chairman. N o w I understand.

(*Burgess covers with a deprecatory cough a lively satisfaction with his own diplomatic cunning. Lexy folds his arms and leans against the head of the sofa in a high-spirited attitude after nearly losing his balance. Candida comes in with glasses, lemons, and a jug of hot water on a tray.*)

CANDIDA: Who will have some lemonade? You know our rules: total abstinence. (*She puts the tray on the table, and takes up the lemon squeezer, looking enquiringly round at them.*)

MORELL: No use, dear. Theyve all had champagne. Pross has broken her pledge.

CANDIDA (*to Proserpine*): You dont mean to say youve been drinking champagne!

PROSERPINE (*stubbornly*): Yes I do. I'm only a beer teetotaller, not a champagne teetotaller. I dont like beer. Are there any letters for me to answer, Mr Morell?

MORELL: No more tonight.

PROSERPINE: Very well. Goodnight, everybody.

LEXY (*gallantly*): Had I not better see you home, Miss Garnett?

PROSERPINE: No thank you. I shant trust myself with anybody tonight. I wish I hadnt taken any of that stuff. (*She takes uncertain aim at the door; dashes at it; and barely escapes without disaster.*)

BURGESS (*indignantly*): Stuff indeed! That gurl dunno what champagne is! Pommery and Greeno at twelve and six a bottle. She took two glasses amost straight horff.

MORELL (*anxious about her*): Go and look after her, Lexy.

LEXY (*alarmed*): But if she should really be— Suppose she began to sing in the street, or anything of that sort.

MORELL: Just so: she may. Thats why youd better see her safely home.

CANDIDA: Do, Lexy: theres a good fellow. (*She shakes his hand and pushes him gently to the door.*)

LEXY: It's evidently my duty to go. I hope it may not be necessary. Goodnight, Mrs Morell. (*To the rest.*) Goodnight. (*He goes. Candida shuts the door.*)

BURGESS: He was gushin with hextra piety hisself arter two sips. People carnt drink like they huseter. (*Bustling across to the hearth.*) Well, James: it's time to lock up. Mr Morchbanks: shall I ave the pleasure of your company for a bit o the way ome?

MARCHBANKS (*affrightedly*): Yes: I'd better go. (*He hurries towards the door; but Candida places herself before it, barring his way.*)

CANDIDA (*with quiet authority*): You sit down. Youre not going yet.

MARCHBANKS (*quailing*): No: I—I didnt mean to. (*He sits down abjectly on the sofa.*)

CANDIDA: Mr Marchbanks will stay the night with us, papa.

BURGESS: Oh well, I'll say goodnight. So long, James. (*He shakes hands with Morell, and goes over to Eugene.*) Make em give you a nightlight by your bed, Mr Morchbanks: itll comfort you if you wake up in the night with a touch of that complaint of yores. Goodnight.

MARCHBANKS: Thank you: I will. Goodnight, Mr Burgess. (*They shake hands. Burgess goes to the door.*)

CANDIDA (*intercepting Morell, who is following Burgess*): Stay here, dear: I'll put on papa's coat for him. (*She goes out with Burgess.*)

MARCHBANKS *(rising and stealing over to Morell)*: Morell: theres going to be a terrible scene. Arnt you afraid?

MORELL: Not in the least.

MARCHBANKS: I never envied you your courage before. *(He puts his hand appealingly on Morell's forearm.)* Stand by me, wont you?

MORELL *(casting him off resolutely)*: Each for himself, Eugene. She must choose between us now.

(Candida returns. Eugene creeps back to the sofa like a guilty schoolboy.)

CANDIDA *(between them, addressing Eugene)*: Are you sorry?

MARCHBANKS *(earnestly)*: Yes. Heartbroken.

CANDIDA: Well, then, you are forgiven. Now go off to bed like a good little boy: I want to talk to James about you.

MARCHBANKS *(rising in great consternation)*: Oh, I cant do that, Morell. I must be here. I'll not go away. Tell her.

CANDIDA *(her suspicions confirmed)*: Tell me what? *(His eyes avoid hers furtively. She turns and mutely transfers the question to Morell.)*

MORELL *(bracing himself for the catastrophe)*: I have nothing to tell her, except *(Here his voice deepens to a measured and mournful tenderness.)* that she is my greatest treasure on earth—if she is really mine.

CANDIDA *(coldly, offended by his yielding to his orator's instinct and treating her as if she were the audience of the Guild of St Matthew)*: I am sure Eugene can say no less, if that is all.

MARCHBANKS *(discouraged)*: Morell: she's laughing at us.

MORELL *(with a quick touch of temper)*: There is nothing to laugh at. Are you laughing at us, Candida?

CANDIDA *(with quiet anger)*: Eugene is very quick-witted, James. I hope I am going to laugh; but I am not sure that I am not going to be very angry. *(She goes to the fireplace, and stands there leaning with her arm on the mantelpiece, and her foot on the fender, whilst Eugene steals to Morell and plucks him by the sleeve.)*

MARCHBANKS *(whispering)*: Stop, Morell. Dont let us say anything.

MORELL *(pushing Eugene away without deigning to look at him)*: I hope you dont mean that as a threat, Candida.

CANDIDA *(with emphatic warning)*: Take care, James. Eugene: I asked you to go. Are you going?

MORELL *(putting his foot down)*: He shall not go. I wish him to remain.

MARCHBANKS: I'll go. I'll do whatever you want. *(He turns to the door.)*

CANDIDA: Stop! *(He obeys.)* Didnt you hear James say he wished you to stay? James is master here. Dont you know that?

MARCHBANKS *(flushing with a young poet's rage against tyranny)*: By what right is he master?

CANDIDA *(quietly)*: Tell him, James.

MORELL *(taken aback)*: My dear: I dont know of any right that makes me master. I assert no such right.

CANDIDA *(with infinite reproach)*: You dont know! Oh, James! James! *(To Eugene, musingly.)* I wonder do you understand, Eugene! *(He shakes his head helplessly, not daring to look at her.)* No: youre too young. Well, I give you leave to stay: to stay and learn. *(She comes away from the hearth and places herself between them.)* Now, James! whats the matter? Come: tell me.

MARCHBANKS *(whispering tremulously across to him)*: Dont.

CANDIDA: Come. Out with it!

MORELL *(slowly)*: I meant to prepare your mind carefully, Candida, so as to prevent misunderstanding.

CANDIDA: Yes, dear: I am sure you did. But never mind: I shant misunderstand.

MORELL: Well—er— *(He hesitates, unable to find the long explanation which he supposed to be available.)*

CANDIDA: Well?

MORELL *(blurting it out baldly)*: Eugene declares that you are in love with him.

MARCHBANKS *(frantically)*: No, no, no, no, never. I did not, Mrs

Morell: it's not true. I said I loved you. I said I understood you, and that he couldnt. And it was not after what passed there before the fire that I spoke: it was not, on my word. It was this morning.

CANDIDA *(enlightened)*: This morning!

MARCHBANKS: Yes. *(He looks at her, pleading for credence, and then adds simply)* That was what was the matter with my collar.

CANDIDA: Your collar? *(Suddenly taking in his meaning she turns to Morell, shocked.)* Oh, James: did you? *(She stops.)*

MORELL *(ashamed)*: You know, Candida, that I have a temper to struggle with. And he said *(shuddering)* that you despised me in your heart.

CANDIDA *(turning quickly on Eugene)*: Did you say that?

MARCHBANKS *(terrified)*: No.

CANDIDA *(almost fiercely)*: Then James has just told me a falsehood. Is that what you mean?

MARCHBANKS: No, no: I—I— *(Desperately.)* it was David's wife. And it wasnt at home: it was when she saw him dancing before all the people.

MORELL *(taking the cue with a debater's adroitness)*: Dancing before all the people, Candida; and thinking he was moving their hearts by his mission when they were only suffering from—Prossy's complaint. *(She is about to protest: he raises his hand to silence her.)* Dont try to look indignant, Candida—

CANDIDA: Try!

MORELL *(continuing)*: Eugene was right. As you told me a few hours after, he is always right. He said nothing that you did not say far better yourself. He is the poet, who sees everything; and I am the poor parson, who understands nothing.

CANDIDA *(remorsefully)*: Do you mind what is said by a foolish boy, because I said something like it again in jest?

MORELL: That foolish boy can speak with the inspiration of a child and the cunning of a serpent. He has claimed that you belong to him and not to me; and, rightly or wrongly, I have come to fear that it may be true. I will not go about tortured with doubts and suspicions. I will not live with you and keep a secret from you. I will not suffer the intolerable degradation of jealousy. We have agreed—he and I—that you shall choose between us now. I await your decision.

CANDIDA (*slowly recoiling a step, her heart hardened by his rhetoric in spite of the sincere feeling behind it*): Oh! I am to choose, am I? I suppose it is quite settled that I must belong to one or the other.

MORELL (*firmly*): Quite. You must choose definitely.

MARCHBANKS (*anxiously*): Morell: you dont understand. She means that she belongs to herself.

CANDIDA (*turning on him*): I mean that and a good deal more, Master Eugene, as you will both find out presently. And pray, my lords and masters, what have you to offer for my choice? I am up for auction, it seems. What do you bid, James?

MORELL (*reproachfully*): Cand— (*He breaks down: his eyes and throat fill with tears: the orator becomes the wounded animal.*) I cant speak—

CANDIDA (*impulsively going to him*): Ah, dearest—

MARCHBANKS (*in wild alarm*): Stop: it's not fair. You mustnt show her that you suffer, Morell. I am on the rack, too; but I am not crying.

MORELL (*rallying all his forces*): Yes: you are right. It is not for pity that I am bidding. (*He disengages himself from Candida.*)

CANDIDA (*retreating, chilled*): I beg your pardon, James; I did not mean to touch you. I am waiting to hear your bid.

MORELL (*with proud humility*): I have nothing to offer you but my strength for your defence, my honesty of purpose for your surety, my ability and industry for your livelihood, and my authority and position for your dignity. That is all it becomes a man to offer to a woman.

CANDIDA (*quite quietly*): And you, Eugene? What do you offer?

MARCHBANKS: My weakness! my desolation! my heart's need!

CANDIDA (*impressed*): Thats a good bid, Eugene. Now I know how to make my choice.

(*She pauses and looks curiously from one to the other, as if weighing them. Morell, whose lofty confidence has changed into heartbreaking dread at Eugene's bid, loses all power of concealing his anxiety. Eugene, strung to the highest tension, does not move a muscle.*)

MORELL (*in a suffocated voice—the appeal bursting from the depths of his anguish*): Candida!

MARCHBANKS (*aside, in a flash of contempt*): Coward!

CANDIDA (*significantly*):I give myself to the weaker of the two.

(*Eugene divines her meaning at once: his face whitens like steel in a furnace that cannot melt it.*)

MORELL (*bowing his head with the calm of collapse*): I accept your sentence. Candida.

CANDIDA: Do you understand, Eugene?

MARCHBANKS: Oh, I feel I'm lost. He cannot bear the burden.

MORELL (*incredulously, raising his head with prosaic abruptness*): Do you mean me, Candida?

CANDIDA (*smiling a little*): Let us sit and talk comfortably over it like three friends. (*To Morell.*) Sit down, dear. (*Morell takes the chair from the fireside—the children's chair.*) Bring me that chair, Eugene. (*She indicates the easy chair. He fetches it silently, even with something like cold strength, and places it next Morell, a little behind him. She sits down. He goes to the sofa and sits there, still silent and inscrutable. When they are all settled she begins, throwing a spell of quietness on them by her calm, sane, tender tone.*) You remember what you told me about yourself, Eugene: how nobody has cared for you since your old nurse died: how those clever, fashionable sisters and successful brothers of yours were your mother's and father's pets: how miserable you were at Eton: how your father is trying to starve you into returning to Oxford: how you have had to live without comfort or welcome or refuge, always lonely, and nearly always disliked and misunderstood, poor boy!

MARCHBANKS (*faithful to the nobility of his lot*): I had my books. I had Nature. And at last I met you.

CANDIDA: Never mind that just at present. Now I want you to look at this other boy here: m y boy! spoiled from his cradle. We go once a fortnight to see his parents. You should come with us, Eugene, to see the pictures of the hero of that household. James as a baby! the most wonderful of all babies. James holding his first school prize, won at the ripe age of eight! James as the captain of his eleven! James in his first frock coat! James under all sorts of glorious circumstances!

You know how strong he is (I hope he didnt hurt you): how clever he is: how happy. *(With deepening gravity.)* Ask James's mother and his three sisters what it cost to save James the trouble of doing anything but be strong and clever and happy. Ask m e what it costs to be James's mother and three sisters and wife and mother to his children all in one. Ask Prossy and Maria how troublesome the house is even when we have no visitors to help us to slice the onions. Ask the tradesmen who want to worry James and spoil his beautiful sermons who it is that puts them off. When there is money to give, he gives it: when there is money to refuse, I refuse it. I build a castle of comfort and indulgence and love for him, and stand sentinel always to keep little vulgar cares out. I make him master here, though he does not know it, and could not tell you a moment ago how it came to be so. *(With sweet irony.)* And when he thought I might go away with you, his only anxiety was— what should become of m e! And to tempt me to stay he offered me *(Leaning forward to stroke his hair caressingly at each phrase.)* h i s strength for my defence! his industry for my livelihood! his dignity for my position! his— *(relenting)* ah, I am mixing up your beautiful cadences and spoiling them, am I not, darling? *(She lays her cheek fondly against his.)*

MORELL *(quite overcome, kneeling beside her chair and embracing her with boyish ingenuousness)*: It's all true, every word. What I am you have made me with the labor of your hands and the love of your heart. You are my wife, my mother, my sisters: you are the sum of all loving care to me.

CANDIDA *(in his arms, smiling, to Eugene)*: Am I y o u r mother and sisters to you, Eugene?

MARCHBANKS *(rising with a fierce gesture of disgust)*: Ah, never. Out, then, into the night with me!

CANDIDA *(rising quickly)*: You are not going like that, Eugene?

MARCHBANKS *(with the ring of a man's voice—no longer a boy's—in the words)*: I know the hour when it strikes. I am impatient to do what must be done.

MORELL *(who has also risen)*: Candida: dont let him do anything rash.

CANDIDA *(confident, smiling at Eugene)*: Oh, there is no fear. He has learnt to live without happiness.

MARCHBANKS: I no longer desire happiness: life is nobler than that. Parson James: I give you my happiness with both hands: I love you because you have filled the heart of the woman I loved. Goodbye. *(He goes towards to the door.)*

CANDIDA: One last word. *(He stops, but without turning to her. She goes to him.)* How old are you, Eugene?

MARCHBANKS: As old as the world now. This morning I was eighteen.

CANDIDA: Eighteen! Will you, for my sake, make a little poem out of the two sentences I am going to say to you? And will you promise to repeat it to yourself whenever you think of me?

MARCHBANKS *(without moving)*: Say the sentences.

CANDIDA: When I am thirty, she will be forty-five. When I am sixty, she will be seventy-five.

MARCHBANKS *(turning to her)*: In a hundred years, we shall be the same age. But I have a better secret than that in my heart. Let me go now. The night outside grows impatient.

CANDIDA: Goodbye. *(She takes his face in her hands; and as he divines her intention and falls on his knees, she kisses his forehead. Then he flies out into the night. She turns to Morell, holding out her arms to him.)* Ah, James!

(They embrace. But they do not know the secret in the poet's heart.)

PART TWO

ESSAYS

Henri Bergson

Laughter: Essay on the Meaning of the Comic*

TRANSLATED BY MAURICE CHARNEY

Let us now note, as a symptom no less worthy of remark, the *lack of sensitivity* which ordinarily accompanies laughter. It seems that the comic can only produce its shattering effect when it falls upon the surface of a soul that is calm and unruffled. Indifference is the natural milieu of comedy. Laughter has no greater enemy than emotion. I do not mean to say that we cannot laugh at a person who inspires us with pity, for example, or even affection. Only, for a few moments, we must forget that affection and silence, that pity. . . . The comic demands, therefore, in order to produce all of its effect, something like a temporary anesthesia of the heart. It addresses itself to pure intelligence. . . .

A man who is running in the street stumbles and falls; the passersby laugh. They would not laugh at him, I think, if they could suppose that the fantasy suddenly came to him of sitting down on the ground. They laugh because he sat down involuntarily. It is not therefore his sudden change of position that causes us to laugh but rather the involuntary nature of the change—his awkwardness. Perhaps there was a stone on the road. He ought to have changed his pace or avoided the obstacle. But because of a lack of flexibility, or by absentmindedness, or by the obstinacy of his body, *or by an effect of stiffness or of momentum*, the muscles continued to make the same movement when circumstances demanded something else. That's why the man fell and that's what the passersby laughed at.

Now consider a person who busies himself with his petty, everyday affairs with mathematical regularity—except that the objects that surround him have been rearranged by a mischievous prankster. He dips his pen in the inkwell and draws it out, covered with mud; he believes that he is sitting down on a solid chair and finds himself stretched out on the floor and goes altogether against the grain and seems to function in a void, carried along by an effect of momentum. Habit had imprinted an

*From *Le Rire: Essai sur la Significance du Comique* (1900), tr. Maurice Channey.

557

impulse. He should have stopped the movement or diverted it. But not at all; he continued mechanically in a straight line. The victim of a practical joke is therefore in a situation like that of the runner who falls. He is comic for the same reason. What is laughable in one case as in the other is a certain *stiffness of the machine* in just the place where one would like to find the attentive suppleness and living flexibility of a human being. Between these two examples, the only difference is that the first happened by itself while the second was produced artificially. In the first example the passersby only looked on; in the second the mischievous prankster made an experiment. . . .

The attitudes, gestures, and movements of the human body are laughable in the exact proportion in which the body makes us think of a simple machine. . . .

We may thus solve the little enigma that Pascal proposes in a passage from his *Pensées*: "Two similar faces, neither of which makes us laugh by itself, do make us laugh by their resemblance when they are taken together." We could also say: "An orator's gestures, none of which is laughable in itself, make us laugh by their repetition." That's because a life that is really alive ought never to repeat itself. Where there is repetition or complete similitude, we suspect that something mechanical is operating behind living matter. Analyze your impression when you see two faces that resemble each other too much. You will see that you think of two copies obtained from the same mold, or of two prints from the same seal, or of two reproductions from the same negative—in sum, of a process of industrial manufacture. This turning of life in the direction of the mechanical is here the true cause of laughter. . . .

From the derived idea of travesty we must return to the original idea: that of a mechanism superimposed on life. The lifeless formality of all ceremonies suggests to us an image of this sort. As soon we forget the grave object of a solemn occasion or of a ceremony, those who take part in it give the impression of being puppets. Their mobility is regulated by the immobility of a formula. It is an example of automatism. But perfect automatism will be, for example, that of an official performing his functions like a simple machine or the unconsciousness of an administrative rule applying itself with inexorable fatality and considering itself a law of nature. Quite a few years ago a steamer was shipwrecked near Dieppe. With great difficulty several passengers were trying to save themselves in a lifeboat. Some customs officers who had bravely come to their assistance began by asking them "if they had anything to declare." I find something analogous, although the idea is more subtle, in the words of a deputy challenging the minister on the day after a crime committed on the railroad: "The murderer, after doing in his victim, must have gotten out of the train on the wrong side, in violation of administrative regulations." . . .

The general law of these phenomena could be formulated thus: *Every incident is comic that calls our attention to the physical aspect of a person when the moral aspect is in question.*

Why do we laugh at an orator who sneezes at the most heartfelt moment of his discourse? From where does the comic derive in this phrase from a funeral eulogy, cited by a German philosopher: "He was virtuous and completely round." It originates from the fact that our attention is abruptly shifted from the soul to the body. Examples abound in daily life: A person whose body embarrasses him—that's the image that is suggested to us in these examples. That's what makes shyness sometimes a little ridiculous. The shy person can give the impression of someone whose body bothers him and who looks everywhere around himself for a place to get rid of it.

The tragic poet also takes pains to avoid anything that could call our attention to the physicality of his heroes. As soon as a concern for the body intervenes, we fear the infiltration of comedy. That's why tragic heroes don't drink or eat or warm themselves. As much as it is possible, they don't even sit down. To sit down in the midst of a grand speech would be to recall that he has a body. Napoleon, who demonstrated his psychological insight at certain times, noticed that we pass from tragedy to comedy by the sole fact of sitting down. . . .

Let us now expand this image: *the body lording it over the soul.* We are going to derive a more general principle: *form wishing to triumph over substance, the letter seeking to quarrel with the spirit.* Isn't this the idea that comedy tries to suggest to us when it ridicules a profession? It makes the lawyer, the judge, and the doctor speak as if health and justice were of slight importance, the main point being that there should be doctors, lawyers, and judges, and that the external forms of the profession be scrupulously observed. Thus the means is substituted for the end, the form for the substance, and it is no longer the profession that is made for the public, but the public for the profession. The constant concern for form and the mechanical application of rules create a kind of professional automatism comparable to the automation that bodily habits impose on the soul, and equally laughable. . . .

Let us return one last time to our central image: something

mechanical stuck on to something living. The living being we are concerned with here is a human being, a person. The mechanical apparatus is, on the contrary, a thing. What thus caused laughter was the momentary transformation of a person into a thing, if we wish to consider the image from this perspective. Let us then move from the precise idea of a machine to the vaguer idea of a thing in general. We will have a new series of laughable images that we will obtain, in a manner of speaking, by blurring the contours of the first and which will lead us to this new law: *We laugh every time that a person gives us the impression of being a thing.* . . .

Let us try to grasp even more closely the image of the spring under tension, released, and under tension again. Let us try to disengage the central point. We are going to observe one of the usual devices of classic comedy: *repetition.*

Where does the comedy derive from in the repetition of a word in the theater? We will look in vain for a theory of comedy that can give a satisfactory answer to this very simple question. The question remains, in effect, unanswerable, as long as we expect to find the explanation of an amusing feature in the thing itself, isolated from what it suggests to us. Nowhere does the current method of explanation betray its inadequacy more strongly. But the truth is that leaving aside certain special examples to which we will return later, the repetition of a word is not laughable in itself. It only makes us laugh because it symbolizes a certain particular play of moral elements, a symbol itself of a completely material game. It is the game of the cat who plays with the mouse, the game of the child who pushes and again pushes the jack-in-the-box back to the bottom of its box, but refined, spiritualized, transported into the sphere of feelings and ideas. Let us state the law that defines, in our view, the main comic effects of the repetition of words in the theater: *In a comic repetition of words there are generally two terms present: a feeling that is kept down and releases itself like a spring, and an idea that takes pleasure in pushing the feeling down again.* . . .

To go far only to return, without knowing it, to the point of departure is to summon up a great effort for a result that is nil. It was easy to be tempted to define the comic in this latter manner. This was apparently the idea of Herbert Spencer: laughter would be the indicator of an effort that suddenly encounters emptiness. Kant had already said: "Laughter arises from an expectation which all at once resolves itself into nothing." We are aware that these definitions would apply to our last examples. Still, we would need to apply certain restrictions to the formula because there are many useless efforts that don't make us laugh. But if our last examples present a great cause ending in a small effect, we have also cited others immediately before, which should be defined in exactly the opposite way: a great effect coming from a small cause. The truth is that this second definition would be hardly better than the first. The disproportion between cause and effect, whether it presents itself in one direction or the other, is not the direct source of laughter. We laugh at something that this disproportion can, in certain cases, make evident. I mean the special mechanical arrangement that it allows us to perceive by a kind of transparency behind the series of effects and causes. Neglect this arrangement and you abandon the only thread capable of guiding you in the labyrinth of the comic, and the rule that you will have followed, perhaps applicable to certain properly chosen examples, remains vulnerable to collision with the first example that will come along to destroy it.

But why do we laugh at this mechanical arrangement? That the history of an individual or that of a group appears, at any given moment, like a game engineered by gears, springs, or strings is undoubtedly strange, but where does the special character of this strangeness come from? Why is it comic? To this question, which we have already asked in various forms, we will always give the same answer. The stiff mechanism that we detect at one time or another like an intruder in the living continuity of human affairs has a very special interest for us because it is like a *distraction* from life. If events could be unceasingly attentive to their own occurrence, there would be no coincidences, no unanticipated meetings, no circular series; everything would unfold in a straight course and move forward forever. And if men were always attentive to life, if we were constantly in contact with others as well as with ourselves, nothing would ever seem to be produced in us by springs or strings. The comic is that side of a person by which it resembles a thing, that aspect of human events that imitates, by its very special stiffness, mechanism pure and simple, automatism, and finally, movement without life. It therefore expresses an individual or collective imperfection that calls for an immediate corrective. Laughter is that very corrective. Laughter is a certain social gesture that underlines and represses a certain kind of distraction in men and in events. . . .

To lapse, by an effect of stiffness or momentum, into saying what we don't want to say or doing what we don't want to do is, as we know it, one of the great sources of the comic. That's why absentmindedness is essentially laughable. That's also why we laugh at whatever there can possibly be of stiffness, of the ready-made, of the mechanical in gestures, attitudes, and even in facial features. Can we also discern this kind of stiffness in language? Yes, undoubtedly, because there are preexisting formulas and stereotyped sentences. Someone who expressed himself always in this style would invariably be comic. But in order for an isolated sentence to be comic in itself, once detached from the person who speaks it, it is not enough for it to be a ready-made sentence; it must also bear a sign by which we would recognize without any possible hesitation that it was spoken automatically. And this can hardly happen except when the sentence contains a manifest absurdity, either a gross error or a contradiction in terms. From which we may draw this general rule: *We will get a comic meaning by inserting an absurd idea into the mold of a familiar and well-established expression.* . . .

"We laugh every time our attention is turned aside to a person's physical being when moral qualities were in question." This is a law that we proposed in the first part of our work. Let us apply it to language. We could say that most words present two senses: physical or moral, depending on whether we take them literally or figuratively. Every word begins, in effect, by designating a concrete object or a material action, but little by little the meaning of the word may have spiritualized itself into an abstract relation or a pure idea. If, therefore, our law applies here, it should take the following form: *We achieve a comic effect when we pretend to understand an expression literally when it was used figuratively.* Or further: *As soon as our attention concentrates on the materiality of a metaphor, the idea expressed becomes comic.* . . .

In a certain sense we could say that all *character* is comic if we understand by "character" everything that is *ready-made* in our personality, that which exists within us as a mechanism, which, once wound up, is capable of functioning automatically. It will be, as it were, that aspect by which we repeat ourselves. And it will also be, consequently, that aspect by which others can imitate us. The comic character is a *type*. Inversely, resemblance to a type has something comic about it. We could have been long acquainted with a person without discovering anything laughable about him, yet if one takes advantage of an accidental comparison to apply to him the well-known name of a hero of drama or romance, for a moment at least he will in our eyes verge on the ridiculous. Yet this fictional character may not be comic. But it is comic to resemble him. It is comic to let oneself be inserted, so to speak, into a prepared frame. And what is comic above all is to let oneself become a frame into which others will easily insert themselves. This is what it means to solidify into a stock character. . . .

Another form of this comic stiffness is what I will call *professional ossification*. The comic character will insert himself so closely into the rigid frame of his function that there will no longer be any space to move, or above all, to be moved, like other men. . . .

But the most frequently used means for making a profession comic is to confine it, so to speak, within the limits of its own special language. This creates a situation in which judge, doctor, and soldier apply to ordinary matters the language of law, military strategy, or medicine, as if they had become incapable of speaking like everybody else. Usually this kind of comedy is rather crude. But it becomes more delicate, as we have said, when it reveals a particularity of character at the same time as a professional habit. . . .

Comic absurdity is of the same nature as that of dreams. First, the way intelligence functions in the dream is indeed what we have just been describing. The mind, in love with itself, doesn't look for anything else in the external world than a pretext to materialize its imaginations. Sounds still come confusedly to the ear, colors still move around in our field of vision; in short, the senses are not completely closed. But the dreamer, instead of calling on all his memories to interpret what his senses perceive, makes use instead of what he perceives to embody his favorite memory. The same sound of wind blowing in the chimney will become, according to the psychological state of the dreamer, according to the idea that occupies his imagination, either the howling of wild beasts or a melodious song. Such is the usual mechanism of illusion in dreams.

But if comic illusion is a dream illusion, if the logic of comedy is the logic of dreams, we can expect to find in the logic of the laughable the various characteristics of the logic of dreams. Here again we can confirm the law that we know well: One form of the laughable being given, other forms, which don't have the same comic essence, become laughable by their external resemblance to the first. It is easy to see, in fact, that every *play of ideas* can amuse us, provided that it recalls, closely or distantly, the play of dreams. . . .

There are also *comic obsessions*, which come very close, so it seems, to dream obsessions. To whom has it not happened to see the same image reappear in several successive dreams and take on in each of them a plausible meaning although the dreams have no other point in common? Effects of repetition sometimes present this special form in the theater and in the novel; some of them have a dreamlike resonance. And perhaps it may be the same for the refrain of many songs: it is persistent, it comes back, always the same, at the end of all the couplets, each time with a different meaning. . . .

But above all there is a madness that is characteristic of dreams. There are certain special contradictions, so natural to the imagination of the dreamer but so shocking to the reason of someone who is awake, that it would be impossible to give any exact and complete idea of them to someone who has not experienced them. We refer to the strange fusion that a dream often makes between two persons who become only one but who nevertheless remain distinct. Ordinarily one of these persons is the sleeper himself. He feels that he has not ceased to be who he is; he has nonetheless become another. It is he and it isn't he. He hears himself speak, he sees himself act, but he feels that another person has borrowed his body and has taken his voice. Or else he will be aware of speaking and acting as usual, except that he will speak of himself as if he were a stranger with whom he has no longer anything in common; he feels himself detached from himself. Would we not find this same strange confusion in certain comic scenes?

Sigmund Freud
The Joke and Its Relation to the Unconscious*
Translated by Maurice Charney

But here we must stop and ask ourselves with what this first result corresponds, either in whole or in part, in the literature on the subject. Obviously with brevity, which Jean Paul calls the soul of jokes. Brevity is not in itself witty; if it were, then every laconic remark would be a joke. The brevity of jokes must be of a special kind. We recall that Lipps has tried to describe more closely the special quality of abridgment in jokes. Here our examination has proved that the brevity of jokes is often the result of a process, which, in the wording of the joke, has left behind a second sign: the development of a substitute. By using the process of reduction, which intends to cancel out the odd workings of condensation, we also find that the joke depends only on its verbal expression, which is produced by the condensation process. Our entire interest, of course, is now devoted to this strange and, until now, not properly appreciated process. We can also hardly understand yet how all that is valuable and everything that brings us pleasure in a joke can originate from condensation.

Are analogous processes, which we have here described as the technique of jokes, already known in any other area of psychological phenomena? They are, indeed, in a field that is apparently very distant from jokes. In 1900, I published a book, which, as its title (*The Interpretation of Dreams*) indicates, attempts to explain what is enigmatic about the dream and to present it as a product of our normal life. I found occasion there to bring the manifest and often strange content of the dream into contrast with the latent but quite correct dream thoughts from which the dream arises, and I explored the processes that make the dream out of the latent dream thoughts as well as the psychological forces that come into play in this transformation. All these processes of transformation taken together I called the "dream work." As a part of this dream work I have described a process

*From *Der Witz und seine Beziehung zum Unbewussten* (1905), tr. Maurice Charney.

of condensation that shows the greatest similarity with the technique of jokes, as this leads to abridgment and creates substitute images of the same sort. Everyone will be acquainted, from his own memory of his dreams, with the mixed creations both of persons and of objects that we encounter in dreams. In fact, the dream even creates such mixed forms from words, which may be separated out in analysis. . . .

Other times, and much more frequently, the condensation process of dreams generates not mixed creations but images that completely resemble a thing or a person except for some additional quality or change that comes from other sources. . . . We cannot doubt that in both examples we have before us the same psychological process, which we may recognize by its identical results. Such a far-reaching analogy between the technique of jokes and the dream work will certainly increase our interest in jokes and arouse in us the expectation that a comparison between joke and dream will shed a good deal of light on jokes. . . .

The interesting processes of condensation with the development of a substitute, which we have recognized as the heart of the technique of verbal jokes, have directed us to the structure of dreams in whose mechanism the same psychological processes are disclosed. This is also indicated by the techniques of jokes that depend on reasoning—displacement, errors in logic, nonsense, indirect representation, representation by contraries—which reappear one and all in the technique of the dream work. Displacement endows the dream with that alienated look that keeps us from recognizing its continuity with waking thoughts. The use of nonsense and absurdity in the dream has prevented it from being dignified as a psychological product and has misled authors to suppose that a disintegration of mental activity and an arrest of all critical, moral, and logical powers are the conditions of dream formation. Representation by contraries is so frequent in the dream that even the popular, completely fallacious books of dream interpretation usually take it into account. Indirect representation, the substitution for the dream thought of an allusion, of a small thing, of a symbolism analogous to simile, is indeed that which differentiates the manner of expression of dreams from our waking thoughts. Such an extensive agreement as that between the methods of joke work and dream work can hardly be an accident. . . .

The power that makes it difficult or impossible for women and, to a lesser extent, men to take pleasure in undisguised obscenity we call "repression." We perceive in it the same psychological process which, in serious illnesses, keeps whole complexes of impulses (together with their derivatives) away from consciousness and which has turned out to be an important factor in the production of the so-called psychoneuroses. We attribute to culture and higher education a strong influence on the development of repression and assume that, under these circumstances, a change occurs in the psychological organization (a change that can also be brought about as an inherited predisposition) as a consequence of which what was previously experienced as pleasant now appears to be disagreeable and is rejected with all one's psychological powers. Through the repressive workings of civilization, the basic possibilities of pleasure, now rejected by internal censorship, are lost. But the human psyche finds all renunciation so difficult that the pointed joke offers a way of reversing the renunciation and winning back what was lost. When we laugh at a refined obscene joke, we are laughing at the same thing that makes the peasant laugh at a coarse dirty joke. In both cases the pleasure comes from the same source. We could not bring ourselves to laugh at the coarse dirty joke; we would feel shame, or the joke would appear disgusting to us. We can only begin to laugh when the joke lends us its support. . . .

We are now prepared for the role played by jokes in hostile aggression. The joke will allow us to use what is ridiculous about our enemy that we, because of the impediments that stand in the way, could not express aloud or consciously. Again, the joke will therefore get around restrictions and make available to us sources of pleasure that have become inaccessible. Further, it will bribe the hearer by its reward of pleasure, without any close investigation, into taking sides with us, just as we at other times have been bribed by an innocent joke into overvaluing the content of a wittily expressed sentence. "To draw the laughers over to one's side" is a perfectly apt saying in our language.

The blocking of insult or an offensive reply through external circumstances is so frequent an occurrence that the pointed joke is used with special fondness in order to allow aggression or criticism against superiors who exercise authority. The joke, then, offers a rebellion against such authority, a liberation from its pressures. This same impulse accounts for the charm of caricature, which makes us laugh even if it doesn't turn out well, merely because we consider rebellion against authority as something worthwhile for its own sake. . . .

Among the institutions which the cynical joke is accustomed to attack, none is more important or more earnestly protected by moral rules (but nonetheless more inviting to attack) than the institution of marriage, against which, therefore, most cynical jokes are directed. No demand is more. personal than that for sexual freedom, and nowhere has culture tried to practice a stronger suppression than in the area of sexuality. For our purposes a single example may suffice, the one mentioned on pg. 62 of *An Entry in Prince Carnival's Album*: "A wife is like an umbrella—eventually one ends up taking a cab."

We have already discussed the complicated technique of this example: a disconcerting, apparently impossible comparison but one which, as we now see, is not witty in itself; further, an allusion (a cab is a public vehicle), and, as its strongest technical device, an omission that heightens incomprehensibility. The comparison could be set out in the following way. We marry in order to protect ourselves from the attacks of sensuality, and then it turns out that marriage does not offer any satisfaction of somewhat stronger needs. This is exactly like our taking an umbrella to protect us against the rain but getting wet anyhow. In both cases we have to look for stronger protection: here a public vehicle; there women available for money. Now the joke has almost completely been replaced by cynicism. That marriage is not an arrangement calculated to satisfy male sexuality we don't dare to say out loud and publicly, except if we are forced into it by the love of truth and the reformer's zeal of a Christian von Ehrenfels. The strength of this joke lies in the fact that, through all sorts of detours, it has nevertheless said what we don't dare to say. . . .

Among the various sorts of inner inhibition or suppression is one that deserves our special interest because it is the most far-reaching. It is called "repression" and is recognized by its ability to exclude from consciousness the impulses and their derivatives. We will eventually learn that the pointed joke is able to release pleasure, even from sources subject to repression. If, as indicated above, the triumph over external obstacles can be traced back to the triumph over inner inhibitions and repressions, then we can say that the pointed joke demonstrates the chief characteristic of the workings of jokes—to free pleasure by the elimination of inhibitions—more clearly than all the other phases of the development of jokes. The pointed joke strengthens the tendencies, in whose service it functions, by bringing support from impulses that are maintained in suppression, or it puts itself generally at the service of suppressed tendencies. . . .

Dealing with pointed jokes shows that under such circumstances the suppressed tendency, through help from the pleasure of the joke, can become strong enough to overcome the otherwise stronger inhibition. The insult occurs because with it, the joke is made possible. But the satisfaction that is achieved is not only the one produced by the joke. It is incomparably greater; so much greater than the pleasure from the joke itself that we must assume that the previously suppressed tendency has succeeded in expressing itself perhaps without any diminution at all. In these circumstances the pointed joke is most heartily laughed at. . . .

We can now express the formula for the workings of the pointed joke. It puts itself at the service of tendencies so that, by taking the pleasure of jokes as a fore-pleasure, it can create new pleasure by the lifting of suppressions and repressions. When we now survey its development, we may say that the joke remains true to its nature from the beginning to its completion. It begins as play, in order to draw pleasure from the free use of words and thoughts. As soon as the strengthening of reason prevents any further play with words as meaningless and with thoughts as nonsensical, the original joke changes into a jest in order to hold on to these sources of pleasure and from the freeing of nonsense to be able to gain new pleasure. As an essential but nonpointed joke it lends its help to thoughts and strengthens them against the attack of critical judgment, in which it is helped by the principle of the confusion of the sources of pleasure. Finally, it joins forces with important tendencies that are struggling against suppression in order to lift inner inhibitions according to the principle of fore-pleasure. Reason, critical judgment, and suppression—these are the powers against which it fights one after the other. It holds fast to the primary sources of verbal pleasure, and it opens up for itself, from the stage of the jest on, new sources of pleasure through the removal of inhibitions. The pleasure that it produces, whether it is pleasure from play or from the lifting of inhibitions, we can always derive from saving in the expenditure of psychological effort. . . .

In laughter, therefore, according to our assumption, the conditions are such that a quantity of psychological energy previously committed to repression is now freely expended. Although not every laugh is a sign of pleasure—but certainly the laugh over a joke is—we will be inclined to attribute this pleasure to the lifting of the previously committed psychological energy. When we see that the hearer of a joke laughs but that the maker of the joke cannot laugh, this may signify to us that in the hearer a commitment of energy has been lifted and discharged, whereas in the formation of the joke there are impediments either to the lifting or to the possibility of removal of this commitment. The psychological process in the hearer, the third party of the joke, we can most appropriately characterize by emphasizing the fact that he buys the pleasure of the joke with very little expenditure of his own. The pleasure is a gift to him, so to speak. The words of the joke that he hears necessarily produce in him a conception or a train of thought that great inner obstacles opposed themselves against. He would have had to make his own effort in order to make it occur spontaneously in the first person, and he would have had to exert at least as much psychological energy as would balance the strength of the inhibition, suppression, or repression. This psychological expenditure he has saved himself.

According to our previous discussion, we might say that his pleasure is in proportion to this saving. Our insight into the mechanics of laughter would rather make us phrase it this way: The psychological energy previously committed to inhibition is now, through the restitution of the tabooed idea through auditory perception, suddenly rendered superfluous, has been lifted, and is now ready to be discharged by laughter. Essentially the two ways of representing what happens come to the same thing because the expenditure of energy that is saved corresponds exactly to the inhibition that has become superfluous. But the second way of putting it is more satisfactory because it allows us to say that the hearer of the joke laughs with the sum total of psychological energy that has been freed by the release of energy committed to inhibition. He laughs off, as it were, this sum total of psychological energy. . . .

We recall what occasion we had during our investigation of the joke to think of the dream. We found that the character and the effect of the joke are bound up with certain forms of expression and technical means, among which the most striking are the various kinds of condensation, displacement, and indirect representation. Processes that lead to the same results—condensation, displacement, and indirect representation—have become known to us as characteristics of the dream work. Doesn't this correspondence bring home the conclusion that the joke work and the dream work must be identical at least in one essential point? . . .

In relation to the processes of condensation, we have so thoroughly discussed the analogy between joke and dream that we may be briefer in what follows. We know that the displacements of the dream work indicate the influence of censorship on conscious thought, and, accordingly, when we meet with displacement among the techniques of the joke, we are inclined to assume that an inhibiting force also plays a role in the formation of a joke. We already know that this is quite generally the case. The endeavor of the joke to win back the old pleasure in nonsense or the old pleasure in words finds itself inhibited in a normal mood by the veto of critical reason, which must be overcome in every individual case. But the manner and style in which the joke work resolves this task show a decisive difference between the joke and the dream. In the dream work the resolution of this task occurs regularly through displacements, through the choice of ideas which are far enough distanced from the ones that are objectionable to find their way through censorship, but which are still derivatives of that idea whose psychological commitment they have taken over through full transference.

Displacements are thus never missing in any dream and are much more comprehensive. Not only distraction from a sequence of thought but also all kinds of indirect representation are to be counted among displacements, especially the substitution of a meaningful but offensive element by one that is indifferent but seemingly harmless to the powers of censorship, something that is the most remote sort of allusion to the first—the substitution through a symbol, a comparison, a small thing. The idea cannot be rejected that bits and pieces of this indirect representation are already formed in the preconscious of the dream—for example, the symbolism and the representation by analogy—because otherwise the thought would never have been brought to the stage of preconscious expression. Indirect representations of this sort, and allusions whose relation to the essential object is easy to find, are also permissible and much-used means of expression in our conscious thoughts. The dream work, however, overdoes the unrestrained use of this means of indirect representation. Any kind of relationship is, under the pressure of censorship, good enough to make a substitution through allusion, and the displacement from one element is permitted to any other. What is especially striking and characteristic of the dream work is the replacement of internal associations (similarity, causal relationship, etc.) by so-called external ones (simultaneous occurrence, spatial contiguity, analogy of sound).

All these means of displacement also occur as techniques of the joke. But when they occur, they observe, for the most part, the limits placed on their use in conscious thought. They can be entirely lacking although the joke also regularly has to accomplish the giving up of inhibition. We understand this lesser importance of displacement in the joke work if we remember that the joke generally has another technique at its disposal with which it protects itself against inhibition; indeed we have discovered nothing more characteristic of jokes than just this technique. The joke does not make compromises as does the dream; it does not avoid inhibition, but it insists on preserving word play or nonsense unchanged. But it confines itself to a choice of cases in which this word play or this nonsense can appear to be permissible (in the jest) or meaningful (in the joke) at the same time, thanks to the ambiguity of language and the many-sidedness of mental relations. Nothing separates the joke better from all other psychological creations than its double-sidedness and double-tonguedness, and at least from this perspective writers have been closest to understanding the joke through emphasis on "sense in nonsense." . . .

Nonsense and absurdity, which occur so often in the dream and which have incurred for it so much unmerited scorn, never come about accidentally through the throwing together like dice of imaginative elements, but it can always be demonstrated that they are intentionally allowed by the dream work and meant for the representation of embittered criticism and disdainful contradiction within the dream thoughts. Thus the absurdity of the dream's contents replaces the judgment, "it's nonsensical," in the dream thoughts. . . . We have now learned, by the resolution of certain pointed jokes, that nonsense in the joke is made to serve the same purposes of representation as in the dream. We also know that a nonsensical facade of a joke is especially suitable to heighten the psychological expenditure in the hearer and thus to increase the sum total of energy available to be freely discharged by laughter. But besides this we don't want to forget that the nonsense in the joke is an end in itself, because the intention of recovering our old pleasure in nonsense is among the motives of the joke work. There are other ways of recovering the nonsense and drawing pleasure from it: caricature, exaggeration, parody, and travesty use the same sources and so create "comic nonsense" of their own. . . .

It still remains for us to present a brief comparison between the joke and the better-known dream, and we will create the expectation that two such dissimilar psychological products would, aside from one already recognized agreement, only show us differences. The most important difference lies in their social behavior. The dream is a totally asocial psychological product. It has nothing to communicate to anyone else; it originates within a person as a compromise among struggling psychological forces; it remains incomprehensible to the person himself; and it is therefore completely uninteresting for another person. Not only does it not need to set any value on intelligibility, but it also must even guard against being understood because it could thus be destroyed; it can only exist in a carnival disguise. It may therefore make unhindered use of the mechanism that rules unconscious thought processes until it reaches a distortion that can no longer be redressed.

The joke, on the other hand, is the most social of all the psychological activities directed toward the production of pleasure. It often requires three persons and its completion demands the participation of someone else in the psychological process incited by the joke. It must therefore be fully intelligible. It may use the possible distortion in the unconscious through condensation and displacement in no further degree than can be corrected by the understanding of the third person. Furthermore, joke and dream have grown up in very different areas of psychological life and must be lodged in places quite far from each other in the psychological system.

The dream is still always a wish, although one that has been rendered unrecognizable; the joke is developed play. The dream retains, in spite of all its practical uselessness, its relation to the major concerns of life. It seeks to fulfill needs by the regressive detours of hallucination, and it owes its *raison d'être* to the one need that is active only during the night—the need to sleep. The joke, on the other hand, seeks to draw a small reward of pleasure from the mere, need-free activity of our psychological apparatus. Later it tries to snatch some pleasure as a by-product of that activity and manages, as a secondary purpose, to achieve important functions directed at the outside world. The dream serves principally to spare us displeasure, the joke for the acquisition of pleasure; but these two goals encompass all our psychological activities.

Maurice Charney
Seven Aspects of the Comic Hero*

1. The comic hero imagines himself
to be invulnerable and omnipotent.

The comic hero is a dreamlike figure who seems oblivious to human limitations. He can easily walk in the air—as in Ionesco's play, *The Aerial Pedestrians*, or *A Stroll in the Air (Les Piétons de l'Air)*—hover, glide, and perform remarkable aerodynamic feats without any effects at all. The weightless, balletic grace is essential to the comic effect, because any hint of exertion—any sweat—pricks the bubble of illusion and makes the comic hero mortal like us. Mortality is an assumption of tragedy, where the identification with the hero generates the sympathy that is indispensable for tragic effect.

In the Harold Lloyd movie *Safety Last*, we see him dangling raffishly from the hour-hand of a clock far above the street, which beckons menacingly like the abyss below, but Harold Lloyd manages to maintain an energetic, altogether businesslike expression. He isn't scared, and the terror we feel has definite limits, since we have ruled out the possibility that he might fall. He is invulnerable, omnipotent—maybe just lucky—and we follow his high-altitude act with the comic exhilaration of danger that will surely be overcome. Of course, it is only a film, it is not actually happening at this very moment, and the dangers have been safely neutralized by the medium: God's in his heaven and the film is in the can.

To make a crosscultural and interdisciplinary comparison, Shakespeare's Falstaff may have much in common with Buster Keaton. Both are totally impervious to the blows of Fortune, not from any stoic fortitude, but merely because both function outside the system of physical constraints, including the law of

*From *Comedy High and Low: An Introduction to the Experience of Comedy* (New York: Oxford University Press, 1978).

gravity (in Falstaff's world, "gravity," meaning sobriety and uprightness, can be misheard as "gravy," as in *Henry IV, Part 2* 1.2.166–68). Both have achieved a kind of weightlessness—if such a paradox can be sustained for a fat man so gross as Falstaff. He may be fat but he is never shown to be ungraceful, and his weightlessness is only a way of indicating his ultimate freedom from the very body with which he is burdened and of which he is so inordinately proud. It must be clear by now that the question posed by Maurice Morgann, the eighteenth-century critic, whether Falstaff is really a coward is entirely irrelevant, since he is so clearly protected from the dangers of military encounter. Like matter, a Falstaff can neither be created nor destroyed: he exists in a timeless continuum. His undisputed status as the comic hero protects him against sword thrusts, bullets, and other hostile and destructive arts. He is literally invulnerable.

2. The comic hero indulges in wish fulfillment and fantasy gratification.

Wish fulfillment and fantasy gratification sound like serious charges to bring against our defenseless, but luckily hypothetical, comic hero. Freud is constantly berating jokesters and laughers for their infantile and regressive impulses, as if, by committing themselves to jokes, they were refusing the rigors of adult life. It's true that the joke-teller demands instant gratification. It won't do to tell him that you will think about his joke and let him know if you find it funny, as in the old saying: "Tell an Englishman jokes when he's young so he will have something to laugh about when he's old."

Physiologists have connected laughter with two other involuntary activities: orgasm and epileptic seizure. All three are muscle spasms, which reach a climax and then subside. The intense climax satisfies the original impulse and purges it, so that one may well say, to twist the adage: after laughter the soul is sad. Weeping is apparently not the organic opposite of laughter or really analogous to it at all. For one thing, it is inspirational (drawing in the breath) rather than expirational and explosive as laughter is. In laughing, we are trying to get rid of some overwhelming and irresistible stimulus. Our response to tickling, which is the most fully studied aspect of this subject, may be protective and defensive: we attempt to withdraw the threatened part from the line of attack (or potential attack). This is like the child's threat: "I bet I can make you laugh," as if the involuntary laughter were a sign of weakness and capitulation. Freud connects laughter, like sex, with the suppressed, repressed, and unconscious activities of the Id, and his book on jokes is an offshoot of his monumental study of dreams. His analysis of joke-material (the inimitable *Witzwerk*) proceeds along the same lines as his analysis of dreams (the *Traumwerk*) and slips of the tongue, with the seemingly random manifest content expressing specific latent meanings.

The basic mechanism of dreams and of comedy is wish fulfillment. The comic hero imagines himself as not only adequate for every situation that may present itself, but infinitely superior to all other men. He is never at a loss for an answer, and this must be central to our understanding of comic superiority. Not only an answer, but a beautiful, witty, eloquent answer. Wish fulfillment implies unlimited versatility and intelligence. The clown's quick rejoinders use the traditional logical forms of *tu quoque* ("the same to you") and *quid pro quo* ("tit for tat"), which are the hallmarks of comic resourcefulness: any answer can itself be answered, the comedian can return and improve on someone else's witty comment, he must always have the last word, and, most importantly, he can never be put down or embarrassed. In our complex social life, this in itself is a form of omnipotence and invulnerability.

The links between comedy and dreams are very specific, especially in the mechanism of free association, by which the dreamer and the comic hero jump from point to point by intuitive leaps and without any necessary, logical connection. There is, of course, a dream logic, as Freud so painstakingly demonstrated, different from the commonsense logic of ordinary waking experience. Dream logic is symbolically self-contained and self-consistent, and the leaps are all generated by a train of thought which expresses important preoccupations. The dream world of *The Wizard of Oz* is a projection of the cozy farm scenes with which the film begins, and Shakespeare's *Midsummer Night's Dream* uses the dream sequences in the wood to play out conflicts in the real world of Athens.

Dream technique allows for a fluidity of movement that is not possible in everyday life. Displacement of real to imagined experience, distortion of visual images, substitution of dream logic for rational sequence and causality, endless repetition and variations of fixed patterns can all be freely used to emphasize a certain mood or turn of thought. Suddenly, everything is possible, and from this unlimited freedom come the startling puns and new associations out of which comedy is created. It is important to insist that the making of comedy is an imaginative activity that seeks to recombine and refashion the raw materials of experience into something different, something created by the mind, something essentially metaphorical. These high claims for the powers of comedy indicate that it is not a "realistic" art at all. It may draw on the humble materials of daily life that tragedy in the high style rejects, but this is only the beginning. The comic imagination uses these materials for its own purposes. As in dreams, the facts are thoroughly transformed by distortion, over-emphasis, imaginary dialogue, wordplay, incongruity, and other personalizing devices, so that the imagined reality has little resemblance to the reality with which we began. To put it simply, the objective reality is fundamentally changed by the churning and turbulent processes of wish fulfillment and fantasy gratification.

3. The comic hero engages in play without any ulterior purpose.

Huizinga, the Dutch historian and author of *The Waning of the Middle Ages*, reminds us forcefully that man is an animal who needs to play, that play is an instinctual impulse that must be satisfied. Man is *Homo ludens* (which is the title of Huizinga's fascinating book on play), and to ignore this is to obscure an essential characteristic of all living creatures. Phylogenetically speaking, how far back would Huizinga be willing to go? Do amoeba play, and are water spiders really skipping and frolicking on the surface of a pond? To what extent do we anthropomorphize and animate the nonhuman creation? We might as well ask if dogs really laugh, even though they can almost exactly mimic human laughter. But play is something more fundamental than laughter, and it satisfies imperative physiological needs. The insistent babbling of small children—sometimes pure nonsense phrases—fulfills a need for expression that cannot be resisted. Or mere high spirits, if there is such a thing, may find an outlet in a purely physical activity like running. There is a sense in which running, or skipping, or even singing in the shower, are completely joyous activities without any ulterior motive. Huizinga's argument depends strongly on animal physiology, where play is a powerful physical drive. Once the theory is applied to human beings, however, complications arise.

Freud, and Freudian critics, tend to stigmatize play as infantile regression, and their theories of comedy are so highly purposive that mere play seems to drop out entirely. But this simplifies and rationalizes motives. If comedy is a way of mastering a fearful, uncertain, and mysterious reality, we may play at roles and positions for some temporary advantages and without being fully committed to them. Freud so thoroughly excludes children from his account of comedy that he fails to see how we may be continuing childlike attitudes and responses in our humor. Even if we admit that aggression is a powerful component in many jokes, we still need to define the exact status of that aggression. We may be playing at the aggressor with a histrionic audacity that may frighten even us, as Charlie Chaplin seemed to scare himself as the Great Dictator. The status of this aggression is ambiguous. It's like a group of children telling ghost stories during a blackout who wind up being terrified. The play element is the part that is difficult to account for. We are kidding around and we are serious at one and the same time, and the exact proportions of each may baffle us. We may not really discern the strength of our own motives until we test the reactions of others. They may either inspire us to go on or dampen our enthusiasm.

4. The comic hero is a realist who celebrates the body and affirms the life force.

Paradoxically, comedy can, at different moments, rejoice in the triumph over the material limitations of the body and also indulge in the equally powerful impulse to enjoy the pleasures of the body. No theoretician of comedy has ever claimed that eating, drinking, sleeping, fornicating, or any other pleasure of the senses was comic in and for itself. Even in the lowest kinds of farce or pantomime, the humor of the senses is derived either from hyperbole or understatement—a skillful exaggeration of what the audience might expect, or a teasing frustration of the expectations that have been aroused. One can imagine the methodical consumption of several hundred pancakes (on the lines of the joke in which the analyst reassures his patient: ''There's nothing wrong with liking pancakes. I have a closet [or steamer trunk] full of them myself''). Or we can picture a striptease photographed in reverse (either in slow or in speeded-up motion), but eating or sex in themselves have no inherent comic force. The point is that the comic hero, by his very nature, needs to declare himself the patron of everything real, physical, material, enjoyable, and the enemy of all abstractions, moral principles, seriousness, and joylessness. This is a matter of basic allegiance to the life force.

In his influential theory of comedy, Henri Bergson separates those who celebrate the life force (and are therefore the makers of comedy) from those who impose a mechanical rigidity on the free flow of experience (and thereby qualify as the butts of comedy). The comic hero is typically someone who believes in daily life and its round of assorted and unanticipated pleasures, who is optimistic about the future, and who, unlike the tragic hero, has little or no interest in the past. He is a hedonist who lives for the moment, and wit becomes a lifestyle that replaces any moral, ethical, or religious commitments. The fat man, if he is fat enough, is himself a hyperbole in the flesh, an impressive "too much," a living exaggeration, a creative overreacher and overdoer. This is the source of his comic strength.

The old joke of the attractive woman disassembling herself in the privacy of her bedroom "After the Ball Was Over" turns on false appearances, but there is also a kind of fascinated horror at the body's standardized and easily replaceable equipment. It is curious that the upper-berth jokes recorded by Gershon Legman in his gargantuan anthology, *Rationale of the Dirty Joke*, all depend on mechanistic and voyeuristic assumptions of the body—always a female body—as a cunning device for sexual gratification. Upper-berth jokes, which have now virtually disappeared with the Pullman car and transcontinental trains (one of Legman's chief sources of material), are inherently simple, because there are only three worthwhile (and completely detachable) sexual parts. The gentleman in the upper berth—and he is always a gentleman and always in the upper berth—may well grow impatient at what he takes to be an excessive series of preliminary and superfluous detachments and unscrewings. One classic punch line is for the upper-berth gentleman to say petulantly: "Hey, lady, stop wasting time. You know what I want; just unscrew it and pass it up here." This is the archetypal comic situation of Bergson's essay on laughter, since it superimposes a mechanical conceit on the free-flowing and otherwise spontaneous nature of human experience.

5. *The comic hero cultivates comic paranoia, as if laughter were an essential defense against a hostile reality.*

Comic paranoia could be demonstrated biographically from the lives of the great comedians, or even from the lives of the second- and third-rate comics who figure in Phil Berger's *The Last Laugh: The World of the Stand-up Comic*. Woody Allen is in a long tradition of sad, neurotic, defensive clowns—schlemiels, nebbishes, misfits—whose wit is the only thing that keeps them going. These are the oppressed anti-heroes, beaten down by bureaucracy, baffled by the intricacies of the Machine Age, nonplussed by the mysteries of women and sex, who find it difficult to perform the simplest acts, but who nevertheless have feverish fantasies of their suppressed heroic potential, as Woody Allen re-creates machismo roles in the style of Humphrey Bogart in *Play It Again Sam*. There are similarly inflated dream sequences in most of Woody Allen's movies.

Admittedly, this is an extreme case, but comedians never seem to find reality warm, comforting, and supportive. Something is always going wrong, mistakes and accidents and unaccountable mishaps are at the heart of the typical intrigue plot in comedy, and the comic hero is usually trying to grapple with a highly resistant reality. He is always on his guard, always on the *qui vive*, always alert to disaster and instant chaos. Wit is a weapon with which to protect yourself, perhaps the only weapon. The sad clown is neither powerful, rich, well-born, handsome, well-connected, or in any way favored by the gods. He must make his way alone, against overwhelming odds, with ridiculously inadequate equipment.

In a typically comic situation of this sort, not only is there a gross mismatch between the comic hero and the gigantic forces he is pitted against, but the comic hero is protected, as it were, by his own imperfect perception, or what may be called either innocence or stupidity. Mr. Magoo's extreme nearsightedness allows him to go through harrowing adventures with only the dimmest awareness of what is happening. He is constantly mumbling the platitudes of mistaken politeness in entirely inappropriate situations, and his hearty appeals to "Dear old Rutgers" usually come at moments of impending doom. Or the comic hero performs some heroic act unintentionally, striving for an effect just the opposite from what actually occurs. W. C. Fields inadvertently captures the robber in the *Bank Dick*, as does Inspector

Clouseau (played by Peter Sellers) in *The Return of the Pink Panther*. The capture is an accidental by-product of something entirely different, but the comic anti-hero quickly adapts to his new status, since comic reality is inherently unstable, unsolid, unsubstantial, with an unlimited tendency to become unstuck. In these sudden transformations the element of surprise is negligible— Chaplin can become the Great Dictator and be changed back to the little tramp without violating our expectations. Comic reality is infinitely flexible, and heroic and unheroic roles are so easily interchangeable because the heroic and the grandiose are only illusions.

The kind of comedian we are talking about never consciously tries to be funny. He doesn't laugh at his own jokes, and he certainly could not be called happy or joyous. He is, in fact, solemn, fearful, and glum, convinced that ultimate disaster is only moments away. Meanwhile, he devises hare-brained schemes that will prolong life for an instant or two longer. It is all futile, but comic ingenuity helps to pass the time. There is a firm conviction that he is the one sane man who remains alive in an otherwise distorted and surrealistic world. Again, "realism" proves to be a totally inadequate criterion for comedy. It is the grotesque twisting of the familiar that is the source of comedy, which cultivates a mood of blurred, out-of-focus perception, in which we have lost our clear vision, firm footing, and sense of rightness and decency. Comic paranoia suggests a certain fixed attitude to reality from which a good deal of comedy springs, although "paranoia" is perhaps too strong a term. It is evident, however, that comedy does not arise from well-adjusted, middle-class persons, decent, hard-working, sane, with what psychiatrists call realistic goals and expectations. Comedy is produced rather from hysteria and frenzy and offers a technique for survival in a mad world.

6. The comic hero may serve as the ritual clown of his society, acting as a scapegoat for its taboos.

The theory and practice of the ritual clown is well documented from the study of various Indian tribes of the Southwest, especially the Zuñi Katcinas. The annual appointment of a ritual clown provides an ingenious safety valve for the pressures, guilts, and accumulated repressions of the society. Like the scapegoat, the clown takes upon himself all the taboos of the society and spends his time obscenely flouting everything decent and sacred. He masturbates publicly, covers himself with excrement, makes sexual advances to virgins and married women alike, utters forbidden words, and openly blasphemes against the gods. His outrageous conduct fills his auditors with emotions of loathing, fear, and terror, since they expect the gods to strike him down at any moment. But the clown plays his carefully assigned role with merriment and abandon. He is a jester, a sacred fool, who has license to break all taboos during the time he is on stage. It is all very histrionic, and the ritual clowning functions like an extended theatrical performance, in which the audience, through catharsis, is released vicariously from its burdensome fears and taboos. The ritual clown acts out a forbidden social role for the general good of the community.

The fool in Shakespeare functions against a background of real fools, who were part of noble households in the Elizabethan period, either natural fools crazed in their wits or professional jesters, or some combination of the two. The fool in *King Lear* doesn't have the sophistication of such professionals as Touchstone in *As You Like It* and Feste in *Twelfth Night*, and his acerbic, eccentric manner seems closer to genuine madness, as Melville certainly thought in his re-creation of the fool as Pip in *Moby-Dick*. At a critical point in the play, Lear can only speak to the fool and Poor Tom, the Bedlam beggar (Edgar in disguise). The fool understands Lear's folly as no one else can, and he speaks by allowance and permission. In a sense, he is totally fearless, despite Lear's continual references to the whip, by which the fool could be officially chastised. The fool becomes the ritual scapegoat for everything that is troubling the old king, but he is also a philosopher and moral instructor as well. Since he is completely outside the social hierarchy, he is free to speak and to act without constraint; it is as if, except for his role as ritual clown, he had no separate being at all. He exists for the sake of King Lear: to mitigate his passion and to offer him an elemental commiseration and comfort, and also, in another sense, to be the lost son that Lear never had.

The fool and the ritual clown are far from any heroic notion of the comic hero, yet they fulfill a necessary and vital function. They are the most humble of creatures, the lowest on the social scale, completely anonymous and insignificant. Yet as truthspeakers they are endowed with a terrifying power. They are not, of course, aware that they are anything so exalted as truthspeakers. They merely act their role according to the prescribed forms and in an unsophisticated and unselfconscious way. Their purposeful folly and licensed wit free them from the restraints of ordinary men, and witnesses have testified to the ambiguous mixture of grossness, stupidity, and awesomeness in the ritual clown. The assumption is that the gods speak through their appointed fool, who is a mouthpiece for their dark and inscrutable wisdom, and who may actually be privy to their secrets. The ritual aspect overrides any personal considerations, and we arrive at the central concept of the sacred fool, who is the gods' minion. In this hypothesis, the gods are not orderly and predictable, but vast, chaotic, incomprehensible, and even obscene forces. Ritual clowning and the role of the fool offer a way of mastering a mysterious and anarchic reality.

7. The comic hero doesn't eventually merge into the tragic hero, but represents an entirely different range of experience.

It is unfashionable, and perhaps even unsporting, to insist that comedy is separate from tragedy and to resist the proposition that all comedy aspires to the condition of tragedy. We must reject the glib assumption that comedy is a lesser form of art and experience that somehow needs to be ennobled and completed by tragedy. Dramatic criticism usually hunts out ways in which comedy may lay claim to darker overtones and a tragic coloring. Shakespeare's "problem" comedies—*Measure for Measure, Troilus and Cressida, All's Well That Ends Well*—are conventionally praised for the wrong reasons, and their supposed resemblance to tragedy immediately elevates their status in the Shakespearean canon. Jonson's *Volpone* has been similarly extolled for its tragic implications, while its comic brilliance is awkwardly acknowledged but minimized. Thus Molière's vigorous and uncompromising comedy, *Le Misanthrope*, is distorted by the tragic perspective, and more recent playwrights like Beckett, Pinter, and Dürrenmatt may suffer from our inability to appreciate comedy—even dark comedy, tragicomedy, tragic farce, or whatever we may choose to call it—without putting in facile claims for the "seriousness" of tragedy.

This is not intended to attack tragedy and the possibilities of true tragedy in our time, but only to insist on some of the differences between comedy and tragedy. Traditionally, tragedy ends in death (or its equivalent, like the blinding of Oedipus), whereas comedy ends in marriage, feasting, dancing, the promise of babies, and a general mood of reconciliation. Death, or the threat of death, is always unreal in comedy, and even more unreal in tragicomedy, where it is only an effect of manipulation. Once death is removed as a possibility, the system of serious punishments and rewards breaks down, and we have to rely on poetic justice. Comedy doesn't allow for grave punishments at all, but it moves towards untangling complications and reconciling enemies. The expected happy ending of comedy still makes a great deal of difference in the kind of causes needed to produce the programmed result.

In Horace Walpole's famous dictum, "The world is a comedy to those that think, a tragedy to those that feel." In other words, human involvement produces tragedy, while the comic hero remains aloof from the events in which he participates. He doesn't feel deeply. In the sense of sympathy and commiseration, he probably doesn't feel at all. The tragic hero is committed, a man of principle, profoundly flawed or mistaken, but still serious, moral, open to the effects of choice and free will, and ready to take the moral consequences of his acts. None of these noble qualities applies to the comic hero, except fortuitously. He engages in adventures and encounters in which chance plays a large role, but he never truly feels sorrow, guilt, compassion, or any of the legitimately tragic emotions.

There still remains a serious theoretical question whether comedy is the obverse of tragedy, with both together defining the whole range of human experience. This dualistic formula sounds comforting, but in practice comedy and tragedy widely overlap. Comedy is not composed of the things tragedy is not—its leftovers, as it were—nor is it a lower form or trivialization of tragedy. These formulations are objectionable because comedy is a different kind of experience from tragedy, and it may well be that, although comedy has innumerable resemblances to tragedy (and also direct contrasts with it), the one form has no essential relation to the other. This statement violates a humanistic assumption about the organic connection of literary forms and genres, but comedy has been so glibly subordinated to tragedy that it becomes important to insist that comedy and tragedy are different entities in their own right.

Comic catharsis is often equated with catharsis in tragedy, and Aristotle's *Poetics*, which formulates the idea of the purging of pity and fear, was cleverly reversed in antiquity to produce his unwritten (or lost) treatise on comedy (as reconstructed in Lane Cooper's *An Aristotelian Theory of Comedy*). The procedure seems highly irregular, since no justification is offered for the belief that tragedy and comedy are analogous systems. Whatever we may think about that question, we may still ask: Is there a comic equivalent for tragic catharsis? Comedy, too, arouses strong and even violent emotions, but the relief and mollification that comedy finally brings seem to lie in the area of beneficial wish fulfillment. We are allowed to work through our anxieties about our limited capacities and powers. Gut laughter provides for the release of primitive drives and instinctual needs that may be suppressed in daily life. It is a ritual release shared with other members of the audience. We are engaged in vicarious play, sometimes with great intensity. Comic catharsis purges inhibitions and obstructions alike and lets us express a grandiose, heroic, and eloquent vision of ourselves—a vision that gains force from being so demonstrably untrue.

Barbara Freedman

Errors in Comedy: A Psychoanalytic Theory of Farce*

The widespread assumption that farce is light, inherently meaningless comedy derives from a no less reputable source than the *Oxford English Dictionary*. Here we learn that farce is "a dramatic work (usually short) which has for its sole object to excite laughter." This definition has been largely responsible for the two major attitudes toward Shakespearean farce. The first is represented by that group of critics who know that Shakespeare never wrote anything solely to make us laugh and so argue that Shakespeare never wrote farce at all. Anne Barton, in the Riverside Shakespeare introduction to *The Comedy of Errors*, observes that "despite its emphasis on plot and situational absurdity, despite the merry violence in many of the scenes, it is not really possible to contain *The Comedy of Errors* within the bounds of farce as defined by the *Oxford English Dictionary*." She therefore concludes that what Coleridge termed "this legitimate farce in exactest consonance with the philosophical principles and character of farce" is in fact no farce at all. E. M. W. Tillyard offers a similar assessment of this comedy's generic status, complaining that "when an example of a lesser literary kind reaches a certain pitch of excellence, it is apt to transcend the kind to which it belongs." The more popular critical approach, however, is to agree that Shakespeare wrote farce, but to consider *Errors* (as well as Shakespeare's other predominantly farcical plays) to be nonsensical *insofar* as they are farce. The plays are pronounced "two-dimensional only, unsubstantial, not intended to be taken seriously." The editor of the Pelican edition of *Errors*, for example, laments that "there is left over nothing really to think about—except, if one wishes, the tremendously puzzling question of what so grips and amuses an audience during a play which has so little thought in it."

The reasoning behind these arguments appears to be that if a

*From *Shakespearean Comedy*, ed. Maurice Charney, *New York Literary Forum*, V-VI (1980).

farce should do more than arouse laughter, it is no longer a farce, and if it does no more than arouse laughter, it is not a serious or viable art form. Obviously, the *OED*'s stipulation that farce's sole object is laughter only makes sense when reworded so as to stipulate that farce's essential aim is laughter. In this way, the definition does not exclude those intellectual, emotional, and aesthetic aims that differentiate a Chaplin masterpiece from the tasteless films of the Three Stooges, or a work of art from a mere simulacrum. The latter complaint is substantive, however; the charge that farce is inhospitable to meaning has riddled, if not undermined, the very concept of farce criticism.

This essay calls for a re-evaluation of Shakespearean farce in light of a psychoanalytic theory of the dynamics of meaning in farce. It suggests that the critical neglect and disparagement of the farces is largely due to the plays' own insistence on their meaninglessness, an insistence which by no means should be accepted at face value. Rather, I shall argue that a strategic denial and displacement of meaning is intrinsic to the genre and essential to the humorous acceptance of normally unacceptable aggression which it allows. I shall confine my proof to *The Comedy of Errors;* those Shakespearean plays which share the same generic background, *The Taming of the Shrew* and *The Merry Wives of Windsor*, would be equally suitable subjects for analysis. A major assumption of this study is that without an appreciation of the role of farce in these plays and a more sophisticated understanding of the dynamics of meaning in farce, the "nonromantic" comedies will never be properly understood.

The association of farce with that which is insignificant and insubstantial is deeply rooted in the word's history. Our use of "farce" may be traced back to the Old French (*farsir*) and the Latin (*farcire*), meaning "to stuff," and appears to be a metaphorical use of its longstanding, and still popular, equation with "stuffing." As early as the thirteenth century, the latinized form of "farce" was used to refer to Latin phrases, and even rhymed passages in French, interpolated in any set liturgical formula. Its use was ultimately extended to include the improvised clowning which was similarly inserted in religious dramas. It was at this point, apparently, that the word became permanently associated with the nature and quality of the matter interpolated, rather than its interpolated status. For most of us, "farce" now signifies the recasting of what we normally consider serious in a foolish and insubstantial light.

While the *OED*'s definition of farce as a drama "which has for its sole object to excite laughter" may be considered historically accurate, it fails to take into account contemporary usage of the term. Briefly, the definition is misleading in ignoring the changes that occur when an interpolated form becomes a full-length play and viable genre, as farce has today. It ignores the distinctions between "farce" and that which is "farcical" (the former striving for much more than laughter), and it ignores the basic, accepted differences between farce and other forms of purely comic drama, such as folk comedy, intrigue comedy, and burlesque. Obviously, farce does more than arouse laughter, and it does so in ways which are recognizably different from other forms of comedy. Finally, the description of a genre solely in terms of affective response is problematic in itself, but particularly so when the affect is laughter. Since there is no critical consensus about the causes of laughter, we are left with a definition of farce as a mysterious response to an undefinable object.

A survey of definitions of farce in dictionaries, encyclopedias, and literary and theatrical glossaries, however, provides us with three basic structural elements to which this mysterious response may be attributed: an absurd situation, normally unacceptable libidinal action, and flat, surrealistic characters. A valid definition of farce might only list these three characteristics; a valuable one would discover what is essential in these elements and why. It would, ideally, determine their relationship as a dynamic, functional modality, which would enable us to understand how farce is constructed and how it can be deconstructed analytically. Considered as interdependent, functional units, the one dynamic element would seem to be farce's normally unacceptable libidinal action. The key to farce, as Eric Bentley reminds us in *The Life of the Drama*, is that we laugh at violence; the unacceptable becomes acceptable, even enjoyable. What Bentley sidesteps in his brilliant treatment of the genre is how the characteristic elements of farce interact in a functional manner to enable us to enjoy the unacceptable.

Fowler's *Dictionary of Modern Critical Terms* anticipates a functional analysis in its suggestion that farce's "encapsulated universe encourages a comedy of cruelty since the audience is insulated from feeling by the absence of motive, and by the response being simultaneously more and less aggressive than real-life response." Fowler thus views farce's absence of cause and effect, its absence of logic and realism, in a functional manner. The first and last terms of our classic definition—an absurd situation (here translated as absence of cause) and stereotyped, flat characters (translated as absence of effect)—may be viewed positively, as making possible a certain type of humorous response determined by the definition's second term: unacceptable aggression.

One might choose, however, to reverse Fowler's ordering and suggest that it is not the encapsulated universe that encourages a comedy of cruelty, but cruelty that encourages—indeed demands— the anesthetizing removal of cause and effect, thus creating comedy. In other words, it is not the absence, but the denial of the cause and effect of farce's violence that enables its expression and renders it safe. Were we not able to disown intent for aggression through error or dissolve remorse for its consequences through denial, the characteristic humor that ensures farce's popularity could never be achieved. On the other hand, were some initial, meaningful aggression not present to be disowned or denied, farce would lack both pleasure and humor. Like dreams, farce couples a functional denial of significance with often disturbing and highly significant content. The union of the absurd and the significant is essential to farce; a mother-in-law is mistakenly barraged with cream pies, a son mistakenly marries his father's mistress, a troop of policemen just happen to chance upon a street lined with banana peels. A taboo is always both broken and not broken.

Clearly, farce cannot function in a moral vacuum; it is not anesthetic, and its violence cannot operate in the absence of meaning. It is the denial of meaning that makes farce work. Yet if it is the denial and displacement, as opposed to the mere absence, of meaning and affect that characterizes farcical aggression, then these displaced elements can be reconstructed to reveal meaningful dramatic action. Illogic, contradiction, omission, and mistakes become signifiers of a functional dislocation of meaning through which the absurd becomes meaningful. Hence, a definition: farce is a dramatic genre deriving laughter chiefly from the denial of the cause (through absurdity) and the effect (through surrealism) of aggressive action upon an object. And hence, as well, a model of analysis.

The argument that farce's aggression is meaningful has long been implicit in the descriptions of anxiety, paranoia, horror, and menace that accompany critics' discussions of this supposedly carefree genre. Bentley, for example, claims to view farce as an exhilarating world of children without parents, action without consequences, id without superego: "Farce affords an escape from living, a release from the pressure of today, a regression to the irresponsibility of childhood." Yet his language points to a sense of malevolent and punitive action, to a sense of the terrors

of childhood as well: "Human life in this art form is horribly
attenuated. Life is a kind of universal milling around, a rushing
from bedroom to bedroom driven by demons more dreadful than
sensuality. The kind of farce which is said to be 'all plot' is often
much more than ingenious, it is maniacal."

The maniacal demons which inhabit the farcical world can,
however, be identified. Bentley offers a clue: "Melodrama and
farce are both arts of escape and what they are running away
from is not only social problems but all other forms of moral
responsibility. They are running away from the conscience and
all its creations. . . ." I would agree only if we add that if farce
involves running away from the conscience, it re-enacts that
chase with the conscience as a strong contender. Bentley's descriptions of being driven from bedroom to bedroom by demons, of a
loss of free will and control to something which "bristles with
menace," something which threatens, in turn, to lose control,
suggest that farce enacts something like a primitive superego
punishment for the characters' libidinal release in the form of a
maniacal plot which both arranges libidinal gratification and
punishes for it. This would explain why the more the characters
lose control in farce, the more tightly the plot is wound up; why
the more the characters seek gratification, the more severely the
plot punishes them for it. The lawless plot aggression in farce is,
paradoxically enough, punitive supergo aggression. Only conscience, primitive conscience, enjoys violence without guilt or
cost. The characteristic sense of anxiety and menace in a highly
elaborated, paranoid plot; the celebrated chase, the hallmark of
farce; the series of blows mistakenly delivered—all are signs of a
comedy of the superego. The secret of the strange enjoyment of
farce may be that although we enjoy fulfilling forbidden wishes,
we enjoy punishing them just as much, if not more, particularly
when we can do so in a plot which is apparently devoid of logic,
meaning, and harm.

Our understanding of farce has shifted, then, from an art form
which simply enjoys libidinal release and gratification to a form
which expresses, instead, a dialectic of gratification and punishment as gratification. (Hence the relation of bedroom farce to
slapstick: the former provides the usual content of farce, the trans-
gression; the latter the informing principle of the action, the form
of farce, the punishment.) Although there is no literature on this
dialectic in farce, Norman Shapiro discusses the theme of punishment in the works of that consummate farceur, Georges Feydeau.
Shapiro is careful to distinguish between two different forms of
punishment in Feydeau's plays: absurd punishment "which de-

lights in recreating . . . the absurdity and inexplicability of everyday life'' and meaningful punishment, which satirizes human pretensions. His examples, however, negate that distinction, because they offer a striking similarity to dream episodes in which the gratification of an illicit wish is coupled with an apparently absurd yet obviously displaced punishment. Hence Shapiro designates punishment in a thinly disguised Oedipal plot as absurd and unwarranted. The only real distinction between the two groups is the degree to which the characters' transgressions, and hence the logic of the punishment, is disguised. Farce is not the typical product of a world view which enjoys contemplating "the absurdity and inexplicability of everyday life," then, but the product of a world in which life is considered all too explicable and moral values are regarded all too seriously—so seriously, in fact, that aggressive action taken both against certain laws and in the name of those laws provides much needed relief in the form of laughter.

What is of chief importance in understanding farce, then, is the recognition that the plot's aggression is punitive, and meaningfully so—a recognition in turn dependent upon the reconstruction of the characters' disguised, denied transgressions. We may gather these perceptions into a working model of farce as follows: farce is a type of comedy deriving laughter chiefly from the release and gratification of aggressive impulses, accomplished by a denial of the cause (through absurd situations) and the effect (through a surrealistic medium) of aggressive action upon an object, and functioning through the plot in a disguised punitive fashion which is directly related to the characters' disguised libidinal release.

The perfect psychoanalytic description of farce is in fact the punishment dream:

In these dreams, as in so many others, the ego anticipates guilt, that is, superego condemnation, if the part of the latent content which derives from the repressed should find too direct an emergence in the manifest dream. Consequently, the ego's defenses oppose the emergence of this part of the latent content, which is again no different from what goes on in most other dreams. However, the result in the so-called punishment dreams is that the manifest dream, instead of expressing a more or less disguised fantasy of the fulfillment of a repressed wish, expresses a more or less disguised fantasy of punishment for the wish in question, certainly a most extraordinary "compromise" among ego, id, and superego.*

There is no better description of the underlying dynamics of meaning in farce. The identification of farcical drama as a type of punishment dream or fantasy explains both the extensive disguise of its characters' libidinal transgressions (whether in content, cause, or effect) and their minimization in favor of audience and author identification with punitive plot action against those transgressions, disguised solely in terms of cause and effect.

*Charles Brenner, *An Introductory Textbook of Psychoanalysis*

BIBLIOGRAPHY

GENERAL STUDIES OF COMEDY AND LAUGHTER

Bakhtin, Mikhail. *Rabelais and His World*, trans. by Helene Iswolsky. Cambridge, Massachusetts: Massachusetts Institute of Technology, 1968.

Bergson, Henri. *Laughter* (1900), in *Comedy*, ed. Wylie Sypher. Garden City, New York: Doubleday Anchor, 1956. Also includes George Meredith, "An Essay on Comedy."

Charney, Maurice. *Comedy High and Low: An Introduction to the Experience of Comedy*. New York: Oxford University Press, 1978.

————, ed. *Comedy—New Perspectives*, in *New York Literary Forum*. Vol. 1, 1978.

Cornford, Francis M. *The Origin of Attic Comedy*. Cambridge: Cambridge University Press, 1934.

Eastman, Max. *Enjoyment of Laughter*. New York: Simon & Schuster, 1936.

Freud, Sigmund. *Jokes and Their Relation to the Unconscious* (1905), trans. by James Strachey. New York: Norton, 1960.

Grotjahn, Martin. *Beyond Laughter*. New York: McGraw-Hill, 1957.

Gurewitch, Morton. *Comedy: The Irrational Vision*. Ithaca, New York: Cornell University Press, 1975.

Holland, Norman N. *Laughing: A Psychology of Humor*. Ithaca, New York: Cornell University Press, 1982.

Hoy, Cyrus. *The Hyacinth Room*. New York: Knopf, 1964.

Huizinga, Johan. *Homo Ludens: A Study of the Play-Element in Culture*. Boston: Beacon Press, 1955.

Kern, Edith G. *The Absolute Comic*. New York: Columbia University Press, 1980.

Levin, Harry, ed. *Veins of Humor*. Cambridge, Massachusetts: Harvard University Press, 1972.

Olson, Elder. *The Theory of Comedy*. Bloomington, Indiana: Indiana University Press, 1968.

Palmer, John. *Comedy*. London: Secker, 1914.

Schaeffer, Neil. *The Art of Laughter*. New York: Columbia University Press, 1981.

Sedgewick, G. G. *Of Irony, Especially in Drama*. Toronto: University of Toronto Press, 1934.

Thompson, Alan Reynolds. *The Dry Mock: A Study of Irony in Drama*. Berkeley: University of California Press, 1948.

Willeford, William. *The Fool and His Scepter*. Evanston, Illinois: Northwestern University Press, 1969.

ARISTOPHANES

Dover, K. J. *Aristophanic Comedy*. Berkeley: University of California Press, 1972.

Ehrenberg, Victor. *The People of Aristophanes*. London: Methuen, 1974.

Murray, Gilbert. *Aristophanes*. Oxford: Clarendon Press, 1965.

Norwood, Gilbert. *Greek Comedy*. Boston: Luce, 1930.

Whitman, Cedric H. *Aristophanes and the Comic Hero*. Cambridge, Massachusetts: Harvard University Press, 1964.

PLAUTUS

Beare, W. *The Roman Stage*. London: Methuen, 1950.

Duckworth, George E. *The Nature of Roman Comedy*. Princeton, New Jersey: Princeton University Press, 1952.

Harsh, P. W. *A Handbook of Classical Drama*. Stanford, California: Stanford University Press, 1944.

Little, Alan McN. G. "Plautus and Popular Drama," *Harvard Studies in Classical Philology*. 49(1938), 205–28.

Segal, Erich. *Roman Laughter: The Comedy of Plautus*. Cambridge, Massachusetts: Harvard University Press, 1968.

SHAKESPEARE

Barber, C. L. *Shakespeare's Festive Comedy*. Princeton, New Jersey: Princeton University Press, 1959.

Berry, Ralph. *Shakespeare's Comedies: Explorations in Form*. Princeton, New Jersey: Princeton University Press, 1972.

Charney, Maurice, ed. *Shakespearean Comedy. New York Literary Forum*. Vols. V–VI, 1980.

Nevo, Ruth. *Comic Transformations in Shakespeare*. London: Methuen, 1980.

Salingar, Leo. *Shakespeare and the Traditions of Comedy*. Cambridge, Massachusetts: Cambridge University Press, 1976.

MOLIÈRE

Fernandez, Ramon. *Molière*, trans. by Wilson Follett. New York: Hill & Wang, 1958.

Gossman, Lionel. *Men and Masks: A Study of Molière*. Baltimore, Maryland: Johns Hopkins Press, 1963.

Guicharnaud, Jacques, ed. *Molière, a Collection of Critical Essays*. Englewood Cliffs, New Jersey: Prentice Hall, 1964.

Hubert, Judd D. *Molière and the Comedy of Intellect*. Berkeley: University of California Press, 1962.

Moore, W. G. *Molière: A New Criticism*. Oxford: Clarendon Press, 1969.

GOGOL

Ehre, Milton, and Fruma Gottschalk, ed. and trans. *The Theater of Nikolay Gogol: Plays and Selected Writings*. Chicago: University of Chicago Press, 1980.

Erlich, Victor. *Gogol*. New Haven, Connecticut: Yale University Press, 1969.

Fanger, Donald. *The Creation of Nikolai Gogol*. Cambridge, Massachusetts: Harvard University Press, 1979.

Maguire, Robert A., ed. and trans. *Gogol from the Twentieth Century: Eleven Essays*. Princeton, New Jersey: Princeton University Press, 1974.

Nabokov, Vladimir. *Nikolai Gogol*. Norfolk, Connecticut: New Directions, 1944.

FEYDEAU

Baker, Stuart E. *Georges Feydeau and the Aesthetics of Farce*. Ann Arbor, Michigan: UMI Research Press, 1981.

Pronko, Leonard C. *Georges Feydeau*. New York: Ungar, 1975. World Dramatists Series.

———. *Eugène Labiche and Georges Feydeau*. New York: Grove Press, 1982. Modern Dramatists Series.

Shapiro, Norman R., ed. and trans. *Feydeau First to Last: Eight One-Act Comedies*. Ithaca, New York: Cornell University Press, 1982.

———, ed. and trans. *Four Farces by Georges Feydeau*. Chicago: University of Chicago Press, 1970.

SHAW

Bentley, Eric. *Bernard Shaw*. Norfolk, Connecticut: New Directions, 1947.

Carpenter, Charles A. *Bernard Shaw and the Art of Destroying Ideals: The Early Plays*. Madison, Wisconsin: University of Wisconsin Press, 1969.

Ganz, Arthur. *George Bernard Shaw*. London: Macmillan; New York: Grove Press, 1983. Modern Dramatists Series.

Kaye, Julian. *Bernard Shaw and the Nineteenth-Century Tradition*. Norman, Oklahoma: University of Oklahoma Press, 1958.

Meisel, Martin. *Shaw and the Nineteenth-Century Theatre*. Princeton, New Jersey: Princeton University Press, 1963.